A Key to a Throne

A Key to a Throne
A Tale of Enadir

Rhydian King

I Mam a Dad, diolch

Enadir

The Midlands and surrounding countries

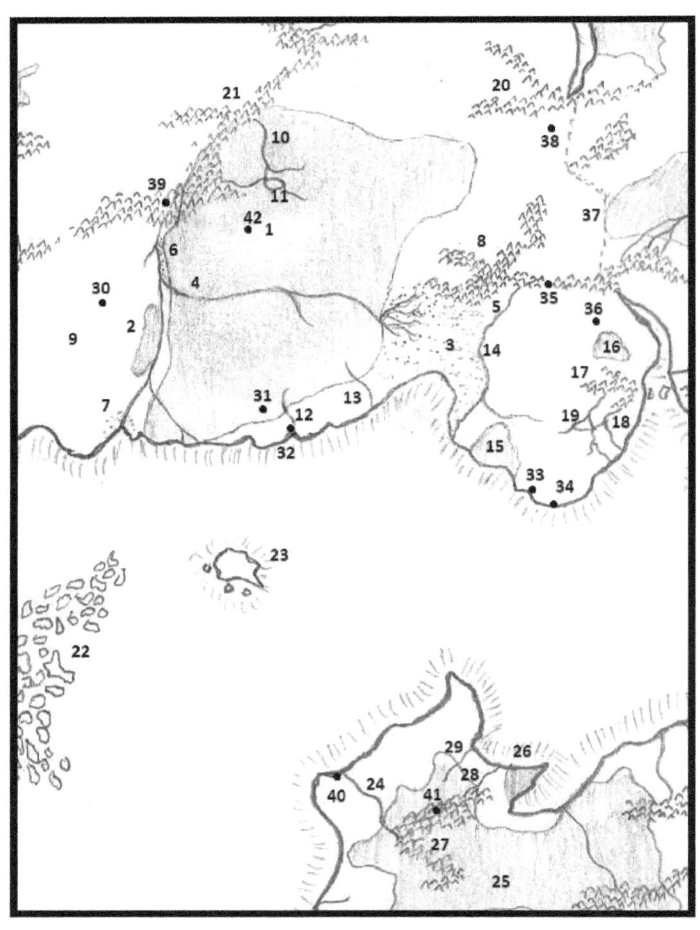

1. Dailas Forest	22. Jagged Isles
2. Pine Wood	23. Sea-neiad Isle
3. Cysgodgors Marsh	24. Werlit River
4. Crisiaddwr River	25. Daiwen Jungle
5. Bramble Plain	26. Coeddu Forest
6. Critanna Marsh	27. Haq-nel Mts
7. Tarin Swamp	28. Ailunel River
8. Tarnegrefur Mts.	29. Silin-ae River
9. Black desert	30. Crastalan
10. Ioer Rivers	31. Council
11. Eoli Lake	32. Morgenal
12. Gwenal River	33. Tonnis
13. Dantwenn River	34. Muranath
14. Atrael River	35. Imhara Pass
15. Saraman Woods	36. Denran (ruins)
16. Pawal Woods	37. Eastern Barrier
17. Cracket Mts	38. Arfan (ruins)
18. Hostaa Rivers	39. Bletta Castle
19. Ahanemis Lake	40. Maralen
20. East Jaws	41. Setarack Temple
21. Mts of Iadden	42. Cadaran

Part 1 - Rebellion

Prologue: Betrayal
Thirty-two years earlier

'Although less gruesome, a stab with a knife can be far more devastating than a cut with a sword, you know. Place it here, next to your sternum, and I can slip between your ribs to cut the vessels supplying your heart. A bit further along and I can collapse a lung, leaving you to suffocate. Or shall we be less obvious? Next to your pubis here, shall I place a finger? Ah! A lovely, bouncing pulse. A little cut there and you'll be drained like a piece of game. Shouldn't take too long with how quickly your heart is going. Try to calm down.'

'Please,' she whispered, old lips trembling.

'Or how about something else?' he moved behind her, trailing the cold blade around her waist and up her spine. 'A bit rougher, perhaps, but a sharp stab between your backbone and skull and I'll sever your spine. It won't take long after that.'

'Please,' she whimpered, keeping her head still against the blade.

'Oh, but it'll make you bleed too much, you're right. How about we go slightly laterally, on either side? We'll have to be careful not to nick the vessels travelling up your neck bones, but with a nice, slim blade like this, I might just get it in the right place to cut the nerves as they come out. At the right level, that'll paralyse your diaphragm, you know. You'll suffocate from two tiny cuts in your neck, but only if I'm precise.'

'Why?'

'You know why,' he snapped. How dare she question him. 'Yes, that might be a good way. Or we might go lower, to your kidneys. They receive a quarter of your body's blood supply with each heartbeat, you know. How long do you think it'll take for all that blood to fill up your belly? I imagine it's quite painful to feel it pump away inside you. You won't lose too much on the outside, of course, but on the inside…it'll be like a wine-skin filled to bursting, sloshing about in there, like all those times you've over-indulged. Or how about I just stick it into your belly, twist it around to really open up all those intestines, let all the excrement out into places it shouldn't go. You might survive for a few hours, maybe even days, waiting for infection to take hold. How does that sound?'

A whimper, incomprehensible.

He grabbed her by the jaw. The whimpers turned into sobs.

'I could break your jaw? Leave the gums open and torn… ever seen a man die of a broken jaw? It isn't pretty. Once the infection sets in, all manner of pus and shit starts oozing out as the bone falls apart. You can taste the rot for the few weeks you have left. The infection gets most, but the others starve, too swollen to chew down their slop.'

'Please don't,' she blubbered, tears streaming from her eyes, slime spilling from her nose.

Pathetic. They knew the risk when they defied him. Now to face the consequences.

Was it really that difficult to wait for his return? Two years, that was all he'd been away for. Two years and they'd forgotten him, turned back to their old ways, abandoned the laws he'd written. Or perhaps they thought he'd forgotten them, that his absence was permanent. Perhaps they hoped it. Hoped to one day come across his corpse, lying in a ditch, covered in loam, maggots eating his limp flesh. Funny how fortunes can turn.

Did he not promise to return? They should know by now that his word was his bond. He would be away for a while on a brief journey of discovery, but that was all. Duty would bring him back, as it did the first time. A leader didn't abandon his people. Not unless they abandoned him first.

History, it seemed, was doomed to repeat itself. These villagers, these scum, they tried to cut him off once before, banished him for no other reason than fear of the change he heralded. Three years ago, the old village elders learned their lesson for standing in his way. Could the rest of them really be so stupid to doubt he might do the same again if provoked? Last time, it was only eight elders he needed to make an example of. This time, everyone would learn.

'I gave you your chance last time,' he sighed, turning back to the old fonex. Her grey skin was dark, like his, drinking in the torchlight, concealing her in shadows. The only difference between them were the scars on his skin to the wrinkles and blemishes that came with her age. Her silver hair was lank, streaked with smoke, dirt, and sweat. A tribute to her failed attempts to crawl from her fate.

Her husband groaned softly beside her, his arms bound in an identical way to hers above his head, suspended from a roofbeam. How he ever thought to place himself as an elder was beyond comprehension. The old snake barely had enough cognitive ability to take himself to the latrine when the urge struck, let alone lead a village. It was an insult. To choose this senile snail as his replacement? He stood for everything Stolach hated, everything he'd cast down when he took leadership three years ago. Tradition, meekness, complacency, lack of ambition. The fool was content for them all to live and die in the few hundred square metres of their village. He didn't care about the rest of the Midlands, he didn't care if they could help bring it back to order. As long as this insignificant village was relatively content, that was enough for them, for all the elders. Sickening.

'Please, Stolach, don't– ' the woman pleaded again.

'Silence!' he snarled. 'You had your chance. You've already been found guilty. The only question is your sentence.'

'Mercy.'

'Mercy? This knife is mercy. You've wounded me deeply, far deeper than any blade can reach. I punish you with a smaller wound than the one inflicted on me. That's your mercy.'

'Stolach, this isn't you!'

'You know nothing of me! You stood aside when they first sent me away, you let them throw me out into the cold. They wanted me dead, you know. All of them, those skeletons in their unmarked graves; they thought banishing me was a death sentence, and you let them do it. You all did. I showed you mercy when I let you live then. How kind am I, to give you mercy again?'

She didn't answer, only stared at him with those tearful, frightened eyes. His stomach lurched. How dare she try to manipulate him with her weakness, her frailty.

'Am I not kind?' he shouted, inches from her face.

She flinched, trembling, but didn't answer. He pressed the knife against her husband's inner thigh, making him gasp as the point broke the skin.

'Yes!' she cried. 'You're kind, and sweet, and honourable. And you wouldn't do this to us!'

'I wouldn't?' He laughed, pent-up emotion spilling over. 'You know nothing. Hiding here in your little homes. Soft. Weak! I have survived the harshness of the wilderness beyond our holes and tree-houses. But I am honourable, unlike you, stealing power while I was away. You know the punishment for thievery in some places? They cut off a hand, so they don't steal again. You stole my village with your words, I think I'll take your tongue.'

She resisted. It was too difficult to keep her mouth propped open, so he forced it with both hands until it popped out of its sockets. Tongue lolling out of her dislocated jaw, it didn't take him long to remove the liar's tool. Her sobs turned to gurgles and splutters as she choked on the blood flooding her mouth. He stared down at her in disgust.

'This seems fitting enough for you. Your husband can watch you drown, and wait for smoke and flame to take him. Justice is served.'

He left them, locking the front door of their home behind him. The rest of the village burned brightly, ash and cinder filling the air. Bodies of dozens of fonex littered the floor, their dark grey complexions nearly invisible in the shadows, blending in with the ash. The smell of burning wood nearly masked the metallic stench of blood and the oddly-familiar scent of roasting flesh. Taking a burning branch from the ground, he set the door alight.

The damp winter night would prevent the fire from spreading, but it wouldn't save the village. It didn't deserve saving. They betrayed him by accepting the new elders. He served justice to them all.

Covering his mouth and nose, he fought through the blaze to the forest, relishing in the cool shadows beyond the fire's reach. Turning one final time to the slaughtered village, Stolach nodded quietly to himself.

'Farewell mother, father. I deserved better.'

Chapter 1

Would today be the day for liberation? From the shadows of the alcove, Lidan narrowed his eyes at the question and stepped into the dwindling light of sunset. Red skies promised the opening of the city gates, but would they be open for him?

He gathered his thin cloak around him and walked swiftly through the narrow streets of Crastalan. The city's black granite foundations radiated with the sun's heat, dampening his armpits and groin with sweat. His worn shoes padded softly along the ground. He kept his head lowered. It was wise to keep his face hidden. The glistening brand on his cheekbone was a beacon to those who understood its significance.

The city was only just coming to life. Crastalan was a nocturnal place, the boiling heat of summer making it nigh impossible to survive the streets in daylight. It was only once the sun was set and the torches lit that the inhabitants came bursting forth from their homes. At this hour, it was just about cool enough to move around, but still so hot that most decided to stay inside for a while yet. That suited Lidan just fine, as he had no desire to be seen.

Of course, it wasn't as though anyone would recognise him. He was nobody; a ghost, a distant memory even in the minds of those who cared, or used to care. Insignificant. Forgotten. A shadow of an unimportant echo. Even so, it was best to go about his business when fewer people were around. Crowds irritated him; too many people spouting rubbish and yelling at each other, and crowds attracted guards, of whom he had no particular fondness.

Four men bustled past, their flabby stomachs bouncing beneath loose tunics, sagging over their straining belts. He shrank back into the shadows, lip curling at their wealthy arrogance. The high stone walls of the building behind him pressed into his back. He glanced through one of the thick glass windows to see shelves of candles and tallow; a chandler. The concept of devoting an entire store to something as simple as candles seemed ludicrous. This place was so different to his home, how could he have ever hoped to survive its complexities?

Weaverlodge had been – and presumably still was – a poor village, far to the south of the capital, in the grassland plains south-west of the Pine Woods. Back then, life seemed so mundane, so dull. He'd give anything to return to it now. Not just him, of course, all of them. Not that he ever could go back, not now. Their faces were a blur in his memory, lost in pain, save for one. Such memories were likely all that remained after their folly.

Leaning forward from the wall, he could see the tower. The keep. Reaching high into the sky, always visible wherever you were in the city. No matter how dark or twisted your alley, how small and enclosed your den, you could never escape its shadow. He turned his head away, tried to ignore it, but it was impossible. To live in Crastalan was to be constantly reminded of the tower, the king, and his minions.

He wandered through the streets, heading for the market square. For as much as was possible, he stuck to the alleys; the twisting, coiling, pathways that snaked through the underside of the city like a thousand streams in a forest. Looking around, he couldn't help but shake his head at calling them alleys. Built by giants in a time lost to legend, the scale of the city matched its former masters. Alleys were wider than the roads of Weaverlodge, roads as broad as rivers, buildings like castles. Running his hand along the walls of the 'alley', his fingers glided across the stone, worn smooth as a sheet of polished quartz by the passing of two thousand years, or so they claimed. For all those centuries, this place had endured. He had hardly endured three weeks before it claimed him for another three years in its dungeons.

His alley brought him to a crossroads. Five paths, each paved in the same black granite that constituted the entire, sprawling city. From the first level to the fifth, to the tower at its heart, there was no exception. It was only the later additions of modern inhabitants that were built of an alien material; wood and grey stone extensions jutting from the higher levels like tumours in an attempt to find more space to hold their wealth.

The alley to his immediate right led to an abrupt dead-end. It served only as the backdoor passage for the stores on its side. The one beside it reeked of sewage and was covered in grime. Even from his limited time here, he knew it led to one of the gateways of the extensive, labyrinthine waste system beneath the city. It was best avoided. Not only because it circled around to completely the wrong direction, but also the stench would soon have his eyes watering.

The second alley to his left looked harmless enough, and would have led to the market, but he shied away. The rolls of cinnamon dangling from twin torches at the alley's corner deterred him. It was the universal mark for the whorehouses of the city. Along with the dried nettles for the fighting pits, and the sprigs of rosemary for the poppy-dens, these marked alleys were best avoided, unless you sought their particular offerings.

To his immediate left, the alley took a detour to the partition wall between the city levels. Again, it was the wrong direction, there were no gates there, nothing but cold stone walls rising thirty metres into the air as a battlemented palisade, one of the many that divided the city into its five distinct tiers, each one encircling the next. This level, the second, was the largest, and where the majority of the inhabitants lived. It had the market squares, the stores, the houses of the wealthy, the inns, the gambling dens, the breweries, everything a city needed to survive. Or at least, if you had the money to do so. Within the second level was the third; the healing level, full of apothecaries and infirmaries. It was one he knew well. Beyond this was a garden level, supplied by natural springs and wells far underground. This oasis, made fertile by the hidden water and massive carts of manure brought from the stables, was not openly accessible to the masses. He'd been through it a few times, but could hardly remember anything about it. Beyond this, was the fifth level. He shuddered. Three years of his life spent in that level. He vowed never to return. Never.

He took the middle alley. It was longer than the one marked with the cinnamon, but he had no desire to come to blows with the men who frequented such establishments. Not for fear of what they might do to him, such violence seemed trivial after what he'd endured, but rather for fear of attracting the attention of guards.

He clutched his money pouch as he padded along, his worn shoes flapping softly with each step. Two men were on the other side of the road, watching his approach. It was perfectly possible they were harmless citizens. But then again… he held his pouch tighter as he passed, feeling their eyes follow his path. It was two days since he'd last eaten anything, he needed this money to pay the innkeeper, and eventually the gatekeepers to buy his passage out the city. It would not do to lose what little he had left.

It was a week since he'd stepped through the partition wall between into the second level from the third. A week of searching for an opportunity to leave this place, at last.

Such an opportunity was yet to present itself. Cautious, weak, and weary as he was, he wasn't sure where the best place to leave the city was, and spent his days waiting by the gates, taking note of the guards. He knew which were observant, and which were nonchalant, looking for the ones least likely to notice the brand on his cheek. Nothing more than a small circle with a bisecting horizontal line. Nothing less than the mark of the damned, sentenced for lifetime imprisonment, or worse.

At first, he considered hiding the mark with a scarf, but his first day of watching put that idea to rest, as the guards checked the faces of anyone leaving the city, and paid even more attention to any who tried to conceal their features. There was also the question of what time to leave. Early in the evening or late in the morning, there were fewer people going through the gates and therefore fewer guards. However, this meant each person was observed more closely, while later in the evening when there were tides of people going through the gates and the guards doubled, they were less attentive. It would be risky either way, he simply had to determine which was riskier.

Of course, there was also the question of what to do once his did buy his way through the gates. Beyond the enormous curtain wall, surrounding the city for miles around, was a sprawling, stinking, dusty shanty town. A town to welcome each new traveller to the city, as it had once welcomed him. Men, hanex, fonex, goblins, juggernauts, dreyads, and satorrs who came to Crastalan with no wealth, and were condemned to live their lives at the foot of its walls. A miserable place. Not only for its physical properties, but for its sense of lost opportunity, of hopeless poverty next to the wealth of the city proper. Most who came searching for a better life ended up there, cursing the four winds for their misfortune. Poor fools, they didn't realise their good fortune, even as they languished in the muck and squalor of the shanty town.

Finally, the alley opened to a wider road leading to a great market square. Four hundred square metres of bare stone floor with four fountains at each corner marking the points of a compass. Even at this hour, when he expected to be the only one awake, the market bustled as traders set up their stalls for another day or trade. From a small kiosk came the delicious, tantalising aroma of hazelnuts roasted in honey and spices in the style of the Jagged Isles. His mouth watered, but he couldn't afford it.

He'd entered the square from the street nearest the southern fountain, bearing a statue of a ship sculpted from red marble, and turned to his right to make for the eastern fountain, marked by a small juniper bush rising from the waters. It was at the eastern face of the great outer curtain wall that the city's gatehouse was situated, and the only way he knew in and out of Crastalan. Naturally, this was the best way out, with the least amount of time spent in the heavily-garrisoned first circle. It was the military circle, housing the barracks, training grounds, smithies, stables, and armouries of the city garrison.

He left the square, keeping to the shadows as much as possible. He passed several servants, hurrying to light the lamps, torches, and candles adorning the walls. Eventually, more and more citizens emerged from their homes and set about their nightly businesses. By the time he reached the east gate, the moon was high in the sky, barely visible over to the light cast by the countless torches.

He kept a fair distance away from the gate so as not to attract unnecessary attention. He watched carefully as countless individuals made their way in and out of the city, their heavily-laden wagons teetering behind. He might have considered smuggling himself through the gates in one of them, but the guards checked each one thoroughly, stabbing spears into wagons of hay and swords into carts of fruit, ignoring the protests of the owners at the damage to their stock.

In total, there were twelve men guarding the gate. He recognised a few of them from his time spying. The man with an ugly pointed goatee was sharp and merciless, while the fat hanex was laughably inattentive, probably dreaming of his next meal as he leaned on his spear. Whether he recognised them or not, they were all his enemies. After three hours, the guards were relieved, and a new dozen stood in their place, in addition to a dozen more for added protection in the swollen midnight crowds. Of these, only one was familiar to him; a short, wiry young lad, around his age. He recognised this one because of his youth and his uncommon pleasure in catching potential thieves. Only two days ago, down at the south gate, Lidan saw him pick up a squirming child, probably a pickpocket, and hack off her right hand with his axe in front of a crowd of onlookers. When he walked back to his inn the following morning, he saw the girl again, sprawled next to a pile of waste, bled to death, as a dog gnawed away at her leg.

He imagined killing him, but knew he wouldn't. It wouldn't accomplish anything, it wouldn't help him in his cause. Indeed, if he were to attempt it, he could expect to end up like the girl, and the wiry young guard would simply go on. He doubted he even remembered her.

It was three years ago when he witnessed first-hand the horror of such punishment, and the rage, the grief, the emptiness that followed. It was an attempted retaliation against such 'justice' that ultimately led to his current situation. Shuddering, he rubbed his hands. Ten fingers, all working. Bless the North winds.

He stayed where he was all night, watching the gate. The guards halved again at four o'clock to the original twelve. Eventually it was time to leave. The city was packed, and he had to shove his way through the suffocating crowds. It took him nearly an hour and a half before he ducked back through the inn's doorway, breathing in the cool air, beautifully fresh and cold after the already scorching heat of the morning sun. He nodded to the landlord, walked up the granite steps to his room, and collapsed on the bed.

*

Somebody shoved his leg. Again. More aggressively this time. Groaning, his eyes blinked awake. He stretched and propped up on his elbow. At the foot of his bed was a woman, perhaps in her mid-forties, a sour expression on her face. She shoved him again, harder.

'Wake up, you. Payment's due. What you gave yesterday wasn't enough.'

Lidan sighed and stuck his hand into the leather pouch at his belt. 'How much do I owe you?' he mumbled.

'Four coppers for today, and another one for yesterday. You only gave us three yesterday.'

He frowned, all that was left in his pouch were eight copper coins and one silver, for the main gate. 'It only cost three coppers yesterday.'

'Price has gone up. Now it's four coppers per night. Pay up, or we'll call soldiers,' she leered. Ever since he arrived, he felt the innkeeper's wife was a foul woman. Now it seemed she'd taken it upon herself to rob him as well. But he had no choice, as she knew, so he gave up the money.

'Now I don't have enough to stay for another night,' he complained.

'Then you'll have to leave, prisoner, otherwise-'

'Yes, I know,' he interrupted. 'You'll call soldiers.'

She gave him a mocking grin and left. He closed his eyes. Fate had spoken. Today was the day. Two coins would have to be paid to get into the first city circle, and then his silver to get through the outer gate, which meant he had one coin to spare. His stomach rumbled. There was only one thing worth spending it on.

He left the inn, earlier than usual, and walked to the market square. Hardly any of the stores were open, but thankfully, the one selling the roasted hazelnuts was. The trader smiled broadly as he flicked him the coin, and shoved a scoop of nuts into a wooden bowl. He sat down at a table in the kiosk, savouring the taste of the sweet ginger and cinnamon, the honey, the crunchy nut at its centre. When he was done, he handed the trader back his bowl and headed to the east gate.

He arrived later than expected, the gate already busy. There were only twelve guards, and he waited for the moment to approach. It came sooner than expected, as a gaggle of scantily-clad women shuffled through, giggling childishly. The guards were distracted by the whores, and Lidan pushed his way through. The soldier hardly looked at him, took the two coppers and pushed him through without a question, eager to stare at the women. He hurried through. North winds be praised for the distraction!

His gratitude was short-lived. Now he was in even greater danger. Totally surrounded by guards. He considered lifting his hood to shroud his face and remain inconspicuous, but nobody else wore theirs. To lift it would draw attention. He kept his head bare, but turned his cheek to the ground, as if suffering from a sore neck. Anything to hide his brand.

This was only his second time on this road, the Eastern Trench. So-called because it was built on granite blocks set two feet lower than the rest of the first city level, so the guards positioned along the sides were constantly looking down on the travellers. It served two purposes. First, it ensured nobody could accidentally stray into the first level, which was strictly reserved for the soldiers. Second, it gave the guards an elevated position, and an advantage against anyone attempting to attack them from the trench. The road was perfectly straight, leading form the east gate to the gatehouse. Travellers were commanded to always keep to the left, leaving two constant streams going in opposite directions.

In front of him were three men, each one fatter than the next, swaggering down the road. Their mail shirts jingled like purses, ornate scabbards bumping their thighs rhythmically. Mercenaries of some description, perhaps hired as the personal guards for a merchant. Such a thing wasn't uncommon, and although no man was permitted to hire any more than four men as bodyguards, there were more than enough merchants to hire the sell-swords. He stepped into their shadows and followed them closely. The watching soldiers were likely to have their eyes drawn towards the three fat men themselves and ignore the skinny, dirty street urchin scurrying along behind them.

It seemed to work. Nobody challenged him. Hope spread like poison in his gut. He might make it.

He reached the halfway point, and his plan failed.

One of the mercenaries stumbled over a stone, and Lidan walked straight into him, nearly toppling him over. The mercenary spun around, glaring. A round face, small blue eyes, a large nose, and fat, wet lips. A sheen of sweat plastered his greasy forehead, and small flecks of spittle gathered at the corner of his mouth.

'What in the four winds you doing?' the mercenary blazed, froth flying from his mouth.

He recoiled, stammering his excuses. 'Forgive me, sir, it was an accident, I didn't see you stumble.'

'Didn't see? You didn't *see*?,' a sweaty fist seized his shirt. 'You're a stupid little swine if you expect me to believe *that*. You were trying to rob me!'

'No!' he shouted, scrambling back, trapped by the fist.

'Pickpocket! I know your games!'

'No!' he cried again, panicking, aware of the attention they were drawing. 'It was an accident! I swear!'

The fat man lashed out. He was surprisingly swift, and vicious. The mailed, gauntleted fist struck hard. His head snapped back, his cheek exploding in pain. He collapsed to the ground, dazed, while the mercenary stood above him, calling the soldiers to make an arrest. Lidan lay where he fell, head spinning. He could already feel his cheek swelling, and there was a dampness to it; either blood or tears, he didn't know.

A soldier pointed a spear at the mercenary. 'Silence! I saw it, clumsy oaf. You slipped, the skinny one wasn't looking where he was going and walked into you.'

'Aye,' barked the mercenary. 'Walked into me! A common trick used by thieves to distract your mind while their hand slips to your money purse! Cut off the cur's hand!'

'Enough, pig,' snapped another soldier. 'I saw it too. You stepped on a slick part of stone, your weight betrayed you, and you slipped. The skinny one was looking at his feet, not at you. Now move along. Move along!' He waved his spear at both the mercenaries and the small crowd gathering at the commotion.

A soldier knelt down and offered the butt of his spear into the trench to Lidan.

'Hold on to this, boy, I'll pull you up.'

He did as he was told, heart in mouth, trying to keep the left side of his face turned away as he was hauled to his feet. He tried to scurry away, but the spear point barred his way. 'Wait now, boy, let me have a look at that.'

His hand shook as the guard grabbed his jaw and turned his head. Tears built up, threatening to burst. This was it. His brand, exposed. The soldier's eyes narrowed. He tensed his legs, preparing to tear away from the soldier's grasp, to flee. He could lose himself in the crowd. He was sure of it. It wouldn't take long to get out of sight. Keep his head down, push into the middle, make his way as quickly as possible to the gatehouse.

The soldier's grip tightened. Too tight. He could never break free. It was over. Back to the fifth level. Back to the dark. The pain.

He saw the soldier's lip curl, and he whistled between his teeth. He waited for the sound of irons closing around his wrists

It never came. Instead, came the rumble of laughter as the soldier patted his other cheek merrily.

'Well the skin's been split like a rotten fruit, and you're going to have a monster lump there, but you'll be fine. Stay away from mercenaries, boy, they're scum. Run along, now.'

He nodded, dumbfounded, and re-joined the flow of bodies moving down to the gatehouse. He lifted a hand to explore his face. It came away bloody. The mercenary's fist had collided directly with the brand, splitting the skin and completely obscuring it. Somehow, impossibly, the mercenary might have inadvertently helped him.

Clutching a hand to his injured cheek, he was jostled along with everyone else, keeping pace with the crowd. Before him now was a trader with an empty cart – and probably a full purse – having sold all his wares in yesterday's markets. To his right were a man and his wife, the woman with a baby in a sling across her front. Both looked worn and haggard, their clothes patched and threadbare, their shoes flimsy strips of leather tied to their soles. He imagined they were either beggars, victims of thieves, or simply a new family who had fallen behind on their taxes and were now being cast out the city, to scrounge a living in the shanty town. He might have pitied them once, but since his ordeal in the fifth level, pity was hard to come by. Not even that little girl with her leg getting chewed to pieces by a hungry dog stirred pity in him, only anger. Only hatred. Only desperate fear.

The traffic of bodies slowed down at the gatehouse, as people clutched their silver coins tightly for fear of pickpockets. Once paid, the guards waved them through the gates and out the city.

The gates themselves were enormous. Ten steps led down from the Eastern trench to the outer wall, but even at the top of those steps, one would have to crane their necks to see the top of the gate. Carved from thick oak planks, studded with iron, and plated on either side by irregular iron plates, they were formidable. In times of siege, massive bars of oak and steel could be slid into racks between the gates to secure them further, and large chains hung down from their entire height, to be secured to iron rings set into the ground. Even to his inexperienced eyes, it was obvious these gates were built to withstand wars he could only imagine.

Both were half open today, to give a space wide enough to let through the large ox-carts two at a time. A unit of fifty soldiers were on the trench floor alone, while there must have been fifty more surrounding the trench, and countless other staring down from the high curtain walls. This wall, built of stone blocks so enormous it held itself together with little more than its own sheer weight, towered above them, nearly forty metres high. Its outer face was even enamelled with riveted iron sheets. Twenty towers, placed at regular intervals around its circumference, added to its formidability, each housing regiments of soldiers guarding their stretch of the battlemented walls, each with a trebuchet or ballista on its highest level. The soldiers scowled at the crowd, daring them to place a foot out of line. He instinctively lowered his head, looking as meek and pathetic as he felt in the shadow of such a force.

As he waited in line, now behind a broad Southlander with a blacksmith's apron and a little barrow full of tools, he heard the cry from behind.

'Pickpocket! Somebody's stolen my silver!'

Panic rippled through the crowd as people hurriedly checked their coins were safe. Lidan didn't move. He clutched his silver ever since he stepped in line, and didn't want to betray its location to anyone. Such was an old trick used by some gangs; one member would pretend to have lost a purse, or item of jewellery, and cry out in a large crowd about robbery, then as the surrounding people checked their possessions, the thieves would observe where said valuables were kept upon one's person, and move to take it with their light, searching fingers. Lidan knew better, but most around him fell for the trick and began patting their tunics and trousers, or reaching into their backpacks. Many would go through the gates a few coins short, he observed quietly. It seemed, however, that some of the guards were familiar with such a con, and two of them jumped into the trench to frogmarch the traveller who'd cried out for questioning. If he was really just an innocent victim, then he'd have nothing to worry about, if he was a thief ... the dogs would not go hungry tonight.

Before long it was his turn to pay, and he deposited his silver into the mailed fist of a disinterested guard, his bristly beard damp with sweat, or maybe ale from the blurred look in his eyes. Head bowed, he hurried along, and was finally through the gates, beneath the great outer wall. It was so thick, the road through was almost a tunnel in itself, the black granite smooth underfoot by the passing of countless feet. Cold, too, the shadowed passage untouched by sunlight. Above him were the gaping mouths of murder-holes, waiting to vomit boiling tar or quicklime on attackers. He shuddered. Woe betides any fool who dared mount an assault on this fortress.

Finally, he was out. Out of the dungeons, the tower, the city, the despair. Freedom beckoned like an old friend. He smiled as the moonlight hit his face, and stepped into a new beginning.

Chapter 2

The moon's promise of freedom was a lie. Now he was locked behind the dangers of the vast, sprawling shanty town, and his poverty. In the sense of being able to walk around unguarded, he was indeed free in this filthy, dry, desolate slum, but free to do what? To die? He had no supplies, no water, and no means of leaving the town to brave the black desert. Two days after walking through the outer walls of Crastalan, he was as trapped as he had ever been, as he realised the city's strongest defence was the land itself.

So far, he had lived from day to day, scrounging for scraps of food in discarded waste heaps, or sitting on the hard sun-baked ground, hoping someone might drop a coin into his lap. Nobody ever did, there were so many beggars here that no-one spared him a second glance.

As he wandered the streets the second night, walking aimlessly, going wherever the crowd took him, his stomach tightened as the aroma of frying potatoes hit his nostrils. Around the corner was the source; a food stall run by a couple of Southlanders, with a little fire heating several steaming frying pans. Two soldiers flanked the stall, scowling. They were selling cheap food for a cheap price. The only thing on the menu was the fried potatoes, cut into large chunks and set in the pans in a bath of grease, to cook until crisp and golden. Lidan's mouth watered, but he walked past, his gut growling longingly at the missed meal. His last proper meal had been those nuts back in the city, and since then it was only a few stale crusts of hard bread and apple cores that sustained him. He was fortunate, of course, that there were several wells in the town, though he'd have to queue up for hours to reach them, and had nothing to store water in, so made do with gulping down as much water as he could from the bucket each time. The key was not to drink so much to make you vomit, as he did on his first attempt. No, drink slowly, only as much as the stomach could take.

But water alone was not enough. Drinking so much and eating so little made his stomach twist. But the heat was too much to abstain.

Bent double, he guzzled bucket after greedy bucket, keeping the heat at bay with his pain.

As the sun rose, he ducked away from the crowd and stumbled into the shadows of the ramshackle buildings. They were made of an assortment of materials, some from wood, others from sun-hardened mud, one or two from thin metal sheets. As far from the regal black granite of Crastalan as an ant to a hydra. He passed a building that had once been an ox-cart, the wood splintered and dusty, with the wheels nailed together and covered in animal-hide to make a roof. Another looked like it started out as a jolly little coracle, but its owners had built up around it with mud to form a crude hut, sensing the boat would never see water again.

He walked and walked, looking for an ideal place to sleep. It wasn't enough to find somewhere shaded now; he needed somewhere to remain sheltered all day from both sweltering sun and desert gales, the latter as much a threat as the former, blowing grit into one's eyes, mouth, and airways. Desert-lung was a killer. He'd met several travellers back at Weaverlodge who'd suffered, traders who'd spent years going back and forth across the black desert between the grassland villages and Crastalan. The sight of their black, bloody sputum hacked up into tavern spittoons haunted him to this day.

He found a likely shelter, a sad little hovel between two huts. Cramped, stinking, and filthy, it would do just fine. As soon as he crawled into the shade, something growled malevolently in the darkness. He beat a hasty retreat. It was probably just some stray dog, but he was in no mood to fight a hungry animal for a place to rest. Besides, the dog would win.

Eventually he found another little grotto of sorts, walled on three sides by huts, with the roof of one hut overreaching its wall to provide shelter. There was another beggar, an ancient satorr with greasy grey hair, thin enough to be a living skeleton. He glanced wearily at Lidan as he approached, and rubbed the sleep from his eyes.

'Can I join?' asked Lidan, standing above him.

The satorr didn't answer, but shifted to one side to make room in the shade. He collapsed gratefully, curling up in a corner.

*

He woke around midday, the sun at its zenith. Sweat trickled down his back and beneath his arms. He groaned and stretched, the old satorr was gone. He coughed lightly to clear his throat of the accumulated dust while he slept, wincing at the sharp burn. His throat was parchment-dry, as if it were scoured with a fistful of gravel. Licking his lips with a dry tongue, he considered leaving his shelter to go to a well, but the day was too hot. Considering the sweltering heat he was suffering here in the shade, he shuddered to imagine the temperature outside.

He lay back. The ground was damp with his sweat, but he attempted sleep. Unsuccessfully. He lay still, drawing ragged breaths, too weak even to pray.

Sometime later, as he still wrestled with sleep, someone walked into the shelter. It was a tall figure, clothed in long robes, a long scarf wound around its head. He watched warily as the figure sat down beside him and unwound the scarf. His sticky eyes widened. The old satorr, returned again. He attempted a smile to greet his company. It was returned with a disapproving frown.

Had he the energy, he would have withered from the look. Instead, he simply closed his eyes. Something pressed against his chest. He opened his eyes. A water-skin. Mustering the energy, he sat up and gulped a mouthful. It was warm, gritty, and had a slightly metallic taste to it from the copper lid of the skin. No doubt it held all manner of scum and muck from the satorr's rotten mouth. How wonderful it felt on his lips, tongue, running down his cracked throat.

He returned the skin to the satorr, wiping his mouth with the hem of his tunic.

'Thank you,' he croaked. 'I was dying of thirst.'

'I know,' the satorr shook head. 'Why didn't you have a drink before?'

'It's too hot to go out. Figured I'd just wait 'til sunset to go to the well.'

'Why didn't you fill up your water-skin last night? Save yourself something for the day?'

'I don't have one,' he should have been embarrassed, but had no room for anything but exhaustion. 'I've been relying on drinking as much as I can at night and sleeping through the day.'

'Foolish. You need a skin. If I had one to spare I'd give it to you, but this is my only one. You'll need to get yourself one if you want to survive the week.'

It was true. He'd never survive this shanty town. But then, that was the point, wasn't it? He didn't *want* to have to survive the town, he wanted to be free of it, to feel grass under his toes, water on his skin, rain on his head. He said as much to the satorr, who shrugged.

'So you don't want to live here, that's fine. You'll still need a skin to get across the desert.'

He nodded. 'Where? I have no money, and nothing to trade for one.'

'Then you'll have to steal it. It's that or death. You should get better clothes. Those rags are letting in too much sun, you'll burn to a crisp if you're not careful. See this long bit of cloth? I wrap it around my head like this. Keeps the sun off me, but doesn't bake my old head,' he held up the scarf. 'Again, I'd give you one if I had a spare, but I don't. You have food?'

'No, do you?' he asked, thirst quenched enough for hunger to pang again.

'A shame. I don't either. I would tell you to steal some, but most of the food stalls are guarded, it'd be death if you tried to steal some. Then again,' he added, thoughtfully, 'I suppose it'd be death if you don't try, so you don't really have anything to lose, do you?'

Lidan looked about him, and sighed. 'Why do people even come here? What's the point? They'd be better off back in their little villages, not here. Empty desert, no food, no money…'

'Speaking from your own perspective. The majority who come have enough money to settle in the town, build themselves a nice home, and sell their wares or skills to make a living. For most people it's decent enough. The soldiers even protect them from thieves and outlaws. I agree, from *our* perspective, as lowly beggars, life is cruel. But that's because we squandered our money, reached too far, or came here without thinking it through, eh?'

'Maybe,' he muttered. Here he thought they were strangers, but the satorr saw right through him. 'What's your name, anyway? I'm Lidan.'

'Alright. I'm Winten.'

'Thanks for the water, Winten, and for your advice.'

'Beggars look out for each other, nobody else will.'

They said no more after that, and turned their backs to one another. Not that it mattered. '*Beggars look out for each other.*' He smiled at the sentence, repeating it a hundred times over. How true. He knew it well enough from before the prison. Admittedly, there were grander alcoves and alleys in the city proper than out here, but the filth and waste of others was the same wherever he slept. But being with someone to look out for you, to watch your back, was a rarity. He thought he was alone, would always be alone. But now Winten was here, perhaps it would not be so. With a smile, he slept, safe in the company of a fellow beggar.

*

The street was dark, crowded, with jeering civilians pressed on all sides. The guards held Zile in their vice-like grips. The sentence was called out. The blade gleamed in the torchlight. A whistle. A thud. A scream. Dark blood on darker stone. He wailed. There was nothing he could have done. Nothing.

*

He woke with a gasp. It was night, and still warm, as always. What little water his body had to spare evaporated from his skin in a stinking sweat. Even in his filthy state, the odour stung his nostrils. Shaking from the painful dream, he sat up. Alone.

'Winten?'

No. Gone. Of course he was gone. An overwhelming surge of grief swept over him. Whether it was from the dream or this new abandonment, he couldn't tell. Not that it mattered. It was the same as before, him against the world, with nobody to watch him as he suffered. He might have cried, but his eyes were too dry and gummy.

Shaking his head, desperate for a clear mind, he left the hovel.

Winten may have left him, but his advice remained. He went to the nearest well and had a drink. The queue was shorter tonight, as the sun had only recently set, so he didn't have to wait for too long before it was his turn with the bucket. His stomach churned as the water filled it, but he ignored the pain. Just enough for the night.

His plan was to head to one of the unofficial market squares, where folk who were either too poor or too lazy to take their wares into the city itself gathered. He was surprised to see how many there were. At least twenty stalls crammed into an area not fifty metres square, completely packed, with crowds gathered around each stall, haggling and exchanging coins for weapons, food, equipment, for fixing saddles and scabbards, buying new clothes. There was even a little anvil, where a stocky youth offered his hand at fixing horseshoes. The smith had a long queue of men before his stall; soldiers, mostly, the outriders and scouts of the king.

Why fix their horseshoes at this run-down place in the slums instead of the stables and blacksmiths of the city proper? Maybe it was cheaper here, away from the eyes of their stern commanders. Maybe they liked to watch the fools like him scratch out a life in the mud.

He lingered by one of the horses, a plan forming in his mind, but he must have been staring too intently. One of the outriders, a thin fonex with light brown skin, squared up to him and demanded what he was doing. Lidan muttered an apology and scampered off, the chuckles of the soldiers ringing behind.

All the stalls in this market square were too closely guarded to try his hand at thievery, so he squeezed himself away and wandered the slums to the next one. This square was smaller, with fewer stalls, though no less cramped. Worse, a guard tower was erected in the middle of the square, housing four soldiers with crossbows, staring vigilantly at the swarming crowds below. This was not the one.

It was not the third, nor the fourth, but the fifth square he arrived at that he deemed safe enough – or dangerous enough, depending on how you looked at it – to steal from one of the stalls. By now it was around two in the morning, and the sky was as dark, with only a crescent moon to illuminate it. This square was badly lit, and the soldiers had mostly gathered around one large food kiosk. It was obvious from its size that this was a permanent feature of this particular square, and the owner probably slept in the back. The owner had also had enough time to build it into a sturdy building, dominating the square. The guards' orientation to this kiosk meant that the other stalls, of which there were many, relied on their personal bodyguards to protect them, of whom there were few.

Lidan looked around. It was not as full as the others, possibly because the early market rush had ended some time ago, with most of the stores' wares sold, but there were still enough people around to be able to melt away into the crowd. Aside from the food kiosk there were a couple of little carts selling planks of wood, presumably for building more of the scrap huts, a man selling jewels from an oaken chest, three stalls selling fabric for making clothes, a satorr with the tools of a cobbler, and another blacksmith farrier. He saw several stalls selling useless odds and ends, from parchment and quills, to bars of iron and bronze, a large group of Islanders selling various tinctures and potions, as was typical of their people and their tropical medicines, and finally a man selling weapons from his ox-cart.

His eye lingered on the cart. It was no water-skin, but a weapon wouldn't go amiss. He could use a blade to threaten someone, steal their skin. It would be easier than pinching one from a stall and risking the guards or mercenaries. He walked past the weapon-smith's guard, advertising his master's wares with proclamations of magnificence. Strange tattoos covered his face and neck. The marks of a former pit fighter.

'Finest-quality weapons you've ever seen! Not a soul in Nefarwy has ever wielded weapons as fine as these. Even the king envies our goods! How about you, marm, care for a dagger to protect you from hungry men? You, sir, a cudgel to cave in the heads of muggers and burglars! You, priest, we have quarterstaves you might like, blessed by the northern winds themselves!'

He raised his brows; he hadn't expected to find a priest in the slums. But there he was, an old man in the brown habit, tied around the waist with a white girdle, wandering about the square. As he passed, he bowed his head in respect. Judging from the medallion around his neck, a tilted semicircle with four spikes, he was a simple acolyte worshipping the north winds. Most people in Nefarwy worshipped the north winds for their power and wonder. He wasn't entirely sure why it was the north wind they deemed the holiest and strongest, but that's how it was. In his current situation, he wasn't going to question it.

Shaking his head, he approached the weapon cart, five paces away from the young guard, still busy praising his master's products. Men with such tattoos made him nervous; they were all too similar to the Hobb, the fierce nomads of Dailas. Over time, the traditions of these nomads seeped into some of the other villages in the forest, even to Crastalan's fighting pits. Any man marked with such tattoos signified their martial prowess. Renowned brawlers, distinguished in blood, it would not end well for him if he got caught.

A fine fighter he may be, but as a salesman, he clearly had a long way to go. There were only three others around the cart, as the young guard's shouting seemed more effective at driving people away than it did at summoning them. His master was currently talking to a hanex, haggling over the price of a sword.

'Five silvers!'

'Outrageous! That's more than I made in three months as a soldier! I'll give you two silvers.'

'Five. The sword is made from good steel, from my forge back in Dailas, and do you see the pommel? The mark of the northern winds. It'll bring you protection. Five silvers is a good price for such a weapon.'

The hanex spat in contempt. 'It'll be my skill that brings me protection, not the wind. Don't try to push your holy nonsense on me, the sword isn't worth five. Looks more like iron than steel to me, anyway.'

The smith bristled, his pale skin flushing. 'Doubting my work? The price has gone up to six silvers, then, for your insult! It's made of the finest steel, heat treated and tempered the *right* way, and folded just enough times for optimal resistance and hardness. You'll be hard-pressed to find a better weapon. Could an iron blade do this?' He took up the sword, held the blade securely at the foible, and flexed it. It bent into a neat half-circle, only to spring back to its original form when he released the pressure. 'See that? No warping, no shattering, as strong as ever.'

The hanex paused. 'Alright so it's good steel. I'll give you three silvers for it. And you'll pay to get it sharpened. It's all I can afford as a bodyguard.'

'Then I suggest you find a better-paid job. The price is six silvers, and you're lucky I'm still willing to sell it to you.'

'You greedy rat. Fine. I'll give you four, and twenty coppers, it's all I have on me. But throw in the scabbard as well.'

The smith paused, thinking, then picked up the leather scabbard, sheathed the sword and offered it to the hanex, who tossed him a purse of money and walked away, grumbling. The smith grinned smugly as he tied the purse to his belt, not bothering to inspect its contents, and moved on to the next customer. Lidan waited as the man before him bought a cudgel, slowly playing with the empty money-purse at his belt. He chewed his lip thoughtfully, and gently kicked at a couple of flat stones by his foot. It would be risky, especially with the guard, but he had no other option.

Finally, the smith looked at him.

'So, young man, what can I get you? A sword? A dagger? How about an axe? An axe will give you some extra muscle in a fight, by the four winds I can tell you need it.'

He smiled thinly. 'What daggers do you have?'

The smith stepped back and rooted about his cart, taking up short blades and cradling them in his arms, then brought them to the front to show him. There were all manner of daggers, knives, and dirks, some curved, some with serrated blades, some single edged, some barbed, others plain, one even had a gilded hilt and delicate silver inlays all over the blade. The smith picked up the gold-hilted dagger and winked.

'Fancy little treasure, this one, much too expensive for you, methinks,' he tossed it to the back of the cart. 'What kind of dagger are you looking for? Nothing too expensive, I'd wager, from looking at your clothes, no offense meant, of course.'

He shrugged. 'None taken, just a simple dagger, if you would. Not iron, mind, steel. I don't want it rusting.'

'Steel still rusts if you don't take care of it,' he warned, as he picked up a couple more daggers and threw them to the back of the cart. 'Alright, so straight bladed or curved, single or double edged?'

He paused to think. 'Double edged, and straight, please. Remember; nothing too expensive.'

The stall-owner nodded, and sorted through more knives, throwing more and more back into the cart, until he had two left, both double-edged straight blades. There was a white knife, about a foot long from pommel to point, and a more expensive-looking rondel dagger with a carved wooden hilt.

'Single-edged, but beautiful, no?' the trader gestured to the rondel.

He considered both, and pointed to the knife. 'Could I have a hold of that one? To get its feel?'

The smith nodded and handed him the weapon. He fumbled and dropped it. As he bent down to pick it up, he grabbed a couple of the flat stones from the ground and concealed them in his palm. He held the knife in his hand, testing its weight, as his other hand opened the drawstring of his purse and dropped the stones inside. He nodded.

'This one's good. How much for it?'

'I'd say... two copper ingots?'

Lidan frowned. 'That would be difficult,' he grimaced, 'I only have three copper coins and a silver in my purse.'

The trader's eyes brightened. 'For that much I'll give you both, and a free leather sheath for one of them!'

He shook his head. 'I'll want a sheath for each, and wooden ones, not leather.'

Now the smith shook his head. 'I don't have a wooden scabbard for the knife, only the rondel.'

'Fine. A silver and three coppers for the two knives, a wooden scabbard, and a leather sheath, and throw in a sword-belt as well, to sweeten the deal.'

The smith narrowed his eyes. Perhaps he'd asked for too much? Four winds, what if he checked the purse? He'd already poked fun at his threadbare clothes, he might not believe he had the money.

The smith scoffed and shrugged, and turned to find the additional items.

Lidan untied the purse, the four small flat pebbles nestled inside, and held it in his hand. The smith returned with the belt, the blades already on it, and handed it over. He threw him the purse, and turned away immediately.

He walked as quickly as he dared, so as not to draw suspicion, and once he was past the tattooed guard, still shouting out to passers-by, he ran as fast as he could from the square. The guards at the food kiosk watched him disinterestedly as he raced by. Turning a corner, he was away from the weapon cart, the square, the guards, and away from danger.

Shaking with excitement, he laughed. Pride mixed with fear. He fixed the belt around his waist and drew the blades, turning them to catch the flickering rays of light from the torches. Looking at them, his excitement suddenly gave way to guilt. It was not the first time he'd stolen. As a boy he pinched loaves of bread from the village baking oven, and fruit from a neighbour's table, even a shirt once, from an older boy whom he disliked. This was the first time he'd stolen anything worth more than a few coppers at most. By the four winds! He even haggled with the smith to get more out of the one-sided deal. But he had to ask for more. Had to. Otherwise the smith might have suspected foul play, as buyers were expected to haggle with prices. The weapons would help him steal a water-skin. Maybe he could trade it for one, or simply press the blade to the bottom of a salesman's spine, to demand his wares. He swallowed hard, burying his guilt. Steal or die. He chose life.

*

He woke in a boiling hovel and sought the nearest well. Thirst sated, for now, his search continued for a water-skin. By midnight he was on his knees, hunger gnawing his empty belly, turned at each junction by the horrified storekeepers.

Dragging himself from food stall to food stall, he pleaded for an exchange; his rondel for a meal. Nobody accepted, a beggar in the slums was lower than mud. He grew desperate, lost, pathetic. Ashamed at what he'd become. But this was not his first time begging for scraps. By the four winds, it was far from his first taste of desperation. Finally, one took pity on him, and relieved him of both the dagger and wooden scabbard in exchange for a plate.

Lidan sat on a high stool at a raised bench and waited for the food to be brought to him, his head lolling around on his neck. Smiling grimly, he thought to himself just how lucky he was that this onset of weakness had only struck him when he had something to exchange for food. Before long, the stall-owner brought him his meal; a plate of tough dog-meat, a bowl of milk, and another bowl full of boiled root vegetables. He ate slowly. Nevertheless, his stomach ached, groaning like a maimed bear as the unfamiliar food stretched its walls. It spasmed, regurgitating into his throat and mouth with a fresh burn, cooled by the milk. The dog-meat was tough and stringy, probably from one of the strays. Funny, he was little more than a stray dog himself. The memory of the dog and the little girl lingered at the back of his mind. Could it be that this animal had eaten off the corpse of a thief as well? He nearly smiled at the turn in fortune.

Draining the last of the slightly-sour milk from the bowl, he thanked the stall-owner, who promptly waved him away.

He was well aware that the dagger should have bought him more food than that one meal. He probably could have paid for ten or more platefuls, but there was nothing to be done, the man was kind to accept his barter, and that was that.

Replenished, he was back to wandering the shanty town, going from street to street, the ground changing from hard-baked mud and rock nearer the outer wall to the soft, black sand blown in from the desert nearer the fringes of the slum. He avoided the market squares, which wasn't difficult, there weren't many near the fringes, it was mostly just cesspits and hovels, with the occasional set-up establishment, which were few and far between. He passed a *Gwrch,* a knowing woman. She might know what to do. The one in Weaverlodge was always full of advice, and the familiarity might be welcome. But he didn't have the coin to buy her advice. Never enough coin, and a gwrch was the last person you should ever try to trick with a pebble.

Pausing at the bottom of a street, he turned to his left and saw the black desert beckoning him, stretching away to the horizon. A barrier he would have to cross, sooner or later, something to put between him and the king's gaol. Lifting his hand, he touched his left cheek. It was still there. Perhaps different, thanks to the fat mercenary, but the mark of a prisoner was still there, no matter how it looked. That mark went bone-deep, branded right into his core. It couldn't be removed so simply.

He turned and walked back to where the slum was more heavily populated, closer to the curtain wall, where the ramshackle buildings had stood for nearly seventeen years.

As he plodded along, he heard footsteps behind him, mixed with the rhythmic beats of horseshoes. He turned and saw four outriders returning from the desert, each on foot, leading their horses through the streets by the reins. The first one raised a hand to him.

'Beggar,' he called gruffly. 'Where's the nearest market? One with a farrier and a stall selling good food.'

'I can lead you there, sir, it's easier than giving directions,' he mumbled, meekly, instinctively turning his cheek.

'I meant for you to lead us, otherwise you'd have felt the back of my blade across your thighs!' the other outriders chuckled. 'I want a place with good food, now, not your beggar's muck. Think you can manage that, boy?'

Flushing, he beckoned them to follow. He didn't have much else to do and was heading that way anyway. Besides, there was a chance they might give him a few coins as reward for leading them.

'Always ask beggars for directions,' he heard the gruff-voiced man tell his companions. 'They all know the secret ways through cities to get you places at fast as possible.'

Lidan pursed his lips. Though a beggar he may be, he hardly knew the shanty town well enough to know any shortcuts. Indeed, he mostly just wandered wherever, normally sticking within walking distance of a well, going without a specific purpose in mind. With a bit of luck, a suitable market place would drop into their path before they came across another, more gastronomically-wise beggar.

His luck held, however, as he caught the scent of food cooking, shouting, the clattering of wares, and the jingle of money. The outrider sergeant – he assumed he was a sergeant, with his gruff voice and air of command – clapped him on the shoulder with a mailed hand. His knees buckled at the blow, making him stumble. The sergeant laughed.

'We'll make our way from here, boy.'

He kicked him hard to the ground. The other three jeered and stepped over him, following their leader. One spat at him, but missed, the gob of slime spattering on the ground by his head. He glared at them as they left and was about to turn away when something hanging from the saddle of the fourth horse caught his eye; a large skin of water, maybe wine.

Later on, he wondered what madness drove him to do what he did next, what kind of desperate rage fuelled his actions, but instead of turning away from the soldiers, he followed them, hand gripping the hilt of the knife thrust through his belt.

Making sure that he was at least two dozen paces behind the outriders, he went with them into the market. He watched them approach a farrier and flick him a few coins to fit new horseshoes to their mounts. The watched them barge their way through the crowd to a food stall, place their orders, and sit at another table full of soldiers, joking and shouting in loud, obnoxious voices. Good. Keep them distracted, boys, keep them distracted.

He returned his attention to the farrier, who tied the horses to a hitching post driven into the ground and struggled to hold its leg to measure its hoof. He wove his way through the crowd and stood by the smith, gesturing to help. The young farrier smiled gratefully, instructing him wordlessly to hold up the horse's leg so he could do his work. Lidan did as commanded. He was used to horses. In Weaverlodge, he was one of the fastest riders. Only Zile was faster. He grimaced. No. Don't think about him.

Turning, he searched for the horse with the bulging water-skin. As it happened, all four had water-skins, among other little treasures. One had a bow and quiver of arrows hanging from the saddle, another had a round oak shield and a sheathed sabre. The other two had long axes hanging from the saddles. So careless of them! Someone was bound to steal such fine arms if they happened to be unguarded.

He waited until the smith had gone back to his little anvil and was busy beating a horseshoe into the desired shape for the horse. Keeping an eye on the table of soldiers, he moved round to the horse with the sabre and shield. Taking hold of the reins, he drew his knife. Licking his fingers, he put them to the beast's nostrils so that she could familiarise herself with his smell. It was years since horse-racing in Weaverlodge. Surely the ability was still there?

Slowly, ever so slowly, he sawed through the rope holding her to the hitching post. He smiled excitedly when the final strand snapped. Returning the knife to his belt, he grabbed the reins tighter and clicked his tongue to get the horse moving. Just walk her out, nice and slowly. Nobody would notice.

At that very moment, the farrier just happened to pause for a breath and glanced over. His mouth dropped open.

'What are you *doing*?'

The cry was loud enough for one of the outriders to turn around curiously. His eyes met Lidan's and he blinked stupidly. He grabbed his companion's arm and pointed.

Lidan didn't wait to see what happened next. He thrust his foot into the stirrup, swung onto the saddle, gave the reins a tug, and turned the horse around. Behind him came a clatter and a yell of fury as the soldiers hurried to stop him, but he dug his heels into the horse's flanks and she galloped out of the square into the streets.

Soon enough, he discovered why the soldiers hadn't been riding their horses in the slums. The ground was too dark to see where he was heading. The buildings were built too closely together and the streets were tight with sharp turns. Luck, however, remained by his side, and he rode his way through the slums without falling.

He broke out of the streets. The ground gave way to soft sand. He flicked the reins again, and the horse galloped faster. Far behind him, he heard the distant sounds of pursuit, but they were too far behind, having taken far too long to unhitch their mounts from the post. Before he knew it, he rode past the final outlying hut and was racing away across the black desert.

*

Two nights after leaving the city, Saviour was walking, her energy spent, her flanks heaving as she panted, desperately trying to fill her lungs with the hot, dry air. Lidan was equally exhausted, sweat dripping from his brows as he plodded along next to her to spare her his weight. That first night of riding had been the most exhilarating night of his life, galloping hard across the desert with nothing around him except darkness. On that night, Saviour was livelier, excited by the sounds of pursuit and Lidan's own anticipation. As the sun rose, he looked back to see if anyone was chasing after him, but there was no one. They'd left any pursuers far behind. He was away, free, and the world beckoned.

Saviour seemed an appropriate name for the horse, and she responded to it as if it were her name from birth. He loved her in those first few hours more than he'd loved any other animal. If he had a stable of hay and a bag full of sugar, he would have given it all to her there and then.

But Saviour started flagging at the end of the first night, and he took a turn for the worse soon after. Perhaps it was the excitement of the chase, perhaps it was the sour milk, or the unexpected large meal, or fouled water, but something set his bowels on fire. The jolting on horseback did him no favours. Any dignity he had left was lost after the tenth bout of squatting over the mud and sand, praying his body would pass whatever poison consumed his gut.

When day came, with the fierce sun blazing, they sheltered in the shadow of a small depression to sleep. The black desert was a peculiar desert, curiously flat, with the black sand often giving way to cracked, rock-hard mud. The mud was easier to ride over, but offered little in the way of shade. Some claimed the entire desert was once a great lake, hence the flat, cracked bottom. He couldn't care less. It was a desert now. There were few sand dunes and the colour of the ground soaked up the sun's heat, making it like an oven by day. By night, the lack of shelter allowed winds to pick up to tremendous speeds, which hammered him and Saviour like a tidal wave, chilling them and knocking them about like leaves.

By the time his stomach recovered, the climate was taking its toll on Saviour. He did what he could to keep her well, only riding her when his legs trembled with exhaustion, even carrying the sabre and shield himself to spare her their weight. He gave her a good share of his water, dehydrated as he was from his illness, and tore up small clumps of desert grass whenever he came across some to feed her. But the grass was gritty and lacked nutrition, and what little water he could spare wouldn't sustain her, so Saviour weakened, and her breathing quickened. To make things worse, he realised she was one of the horses in need of new shoes. Two threatened to fall off at any moment, and the overgrown heels were clearly a source of discomfort to her. He was half tempted to wrench them off himself and get it done with, but knew little and less of how to trim it down after, so he left them, muttering apologies to her. She was an understanding beast, and nuzzled his shoulder at every opportunity. It was good to have a friend again.

He shifted the shield across his shoulder. It was a heavy thing, made of oak and covered with a thin sheet of steel. Resilient as a stone wall, but half as heavy as one too. The sabre was more to his taste. Before his imprisonment, he had always preferred single-edged blades such as sabres, scimitars, and backswords. It rested on his left hip, tapping against his thigh with each step. Like a proper warrior. He could pretend, at least.

The darkness seemed to stretch on for an eternity. Two different kinds of darkness. The complete, pure black of the ground, and the prettier navy of the sky, illuminated by the moon and a thousand stars. As they trudged along the ground, he often found himself looking up at the sky, marvelling at the stars, amazed at how he'd never seen them in Crastalan. The city's shadow blotted out such beauty, and here, like him, they were free.

Freedom. The word kept him going. The lie he kept repeating to give him strength, hope, the will to continue. His plan, if you could consider it a plan, was to walk as far as he could from Crastalan.

Maybe then, when he was at the farthest point in Nefarwy, he would taste the sweet elixir of freedom.

His dreaming was cut short when he turned his attention back to the ground. A star appeared to have fallen. It twinkled feebly about a mile ahead. He gave Saviour's reins a pull, and she slowed to a halt, nickering tiredly. Staring at the light, he ran his hand along Saviour's neck, whispering to her how well she was doing, how proud he was of her. Should he bypass the light, or go to it? Who was it? Friend or foe?

He looked at Saviour again, at her overgrown nails and loose shoes. Maybe they'd be able to help? But if they were bandits or worse, goblins wandered from their Pine Wood, what would he do? He hefted the shield. He wouldn't last too long with it, it was so damn heavy, and he was so weak. But what if they had food?

In the end, hope overcame caution, and he gave Saviour some grass, a drink from his dwindling skin, and mounted. This way, he could make a quick getaway if the light was evil. He dug his heels into the horse's flanks, and she shambled along in the required direction.

The light was, of course, a little campfire, betrayed by its orange hue and faint wisp of smoke.

He was nearly within fifty metres of the fire when he realised he was being watched. It was an eerie feeling, a cold shiver in his limbs, a prickling at the back of his neck. Saviour felt it too, and she whinnied unhappily, flaring her nostrils to catch the scent of the watchers. He reined her to a halt and drew the sabre with a dull whish, the light of the fire catching on the blade.

Man and horse stood still for a few seconds, scarcely daring to breathe. He saw eyes around them. Three pairs of eyes, staring, set low in the ground, not twenty feet away. The watchers realised they'd been seen and rose together, revealing themselves in the dim light. Dreyads. Grey dreyads.

His heart fluttered. The king's scouts. Merciless, utterly deadly, and he had ridden straight into their camp. He couldn't move. They would take him back. To the dark. The pain.

One of them approached silently and held out a hand to take Saviour's reins. It was enough to snap him back to reality. He cried and swung the sword. The blade bit deep into flesh and bone. The scout grunted and dropped to the floor. Wide-eyed, he tugged hard at Saviour's reins and kicked her flanks. She galloped away from the fire, the sand streaming behind her.

Chapter 3

Lidan gasped for breath as he plunged headfirst into a line of shrubbery. He gritted his teeth as whippy branches tore through the skin of his cheek. He was being hunted. Thorns ripped open his already torn clothes, adding to his desperation as the forest pulled him back. No! Not after coming so far. Please no. The branches relinquished, and he crashed through.

He paused for breath beneath a great sycamore, what little bark that showed through the choking noose of ivy rough against the back of his head. His eyes peered through the surrounding foliage for any sign of his pursuers. When would they end this game? It had gone on for far too long. They must be tiring from it. It would soon be over. It would all be over.

He stroked his left cheek, now an ugly mess of scar tissue. A surge of relief rushed through him as he considered how fortunate he'd been to make it this far. But he wasn't free yet. The Dailas Forest was simply a barrier between him and Crastalan, one easily penetrated.

He bent low and rushed to the safety of an oak, where he took another moment's pause in the giant's shadow. He needed to keep moving. The dreyads couldn't be that far behind him. Should they catch him they'd drag him back. Then *He*'d sling him into a dungeon to await torture and torment. Not death, though. Never death. That was too kind.

He'd been running from the dreyads for well over a week. Fuelled only by a burning will to survive. Every night he would collapse exhausted into a hollow tree, or a shallow ditch, or a damp cave, and pray the trackers wouldn't find him. They were gaining, though. Each day brought them closer, and today would be his last; his pathetic few weeks of freedom now over. He snorted, 'freedom' he called it, but what kind of freedom was running for your life, living in fear of being caught again? His cell was all around him, the invisible bars made of terror. As much a prisoner as he ever was. A prisoner for life.

Saviour died eight days ago. After fleeing from the dreyads' camp, they tore across the desert without rest, both frightened, both desperate for escape. Resting only when was absolutely necessary, they allowed themselves to be driven by their need to be away from the fire. Finally, the mud and sand gave way to short, pointy grass. It fed Saviour for a while, gave her at least something to live on. Things started looking up. At times, he hoped they were no longer being followed, but he'd wounded one of them. They wouldn't let him escape out of principle. Once, when they rested on a hill for a few exhausted hours, he saw the glimmer of a fire in the distance, confirming his fears. More than that was the *feeling* of being hunted. The constant fear felt by all prey in the forests and flatlands of Enadir. They left the desert a few leagues north of the Pine Wood, but never ventured far enough south to see it. Finally, he and Saviour braved the currents of the Crisiaddwr River. It nearly killed them. Swept miles downstream by the current, they were finally deposited at the concavity of a meander. It took time to recover from the ordeal. Time enough for the dreyads to gain on them. By the river he felt watched. Perhaps not by the dreyads, but by something. A group of creatures lurking in the water, spying on him.

When Saviour finally recovered, he swung up into the saddle once again and pushed her further east, away from the staring, invisible eyes. As they raced across the flatlands separating the river from the Dailas Forest, Saviour tripped. She crashed down hard on the ground, legs sticking out awkwardly, eyes rolling as she screamed. He was thrown off her as she fell, sprawled a few paces away, and lost consciousness. He remembered the terrible silence when he woke. He remembered leaving his poor friend on the grass, dead from exhaustion and her injuries. He left her there and ran for his life into the forest. Sometime after reaching the cover of the trees, the dreyads caught up with him and began their cruel games.

Resting his hand on the hilt of his sabre, he scanned the area. The worst thing about it was the dreyads could have caught him days ago. He was sure of it. They were just toying with him, playing with him as a cat would a terrified mouse. Once they were done with him and had him in their chains, he'd be dragged back to Crastalan for more sinister games. It couldn't happen. When they finally revealed themselves, he had to die. With sword in hand, preferably, but if not, he could try to eat enough mud and stones to rip himself open from the inside. Bleed to death out of his arse on the way back. That would show them.

He froze as he heard a rustle in the branches ahead, followed by a cry. Not of surprise, of relief, of joy, or even victory. A cry of pain. There was no mistaking its lingering note.

He felt the cold fingers of panic grip his heart. Someone else had fallen foul of the trackers. Judging by how close the cry had sounded, they were only a few moments away. Death or capture was only a few moments away.

The wind died. Silence settled its choking grip on the forest. Not a sound could penetrate the deathly stillness, not a birdsong or the screeching of an insect, it was as if the whole forest held its breath and counted the seconds he had left to live. He heard his blood pounding in his ears. His eyes watered. His fingers twitched. He crouched low to the ground, readying himself for the imminent skirmish. For the tenth time during the chase, he vowed that if this was his end, he would make it an end worthy of remembrance. Or however worthy of remembrance as an insignificant escaped prisoner could be. He gripped his sabre tightly as the rustling came nearer, and out of the gloom came a shadow.

He gasped. In front of him was not a scouting party of dreyads, but a person. An individual with large dark eyes set widely apart in his skull, and no nose to speak of save for two slit-like nostrils set above a narrow mouth. He had sharp cheekbones and a pointed chin, narrow shoulders tapering to even narrower hips. It was the lithe, slim figure of a runner, a scout, an individual capable of walking for days on end while still having enough energy to wrestle a boar when he reached his destination. His skin was a startling reddish-brown colour, while his clothes were crimson, white, and black, made of wool and tough leather. Through his belt was stuck a long, slim dirk, beside which his hand hovered in caution. Strung to a loop at the back of the same belt was a small pipe, the kind a minstrel would carry. A chill ran down his spine. A daemon.

Suddenly, it looked up and turned its angular face to stare directly at him. How could it tell? He'd never made a sound. Swallowing a lump in his throat, he stepped out from his hiding place.

He stared at the creature. The daemon cast a casual eye back. He forgot his pursuers, completely captivated by the new arrival. When he was young, the village elders often spoke of the races of Enadir, from the juggernauts to the troglodytes, the fonex to the calefs. Sometimes they spoke of daemons. Any conversation about daemons always held a sense of mystery and wonder, with their curious names and hidden past, always at the heart of the greatest adventures in history. He'd always been warned against them, not to trust them, to shun them, to fear them, for none of those tales ever ended happily. However, those stories were always filled with excitement and adventure, stories worth listening to ten times over, stories that few had the honour of living. A dying race seldom seen beyond the shadows of rulers.

'Boy,' the daemon greeted, its voice soft.

'Daemon,' replied Lidan, a new excitement causing his own voice to quiver.

'What brings you here?'

'Freedom from the king,' he raised his sword sheepishly. 'I'll fight for it if I must.'

'Put it away,' smiled the daemon. 'Stolach's no friend of mine. You seek freedom? Those dreyads were for you?'

'Are they coming?' he gasped, spinning to face the trees behind, gazing into the shadows of the dense foliage.

'Relax, the dreyads are dead. They won't ever hunt another soul.'

'You killed them?' asked Lidan, unable to hide the awe in his voice. 'I thought there were at least five!'

'Four.'

'Impressive,' cooed Lidan. 'Although, we still haven't introduced ourselves. My name is Lidan.'

'Gwahl.'

'Pleased to meet you'

'Indeed. Please excuse me but I have business to attend to.'

'What business?'

'One that doesn't concern you.'

'I'm sorry. I was just curious.'

'Have you ever heard the phrase "curiosity killed the cockatrice"?'

'Yes, though I never paid it any heed,' he grinned sheepishly.

'That may explain the dreyads,' smiled Gwahl back.

'They chased me because I was a prisoner and I escaped.'

'Interesting... so were they taking you to the king and on your way there you managed to break free of your bonds?'

'No, I was a prisoner in Crastalan and I escaped,' he was reluctant to say any more. He disliked telling stories, he never thought himself a good-enough story teller to do justice to the tales. Perhaps one day he would be a better orator, but not yet. Besides, there were stories worth telling and his was not one of them, certainly not for enjoyment.

'Impressive,' echoed Gwahl. 'You managed to make it all the way to Dailas Forest. That's a tale I would very much like to hear...' he paused in thought, then said almost to himself, 'but I must reach the Council.

'The Council?' asked Lidan

The daemon shot him a look of annoyance. 'Yes, now if you'd excuse me.'

He brushed past Lidan and walked into the forest behind him. Lidan paused, watching him leave. Zile and the others, then Colrick, then Winten, then Saviour... he wouldn't, couldn't, lose another companion. He couldn't be left alone again. He followed.

He'd barely walked ten paces before the daemon disappeared behind a birch. Lidan followed as silently as he could, his flimsy shoes treading lightly on the leaf-strewn ground as he approached the tree. He looked behind it and saw nothing. Confused, he turned around swiftly, peering into the surrounding forest. Gone. Daemon magic. The elders were right. Tricky and sly as his reputation promised, Gwahl had disappeared

A hand clamped his shoulder.

'If you try to follow me, I'll have to kill you, boy.'

Lidan shrugged his shoulder away. 'Why can't I come? You said you were an enemy of the king – have *you* not heard the expression "the enemy of my enemy is my friend"?'

'You can't come because I don't know who you are, I don't know where you came from, and I don't know anything about you! How do I know the Council needs you?'

'Because I hate the king's rule…and his servants… I escaped from Crastalan, fought his soldiers; surely you don't know many others who've accomplished similar?'

'Many prisoners escape Crastalan, boy, what's impressive – and suspicious – is that you had the stamina to run so far.'

'So, I could be used for something, a scout, a runner, something useful to you?

'Unlikely.

'You don't know.

'I can guess.'

He paused, irritated by the flat refusal, frightened to be abandoned again. 'Won't you consider it?

'Why should I?

'Why should the king wish to find your little council?

'You really don't know?' asked Gwahl suspiciously.

'No, but if they oppose him I'm more than willing to join you!'

Gwahl chuckled. 'You should not be so ready to give your allegiance to an organisation you know nothing about.

'You oppose the king, it's all I need to know.'

The daemon thought for a moment. 'Very well. I'll take you with me. They can decide what to do with you.'

'Thank you!' he shouted his relief. 'Now I have something to do other than run from soldiers.'

'Indeed,' said Gwahl, before turning sharply and setting off through the trees in an easterly direction. 'Just so you know,' he said over his shoulder, 'although your stamina is apparently great, it isn't nearly good enough to be a scout or runner for the Council. A common soldier, however, you might make. Or a servant. Probably a servant. Always handy to have a few around the place.'

Lidan smiled at the remark but said nothing. The slight smirk Gwahl wore as he said it suggested it was a jest, but he couldn't be sure. Teasing, joking, playful conversation were all part of having someone with you. All part of companionship.

As they walked, Lidan asked Gwahl about himself, but the daemon wouldn't answer in any depth

'I am a daemon. I do as daemons do,' he said

'Which is?' he prompted.

Gwahl shrugged. 'My people are from a forgotten island across the seas. I spent a good deal of my life wandering Enadir, mostly here, Nefarwy, and I am sympathetic towards the cause of the Council. Some time ago it was brought to my attention they were gathering troops, and my presence was asked for, so now I go.'

'This Council, what is it?'

'An enemy of Stolach.'

'Yes, but what *is* it? What does it do? When was it formed? How does it oppose him?'

'As all rebellions do.'

'Like outlaws?'

'No, outlaws have only personal agendas. We fight for change.'

'What kind of change?'

'Change from Stolach.'

'In what way?'

'Every way that matters.'

He tripped over a tangle of roots. Recovering, he skipped to catch up with Gwahl, who hadn't slowed down.

'Can we change our path? I was avoiding roads while the dreyads were after me, now they're gone, won't it be easier to get there on a beaten track?'

'Perhaps, if you don't mind the rogues and outlaws.'

'But isn't that who we're looking for?'

'No, we're going to the Council.'

'Aren't these rogues with you as well?'

'No!' he nearly shouted. 'Don't you listen? Gorgon's teeth! We aren't common outlaws or highwaymen, we are an opposition, a rebellion. The roads are full of bandits and rogues, they'd pounce on the two of us without hesitation.

'We could stay on the safe ones?'

'They're only safe if they're regularly patrolled by the king's soldiers. I can't imagine you'd like to run into them, would you?'

He shrugged. 'But it's difficult trudging through the wild forest.'

'Then turn back.'

He glared at him. 'You know I can't.'

'Then don't complain,' he softened his tone. 'It is for our safety we stay away from the beaten tracks. The brigands and thieves of the unguarded roads are ruthless. Rebels without cause. You wouldn't want to run into them.'

'Rebels without cause?' he repeated.

'Indeed.'

'What's the Council's cause?'

Gwahl rolled his eyes. 'If it'll keep you quiet... it is an organised rebellion, a group of free creatures who have renounced the crown in favour of the high chancellors, their leaders.'

'In what way are they more organised?'

Gwahl paused, considering the question. 'I suppose in their breadth, their reach. Nowadays, very few corners of the Midlands are ignorant to their name. You must be one of the special ones.'

'Lucky me.'

Gwahl snorted. 'Perhaps I should take it as a humbling thought, that there are still untouched villages in Midlands to recruit from. Clearly our influence is not as far-reaching as we hoped.'

'The Council, the chancellors, how are they better than the king?' he asked.

Gwahl looked as though he might smile for a moment, but didn't. 'They are elected by the members of the Council, and as the rulership would be divided between them, no single individual can stand above others as a tyrant.'

'How many chancellors are there?'

'There are usually around four leaders, though the number isn't constant, sometimes there are more, sometimes fewer. It once dropped to be as low as two, when the rebellion was nearly destroyed by Stolach, but it clung to life, and has grown ever since.'

'Who are they?'

'A secret. To protect them.'

'And they're definitely better than the king?'

'That is for the people to decide, I suppose. But, they have vowed to listen to the pleas of all, no matter who they are or where they are, as Stolach once promised, but ignored.'

'So, they are trying to usurp the throne, not destroy it?'

Gwahl frowned at Lidan. 'Why would they want to destroy it? The land needs ruling. If the people of the Midlands were to live with no governance, then the land would eventually collapse into anarchy, and return to the chaos that swept over the lands before Stolach came to power. The Council understands that such a power is needed, though our current tyrant has abused that power, or directed its potentials incorrectly. Is that not the answer you were expecting? Because if you want to remove everybody from any sort of rulership, I fear that the Council is not the place for you to be, boy.'

'No, it's just that, when you said you opposed the king, I assumed you meant you were fighting for freedom.'

'I am fighting for freedom, for liberty, as is the Council; liberty from a fonex who isn't ruling as he should be. What you perceive as 'freedom' is chaos. Should we abandon the people of the Midlands to total unrestraint, then you would be begging for some kind of rulership.'

Lidan clicked his tongue against the roof of his mouth, and thought over what the daemon had said. The creature seemed to know what he was talking about, although he thought that the inhabitants of the Midlands were of a better quality than to descend into total madness. He said as much to Gwahl, who actually *did* smile this time.

'You are so young.'

Lidan huffed at the condescension, but had more questions. 'So when did it start? The Council, I mean.'

Although he himself hated accounting any tales, he adored listening to them, and whenever an opportunity presented itself, he would be the first to drop what he was doing to listen. People had told him in the past that he had a talent for drawing out stories, like prising a snail from its shell he could twist and tug them out of the speakers. Most people were all too happy to tell stories, to listen to the sound of their own voices as they recounted their adventures. Gwahl was not like these people, and spoke with a hint of boredom, as if he were filling Lidan in on an uninteresting military report.

'It was formed around fifteen summers ago, quite soon after Stolach completely took over the Midlands.

'Who started it?

'Aren't you full of questions.'

'I want to know!'

'I can tell. It's not especially interesting.'

'It is to me!'

'Well, there's no harm in learning history. They began as three individuals, two old men, and a brave woman. It was they who first brought people together, travelling from village to village, showing the people the poisonous reality of Stolach's rule. Years later, the rebellion had spread throughout the majority of the villages in Dailas. Obviously, not everyone in each village joined, the majority were satisfied with bending their knees to Stolach and saw the Council as common outlaws.'

'So it wasn't just me. If you say you oppose the king, then "outlaw" is what people will think.'

'Perhaps once. In the near future, they will think "liberator". Or at least they will when speaking of the Council.'

'Maybe if they weren't so secret, more people will know who they are, what their intentions are. More people might be inclined to join.'

'That's exactly what's happening now. And as I said, it isn't such a secret, not these days. Do you want to know how it was formed or not?'

He nodded, reprimanded.

Gwahl sighed and paused for rest against the rotting trunk of a fallen chestnut tree.

'Eventually the king tracked down the three pioneers to the rebellion and slew the two men. The woman set about with a renewed enthusiasm, and the numbers swelled. She organised them, held secret meetings and gatherings, always in the shadows, in the darkness, out of sight. When they had the basis of a militia, they banded together in the Dailas Forest and started attacking the king's soldiers. Eventually she was caught and killed, and the rebels elected four members amongst themselves to stand as the first high chancellors, and they melted away once more into the shadows. They continued her work gathering troops and members, and more and more people came to join. In recent months they once again stepped out of the shadows and began launching raids. Now, they seem to have decided to gather everyone, all their members across all of Enadir, from over mountains, rivers, and seas. I don't know why, before you ask, I just know that's what's happening. The secret is very much out for the world to know.'

Gwahl waited for a response, but Lidan had none, considering the tale carefully. It all seemed so exciting, so much grander and meaningful than his own little rebellion. One thing was for sure, something so organised and far-reaching would never meet such a disastrous, awful end as his attempts.

Lidan noticed the only weapon Gwahl carried was the dirk through his belt. And although it was indeed elegant, nearly eighteen inches long with a glittering emerald pommel stone and an intricate scabbard, he doubted Gwahl would be able to hold his own against an opponent armed with a longer blade. When asked if he had any other weapons concealed in the folds of his cloak, Gwahl smiled.

'It's my only one, made by my own hands. It's one of our traditions to make our own weapons. Besides, I don't need any other.' Lidan snorted, earning a disapproving look. 'I don't jest, Lidan. I tailored this weapon to fit me perfectly; it's as much a part of me as my arm.'

Again, Lidan shook his head. 'I bet I could easily beat you with my sabre.'

Gwahl's eyes twinkled. 'Is that so? If you ask me, that particular sabre is more of a weapon for a mounted man, it won't serve you as well on foot. All that weight in the foible? Slow and cumbersome. Get an arming sword, it'll serve you better.'

'I prefer single-edged swords. Besides, if you only have that dirk you could never stand up to an enemy with a longer blade. You'd never get close enough to kill them.'

Gwahl laughed. 'Very well, strike me with that ungainly blade at you belt!'

He made as if to turn away, but at the last moment, whipped out his sabre and slashed at Gwahl's unprotected flank, trying to catch him off guard. Gwahl simply swayed to one side, expertly evading the flailing blade. Time after time Lidan lunged and hacked and slashed at Gwahl, and each time the daemon merely swayed slightly and allowed the sword to pass within a hair's breadth of his body, the faint smirk ever present on his lips. Anger bubbled up inside his chest. He'd show him the price of arrogance. He'd show him he deserved respect.

Drawing back his arm, ready to deliver a crushing blow to his head, and the daemon made his move. With a swiftness that would make a falcon blush, Gwahl darted around, disarming him in the process with a quick tap to the back of his hand. Gently, he pressed the jet black, double-edged blade of his dirk to the small of Lidan's back.

'So how much did you bet?'

*

Night soon fell, enveloping the forest in gloomy shadow, and Gwahl announced an end to the day's travels. They made their camp under a willow beside a trickling stream of crystal-clear water. Gwahl sat himself down beside the gnarly trunk and closed his eyes. Still smarting from his ignominious defeat, Lidan slumped next to him, glaring moodily at the stream.

Gwahl opened an eye. 'Don't sulk like a spoilt kitten, Lidan — you should embrace your defeat as a chance to improve your swordsmanship. You didn't really do that badly, some of your strikes were quite skilled. Besides, when we reach the Council there'll be plenty of time to improve. Captain Spotal might be there, and I assure you that after a few lessons with him your prowess with a sword will blossom.'

'Who?' he asked sullenly, not entirely convinced that defeat should be embraced.

'Captain Spotal, an old friend of mine,' replied Gwahl. 'Possibly one of the greatest swordsmen within recent generations, save perhaps for Stolach himself. He's beaten just about everyone who's ever challenged him.'

'Did he beat you?'

'The first time I sparred with him, he disarmed and beat me in a grand total of two minutes. I got closer the second time- I lasted three and a half.'

Lidan smiled. Perhaps the daemon wasn't as invincible as he seemed. 'How many times have you duelled?'

Gwahl paused for a moment. 'We've sparred quite often, more times than I can remember, but I know I've only beaten him ... four times?'

'He's that good?' he groaned.

'Don't worry,' chuckled Gwahl. 'Give yourself time and you'll be more than a match for anyone. Now get some sleep, we won't reach the Council anytime soon.'

*

He was chained to a cold stone wall. Before him was a rusty iron door. The manacles dug in, raw flesh at his wrists blistering and chafing against the rusted iron. Screams and moans of other prisoners echoed all around, waxing and waning like the tides of pain wracking his body. A bowl of muddy water lay in one corner of his cell, too far to reach. He could only watch the glimmering liquid with thirsty eyes. Scraps of food lay across the floor, all in different stages of decomposition. Strung up like game, ready for slaughter. A wound on his flank throbbed, burned. He could feel the stretch of swollen skin, the ache of infection, the stench of pus intermittently discharging from its depths. One wound of many.

Another rasping breath from his parched throat, an ugly guttural sound that echoed from the bare walls of his empty cell. His clothes hung in rags around his skeletal frame, clinging limply to his lifeless limbs.

Diseased. Tortured. Pathetic.

Deserved.

The cell door opened. A man entered. His gaoler. Burly body swaying on tiny sticks of legs, trailing behind a cat o' nine tails, small copper balls at the end of each strand clinking as he swaggered. He groaned. Was it time already?

The gaoler reached up to unshackle him. He stank of unwashed sweat and onions. The manacles clicked open, sending him tumbling to the ground in a heap, legs devoid of any semblance of strength. The gaoler growled something. Too weak to care, he lay as he was. The whip clattered against the ground by his face, sending a shower of sparks as copper met stone. He didn't move, vision clouded by the after-glow of the sparks, a thousand blissful dots of colour in the darkness. Strong hands caught him beneath the arms and dragged him across the floor, scraping knees and feet as he went. The gaoler hawked and spat on him, the trickle of slime on his neck familiar, almost cooling. Through a corridor, dark as his cell, past barred doors, to the correction room.

Heart quivering with a fear his body was incapable of responding to, he merely whimpered. The gaoler sniggered at the sound. Adjusting his arms around his waist, he held him tighter. A firm hand pressed against the festering wound on his flank, sending a new spasm of pain shooting up his body. Something burst, a strange relief. The gaoler cursed and dropped him, pus and blood covering his hand.

'Dirty bastard! Slug! Got your stink on me!'

He lay panting on the cold stone floor, the ache in his flank subsiding. Better. Momentary relief.

'You'll pay, scum,' the whip clacked again. He didn't flinch. 'You'll pay.'

Hands around his armpits again, hauling him up. The damp chill of the dungeons faded as he was dragged to an oppressive heat, as unpleasant as the chill that preceded it. He wilted as the roar of the furnace grew loud. Terribly familiar.

Whimpering, he was flung into a chair.

Lips moving wordlessly, his throat too raw to make a sound, his head followed the gaoler as he circled. It wouldn't have mattered. Scream, whisper, beg, bargain. It all ended the same way.

The gaoler approached the furnace, heat-proof apron over his bulging stomach. He reached into the glow and pulled out a long poker, circular head glowing like a star. He twirled it around his wrist, grinning like a twisted child. He brought it to Lidan's flank.

Skin sizzled, bubbled, popped like bottles of wine. At first nothing, then the burn as the heat of the poker found healthy flesh.

He gasped, breath catching, ribs aching, the stench of scorched flesh and burning pus rancid in his nostrils.

It withdrew, back to the furnace. The gaoler looked at him over his shoulder, a wider smile on his broad face.

He approached again, tip of the poker smoking faintly.

His hand closed around his face like a vice, too strong to struggle against. He could only roll his eyes as the poker approached again, not his flank. His cheek.

Skin spitting, churning, he finally found his voice to scream.

*

Lidan woke panting. He looked around in panic. Dailas Forest, not Crastalan. Not the gaols. Relaxing, he saw Gwahl observing him with calm eyes.

'Bad dream?' asked the daemon.

'Yes,' whispered Lidan. 'A terrible nightmare.'

'Crastalan?'

'Yes,' repeated Lidan. 'The dungeons. I'm sorry if I woke you.'

'You didn't,' smiled Gwahl. 'I was already awake. Will you need more sleep?'

'No.'

'Very well, we may as well start off again, not much else to do around here,' Gwahl got up and stretched. 'I'll find us some food on the way.'

They trudged through the undergrowth for some time, munching on the multitude of berries Gwahl harvested. He was grateful the daemon hadn't asked him for details of his dream. Some-memories were better left unexplored. They walked for hours in silence, broken by the occasional muttering of Gwahl as he navigated his way through the wood. Lidan remained silent, lost in his memories, the scar on his cheek throbbing all the while.

Around midday Gwahl stopped abruptly. He did the same. The daemon stared at the silent forest for a few seconds, then turned and dived on top of him, dragging him to the floor.

He pressed his hand to his mouth.

'Don't make a sound. There are a group of creatures close by, they haven't seen us yet. I'd rather keep it that way.

'Now, you see that log to your left? In the middle of those nettles? Good. When I say go, you'll crawl across and lie under it. You'll stay there until I give you permission to move, do I make myself clear?'

'Where will you go?' he whispered back as the hand relaxed from his mouth.

'I'll be right behind you. Don't panic if you lose sight of me for a while, just stay quiet and keep your head down. Now, go!'

He crawled on his stomach to the log, ignoring the bite of the nettles. As promised, Gwahl was nowhere to be seen. He waited.

He lay as he was for a good ten minutes, gripping his knife and straining his eyes and ears for the slightest sign of his companion. Suddenly he heard a loud yelp followed by harsh shouts and the unmistakable plucking of bowstrings. After thirty seconds of clamour, silence settled back over the forest. His heart kept hammering. Where was Gwahl? He didn't dare move. An earwig crawled over his cheek, but he couldn't muster the courage to brush it away. Where was he?

Without warning a voice sounded from atop the log.

'Come out, my friend, danger has passed.'

He jumped. He hadn't heard anyone approach. Cautiously, he ventured from his hide. Gwahl was lying nonchalantly on the log, idly chewing a stem of grass.

'For how long have you been there?' he demanded, shaken.

'A minute, maybe. I wanted to see how long you could stay under there and not give yourself away. I applaud your stealth. Had I not known you were there I would've walked right by.'

'What was that noise?' he asked, curtly. Was everything a game to the daemon?

'Nothing. Just a wandering group of thieves, walking in the wrong part of the forest. I frightened them away.'

'I heard bowstrings.'

'Of course, nobody's foolish enough to travel through the Dailas Forest without some sort of protection. Besides, as I said they were thieves, folk like that need weapons, eh?'

'How's this the wrong part of the forest?'

'A bit close to us for my liking, and heading in the same direction. Rogue bands of defected soldiers and gangs of thieves like that are dangerous, not to be trusted or associated with. They only make things difficult for all of us.'

'How so?'

'By robbing provision trains and travellers between villages, killing Stolach's soldiers out on patrol, harassing folk coming to join our cause, generally making a nuisance of themselves.'

'If they're robbing from the king surely that's a good sign? They might help the Council if you asked?'

'Weren't you listening? They're rogues – out for themselves and their own little gangs, they are as against us as they are against Stolach. They attack our scouting parties and steal our food. I'd normally pursue and kill them but I thought you'd prefer it if I remained with you.'

'Are there really that many of them?'

'Far more than you might think. You're lucky you didn't run into one before I found you, seeing as you don't have much worth stealing they might have simply cut you down where you stood. As I said, best to stay away from the roads. Anyway, we still have far to go.'

Chapter 4

For three more days, the daemon led him through the woods, strolling through the trees seemingly without a care in the world. Lidan enjoyed it, the peace, the confidence of the daemon. Something about his manner promised safety, and despite his frequent warnings of danger in the forest, it all seemed distant next to Gwahl. He needed this respite, this peace, after everything he'd been through, the peacefulness the daemon exuded was like a balm to blistered skin. Watching him now, ambling so casually, it seemed this curious creature was almost a part of the forest, as if he knew instinctively everything that was going on around him.

Once, the daemon played a tune on his pipe, a merry little jingle as they walked through the trees, answered gaily by the blackbirds in the boughs above their heads. It was a wonderful instrument, delicately carved from cherry-wood, with a beautiful copper fipple and decorative bands. The notes that sprung forth from its six holes were piercing but gentle, lifting his spirits as he trotted behind his companion. All too soon it was over, the daemon tied the pipe to his belt, and he was left to wait in anticipation for the encore that never came. As he followed Gwahl, he studied the instrument, and eventually realised the intricate patterns of lines, loops, and half circles along its length were runes of a foreign language.

'Where did you come from, Gwahl?' he asked, breaking the normal silence of their walk, keen for another story.

'I told you, I come from an island far away.'

'No, I meant where did you *just* come from.'

'What do you mean?'

'As in, where were you when you decided to go back to the Council?'

'Oh, I see, I was wandering the woods, as I normally do. I first heard the chancellors were gathering everyone together when I was much further north, around the foothills of Iadden, that's when I started south to reconvene.'

'You've come a very long way!' he exclaimed.

'I'm used to travelling,' Gwahl shrugged. 'It's my life.'

'Your entire life is just travelling across Nefarwy?'

'Nefarwy and all of Enadir.'

'Why? Why don't you find a home to stay?'

'Enadir is my home! I have the best, biggest home anyone could ask for, why should I shut myself away into one corner of Enadir when she has such wonderful places to visit?'

'To have a place to call your own, to raise a family and grow old?'

'I'm already old. Besides, that life doesn't appeal to me. I prefer to go places, be everywhere and anywhere my heart takes me.'

'But why? What's the point of it?'

'What's the point of living in a little house and having a family? Does there have to be a point? Can we not just live our lives as we wish and watch it open up before us? Just because you want to shut yourself away from the wide world and raise a family – a noble life, don't get me wrong – it doesn't mean everyone does.'

Lidan shook his head, 'That's not what I want, perhaps I wanted it once, but not anymore, not since everything fell apart. At least not right now.'

'So, what do you want now?'

'Freedom.'

'Well congratulations,' Gwahl gestured to the open forest, 'freedom is yours!'

'No, this isn't freedom,' he paused, struggling to find the words. 'When I escaped the dungeons, I thought I was free, but then I realised Crastalan was as much a prison as my old cell. Once I left the city, I was trapped in the slums, the sand dunes the bars to my cage. When I finally left the town and set out across the desert, I still wasn't free,' he paused again. He wanted to share it with Gwahl, the burden. He wanted to trust someone again. 'I realised no matter how far away from my cell I travelled, I'd never be free of what happened. I'm still afraid. Still… guilty.'

'You think your goal unobtainable, your fear unconquerable? It's only through holding such thoughts that they grow in power.'

His thoughts turned to Zile and the others from Weaverlodge; Ledahaf, Zuk, and the others. He remembered the hope, the reality, the desperation. He remembered the grey-eyed general. The gaol. His nightmares.

He swallowed, looking at Gwahl again. 'No. I know how to reach my goal. I'll never be able to outrun my fears, but I can fight against them. By joining you, the Council, I can actively battle the cause of fears, and once we win, I'll reach my goal, have my revenge, and find my freedom.'

Gwahl nodded and smiled. 'Alright you've already convinced me to bring you to the Council, no need to give me these inspiring speeches.'

He blushed. 'No, that's not what that was, I meant it. The only way I can truly have my freedom is if the king is overthrown, and his generals and soldiers all gone. Right now, what I want is to fight him.'

'Excellent, you'll fit right in with the others. But let me ask you, what will you do after that? Once Stolach is defeated and your freedom is won, what then?'

'Whatever I want. I suppose I'd like that life that you hate so much; a home, a family, and land to work on. It'd be good to live like that.'

The exact life he'd abandoned. If only he'd known how precious such a life was he might not have thrown it away in childish pursuit of something more.

'That's exactly my point. Once you have true, uncompromised freedom you can do whatever you want with your life. When you have your freedom, you'll live in peace and raise a family. When I have my freedom, I'll do what I want, and keep wandering Enadir, because that's what freedom is to me.'

Lidan paused. '"When" you have your freedom?'

Gwahl smiled wanly and looked at him. 'Very observant. This may surprise you, Lidan, but you're not the only one whose life is dependent on Stolach's defeat. Everyone in Nefarwy will soon be imprisoned by this war. I wasn't wandering the woods in my usual idle way, I've not done so for a good thirty years, not since Stolach,' he paused, then added quietly. 'Not since before him, even.'

'So what were you wandering the woods for?'

'For ways to defeat him. Clues, secrets, allies, anything that can help us in our plight. I was away for a while a few years ago for other reasons, but now I'm back to focus on this.'

'Other reasons?'

'Daemon business.'

'Sounds intriguing.'

'Not a topic for discussion.'

His tone suggested there was no debating the matter. A hardness to his voice, killing that topic of conversation before it had time to flourish. Upsetting the daemon was the last thing he wanted to do.

'Does the Council send you on quests?' his asked after a second.

Gwahl laughed, relaxing. 'No, I am something of a free agent, you might say. I act of my own volition.'

'Oh,' his excitement waned. 'Then why fight? Do you have something against the king?'

The daemon smiled. 'Something against the way he's ruled the Midlands, that's all.'

'I suppose I'm the same, in a way.'

'But you have a very good, very personal reason to be against Stolach,' frowned Gwahl. 'He shut you away in a cell, after all.'

'It was one of his generals who sentenced me, not the king himself. Sure, I'd like a personal sort of revenge against that general, but King Stolach needs to go. If it weren't for him, many things would be different.'

'Honestly, they'll make you a high chancellor with all of these inspiring quotes,' chuckled Gwahl.

He smiled, embarrassed, 'So anyway, you were in the Mountains of Iadden looking for allies, heard the Council were gathering their troops, and decided to come back?'

'Indeed.'

'How did they know where to find you? If you wander as much as you do, and weren't sent up to Iadden, how did they know where you were?'

'They didn't. I passed through a village which had just received word of the Council gathering, the elder being a long-time supporter of the cause. They were preparing to travel down south. I kept myself hidden away, as I have to nowadays, so none of them saw me, but I heard what I needed to.'

'Why did you have to keep yourself hidden?' Lidan frowned. 'Surely they were allies?'

'Not because of my allegiance to the Council,' Gwahl smiled.

'Then why?'

He gestured to himself. 'Daemon. Folks tend not be too warm to us these days, even among allies.'

He thought back to the warnings given by his village elders on daemons. Never trust them. Yet here he was, revealing all his hopes and fears to one he'd just met. Foolish? He looked at Gwahl again. No. He *could* trust him. He'd saved him, after all.

'I honestly didn't realise how big the Council was,' he shook his head, changing the subject. 'All the way to Iadden. If only I'd known sooner.'

'So you can imagine my surprise you hadn't heard of it,' Gwahl smiled. 'Where are you from again?'

'Weaverlodge. It's in the grasslands plains south of the Black Desert.'

'I see, makes sense now. There are quite a few villages down there, some friendlier than others.'

'Yes, but the plains are vast, and we're quite isolated from each other.'

'I know, which is why it makes sense that you didn't know about the Council. It's likely our agents never reached your village, especially considering its proximity to Crastalan. Why did you leave?'

He flinched at the question. 'We were poor,' as if that were explanation enough. He shook his head. It would be good to explain himself, cathartic. 'Our and the main trades were in farming crops and selling hay, woven baskets, or linen made from the dried grass and flax of the plains. A group of us decided to leave for Crastalan in hope for a better future, riches and the like, same old story I'm sure a thousand other fools have told on their way to the city, but it wasn't to be. We were poor, and in our desperation, did… foolish things,' he took a breath, willing himself to share the full story. He could trust Gwahl, reveal his secrets, confide in a new friend.

Except he couldn't even face it himself.

'We were imprisoned for it. I'm the only one left.'

'Will you return, do you think? To Weaverlodge?'

And face the villagers? His aunt and uncle? To lay bare his failings and tell them why it was him, and him alone who returned from Crastalan? He shuddered.

'Never.'

Gwahl nodded. He didn't press the matter further. The conversation ended, and they lapsed back into their steady, silent walk.

Part of him wished he could go back, but not as he was now, rather as a returning hero, laden with glory and riches from his journey, bringing a new age of wealth and prosperity to the village. Not that it would ever be enough to compensate for their loss. All the gold in the world would be nothing but cold metal in the face of his failures, of the emptiness of the village. So he'd stay away, take the cowardly route, hide from their judgment, and seek retribution by fighting the root cause for their troubles.

As they trudged in silence, Gwahl handed him a fistful of blackberries. Exactly when and where he'd found them was anyone's guess, but he took them gratefully. A master forager, it seemed, but of course he would be, if he spent his life wandering the woods, he'd have plenty of experience finding food. In fact, he was so good at it that Lidan suspected the daemon was purposefully leading them from one food source to another. After the fifth handful of blackberries seemingly from nowhere, along with two apples, a bunch of mushrooms, and even a wild onion, it was getting a bit much. As they rested for a late lunch, Gwahl handed him yet another handful of walnuts, skilfully prised open with the aid of a sharp stone. He held up his hands in protest and patted his stomach,

'Please, no more, I won't be able to walk if you keep feeding me like this!'

'You're too thin, you need to eat more to regain your strength. At our pace you shouldn't get any cramps, it might actually help with digestion.'

'I'll go to sleep if I eat too much.'

'You'll collapse with exhaustion if you don't. There's nothing to you. After the journey you've had as well, lugging that big old thing,' he leaned over and tapped the oak and iron shield. 'I'd leave it here if I were you, it's not doing you any good.'

'But I've carried it all the way from Crastalan!'

'You've also carried your fleas all the way from Crastalan, do you want to keep them too?'

'But I'll need it when we reach the Council, for fighting the king.'

'I doubt you'd be able to lift it high enough for it to do you any good in a fight. You'll be provided more suitable weapons once we reach the Council.'

'I don't care, it's mine, it means something to me. Besides, I'm stronger than I look. I might not be the biggest in the world but I have a strong body. Everyone always said that. The shield will serve me well.'

Gwahl made a humming noise, clearly unconvinced, and handed him another handful of nuts. 'So where did you learn how to fight?'

'Back home, in my village.'

'Obviously, but who taught you?'

'There was a man, a retired sailor, he lived alone in a little hut. My friends and I would go and listen to his stories of his adventures on the Great Waters, battling pirates and seeking treasures. He still had his old weapons; some daggers, sickles, a couple of cutlasses. Twice a week, after doing our daily chores, we'd go and spar with each other while he watched and gave advice.'

'Your only experience of fighting is with untrained youths using old cutlasses from a washed-up seaman?'

'He was nice, and I learned a lot! You said earlier that some of my attacks were skilful! And besides, that's not my only experience. Several times I went with some of the men to another village, at the estuary of Crisiaddwr. The journeys brought us close to the Pine Woods, and we were sometimes attacked by goblins. I always helped the men fight them, and we never lost a battle. I've even killed a couple, so I know what it's like.'

'Ah, so you have at least *some* experience of combat. At least the cutlasses explain your preference for single-edged blades. As I said before, you'll get taught more refined swordsmanship when we arrive. We can't have you going into battle without proper instruction.'

*

That evening, they rested near a shallow cave, its walls and floor covered in a soft moss to rest their heads against. They ate and chatted, watching the weather turn first to a light drizzle, then a heavy downpour as the grey skies above emptied their load on the forest below. Safe inside their little cave, they watched the falling rain.

He enjoyed watching rain, especially when he was nice and dry under a shelter. When he was younger, he would sit in the doorway to his home and gaze at the falling sheets of water, his back warmed by the fire inside. He leaned back and removed his shoes, relaxing against the soft cushion of moss. Gwahl, however, refused to light a fire, worried the smoke would draw unwanted attention. Looking at the daemon now, he seemed on-edge, agitated, perched on a rock, peering through narrowed eyes at the cave entrance.

'Is something wrong?' asked Lidan

'Just a feeling,' he replied, never taking his eyes from the rain.

'Don't you like the rain?'

'There's nothing wrong with rain, only what it might bring.'

He looked at the daemon. 'Do you mean like a cold? As long as we stay in the dry, we should be alright.'

'No, Lidan, not like a cold. We should leave, spend the night under the trees. Come on.' He jumped off the rock and began gathering his things.

Lidan stood. 'Why? We'll be drenched if we go outside! It's nice and dry here.'

61

'Exactly, which means others will come for shelter. It's safer for us outside. You might get a little wet, but a disturbed sleep is better than a permanent one.'

'There's nobody around,' he said, beckoning to the drenched trees outside. 'And look, it's nearly dark. I don't particularly want to wander around the forest at night.'

A soft breeze blew directly into the cave, sending a few raindrops pattering against their legs as they stood together in the entrance. Gwahl's head whipped around and he stared outside, before picking up Lidan's shield and thrusting it into his arms.

'People *are* coming, my friend, and I don't want them to see us. There's no time for arguing, just come.'

'Alright wait a minute,' he replied, miserably. 'Just let me get some things together.'

'Hurry up,' hissed Gwahl. Lidan moved slowly, taking time to put his shoes back on as he attempted to delay leaving the crisp dryness of the cave. Gwahl looked at him, pointedly.

'Alright I'll be just outside, I'm going to give the area a quick scout. When I come back we're leaving straight away, understood?'

He nodded, and the daemon stole away into the rain. In the receding light, he was almost immediately lost from sight. Gathering his belongings, he struggled to make everything as waterproof as possible.

He froze at the sound of unfamiliar voices outside, approaching the cave. It was difficult to hear what they were saying over the thrumming of the rain, but there were at least three of them. Three strangers. Frightened, he whipped his head around, searching for an escape route. None but the cave mouth. Shadows of strangers were silhouetted against the rain outside.

Afraid, he shrank to the back, drawing his sabre and raising his shield. Where was Gwahl?

A gruff voice cut across his thoughts. 'By the four winds! Bloody weather! Look at me, I look like a filthy, sodden rat!'

'Nothing new there, then,' said another in a drawling slur.

'Shut your filthy mouth,' said the first voice, 'or I'll shut it for you. Disgusting creature.'

'Both of you be quiet, just get into the cave,' said someone else in an annoyed, but authoritative tone.

Four figures strode through the curtain of falling rain into the cave, shaking themselves off. There were two hanex, a satorr, and a large hulking juggernaut. All of them carried bags filled to the brim, and all carried an assortment of weapons. The juggernaut had a large warhammer, the satorr and one of the hanex carried swords, while the other hanex had a shortbow. He watched them with wide eyes as they lounged about the cave's mouth. The satorr spoke, and Lidan recognised him as the source of the first voice.

'Koli, why does Heren have to come in here? This cave is small enough without him taking up half the room, and he stinks too. I'll never get any sleep with that odour filling the air.'

The juggernaut glowered at him, and muttered something unintelligible, before taking a massive swig from a water-skin, presumably filled with some sort of liquor judging by the juggernaut's drunken slurs. The satorr looked at him with an expression of disgust and turned to one of the hanex.

'Why is the drunken fool here? Just send him outside.'

The hanex, presumably Koli, approached the juggernaut and gently took the water-skin away from him. The juggernaut growled in protest.

'Give it to me,' he said – revealing himself to be the third voice. 'You've drunk enough for today.'

The juggernaut bared his teeth at the hanex and knocked him away with a sweep of a mighty arm. The water-skin snapped off its strap and flew through the air to land at the satorr's feet, who kicked it forcefully outside. Heren roared again and rushed outside to search for it.

Shaking his head, the satorr helped Koli to his feet.

'Honestly, that brute is no good for us, none at all.'

'He has his uses. I'd sooner have him as a friend than an enemy.'

'I'd sooner be rid of him. Why did you bring him? Us three could have slipped away easily enough without him slowing us down.

Had I known I'd be living with that stink I would never have left the others.'

'And go head-to-head against Council soldiers? Don't make me laugh. Pahag's mad if he thinks anyone will follow him against them, or the king. We were wise to take our chances on our own.'

'I still reckon we'd have a better chance without that damned drunk.'

'Just get some rest, will you? And don't provoke him anymore; you don't want an angry juggernaut at your throat. Dirdin, what's the matter?'

Lidan looked at the second hanex, the one with the shortbow. His heart skipped a beat as he realised that he was staring at him, an arrow drawn in the bow and pointed at his chest. Trembling, he crouched lower behind the shield.

'Well, what do we have here?' the satorr grinned evilly, drawing his rusty sword. 'A trespasser, loitering around the back of our cave.'

'What's your name?' asked Koli, whose hand was creeping towards his own sword as he eyed Lidan's sabre.

Lidan said nothing, but watched them fearfully as they slowly crept towards him. He knew there was no escape. He'd been cornered from the moment they stepped in from the rain. Carefully, he moved back to a little corner, so that rock was on both sides of him. In this position, he was completely protected on both sides, and the only direction they could come at him was from the front, and so long as he had his shield, he should be able to live for long enough for his friend to come back. His eyes jumped between the three and the cave's mouth, hoping to see Gwahl charge through and save him.

'Do you have anything valuable?' the satorr stepped closer. 'If you give them to us we might let you leave, we're kind like that.'

The shortbow-armed hanex looked him up and down, lip curled, and said in a slightly nasal voice. 'I don't think that he has anything of value. Look at him. Bloody beggar.'

'He has good weapons,' said the satorr. 'I quite fancy that nice-looking sabre. Shield might be a bit heavy for me, but Heren might like it. I'll give it to him as an apology for the name-calling.'

'No, I'll take the shield,' said Koli. 'I've been in need of a new one for a while.'

They were now within three paces of Lidan, and he lunged forward half-heartedly, swinging his sabre in a wild slice through the air. That made them jump back a little, but he knew they would soon attack him properly.

'Stay back!' he cried, trying to sound brave and strong. 'This cave is mine. My companions will be returning soon, and they'll cut you down should they find you in here!'

The satorr laughed. 'Nice try, so how many companions do you have with you?'

'Five,' he lied, in as gruff a voice as he could muster, 'all of us armed and experienced soldiers of the Council. You don't want the entire force of the Council coming down on you, do you?'

That made them pause, if only for a moment, but then the satorr laughed again. 'You're a poor liar. You're all alone here, with only us for company. Come on, now, just give us your things and we'll let you live.'

He stepped forward and grabbed the edge of his shield. He yelped and slashed at the hand. The cut wasn't deep, but it was enough to make the satorr cry out and step back. He brandished his sabre before him, glaring at his three assailants from his little rocky crevice.

The satorr spat. 'That's the end of it now. We really would have let you live, but now I'm going to kill you nice and slow.'

Suddenly the light in the cave diminished as a large figure stood in the entrance.

'Come in, Heren,' said Koli, keeping his eyes on Lidan. 'We need you in here,' he turned his head slightly to address the satorr. 'Now you'll see one of Heren's uses; prying little insects out of their holes with his long sharp claws.'

Heren, however, did not move, and the figure at the cave's mouth stood where he was, motionless. The satorr turned, annoyed, and walked back to shout at him. Suddenly Heren crashed through the curtain of rain, and fell flat on his face, half-in and half-out of the cave.

'You stupid drunken clout,' shouted the satorr, walking back to kick the juggernaut in the head. 'Get your ugly head-' he stopped suddenly and gasped, stepping back in horror.

Lidan saw why. A puddle of dark red blood was spreading over the cave floor, soaking into the moss as it pulsed from the creature's neck. He looked back at the satorr, who sat down in shock, staring at the grisly quagmire surrounding the massive body.

Another figure walked into the cave, and he nearly wept for joy.

'Good evening, gentlemen,' said Gwahl as he bent down to wipe the blade of his dirk on some moss. 'It seems you've apprehended my companion. I'd be glad if you let him go, unless you'd rather end up like your friend.'

The satorr got up to his feet, bellowing incomprehensively with rage as he charged Gwahl.

The daemon dodged to one side and slashed with his dirk, cutting deep into his opponent's back. The satorr howled in pain and staggered to one side to support himself against the wall.

Koli left Lidan to engage this new threat, hacking away with his sword. All of his blows were parried by Gwahl, whose dirk spun before him in a dark blur as he turned aside the hanex's strikes.

They exchanged blows and duelled around the carcass of the juggernaut. It was painfully obvious that Gwahl was vastly superior to Koli, and was, for some reason, just playing with the hanex. His arrogance, however, soon proved to be a weakness, as the satorr finally recovered enough to join the hanex in his assault, and Gwahl was beset on both sides, his dirk a dark streak flying through the air as he dodged and ducked and parried for his life.

All of a sudden, for no apparent reason, Gwahl stumbled slightly. Perhaps he slipped on a particularly damp patch of moss, perhaps the force of one of his enemies' blows had been too great, perhaps one of his own strikes had been too haphazard, or perhaps he was simply tiring. Whatever the cause, he stumbled, and the satorr saw his opportunity, jumping forward to grab his arm. Being too close to use his sword, Koli did the same, and Gwahl was held tightly between the two, straining his muscles to break free.

'Shoot him, Dirdin!' shouted Koli.

Dirdin, who'd been watching the fray with Lidan, turned his bow to the daemon and sighted down the shaft.

'No!' yelled Lidan, charging forward and sweeping his sabre in a wild arc. His arm jarred as the sword bit deep into the flesh of the archer's neck, coming to a sudden shocking halt when it met bone. The arrow shot from the bow to clatter harmlessly against the rocky wall. Shaking, he placed his foot against the gurgling hanex, clutching desperately at his mangled throat. He wrenched his sabre free. It came out with the sound of a boot tugged from a bog, and the patter of raindrops on wet leaves. Blood spurted out and splattered over him, and he recoiled in horror.

On the opposite side of the cave, the other thieves were staring at him, giving Gwahl the opportunity to wriggle free from their grips. Lidan turned to face the other opponents, just in time to see the daemon cut the satorr's throat and stab Koli in the chest. Both fell to the ground, dead and dying. Gwahl nodded at him and gestured to Dirdin, who was still writhing in agony on the mossy floor.

'Put him out of his misery.'

He nodded dumbly and stabbed the hanex in the chest, where he hoped his heart was. His first strike clacked against the sternum, skimming off to lacerate his chest, adding to the pooling blood. Dirdin gazed at him in a mixture of shock and agony. Shaking, he returned the blade to his chest, and slowly pushed it through the space between his ribs. There was more resistance than he expected, and the horrible crackling of steel against bone and sinew seemed deafening. The sorry creature's eyes bulged one last time before the life faded from them, and he was still.

'We should leave. This place is full of death, no good to sleep in. Follow me outside, and we'll wash ourselves of blood in the rain.'

He nodded, and stumbled after the daemon into the downpour, not looking at the carcasses on the floor. They walked through the soaking wood for some time, letting the water wash away the stain of blood from their clothes, their weapons, their faces. They kept walking even when they were clean, stumbling in the darkness through the undergrowth. Finally, Gwahl stopped beside a large oak, whose strong boughs and thick foliage had retained some modicum of dryness in the ground beneath its leaves. The daemon sat down and closed his eyes in weariness.

He sat beside him and put his head in his hands.

'I'm sorry, Gwahl,' he said in a whisper.

'What was that? I can't hear you over the rain.'

'I'm sorry,' he said, louder. 'Had I been swifter then we might have gotten away.'

'We might, but we got away with our lives and all our possessions anyway, did we not? No harm done.'

'No harm?' he looked at the daemon incredulously. 'We killed four people, we were nearly killed ourselves!'

'But we weren't. I saved you and you saved me. We came out of the cave safe and sound. You did well, Lidan, now get some rest.'

'From now on I'll do as you say, Gwahl, I won't do anything that might put us in danger.'

To his surprise, the daemon chuckled, as if they were discussing nothing more than a spoiled meal in the kitchen, as opposed to a lapse that nearly led to their deaths.

'I'm glad to hear it, my friend. Now please, get some rest, you performed admirably in the cave and I'm glad to have you with me. Just try to trust me next time.'

'I will, I promise.'

He heard the daemon grunt in acknowledgment, and then settled his back against the tree trunk, waiting to go to sleep.

*

The next day they woke up early. Rain was still falling, but now only a light drizzle, with clear skies ahead promising a drier day. Lidan's mouth and the grass next to him was crusted in the vomit he'd been retching up all night. Each time he moved his arm he felt the impact of his sword biting into flesh and bone, and the effort it took to jerk the blade free. Once again, the crack of steel on bone set his stomach turning, and he bent over, breathing heavily as he willed his stomach to settle.

He knew the blinding agony of cold steel cutting into raw flesh. He knew the burn of its frozen edge, the weakness of lost blood.

He knew how long it took for wounds to heal, how they scarred, how the flesh distended and wept and sloughed away when infection set in. It was one thing to suffer flesh torn apart by a blade, but another thing entirely to deliver its cruelty. Not that such things would concern the hanex. There'd be no puckering of scar tissue, no picking at pus-filled scabs, no relief when wounds finally stopped aching.

Thankfully, Gwahl didn't bring up the events of the night before. The daèmon offered Lidan a concoction of herbs infused in rainwater, stating it would help with the vomiting. He took it gratefully, and within minutes, his vision cleared and his stomach settled. Gwahl nodded approvingly and went about the normal business of the day foraging for food.

The daemon's indifference was chilling. The hanex's death weighed heavily on his conscience, his name, Dirdin, still present in his mind, he doubted Gwahl even remembered what they looked like. He shivered. However kind, however wise, however thoughtful his companion may be, he was a killer, the likes of which he'd never met before. At least not in a companionable way.

The general who sentenced him, the grey-eyed nightmare, was also a killer.

Clearly, his brooding mood was noticeable, and Gwahl soon called him up on it.

'They were bad people, Lidan,' he said to him as they walked, breaking a silence of hours. 'Don't worry yourself over their deaths.'

'How do you know that?'

'Did they not threaten you with death?'

'Only if I didn't give them my things. They were just thieves.'

'"Just thieves"? You know nothing of this forest, these lands, these times. They would have robbed you and killed you, Lidan. Or if not us, then some other traveller, a passing family, a young child. I warned you about the rogues in this forest; they have no honour, no compassion, and no sense of purpose other than to keep robbing and spreading their selfish anarchy until the entire world burns in their malicious games. We rid the forest of an evil, my friend, and we saved each other's lives.'

'His name was Dirdin, the hanex I killed. What if he was only robbing to get money to support his family?'

Gwahl sighed and put a hand on his shoulder. 'I thought you'd killed before?'

'I have, I've killed goblins.'

'By yourself, with your own hands?'

'Yes,' he paused. 'No. I've killed once with a bow and arrow, but whenever it came to hand-to-hand combat, all I would ever do was incapacitate them, distract them, injure them, and then one of the men would come and end it.'

'This is the first time your arm has felt the touch of death?'

'Yes.'

Gwahl sighed. 'I suppose the first time is difficult. I probably felt the same way, if I could remember it. There shouldn't be any difference between killing with a bow and killing with a sword, both result in the same outcome.'

He shook his head. 'There's a difference. I felt my sword sink in, and when I wrenched it out, it was as if I were wrenching out his very essence. He might have been a good person.'

'And you never felt this remorse after killing goblins?'

'No, but they're monsters, they raid our villages and kill our people.'

'How was this hanex any different from them? The rogues raid and murder too. They are no different from the goblins who would attack your trading caravans. In fact, I would go so far as to say that these rogues are worse. At least the goblins attack to steal supplies to feed their colonies and villages, and only strike at those who stray close enough to their wood to be a possible threat to them. These gangs of thieves have nobody. They have no villages, no families to feed, only themselves and their little gangs of lawless savages. Anyone can become a monster, Lidan. Men, goblins, hanex, daemons. One's race does not dictate their character, only their actions. I appreciate the fact that this was the first time your hands have ever been literally stained with the blood of your fallen foe, but to kill is to kill, the same blood will stain you no matter how you do it.'

He nodded. 'I'm sorry, it's just easier to kill from far away, and to kill things that look like evil savages.'

The daemon smiled. 'You must learn to see past appearances. I know more than a few brave goblins, and countless savage men who dress in finery. Forget the hanex. Plenty more will fall to your sword before this war is won.'

They fell silent after that, but he knew he wouldn't forget that name. He might want freedom, he might want vengeance, but after it was done he knew he wanted to return to a peaceful life. As soon as he forgot that name, 'Dirdin', then he was as cold-hearted a killer as Gwahl, as the general, and after that there was no going back.

*

Three days later, they were resting beneath an impressive silver birch, jutting out the ground like a standard. Waiting, apparently. He crunched an apple. Things had been relatively muted between them since the skirmish with the thieves. The veil come away, revealing deeper truths about the daemon, about what this fight would entail.

He was ready for it, he was sure of it. After the dungeons and the tortures, after escaping Crastalan and meeting Gwahl, he was ready to fight back.

In the distance came the sound of marching footsteps.

Gwahl stared at the point in the trees where the sound came from. Lidan stared with him, the apple in his hand suddenly bland on his tongue. This was what the daemon was waiting for. It must be a column marching in formation, judging from the regular tramping of their boots. The faint jingle of metal suggested armour, so presumably this wasn't just another band of rogues come to attack them.

All of a sudden, a column of twenty soldiers, a few of them Islanders, clad in shining mail armour and rich green tunics strode into view. Each bore a high helmet upon their heads and spear in their right hands. One stepped forward, a bright red sash over one shoulder and a sword at his hip, his eyes wide in surprise.

'Gwahl!' he exclaimed. 'I didn't expect to find you here! Last we heard of you, you were around Cysgodgors? The patrols out east are on the look-out for you.'

'Well, the marshes are far too unpleasant to be around, can't stand the stench for too long,' Gwahl grinned as he rose to his feet.

'No, that's true,' laughed the Islander. 'My name's Major Nakatar Haweis, second battalion, second regiment, I'd be honoured to escort you to the Council.'

'How kind. We're not distracting you from other duties, I hope?'

'We were just doing a final sweep, on our way back to be relieved now.'

'Perfect! Lead on, Major.'

The major paused and looked Lidan up and down. 'Forgive me, but your companion is…'

'Oh, he's no bother, a friend. New recruit. I'll be keeping an eye on him, don't you worry.'

'New recruits are always welcome,' Nakatar smiled. 'Are you sure he's not just joining for the food?'

Several of the soldiers laughed, and Lidan blushed, looking at his feet shyly. Gwahl patted his shoulder reassuringly. 'Can't blame him, he needs some more meat on his bones if he's to terrorise Stolach's soldiers with the rest of you lot!'

'As long as he does his part, he can eat all he likes, I'm sure,' chuckled Nakatar. 'By the four winds, I'll give him half my pudding if it means another fighter for the cause.'

'Naw, Major, you'd never share your pudding let's be honest,' said one of the soldiers.

'Cheeky blighter, but he has a point,' Nakatar winked at Lidan. 'Alright you lot, back to base, all this talk of food's got my belly rumbling.'

Chapter 5

They left the birch and the undergrowth, and he finally walked on one of the roads through the forest. 'Road' was quite complimentary to the overgrown, bumpy, unkempt path through the trees. More of a glorified game-trail than anything, but certainly easier than picking his way through and around the trees. He followed them through the densely packed woods, clambering over branches and fallen tree trunks across their path, trudging through mud and slogging up hills. It was about as far from the stone roads and avenues of Crastalan as you could get. Even the dusty roads of Weaverlodge were a luxury compared to this.

As he marched, he explored the faces of the soldiers. Each bore the same stern expression, their faces laced with ugly cuts and jagged scars. He must have been staring and Gwahl soon leaned over.

'Each of them has fought many battles. This lot,' he motioned to the green-clad soldiers, 'are a unit of the Council Guard, our elite troops. Along with the militia and brigades, they make up our army.'

Soon, the Council Guard led them into a vast encampment. No, more of a town, even a city of countless makeshift tents slung across low hanging branches. Paths were beaten into the ground with the passing of hundreds of feet. In the middle, a great pavilion rose up into the surrounding canopy. Weapon racks dotted the camp, to which soldiers constantly came and went, picking up bows, spears, battleaxes. The soldiers themselves were made up of all manner of creatures. There were men, hanex, satorrs, calefs, dreyads, neiads, even a great black juggernaut who towered over all. As they walked down the paths, he noticed many different stalls. There was a Southlander working as a blacksmith, beating out a sheet of metal on his iron anvil. There was an apothecary in the form of a hanex, an armourer fitting a man with a new hauberk, leather-workers tanning and boiling leather, knowing women with their cunning eyes, stables full of snorting horses, all the makings of a busy town.

The major led them onward, passing more and more tents and stalls and makeshift huts as they went. In a way, it was similar to

Crastalan's shanty town, only cleaner, fresher, more pleasant. Some had built their settlements around the ruins of ancient buildings, their stone and mortar crumbling away, leaving only the remains of their foundations to build upon.

Weaving through the hustle and bustle of the bubbling town, they finally reached the pavilion. Outside the entrance was phalanx after phalanx of Council Guard, their polished helms glinting in the sun. Nakatar turned, and told Gwahl to enter. He walked in without hesitation. Lidan cautiously approached the entrance and peered inside, but it was darker than pitch. He turned and looked at Nakatar, but the major shook his head, and motioned for him to remain. He frowned, and shuffled around on his feet awkwardly, unsure what to do. A few minutes later, Gwahl stepped back outside.

'I'm sorry, Lidan, wait outside for now.'

'Why can't I come?'

'This gathering isn't for spectators. I'll call you up when other matters have been seen to.'

'Will you be long?'

'Maybe. Ask Nakatar for some water and food while you wait.'

'Aye, I could do with refreshments,' nodded Nakatar, looking around for a servant.

'You'll be fine,' Gwahl reassured.

He forced his lips to smile briefly, but it was lost as soon as Gwahl disappeared back inside. Leaning against a tent pole, he waited for his return.

*

Gwahl paused just inside the entrance, waiting for his eyes to adjust to the gloom. A wooden stairway to his left, winding around the thick trunk of a centuries-old beech. How elaborate. How long did this take them to build? No doubt time better spent on fortifying the perimeter, but who was he to judge? As ever, his was the work of an advisor, not a leader. To make a recommendation and see it disregarded, then pat them on the back for the disaster of their mistake. Such was a daemon's place, unless you were called Deia. Deia could do no wrong, or so he seemed to think.

The first level was a library, full of scrolls and ledgers, complete with a multitude of small study desks occupied by ageing scholars. Such tomes and scrolls in the Council's possession were of a lesser quality, found in the ruins of settlements of an earlier age. Any works of importance were safe in the libraries of Crastalan or the halls beneath the Rhetta Mountains in the far north. The second level was nothing more than a barracks for the Council Guard stationed outside. The third level was a small infirmary, filled with crisp white hammocks and fresh blankets. A few medics in white habits hurried about, tending whimpering patients, wounded from who-knows-what skirmish. He stepped inside to scan the occupied beds for familiar faces. None, thank Enadir. The fourth and final level was enclosed by a pair of thick curtains. Pausing momentarily to catch his breath, he entered.

A dark room with two tables, one small and oval, set upon a raised platform, the other large and crescent shaped, facing the platform. He walked around the latter to find a seat.

Most of the seats were already taken. Some he recognised, others he did not. Whether or not he knew them, they all nodded politely as he passed and he returned the gesture. First was a tall red-faced man with a great polearm resting against the table in front of him. Tanor, commander of the Council Guard. Beside him was a smaller dark-skinned Southlander with a battleaxe resting on his lap, deep in muttered conversation with a pair of neiads, both of whom bore crossbows upon their backs. He didn't know them, but they had the air of capable fighters. Beside them was Noswen, silently observing the daemon whilst honing the blade of her falchion. Pwtrek towered over her, the juggernaut's arms crossed and frowning down his nose at the hanex. He clasped Pwtrek's shoulder and smiled at Noswen. It was years since he'd seen either of them. At the far end was a slender calef with shoulder-length brown hair, his hand resting on the hilt of his precious jian. The calef smiled at him and motioned to the seat beside him.

He sat and clasped his friend's hand. 'Good to see you again, dear Spotal!'

'Been far too long, my friend! I hope you know you've been keeping us all in suspense.'

'Have I?' he laughed. 'I must apologise! How long have you been here?'

'Personally? Two days, many of this lot have been here for longer. Nothing's really happened yet, don't worry. We were waiting for everyone to get here before we began.'

'Began what?'

'Don't know, only that it's a matter of some secrecy. Apparently, you were the last one.'

'I see...' he murmured. 'Who are they?' he asked, looking over at the neiads and the Southlander, 'Never met them before.'

'No idea. The neiads presumably from Commander Afarn, the Southlander from... the southern branch?'

Gwahl raised his eyebrow. 'Southern branch?'

'Winds! I don't know, do I? We'll all be introduced before long. What took you so long to get here?'

'Chance. Didn't even know I was supposed to be here until a few weeks ago. I was in Iadden's foothills when I heard the Council were gathering forces. Have you just been sitting in this room all this time, waiting for me to arrive?' he winked.

Spotal snorted. 'You think a lot of yourself. No, a runner arrived a short while ago to say the Guard were bringing you in, so they sent for us.'

Further conversation was halted as a bell tolled, silencing the table. Five hooded figures entered from the far end and took their seats at the oval table; the high chancellors. Rising as one, the occupants of the crescent table, Gwahl included, gave a short bow and sat down again.

Under their hoods, the individual chancellors were difficult to distinguish. Then again, that was supposedly the point; while in office, they all spoke as one. Or something along those lines. Pomp and ceremony, it seemed even rebels hiding in a forest needed some. There was Tuulik Salpens, an old scholar, Denil Imein, a former village elder, General Widrias Gesharr, the satorr, Chaplain Stegil

Mawein, of the Order of the Mountain Air, and finally General Agral Opens.

One of them rose and looked down at them. The Council was about to begin.

'Welcome,' he toned in a deep sonorous voice, 'to our Council. Before we discuss the true reason why we have called you here, let me hear what news you have of our allies in other lands. Auran, make your report.'

The Southlander rose, keeping his eyes on the chancellors.

'The king has invaded my country, slaughtering my people. He formed an alliance with men of the Jagged Isles, and now controls the Great Waters,' his voice was deep, though softly-spoken, and bore the characteristic sing-song accent of the Southlands. 'As you know, our country's armies were all but massacred. I was sent here by my Lord Belia-stobai with forty others to show our support, though honestly we can hardly afford to lose so many men.'

'Thank you, Auran. I am sorry for the grave news you bring of your lord. Have all the rulers of the Jagged Isles sworn allegiance to the crown?'

'Not all, but many. Most. There are a few small islands still resisting, but I cannot see their plight lasting long. All are too proud to join together and form a united force to confront him, so these divided states will be easily consumed.'

'Let us hope they hold out for a while longer... Spotal, what news of our allies to the east?'

Spotal rose. 'My General Teig has been keeping our borders safe from invading troglodytes from the Cysgodgors Marshes. There's something peculiar about this. Normally we only have to battle one or two tribes a week to protect our lands, but now they attack constantly across our whole southwest border. We fear Stolach has somehow managed to gain their trust and they now act under his orders. It sounds absurd, I know, but it would explain their new-found enthusiasm. As you can imagine, our armies are stretched thin. We have hardly enough troops to defend our own lands. For that reason, my general could spare no more than three score calefs to aid you. I am sorry, but if we were to send more the troglodytes would overwhelm us. However, we were able to bring with us a very large amount of Harandale roots from our northern farms as provisions for you.'

Gwahl blinked. How surprising. Harandale root was a plant native to the Eastlands, a very difficult thing to farm, guarded jealously by the calefs. One small root would provide a man enough energy to walk for a whole day; they were truly mystical things, protected with much pride. As far as he knew, to steal from the Harandale crops was punishable by death, they were so hallowed by the calefs. It was a great honour for them to provide the Council with such a gift, more so than had they sent them their entire army.

'My general also wanted me to tell you that our scouts have reported juggernauts coming from the north, bearing the crest of the king. They are heavily armed and well trained. Our northern forces will not be able to hold them forever.'

'Disheartening news, Spotal, if our allies to the east should fall, we would find ourselves surrounded with no way out. General Teig is a great commander, if she cannot hold off the king's forces, no-one can,' the chancellor's voice trailed to silence, quietly musing over Spotal's news. As he sat, silent, another stood and addressed Spotal.

'Captain, we heard rumour of an attack on King Lleunedd?' she asked. Denil. Betrayed by her voice and slight stature.

'Yes,' Spotal shook his head. 'Three weeks ago an assassin infiltrated Muranath and crept into King Lleunedd's chambers. Our king is a light sleeper and woke to find the foul creature poised above him, dagger in hand. They wrestled and the king eventually strangled him, but not before he was scratched by the tip of the assassin's poisoned blade. He now lies in his bedchambers, our finest healers tending him day and night. The poison, however, is an unknown toxin. We cannot find an antidote.'

'King Lleunedd might die?' asked Tanor, brows raised.

Spotal sighed. 'As I said, we cannot find an antidote.'

'Noswen?' Denil asked, hesitantly.

The hanex shrugged. 'I have no way of knowing which cocktail this assassin used. There are a thousand different combinations.'

'Half of them written by you, I'm sure,' muttered Pwtrek, under his breath.

Denil sighed, wisely ignoring the comment, and turned back to Spotal. 'Who's currently commanding your kingdom, with the king so impaired?'

'Muranath's court is more than up to the task of day-to-day comings and goings. We have plenty of nobles and politicians for that. In terms of defence, that has always been General Teig's responsibility. Eventually, Prince Denall will take his place in stately matters.'

'Nevertheless,' murmured Pwtrek, 'it is worrying this assassin was able to get into the king's chambers so easily,' his eyes flicked around the room, resting on Noswen for a few moments, before turning back to the oval table. 'These scum that call themselves assassins should be stopped before they get within ten leagues of any commander, then hanged for the crows to feast upon their living bodies.'

Gwahl rolled his eyes, a petty jab, but unfortunately not unexpected. An uncomfortable silence settled, the sound of Noswen's whetstone providing the only relief. Spotal cleared his throat.

'Well, we do everything we can to stop them – and I can assure you, those assassins who are caught are treated with the judgement they deserve.'

Auran looked at Spotal. 'You, Spotal, is it? You said the troglodytes are only attacking from the southwest border of your lands. Why don't they attack from the northwest? The marshes go all the way up to Tarnegrefur, don't they? Or are troglodytes only in the south?'

Gwahl frowned. Surely that was common knowledge? Then again, he was from the Southlands, and Nefarwy's geography was probably unfamiliar.

Spotal blinked. 'They can't. The bramble plains, an impassable barrier, separate the northwest border from the Marshes.'

'Brambles?' repeated Auran, flatly.

'Aye, brambles.'

'How are they impassable?' Auran shrugged his shoulders.

Spotal's mouth dropped open, apparently at a loss for words. Gwahl rolled his eyes at the calef. It really wasn't that surprising. How much did Spotal realistically know about the Southlands, after all?

'There are many different kinds of plants growing on the plains,' he explained, patiently. 'Each one bears long thorns, some needle-thin, others broad as daggers. All secrete potent poisons from their tips. Most are long enough to stab a man clean through. If that doesn't kill you, the poison will.'

Auran nodded slowly. 'But if you were careful and cut your way through with axes, that would surely work?'

Gwahl smiled. 'You would need to be a skilful woodsman indeed to cut through the thorns. Even the sap is deadly poison, and any breaks in the skin are passages to spread through the blood. Splinters or woodchips flying through the air while chopping can be deadly.'

Auran nodded again. 'I see. There are no woodsmen capable of this?'

Spotal found his voice again. 'Are you suggesting the troglodytes might somehow find it within themselves to cut through a barrier that has stood for centuries? Be sensible. They are savages, they don't have the means for such a thing.'

Auran raised his hands placatingly. 'I was only voicing my concerns for your lands, but if you say the northwest border is safe, I shall believe you. I do not know these lands. I was unaware of the formidability of this wall. I'm sorry if I offended you, but I would be grieved if the savages overran your country.'

Gwahl smiled. This southerner was growing on him.

Spotal nodded. 'Thank you for the sentiment. I assure you, no troglodyte has ever, or will ever, cross the bramble plains.'

The chancellor who spoke first nodded. 'Don't worry, Auran, the calefs know how to defend their home. Pwtrek,' he turned to the juggernaut. 'Spotal mentioned your kin, do you know of anything?'

He rose with a grunt, wincing as he stretched his legs. 'I knew nothing of this,' he growled, 'but it wouldn't surprise me if a great number of my people threw in their lot with Stolach. Remember Tomon. With a juggernaut as Stolach's second, he's respected by my people. As for my report, the northern Dailas Forest is overrun with satorrs, men, and grey dreyads, all of them going to join Stolach's northern armies. They are being trained and armed, and the king's northern forces have never before seen such strength in numbers. Field Marshal Strikk, commander-in-chief of the king's northern armies, must be jumping for joy right now. Word has it that it's an invasion force, probably to purge Dailas of resistance once and for all.'

'How long before they're ready?' asked Tanor.

'Quite some time yet, possibly as long as two seasons,' replied Pwtrek. 'It takes time to arm and train all the troops. But once this horde is ready I can see no easy victory against them. Commander Afarn will be hard pressed to keep this force from crossing the Crisiaddwr. Should they reach the southern forest, it's only a matter of time before we are destroyed.'

'We may have to send a large portion of our army up there to help Afarn in that case,' muttered the chancellor, turning to the two neiads. 'What have you to say of this, my friends?'

Both neiads rose as one. Man and woman. Siblings, from the looks of them. The woman spoke first. 'Although the news of this invasion force is new to us, we can assure you the army will never cross the river. We will not be defeated.'

'We continue to intercept most scouts attempting to cross the main flow of the Crisiaddwr, although some will inevitably manage to do so,' the other continued the report. 'Also, we are in the midst of a guerrilla war with both the pine goblins in the Pine woods to the west and roving bands of Hobb and rogues to the north. A war, I'm pleased to announce, that results in many victories for us. That being said, the new bridges the king built across the Crisiaddwr – South Bridge that spans the river from the Pine Woods to the flatlands, and North Bridge that is a few miles north of Critanna Marsh – are both completed. They are reasonably garrisoned, a few hundred soldiers to each. Unfortunately, we don't have the means nor the forces to attack either. At least not for now.'

'In addition, Afarn has sent a grand army of five hundred neiads to you, in case you need them,' the woman concluded.

'Thank you Depani, and thank you Chekry. The troops Afarn sends will be greatly appreciated, although from Pwtrek's report I fear that you may need them in the future. Let's hope you continue to harass the king's armies with your guerrilla war.'

'What about the bridges?' asked another chancellor, his voice quavering. Gwahl guessed this was Tuulik, the oldest. 'Is the king sending troops over them to strike at us?'

'No, sir,' replied Chekry, the brother. 'The forces sent there simply hold the crossings, a few hundred soldiers at most. It just makes it easier for Stolach's scouts to cross the river and get into the forest. Opens up trade between Dailas and Crastalan, that sort of thing. Not a bad idea, really, unifies the Midlands a bit more... We stop the patrols we can, raid a few caravans if it's safe, but we dare not attack the bridges openly.'

'Bridges across the river, gathering forces in the northern forest... really does sound like he's preparing for a purge,' muttered one of the chancellors, gruffly.

'Maybe,' nodded Spotal. 'Then again, it might just be to make it easier to travel across the river. Before the bridges, people relied on the little ferries, which you neiads could destroy all too easily.'

'As was our duty to keep away the king's soldiers,' said Depani, edgily.

'I'm not saying it wasn't,' said Spotal raising his hands. 'I'm just saying maybe he felt he needed a way to connect his lands together, as you said. The garrisons are probably just there for protection.'

'You don't think that he's preparing an invasion? We're telling you he's moving more troops into the forest. Pwtrek's seen a whole load of them in the north. That's no coincidence,' said Depani.

'I don't know. I'll admit, the north doesn't look good, and the bridges makes a strike from the west pretty likely too, I just don't want anyone jumping to conclusions. All we know so far is that the king's bridges are built, and they are guarded,' Spotal shrugged.

'Aye, and he's got a whopping big army in the north,' Pwtrek laughed sarcastically. 'Pretty much surrounded, and not much chance of help from your lot because he's cajoled the bloody trogs into fighting for him. Doesn't look good for any of us.'

'Alright, thank you all,' The deep-voiced chancellor turned to Noswen, still sharpening her blade.'Noswen, you've already briefed two of us chancellors on your mission. Can you repeat it for the benefit of the rest?'

She looked up from her work for a moment, before returning her concentration to her whetstone. At first it seemed that she would remain silent, but then she spoke. As flat and toneless as ever. Gwahl shook his head. Poor thing, hiding behind her mask.

'Last month I managed to infiltrate the Pine Wood. I remained there for a week. The goblins have a vast army, numbering at least ten thousand troops, each of them fierce and eager to earn whatever reward the king promised them. As ordered, I assassinated three of their chieftains. Unfortunately, that will not do much to their morale, they will simply elect new, stronger leaders, of that I am certain. You also sent me to kill the king's advisors. I regret to announce I failed. Although I managed to gain entrance to Crastalan, the chambers of the higher commanders and advisors were too heavily guarded to infiltrate. I was nearly discovered and retreated back to Dailas. That is all.'

'Your report is grave, Noswen,' Tuulik muttered, turning to his fellow chancellors. 'Did I hear you correctly when you said there were ten *thousand* pine goblins under the king's command, in addition to his previous forces?'

'Correct, sir.'

'How could they have amassed such an army?' asked Denil, her delicate voice quivering.

'I don't know. The pine goblin population has increased drastically over the past few summers in those woods. Also, all the different tribes in the wood have united under Stolach's banner. Instead of a scattering of villages throughout, there is now a vast city in the heart of the forest, and each day more tribes flock to this wooden citadel.'

'If there were ten thousand when you left, how many would you say there are now?'

Noswen exhaled softly. 'I cannot be sure, but were I to hazard a guess, the army could have easily grown to be nearly twelve thousand strong.'

Denil put a hand to her head, stunned. Gwahl noticed the neiads' discomfort as Noswen spoke, averting their eyes, shifting uncomfortably, sneering. He sighed, not just Pwtrek, then. She didn't deserve such treatment. To her credit, she ignored them.

The deep-voiced chancellor turned to Spotal. 'Maybe the bridges *are* made for invasion, then,' without waiting for an answer he addressed Tanor. 'As commander of the Council Guard, is there anything to report to this council?'

Tanor shook his head. 'No, sir, apart from picking up a few more wandering soldiers and the constant skirmishes with rogues or Hobb, there's been nothing sufficient to report, apart from the consistent increase in these incidents.'

'Thank you, Tanor. Gwahl, your face is one we haven't seen for many moons. I'm glad our invitation finally reached your ears. We weren't sure whether you'd come. Do you have anything to say, old friend?'

Gwahl rose and smiled and the figure. 'It is mere fortune – or fate – that brought that invitation to my attention. My report is much the same as everyone else's. The king controls the Great Waters to the south, in addition to most of the lands across it. When I was roaming the Northlands, near the Mountains of Iadden, I saw minotorrs bearing his insignia. Surprisingly, the men from beyond the black desert, of the Westlands, have journeyed from their homes to here as well. I was around Crastalan when I saw a regiment on patrol, heading from the city. Somehow, he's managed to recruit them. He's clearly gathering forces from the surrounding lands.

'On the way to the Council I also saw a hunting party of the king's grey dreyads on course to our base. Fortunately, our location remains hidden, they were just chasing an escaped prisoner. He's waiting outside, actually, a keen new recruit. I also ran into several gangs of rogues on my way here, but I dealt with them the same way as the dreyads.'

'Hold on, let's back up a bit here,' cried Spotal. 'Stolach has the minotorrs under his command now?'

'Afraid so, and it's no small legion either. He's been to the heart of the mountains, Bletta Castle, and managed to cajole High Marshal Nostiir into joining him,' Gwahl nodded, lips pursed.

'Never did I think the day would come when minotorrs would take orders from a fonex,' grumbled Pwtrek darkly.

'But these are dark times, Pwtrek, and Stolach's shadow blots out the sun shining over the heads of all creatures, even the minotorrs. But I fear these men from the west more than the minotorrs. They are a mysterious folk of whom I know little. Could you enlighten us, Gwahl?' asked the chancellor.

He rubbed his chin, picking his words carefully. For so long, the Westlands had been isolated from the rest of Enadir, a testament to the benefit of having daemons guide a people to success not seen since the giants. But despite all their best efforts, the taint of the rest of the world was reaching them, or perhaps they were reaching it. Gogofaint would be disappointed. So would Deia.

'They are strong, hardy, disciplined. Their villages have learnt to live in the harshest of conditions. A resilient people. Their wisdom and nobility is truly impressive, as is their courage. In the past, several of my kin journeyed to their lands and helped establish order following the War, and with the guidance of my fellow daemons they have become a powerful people. From what I know, they fight well. Each child is given a bow at four and taught to use it until adulthood. I would not take them lightly.'

'Mighty opponents, to be sure,' nodded Depani. 'Why is it only now that we hear of them?'

'For the most part they keep to themselves. Clearly Stolach never thought to approach them before now,' he said. Partly true.

'Why did we not approach them?' asked Pwtrek.

'We did,' said one of the chancellors, bitterly, 'but they turned our messengers away. They saw us as warmongers and agents of discord. They said the war was a matter for our country, not theirs.'

A fair enough response, truth be told. There was more than just a taste of Gogofaint in that response, but he didn't blame him. Keeping them isolated from the poisonous Midlands was wise, but as always, people would only listen to the wisdom of his race for so long before turning to their own guidance. It was just bad luck they turned when Stolach went calling.

'Clearly their opinions have changed,' said Spotal. 'Stolach must have a silver tongue to coax them out of their homelands to fight for him.'

'It's worrying that they were willing to take such a perilous journey to fight at Stolach's side,' muttered Pwtrek, frowning even harder.

'Perilous how?' asked Auran.

'The Burning Eye of the West – a fire-spitting mountain, spouts massive gouts of liquid flame and acrid smoke that makes passage from the black desert to the Westlands extremely dangerous. There is a natural border between the two countries of smoke, fire, and ash, stretching for many leagues north beyond the Burning Eye itself,' explained Gwahl. He should know. He'd made the journey himself. Going all the way round Iadden was a pain, but one far kinder than the suffocating columns of ash and sulphur of the direct passage.

'Precisely,' continued Pwtrek, 'and the fact that they were willing to cross this barrier shows their conviction.'

An uncomfortable silence followed as they reflected on the potential danger of this new enemy. Suddenly, one of the chancellors clapped his hands and stood tall, fist raised in defiance. He'd remained silent for much of the meeting so far, and seemed to relish the opportunity to finally have his say.

'No matter how strong their conviction, it cannot be equal to our own. Remember, no matter what they believe themselves to be fighting for, as long as they bear Stolach's standard, they will be fighting for tyranny, a pale notion compared to the dazzling gleam of freedom that is ours!'

Well, good to see someone had some optimism! Gwahl settled back into his chair. Reports all done, now for the meat of the meeting. The chancellor continued.

'So! Thank you all for your reports, but now to work. I'm sure we all recognise the looming threat. The king has become powerful, powerful enough to rid himself of all who oppose him. As was alluded to from your reports, he plans to purge these woods of resistors once and for all, to expand his kingdom to other lands, to rule all with a vice-like grip that will never grow weak!

'It is our duty to defend ourselves from his wrath. We called you here to underline our plan to rid us of this tyrant, this false king. Be under no false impressions, the mission that we propose is dangerous, it could be described as downright foolish. It must not be undertaken by the faint-hearted, the weak of mind or the foolhardy. We propose to launch an assault upon Crastalan. We propose the Council will no longer skulk in the shadows. We propose to engage the king in battle, and fight for the freedom of all creatures from this fonex scum!'

Gwahl raised his brows. Bold indeed. Good thing he was sitting down. The stunned silence echoing around the chamber suggested the others felt much the same, broken only by the faint scraping of Noswen's whetstone. It stretched on. And on. Uncomfortably long. They all knew the facts. Launching an attack on such a formidable fortress was foolish to the point of suicidal. He glanced around the table. Lots of doubt on those faces. Lots of fear.

Tanor cleared his throat, breaking the silence. 'Sirs, although what you propose is indeed valiant, it will come at a heavy price. The walls of Crastalan are higher and thicker than any other fortress in Nefarwy, not just Nefarwy, all of Enadir. It's foolish to launch such an attack with our current forces.'

The chancellor nodded. 'You're right, of course, an outright charge would result in the deaths of many, with only the slightest chance of victory. But as mentioned before, there is a mission that the Council wish to send a select few upon. This mission will allow the main bulk of the army access to the fortress.

'Crastalan is an ancient city fortress, built long before the king claimed it as his own. Built by giants and daemons. It has many secret passages and doorways, all of which the king has found and securely locked to await his own uses. Except for one. There is a single entrance to that remains open. The king found every other key to the city, the eagle key, the stag key, falcon, ox, stallion, and lion keys. Some of you are more familiar with this fact than others. Since acquiring the lion key, they are all in his possession. All save one. It was lost from all hope, until now. If we were to find it, the passage would lead us to the heart of the fortress, and to near certain victory.'

The skin at the back of his neck prickled. After all this time, this was it. He realised he was holding his breath. Sixteen years on, now it was happening.

'It is rumoured the king almost found the fabled artefact, but its guardians sold their lives to defend the secret of its location. It's rumoured it was lost in the middle of the Tarnegrefur Mountains. And it is there that we will send our brave soldiers, to find it and return it to the Council.'

'Rumoured,' snorted Pwtrek. 'I heard a rumour once that my cousin bedded a goblin's wolfhound, doesn't mean it was true. Who told you this rumour?'

'A reliable source,' said the chancellor.

'Do we know this reliable source?'

'I cannot say.'

'Of course you can't... The Tarnegrefur Mountains are a great distance away, and they cover a massive area of land. You propose to search every crevice and every gorge in those mountains to search for something we don't even know exists? It's foolish! Noswen said she'd managed to get in to Crastalan, why don't we all use the same way?'

'I got in by scaling the wall of the fortress with rope and grapple,' said the black hanex. 'It took all my skill not to be seen or fall. I don't know many people capable of doing that, and certainly none of you here today. It would be impossible for a whole army to do it.'

'Then why don't you go in and open the main gate for us?' asked Pwtrek. 'That way we could storm the fortress without the hassle of going to the mountains.'

'The doors to the gatehouse are guarded by a battalion of soldiers. I'd be killed before I got close.'

'You see Pwtrek?' said the chancellor. 'If we find this key, we can get our men into the city. If we get this key, we can open up his fortress. I know it sounds desperate, but it's our best chance.'

'Why can't we pick the lock? Or create another key to fit the keyhole? I'm just pointing out the enormity of the task you're setting whoever you send out there. If the king couldn't find it, why should we?'

'Impossible. No lock-pick alive could ever dream of getting past the intricacies of Crastalan's locks, such technology is lost to us,' the chancellor shook his head.

'Nonsense, you said Crastalan was built by giants and daemons, we have a daemon here,' Pwtrek gestured to him. 'Can you not give us some insight, Gwahl? How do we pick it?'

Gwahl cleared his throat lightly, but Spotal cut across before he could answer.

'Crastalan Tower was built over twenty centuries ago, why would Gwahl know anything about its construction? Besides, with deepest respect, chancellor, the city was built by giants alone, the daemons had nothing to do with it,' he shrugged. 'It's been a while since I opened a history book, but I still remember one or two facts.'

Gwahl smiled despite his building nausea. 'Besides, that sort of crafting was never my area of expertise. I'm a wanderer, not a builder. As they said, the technology is lost.'

'Alright, so there's a secret tunnel through the city, how big is the tunnel? Big enough for an army to march through? Where does it open up? Sounds like a fantasy to me.'

'We cannot know the size of the tunnel until we stand inside it,' said Denil, 'as for where it opens up...'

'This I can answer,' said Gwahl. 'The tunnel will wind through the city and up to the tower itself, eventually opening up into the seventeenth level; Crastalan's library.'

'The seventeenth level! I can see why you want to believe this rumour,' laughed Pwtrek. 'Alright, assuming it exists, this key, what does it look like?'

'Each key was fashioned after a different animal,' said the chancellor. 'This is the serpent key, and it will win us the war.'

Gwahl gripped the armrest to stop his hands from shaking. Sixteen years of sitting on in, now it was time to act.

'Who do you propose will go on this journey?' asked Tanor,

'I don't think you need too many individuals on this kind of mission,' said Spotal, thoughtfully,

'There's a reason why we summoned you here,' continued the chancellor. 'Each of you represent one of our allies; the neiads, the calefs, our Southland and Northland friends, and the heart of the Council Guard. The quest that we propose is one that all of our allies should have a hand in, a victory that we should all share. So, my proposition, as general of the Council's armies, is that you, sitting at this table, will see this task complete.'

General of the Council's armies? Either Widrias or Agral, then. He smiled. Widrias. He should have recognised his old friend sooner. It would be Widrias who proposed such quest as this one, he had always been intrigued by the tale of the serpent key. Nausea gave way to a glimmer of excitement. It seemed the chancellor caught his eye beneath his hood, caught his smile. He thought he saw a smile returned from within those shadows. Finally, it was time.

'I can understand you sending Chekry and Depani, Auran, Gwahl, and even I,' said Pwtrek, 'but Spotal and Tanor should not leave the main force of the Council.'

'Why not?' asked Spotal.

'You're the ambassador for Lleunedd; you can't just leave here and go chasing after a dream! What if an urgent matter with the calefs should arise? Who would we turn to for advice? And Tanor is the head of the Council Guard! He can't leave the chancellors.'

'What's the role of the Council Guard, Pwtrek?' asked Widrias,

Pwtrek shifted awkwardly in his seat. 'They form the elite of the Council's army, our hammer to the anvil of the brigades, they have the main responsibility for defending us and the high chancellors.'

'Defending the high chancellors,' repeated Widrias. 'As *I* will also be joining you on this journey, I'll feel far safer knowing Tanor is there by my side.'

Gwahl snorted. Typical Widrias. But the others didn't know him as well as he did, and a murmur of discontent spread along the table. It was unheard of for any chancellor to embark on any mission. Normally they would lead from behind, from the shadows, lest they be struck down in battle. Of course, this was Widrias, as courageous and valiant a leader as one could ask for, always at the fore of his armies, leading by example in the midst of the fray. It was a sign of his military genius that even in the heat of battle he could observe the battlefield in its entirety, knowing when to draw back or push forward even as his foes closed in around him. This was not a chancellor to remain at the rear while his men fell. He was one to sweat and bleed with them.

'I won't allow it,' declared Tanor, rising to his feet and looking past Widrias at the other chancellors. 'I'll gladly go on this journey if you command me to go, but I cannot accept the risk to a chancellor's life.'

'I second this,' declared Pwtrek,

'Aye, agreed,' nodded Depani.

'It should probably be reconsidered,' murmured Spotal.

Denil raised her hand. 'There's no use in debating this, my friends, the decision has already been made. All that remains is to see whether you'll accept the task.'

Tanor shook his head. 'This is a mistake. From the reports you've just heard, surely you must see that now is a time for you all to stand together in safety, not split apart and put one of you at risk?'

'On the contrary, Tanor,' said Tuulik. 'This actually brings us to a matter we have been considering for a while. We believe it would be better if one chancellor should remain away from the rest for most of the time, that way if we should face a catastrophic attack on our camp in which the others all perish, there will be one hidden away somewhere in the land to revitalise our organisation. This mission is a method to put this idea into place, to see how it works out.'

'Not a bad idea,' mused Gwahl, 'provided the chancellor who is away can keep themselves safe.'

'As long as I have a company of strong, loyal companions by my side, there's no question I'll be safe,' said Widrias. 'What do you say?'

'I'm with you until the end, Wid- chancellor, even though I don't like this,' said Tanor, catching himself before he broke the formality of the meeting.

One by one, those sitting at the crescent table all voiced their commitment.

'By what route will we go to the mountains?' Tanor asked, glumly. 'I suppose Pwtrek's report on the recent activities in the northern woods puts that path out of question.'

'Indeed,' agreed Widrias. 'It was our initial plan to take the northern path, but clearly that's no longer viable.'

'We could go by sea?' suggested Depani. 'Go to Afarn, take a ship, sail down the southern branch of the Crisiaddwr to the Great Waters, and then east to Tonnis Harbour, and up the Atrael River to the mountains?'

'A bit of a round-about way to reach our destination,' grimaced Tanor. 'It would take us far too long, going north and west in order to go east, there are far easier paths.'

'Depani's right that we should go by sea, though,' agreed Pwtrek. 'Perhaps Spotal could get some message to Tonnis Harbour and ask for a ship to come to Morgenal to take us up the Atrael?'

Spotal shook his head. 'They won't come, when I arrived with the reinforcements, we didn't venture into Morgenal, we anchored at the estuary of the Crisiaddwr and disembarked in longboats. The barons have no love for us. Besides, it would take a lot of convincing to spare one of our ships, and again, it's another matter of going west to go east.'

'We could try to buy passage on a ship in Morgenal?' suggested Auran. 'There must be someone sympathetic to our cause in the city?'

'I'm sure there are many,' agreed Tanor 'but I doubt the barons would let them aid us.'

'There is one who might,' said Widrias, thoughtfully. 'Yes, there is one we could turn to as a last resort… Very well, we shall journey to Morgenal, find ourselves our captain and ship, sail to Tonnis Harbour, and then proceed to the Mountain through the Kingdom of the calefs. That seems the safest way to me, unless anyone has any further suggestions?'

Nobody did.

'One final question; is it only us here who will go? There is secrecy in fewer numbers, but protection with more bodies,' Auran looked around. 'I'm sure everyone here is more than capable when it comes to combat, but I know I'd prefer to travel with some additional support. Besides, we don't know what difficulties we may face on our journey, perhaps a large force will stand in our way and we'll have no choice but to fight them?'

'No, you're right,' nodded Widrias. 'Fifty soldiers from the Council Guard will also join our company.'

Auran nodded, satisfied.

Food was brought up soon after. Simple things. Berries and bread, roast meat, hard cheese. Gwahl grinned at Widrias again. He couldn't help it. He'd almost forgotten about it, hadn't strayed close to the mountains for all that time, away on missions set by Deia. Now was his chance to get back to it. But beneath the excitement was something else, something that soon had the smile fade to a sour grimace as he chewed his crust. What was it? Nerves? Dread? He finally had time to go there, he should be as excited as he first felt. Why instead did he feel like he'd just run out of excuses to stay away?

'What's up?' Spotal asked.

'Nothing, just strange, haven't been on a quest like this for a while,' he smiled fleetingly.

'We'll be a good company,' nodded Spotal.

Company…

'By Enadir! I forgot!' he stood suddenly and cleared his throat, catching the attention of the chancellors. 'Sirs, another matter has slipped my mind. Outside the tent is a young man whom I met on my way to the Council, he wishes to join with us.'

'Very well, what do you know about him? Is he trustworthy?' asked Tuulik.

'He seems it. I met him a couple of days ago, running from the king's dreyads. Apparently, he escaped Crastalan's dungeons and managed to flee all the way to Dailas.'

'Quite a feat,' nodded Widrias. 'But why bring this up with us? Send him over to the recruiting sergeants, they'll give him a place in our ranks.'

'If I may, sir, I believe him to be better than a mere rank-and-file soldier. He has a certain quality about him, I can't explain what, but you'll see it when you see him.'

'He's can't join the Council Guard, if that's what you want,' muttered Tanor. 'My soldiers are hand-picked out of the masses, only the best and most trusted.'

'No, I know he won't join your men, Tanor,' smiled Gwahl. 'Neither should he join the militia or the free company or even the general brigades or divisions.'

'Then who should he join?' asked another hooded figure

'He should join us, on our quest.'

Eyebrows were raised, glances exchanged, and Widrias grumbled disapprovingly. 'What makes you think that he can be trusted?'

'On the way here, we were assaulted by some rogues. I purposefully put myself in a position of danger, a situation in which I would surely die – or so it seemed, at least – unless he intervened. He did exactly that, and "saved my life" through his actions.'

'What exactly did you do?' asked Pwtrek, smiling.

'I let my enemies close in on me and catch me, then when one was about to shoot me with an arrow, my companion killed the archer.'

'What if he is a spy, and only saved you so you would lead him to us?' asked Tanor.

Gwahl shook his head. 'I don't think so. We spoke at great length on the way over, I know a lot about the boy's character. He's no spy.'

'Very well,' said Widrias. 'Send him up here so we can judge him for ourselves.'

Gwahl smiled and sat down again. Hopefully, his new friend would answer their questions honestly. If he did, they would accept him. After all, another friend on the journey would be welcome.

*

Lidan stumbled through the curtains. Clothes torn and stained, mud coating virtually every part of him, he felt exposed, vulnerable in front of so many prying eyes. The guard led him to stand before the oval table at the centre of the room, crescent table at his back. Glancing around, he caught Gwahl's eye. The daemon nodded reassuringly.

One of the figures on the oval table cleared his throat and stared down at him. Although a hood covered most of the figure's face, he could see the creature's eyes reflecting the candle-light. A shadow with flaming eyes.

'So, what's your name?'

'Lidan, sir, Lidan Dimarr' he replied quietly.

'Why are you here?'

'I want to fight the king. Gwahl said you opposed him, so I asked if he would bring me along.'

'Gwahl said that you hadn't heard of us before, and yet you were very keen to join us. Perhaps that wasn't a wise move? For all you know we could be worse than Stolach.'

Lidan shook his head. 'No. The king is my enemy, cruel and hard. I've... suffered because of him, living under his rule, being tortured in his name. I want to fight him, him and his cronies. You lot seem like the type to bring the fight to him.'

'Aye, we might just...' the figure paused. 'But how do we know you're not a spy? You escaped Crastalan, then somehow made it all the way to Dailas without being caught, with dreyads on your tail the whole way? Seems convenient.'

'I'm not a spy,' he said, firmly. 'As for my escape, it was far from convenient. I got lucky, lucky enough to find friends, weapons, a horse… lucky enough to be a single prisoner or little importance to the king and his generals. That's how I made it this far. I'm a nobody. A beggar in rags, why should he waste his time searching for me?'

'And yet he sent his dreyads after you, and you somehow managed to evade them?'

'No, sir, I ran into them during my escape. I walked into their campsite by accident, struck one of them and ran, then they hunted me for fun I think.'

Silence after that, the hooded figure stroking a shadowed beard. Then he sighed and turned to Gwahl. 'Very well, Gwahl. You trust him and his answers were satisfactory, he can come. I would warn you though, he is *your* responsibility, *your* charge. If he does anything stupid, you will both be held accountable, if he betrays us, you shall both be severely punished. We'll take him with us, to keep an eye on him if nothing else, he couldn't possibly report back to Stolach from where we're going. Now, everyone leave, make your preparations for the journey ahead.'

A scuffle behind him as everyone stood and bowed to the table. He followed suit, clumsily, then Gwahl and a tall calef were beside him, smiling as they ushered him back to the stairway.

'Did I do alright?'

'Wonderfully. You're now an official soldier of the Council,' Gwahl led him downstairs, hands around his shoulders.

'Aye, stirring words,' the calef smiled.

He blanched at the mouthful of sharp, glistening fangs. He'd only seen calefs a handful of times before, and never this close. It was unusual how different they were to men. They had the same features, of course, but they were all exaggerated in a way. His eyes were abnormally large and almond-shaped, his nose sharp and pointed, high cheekbones, a pointed chin, a wide mouth. The most startling differences were his ears, set higher than a man and tapered to a long point, and his teeth, like the fangs of a cat.

'So, Lidan, I'm pleased to make your acquaintance. My name's Spotal. Gwahl here tells me you'd like a few lessons from me in the art of swordsmanship?' His voice was fair and musical, as if it were made for singing.

'Well, if that's alright with you,' spluttered Lidan, still eyeing his gleaming teeth.

'Of course!' he smiled more broadly. 'I'd never dream of refusing, I take it that you sparred with our friend here on the way over?'

'Yes,' nodded Lidan glumly.

'Fast, isn't he? I had a hard time placing a blow on his miserable little body the first few times we fought! He just kept ducking and jumping around like a little insect.'

'Hah! But once you did hit me you made it count!' laughed Gwahl, gingerly rubbing his right flank in memory of the duel.

As they walked down the stairs Gwahl gave Lidan a brief summary of the task at hand. His eyes widened with each sentence. By the time the brief summary was done, he was practically dancing. Despite Pwtrek's thoughts on the matter, it sounded too exhilarating to question. How often had he heard tales of Tarnegrefur Mountains, stretching so high into the sky that their tips stood above the clouds? Or Morgenal Harbour, the ancient city port where so many voyages began? Or Muranath Castle, jewel of the Kingdom of the calefs? As he wondered what General Teig might look like, he regarded his new companions, each one a loyal servant to the Council.

Beside him was Gwahl, smiling, laughing, at ease with everyone. Despite the short time in his company, he respected the daemon more than anyone he'd ever met. Hopefully, Gwahl felt the same. Without him, he'd be dead in the woods, victim of the dreyads. Bless the north winds he found him.

Standing by the doorway was Captain Spotal Lasaai, the calef, one of the greatest swordsmen of their time, or so they claimed. His lithe frame was that of a hunter, a dancer. He wore light white armour made of toughened leather. He caught Lidan looking at him and gave him a smile and a broad wink, patting the hilt of his jian lightly.

Beside Spotal was the hanex, Noswen Aikass, with her falchion in a scabbard across her back, a long dirk strapped to one thigh, blowpipe and darts to another. Her cloak was black and her armour sparse. Strong shoulders and powerful legs, like a panther. He averted his eyes when he saw her watching him. Something about her expressionless face was unsettling.

Auran Meerl sat outside. He supposed his silence was because he missed his home, where the sun shone for eighteen hours a day and water was scarce. His armour was simple; a padded linen coat that hung down to his knees, fastened with a belt; a gambeson. Studded leather chaps protected his lower legs. They looked uncomfortable over his linen trousers, but he wore them like a second skin. A pair of steel gauntlets dangled from a thong at his belt. There was something familiar in his silence, a contemplation over past misgivings that reflected his own. Auran stroked a slender finger over the head of his magnificent battleaxe, its long steel blade glinting in the fading sun, and a shaft of black, polished wood with tight leather binding that served as a handle.

The great black juggernaut, Pwtrek Mestax was talking to Gwahl, his spear leaning against his shoulder, and a mighty long-sword in a scabbard at his side. His legs were protected by heavy plate armour; greaves, cuisses, and chausses, but his torso was unarmed, covered instead in his long, coarse, black pelt. He could tell that Pwtrek would be a fearsome opponent in combat with his claws alone, but with spear and sword...

The neiad twins, Chekry and Depani Hemwr were a playful pair, always with smiles on their lips and never without a cheery comment. The brother bore a great crossbow, whilst the sister held a much smaller one, designed to be loaded and shot more swiftly, at the expense of range and power. Both wore long, slender rapiers in ornate sheaths at their sides. Neiads were generally considered one of the finest warrior races in the lands, and one look at the twins' powerful frames told him no different.

The tall red-faced man, Tanor Lamein, stood at the bottom of the walkway, polearm in hand. He was probably the biggest man he'd ever seen, with a broad back, a strong chest, and shoulders like cauldrons. This was the first time he'd seen the polearm up close, and nearly gasped in awe. The aged oak shaft was as long as Tanor was tall, with a rich red leather grip covered in pale gold studs. The head was no less magnificent. One side was a rectangular hammer, fiercely spiked along its length, while on the reverse side was a hooked spike, like a hydra's claw. At its head was another spike, squarer in cross-section than a spear, perfect for punching through plate armour, with a twin at the opposite end of the shaft. Twin steel langets riveted the head to the shaft, tempered steel inlaid with intricate filigree. As Lidan gazed at the polearm in the man's gauntleted hand, carrying it as though it weighed no more than a small forge hammer – though it clearly weighed more than ten such hammers – he knew Tanor was not a man to be taken lightly. He wore the chainmail and green surcoat of the Council Guard, scarred and battle-damaged.

Finally, was the member of the Council joining them, General Widrias Gesharr, the chancellor who questioned him most during the meeting. He still wore the same hooded cloak to obscure half his face, revealing only a bearded chin and stern mouth. Underneath the robe was a fine coat of mail and dark green jerkin, adorned at the hems with a delicate golden trim. Jutting from the bottom of his cloak was the scabbard of a greatsword, carried on his back. Impractical if needed to be drawn for battle, but more comfortable for travelling. The hilt extended above his right shoulder, but was similarly covered in a protective leather sheath. As the general appeared from the walkway, all present ceased their chatter and saluted, respectfully. Lidan followed suit awkwardly. Widrias acknowledged their gesture with a nod, and stormed out the tent in a flurry.

Chapter 6

Despite his lofty hopes and ambitions of setting out at once, it was not to be. Planning such an expedition apparently took a lot of time and effort, or so Gwahl claimed. There were provisions to organise, weapons and armour, maps, medical equipment, spare clothes and all manner of technicalities and unexpected bureaucracy to be seen to. Apparently, even rebellions had a staggering amount of paperwork to keep track of who went where, for what, with whom, and why. Lidan spent the days trailing behind Gwahl as the daemon attended various meetings, then took to wandering through the camp when this got too dull. Disappointingly, Spotal was too busy for those lessons, so he sought other instructors. Despite his initial apprehension, most were happy enough to accommodate his questions, and he spent several hours sparring and practicing with the other new recruits.

On the third day, he was returning to his tent from a reasonably disheartening sparring session when Spotal beckoned him over. Nothing else to do that day, and he wasn't going to miss out on this, whatever it was. Navigating their way through the labyrinth of tents, chatting aimlessly, Spotal led him to one, chests and empty rails outside.

'Go on, a surprise for you,' the calef gestured to the door.

'A nice one?'

'Hopefully.'

A wizened old man greeted him from the gloom, his skin a maze of wrinkles and liver spots, his thick sleeves full of pins and needles stuck through at various angles for safekeeping. Lengths of cloth spilled out of half-open crates stacked around the tent's circumference. A tailor. He looked down at his tattered shirt and grimaced. Like walking into a top bakery carrying a soggy-crusted pasty you attempted at home.

'The calef captain told me your clothes were in a poor state,' cracked the old man's voice. 'I never imagined they were this bad!'

He grinned. 'After all I've been through, I'm surprised they're still holding together.'

'Only just,' he circled him, picking at the threadbare shirt. 'The calef said your clothes hurt his eyes, and I'm inclined to agree! Our boys should look good, makes them look more professional, like a proper army.'

Bitter memories were stitched into the fabric of these clothes, ones he'd be better off without. He nodded to the tailor.

'Alright. Might be time to get rid of them.'

'You'll look like a proper soldier by the end.'

'Might be a while before I feel like one.'

*

He emerged a few hours later. Gone were the rags, replaced by sturdy leather boots, dark green trousers with black leather chaps, a fine wool shirt and a brigandine of toughened leather, inlaid with thin iron plates within the fabric. He caught his reflection and smiled. Professional indeed.

Spotal looked up from the book he'd been reading, idly playing with some talisman or charm about his neck. His lips broke into a smile and he yelped with delight. Returning the talisman to the folds of his tunic, he clapped his hands.

'Out of those rags! Finally! You look like the perfect soldier, my friend.'

He flushed and mumbled his thanks, before looking up at the calef and grinning. 'Hurt your eyes, did they?'

Spotal smiled. 'Well, I'm used to being surrounded by elegance – the sight of an impressionable young man wearing filthy rags appalled me! Besides, this is armour. Strong and resilient. I did you a favour bringing you here.'

Lidan nodded and started down the path back to his tent. 'I'll thank you when it saves my life and only then. Otherwise your head won't fit through your shirts.'

Spotal laughed again as he followed. 'Not so fast, we need to see to your weapons before we set out. What do you have?'

Lidan pointed in the direction of his tent, shared with Gwahl. 'Sabre, dagger, shield. Standard stuff.'

'A sabre is hardly the standard weapon for a simple foot soldier,' smiled the calef. 'Most of our lot have spears in formation or daggers and axes for skirmishes. Get your things and come with me to the armourers.'

A few minutes later, he handed him his weapons. Spotal, joined by a burly, bearded armourer, scrutinised them.

'A cavalry sabre,' barked the armourer. His gruff accent characteristic of a northerner. 'Not really suitable for a man of your stature, or rank. Mounted weapon, that one.'

'Aye,' agreed Spotal, 'the curvature of the blade, the broader foible, the overall length, they all make it difficult to wield on foot. The knife and shield are good enough. The shield especially, oak and plate. Explains its uncommon weight, but it'll offer you considerable protection. A bit overkill, perhaps, but at least you'll be safe, provided you can lift it. Might I ask where you got them?'

'I stole the sabre and shield from the saddle of one of the king's outriders, the dagger I took from a stall in the town outside Crastalan,' he said.

'You'd be better off with this arming sword, it's easier to use on foot,' said the armourer, taking a straight-bladed sword off a weapon rack and offering it to him.

He shook his head. 'I'd rather keep my sabre, thank you.'

'It's for your own benefit, Lidan,' warned Spotal. 'By using this sabre you'll be slow, cumbersome, easier to deal with. Or you will as a beginner, at least. Its weight distribution is too imbalanced for you. Use one of our arming swords, it'll be easier for you to wield. A quicker point, swifter, easier, and more controlled in the lunge. You'll also have the benefits of having the true and false edges of your blade,' he looked at Lidan's blank expression. 'Don't worry, I'll teach you about them.'

Lidan nodded. 'Thank you, but honestly, although quick lunges might be good in a fancy duel, I can't see me doing any of them. I'll just be hacking away in the heat of melee, and I'm already used to sabres and cutlasses.'

The armourer snorted. 'You're right. Against the common, untrained brawlers you meet in the forest, slashing about is generally their way, but consider going against an elite soldier, trained in swordsmanship. They'd turn away your blows and skewer you. Listen to the Swordmaster Spotal, he knows a thing or two.'

'If I find myself fighting an elite soldier, I doubt I'd be able to defeat him, no matter what sword I use,' he shrugged.

Spotal sighed. 'All the more reason for us to have these lessons, I suppose. All I can do is advise,' he shrugged and turned to the armourer. 'Would you be able to sharpen and improve his sabre for him? Make it easier to wield?'

'Of course, Captain, I'll do my best.'

'My thanks,' Spotal turned away and called over his shoulder as the armourer measured Lidan's arms and legs. 'You're stubborn, are you not, Lidan? Never mind, you'll learn your lessons, hopefully not permanently.'

*

The stories he'd been told about grand quests normally started with a magnificent sunrise to see the heroes off, bugles and drums, cheering crowds, songs of triumph and courage, joy and jubilation all around.

Reality was a more muted affair. Early hours, dawn not yet peeking above the treeline, the morning mist curling around the boughs. No fanfare but the trudge of boots in mud. No songs but the call of a wren.

Not that it mattered to him. He could have jumped, sang, cried out his thanks and laughed for them all, but he didn't. he kept his excitement hidden as best he could, but couldn't keep the smile away. His first quest, his first time living a proper adventure! Hopefully not his last. He checked his gear for the tenth time since beginning the march. Sharpened and shortened sabre, knife, shield, water-skin; he ticked each of his possessions off his fingers. Nothing lost in the past two minutes of walking.

Shifting the weight of his hefty pack of provisions, made mostly of the mysterious Harandale Roots of the calefs, he looked ahead. No need for sunshine and crowds, this was all he needed. No need to watch a company out on their quest, better to live through it, shoulder to shoulder with his brothers in arms. This is what it was to belong, to have someone by your side.

Pwtrek marched next to him, his mighty spear doubling as a walking stick. Even among juggernauts, he was big, towering above him like a redwood to a sapling.

Pwtrek caught him looking and smiled. 'So, little one, this is your first time marching in a regiment?'

'How did you know?' he marvelled. Such insight!

'Because, my friend, your feet are topsy-turvy to the rest of the regiment. Left-right, not right-left!'

Lidan cursed under his breath and shuffled to correct himself.

'That's better, little one,' exclaimed Pwtrek. 'Now try not to lose your step again, makes the whole regiment look sloppy!'

'I'll try not to, sir,' he grunted.

'Don't worry, I was only teasing. You'll do fine. You've got the look of a capable soldier about you!' he smiled again. 'So, tell me, how did you end up here in the woods, marching around with old veterans like me?'

He quickly gave a brief outline of his journey from Crastalan to the Council. Pwtrek in turn recounted his own tale.

'I've never found the prospect of one man commanding all these lands appealing, you see,' he began. 'I prefer the Midlands as a democracy, and when this Stolach began conquering tribes and proclaimed himself king, I knew it was for the worse. Winds! Even the fragmented, fractured lands before Stolach came about was better than this tyrant's reign, at least then we had control over our own villages!

'Anyway, I'd been in quite a few small skirmishes with the king's troops before I met the general,' he pointed to the front of the column of soldiers, where Widrias marched with Tanor and a few others. 'He assisted me in eliminating a few filthy men who were terrorising a small family of hanex. We destroyed the vermin and he asked me to join his rebellion. Much as you did, I agreed and soon became quite an important figure in the Council, if I do say so myself,' he chuckled.

'What did you do?'

'Well, they often sent me northwards, near my old home, to keep an eye out for the king's meddling beyond the Midlands. I was a sort of scout or spy, I suppose, reporting back every few months. It was on my way back a few summers ago a band of goblins ambushed me and wounded my leg horribly. After that my days as a scout were basically over. Now you must understand, a band of goblins would normally pose no threat to me, all skinny limbs and puny weapons, the lot of them, but I've had a tricky leg for many years now, and the ambush finally did it in. Happened in those vicious southern winds eight years ago, I'm not sure if you remember them?'

'I do!' he exclaimed, 'the winds were so strong they tore down a quarter of the buildings in the village!'

'Aye, yours wasn't the only village to be hit hard by those gales. A fir tree fell on me, blown clean from its roots, all thirty feet of it, crashed into my knee. Then a few years later a hairy little goblin hits the same knee with a club, can't say it ended well for him. Anyway, I returned to the Council to file my report, and then I wandered north to scratch out a living in relative peace.

'Of course, Stolach soon made sure that plan would fail,' he growled. 'Recruiting forces in the northern forest, it was mere days after I saw the great armies to the north when Council scouts came and requested my immediate return. So I came, and here I am.'

They continued to talk and march long into the evening before Widrias called the column to a halt. Lidan collapsed gratefully under a yew and nearly fell asleep as soon as his eyelids met. His rest was disturbed when Gwahl shook him awake.

'Getoff,' he grumbled.

Gwahl snorted and kicked him lightly in the flank. 'Food. Sleep later.'

It was all he needed to chase away the tiredness and was soon up and running to the food carts.

The company sat munching on warm bread heated up over a fire pit. The rations in their packs were to be consumed only after the few wagons accompanying them returned to the Council. They chatted and laughed and joked until sleep finally caught them in its lulling snare. Silence settled, broken occasionally by the sniffles of the soldiers on sentry duty. Lidan slept a dreamless sleep, allowing him to be engulfed by the darkness as it soothed his aching muscles after a long day's march. It was a peaceful night, a fine night. Safe with his new companions.

*

The dawn sun swept its warmth through the forest below. The morning dew shimmered as it caught its rays, illuminating the wood in a sparkling golden glow. Lidan brushed the glistening droplets from his brigandine. He breathed in the warm air. Another day's march. He could get used to this. He lay back and imagined the potential breakfasts that awaited. Warm porridge, maybe roast chicken, more bread toasted over the fire. Things had turned out so well. To think where he was but three weeks ago. Zile would have enjoyed this life too. They all would.

His dreams of a hot meal came to a sudden, unsatisfying end. Gwahl forcefully threw an apple at his stomach, ordering him up before the entire army left without them. Lidan moodily voiced his wish of a warm breakfast to the daemon, and was greeted with a roar of laughter.

'Really, Lidan!' cried Gwahl. 'A warm breakfast! Would you like us to run you a bath as well? Carve you an armchair? Stitch a lovely warm blanket? Hot breakfast. Enadir spare me.'

He trudged behind the daemon with a foul expression. Nothing wrong with hoping for something warm. It was perfectly reasonable to anticipate a hearty meal before a hard day's march. He munched on his apple and pulled a face. Sour apples were hardly what he'd dreamt of.

Surprisingly, the march was far more tolerable than expected and he found some comfort in the column, flanked on either side by seasoned soldiers. That being said, Tanor's shout to make camp in the evening was more than welcome. The food carts were long since returned to the Council, and he contented himself with a simple supper of a single Harandale root. It was small, bulbous, and unappetising in appearance. Light blue and flecked with yellow specks. It tasted similar to pumpkin, with a slightly nuttier scent, and a surprisingly dense texture. His jaw ached once he'd finished, and

106

he lay beneath a beech nursing his cheeks, wondering how long it would be until he ate another hot meal.

When morning came, he was surprisingly refreshed. The ache in his muscles gone, leaving them supple and strong. Mentioning this to Gwahl, the daemon smiled and pointed to his pack of Harandale roots. Apparently the calefin plant had been specifically bred for soldiers on the march, and was renowned for its ability to rejuvenate. Gwahl said that in the infirmaries throughout the kingdom of the calefs, wounded soldiers were served nothing but mashed Harandale roots, which allowed them to heal and return to the field far sooner than any other army could manage.

Even so, mysterious and useful as they may be, they were a far cry from roast chicken.

It was his desire to find more meat that led to disaster that evening. As they threw down their packs to rest, Lidan borrowed a bow and quiver from one of the Council Guards on the promise he wouldn't lose or damage any arrows and went to hunt. He was not an experienced hunter, and had no clue how to track animals through a forest, but it surely couldn't be that difficult? He was optimistic. At least a couple of pigeons, maybe even a rabbit or two.

Often, the luck of the inexperienced gives them opportunities that seasoned veterans would scarce believe. So it was that evening as a fat pigeon landed on a bough not twenty feet from him. He blinked. By the north winds! A smile to envy a child stealing honey spread over his lips as he nocked an arrow to the bowstring. The pigeon watched him curiously, cooing softly as she bobbed her head back and forth. As he drew, the motion seemed to frighten her. She flew away in a fluster. Thinking himself a rather fine shot, he released the arrow anyway. Missed. Miserably. He cursed. Now he had the problem of finding the damned arrow. By the time he did that, it would be too dark to do any more hunting. Bloody pigeon.

As he trudged away, searching, an unfamiliar smell hit his nostrils. Smoky and intoxicating, like the smell of a heavily-scented candle on a hot day. His head spun. The forest started undulating before his eyes and placed his hand on a trunk to steady himself. He shook his head to clear it, but the smell lingered, clinging to his nostrils like a limpet on a shipwreck.

Shaking his head in a near frenzy, he caught a glimpse of someone staring at him. It was him who'd frightened the pigeon away. He was the source of the stink, pulsing from his skin in cloying waves. A man, worse, a Hobb, judging by his tattoos. Pushing six feet tall and built like a stone wall.

Lidan swallowed. He'd heard plenty of tales about the Hobbs of Dailas. Fearsome warrior nomads, covered in intricate tattoos marking each kill. Their culture and customs set them apart from other men. Most notably, their use of narcotics. It wasn't just the essence of poppy seeds, or powdered crystals from the Jagged Isles, or even the deadly leaves from the Southlands. From birth, they indulged in all manner of stimulants, changing their behaviour, warping them into something more animal than man. But among all their ingestions, it was Vapour that was deadliest. A toxic smoke, a cocktail of substances, both natural and man-made, each recipe individual to that clan, all of them ending in the same result. It induced states of both euphoria and fierce aggression, depending on the dose. Supposedly more addicting than even Azag syrup from Azagin in the Jagged Isles, the thirst for Vapour was all-consuming, ravenous, uncontrollable in its later stages. It was no accident there were few Hobbs over the age of fifty. Most died from overdosing or were 'honourably' rejected from their clans when the thirst for Vapour, or 'the Desire' as they called it, took hold. Such rejection was for the sole purpose of finding a suitably violent death to quell the Desire and find the bliss of passing.

From the looks of this one, he was desperately Desired. His chest heaved and his nostrils flared, glaring angrily at Lidan.

Wide-eyed, he weighed up his options. At present, the Hobb was about thirty metres away from him. Theoretically, far enough to shoot. However, following his recent mishap with the pigeon, his confidence in his archery was somewhat diminished. That left running or fighting, and judging from the Hobb's powerful legs, running was not such a good idea. That being said, fighting didn't seem too appealing either.

His hand shook as he eased it over to his sabre and grabbed the hilt, white-knuckled. The Hobb growled and drew a backsword from his scabbard, his mouth frothing in his drug-crazed state. A moment later, he charged, screaming incomprehensibly as he bore down on him.

Lidan balked, searching for his shield, but of course he left it back at the campsite. Heart racing, he drew his sabre with a flash and braced himself for the clash. The pounding of the Hobb's feet on the grass sent a dull tremor through his boots.

At twenty paces he could taste the smoke oozing from his skin.

At ten paces he could see the mad glimmer in his eyes, a cruel light dancing behind the pupils, like a primal hunger for blood, battle, and death.

At five paces he braced his feet, doing all he could not to lose control of his bladder.

He hit him with a crunch, dipping his shoulder to barge him to the ground. Lidan went flying, landing heavily on his back as his foe overran a few paces, giving him time to get up and ready himself again. He considered calling for help, but what if there were more of them around? He didn't fancy his chances against one, let alone two or three.

No more time for thought. Sabre above his head, he received a barrage of blows. A high guard, like they taught him in the Council. The sword blade raked against his sabre, jarring his arm and forcing him back. He realised the Hobb's intention, to force him into a corner where there'd be no escape.

Fight back! Fight back or die a fool's death.

He threw himself sideways, catching the Hobb off guard. His foe stumbled and nearly lost his balance. Lidan slashed at his unprotected back, but his enemy rolled forwards, anticipating the blow.

The two circled each other cautiously, oblivious to everything except each other. Lidan shrugged off the bow and quiver. Might not make much difference, but better than risking it getting tangled up in his legs. He lunged half-heartedly at the Hobb's left flank. Easily parried. His enemy smiled, a string of drool hanging from his lower lip. Four winds! This was bad. A few days into the quest and he was already going to die.

Think! What to do? Nothing. Those few basic lessons at the Council were buried beneath ten feet of hard-packed fear. He could barely keep his legs from trembling, barely keep his sword in his hands.

He resolved to the one thing that was stuck in his memory, *'The strongest defence is a powerful offence.'*

Springing forward with a frankly pathetic roar, he swept his sabre in a blurring figure-of-eight. The Hobb seemed unimpressed and casually sidestepped his clumsy charge, letting him pass by. Lidan turned quickly and advanced, twirling his sword around his wrist. Their blades met in the air with a clang. Shockwaves rushed down his arm. Almost enough to drop his sabre. But he clung on. Just.

The stocky brawler struck at his right flank, he parried the blow and quickly twisted aside to avoid the stab to his stomach. He returned the gesture, but his flailing blade was easily knocked aside.

They went blow for blow for what felt like hours, but was in reality mere minutes, before he made his critical error. Wrist aching from swinging the blade, he was desperate for an opening, something to finish the fight. Right on cue, an opening in his foe's defences, a gap that appeared after he swung wildly at Lidan's head. He lunged, aiming for the chest. The Hobb swayed to his left and caught his weak wrist. He tried to pull away but it was no good. Too strong. The Hobb wrenched the sabre from his hand and kicked him to the ground.

He groaned as he hit the grass. Tricked! By a drug-addled oaf. Sneakily leaving a gap for him to try to exploit, while all the time the monster knew he was in perfect safety. The Hobb glanced at the sabre and threw away his backsword, selecting it as his new weapon. He smiled again, his facial tattoos contorting foully as he bore down on him. His entire body quivered in its drugged-up excitement, anticipating the blood to be spilled. If ever there were a time to lose control of your bladder, this was it. He just hoped they wouldn't judge him when they found his bloody, piss-soaked corpse in the mud.

'Lidan!'

Both turned. Blessed winds! Gwahl and Spotal approached, weapons drawn.

'Help!' he squeaked.

Spotal sprang forward, his jian flashing a wonderful silver as he engaged their foe, giving Lidan time to find his feet and scramble to Gwahl. He watched the calef duel the Hobb, his strong arm turning aside the foe's clumsy strikes with the poise and grace of a dancer.

Hiding behind Gwahl's reassuring presence, he drew shuddering breaths of relief. Safe again. Four winds! Safe again.

Spotal fenced the Hobb coolly, almost disinterestedly, even glancing over his shoulder at the two of them. Their eyes met, and he did something unexpected.

With a quick flick of his sword, he disarmed the Hobb and kicked him hard in the stomach, winding him.

As his foe staggered away, clutching his midriff, Spotal picked up the sabre and handed it back to Lidan.

'Now, attack again.'

'What?' Lidan stared at him. What was he talking about? 'Why can't you kill him?'

'Why can't you?'

'He's too strong for me,' said Lidan, facing their foe, backsword recovered.

'I'll guide you. This here is the most important lesson I can give you.'

'I can't.'

'You must. This is your most important battle. Back down now and you'll never recover your confidence.'

'My wrist is too tired,'

'Aye, your sword is too heavy. No use crying over it. You've made your decisions. Use the weight to your advantage.'

He shook his head and looked over at the Hobb, glaring at Spotal. 'How?'

'Just do as I say. Now go! This is battle! There's no room for hesitation!'

Definitely not how he expected this to turn out. He stepped forward reluctantly to meet the Hobb, sabre heavy in his hand. The

Hobb's eyes snapped from Spotal to him and came charging in, sword swinging and howling with rage.

'When I tell you, step to your right, with your sabre held vertically across your body. Hilt high, Lidan. High. Point down. Good. As he passes, follow him with your sword.'

He tried, but stepped too early, before Spotal called out. The Hobb adjusted his charge and hit him. It wasn't a clean hit, only a scratch on his arm, but it was enough to throw him off balance.

'Take a step back!' shouted Spotal. 'Regain your footing. We'll try a different guard. Stand with your right foot forward, your hilt at waist-height with the blade pointing upwards! Sword up, Lidan! Here he comes! Parry! Parry! Cut to the right! No! Step back now! Now! Good, recover. Watch your head, he's going for- Duck! Blast it, Lidan, take more care! Now, riposte! Riposte!'

'He doesn't know what that means,' he heard Gwahl mutter as he scurried back. Spotal muttered something back and continued his coaching.

'Alright, he's coming at you from your left, adjust your footing, swing your left foot round behind you, good. Always keep your enemy to your front, facing them sideways on. You're fighting without a shield right now, things are different to what you're used to. Parry! Good! Try turning the blade aside instead of just knocking it away, it gives you an opening for attack. Circular motions, Lidan, they take away the force of the blow. Not like that! Step back! We'll leave that for another day. Now, when the opportunity arrives I want you to start your own attack, instead of reacting to what he does. Let him swing, now step forward! Press on! Good! You have him now! To his right! Again! No, retreat! Back! The opportunity has passed. Step back! Parry!'

So it went on, he duelled his opponent furiously, all the time following Spotal's instructions. He could feel the tide of battle shift. Whereas before he'd been getting bludgeoned, now they were locked in a fierce duel. Both bled from several cuts, none of them serious, but wounds nonetheless, and Spotal instructed Lidan how to protect those wounds while targeting his opponent's.

He made his second critical mistake. Buoyed by the shift in momentum, he ignored Spotal's instruction to adjust his footing before lunging forward, aiming for his enemy's chest. His sword was knocked aside. Off-balance, he was pushed off his feet while parrying the following counter.

Lidan recoiled. As he tried to crawl away he felt something hard press into the back of his spine. Reaching behind, he felt the handle of his knife, forgotten in its sheath at the back of his belt. In a flash, he whipped out the blade and threw. The Hobb's eyes bulged as he saw a gleaming blade rush towards his chest. He tried to deflect it with his sword but was too slow. His throw was poor, and the handle glanced off his collarbone, spinning around and driving the point up into his throat. Damn lucky.

The barbarian sank to the ground, breathing heavily, spluttering through the wound. He tried to support himself on the backsword, but the blade couldn't hold his weight and he fell to the floor. Staring up at the sky, he spluttered a final mouthful of blood, gurgling softly.

Lidan approached shakily. He glanced over his shoulder. Spotal and Gwahl nodded him on. The Hobb's gurgles trailed away. He placed his sabre just below the collarbone and pushed is weight onto it. The gurgles were silenced.

Spotal clapped him on the shoulder. 'You certainly made things difficult for yourself, but in the end, you did well.'

'How did you know I was in danger?'

His voice quivered. It seemed only a couple of days ago he'd killed the thief, now here was another to his tally. How many before this quest was through? He needed to sit, to have a moment for himself.

'We knew you'd gone hunting, so were listening out for you. We heard shouting and came to help. Was the hunt successful?'

'No,' he swallowed. Now wasn't the time to retch, not in front of Spotal. 'And I lost an arrow.'

'I'm sure you'll be forgiven.'

They returned to the campsite, Gwahl and Spotal chatting a whole load of nothing. Perhaps they did it on purpose to distract him from the ordeal, perhaps they were so detached from death it was as mundane as their conversation on hunting game and favourite sauce to complement seasonal pheasant. Too much for him. As soon as they returned to the others, he curled into a ball in a patch of tall grass, shivering despite the warmth of the evening. The long blades cradled him as he returned to his fevered dreams.

Chapter 7

Crastalan dungeons. Dark. Damp. Alone. His only company the algae and mosses filling the cracks in the wall. The only source of light was the torch outside his cell, shining in a miserable yellow pool through a crack under the iron door. He stared at the light, hungrily taking in its golden glow.

His gaoler stormed in, trailing behind the barbed whip. He flinched at the sight, covering his eyes with a bony arm. The scars across his back tingled as the barbs scraped across the cold stone floor. The gaoler hauled him up by his elbow and dragged him into the corridor. A young prison-hand took over, shoving him up a short flight of stairs to an open door. Thrown again, he lay on the floor, shivering. He didn't know for how long he stayed there, curled in a ball, wishing he were invisible. But he wasn't. A guard came, as he always came, and took him by his iron collar to the streets.

Stumbling and weeping silently, he was led by the neck through a pungent garden, quiet alleys that smelled of bitter medicine, and finally into the bustle of a crowd. Dimly aware of distant taunting as people tossed mud and rotting waste over him. He kept his head bowed, letting the shower of filth wash over. If only he could grab some of the food to eat later. The scabs on his knees were torn off anew. A crimson wake on the black stone steps. A child skipped up to slap him forcefully around the ear. Laughter. Once upon a time he might have wept at the shame, but no longer. Just let it end. Let them slap him, piss on him, throw him into the cesspits. Anything to make it stop.

Humiliation accomplished, he was forgotten, discarded, even by the taunting crowd. Only good for a few minutes' sport before he became too pathetic even for their tastes. The next prisoner was brought up. He was thrown aside.

Taken again by the collar, the guard half-dragged him through the gutters and up a flight of stairs. He cried out as he landed heavily on the stone steps. When morning came, new bruises would decorate his frail body. Through a heavy door into a building. Handed over to two other servants, nothing but a sack of meat, an inconvenient package for the servants to deliver.

They took him through cold stone corridors to a grand, black doorway, steel spikes jutting from the black wood. The doors opened and the servants threw him inside. Unconsciousness beckoned. Old friend with your gentle numbness. He didn't hear the boots until they were right in front of him. Someone dragged him to his feet. Grey eyes.

He whimpered. The grey eyes.

The grey-eyed monster carried him across the room by the collar, its hard edges digging into the sores of his neck. A piece of cloth soaked in something sharp was held against his nose. Unconsciousness retreated, bringing back unwelcome lucidity.

He opened his eyes. Five others slumped against a wall. He tried calling out to them, but lacked the energy. Grey Eyes sat him down facing them and walked away, out of sight. Lidan stared at the five, some faint recollection of their faces. His dulled mind ached with confusion. He knew them. He was sure of it. But who?

As he struggled, one of them flew up into the air sharply. He dangled, legs twitching. Lidan stared dumbly. A noose around his neck. That much, he understood. The other four followed. Two died immediately as their frail necks cracked and popped. The other three twitched and gasped, pungent urine trickling down their legs. The nooses released and they fell in a miserable bundle, coughing, spluttering, vomiting.

Grey Eyes returned and approached the first of them. He held him up by the neck. He drew a knife and cut slowly across his chest, first from the base of the neck to the fork of the legs, then from armpit to armpit. The man groaned as what little blood he had in his body gushed out, pattering on the floor to mix with the urine. Like raindrops, or cider from a barrel. He watched the droplets run down the bare chest. Little lines, like ink on a parchment. What were they spelling?

The second man was stuck through the chest. Gasping. Suffocating. Silent. The third tried to crawl away, wheezing on all fours. Grey Eyes stepped over and pulled a mattock from a rack on the wall. He stepped on his foot to stop his pathetic attempt at escape. The mattock lifted and crashed down on the his back. Vertebrae snapped and ribs shattered. The wheezes turned to surprised splutters, like a little mountain brook tinkling around stones. Grey Eyes approached Lidan.

'Now, scum,' Grey Eyes held his chin in his hand. His voice was calm, almost kind. 'You see the price of treason.'

He grabbed him by the back of the neck again, like a stray dog, forcing his head around to the corpses. His dull eyes stared dumbly at the spreading puddles of crimson. Something about it told him it was bad. Unhealthy. It's what stopped them from moving.

'Such mercy will not be yours.'

The grey eyes were as calm and cold as when he'd first entered the room. He stared back into the shining orbs. They changed colour, became a softer, darker brown. The figure grew larger, bulkier, the city dissolved.

*

He woke. Pwtrek gazed down at him, face creased with worry. He smiled weakly up at him, and the juggernaut sighed with relief, sitting back on the forest floor.

'Thank the north winds you're awake. You were thrashing about in your sleep. Thought you might do yourself some damage.'

'Thank you, Pwtrek,' said Lidan, voice shaking. Just a dream. All over. 'Do I have time to close my eyes or are we moving on?'

'Sorry, little one,' smiled Pwtrek. 'No more sleep. Unless you can snooze on the go?' he paused, looking him up and down. 'These nightmares… they happen often?'

'Often enough,' he muttered. As cruel as these memories may be, there were far crueller ones to revisit. Of Zile. He shook his head. It would do him no good to linger on it.

Groaning, he stood, a new ache in the small of his back. A rough stone under the grass was the culprit, kicked away into the undergrowth as punishment. That'll teach it.

They set off again, Lidan in the rear ranks, marching stiffly from his sore thighs and buttocks. Who knew swordsmanship took so much out of your legs? Not him, that's for sure. He looked around for

Pwtrek but he was at the vanguard with Gwahl and the neiad twins. The Council Guard were pleasant enough but far from chatty. A march in silence, then.

He tried enjoying the sights of the forest, the sight of the lush canopy swaying in the breeze, the sound of its gentle rustle. He smelled the rich, deep fragrance of the dark earth and he enjoyed the feel of a warm breeze against his skin. He threw his head back and closed his eyes, letting the morning sun warm his eyelids.

Despite his efforts, the pretence of relaxation, he was still shaken after the skirmish with the Hobb. His arm still throbbed from the endless crashing blows against his shield, and no matter how hard he scrubbed his hands, he could still see the stain of blood on his palms. Closing his eyes, he shuddered at the thought of the man's snarling face, his shocked expression when the dagger pierced his flesh.

'Dirdin,' he whispered to himself, recalling the name of the hanex in the cave.

A chill down his spine. A movement in the corner of his eye. He snapped his head around. Noswen. Hardly making a sound as she stalked through the woods. Damned impressive. Gliding over the grass rather than walking. She must have come into his peripheral vision on purpose, no way would he have noticed her otherwise. She turned to him, flicked her eyes up and down, examining him as a butcher might examine a carcass. Her eyes were blue, cold as a crisp winter morning, twin orbs of ice. He turned away, uncomfortable.

'I've been watching you,' she said, her voice as calm as ever. He suppressed a shudder. Flat and emotionless, a voice that would sound the same should she compliment your clothes or ordered you to beg for your life before her blade.

'I hear you're a capable fighter, considering your gross inexperience. Rumour has it that you can hold your own against a Desired Hobb. Possibly even one of the king's dreyads?'

'Spotal helped me. Just did what he told me,' he mumbled.

'The king's prisoner? Escaped and made it all the way to the Council? A remarkable feat for one of…how many years?'

'I'm not sure, three, perhaps?'

'Three years. Three years of torture and suffering, but you had the resilience to make it all the way here. The horrors you must have faced. As I said, remarkable. I wonder how you did it?'

The hanex paused for a second. Perhaps she expected an answer. He didn't have any to give. What did she want? Somehow, a conversation with his old gaoler seemed almost appealing.

'Don't want to talk to me about it,' she shrugged. 'For your sake, talk to someone. Your nightmare last night was of your time in the dungeons?' he nodded in reply. 'I wonder what you did to deserve such terrible punishment?'

He kept his eyes fixed on the ground in front of him. Why was she here? Couldn't she just leave him alone? The others in the column were already shying away, keeping their distance. As if he weren't already enough of an outsider, now they were going to associate him with her.

'Fear is a powerful thing. It is the poisonous fuel that drives you to things that are quite out of character. Theft, spying, *assassination*. If this fear is left unchecked, then you may lose yourself in that new persona moulded by terror.'

'What are you suggesting?' he whispered, trying to catch the eye of a satorr. The soldier ignored him. Nobody wanted to come close to her. Said a lot when trained soldiers were scared of a person.

'Nothing,' she never took her eyes off him. 'Just a warning. Fear is powerful. Don't let your fear of the king and his servants drive you to do anything foolish, anything you might regret.'

'You think I might kill someone? That I'm an assassin sent after you?'

'No, you don't possess the skill of my guild. But you might be frightened enough to try and kill someone important, to present their heads to the king as a way of escaping his wrath? I'm warning you that such a path leads only to despair.'

'It never entered my mind.'

She nodded, still staring intently into his eyes, but said nothing more, flitting next to him in silence. It was almost worse than her questioning, knowing she was there, just out of eyesight, watching.

Gwahl saved him. The daemon came trotting along, all grins and good graces to the men. He beamed at Lidan, even wider to Noswen, calling her over out of the shadows.

'Tanor reckons we'll break out the forest in a bit, the trees are thinning out and there's more of a breeze in the air,' said Gwahl, Lidan smiled and nodded in acknowledgement. The daemon turned to Noswen. 'Care to join me and Tanor at the vanguard? We can catch up properly, share tales and reminisce of past glories.'

'I'd like that,' she nodded, gliding up the column to Tanor.

Gwahl turned to Lidan. 'I saw you two from up ahead. You seemed a little... surprised? Thought I'd better rescue you.'

'No, no,' Lidan chuckled. With her gone the air seemed that much clearer. 'Well, yes, actually. Startled me a bit when she accused me of planning to kill someone.'

'Really? I'll have a word with her. Reaffirm my trust in you.'

'She kept talking about how my fear of Stolach could drive me to do it.'

Gwahl nodded. 'Understandable. You see, it was her own fear of Stolach that led her so deeply into his service. Noswen was a fine swordsman when she was young and enjoyed challenging people to duels. One day a regiment of the king's soldiers visited her village, and she challenged one of them to a fencing match. Noswen won easily, but accidentally drew blood from the soldier's hand as she disarmed him. She was beaten and arrested. They took her back to Crastalan and presented her to the king. Stolach saw potential in her and indoctrinated her into his Guild of Assassins. I don't know the full extent of the horrors she was subjected to during those years, but when everything was done she was a broken puppet for him, terrified of his rage. So began her time as the fonex's greatest assassin.'

'Why did she leave him?'

'She overcame her fear, and let herself become the good person I know she is. But don't let what I or anyone else says about her influence your opinion, that's for you to decide.'

'I think she's... unique,' smiled Lidan.

Gwahl laughed and clasped him on the shoulder. 'Aren't we all?' he glanced up the column and nudged him. 'Ah!' he exclaimed. 'Perhaps Noswen wasn't the suspicious one?'

He followed the daemon's gaze and saw the hanex muttering something in Widrias' ear. The satorr nodded and glanced over his shoulder at Lidan, who quickly looked away. When he looked back, the general was once again facing forward, and Noswen was marching with Tanor.

'The general?'

'Apparently so,' Gwahl chuckled. 'You can't blame him, he's cautious, and the circumstance of your recruitment is unusual.'

'So he doesn't trust me?'

'Nonsense, it's me he doesn't trust,' he laughed again. 'But if Noswen assures him of your character, he'll believe it.'

'Do you think she will?'

'Were you honest?'

'Of course!'

'Then she will,' he shoved him lightly. 'Now get back into rank, can't have you wandering off on your own again! The Hobbs of Dailas shudder at the mention of the lone Council soldier, I'm sure.'

The daemon winked and jogged back to the front. He watched him speed away. They'd barely know each other for more than a couple of weeks, but he seemed to know him so well. His smile faltered as his thoughts returned to Noswen. Mistrusted by the masses for her past actions. Only a few friends, even here. Perhaps he was being too judgmental.

He was still thinking about her when Pwtrek fell in line next to him, offering a rosy apple and a flask of water. He took the food and drink gratefully, tearing through both.

'How've you been finding the march?' asked the juggernaut as they climbed over a fallen tree-trunk.

'Tiring,' he admitted. 'But interesting.'

'How so?' Pwtrek raised an eyebrow. 'Apart from your scuffle, of course.'

'I was talking to Noswen earlier, and she told me-'

'Don't talk to me about that murderer,' he growled. 'Believe me, Lidan, you'd do well to stay away.'

He blinked, taken back by the outburst. But Pwtrek wasn't finished.

'Her name is spat upon. A traitor, an assassin, Stolach's pet. What she did to us cannot, should not be forgiven.'

'What did she do?'

'A story for another time, my friend.'

He nodded, the juggernaut would tell him in time.

'Pwtrek, last night, why was the Hobb like that?'

'Vapour.'

'Yes, I know, but why? Why do it? Why let yourself get to that state?'

The juggernaut shrugged. 'Because that's their culture. They ingest those drugs from the moment they take their first breath, the Desire is inevitable.'

'It's like he wasn't even human, the way he snarled.'

'I agree. They've lost their humanity. I suppose it helps in their fight for survival as nomads. You're lucky, in a way, he was truly Desired.'

'How do you mean?'

'Well he'd reached the point of rejection, hadn't he? A loner. Had it been a clan, you'd have been in a world of trouble.'

'Are there many of them in the woods?' he peered into the trees.

'Not usually, no. They normally keep to their own territories. But regrettably, in recent times, with the Council concentrating on fighting the King's forces and vice versa, the wilder inhabitants of the lands have thrived. Not just Hobbs, rogues and ruffians. Bandits. It's an issue I hadn't considered until very recently.'

'Will it be a problem?'

'Maybe. Probably. Hard to tell. But if I had to guess, I'd say there are far more than we would like, and as long as this conflict with the king continues, their numbers will probably grow. If we're not careful Enadir might well return to the state it was many decades ago.'

'What state is that?'

'Again, that's a story for another time. If I'm not much mistaken I can see the end of the forest nearing, and the first step of our journey will almost be over.'

A few minutes later and they left the cover of the trees. He took his first eager steps onto the southern flatlands. They stretched for miles ahead, a sea of green hills and grey skies. Somewhere to the south were the Great Waters, and to the south-east was a well-trodden road leading to their next destination. Morgenal Harbour.

Chapter 8

Rain lashed Gwahl's face like the sting of a thousand pinpricks as he stumbled through the streets. He was near the docks, where towering ships made port. They reached the town after four days of solid marching from the southern fringes of the forest, and the weather worsened with each step.

Most cities had a hierarchical structure with the richest living in fine houses near the centre, while the quality of living worsened as one neared the fringes before reducing to slums. The city of Morgenal Harbour was not so. The whole damned place was a slum. If a fool arrived with vast riches and a mind set to live out his life in peace, within a week he'd be dead, living on the street, or sleeping in cramped conditions with several other unscrupulous creatures. The city was a mess. A sprawling shanty town. A literal harbour for all the lost, damned, and otherwise unsavoury. Many of the laws held and followed by one would conflict entirely with the laws held by another, or indeed, any laws he may have followed a few minutes beforehand, as the citizens would change their stances on legality to suit their needs. 'Hourly orders' as they were called, maintained by Morgenal's constables, one of the most respected, albeit difficult, professions in Nefarwy.

Despite the general squalor of the place, near the seafront, order cleared the chaos. Neat jetties jutted out into the sea to calm the waters near the wharves, where numerous ships loaded and unloaded their wares, to be taken on barges up the Gwenal River to Dailas. It was at the precious waterfront that the king mostly tried to make his presence felt, as several units of his soldiers raised taxes on the imports and exports. On the waterfront was also where a select few men and women clawed their way into positions of relative power. Having gained ownership of the docks and wharves, these chosen few could demand payment from the captains berthing their ships at the ports. Of course, a large portion of the coin would be taxed by the king, but enough remained for these ruthless individuals to rise higher than other citizens, and go about enforcing – and breaking – the hourly orders of Morgenal. These individuals were the barons, and were in a constant struggle for power with each other.

Widrias made the wise decision to avoid the barons, as meddling in their affairs was asking for trouble. Gwahl knew, of course, that the barons' loyalty to the king was practically negligible. If they had their way, they'd kill every soldier in the city and claim independence. But who could take that risk? They'd only manage it if they all banded together and worked as one, and none of them trusted each other enough to propose such an alliance. Indeed, the one who proposed it was probably the likeliest to betray the others. No, no baron would seize the Council army out of loyalty to the crown. Instead, they would turn them over out of loyalty to *gold*, as a prize would be expected for any man who handed over to the king a member of the rebellious Council. As Widrias said, it was safer to stay away from them, and go about their business without announcing their presence to the world. More easily said than done, of course, as approaching the docks meant marching straight into the barons' territories. A bit of guile was needed, and they set out in small groups of twos and threes.

Morgenal was an old city, and although the outside world had changed many times in his life, this settlement had remained much the same since its founding. That is, until this recent age of order proclaimed by the king. His rulership was met by a surge in prosperity, and the city grew ever larger and ever richer – though none the cleaner – as more and more ships sailed in from the Southlands, Jagged Isles, and beyond.

With its riches came people. A steady stream of migrants from all four corners of the world. Some came with the intention of passing through, only to be caught in the city's snares. Others came because they had nowhere else to go. A few came out of some twisted hope for a better life. Amid the desperate, the foolish, and the damned, the beggars, the thieves and the outcasts, the proud, the meek, and the cunning, amid the hundreds of thousands who crawled through this hive, was the one they sought. A captain who would take them to Tonnis Harbour.

For two days, they'd dispersed themselves about the city, approaching ship's mates, bosuns, captains, asking for passage to the kingdom of the calefs. Two days of bribery, cajoling, and coaxing. Two days of fruitless search. They claimed the journey too hazardous, too long, too inconvenient, especially in recent times. After wearing away the soles of their boots, tramping up and down the piers and quays, nobody was willing to take one man, let alone an entire company, to their destination.

On the third day, however, their luck took a sudden turn. In a gambling den not a hundred feet from the waterfront controlled by Baron Pesk, he overheard two old sailors whisper a name. Not a person, but a ship, arrived at port late at night, and berthed in one of the more secretive, secluded wharves owned by the ruthless Baron Allut himself. The baron was a fierce man, openly defiant to Stolach, the other barons, to everyone but himself. His wharves and jetties were closely guarded and gated off from the others, especially the easternmost jetties, where the waterfront meandered into a natural cove. In this dark, isolated corner of the harbour, came whispers of docks where the more unscrupulous vessels made port. Vessels such as the *Seascale*.

When he heard the name, whispered under the drunken breath of these two sailors, he knew they'd found their captain.

The news silenced Widrias. Gwahl knew well enough of the satorr's turbid history with the *Seascale*'s Captain Mostyn. He knew all about the bad blood. To his relief, however, Widrias put aside that animosity. At last, they had a name to hunt.

Today, in the pouring rain, the hunt continued.

He skipped into the street at the sound of shutters opening above. Sure enough, it was followed by the splatter of a chamber-pot's contents barely a foot behind him. His escorts cursed. He smiled. It would teach them to mind their surroundings. Competent as they may be in battle, the soldiers weren't particularly well-versed in Morgenal's infinite charms.

One such charm was the loyalty of its citizens. If anyone knew where Mostyn was hiding, they weren't willing to say anything. Be it out of fear for Allut's vengeance, or fear of betraying the captain and being branded dishonourable, those who knew kept the information to themselves. For the others, they frowned at being questioned, turned their backs, and muttered barely-discernible curses under their breath. Rumours may spread like wildfire throughout the city, but not between strangers.

He scowled as he turned down yet another street, grimacing as the filthy sludge oozed around his boots. Scanning the street, he found his next target. Squatting next to a run-down shop selling hand-made fishing nets was a beggar, hunched over a tin. Beggars always kept a close ear to the ground, and Morgenal had plenty to offer.

As he neared, he saw the beggar was sitting on a thin stained blanket and clothed in nothing flimsy rags clumsily stitched together to make a crude tunic. He must have been painfully cold.

Four paces away, he crouched before him, signalling to his escorts to stay back.

'Good day, my friend,' he began, cheerfully. 'Terrible weather, no?'

'Weather's weather. It's all the same,' he mumbled.

'Cold though, all this rain. Need a good cloak to keep it from getting into your bones.'

'Try sailing in the northern seas, then you'll know cold.'

'True,' he nodded. 'I remember sailing around the Two Axes when one of the crew fell asleep on watch. Woke up with his legs frozen to the deck. Had to crack his shins clean through to get him below to the infirmary.'

The man hardly batted an eyelid at the tale, but kept his eyes fixed on his tin of copper coins. 'Nobody sails to the Two Axes.'

'Not anymore, no.'

No reply. He changed tact.

'I was wondering…I've lost one of my friends in the city, and for the life of me I cannot find him…'

His voice trailed off, suggestively. The man didn't reply. Gwahl continued.

'Is there any chance you've heard of him? Mostyn Neweit. My friend. The one I'm looking for.'

He shifted a little on his blanket and shrugged.

'Brave sailor,' he finally replied.

'Ah, you know him! Happen to know where he is?'

'He's in a lot of trouble with the king, is where he is,' he muttered.

'I'm sure he is, one of the reasons why I need to find him. Can you tell me where he's staying, what tavern or inn he'll be sleeping in tonight?'

'He should stay away from you, daemon, if he had any sense,' the beggar finally looked at him, glowering under heavy lids. 'I know well the curse of your race, the ruin you bring on your companions. I've met a few of you before, no good ever came from those encounters. Used to think it was just superstition. Now I know better.'

'I bear you no ill will, and it's no fault of mine that life has led you to this end, but if you help me now, then I can surely help you back to your feet.'

The beggar laughed, and uncrossed his legs from beneath him. Two stumps, nothing beyond the shins. 'Poor choice of words. It's because of one of you I ended up like this. On my knees in the filth. You're all alike. Even look similar. Bastard daemon! Death's too good for the lot of you!'

'Alright, enough now,' he stood. A lost cause. He'd played it poorly, now was time to leave before the shouts drew unwanted attention.

'Enough? I've had more than my fair share. Still you force more pain onto me! There'll never be enough destruction to satisfy you. Know this, daemon, I would never betray the great captain to the likes of you. I would sooner lose all of my remaining limbs than tell you where he is.'

Gwahl smiled emptily. 'Never betray him, you say? You already have,' he rummaged around his pouch and tossed a gold coin into the tin. The beggar realised what he'd done and wheezed in horror, pulled himself to his knees and scurried away, but not before throwing the coin back at him. Gwahl watched him leave.

Prejudiced fool. But no different to a thousand others. He was long since accustomed to the fear and suspicion he aroused whenever he walked into a town or village. Perhaps his kin deserved their stigma, given their past transgressions? Then again, at least they still tried to help Enadir, which was more than could be said of others. He spat and returned to his escort.

'Any luck?' asked one of the soldiers.

'Not much, but still useful.'

'Why did he throw your coin back? Idiot should've been grateful.'

'He gave me information about Mostyn. He didn't realise that we didn't know for sure whether he was here. He saw the coin I tossed him as payment and didn't want to be known as a traitor.'

'Seems daft to me, Gwahl, that gold could have gotten him food, shelter, clothes.'

'All of which would have been paid with tainted money. Even beggars must obey the laws of the city. Come, let everyone know that Mostyn certainly *is* hiding here, somewhere in this cesspit.'

*

Spotal peered over the rim of his mug at the other drinkers. He'd been trying to stomach the disgusting ale for half an hour as he tried to weasel some information out of the drunkards around him. Five hours of wandering from tavern to tavern searching for any clues concerning Mostyn's whereabouts after word from Gwahl reached him. This was the latest in a string of equally decrepit establishments.

'So, there I was, fighting an entire horde of them horrible troglodytes,' slurred a man next to him, 'and I was hacking away at them left and right, but they kept on coming! So I let them get close before I unleashed my secret weapon.'

'And what, may I ask, would that be?' he sighed.

The man ducked his chin, before raising it high and belching loudly. 'The smell of a bastard's breath after seven pints of ale!' he proclaimed loudly. Drunk sailors fell about laughing, many of them toppling of their bar stools onto the ground, taking the laughter to a more hysterical level.

Spotal sighed again. 'Hilarious.'

He turned his back to the sailor. Not an uncommon encounter. He scanned the tavern room. Drunkards filling every corner. Some slumped into their tankards, some sipped at glasses of rich wine.

Some were dressed in rags, some in finery as intricate as Muranath's courtroom balls. Some drank alone, others in groups of ten. Groups of whores wandered between tables, men and women, leaning against chairs, bouncing on laps. Sailors, soldiers, merchants, travellers, whalers, fishermen, thieves, and curs. Deals were made, goods bought and sold, suspicious eyes met his own. In one of the booths a group of degenerates passed around an opium pipe, in another they shared a vial of Azag syrup. On a small stage, a group of minstrels struggled to make their voices heard over the hubbub of the patrons, many of them lost in their own songs, competing tunes adding to the din. His eyes searched, finally rested on the form of a solitary calef sitting at a table scattered with empty mugs.

He left the bar and strode over. Without waiting for an invitation, he sat down, casually leaning back in the chair. The calef glared at him through bloodshot eyes.

'What do you want, scum?' he growled.

'Nothing much, brother. Just need some information.'

'Well you're looking in the right place. Bastards from all over Enadir in this filthy city, all of them with some sort of information. But you won't get any from me – stay away.'

'You would refuse innocent information to your brother calef? What of the honour of our race?'

The calef laughed bitterly and gulped what was left of his drink. 'Garre!' he called to the barman. 'Get me more drink! No, not ale get me some brandy, you fool!' He sat scowling as the old man hurried over with a large bottle and a glass. He began pouring the fiery liquid when the calef grabbed him by the shirt and held him close. 'What do you think you're doing?'

'Pouring you your brandy, sir, as you asked,' whimpered the poor man.

'I want the bottle. Now get out of my sight,' he released him, sitting back in his chair, bottle between his lips. He sighed contentedly and looked at Spotal. 'You still here?'

'Until you give me what I want,' he replied, levelly.

'Then you'll be here for a while, and I don't like company, especially not other calefs. Get out of here or feel my claws around your neck.'

'Have you seen Captain Mostyn?' asked Spotal.

'Didn't you hear?' barked the drunk 'I won't answer any of your pathetic questions; I don't care about you, or this Mossy, or anyone! Our *great race,*' he said drily, 'took from me my pride and honour, then this wretched city took everything else, so now *I'll* take all its alcohol!' he laughed hysterically for a moment, before his face turned to stone. 'Why should I care? Why should I care for her? If my name was all she cared about, why waste so many years together…?'

Spotal leaned forward. 'Please, I need your help. Tell me where the captain is.'

'I don't know,' whispered the calef. 'Leave.'

'Please, you must have heard something.'

'*Leave!*' he roared, launching himself across the table.

Spotal punched him in the temple, knocking him down. Instinct, nothing more. The blow shouldn't have knocked him out cold, but with so much alcohol in his system a mere flick would have probably floored him.

He stared at him, chewing his cheek. What led him to this? What drove him to such a sorry state? Lost pride and honour? An all too familiar story. Was this the life that awaited a disgraced calef? He shuddered. A second chance like this quest would not be wasted. Lleunedd would not regret sending him to the Council. Wasting away in a sad, ramshackle tavern was not his fate. Death was more welcome.

Gathering himself, he signalled to the soldiers dotted around the tavern to meet him outside. He didn't see Garre slide up to the unconscious calef, sprawled across the table. He never saw the glint of the rusty knife. He never heard the gurgle of blood from the lacerated throat, or the jingle of coins in the stolen purse. He couldn't smell the blood soaking into the old oak table over the fresh sea air outside. He never saw the other patrons ignore the carcass. He never saw anything. Or so he told himself.

He leaned against the tavern wall, listening to his men's reports. It was generally thought that Mostyn was hiding in the more crowded streets nearer the centre of the city, away from the barons' territories, a few miles from his ship. Damned unusual for a sailor. Then again, nobody ever accused Mostyn of being usual.

*

Lidan was jolted from his absent-minded daydream by Widrias' cough. His chin slid from his upturned palm as he blinked rapidly to clear his bleary eyes. Plumes of dust swirled hypnotically in the dying beam of light from the leaded window, combining with the warm crackle of flames at his back to send him tumbling into the world of his thoughts. It was little wonder he'd spent the past hour daydreaming.

He yawned and turned to the satorr, pacing across the room to an oak desk. This ramshackle inn, 'The Golden Smuggler', had been their base for the past few days, every single bed now occupied by one of their company. To be fair, the bedbugs weren't nearly as vicious as he'd feared, the food was mostly edible, and the grog was on the more mellow side. All in all, he'd been in far worse.

'Any developments on his whereabouts?' asked Widrias, leaning forward in his chair.

'Not on my part,' admitted Gwahl, sat next to the window with Pwtrek. 'I know he's here somewhere, but beyond that,' he shrugged.

'Pretty much the same on my part,' agreed Pwtrek. 'Nobody talking.'

'I heard a rumour that might help,' began Auran, 'but it's just a rumour.'

'Go on.'

'Apparently, he's become rather paranoid, insists his crew stay with him wherever he goes. Might make it easier to find him? If we find one of the *Seascale*'s crew, then we'll find him.'

'What's he scared of?' asked Pwtrek. 'Does he know we're coming for him?'

'I doubt it, probably afraid of Stolach and the other barons?' suggested Gwahl, glancing at Widrias for confirmation.

The satorr nodded. 'Probably. The king, the barons, rival captains, he has plenty of enemies to hide from. Where did you hear this rumour, Auran?'

'A sailor from the Southlands, seemed trustworthy enough. I think he believed he was telling the truth, at least.'

'Fair enough,' Widrias shrugged. 'Anything else?'

Lidan looked around doubtfully. Each day brought only a trickle of information, nothing substantial enough to satisfy his building frustrations. Evidently, this Mostyn had chosen a fine hiding place in coming here.

'Yes.'

He jumped, nearly falling from his chair as Noswen's voice sounded from behind. He never saw her enter, and could've sworn by the four winds that she wasn't there before. From his companions' reactions, he wasn't the only one to find it unnerving. Pwtrek scowled, a couple of the men murmured curses, Spotal giggled.

'I found the *Seascale*,' she continued, gliding around the table and taking a seat next to him. He subconsciously withdrew, shuffling his chair to make space. She seemed to ignore him.

'Good,' nodded Widrias. 'Anyone on board?'

'Yes, a few. Guards.'

'You're sure it was the right ship?' asked Tanor.

'Her figurehead and nameplate were covered, and she bore no colours, but it was her. In one of Allut's secret wharves.'

'Did the guards go anywhere?'

'When they were relieved, I followed them to an inn. Mostyn wasn't inside.'

'You're sure?' growled Pwtrek. 'Auran said they'd be together.'

'I'm sure.'

Pwtrek snorted, drawing a disapproving look from Gwahl. Lidan shifted again in his seat, unable to ignore the rising tension in the room. Glancing back and forth between the two northerners, he wringed his hands under the table.

'There is a situation that explains the two conflicting accounts?' suggested Spotal, catching Lidan's eye as he looked around the room. His smirk suggested he'd also picked up on the strained atmosphere.

'That one of us is wrong?' said Auran, his chuckle lightening the mood.

'Well, apart from that,' smiled the calef. 'Could it be that these guards were among Allut's men, and Mostyn and his crew are elsewhere?'

He saw Noswen nod slightly from the corner of his eye. 'Possibly. The inn was but a stone's throw from Allut's stretch of the waterfront.'

'Quite,' agreed Widrias. 'Whatever the reason, it's the best lead we have so far. Tomorrow, take the men to this inn and question the guards inside. We'll find him, sooner or later.'

*

Tanor dragged his feet miserably. The alley stank of excrement. Judging by the looks of it, it was likely made up of what it smelled. Pushing down the lump in his throat he continued through the slime. As his eyes watered from the stench, he caught sight of his quarry of the past ten minutes.

The alley opened up into an empty street, all boarded windows, smashed glass, and broken bottles. A sound to his left. He turned, nearly twisting his ankle as he spun, catching the edge of a heavy coat disappear around a building. He chased, kicking up filth with each step. Another alley. More grime. He followed.

Beyond the decrepit beggars and degenerates sprawled about in the filth, he caught another glimpse of his enemy, now scrambling up a ladder to the rooftops. He followed. Past a man lying naked on the floor in a puddle of vomit, past an overweight woman grunting like a hog in the embrace of a whore, past two opium-addled children, vacant smiles on hollow faces as they sprawled in a gutter of sewage. Corpses and future corpses littered the shadows. He ignored them. All that mattered was his foe.

Reaching the ladder, he heaved himself up to the roof. Something crashed down on his arms. An old chimney-pot. Crying out, he fell to the floor. A chuckle from above.

Bastard.

134

Back on his feet, he wiped a handful of mud from his front and jumped up, his fingers latching onto the rim of the roof. He snarled as he hauled himself up. Pausing to catch his breath, he took stock. From the rooftops, Morgenal looked very different. Poorly made roofs of wood or slate stretched back for miles, no rhyme or reason to how tall or broad each one was built. Somewhere behind him would be the wooden roof of the inn that Noswen led them to. It was a large building, built from the remnants of an old merchant-ship, its warped planks of wood creaking and groaning in the wind. The guards had left the inn at dawn and he followed with ten others, but they soon noticed them and attacked. Their ambush was clumsy, hasty, easily beaten back. One, however, fled when his companions attacked, and it was Tanor who gave chase.

Had he been a new arrival at Morgenal, he might have been baffled when nobody reacted to the slaughter in the street. They probably assumed it was a dispute over some hourly order, or perhaps a dispute between the barons. As such, the only citizens who watched them did so with dull, disinterested eyes.

He looked up as a drop of rain fell into his dark hair. Black rainclouds loomed ominously overhead. Rain again. He shouldn't be surprised. Not a day went by without a bit of it. From the looks of it, they were in for one of the city's famous storms.

But there he was! Jumping from roof to roof some distance away. Taking a deep breath, he resumed his chase.

He leapt from building to building, the roofs under his feet creaking and groaning with every step. The ones made of slate were slippery, the ones made of wood lurched and sagged. His foot crashed through one, only narrowly avoiding a blade as he tore it free. A voice yelled at him from beneath, but he took no heed. He was gaining on him.

His enemy knew his time was short and jumped back to the streets. He followed, landing hard, rolling over his shoulder in the muck. Keep going. Chest heaving, shoulders aching. His feet were caked in sludge and his knees buckled with every other step. But after pursuing for so long he wasn't about to let his prize get away.

Another whore called out to him from a window, paint-caked face unable to conceal the welts and sores around her diseased mouth. A hooded man offered cut-throat deals on Azag syrup and Vapour, flanked by burly bodyguards. He pushed past an old man, undressed from the waist down, yelling incomprehensibly at his reflection in a window. A priest stood tall over a congregation of three, studded paddle in hand, flogging them to repent for sins committed as a crowd of zealots cheered on. Two constables beat a screaming girl with their batons until she relinquished a burnt crust of pie as a bereaved baker looked on, greasy face etched with grim satisfaction. A woman squatted against a building, trousers about her ankles as she defecated against a shop wall, giggling as the owner chased her away with a broom.

His foe shot a quick glance over his shoulder, yelping when he saw how close he was. He dived through an open doorway. It slammed in Tanor's face. Snarling, he kicked it open off its flimsy hinges. An old woman wrinkled her nose and squeaked incomprehensively. He swivelled his head at the sound of a second door slamming and pushed the old maid aside as he followed the sound to a back door.

He opened the door and there was the guard, dragging himself up over a wall. He jumped up at the top and turned to stare at him, bowing sarcastically and taking off his tricorn hat, revealing his filthy, ugly face, covered in dirt.

Quick as a flash, Tanor whipped out a small dagger from the back of his belt and threw. It hit his target in the shoulder. The man squealed and dropped to the floor on the other side of the wall.

Smiling grimly, Tanor pulled himself over the wall, expecting to find him lying on the other side. An empty alley, the guard staggering along at the other end. He clenched his teeth and continued after his tenacious foe.

Fat droplets of rain fell on his head and shoulders as he splashed down each new street, slowly gaining. The ground turned to slime. At times, he was close to wading through a mire that rose to his knees.

Finally, after what seemed like an age of pursuit, he was within grabbing distance. Mustering up his strength he dived forwards and tackled him to the sludgy ground. He landed on top of his foe, cushioning his fall into the filth.

Tanor heaved him up and roared over the pounding rain. 'Where's Captain Mostyn, filth?!'

The man laughed haggardly and coughed. 'Who?'

'Don't play dumb with me, scum! Tell me where he is!'

'Never heard of him.'

Now it was Tanor's turn to laugh. 'You just happened to be guarding his ship? Tell me!'

'I don't know what you're talking about,' he snarled, revealing front teeth filed to points in a crude mimicry of the calefs. 'Let go!'

Tanor said nothing. Instead he scooped a handful of sludge with his free hand and rubbed it into the wound in the man's shoulder. As he squirmed in discomfort, Tanor punched him repeatedly in the shoulder until he screamed for mercy.

'Are you willing to cooperate? Or do you want more?'

'No!'

'More?'

'No! I don't know where he is!' he screamed. 'All I know is he's in the city somewhere. I'm not even a part of his crew! Allut just paid me a few coins to guard the ship for a few days with my mates. I'm not even one of the baron's men! Please! I've only been here a week.'

'Your mates? The ones you abandoned? We might give them over to Allut, strike a deal. Cowards for information, how does that sound?'

'No!' the man squealed, eyes bulging.

'Information! Specifics!' Tanor raised his fist again.

The ugly face paled. 'He's somewhere in the dregs, the centre of the city, to the western side, I think. I swear that's all I know!'

Tanor grunted and threw him to the ground, where he lay moaning with his back to a wall. He nodded to his shoulder. 'You should get that seen to, unless you want it infected. Better stay away from Allut. He won't be happy about this.'

Turning, he walked away, leaving the guard to nurse his shoulder, sobbing alone in the sludge.

*

Lidan was still in the tavern. Yet again, awaiting the return of those searching the city. According to Widrias, he was too inexperienced to search the city, and would 'Probably get lost without anybody there to hold his hand.'

That last comment stung, and he'd been sulking all day, imagining scenarios where he found Mostyn and brought him to Widrias as a conquering hero. It was a nice daydream, up there with the better ones.

As he fantasized, the tavern door opened and in strode a soaking Tanor. As he walked past, soldiers covered their noses, retched, and glared at the wet, red-faced man. As soon as he passed him he realised why. The man reeked of filth.

Once Tanor reached Widrias's table, he threw a quick salute.

'Sir,' he said. 'Noswen led me and my men to the inn, we waited outside, and when they emerged we followed. They soon noticed us and attacked. One ran away, I gave chase as the others were dealt with by my men. When I finally caught him, I managed to glean some useful information from the cur. Mostyn is hiding somewhere in the western part of the city centre. I think I know where, although I hate to go there. The guards won't talk. They'll be too scared of Allut to admit to their failings.'

'I believe I know which street you're referring to, Tanor,' said Widrias. 'It seems logical he'd hide there of all places, although I hoped it wouldn't come to it. I assume it's that disgusting tavern that he's staying in?'

'That's what I thought, sir.'

'Very well, we leave now – rouse the soldiers, and for the love of the four winds change your tunic.'

Tanor smiled. 'An unavoidable tragedy when running through these streets in heavy rain, sir.'

Within the hour, they were on their way. Finally free of the tavern, Lidan had little time to rejoice in the change of scenery. The rain dampened his spirits enough to wipe the initial smile from his face and he was soon scowling at the raindrops trickling down the back of his neck. For the most part, they stuck to the main roads, some of which were even complete with cobblestones and gravel. Judging the state of Tanor's surcoat, he was glad to stay away from the filthy backstreets.

Weaving their way through the twisting streets, they eventually stopped at an arcade. The change in atmosphere was as abrupt as stepping into the sea from the shore. Its floor, secluded as it was beneath its ominous wooden roof, was dry and dusty, blissfully firm underfoot after the otherwise soft ground of the city. Dark, dancing shadows flitted across the walls from the smoking, spluttering torches set in sconces along its length. Hardly a breeze stirred the heavy air. A stifling atmosphere suffocated him with its silence. It reminded him of the dungeons, overwhelmed by the general aura of death. Too far from the waterfront to be under the barons' influence, too wild and fierce to be controlled by the king, it was left to the citizens.

They gathered outside one of the buildings. He could sense the others holding their breath, just as he was. It was a tavern, of sorts. Perhaps tavern was an overstatement; 'hovel serving alcohol' would be more appropriate. Its nameplate creaked overhead in an undetectable breeze, 'The Serrated Fang' picked out in gilt letters. Morgenal's storms were legendary, and not even the roof of this alley had spared these buildings completely, with rainwater finding its way through the cracks and holes and rotten pores of the roof to play its hand on the foundations of the building. Weather-warped planks of wood leaned heavily against each other like the twisted spine of a crippled old man. A doorman stood outside, his biceps bigger than Lidan's head. As the company approached, he looked them up and down and stepped inside, slamming the door behind him.

Tanor and Widrias consulted in hushed tones outside the door. Eventually, Tanor reached up and rapped the door with his knuckles. The spyhole drew back, and a gruff voice greeted him, presumably the bulky doorman. He was too far away to hear the conversation, but there was a lot of gesturing and smiling on Tanor's part.

He waited with the others, fidgeting at each creak of wood, at each flicker of the torches. Finally, Tanor nodded, and the spyhole snapped shut. He pointed to ten soldiers and motioned them to follow. Widrias, Gwahl, Spotal, and Noswen went with him. Just before stepping through the door, Gwahl paused and looked over his shoulder. He must have looked desperate, as the daemon rolled his eyes and beckoned him to follow.

He scampered after them to the ramshackle bar, while Pwtrek, Auran, the neiads, and the remainder of the Council Guard waited outside.

His eyes took a few seconds to adjust to the gloom. As dark as the arcade was, the room was even dingier, if that were possible. The ceiling was low, low enough for his hair to brush against the rafters. To one side crackled a miserable little fireplace, trying its best to illuminate a deceptively large room adorned with several heavy tables. Sitting around each one, murmuring softly, were an assortment of drinkers, each wearing their heavy waterproof coats, holding large, frothing steins of grog in their calloused hands. To his right was the bar, behind which an old man stood, wiping away at cloudy glasses with an old rag. Behind him were vast barrels of grog, caskets of wine, and bottles of liquor. A minstrel sat on a high stool in the corner, plucking aggressively at his lute. He wasn't very good, tripping over notes and slurring the words of his song. The drinkers didn't seem to mind. The salty smell of the sea tickled his nostrils, mixing with the pungent grog and smoky fire into a cocktail of aromas that set his eyes watering.

Behind him, the doorman closed the door with a slam, making him jump. He stole a glance, and the burly thug scowled, crossing his arms and puffing out his chest. He couldn't fail to notice the gnarled cudgel dangling from a noose at his belt. Gulping, he turned away. Perhaps he should have stayed outside.

Tanor approached the bar and sat himself at one of the high stools. Lidan followed Gwahl to a nearby table to watch. At the bar, Tanor called the barman. He grumpily trotted over and acknowledged the ordered drink with a nod.

From his table, he did his best to assess the drinkers. It was difficult. From what he could make out, there were two groups. A few scattered individuals or pairs, and a tightly-clustered throng. The individuals had the appearance of regular drinkers. He'd been in Weaverlodge's tavern plenty of times to recognise these individuals. Glazed eyes, bulging stomachs, spittle gathering at the corners of their mouths, the yellow tint of their skin and eyes. They played dice, cards, some listened to the incompetent minstrel, some frowned at them, others scowled at the second group. These were more noteworthy. Crowded around the tables nearest the fire, hunched over their drinks, keeping their backs to the rest of the tavern. He could only ever catch the briefest glance of faces cast in shadow. Of what he could see, it was all embellished ears, tattoos, scarred cheeks. He glanced at Gwahl, but he was watching Tanor. He turned back to the bar.

The barman held forth a tankard of frothing grog. Tanor flicked him a copper coin and took a sip. He nodded appreciatively.

'Tell me, friend, do you know any sailors staying around these parts?'

'It's a harbour, innit? What do you think?' the barman grumbled.

'Aye, aye. Any recent arrivals?'

'Check the docks, not here. The notice posts.'

'Aye, good idea. Thought you might know about one, mind?'

'That so?'

'Aye, that's so.'

A pause as they looked at each other. Tanor continued.

'Someone told me a captain was staying around here. Famous one, at that.'

'That so?'

'You tell me. Ever heard of a captain that goes by the name Mostyn Neweit?'

It was clumsy. Even Lidan could tell. The barman froze, glancing to the closely-knit group of drinkers. He licked his lips.

'Never heard of him,' he croaked.

Tanor smiled patiently. 'Come now, tell me where he is and we'll be off!'

'As I said, I've never heard-'

'Perhaps I didn't make myself clear,' Tanor cut across. 'Tell me where the captain is, and I won't punish you,' he lifted his polearm off the floor and smiled emptily.

Lidan's ears twitched. For a second, he couldn't place his discomfort. Then it dawned. Silence. A hundred eyes bored into the back of his head. He didn't dare turn to look at the drinkers, but stared at the bar.

He saw Tanor twitch, before taking a gulp of grog and climbing from the stool. He faced the deathly-silent drinkers.

'Any of you lot know where he is? We need to see him.'

'Closing for the afternoon,' announced the doorman suddenly, in a surprisingly nasal voice for a man so large.

The individual drinkers, the apparent regulars, rose from their seats. Some left their half-full steins at their tables. The majority downed the dregs and stumbled out, leaning against one another. None looked at them as they passed.

'The Rose and Keel is open,' reassured the doorman as they filed out. 'We'll be reopening...' he glanced at the barman, who shook his head. The doorman shrugged. 'We'll be reopening before you know it.'

When the last staggered out, followed closely by the minstrel, the body of his cheap lute stuffed unceremoniously under his arm, the doorman shut the door again and stood before it, scowling deeper than ever.

Tanor raised his eyebrow at the drinkers around the fire who hadn't moved a muscle, save to lift their steins to their lips.

'His crew, I assume?'

Chairs were suddenly pushed back from tables. Weapons were drawn. Tanor took a step backwards and lifted his polearm. Lidan followed suit. At Widrias's signal, they moved up to stand by the bar. His fingers twitched, a cold sweat dampened his armpits. His cheeks felt hot. His ears burned. The drinkers, the sailors, the pirates, the crewmen, whatever he might call them, faced them with curved cutlasses and cruel boathooks. Muscles coiled. Fingers tightened around hilts. Eyes blazed.

The first one to move was a thin hanex, his bony frame swallowed up by his heavy coat. He jumped over a chair and charged at Tanor. He swung his polearm. The hammer-head connected with the hanex's skull, shattering bone and sending gore raining down. Raising his blood-splattered weapon, Tanor charged.

Lidan side-stepped behind a table, avoiding the swinging cutlass of an old, grizzled neiad, the salt in his hair glinting in the firelight. The pirate growled and took another gulp from his frothing tankard, tilting his head back and letting the liquid flow down his throat. He seized the opportunity to scurry away behind another table. The neiad looked around confusedly for a moment before spotting him. He roared and charged again. This time, Lidan jumped onto the table and kicked an unlit candle into the neiad's face. His enemy howled as a lump of solid wax thudded against his snout, drawing a faint trickle of blood his nostril. He punched him in his eye, knocking him to the ground, before jumping down and kicking him in the temple, stunning him.

Something hit the back of his head. Cursing, he turned. A tankard. He winced. Blood on his fingers. Glancing across the room, he barely ducked in time to avoid another. The barman launched a third mug at him. He dropped to the floor. The tankard flew over his head. He rose cautiously, watching the bar, assessing the best way to reach it unscathed. He needn't have worried. Even as he watched, his assailant disappeared, dragged into the darkness between the grog barrels as a shadowed figure dropped from above to drag him down. There was a crash and a faint spray of blood. The shadow jumped back up to the barrels and nodded to him. He nodded back and reminded himself to thank her once the brawl was done.

*

From her vantage point behind the bar, she spied a flight of stairs, partly hidden behind the barrels. She turned, catching Tanor's eye. He was standing on a table, brandishing his polearm like a quarterstaff, crushing the bones of anyone who came within striking distance. She jumped from behind the bar, slithered through the fray, and came up behind him. Leaning forward, she whispered in his ear.

'There's a flight of stairs behind the bar. He's probably upstairs. Should I go now or help down here?'

'No, go now,' panted Tanor, still sweeping his weapon around him. 'We'll follow once we've finished down here.'

'Very well,' she whispered, and leapt back behind the bar to ascend the stairs.

Padding softly up the wooden steps, her eyes searched the semi-darkness for anyone who might offer resistance. She reached a dark landing with two doors on each side. Drawing her dirk, she opened the first door, crouching low. Her caution was unnecessary. Just a small storeroom, filled with buckets, mops and various cleaning equipment. The second room had nothing inside save a small desk and wooden chair. She spent half a minute scouring it for hiding places, but it was just an empty study. The third was a bedroom, three drunk crewmen gambling in candlelight. One stood up and pointed at the open door, reaching for the knife at his belt. She slithered in, keeping to the shadows. Manoeuvred herself behind the drunkard. Unseen, it was all too easy.

A well-placed dart from her blowpipe felled the first, its venom-coated needle working in seconds. She used the thump of his crumpled body to mask her approach to the next two. Their throats were silently cut as they stared stupidly at their fallen colleague. The murdered bodies slumped over the table, empty eyes frozen in an infinite stare.

Her hands were slick with blood, sticky and hot. She wiped them clean on their coats. She paused for a moment to consider their bodies. It was instinctive now, to slide into a room and deliver unseen death. Whether it was with poison, bow, or blade, it didn't require any thought. Perhaps one day it might. Perhaps one day she could pause and think, consider whether they needed to die. One day, she would leave fewer carcasses in her wake. Perhaps.

Another thorough search proved fruitless, and she left the room to open the fourth door. This had another stairway, leading to another floor. She ascended.

At the top of the stairs was a wooden door. She reached for the handle. Locked. She kicked it off its hinges. She walked in, not bothering to conceal herself. It was a large room, a bed in one corner, a large wooden chest, a wardrobe, and a desk under a window. She walked over to look outside. A perfect view of the arcade, she could see the entire Council company. Whoever slept in this room knew they were here. What's more, the window was heavy, its sill covered in a thick cushion of undisturbed dust, and no other way out. Whoever lived here was still in the room. She studied some of the papers strewn across the desk and nodded knowingly. Sea charts. She turned and peered into the semi-darkness, searching. Her eyes settled on a small form in a corner, trying in vain to remain hidden.

Rolling her eyes, she hauled him from the floor and threw him across the room. He crashed against the wardrobe and fell to the ground with a cry. She bounded after him. He drew a cutlass from the scabbard at his hip. She disarmed him with a flick of her dirk. Gripping him by the neck, she held him to the flickering light of the dirty window.

In her hands was a thin man with greasy black hair and a face ravaged by scars. He was clothed in waterproof jacket and trousers, with a loose light blue shirt and a gaudy pink sash around his waist, both made of silk. Oiled sea-boots covered his feet. His ears were pierced with gold hoops and jewelled studs, and his arms were covered in tattoos of ships, animals, weapons, ancient symbols. Calloused hands gripped feebly at her forearms as he tried to tear himself away, to no avail. He was stronger than he looked, life at sea demanded such strength, but she was stronger, and her hands held him like vices. A pirate. His general demeanour confirmed it, the outrage at being caught, the look of defiance in his bright eyes. She pressed her blade against his scrawny neck.

'We've been looking for you for a while, Captain.'

He gulped and laughed nervously, cut short when she dragged him across the floor and threw him down the stairs to the landing below. She jumped down after him and took him by his collar, dragged him across the floor, and threw him down the second flight of stairs to the main tavern. He crashed to the floor and lay whimpering under the bar, splinters and smashed mugs covering his pitiful frame.

She followed. Her companions fared well in the tavern brawl. The majority of their foes were huddled together in a circle in the middle of the floor, under close watch by the Council guard. The others lay still, surrounded by crimson puddles. Spotal stood triumphantly behind the slumped doorman, sword held against his stubbled neck.

They turned to her when she entered, nodding with satisfaction as they glanced from her to Mostyn, and back again. He whimpered at her feet. Gripping his arm, she hauled him up and frogmarched him to Widrias. The satorr nodded to her gratefully and motioned to the chair at a table. With a steady push, she sat him down in the offered chair.

'Thank you, Noswen,' said Widrias. 'I didn't expect to find him in such a sorry state. Lidan, fetch our friend a mug of grog to lift his spirits a little!'

As Lidan scurried away to fetch the drink, Mostyn raised his head. In a throaty, guttural voice, a voice broken by years of heavy drinking and abusive shouting as it struggled to be heard above the roaring storms of the Great Waters, he spoke.

'Why did you come here, Wids? I thought the last time we met would be the last. I thought you'd leave me to die in peace.'

'I'm sorry, Mostyn. But I'm afraid that certain events forced me to seek you out once more. I have a favour to ask.'

'A favour?' asked Mostyn, surprised. 'Whatever could it be that I, a humble captain of the waves could do to aid you, the most famous general of our time?'

She frowned, his tone was impertinent. Widrias caught her eye, and tilted his head to the right. Her hands remained at her sides, for now.

Mostyn continued.

'Could it be that I have a fine ship and crew whose services you've abused many times before, and you've finally decided to pay us for our expenses? No? Too much to hope for, I suppose, especially from scum like you.

'So why else? It can't possibly be that you wish to fight me again, to carve a hole in my gut and leave me to bleed to death? That seems far likelier,' he laughed sarcastically, and his tone turned dark. 'After all you've done, how could you possibly expect me to grant you a favour?'

'Look, Mostyn. I have a company waiting outside this tavern. We need to get across the Great Waters to Lleunedd. Will you lend me your ship? I promise you, the rewards will be great. Nobody else will take us. I know you hate Stolach, why else would you go to Baron Allut? Help us, and you'll be helping yourself by bringing us one step closer to defeating him.'

Mostyn considered this for a moment, taking the occasional sip from the mug that Lidan handed him. He met Widrias's gaze.

'No.

'Excuse me?'

'No. As I said, the memories of my past encounters with you are far too harsh to be put aside. I refuse to have anything to do with you or your friends.'

Widrias bristled with anger. She stepped forward, to placate him, but Gwahl beat her to it. Rushing to his side, he tried to calm him down, whispering frantically in his ear, to no avail. Widrias's anger burst forth.

'You're a disgrace!' he bellowed. 'You say you oppose the king, but by refusing to aid us you are helping him more than any of his servants! You're ensuring victory to Stolach because you're too stubborn, too petty to set aside our differences and work together! You're one of the finest seafarers I've ever met, but you damn infuriate me! Believe you me, if there were anyone else who could help us, I'd go to them, but there isn't. I need your help, Mostyn. I need you ship, your crew, damn it I need you.'

Mostyn looked embarrassed for a moment, before taking a huge swig of his drink and wiping his mouth with the back of his hand. He sighed and leaned forward in his chair. 'Sorry, Wids, but it's still a no.'

Widrias glared at him, as if his gaze were enough to quell the man's insolence. Mostyn remained calm.

'You hate me,' Mostyn shrugged. 'I assure you the feeling's mutual. You swore that our last voyage together would be that – our last. That's the only reason I agreed to it, but here you are once again, demanding things from me and insulting me. I refuse to sell my services and my ship to your cause.'

'I cannot accept that answer, Captain. You *will* let me and my army on your ship and you *will* sail it to the Kingdom of the calefs!'

'Are you serious? Can you actually hear yourself? Sail to King Lleunedd – I hate that calef more than I hate you… no offence,' he added, with a glance to Spotal, who shrugged. 'Besides, even if I were to agree, it would take days to prepare for such a voyage, to stock up on food, plan the course, ready my crew. Speaking of which I see that you've successfully slaughtered some of them and are holding the rest as captives! Have you no sense Wids? That mush of a skull by your feet was Bobo, our cook. Look, lads! Wids killed our bloody cook! No more pudding for us.'

'Bastard,' grumbled one of the crew. Angry murmurs returned the sentiment.

'Bastard indeed. Damn you, Wids. Damn you to the depths.'

He paused, letting his words sink in. Noswen shifted forward and rested her hands on the back of his chair, ready to grab him at Widrias's command. But he seemed to have forgotten her, Gwahl, the men, the crew, the tavern, everything but the pirate in front of him.

'Why would I do business with the man who killed my crew, fought and hurt me in the past and wishes to sail to yet another of my enemies?' Mostyn asked quietly. 'I'm safe here. Allut knows and respects me, pays me well for the treasures I bring him from my raids, gives me shelter from the king. I don't need anything you can give me.'

'Safe? Don't make me laugh. I found you, didn't I? You're at my mercy. Believe me, if I can find you, the king's men will find you too, and they won't give you the chance I give you now.'

Mostyn belched, and grinned.

'I'm far safer than you think. I can see your company outside in the street, is that Pwtrek? How nice. If I see you, half the other men in this area have seen you as well. Everyone knows you're here now,

Wids, and people will go scurrying away to the king's men to tell them how the great general himself is in the Serrated Fang. Either that or they'll go to the barons, who'll send their men to take you away. You were a fool to come here.'

Now Widrias laughed. 'You know as well as I do that the influence of the barons ends half a mile away from here. They can't save you now. As for the king's men, they'll never come here, they know the mobs rule this street and will set aside their differences to protect their own.'

'Well done, Wids, the mobs protect their own. What am I if not one of them? A piece of scum born in the filth of Morgenal and bought his way onto a ship, and eventually became the most feared pirate on the Great Waters. They protect me, Wids, they won't protect you when the king comes-a-running.'

The satorr paused. 'Even so, if I were you, I wouldn't be hoping for the king to come. As you said, you are a feared pirate and wanted by the king. Don't try to threaten me. We both know that neither of us want the king's soldiers anywhere near us, and we both know that you're at my mercy. You'll do as I say and help us.'

'I will not.'

'Mostyn. If you don't, I'll make it very painful for you, then I'll slip into the wharf, steal your ship, and sail to the Kingdom of the calefs without you. Noswen here is quite adept at slipping past and killing guards, we can take that ship whenever we want to. It would be far easier for both of us if you gave me your crew to sail it.'

The captain turned to glance at her, leaning over his chair threateningly. His throat bobbed up and down nervously.

'I'm sure your little assassin is very skilled, but you're wrong. You could never take my ship, Allut has too many men. You'd never make it out the harbour. You *swore* that our last voyage would be our last. You *swore* it. In this city, an oath is a sacred thing, you have no honour if you break it, and if you have no honour in Morgenal, then you have nothing. No opportunity, no money, no power, no allies.'

Widrias glowered. Noswen knew they'd never be able to take the ship by force, the men were soldiers not sailors. Time was running out. For all Widrias' threats, Mostyn told the truth when he warned of people going to Stolach's soldiers. They were running out of time.

'You insult me.'

'Good. I meant to insult you, you overgrown goat.'

Widrias was, by now, nearly purple with rage. His body shook and his eyes blazed. Mostyn, on the other hand was his exact opposite, despite the many fresh cuts and his recently torn clothes, he was calm and relaxed, daintily sipping his grog. Without warning, Widrias bounded across the table, knocking the tankard to the floor and grabbing Mostyn around the neck. He pulled hard and slammed his face on the table, pinning him down. It happened quickly. Too quickly for Noswen to interject. She raised her eyebrows. It was easy to forget how fierce he could be.

He drew a small dagger from his belt and pressed it to the base of Mostyn's neck. Gwahl stepped forward as if to intervene, but she frowned and raised her hand. Widrias was in control, there was no need for him to get involved.

'How about this, my *friend*,' hissed Widrias through clenched teeth. 'You can offer me your services, or I kill you and your crew right here, right now?'

Mostyn's eyes were wide. He struggled to break free of Widrias's grasp, limbs flailing, fingers clawing. The satorr maintained his grip.

'The mobs, the citizens will protect me!' he spluttered. 'The baron's men will kill you if you harm me!'

Widrias increased the pressure on the blade. 'I don't see anyone coming to save you, captain.'

The captain whimpered and struggled for a few more seconds, clawing at the stained wood. His hands fell limp, littered with splinters.

'Get your hands off me, Widrias,' he said in a small voice. 'We can retire to my room to discuss our heading.'

Widrias released his grip and walked up the stairs. Mostyn, beaten and shaken, followed, head bowed in defeat.

*

Lidan walked across the wooden jetty to a towering ship, dark waves splashing against its polished hull, gleaming in the moonlight. From stem to stern the ship was roughly eighty feet long, with a tall aft castle, three masts, gargantuan sails, and a figurehead hidden by a spare sail. He could barely contain his excitement at the thought of sailing it. Aboard a proper ship, just like the ones old Darran back in Weaverlodge used to sail. Finally, he'd live out the imagined adventures of his youth. At times, he was the dreaded Captain Lidan, scourge of the Jagged Isles, laying waste to the fortifications of his foes. At other times, he was the courageous Captain Lidan, battling fierce corsairs to defend the lands. Most often, he was Captain Lidan the discoverer, sailing to uncharted waters, seeking new lands and adventures, the first civilised man to set foot on a thousand different isles of his racing imagination.

His excitement soon turned to dread as he neared the vessel. The sails were torn and dirty, plastered with grime and patched up like a homespun quilt. The wood of the decks, the hull, and the masts was so dark it was nearly black, and it was only by the light streaming from the windows of the captain's cabin that he could even see the ship. As the wind blew, the sail covering the figurehead flapped and he saw a grotesque, screaming serpent, coils straining and mouth wide open in a permanent screech.

He shuddered and climbed the gangplank to mount the deck, suddenly dreading the coming voyage. He gawped, despite himself. A floating fortress. There were ballistae behind the bulwark covering each side of the ship, in addition to the eight arbalests on the aft castle. This was a ship built for battle, for plunder, for pirates. On the larboard hull was the ship's proud nameplate, reading '*Seascale*' in pale gold letters, although this, like the figurehead, was hidden by a loose sail to conceal the ship's identity.

Mostyn had done exceedingly well in preparing the ship for the voyage, loading it with enough food and water in only four days and nights, calling on his many contacts in the harbour to aid him without asking any questions. During that time, the Council company laid low at an inn a few doors down from the Serrated Fang, after

Mostyn had a few words with the landlord. He was happy enough, the beds were full, the drinks flowed, and the coins filled his purse.

Somehow, their presence remained a relative secret, the arcade too unpleasant for the general populace to approach. His only regret was not being able to explore the city, to discover the source behind the wails, the cheers, the raucous laughter. Each night, the crashes and clatters of countless curiosities teased him in his dingy cot, beckoning him to join them in their wonder. Of course, he wasn't allowed. Not even with Gwahl on his wanderings through the city. A prisoner in the inn. Even today, their route from the arcade to the hidden harbour was a secluded one, as Gwahl and Tanor led their company from quiet street to deserted alley in groups of three or four, avoiding contact where possible. What little he saw of the city was darkness and grime, always a few streets away from the cacophony of joy and despair, always around the corner from the excitement. The sight of the *Seascale* was his first taste of adventure since the violence of the tavern brawl. The imminent voyage promised so much more.

Finally, they were off, leaving behind the miserable city called Morgenal.

Pwtrek appeared beside him, and motioned below deck, dodging the sailors scurrying around the ship, climbing up shrouds and heaving on ropes. He rubbed his hands together, staring at their calloused fingers as they prepared the ship.

Crossing the deck, he noticed dark stains on the wood, a muddy-crimson colour. Each time he passed one, he averted his eyes, knowing exactly what it was. They made their way down to one of the lower decks and a vast forest of hammocks, strung up and waiting to be slept in. The two friends followed the rest of the company to their beds and settled down, rocked to sleep by the ebbing tide.

Before his weariness took the better of him, he saw Widrias ordering five soldiers to stand guard. He nodded to himself and closed his eyes. Mostyn seemed far from trustworthy.

Chapter 9

Three days into their voyage and his sea-legs were finally developed. To an extent. Better than three days ago, at the very least. The spew-bucket was no longer attached to his person, the overwhelming nausea no longer hampering his every movement. There was beauty in the fresh breath of freedom of the main deck, the gentle kiss of saltwater on his cheek as the ship met an oncoming wave, the joyful cry of an albatross.

The Great Waters stretched out before them and Morgenal Harbour was many, many leagues behind. Leaning as he was against the bulwark on the forecastle, the hideous figurehead lead the way through the waves. A wondrous piece of work, far beyond anything the carpenters at Weaverlodge could produce. Each scale meticulously carved into the wood, the bunched muscles and the curved fangs, detailed enough to come alive with the rocking ship.

He turned away, watching the crashing waves against the hull. The endless stretch of water glittering to the horizon, nothing but grey skies and greyer seas. Like standing at the precipice of a bottomless chasm, at the brink of eternity.

Brushing a stray droplet from his cheek, he closed his eyes, warm sun breaking through the clouds against his lids. A touch on his shoulder made him jump. Only Pwtrek. The juggernaut joined him against the railing. He waited for him to say something, but a pondering silence remained between them. Fidgeting, he cleared his throat. Pwtrek closed his eyes, as if reflecting on some memory.

'Enadir has changed, Lidan. I can remember the times of wilderness in these lands, the time before this so-called "order". I remember how it all ended, how it all began.'

'How?' asked Lidan, eager, as always, to hear a story.

He sighed and looked up to the sky, staring solemnly at the clouds moving to obscure the sun again.

'Our world, Enadir, is ancient, its massive mountain ranges and fast-flowing rivers. It was a wondrous world, and the most wonderful were the Midlands of Nefarwy, now "The Lands of the

King". With the Great Waters to the south, the black desert to the west, the bleak Northlands above the Kingdom of the calefs to the east. Countless ages ago, many centuries, millennia even, before you or I were born, this land belonged to the giants. They were magnificent and majestic and proud, the true masters of the world.'

Lidan nodded, familiar with the story. It was one he'd heard countless times as a child, of the fall of the giants and the desolation of the Cataclysmic War. Of course, each storyteller had their own iteration of the tale, and he was happy to hear Pwtrek's.

'However,' continued the juggernaut, 'there was another race who matched their strength: The cockatrice. Great winged serpents with eyes reflecting the doom and darkness of existence. It is said that to meet a cockatrice's stare was tantamount to suicide as the vision drove you insane. These creatures flew over the Great Waters from the desolate isle of Uffernen and waged war on the giants, for reasons we cannot imagine, reasons lost in the mists of history.

'The war between these two races desecrated the ground and set fire to the sky, the bodies of these titans piling up to form great mounds. Calefs, men, minotorrs, daemons, and all of Enadir's races fought alongside the giants to aid their masters in this struggle against the terrifying cockatrice, and finally the great enemy was defeated, but at a terrible price. The last of the giants were slain.

'After so many years, decades, some say, of war, the races of the world had forgotten peace and fell upon each other. The land fell into ruin. The daemons, ever few in number, retreated over the sea. The calefs, being the strongest race at that time, secured the east for themselves. The minotorrs took refuge in the mountain ranges of the Northlands. As for the rest, they crawled into caves and hovels and dark crevices. The land was wounded and would bear no fruit. Life was harsh.

'According to the myths, there came a year of terrible storms and earthquakes, as if the very spirit of Enadir were being torn apart. But then, suddenly, Enadir forgave her people for the wars and the damage they had done to the land and bore fruit once more. The great forests of the world swelled and grew, larger and deeper and darker with each passing day, the trees feeding off the soil enriched with the blood of countless corpses. They grew at such a rate that a man could fall asleep a hundred metres from the edge of the forest and wake up in a grove of pines. But although the land itself had healed, its people were still broken.

'Centuries passed since the Cataclysmic War and the Midlands was still nothing but a land of tribes and villages. Each their own little country, the village chief living as king. It was a difficult land to live in, with many fragile alliances between each settlement, broken at a moment's notice to spark off another feud. They fought for the right to farm in a certain place, to drink from a certain river. They would fight if someone felled one of "their" trees for wood to build houses. It was a terrible time to live in. You had to swear allegiance to a tribe for protection and within the boundaries of their lands you lived in fear, but also in some relative safety. Outside of these borders total anarchy reigned. It grew worse and worse over the passing years, trade between villages ground to a halt as rival tribes and rogue thieves intercepted supply trains. Gold was scarce. Creatures were driven to a more feral nature. It is during this time the Hobbs came together. Nomads banded together out of necessity, united in a brotherhood. Their influence spread, and soon enough there were thousands of clans roaming the world. If you had no village, you could join the Hobbs, set about as a rogue, or invite your own early grave. Honest folk had no place in the wilderness.

'Despite the danger, the wild, some creatures held a degree of sanity, and used it to gain power. Some of them combined forces and led their villages south from the forest to the seafront, where they built the first city by men. Morgenal. Centuries later, some individuals in the northern Dailas Forest banded together and sought the help of the minotorrs of Bletta Castle to build their own northern city in the forest. The minotorrs saw potential for the beginnings of an organised civilization in the forest and agreed to help. They led the mining expeditions for stone, and lent them their armies to keep away the chaos of the land. They built the great city of the north, Cadaran. However, those ambitious men had grown arrogant and refused to repay the minotorrs for their assistance. They locked the great gates of the city. Those still inside were clapped in irons by their soldiers, even the minotorrs there were made slaves. It sparked the great war of the north between the masters of Cadaran and the minotorrs of Bletta Castle. A war that raged for decades, perhaps as long as a century. Many village leaders in the northern forest flocked to the city, to seek safety behind the walls. Safety they found, but not the kind they expected. The strong were forced into the city garrison and the weak were made slaves. Cadaran City was, is, a dark, terrible place, but it showed the inhabitants of the Midlands that an establishment of order, however cruel, was possible. Many creatures aspired to be the founders of such an order. One such creature was a young fonex, the fonex that would soon take the entire lands by force. Our great King Stolach Palharr.'

Lidan leaned forward, listening intently. The account of the age of giants was a familiar tale, but this was new. The account of how Stolach became king was always muddled and confused by his village elders, with conflicting tales and contradictions within each story. Perhaps Pwtrek knew the truth.

'He was born and lived his first few years with his people in Dailas. He was an accomplished fighter, and soon became the village champion, commanding more respect than the village elders with his charisma, courage, and intellect. What could have been a shining example among us, tarnished by his pride and ruthlessness. Angered by the change this young fonex brought to the village, they banished him for some trivial insurrection. As a race, fonex possess a high level of cunning, and Stolach was one of the most devious, canny creatures to have ever set foot on this earth. After weeks in the wild, he had his revenge. One night, he returned to the village and crept into each of the elder's houses, gagged them and skinned them alive, before hanging their carcasses from the boughs of a tree in the middle of the village. He appointed himself the new leader, and challenged anyone to deny him this prize. Nobody was stupid enough to do so.

'Stolach seemed content enough for a few months leading his people, but soon grew restless. He yearned for adventure, and one night, departed. He wandered the Dailas Forest for two years, seeking adventure and knowledge, surviving the wilderness, thriving in the chaos. Along the way he came upon a solitary blacksmith in a cave in the ground. He commissioned the perfect sword. The poor fellow slaved for twenty days and nights on the weapon, creating the finest blade Enadir has ever seen, or so they say. As Stolach held the weapon up to the light, he noticed a tiny scratch on the steel where one of the smith's tools slipped. He ran him through and left him to die.

'After two years wandering the wild, he returned to his village and found they'd elected new leaders in his absence. Furious at the perceived slur, he killed them all and left them to rot. His own people. The ones who'd raised him from the cradle.

'He began his travels again, wandering aimlessly through Dailas, slaughtering anyone he met. For the most part, he avoided settlements, the ones he approached chased him away as the half-mad cur that he was, probably assuming he was a Desired Hobb. Eventually, he picked up a companion. A wise old sage. The creature taught Stolach how to conquer, how to think like the enemy, how to pin down his weaknesses and eventually deliver the perfect killing strokes. The two friends, if that's what you can call them, wandered the land for months on a bloody pilgrimage of death and torture. One day, Stolach and his teacher walked into a village of juggernauts, like me, each one towering above them, and began their slaughter. Despite the strength, ferocity, and numbers the juggernauts possessed, they couldn't kill this lean fonex or wily ancient, and as Stolach carved his way through the village one of the inhabitants stepped forward and pleaded with him to stop. He offered his tribe to Stolach as an army to fight under the fonex's command. Stolach considered for a moment and sheathed his sword. This was the start of his great army, the one that would soon rid Enadir of the madness and division that reigned for so long.

'That juggernaut is now his chief advisor and second in command, Tomon Jomein. I personally believe it was Tomon who convinced Stolach to start conquering and unifying, otherwise the fonex may have simply wandered the Midlands, killing and living his baseless life before death finally claimed him.

'Nevertheless, his army was begun. Where he used to destroy villages, he now recruited, and where he used to wander aimlessly through the lands, he now conquered, demanding payment for protection and loyalty.

'As I said, he was not the first soldier to begin such a campaign, following the idea of order set by the masters of Cadaran and Morgenal. In the centuries of division and isolation beforehand, many ambitious leaders had attempted the same thing, conquering other settlements and expanding their little kingdoms, but each were defeated by the forest itself. Too many villages, too many roads, too many trees for rogues and thieves to hide. Stolach knew he needed a capital to sit his bloody throne, so he searched for a palace. Morgenal was filthy and treacherous, and held too many mobs and cunning, aspiring individuals. Besides, it is mostly slums and mud, too base for someone as proud as Stolach. Cadaran was locked in its struggle with Bletta Castle and Stolach knew of the horrors of the city, so he decided against it for the time being. Years after beginning his conquest, he crossed the Crisiaddwr River to go west. He fought his way through the goblin colonies of the pine woods, swept through the southern plains where you're from, then turned north into the black desert. In Crastalan, former home of the giant kings, he found what he desired. At the time, the city was commanded by a small clan of nomads. They resisted the king for two hours before the vast fortress city was overrun by his troops.

'Once he established the city for himself, he led his armies out to the others. Morgenal was easiest to conquer, but to this day most difficult to control. The battle for Cadaran was bloody and exhausting, the siege lasted two years, but he triumphed. The masters of the city bent their knees. He accepted their surrender, then immediately executed them for their crimes, placing his most favoured commanders as lords of the city. You must understand, this victory was possibly the most important of his entire campaign, as the minotorrs completely ceased their attacks on the city now that the old slavers had been removed. This peace between Bletta Castle and Stolach eventually evolved into the alliance we learned about at the Council. A damned outrage.

'Anyway, after taking over both Morgenal and Cadaran, Stolach could declare the Midlands conquered. He returned to

Crastalan to rule. However, each day Stolach spent in the tower heralded the discovery of yet another secret passageway or hidden doorway, chinks in the armour to be exploited. When he interrogated the prisoners, the previous owners of the city, he learned that the keys to each passageway were hidden throughout the lands. Stolach had another quest to complete.

'He tortured each prisoner until he identified the last recorded whereabouts of each key, and left the city with an army to search for them. His quest took him across many lands, across the Great Waters to the Southlands, through the Jagged Isles, and deep into the Northlands. On many occasions, the keys had been moved, so the black-hearted fonex killed and tortured anyone he found for information. It only took half a year before he found them all, save for two. One, the serpent key, was supposedly guarded by a caravan of dreyads, relatives of the nomads who'd initially inhabited the city, constantly travelling through Nefarwy. Stolach knew this would be the hardest to retrieve. The second, the lion key, was locked in a vault in Muranath Castle itself.'

He glanced meaningfully at him, and frowned at what must have been a blank expression.

'Why was it there?' Lidan asked, shaking his head.

'It was taken there for safe keeping, many decades ago.'

'For safe keeping? Did they know Stolach was after the keys?'

'Possibly. Exactly when it was brought to Muranath is unclear, perhaps the calefs took it from Crastalan after the fall of the giants in case they ever wanted to return? Maybe the key's guardians brought it to Lleunedd when Stolach started hunting for them. I don't know.'

'I'll ask Spotal,' he shrugged.

'Best not to, actually,' Pwtrek shook his head.

He cocked his head questioningly, but Pwtrek waved the question away; it would be answered soon enough.

'For months, Stolach sent emissaries to Lleunedd requesting the key be returned to him, its rightful owner. Lleunedd knew its importance and flatly refused each time, knowing possession of this key would give the fonex a nigh-impenetrable fortress. The calefs, unlike the minotorrs, clearly recognised Stolach as an unsuitable king and wanted to keep their weapon. Stolach grew increasingly desperate and in the end, turned to his guild of assassins. Their task? Infiltrate the castle and steal the key from under the calefs' noses.

'Veiled by darkness, a score and a half of men, hanex and fonex infiltrated the city and began their journey to the vaults. Not much is known about what exactly happened. What we *do* know is twenty-nine were caught and killed by Major Cetril Lasaai, father to Captain Spotal. There was a fierce battle in the tombs of the vault, and in one of these stone cellars, Cetril was slain by a knife buried in his back. The assassin escaped and delivered the key to the king, like a faithful mongrel. I'm sure you've guessed by now the identity of this murderer. Stolach's old pet and trusted friend, the greatest assassin of his guild, our travelling companion. Noswen. This act was the final straw that led to the enmity between King Lleunedd and Stolach, which continues to this day.

'It is rumoured that with only one key left to find, Stolach went on a murderous rampage through Dailas, destroying every caravan he came across, mirroring his actions many years before. He eventually found them, but they escaped to Tarnegrefur Mountains. Stolach knew he had them penned in and followed. The rest of the tale you probably heard during your time at the Council. Rumour has it the dreyads sold their lives to protect the whereabouts of the key. Stolach never found it and departed the mountains, apparently assuming that if he couldn't find it with his army, nobody could.

'He returned to Crastalan and locked all the tunnels with his hoard of keys. As for the one missing its key, I would think that Stolach filled it with soldiers, collapsed it, flooded it, anything. Anyhow, he reassumed his throne as a self-proclaimed king, led his armies against any rebellions or insurrections, collected taxes, made deals with the other lands, everything a king does. The Midlands were united under his banner, and its inhabitants suffered the consequences of his iron hand. Taxes, tolls, restrictions, oppression, tyranny. You know the rest, you've lived with it all your life. Villages burned and families killed. The crown and throne only worsened the basest, vilest parts of his character.'

*

He turned away from Pwtrek, sensing the story was over.

It was long, no doubt, and even though he knew the ending, there were parts he'd never anticipated. He'd never even thought of Stolach's youth, how brutal it must have been to produce such a tyrant. But out of everything Pwtrek said... Noswen. Could she really be the one who murdered Spotal's father? If so, why did Spotal tolerate her company? Why did any of them? Now he understood the hateful glares, the shunning. Had she not given Stolach the key to his fortress, robbed the calefs of their greatest weapon against him? Was it not on her account that he was safe and sound behind Crastalan's high walls?

On the main deck behind them, Gwahl took out his pipe and played a merry tune. A sailor joined in with his violin, and together they played a lively jig that soon had the crew jumping and dancing in delight. He watched for a while, foot tapping with the beat. He laughed with Pwtrek when one of the ship's boys, barely twelve years old, began a furious tap-dance to the encouraging cheers of his companions. He turned back to the juggernaut.

'If the final part of the tale, the part with the serpent key, is a rumour, why don't we just ask Noswen if the key exists? Surely she must know after already retrieving one?'

'The other keys existed, that's a hard fact, but this one... seems too good to be true to me. But Widrias and the Council believe it. Gwahl does too. If the chancellors want it to be real, Noswen will say whatever she needs to please them, to get into their good books. We quest after a story, nothing more.'

'But why would Noswen allow us to waste our time chasing this tale?'

'Your answer is in your question Lidan. She probably did it in order to buy some time for her allies in Crastalan, split up the Council, send a chancellor on a wild goose chase to keep him occupied for months, or better yet, killed. It'll bring Stolach time to mobilise a force against us. Stamp us out like he's done to dozens of other rebellions.'

He thought for a moment. Could it be? It made sense, now Pwtrek said it. A spy sent to sabotage their efforts. It was the kind of cunning and deviousness he should expect from Stolach. But Gwahl trusted her. So did Spotal, Tanor, and Widrias. Surely that counted for something?

'You really believe that?' he asked, hesitantly.

'Yes. The only reason I allowed myself to be led away from the Council was to keep an eye on the bitch, to ensure she doesn't try anything on the general. I don't trust her, Lidan, and neither should you. In fact, in these times I would advise you to trust no one save for those you are sure are your friends, and even then, be careful about what you say.'

'Do you trust me, Pwtrek?' only half-joking. 'I've only been around for a few weeks.'

'Of course I trust you, little one. You don't have the capacity to be a spy. The way you jumped at shadows, trotted behind Gwahl like a lost cub. Most importantly, the fact that you couldn't march in a column for a bag of blackberries! The king would never even consider sending such an inexperienced soldier to the front line!'

He smiled weakly, unsure whether to be insulted or grateful. Best not to dwell on it. Pipe and violin harmonised merrily behind. They remained as they were, staring across the waves, ignored by the crew. Like a swarm of bees, they bustled around them, raising sails, scrubbing decks, oiling the heavy weaponry, eager to join the dancing on deck.

Recalling a detail of Pwtrek's story, he turned to his friend.

'The old sage, the one who taught the king, what happened to him?'

Pwtrek frowned. 'Nobody knows. Many say that after Stolach learned all he could, he killed him and hung his carcass from Crastalan's battlements. Others say he still lurks at Stolach's side, forever concealed by shadows and whispering silent advice to his pupil. I don't know.'

Unsatisfying, but no matter, no point pursuing it. He watched the sailors, tapping his foot to the rhythm of the lively shanty.

Before long, Spotal joined them and nudged him sharply in the back with a stick.

'Fancy one of those lessons?'

'Lessons?' Pwtrek raised an eyebrow, looking back and forth between the two and the sticks held in the calef's hands. 'Swordsmanship lessons with Spotal?'

His cheeks flushed as Spotal replied. 'Indeed, my newest student, guaranteed success. You should've seen him duel the Hobb back in Dailas. Like looking in a mirror.'

He laughed. 'Go easy on me, I'm only a beginner.'

*

Three hours later and he was sprawled on a pile of old sails under the main mast. He hissed through his teeth as Gwahl applied cooling salves to the various bumps and welts developing on his skin.

Lessons with Spotal were not what he expected.

Skilled warrior he may be, but he was a damned abysmal teacher. Half an hour of scolding for the way he held his sword, then sparring for another two and a half hours. A painfully infuriating time, as he found himself desperately defending himself for the entire session, flinching every few seconds as the calef's weapon clacked into his limbs, torso, head, and neck. The small crowd of giggling, wincing spectators didn't help the ordeal.

Now, he lay exhausted in the middle of the deck, a new crowd gathered around him, laughing and joking in an attempt to cheer him up, all the time cooing as Gwahl uncovered yet another ugly mark on his skin. Spotal himself was completely oblivious, and set about with the light-hearted attitude of a teacher who thoroughly believed his students were enjoying their lesson. At the end, barely able to stand, he'd been too polite to tell him otherwise and thanked the beaming calef for his time. Perhaps that was why the calef kept shooting confused glances at him from his vantage point on the quarterdeck.

Not that he wasn't grateful. It was just… unexpected. Next time might be better. He jumped as Gwahl pressed slightly too firmly on a welt. The concept of 'next time' came less and less appealing every second. The daemon patted him on the head, smirking.

'You'll live.'

'Haven't been this sore since Crastalan, I swear,' he groaned.

'Wait until tomorrow, you'll be even stiffer'

'Something to look forward to,' he muttered.

Gwahl chuckled and motioned for him to turn over, to work on his back. He blushed as he rolled up his shirt. He'd be surprised if the ugly mass of scar tissue had the capacity to bruise. But no, probing fingers sent sparks of a now-familiar ache. How in the four winds Spotal managed to wallop him on his back so many times was a mystery. He watched Spotal, standing with Tanor and Widrias, gesturing animatedly at something in the distance. Suddenly, Widrias turned and sprang away, followed closely by the other two.

He frowned. What could have startled them?

Chapter 10

Spotal massaged his wrist. A bit stiff after hours of sparring. Perhaps he was getting old, too old for this game. Not that he had much choice. May as well do something useful with his time, and passing on the knowledge of his craft seemed noble enough. The youth was untrained, clumsy, sloppy, but enthusiastic. His eagerness reminded him of himself in his early years. Swinging away with his stick like a windmill, it was like fighting a child, all too easy to dart inside the blows and strike. To his credit, by the end of the session he'd learnt to hold back, to recover, to defend slightly better. Only slightly. It would take time to develop into an adequate soldier. By the looks of things, it would also take time to bounce back from their lesson.

'Must have been too hard on him,' muttered Tanor.

'Apparently so,' he sighed, watching Gwahl slather salves on Lidan's welts.

'Did he complain?'

'Not once. I would have ended it sooner had I known he was in pain.'

'He's hardy,' nodded Widrias. 'Has the makings of a good recruit.'

'Only if he knows not to push too hard,' said Tanor, leaning on his elbows against the rail. 'Won't be any good to anyone if he breaks himself trying to get better.'

'Well it's up to us to guide his learning,' said Widrias, 'and he certainly needs to learn. I did wonder why Gwahl brought him to us, but perhaps I can see his potential.'

'He's not had a minion for some time now, has he?' Tanor nodded at Gwahl. 'It's been a couple of years since the last one.'

'Goes through phases, doesn't he?' shrugged Spotal. 'Few years ago he went through about five different ones within as many months.'

'Just drift apart, don't they?'

'The lucky ones...' Widrias trailed off. 'I do wonder why he took this one on, especially now.'

'I like him,' he smiled. 'I can see why Gwahl invited him.'

'You think that's why? Because he likes him?' the satorr snorted.

'Well, it certainly helped,' he said.

'He seems decent enough,' agreed Tanor. 'Young and honest.'

'Noswen thinks so,' said Widrias.

'Don't you?' he asked, surprised.

'I trust Noswen's judgement, and yes, yours too. Both of you. As I said, he has the makings of a good recruit.'

He nodded, smiling when he caught Lidan's eye. He smiled back, in between grimaces at the daemon's touch. Laughing silently at the situation, he watched the crew for a second, fingering the pendant about his neck before turning to Widrias again.

'What is it, Spotal?' asked the satorr, keeping his eyes fixed on the horizon. 'Share your thoughts.'

'I was just wondering... can we trust Mostyn?' he said, keeping his voice low. 'They seemed happy enough to kill us in the tavern and you were quite heavy-handed with him. How do we know they won't turn on us?'

'Relax, Spotal. I know Mostyn. I never trusted him even when we were friends. It's why I never walk around without the company of you or Tanor, it's why Noswen follows him wherever he goes. Just to keep an eye on our salty friend. I've taken all necessary precautions.'

'Have some faith in the Council Guard,' added Tanor. 'This lot are little more than violent sailors, my men are trained soldiers. They're more than capable of taking on ten times our number. We may not be your snooty Calefin Guard, but we're not bad,' he winked.

'Not that snooty,' laughed Spotal. 'Even if we are, it's with good reason!'

'Don't think anyone loves the Calefin Guard as much as themselves,' Tanor shook his head with a smile.

'Ah, well, not really one of them anymore, am I?' he shrugged away the looks of sympathy. 'It's fine, probably wouldn't be here with you lot if I were still in the ranks, would I?'

'True,' Widrias nodded. 'Anyway, as I was saying, I have no reason to expect Mostyn to leave us alone throughout the whole voyage. By the four winds, he'll try to double-cross us before the end.'

'What do you think he'll do?' asked Tanor, concern deepening his voice as he glared suspiciously at the nearest sailor.

'I don't know, but I have a few guesses...' Widrias's voice trailed off to silence. His eyes narrowed, peering across the sea.

Spotal turned, following his gaze. At first, there was nothing, only endless waves. No, there it was. A tiny black speck on the horizon. Another vessel. He pointed and turned to the others. Tanor couldn't see it, but trusted them enough to know it was there. Widrias bolted down the stairs. They followed, hot on his heels to the captain's cabin.

They jumped onto deck and pushed past the startled crew. He spat in an attempt to clear his mouth of the foul taste building up. Was there no peace to be had nowadays? He turned again. The speck was already bigger. From the speed it was approaching, it would reach them within a few hours, perhaps less. On the bright side, it was more than enough time to organize their company into battle formations, should it come to it.

Widrias stormed into the aft castle, throwing the doors open with a crash. Through the vestibule and into Mostyn's quarters. Sprawled in his high- backed chair, mouth hanging open, a spilled bottle of rum rolling along the table before him with the tide. The cabin itself was vast, spanning the entire width of the ship. Four large windows composed the rear wall, providing a fine view of the foaming waves behind the mighty vessel were they not covered by heavy curtains. To one side was a weapon rack populated by an array of cutlasses, maces and boathooks. To the other side was a large hammock, blankets strewn clumsily across it as it rocked with each passing wave. Small candle-lit lamps dotted the walls to cast small patches of golden light throughout the crowded room, overflowing chests of sea-charts, ledgers, and all manner of tat strewn haphazardly over the velveted floor. In the shadows behind Mostyn, he noted Noswen's shaded silhouette, her clear blue eyes staring at them.

He nodded to her. Did Mostyn know she was there? Perhaps, but probably not. The hanex's reputation was well-earned. He knew all too well just how stealthy she was.

Widrias raised his hand, signalling her to remain. Striding across the stained carpet to the sleeping captain, he slapped him swiftly across the face to revive him from his drunken slumber. Mostyn woke with a cry and drew a concealed knife, holding it to the satorr's throat. Spotal jumped forward, but Widrias was unconcerned, sneering as he slapped the blade away.

'Are you so afraid of betrayal that you sleep with a knife hidden on your person? It doesn't matter. There's an unknown ship sailing towards us and gaining fast. Your incompetent crewman in the crow's nest has failed to notice it still. Had I not seen it approaching, we'd have had even less time to prepare for an attack.'

'What makes you so sure they'll attack?' he mumbled.

'It's heading straight towards us with all sails raised. I don't know but I certainly don't like it.'

Mostyn cursed foully and hurried to the weapon rack to select a cutlass, which he shoved roughly through the silk sash around his waist.

'Save your curses and organise your crew. Prepare them for battle, unless you wish to be captured,' said Widrias as he walked out the cabin and galloped up the stairs to the poop deck. Spotal followed. On deck, Pwtrek was there, glaring at the flag fluttering from the mizzenmast. He pointed a curved claw at the cloth and spat.

'Fool's been flying his colours throughout the journey. Every passing ship would know it's Mostyn, friend or foe. I didn't even realise. Didn't think to look.'

Widrias's face remained impassive, but his eyes blazed with cold fury. Spotal shook his head. Clearly Mostyn's wits were dulled with the passing seasons and countless bottles of rum. The man in speaking staggered into the sunlight, eyes watering at the sudden brightness. He climbed the stairs groggily to the poop deck and fished a spyglass from his heavy sea-coat. Ignoring Spotal and the others, he walked to the bulwark and peered through the ornate scope.

Spotal watched him swing his gaze back and forth, before settling on the ship. For a few painful seconds Mostyn stood as he was, stock still. He saw the blood drain from his face. Worrying. Just like Noswen, Mostyn's reputation was well-earned. True, he was not the man he once was, but was still formidable. If whatever followed them was enough to make him blanche, it was surely a cause for them to be equally worried.

Finally, he spoke, his voice quiet, timid, like he'd sounded after Widrias fell upon him. The awful voice of a beaten man.

'Sea-neiads.'

'You can see them?'

'Don't need to. The quality of the ship, its size, their sailing. Must be. It's a monster galleon crewed by sea-neiads.'

He glanced at Widrias, but the satorr showed no emotion, simply nodding at the declaration.

He wished he had his composure. Inside, he was screaming. Not even his kinsmen could equal the sea-neiads in naval battles. It was only the fact their navy was larger that they could contend for control of the waves.

The sea-neiads were among the first to sell their allegiance to Stolach. It was they, along with the inhabitants of the Jagged Isles, who secured his grip on the Great Waters and the Southlands with their awesome sailing prowess and fearsome combat skills. Their mighty ships were built for a single thing; interception. By annexing trade between the Jagged Isles, it didn't take long for the islanders to sell their allegiance, or for the Southlands to suffer from lack of trade. Each vessel was lovingly crafted by the best carpenters in the land and was capable of outrunning even the swiftest and lightest ships. It was foolish to attempt to outrun or out-manoeuvre them. The best course of action would be to stand and fight, to trust the Council Guard.

He shared a quick glance with Widrias and rushed down to the main deck to bellow orders.

*

Widrias ran around the deck, organising his men. His men. They would not let him down. He paused as he passed Lidan and turned to Gwahl.

'My friend, I need you in the crow's nest. Replace the incompetent swine up there.'

'Keep your ears peeled,' nodded Gwahl.

He watched the daemon ascend the shrouds, unconcerned by wind or wave, as happy on a ship as he was in the forest. Someone he could trust. Lidan stirred, lying bruised and battered on his bed of sails.

'You able to fight, Lidan, or would you rather stay below deck? I saw Spotal land a few blows.'

'Had far worse in Crastalan. The aches after a sparring session are nothing. I can fight.'

Widrias smiled. He certainly had potential. Hopefully it wouldn't be cut short today. He ran from stem to stern bellowing at his soldiers to form ranks until a phalanx was formed in the middle of the ship. Four men deep and ten wide, each side of the phalanx facing a different railing. The two middle ranks were made up of archers, while the outer ranks on either side were solid walls of spear and shield. The remaining men were to guard the poop and quarter decks.

A cry came from above as a pirate was flung from the crow's nest. He hit the shrouds and clung on by his fingertips, cursing the daemon above. A presumably empty bottle of rum followed seconds after, dropping into the sea with a plop. Despite the situation, he smiled, imagining Gwahl's reaction as he found the drunkard. The smile soon faded. How many more were drunk? Sailing and fighting were unfortunately second best to these pirates' ability to drink, gamble, and drink again. He could only hope they wouldn't get in the way of his men.

'Ship at two thousand metres and closing!' The daemon's voice drifted down to him.

He raised his hand in thanks and sprinted to Mostyn on the poop deck.

'What's the range of your ballistae?'

'Around five hundred metres. But they're more reliable at shorter distances.'

'Very well. Gwahl will tell us when the ship is within range, and you can give your crew the order to fire. How accurate are they?'

'You know how good we are.'

'I remember your crew's talents well enough. I only wonder whether the gallons of liquor they've consumed over the years might have affected their aim.'

'Still good enough to storm a fort in the dead of night,' Mostyn sneered.

'Better than that, I hope,' he said, coldly. No use bringing up sour memories, not on the eve of battle.

He walked away and leaned against the railing, his eyes fixed on the fast-approaching ship.

*

Lidan flexed his back in anticipation. The timing couldn't be worse. His sparring session left him exhausted. He'd been placed in the front rank on the starboard side. Was it better to face the enemy ship and be first to exchange blows, or wait for them to circle around but have his back exposed? Neither, preferably. At least Pwtrek was with him, mighty spear in hand, bracing himself for the clash. Further down the line stood Auran, his battleaxe held in an iron grip, staring silently at crashing waves. With luck, the soldiers on either side would compensate for his injuries.

'How do they know it's us?' he asked Pwtrek. 'How can Stolach possibly know we've set out to find the key after so little time?'

'He doesn't, Lidan,' said Pwtrek. 'But the neiads know it's Mostyn, which is enough. Don't worry, Stolach has no idea we're out here searching for his key, whether it exists or not. He'll know after,' he smiled ruefully.

'What do you mean?'

'Why else would a company of Council Guard be here, with so many important individuals accompanying them? If the neiads make it back to the king, what hope we had in secrecy will be destroyed. We must kill each and every creature on that ship to save the mission.'

*

Gwahl watched the enemy vessel with pursed lips. It was a long time since he'd seen such a fine vessel, even longer since he'd seen one handled so well. Its size and speed allowed it to accomplish feats of sailing the *Seascale* could never dream of, crashing through towering waves with arrogance, proclaiming itself master of the waters. Recalling his duties, he leaned over and called to Widrias.

'Ship at five hundred metres!'

*

Widrias looked over at Mostyn, but the captain had already heard Gwahl's cry. He bellowed at his crew to ready the ballistae, ordered the helmsman to bring the ship about, and strode over to one of the mighty crossbows fixed to the railing of the poop deck. Widrias grabbed the rail as the ship slowly swung around, cloak flapping as the wind turned. They drew perpendicular with the enemy, their starboard facing the neiad's bow. When Gwahl's next cry came floating down, Mostyn gave the order.

Missiles sailed over the waves and crashed into the galleon. A boulder glanced off the hull, another flattened a crewmember. They were followed by the bolts from the arbalests, thudding into the crew, killing five and wounding three more. But the neiads were not without war-engines of their own and returned fire with a catapult on the forecastle. The boulder crashed into the *Seascale*'s starboard hull, nearly knocking them off their feet. A volley of arrows followed. Most fell far short of the mark but some found their mark.

The ranged battle continued for agonizing minutes. The ships circled each other like bare-knuckle fighters in a ring, Mostyn's helmsman keeping them out of reach of the galleon. But the foe had the advantage. Every turn, they came closer. Barely ten metres away, Widrias was forced to duck as leering sea-neiads threw javelins and sling-stones at the poop deck, then the helmsman heaved on the wheel again to turn them aside. A final volley of bolts, boulders, and arrows flew between the vessels and they could turn no more.

172

Grappling hooks were hurled, catching ropes and shrouds. Boarding-hooks were cast, thumping over the *Seascale*'s rail. Gangplanks were set, spanning the precarious distance between the convex hulls. They boarded.

As the first corsairs landed on the vessel, a volley of arrows from the Council Guard peppered them, sending those over-enthusiastic boarders into the depths. But the galleon held many men, and the carcasses were cleared to make way.

*

Mostyn stood firm on the poop deck, firing bolt after bolt from his arbalest into the enemy. No matter how many he struck, it did nothing to diminish their numbers. He ducked down behind the bulwark as a volley rained down. Enemy marksmen on the foretops. Hopefully their own would pick them off. As he sat panting beneath his mounted crossbow, Widrias came sliding over. The satorr was shouting something, but over the din of the battle he couldn't make out what he was saying. Finally, after bellowing in his ear for so long, he heard the satorr's cries.

'For the love of the four winds, Mostyn. Take out the captain! The captain! Kill him!'

Mostyn nodded and crouched behind his crossbow. He swivelled the weapon around until he found his opposite eye. A barbaric bastard in an eye-patch and a bandanna, bellowing orders until he was blue in the face. Bloody poser. Probably wasn't even missing an eye. He took aim. His calloused hand tightened over the trigger. He slowly exhaled and squeezed. The bolt raced towards the enemy captain. It would take him in the chest. Just before impact, a wave struck, the galleon dipped and the bolt buried itself in the throat of the crewmember behind. Mostyn cursed and quickly loaded another bolt, but was pinned down as another volley peppered the deck.

*

Gwahl observed the battle below. The neiads had managed to overrun the forecastle and were now attempting to outflank the Council Guard, who were already engaged with neiads sweeping in from the starboard side. They reorganised the phalanx, moving the spearmen to reinforce the stem and starboard sides of the formation, leaving the archers with their backs to the unengaged larboard rail. Mostyn's crew were as chaotic in combat as he first feared, showing little finesse, instead relying on ferocity to overcome their attackers. But they were as experienced fighters as they were sailors, making good use of the shrouds, the mast, the tops, and the sails to defeat their enemies. The *Seascale* was their home, their lives, and they fought with the passion of a defending nation to save their ship.

He should go down to help his companions. Equally, his duty was here. Damn Widrias for banishing him to this task. The nest provided a unique view of the battlefield and he could relay precious information to his friends. But only if they could even hear it over the battle. Stay or go?

His question was answered as another wave struck. A new gust of wind rocked the ship, followed by the faintest kiss from the west. With a sigh born of past experience, he turned to face the larboard side expectantly. There it was. The horizon a mass of boiling storm clouds racing towards them.

*

Widrias groaned on the deck, left leg pinned to the wood by an arrow. Tanor leaned over him, protecting his body from further harm as Spotal desperately tried to remove it. Widrias screamed in pain as Spotal twisted the shaft and wrenched it free. Tanor looked at the arrowhead. They were lucky it was long instead of barbed, otherwise Widrias may well have been trapped. Spotal tore a length of cloth from his cloak and wrapped it tightly around his leg to stop the bleeding. The satorr patted Spotal weakly on the shoulder in thanks as the calef dragged him to lean against the bulwark for protection.

Tanor joined them, raising his arm as a pitiful shelter from the missiles. An arrow thudded into the deck by his foot, prompting him to scramble for better cover. Beside him, he sensed Widrias turn his attention skywards, to the crow's nest. He glanced up and saw Gwahl waving and pointing frantically to the sky. He looked beyond the nest and froze.

174

The thunderclouds rolling towards them were magnificently dark and forbidding, blotting out the sun and covering the sea in an impenetrable darkness, its only relief the occasional flash of forked lighting that lit up the sky. He felt the first raindrops fall. Beside him, Widrias winced as the rain pattered on his bandaged leg. The wind died down, then suddenly rose to hurricane force gales, straining the sails of both ships to their fullest.

Widrias whispered a warning of the coming storm to Mostyn, crouched behind the bulwark, completely pinned down by the raining arrows. Unheard, he closed his eyes with a sigh. His head rolled to one side as he passed out in the middle of battle.

Tanor looked at his general. He'd fought with him enough times to know his limits. It would take a lot for him to pass out from pain. He quickly looked around for Noswen to send her over to kill the enemy captain, but the hanex was already engaging multiple neiads at once, battling for her life. Spotal followed his gaze and rushed to her aid, leaving Tanor alone with Widrias.

He looked around in hope of finding someone else to kill the sea-neiad captain. Nobody. Only him. Tapping a young soldier on the shoulder, he gestured to Widrias. Once the steely-eyed youth was crouched next to the satorr, Tanor made his way down to the deck to find a way over to the enemy ship.

As he scurried across the deck, dodging blades and shoving past battlers, he finally found what he was looking for. A discarded rope and grappling hook. He ran as close to the forecastle as he could and threw the hook over to the other vessel. It latched onto the railing of the ship's main deck. A pause as he lined up. He clenched his jaw. He threw himself off the *Seascale*, desperately gripping the rope in both hands. As soon as he was in the air, he realised he'd misjudged his swing completely and fell heavily into the freezing, crashing sea.

He surfaced with a gasp. Somehow, he'd managed to keep hold of the rope. He stuck his feet out straight behind him, kicked as hard as he could, fixed his polearm under his arm, and hauled himself along the rope. He reached the side of the ship and began to climb. Unseen, he passed the first level of oars. As he came to the second level, an idea struck him. Peering into the gloom inside the oar hole, he expected to see a neiad there, ready with a bow to shoot him down. Instead, he was faced with an empty deck. He swung himself in through the oar hole and crept slowly to the small flight of stairs at one end of the deck. All quiet. He scurried up to the third level.

Disgusted, he shook his head. Filled with sorry creatures with limp hair and dead eyes, chained to the decks. Slaves. His jaw tightened. He could free them. Lead them out and attack the neiads from behind. But no. It would take too long and these sorry creatures were no fighters. Their dull eyes watched him, chests heaving in exhaustion. Forget them. Reach the captain.

Heart wrenching itself apart with guilt, he turned away from the slaves and climbed to the next level.

He found himself in a small corridor with three doors leading off it. The furthest door led to the main deck, filled with yelling neiads, eager to board the *Seascale*. He closed it carefully. Bloody lucky he wasn't spotted. If he wanted to reach the poop deck, he'd have to find another way.

The second door led to an empty galley. No point searching amongst the pots and pans. Just the one door left. He turned the knob. Locked. Quickly checking the door behind him was still closed, he lifted his polearm and smashed the doorknob with the spiked butt of his weapon, flinging it open.

Cautious, he entered, polearm held at the ready to repel any unseen assailants. None came. He was in the captain's quarters, directly beneath the poop deck. It was a majestic cabin, greater even than Mostyn's, filled with riches and luxuries. There were silk robes and sashes, gilded weapons and armour, scented candles and oils, paintings and tapestries, each treasure the profit of a raid on another ship or unsuspecting coastal town. He ignored the profits of blood and walked to the great windows at the rear. He forced the window to the far right open. The climb up looked easy enough, even with his polearm. Although he couldn't see him, he could picture in his mind the captain's exact location. Jumping onto the windowsill, he eased his body out the cabin, gripping his polearm in one hand and the ship herself in the other. He began his ascent. Levering himself upwards and using his free hand and both feet to grip the woodwork, he quickly found himself peering over the railing at the captain's back, surrounded by loyal neiads as he bellowed orders at his crew.

He took a deep breath to steady himself, to prepare for the battle to come, and jumped onto the deck. At first the neiads didn't notice him. Eyes narrowed against the howling rain, he brandished his weapon. The movement caught one of their eyes. A crewman turned sharply, eyes wide. His mouth opened to warn the others, but the polearm's hammer-head crushed his face before he could make a sound. Now they saw him. Howling with rage, they swarmed over. Young and wild, all vigour and no restraint. Easy foes. He soon stood waving his polearm over a growing pile of casualties, broken bones and weeping wounds the price of their impetuous charge.

Free of the chaff, he faced the captain. The captain eyed him nervously, gripping an ornate scimitar as he bellowed for aid from the crew on the main deck. His men were too excited, too eager to join the slaughter on the *Seascale* to pay heed to their captain's cries.

He faced him and raised his beautiful sword in salute. Tanor lifted his polearm and stepped over his fallen foes for better footing. The rain-slicked wood was slippery underfoot. The waves climbed ever higher as hurricane winds swept over the water. Swollen drops of rain thudded against his head, dripping down his nose and freezing his bones. He braced his feet balance and swung his weapon in a slow figure of eight, both hands holding the oak shaft. His enemy stood still, watching the head of his weapon swirling before his face. Drops of water gathered on his eyelashes and he twitched his broad nose as water ran into his nostril. With a roar, the sea-neiad lunged.

He brought the shaft of his polearm crashing down on the searching blade, knocking the neiad off guard and drove his knee into his adversary's stomach. As he doubled over, he brought the shaft back up, smashing the oak into the neiad's nose.

The neiad turned and wiped the blood from his nostril, twirled his scimitar again, beckoning him on. Tanor jumped up on the railing of the poop deck and hurled himself at the neiad. Another heavy wave rocked the ship, making it dip suddenly. For a moment, he was suspended in mid-air, the storm letting him defy gravity. The captain miss-timed his parry, sweeping his scimitar a foot beneath him. He barely had time to cry out before Tanor smashed into his chest, sending him sprawling. Tanor picked himself up, raised his weapon and brought its top spike crashing down on his adversary's face.

Or he would have, had the captain been slower. The neiad rolled out the way just before impact and his polearm crashed into the wooden deck. The entire head exploded through the wood in a shower of splinters. He tugged, but it was no use. Stuck. The curved hook on the reverse side of the head trapping it in the wood.

What a time to lose his weapon! Damn thing! He barely had time to duck as the scimitar flashed at his neck. He recoiled, but the edge caught his cheek, knocking him down. He groaned as he hit the floor, tasting blood. The captain twirled his scimitar and advanced, sneering. Unarmed, he would meet his end.

Tanor scrambled to his feet and circled, trying to stay in the middle of the deck, away from any corners where he could be hemmed in. As he backed away, his foot caught on the sprawled leg of one of the corpses. He tripped, landing heavily on his back. The wind left his lungs. The captain seized his chance and charged, eager to run him through. Unable to breathe, he acted on instinct, rolling to the left and heaving one of the carcasses over him. With too much momentum on the slippery floor to adjust his course, the neiad's scimitar buried itself deep into the carcass. Tanor tossed the corpse aside, scimitar embedded inside. With both of them disarmed, it would be a wrestle.

The neiad kicked out. Tanor swayed backwards, avoiding the attack, the studded boot sweeping in front of him. The momentum of the kick threw the neiad off balance. He saw his opening.

Tackling him to the ground, he landed on top. Pinning him down with his legs, he pummelled him with punches. He grabbed at his neck, but the captain managed to kick him away and sent him skidding across the deck to smash into the bulwark. He got up in time to see his foe rushing towards him, teeth bared and fists clenched. He waited until he was almost upon him before stepping to one side and sticking his leg out low on the ground. Once again, the slippery surface of the wood proved the captain's undoing and he clattered head-first over the makeshift tripwire.

Tanor was on him in a flash. His hands grappled the neiad's neck. Squeezing. He bared his teeth. Squeeze. Strangling the life out of him. Squeeze. His adversary's eyes bulged and his limbs flailed. Squeeze. He pressed his thumbs together into his gullet. Squeeze. The neiad's face turned blue. Squeeze. His thumbs met together with a squelching crack. The neiad's arms fell limply to his side.

He let go, sliding off the neiad's chest to sit on the deck. Deep breaths. An ugly death.

Rain continued to fall. The wind shrieked as it raced between the battling ships. Above him, the clouds continued to boil and turn in the air. Lightning flashed and thunder clapped, the storm the only audience to his grisly victory.

He dragged himself over to his polearm and tore it free. He walked over to the railing facing the *Seascale*, leaning against it to assess the best route back.

At that exact moment, a massive wave struck the opposite side of the ship, lurching her violently. He was flung from the poop deck and sent hurtling into the chaotic sea.

Crashing into the water, the otherworldly cold caught his breath. Surfacing, it took a moment of desperate splashing to wrestle a breath from the violent air. The storm had worsened, the waves rose ten feet into the air and underwater currents threw his battered body like a toy, dragging him under and spitting him back out. When he finally recovered enough to tread water, he nearly sobbed. Fifty metres from either ship, dragged further away with each second. He opened his mouth to scream for help, but sea-water rushed in. A crashing wave dragged him under. The current and the weight of his weapon kept him there. He caught one final, fleeting glance of the *Seascale* and was dragged into the depths.

*

Lidan cowered behind his shield. His boots had no purchase against the slick boards and the neiad's pummelling blows with sword and dagger pushed him back, inch by painful inch. He was going to die.

The assault ceased as the neiad was lifted into the air, skewered by an enormous spear. Lidan nodded his thanks to Pwtrek and re-joined the line. His limbs shook from a mix of terror and exhaustion. This was worse than the Hobb. Far worse. No end to them. All of them trying to kill him.

Of the unit of Council Guard who originally held the deck, only sixteen remained, clustered around the main mast in a phalanx, two men deep and eight wide, repelling the neiads as best they could. It was only thanks to their efforts he was still alive.

He hacked wildly from behind his shield. Its curved surface had already saved him countless times, the few blades that snaked past clacking harmlessly against his brigandine. He owed Spotal his thanks, after all.

His blade bit into something, someone. He could hardly see. Just shadows and screams, blood and gore. He'd pissed himself long ago, the warmth against his leg long replaced by the freezing rain. But there was no place for shame. Only terror.

He stumbled against a body, eviscerated guts stinking. Some men soiled themselves when they died. Nobody mentioned that in the stories.

Another flurry of blows against his shield. He whimpered, willing his arm to keep strong. He lunged again with his sword. Another grunt as it hit something, a terrible weight against his arm. He withdrew with a grunt. Something hit the deck in front. Their eyes met under his shield, agony etched across the neiad's face as blood pumped through fingers clutching his thigh. The Council guard beside him finished the job with a savage thrust of the spear.

The ship rocked perilously. Wave after wave crashed against the hull, spraying them with icy salt-water. Were winds like this even possible? Sweeping gales throwing men across the deck like dry leaves. A lurch sent him skidding to the bottom of the stairs leading to the quarterdeck. He wiped blinding water from his eyes, lifting his shield in time to block another cutlass. He swung wildly. Hit nothing but air. Pwtrek's spear saved him again. Arrows punched the shield, clattering away. They fell like rain. It was luck, nothing more, that kept him alive.

Trembling, teeth chattering, he barged his way back to the main mast. Was it tears or rain against his cheeks? Did it matter?

He reached the safety of their line. Locked shields again to reform the phalanx.

The storm raged on.

*

Auran ducked low, avoiding the cudgel, and jumped high to bring the blade of his axe down against his enemy's neck. At the sight of the decapitated corpse, the surrounding foe withdrew a few feet before throwing caution to the winds and charging. They should have kept their distance.

Wiping water from his head, he patted it on his soaking gambeson in disgust. How he missed his home! He missed the sun on his back, hot sand running between his toes, cool breezes on desert plains. Here there was only rain, freezing winds, and grey skies.

He scowled and gritted his teeth as another soldier fell, a jagged hole in his chest and a sneering neiad stooped over the bloody carcass. Charging, he hit him in the chest with the shaft of his axe, wrenched a knife from the pirate's belt, and thrust it up into his neck. Blood dribbled down the neiad's chin and onto his gauntleted hand. Kicking him away, he twirled his axe, ready for another.

*

Gwahl stared at the battle raging below, tapping the pommel of his dirk. If ever there were a time to intervene, it was now. By the bane of the giants, they needed help. The neiads had captured most of the deck, with the remaining Council Guard huddled together in a tight formation around the mast. The enemy were concentrating on the poop and quarter decks, cutting down the guard, overcoming their skill with numbers. He searched the ship for his companions.

Widrias was still lying behind the bulwark with a single soldier and Mostyn, pinned down as arrows peppered them. Spotal and Noswen stood on a pile of dead neiads, their combined blades making short work of any who approached. Chekry and Depani held the quaterdeck, sending bolt after bolt into the ranks of their cousins, felling many but not enough to stem the tide. Auran, Lidan and Pwtrek were in the group huddled below. Tanor was nowhere to be seen.

He turned away from the bloody spectacle and cast his eyes across the towering waves. The storm showed no sign of ceasing, the clouds stretched far away into the horizon. His eyes narrowed. Something else. Headed straight for them. No, they were heading to it.

His breath caught. Blood froze.

A few hundred metres in front of them was the wave. Vast beyond measure, its peak still building as it gathered more water into its belly. Fuelled by the roaring storms and surging currents, it barrelled through the sea, ready to batter them into oblivion.

In years past, before the Cataclysmic War, in the ages of discovery, he knew of entire fleets upturned in an instant as one of these threw them down. It was said that nothing could escape it once it had you in its fearsome grip, even the great wyrms of the sea would cower at their mention. On past adventures and journeys, he had seen similar waves, but none as frightening as this, not in these waters. As large and violent as the ones surrounding his home island, so far away to the west.

But they weren't in the beast's grip. Not yet, but they'd have to act quickly to avoid it. He stuck his head over the edge of the crow's nest and bellowed his warning.

'Wave at six hundred metres and closing! Captain! Heed me! Wave!'

A brief lapse in the wind let his voice carry to their ears. His final warning was heard. All action ceased as friend and foe turned to him, so high above them in the crow's nest.

'Wave!'

The ships exploded with activity. Self-preservation trumped thirst for victory and the sea-neiads scrambled back to their vessel. The surviving crew of the *Seascale* scurried about, lowering and raising various sails to catch the slightest gust of wind to draw them away from their approaching death.

As he watched, Mostyn rose from behind the bulwark and reassumed his position on deck, ordering his crew about to break out the oars, to cast away everything they didn't need and to pray to the sea to spare their lives.

Everybody moved. Now the *Seascale's* crew proved their worth. With the experience of masters, they took to their tasks, sobered by storm and battle. Mostyn brushed aside the helmsman, shouting to his crew one minute and whispering prayers to his ship and the raging winds and waters the next.

Gwahl clenched his jaw. Despite the efforts of the crew, inch by inch, the sea was dragging them in. He snarled in frustration. The wind turned again. A powerful western gale filled their sails, battling the currents for claim of the *Seascale*.

Suddenly dizzy, he looked again at the wave. They were drawing away. The neiads, on the other hand, were in trouble. Milling about the deck, raising and lowering random sails in an attempt to escape their deaths.

Then it had them.

The galleon climbed its steep slope. Despite their struggles, they were caught like a fly in a web, with the spider slowly approaching. The great, beautiful ship was dragged ever higher, its angle growing ever steeper. Finally, it overbalanced. The scream of its sailors echoed across the waves as it capsized, its vast weight finally working against it. The ship was thrown into the maw of the beast, obliterated by the weight of the water.

He frowned. It was unlike neiads to be so panicked, even by a freak wave. They were masters of the ocean, their captain should have been able to rally them, organise them, take charge of the ship. If Mostyn could steer it away, so could any self-respecting neiad. He exhaled, light-headed. Whatever the reason, at least one enemy was dealt with.

His relief was momentary. Although Mostyn was directing his ship away from the wall of water, he wasn't paying any attention to the rest of the storm. The captain stubbornly sailed his ship directly away from the wave, desperate to get as many leagues between them as possible. He didn't realise the southern wind swiftly picking up on his starboard side, he paid no heed to the rising waves buffeting his ship. It was only when the entire vessel gave a sickening lurch as the south wind blew stronger that he looked around to see what was going on around him. The storm reached its final, raging peak. Perhaps safe from that which had killed the sea-neiads, but death still stalked the *Seascale*.

Gwahl growled as wave after powerful wave buffeted them. From his vantage point, high on top of the mast, he could see it all unfold. The sails tore and flapped as the competing winds ripped the toughened fabric. Men were tossed overboard and were drowned in seconds as the water crashed down. Up where he was, each creak, each wave, each turn of the ship was amplified a thousand times. He braced himself in the nest, waiting for a lull in the storm to make his way down. His muscles strained. His joints ached.

All the while, the wind rose.

*

Lidan screamed as a wave threatened to throw him overboard. Instead, he crashed against the railing and managed to cling on for long enough for Pwtrek to save him. Auran came skidding by, a rope tied around his waist. He threw one end to Pwtrek and the juggernaut tied it around his waist, then around Lidan's, ensuring they wouldn't be separated.

The ship groaned like a sick dog as the storm hurled it across the waters, but still it stayed afloat. He gripped the rope, all memory of the battle forgotten, concentrating on holding on.

One by one, the screams of the wounded were silenced as they were swept away, the deck clearing of carcasses. One battle may be over, but another was before them. Against a far more terrifying foe.

Gasping between waves, he spied the poop deck. Mostyn was there, holding the wheel with arms of steel. His reputation portrayed him as a skilled sailor, apparently the best, but was he skilled enough to sail them out of this? It was clearly a challenge, his grim expression was testament to that. He was sure a lesser sailor would have succumbed to the waves a long time ago. Thank the north winds Widrias chose him as their captain.

A splintering creak came from the main mast. The main sail strained as the winds filled its canvas, drawn as taught as a bowstring. The creak intensified, shook the ship, and ended in a splintering crescendo.

At the base of the deck, the oak mast gave way to the wind and broke. Ripped in two by the terrible force of the gales. Ropes snapped, the decking splintered, and the ship tilted crazily to one side. Slowly, as if struggling to remain standing, the enormous piece of wood fell to one side, the shrouds ripped from their holdings. As it tilted, a small figure jumped from the crow's nest, bounced and spun between the remaining ropes, thudded down to the main deck, right in the middle of Lidan's old pile of sails. Finally, after an age of falling came the deafening crash of the mast falling into the spitting, snarling sea. Sailors scurried over to cut the remaining ropes and free the ship of its drag.

Straining at the rope about his waist, he rushed to the figure. Despite landing in the sails, it was still a hard fall. Cursing, he shook him, praying he'd survived. By some miracle, he was alive. Battered and bleeding, he moaned softly. Ignoring his feeble protests of pain, Lidan tied the loose end of the rope around Gwahl's waist, securing the daemon to him. Satisfied, he dragged him back to Pwtrek and Auran, crouched against the bulwark, hands covering faces in despair. Gwahl gave a final whimper before his head rolled back and lost consciousness.

The west wind suddenly failed, and the south wind blew stronger, buffeting the ship with sledgehammer gusts. The *Seascale* rolled, struck time and time again by waves taller than Crastalan's walls. Sailors who'd been stationed below suddenly poured from the hatch to the lower decks, soaked to the core. Presumably the hull was punctured below. Mastless, taking on water, caught in a storm. He was no sailor, but he knew it was the end. The storm damage was too severe. Their lives were in the hands of Mostyn, struggling to steer the creaking lump of wood to safety.

Together with Auran and Pwtrek, they watched the captain as he battled with his own ship. He roared in defiance as the wheel tore itself free of his iron grip, spinning like a sycamore seed caught in the wind. Somehow, he grabbed hold, and the ship lurched. Back under his control, to an extent. Lidan gripped Gwahl's hand. Pwtrek took his other. They stared at each other, wishing one another a silent prayer of safety.

The *Seascale* lurched again. He stole a glance behind them. Following the damages to the ship, they'd lost momentum, lost a leg in the race. The towering wave rose above. The crest was too far above to see, lost in the darkness of the purple sky. It drew them up with its underwater arms, climbing, climbing. Reaching the crest, they teetered on the edge of the world, and fell.

His world was turned upside down. He looked up, but the ship was tilting, rolling, capsizing.

His final sight before being submerged was the scorched sky, filled with flashes of lightning and crescendos of thunder.

Chapter 11

The morning sun shone merrily on his back. He stirred in the soft sand of the beach. His lower half was still in the water. Gentle waves lapped over him, soothing the ugly bruises covering his body. His eyes opened slowly. He tried to push himself up from the ground, but failed. The muscles in his arms creaked and strained and he collapsed back on the sand. His eyes closed again. He slipped back into unconsciousness.

*

He woke again at midday. Alive. Thank the four winds. Still alive. He forced himself up, world spinning. Too quickly. He nearly fell back from the rush of dizziness. Clutching his swirling head in his hands, he whimpered, his temples throbbing painfully. Gradually, it settled. He took stock of his surroundings.

A white, sandy beach, gentle waves, strewn with all manner of debris, wreckage, and countless bodies. Visions of the battle came flooding back. These meagre planks were all that remained of the *Seascale*. The mighty ship undone by the sea's fickle nature.

Something stirred inside him. His stomach lurched, his eyes watered, and he heaved the contents of his stomach onto the sand. So many people died, by sword and sea, storm and arrow. Yet he remained. Somehow, he remained.

With a grunt, he tried to get up but something pulled him back, coiled around his waist. The rope. Still bound. Survived where the ship was destroyed. Like him. The bonds led to three others, each of them lying face down on the sand as he had only minutes ago. He staggered over. Please be alive.

Collapsing by the first, he rolled him over. Gwahl. Still, silent, a black eye and scabbed cheek. Please be alive. Warm breath against his palm. He sobbed with relief. One companion, at least.

Next was Pwtrek, resembling more of a mountain than a person. He crawled over to his friend and rolled his head to one side. Once again, he was rewarded with warm breath against his hand. The third, Auran, stirred when he rolled him over. He blinked stupidly at him with blurry eyes. The southlander rose slowly to a sitting position and rolled his head around his neck whilst rubbing the small of his back. He looked up at the sun and grimaced.

'Looks like it's around noon. We've been blacked out for almost an entire day,' he gave his signature forlorn sigh and turned to Lidan. 'Anyone else make it?'

'Don't know,' he mumbled, nodding to the strewn bodies. 'There's the rest of us. Most look drowned.'

Auran was silent. Perhaps he thought the same.

'What do we do?' he asked.

'Check the others,' Auran stumbled to his feet. 'Wonder where we are.'

'Don't think this is the Kingdom of calefs,'

Auran snorted and pulled his axe from the strap on his back.

'You see to those two, I'll look for other survivors.'

Slicing through the bonds, he strode over the beach, using the shaft as a walking stick whenever he swayed on the shifting sand. Each body he passed, he checked for signs of life. More often than not, he left them where they lay.

He watched him work. He didn't even flinch, just went about his task. Like he'd done it a thousand times before. Yet here he was, in stark contrast, barely able to work himself up to rouse his friends. He'd been useless in the battle. A liability. Weak and scared. Not like Auran and the others. They'd fought like heroes. But at least he'd survived. Now he could help. Earn his place in the company. He had to.

He cut their bonds. Pwtrek stirred within moments. Eyes snapping open with a touch, only to close again in the glaring sun. The juggernaut shook his head vigorously and rose, waving Lidan away when he came to steady him. Wading in to the sea, he dunked his head under. Lidan watched. Gone mad, perhaps? Driven insane by the carnage? He wouldn't be surprised. But no, of course not. Pwtrek was a veteran, another hero. He burst from the sea and jogged back.

'Winds! That'll cure any headache, I'm telling you now!'

Lidan smiled weakly. Praise the winds, indeed. Now for Gwahl. But where the juggernaut was easy to wake, Gwahl was worryingly difficult. The daemon lay still, unresponsive to his name. Pwtrek lifted his eyelids, exposing black sclera, but still no movement beyond the gentle rise and fall of his chest.

He slapped the daemon across the face in frustration, tearing the scabs from his cheek, drawing blood. He felt sick. What if he never woke? Unseeing, unresponsive, dead to the world. He'd seen people end up like that after far lesser falls.

Grumbling, Pwtrek gripped his finger, pushing firmly into his nailbed. Gwahl snatched his hand away. Pwtrek gripped his shoulder and squeezed.

Gwahl sprang up, drawing his dirk. He groaned and clutched his head, collapsing back to the sand.

Pwtrek grinned and carried him up the beach to the soft dunes and sharp grass above the beach, Lidan trotting at his heels. The juggernaut patted Lidan on the shoulder and joined Auran on the beach.

'How are you, my friend?' asked Gwahl, stirring.

'Me?' he cried. 'I'm fine! What about you? You jumped off the main mast. Did you hit your head?'

'No, the storm just took a lot out of me.' Gwahl smiled, his voice soft, tired. 'Sorry I scared you. Ship's gone, then?'

'Gone.'

'Vicious storm.'

'Yes.'

'A lot dead.'

He paused. 'Yes.'

Gwahl nodded weakly, resting his head back. 'You don't mind if I take a few moments, do you? Getting too old to be jumping off masts and enduring typhoons.'

'Not at all.'

'You did well to survive,' Gwahl reached out and squeezed his hand. 'Battles are always terrible.'

'Aye,' he breathed, tried to change the subject. 'How old are you, Gwahl?'

'Older than you...' murmured the daemon.

No use asking anything else. He left his friend lying on the dune and trotted over to Pwtrek and Auran. They'd established a system, with the living dragged up to the dunes like Gwahl, the dead left rolled over in the sand.

He stopped behind Auran, hand held to a sailor's mouth. Moments later, he shook his head and turned the pirate over.

'How many of us made it?' he asked, over Auran's shoulder.

'Not sure yet. Tanor's gone.'

'Dead?'

'Gone. No body. Lost at sea.' Auran stood still for a moment and shook his head. One of the revived Council guard staggered over.

'Commander Tanor's gone?' he asked, his voice hoarse from swallowed sea-water.

'I'm sorry.'

The soldier sat down hard on the sand, his sobs competing with the calls of the gulls. Lidan bowed his head as he stood over the weeping man, unsure of how to console him. In the end, he simply stood by in a respectful silence, listening to the soldier's mournful whimpers. Auran patted him awkwardly on the back, whispering what empty condolences he could. When the soldier recovered somewhat, Auran walked away.

He followed. 'Where are the others?'

'On the dunes, waiting for us to wake them.'

He clasped Auran's shoulder and walked up to the dunes, leaving his companion to keep checking the remaining bodies for signs of life. He didn't know Tanor. Personally, it was no more of a loss than any other. But from the soldier's reaction, he was clearly loved and respected. His loss would be hard felt. He stared at the bodies strewn across the sand in front of him. Despite the warmth of the midday sun, a chill crept up his spine. Never in his life had he met such a fearsome foe as the sea. She couldn't be bargained with or reasoned with – if she deemed you unworthy of life, there was no escape from her judgement. Those who were alive were fortunate indeed to have survived her rage.

The first one he came to was an old man, clad in the tattered remnants of his green surcoat. He bent over and shook him lightly. His drooping moustache twitched and he lifted a grizzled hand to swipe his hand away. He shook him again, this time waking him. The veteran looked around confused for a moment before settling his head back down.

'That's why I hate travelling by sea,' he muttered.

He patted him on the back and moved on to the next man, and the next, and the next, until only a few dozen remained to be woken. Pwtrek joined him, and the number of survivors blinking into consciousness grew each minute. Soon enough, he came across his friends. First, he woke Chekry and Depani, tied together like he'd been. He only had to shake one for both to rise sleepily and smile at him in gratitude. Next, he found Spotal, his hair puffed up like a lion's mane. Lidan hardly touched him before he slapped his hand away.

'I'm not unconscious, Lidan. Just enjoying the sun for a moment.'

'Well you can stop enjoying the bloody sun and start helping us!' grumbled Pwtrek, in the process of shaking Mostyn awake.

'Quite right, Pwtrek' said Spotal, rising groggily from the sand. 'I was neglecting my duties as an officer, lying down while my friends were still lost.'

He smiled weakly at his wink, knowing full well the calef had been as unconscious as any of the others, before he ran off to assist the juggernaut. Lidan approached a sorry looking bundle wrapped in a heavy cloak. A crudely bandaged leg jutted out from beneath his cape beside the scabbard of a mighty two-handed sword.

He rolled him over. Widrias. Salt crystals lacing his hair and beard, gathering around the base of his horns. He called Pwtrek over. He didn't fancy waking him alone. On seeing his wounded general, the juggernaut cried out in shock.

'There's a wound in his leg,' Pwtrek shook his head. 'I can't tell how serious it is, not until we remove the bandage.'

'It was an arrow,' said Spotal, coming to investigate. 'Had him pinned to the deck. I took it out to get him into cover and bandaged his leg as well as I could.'

'Alright, well done,' said Pwtrek hurriedly. 'Go and get Gwahl, he'll know what to do. He's lying over there somewhere,' he motioned his shoulder. 'But be gentle with him, he took quite a fall on the ship.'

*

Spotal sprang away to find Gwahl. Sure enough, there he was, nestled between tufts of long, sharp grass. Urgency hardening his touch, he shook him awake and dragged him over to Widrias. Muddled by the sudden awakening, it took the daemon a few moments to gather his thoughts. Spotal looked on, chewing his cheek. Finally, as if emerging from a haze, he sprang into action.

'Hold his leg high, Pwtrek, I need to see the damage.'

All too-familiar with battle-wounds, he looked on. Beside him, he saw Lidan wince at the sight of the gaping wound, through and through, exposing fat, muscle, and tendon. Gwahl explored the wound, revealing the white glimmer of bones broken on impact. An especially ugly wound, he didn't blame the boy for averting his gaze.

'All right,' Gwahl nodded, thoughtfully. 'Lidan, go and collect some dry wood to burn. Auran, go and fill a helmet with salt-water, someone else get me a hammer of some sort.' As they ran away, Gwahl turned to Pwtrek. 'I can't heal this, I'm not a surgeon. I can clean and bind it, make it as comfortable as possible for him, but that's all. It'll have to do until we come across a friendly healer. I take it none of our medics made the voyage?'

'No,' replied Pwtrek. 'They're all lying on the beach over there, waiting for the sea to wash them away.'

'A grim voyage. Any idea where we are?' Gwahl asked.

Pwtrek shook his head. 'No. Nowhere near our destination.'

'Well we can at least take the medicine packs, could you go and fetch them for me, my friend?'

Spotal nodded and trotted down the beach. Finding the drowned physicians, he gently removed the packs from their waists. Auran returned a few moments later, carrying a helmet filled with water. He was followed soon after by Lidan, a large pile of sticks and dried leaves in his thin arms. Dropping the wood at Gwahl's feet, he turned breathlessly and gestured inland.

'I think you should come and see this!'

'Not right now, Lidan,' said Gwahl, impatiently. 'Spotal, can you get a fire going?'

'Yes, I have some flint with me, wait a minute,' he knelt and struck flint to steel, showering the dead leaves with sparks.

'Pwtrek? You'll want to see this!' Lidan insisted.

'Not right now! We need to see to Widrias,' said Pwtrek.

He sensed Lidan dancing impatiently behind them. Why was he so excited? Perhaps the wreckage made him delirious? Perhaps it was sunstroke. With more pressing matters at hand, he ignored him and turned his attention back to the fire.

Gwahl set to work. First, he tore off a piece of the satorr's cloak and soaked it with water. He dabbed the wound, cleaning it of its crust of congealed blood. He turned and looked around.

'A hammer, anyone?'

'Why?' asked Pwtrek, worriedly.

'Both bones are broken. The ends are displaced. I need to reset them for them to heal properly. I need the hammer to push them back into place.'

Spotal raised his eyebrows. 'How did he do that? It was just an arrow.'

'Must have twisted when he fell, perhaps the arrow hit them directly, perhaps when you took the shaft out, doesn't really matter at this point,' Gwahl shrugged.

'Are they badly displaced?' he asked.

'Not too badly, but still need resetting. They'll probably be too firmly locked in for me to put back by hand. Now, a hammer?'

Nobody had one. In the end, he used the hilt of Lidan's sabre.

'You'd best hold him down. This might wake him,' said Gwahl.

Spotal held down Widrias' chest and arms while Pwtrek pulled on the satorr's leg to produce the necessary traction and counter-traction, first reproducing the direction of injury at a stomach-curdling angle, then bending it back to correct it. Gwahl opened up the wound further, making a long incision down the inside leg. Spotal blinked. The daemon claimed he wasn't a surgeon, but it was a damned neat job, peeling through tissue layers, fishing out little splinters of broken bone and arrow.

Not that the satorr appreciated his skill. Widrias's tortured scream tore the air. He thrashed wildly, flailing and kicking, but the combined strength of juggernaut and calef kept him firmly pinned.

Gwahl completed the setting with the makeshift hammer. The crunch of steel pushing the ends of the fractured bone back into place made his eyes water. What was worse, it took him several attempts before he was satisfied they were appropriately aligned. All the while, blood dripped from the reopened wounds, staining the sand crimson as it pulsed from the leg. Each grating beat of the hilt made him cringe, and he breathed a sigh of relief when the daemon handed the sabre back to Lidan.

Gwahl washed the wound again with salt- water, drawing even more screams from the satorr. Finally, he cut a length of linen from one of the medicine pouches and used it to lightly bandage the wound. He sat back on his haunches and motioned for them release him.

Widrias writhed in agony, tears welling, gingerly touching his bandaged leg. A bloody stain was already spreading from the wound, but Gwahl refused to suture it, muttering about risks of swelling and loss of limb if anything was bound too tightly.

'We'll see how it heals,' Gwahl scratched his chin. 'If we're lucky, you'll avoid an amputation. Satorr bones heal well, in general, but we'll have to wait and see.'

Widrias finally calmed to agonised whimpers. Gwahl attached a crude splint to his leg and they finally turned their attention to Lidan. Patience was never one of the boy's virtues and he practically ran in his excitement to show them his discovery, forgetting Widrias' recent bludgeoning. He led them over the sand dunes and up a small hill. Spotal gasped. So that's what got him so worked up.

A few hundred metres before them, the horizon disappeared into a thick, grey mist. Sandy ground turned firm, before giving way to thick sludge and mud. Forests of reeds grew in thick clumps, and large pools of stagnant water covered in thick layers of algae dotted the ground. They could see the occasional small, dry bush, the source of the wood Lidan found. A sign, possibly. A sign that death was all that awaited those foolish or desperate enough to venture through the marsh. The barren sludge surrounded them as far as they could see. Even from this distance they could smell the putrid stench of the bog.

They walked back to the beach and sat heavily in the soft sand, trying to forget the haunting smell.

'At least we now know where we are,' said Pwtrek lamely.

'Where?' asked Lidan.

'We're somewhere to the south of the Cysgodgors Marshes. I was right. We're nowhere near our destination. We have difficult times ahead of us.'

Spotal nodded. He caught Lidan's eye. The boy had the same misplaced look of excitement. He didn't realise the danger. He would learn. Or he would die.

Chapter 12

They filed back to the seashore, slipping and sliding as the soft sands gave way beneath their feet. As soon as they were out of sight of the mist, their collective mood lifted. They watched the waves ripple up the sand in its constant rhythm. It was a peaceful setting, gazing out to the horizon, where sea and sky blended in a barely-distinguishable navy line. A soft breeze blew into their faces, pleasantly cool against the warm sun. Lidan absent-mindedly traced patterns in the soft sand, waiting for something to happen, enjoying the momentary stillness while it lasted.

'Alright,' said Widrias, breaking the silence, his voice strained. 'The first thing we need to do is get a better idea of where we are. We all know how vast the marshes are, if by some miracle we've been washed up near the edge, then I'd rather find out now to avoid them.'

'I'll head west,' said Gwahl, 'look for any signs of them ending.'

'If you wouldn't mind, I'd rather you stayed with me for a while longer and tend to our wounded? Myself included,' Widrias attempted a sickly grin. 'Spotal, you go west with Noswen and Pwtrek. Auran, go east with Depani and Chekry. You can go with them, Lidan, keep you busy.'

'I think it's best if I stay with you, sir,' said Pwtrek, clearing his throat. 'To make sure none of that lot get up to any mischief,' he motioned to Mostyn's crew.

'Very well, thank you, Pwtrek. On that note, could you send any of your crew out as well, Mostyn?'

The captain shook his head, eyes red. He'd been quiet since he woke. 'Too much "mischief" to get up to,' he spat. 'We're in no state to go gallivanting around on your little scouting missions, Widrias.'

Widrias rolled his eyes. 'Childish. Have it your way. Now, I want you to look out for any sign of the marshes thinning, any settlements that might save us, small ports or fishing jetties, anything that might suggest civilisation. Keep going until night, then return tomorrow morning with your reports. I want to know everything about where we are.'

'What if we run into trouble? Should we engage?' asked Spotal.

'By the north winds, no! Keep a low profile, if someone, or something, attacks you, by all means run away. No point risking your lives.'

'Should we just follow the beach?' asked Depani.

'Yes, when it runs out, just keep to the shoreline. The marshes come quite close to the shore, so there shouldn't be too much room between you and the mists. If it looks like it's retreating, it's a good sign. Shows we're quite close to the edges. Either Dailas or, hopefully, the Kingdom of the calefs.'

They nodded and set off. Lidan would have preferred to spend more time with Spotal, but Noswen was still a mystery to him, and he was too shy to approach her. Waving goodbye to Gwahl and Pwtrek, he followed the neiads and Auran, trudging away along the beach.

Chekry patted him on the shoulder. 'That your first battle?'

He nodded. 'Can't say I want to be in another one.'

'Nobody does,' Chekry shook his head. 'You did well.'

'Doesn't feel like it. I was scared the whole time,' he admitted, quietly.

'So? So was I. Depani was shaking in her boots. I bet Auran was too.'

'Always,' nodded Auran.

'You'd be mad not to be,' Chekry continued. 'Thing is, you kept fighting. Held the line. That's all you needed to do.'

'Doesn't feel like I did too well,' he mumbled. Shame at the memory of the battle washed over. As scared as the others may have been, he doubted any of them pissed themselves like he did. Like a child.

'You stood with us and fought. You did bloody well, Lidan. Don't think I'd have stuck around for half as long if that was my first battle. Bloody storm as well,' Chekry blew his cheeks out.

'Last time I want to be on a ship, too. First and last,' he tried to change the subject.

Chuckling, the neiad gave him a friendly push. 'Nonsense, they're not always that bad. A freak storm, a big wave, and a galleon full of angry neiads is hardly a normal voyage.'

'You ever been sailing up a river?' asked Depani.

'No, I've crossed the Crisiaddwr on a raft, but it was more of a ferry from one side to the other than an actual journey.'

'Ah the Crisiaddwr,' she sighed longingly, 'most beautiful river ever. You've never seen it have you, Auran?'

'Never,' Auran grunted.

'Shame. Well, you'll see it eventually, I'm sure. Crystal clear waters from Iadden, purified a thousand times over by crashing waterfalls as it goes down their slopes. Biggest river in all of Nefarwy, don't you know?'

'I might have heard that before,' Auran shrugged.

'More than half a mile wide by the time it reaches its estuary,' she continued. 'If you look into the water from the shore, you can see the weeds growing at the bottom from twenty metres away, that's how clear it is! Much nicer than this sticky sea-water,' she looked distastefully at the sea. 'Can't imagine why any neiad would choose that big old puddle over a nice river.'

'It's not so bad,' said Auran.

'Oh, by the four winds it's not bad at all! If it came to a choice of sea-water or no water at all, I'd be diving in there faster than an osprey, but a river is still better.'

'What about swamp water?' asked the southlander.

'I'd rather leave that to the troglodytes, thank you. It's more mud than water, anyway.'

Auran snorted. 'Well, you might have to get used to it,' he paused. 'Ever been to the Southlands? We have some good rivers there.'

'Never made the journey,' Chekry shook his head. 'What's the water like?'

'Warm,' said Auran. 'Especially the Werlit River. It's funny,' he smiled at some memory, 'you get tributaries of different colours, one crystal clear water, one so brown and full of sediment it's impossible to see beyond an inch into the depths, and they mix together so quickly and acutely that there's a line, as clear as land and river, delineating the two branches.'

'Comes from the jungle, doesn't it, the Werlit River?' asked Depani.

'Yes, the Daiwen, one of the many rivers coming from those trees.'

'I thought the southlands were dry?' asked Lidan, innocently. Thank the winds the conversation was steered away from the battle.

'They are, it's quite a polarised land. You have your lush jungles and raging rivers, and then arid deserts a few miles from them,' explained Auran.

'Which do you prefer?' asked Depani in a way that suggested there was a right answer.

'My home was on the bank of the Werlit, but I loved the simplicity of the deserts surrounding us.'

'Are there many neiads in the Southlands?' asked Depani.

'Not sure. If there are, they must keep to themselves.'

'I wonder what they're like?' she mused. 'Growing up with a jungle and a tropical river, they must be quite different to us.'

'I don't know,' Auran shrugged again.

'Did you go sailing much up the Werlit, if you lived on its banks?' Chekry asked.

'From time to time. Preferred walking into the Daiwen if I was going there, but the capital was easier to reach via the Werlit.'

'Isn't the jungle dangerous?' asked Lidan, recalling stories from long ago.

'It's wild,' Auran nodded. 'Less inhabited than Dailas, full of animals.'

'But there are people there?' Lidan asked.

'Of course, mostly isolated tribes. Like I said, they keep to themselves.'

'Shall we go further inland? Ground's firmer away from the sand,' suggested Depani, and they followed her to the sharp, cutting grass just beyond the sand.

Glancing behind him, Lidan could just about still see the remainder of the Council company and Mostyn's crew as a faint blur on the golden sand. From his new vantage point, he could see the billowing mist of the marshes, pulsating eerily like a grey, beating heart.

'Have you ever been in there?' he asked.

'Not properly,' replied Chekry. 'I've been to its borders enough times, gone into its peripheries, but never into the heart of the swamp. Commander Afarn never wanted us going too far in, said it was too dangerous. From the stories I've heard, the looks on the faces of people who survived it, I'm inclined to agree. Nastiest swamp in Nefarwy, Cysgodgors. You can forget Tarin Swamp or Critanna Marshes, they're puny compared to this monster.'

'What kind of stories have you heard?' he breathed.

'I don't believe half of them,' the neiad shook his head. 'I certainly don't want to.'

'What?' he insisted, itching to know. He'd heard stories himself. The older children used to scare them with horror tales about the monsters in the swamp. Had the neiads heard them too?

'No,' Depani interrupted. 'It won't do you any good to frighten yourself. Hopefully we'll never have to find out whether they're true or not.'

'What if they are, though?' he asked, urgently. 'I'd rather know now and prepare myself!'

'Personally, I'd rather not know,' smiled Depani.

He paused and took a chance. 'Is it to do with the troglodytes?'

Chekry nodded. 'They're only half of it. Troglodytes are bad wherever you go, but in those marshes… I heard the air itself gnaws away at your spirit.'

'Well, by the looks of it we'll find out by tomorrow,' said Auran, craning his neck. 'Come on, let's keep going. Plenty of daylight left.'

'No need to encourage us,' assured Depani. 'Chekry and I are well used to scouting. Swimming, usually, not walking, but I dare say we'll be fine. Not like we've ever made such an exciting journey as you did, Lidan. All the way from Crastalan to the Council, you've got some hidden muscles in those skinny little legs!'

Lidan grinned as the burly neiad shoved him playfully.

'So, what did you do before getting thrown into Crastalan's dungeons?' asked Depani.

'I'd rather not talk about it,' he replied, quietly. 'Something only a fool would try.'

'What? No!' the neiad exclaimed, shaking her head. 'No, not what you did to get imprisoned, but what did you do in day-to-day life? You must have had a profession of some sort? Smart thing like you? Books and papers I'd bet. A proper little scholar.'

'Oh, my village were traders,' he smiled. He wouldn't have to relive it. Leave the memories where they were. 'We'd farm the grassland plains, collect the blades, dry them, fashion them into things.'

'What kind of things?'

'Anything! Baskets, mostly, all different sizes and shapes, but also sandals, rope, some light shields, those kinds of things. A few of the older, more skilled craftsmen could make linen from flax, so whenever it was in season we'd sell loads of that as well.'

'Interesting, and you would help them with crafting these baskets and such?' Depani asked.

'Not really, I was never dextrous enough to weave the dried grass properly, I always broke it. Definitely not with the linen, especially not the higher quality stuff. I just helped with farming the crops, harvesting it, bundling it, storing it, and guarding our trading caravans from time to time.'

'Bit skinny for a farmer, aren't you?' Chekry wrinkled his nose.

'Well, I lost a bit of weight in the dungeons,' he mumbled.

'Ah, sorry,' Chekry mumbled awkwardly.

'Idiot. He just said he didn't want to talk about it,' Depani shoved her brother.

'You're the one who asked in the first place!' Chekry punched her shoulder.

'No, it's fine,' he reassured. 'It's nice to remember how things were before it all. Harvest was always a good season.'

'A good life,' nodded Auran. 'A simple, honest living.'

'It was,' he admitted, recounting those simpler years with a pang of longing.

'It's easy to ignore your fortunes, and only appreciate them once they're lost,' said Chekry, sensing his morose. 'But you shouldn't regret your choices, whatever they may have been.'

Lidan smiled gratefully, but the kind words were meaningless. It was easy to say, to never look back, to concentrate on what lay ahead, but after suffering such loss it was impossible not to wish things had been different. After all, if he ignored what lay in the past, what was there to stop him from making the same foolish mistakes again? It was better to dwell, to scream on the inside every night before sleep, to fight back tears at each happy memory of times lost.

'He doesn't believe you,' said Auran, reading his expression.

'I don't doubt it,' smiled Chekry, sadly. 'Maybe you should have kept to that life, never taken the paths that eventually lead you here, but the fact is, the choices have been made, history set in stone, no point wasting your life with regret.'

Lidan shrugged, wishing the conversation would end. The others sensed his reluctance and fell into silence. Not for long. The neiads picked up their lively conversation once again.

'Look there,' Chekry pointed to the distant shoreline. 'Looks like the beach runs out.'

'Is that a good sign? Widrias said if it ran out it meant we were close to the edge of the marshes?'

'Afraid not, Lidan, it's the mist of the marsh that demarcates its edges. The beach running out is just a feature of the shore,' Chekry shrugged.

'Oh, of course,' he mumbled, disappointment replacing the excitement, 'sorry that was silly of me.'

'Not particularly,' chuckled Chekry. 'Nothing wrong with a bit of hope, especially if you're unfamiliar with the coast.'

'No, that's the point,' he smiled, embarrassed, 'my village was barely half a mile from the coast! Not this one, but still.'

'Well in that case you are certainly not forgiven! How dare you make such a mistake!' teased Depani.

Lidan laughed, feeling the colour rush to his cheeks. Chekry shaded his eyes with his hand as he looked east. 'Looks like rockpools, we may as well have some food when we get there.'

Less than an hour later, they wandered over the rocky plateau, made smooth by centuries of sea-water polishing it to a glassy glaze. Lidan slipped more than a few times, bruising his elbows and knees. It was years since he'd last been rock-pooling with his cousins and friends out on a week-long trip to the nearest beach. He remembered how long the journeys took, a day and a half of walking, a few days on the sand and playing amid the dunes, searching the rock pools for crabs, screaming in delight when it tried to pinch his fingers, and then the long journey back to reality in his village. Smiling sadly, he followed after the others. Once they were right at the heart of the rock pools, Depani stopped and looked around, nodding approvingly.

'Alright, first thing is to get a bit of a fire going. I'll go back to the marshes and collect as much wood as I can, you lot start hunting for some little critters.'

'Perfect,' smiled Chekry as his sister wandered back inland. 'You two know what to look for?'

'It's been years since I did this,' smiled Auran.

Lidan smiled as well. 'I used to go rock-pooling every summer, used to love finding the little fish and crabs and such.'

'Crabs and fish? A delicacy when rock-pooling. Don't bother with them, just concentrate on the limpets and periwinkles.'

He couldn't help the look of disgust at the thought of eating limpets. Chekry laughed. 'When you went, were you just there to look at the little creatures, or were you there hunting for food?'

'I was only a child. We used to take enough food with us to last the week! I didn't know you could eat limpets? Aren't they a bit crunchy?'

Chekry nearly doubled over with laughter. Even Auran chuckled. At first, he was offended, but their laughter was too infectious, and he was soon giggling as loud as them. Chekry laughed so hard he slipped and fell into a pool with a splash. The sight of him emerging from the water with a mop of seaweed clinging to his nose was too much. Tears poured down his cheeks. Auran, still shaking with glee, eventually helped the neiad to his feet.

'Don't eat the shells!' cried Chekry, recovering enough to splutter the words.

'I did wonder,' laughed Lidan, massaging his aching cheeks.

'Alright, alright,' Chekry wiped the tears from his eyes. 'Look for mussels, limpets, and periwinkles like I said. You have to creep up on the limpets to get them.'

'Why? I'm pretty sure I can outrun them,' he sniggered.

Chekry whooped and spluttered, Auran shook his head, grinning from ear to ear. They were still giggling when Depani returned, her arms full of the same spindly type of wood as Lidan found earlier that day. One look at them, red-faced and heaving, was all it took for her to start giggling as well, and it all started again.

'Honestly, I expected at least a few morsels by the time I got back,' she laughed. 'Seems like I have to do everything myself,' she winked.

'Limpets can feel you approaching by sensing your footsteps,' explained Auran. 'Once they sense you, they clamp down hard on the rock.'

'So, if you sneak up on them and whack them off quickly with a stone, they come off nice and easily,' smiled Chekry. 'It's not because they're going to dash away!'

'Alright, alright, I understand now, so limpets and the little snails, leave the crabs.'

'I mean, if you happen to find a big crab, you may as well pick it up as well, but don't go looking for them.'

He nodded and wandered away. As Auran said, the first few limpets he tried to prise away from the rocks were clamped down too tightly and wouldn't budge no matter how hard he bashed them with the pommel of his knife. Once he adopted the advice to approach them with light footsteps, he soon had a hoard of the little creatures cradled in the fold of his cloak. He even found a few mussels, several periwinkles, and a bunch of the seaweed one of the old women in his village always ate. In one of the deeper pools, he could see starfish at the bottom, inching their way across the floor, and the flashes of shrimp shooting around from crevice to crevice. He didn't bother trying to catch the shrimp, far too nippy for his clumsy snatches into the water. To his childish delight, he actually did find a crab, and carefully picked it up by the sides of its shell to protect his fingers from its flailing pincers. Its green shell glinted like emeralds in the sun. He sat there for a while, staring at the little creature as it eventually settled down. Far too small to even consider eating, he eventually placed it back into the pool, smiling as it scuttled into the shadows. Crabs were always the highlight of any rock-pooling venture. Always a valuable discovery to show off to his friends.

Careful not to drop any of his haul, he made his way back to his companions, lounging next to the smoky little fire Depani prepared.

'Well done! Lots more to add to our pile. They only take a couple of minutes to cook so they'll be ready in a moment.'

By placing the limpets upside down at the edges of the fire, they sizzled away and cooked within minutes, as promised. Auran showed Lidan how to scoop them out of their shells, remove the edible foot from the black intestines, and get them ready to eat. The first few were overcooked, and Lidan scrunched up his face at the rubbery texture. Salty and tough, they were foul. Seeing their faces, Depani tried one as well, and spat it out in disgust.

'Apologies, they could do with a few minutes less! They'll always taste a bit salty, but at least these next ones should go down more easily.'

As promised, from then on the limpets were cooked perfectly, soft enough to bite through, but solid enough to avoid any slimy textures. The periwinkles were slightly better, the mussels quite delicious. Somehow, Chekry managed to catch a few dozen shrimp, which they toasted over the fire and ate whole. Lidan's seaweed was eaten raw, and had the taste and texture of salty cabbage. Auran produced five oysters and cracked them open. Lidan declined, grimacing as the others poured them raw down their throats.

'All satisfied?' asked Chekry playing with the empty pile of shells. Nodding as one, they got to their feet and continued on their journey. On the way, Lidan scattered the empty shells into each passing pool. Any hermit crab thinking of moving house might thank him for the gift. It was a nice thought.

Once they cleared the rockpools, the beach began anew, prompting them to follow the sands at a leisurely pace. Comfortable in each other's silence, they listened to the lapping of the waves against the sand and the feel of the breeze against their skins. The further east they walked, the more the terrain gradually changed, with the ground inland climbing higher and higher, until there were cliffs more than twenty feet tall between the soft sands of the beach and the firmer ground inland. Depani initially suggested it might signify the end of the marsh, but half a mile later, a break in the cliffs formed by a stagnant, foul-smelling creek provided them a view of the lands beyond the cliff. Marshland and mist, as far as the eye could see. With a shrug, they turned back to the beach and continued onwards.

Eventually, the cliffs grew tall enough that their tops were completely lost from sight, no matter how far one ventured into the sea. Walking with the stifling, towering rocky wall on one side, and the rhythmic waves of the Great Waters reflecting the sun from the other, Lidan was soon sweating buckets beneath his clothes. Their salty lunch was no help either, and his mouth was soon dry and claggy. Auran handed him a smooth, flat stone to suck on, stating it would help with the thirst. To his surprise, it actually did, although he suspected it probably had more to do with the sparing sips of water he took from his water-skin.

With only a few hours of sunlight left, the beach eventually ran out again, coming to a sudden stop as the cliffs cut across their path and jutted out into the sea, like a natural pier. From the top, Lidan could hear the wailing squeak of puffins and watched them pop their heads over the edge of the cliff to stare at the four companions below.

'I suppose we could just set up camp here,' said Chekry. 'Although it's a shame to waste so many hours of daylight.'

'We could look for a way to climb up the cliffs?' suggested Auran.

'I'm about as poor a climber as you can find. Going up a slope with nice big hand-holds isn't too much of an issue, just like climbing a ladder, but don't make me go down anywhere!' chuckled Depani.

'It's too far to double back and get back up to the top of the cliffs,' muttered Chekry. 'I suppose you two will have to jump on our backs, we'll swim around the cliff and see what's on the other side.'

'Sounds good to me!' exclaimed Depani cheerily, wading out until she was waist-deep.

'Why don't you go first to see how far it is to swim,' suggested Auran. 'If it's too far to carry us then we won't bother. No point drowning ourselves.'

'A fair point,' shouted Depani, diving beneath the waves. She swam through the water with powerful kicks of her muscular legs, as silent and sleek as an otter. Lidan blinked and the neiad was already nearly fifty metres away, rarely breaking the surface of the water for quick gasps of air. Barely a minute later, he saw a dark shadow materialise in the shallows near the shore, and Depani jumped out again, blowing droplets from the tip of her wide nose, grinning broadly.

'Bad news for you Auran, the beach starts again a few steps after the cliff!'

'Can't we wait until the tide goes out and just walk around it?'

'No, I dived down to gauge the depth of the seas around it, and the ground sinks down around the cliff in a little ditch so it's always underwater! No choice but to get a little bit soggy, I'm afraid!'

'I can swim myself, you know?'

'If you had a horse, you'd ride it to get to your destination faster,' said Chekry, wading out to join his sister. 'Same principle applies here, except these two horses are a bit chattier, and aren't quite as enamoured to carrots.'

'Shall I hold onto your shoulders?' asked Lidan, stepping into the sea after them, frowning as the cold water drenched his feet.

'Yes, that's the best way. Here, I'll take your shield, just watch your legs don't get in the way while I swim. Don't want to bruise your shins with my kicks.'

'Come on Auran, I won't let you sink.'

'I won't let myself sink, I don't need you for that,' replied the Southlander grumpily, but took hold of Chekry's shoulders as Lidan took hold of Depani's.

'Alright, hold on tight now, take a couple of deep breaths. Good. We'll keep above water as much as we can, but sometimes we'll slip beneath the surface. Force of habit, you know how it is.'

They waited a few more moments to prepare themselves, the twins ensuring their crossbows were secured in their waterproof covers. After sharing a nod, they slowly waded out further and further until the water was around their shoulders and Auran and Lidan were treading water to keep their heads above the waves. Quick as a flash, they plunged their heads underwater.

He nearly lost his breath. Arms nearly torn from their sockets as Depani surged through the sea. Tightening his grip, he did his best to keep his legs clear, but it was difficult to maintain a stable position and received more than a few clips to the shins. Screwing his eyes tight to avoid the stinging spray of the spongy water, he clung on as the neiad ploughed ahead. As warned, they were occasionally dragged under, but the twins would always resurface within a few seconds, to the appreciative gasps of their companions.

Astonishingly, they were swimming for less than a minute before Depani straightened. He opened his eyes and saw the cliff to his left. Chekry and Auran were ahead of them, stumbling the last few steps onto the shore. Releasing his grip on Depani's shoulders, he swam the final few metres to land. She handed back his shield.

'More awkward than I thought it would be, swimming with that in my hands,' she commented.

'Sorry, I'll keep it on my back when we return.'

'No, don't worry it wasn't that bad,' she reassured. 'Just a bit annoyed that fat trout beat me. Normally a much quicker swimmer than he is.'

'Fat trout? Slimmer than you'll ever be, you podgy flounder,' Chekry called. 'Don't believe her, either of you.'

Lidan smiled, shaking his head. Absolutely incredible swimmers. The tide, the currents, the added weight of their passengers, each of these would have made any man pause before making the journey, but to the neiads it was nothing. Even Auran was impressed by their speed, and reluctantly admitted it would have taken him ten times as long to swim the distance on his own.

'I have that stickiness again,' complained Depani half an hour later. She pouted childishly as she rubbed her hands. 'Nasty seawater. No river would ever give you this horrid feeling.'

'And these tiny bits of salt in my pelt,' continued Chekry, picking out the minute crystals from the fine hair covering his body. 'I'll need a bath to get it all off.'

'Well it looks like you'll be in for a nice mud bath in a few days,' muttered Auran. 'Look there, the cliffs finally come back down to sea level. Mist is still there.'

He was right. With the sun gradually sinking in the sky, it cast its rays directly into the mist, staining it a pale yellow as it spilled forth from the swamps, almost like the tongues of fire, lapping greedily at the surrounding land.

'Let's just get to there for today,' said Chekry. 'Tomorrow we can head back and just follow the edge of the cliffs all the way back to the others. No point getting soaked in seawater a second time.'

By the time they reached the mists, the sun was well on its way beneath the horizon and all that remained was a half circle of dazzling scarlet above the silent seas. As the others made camp, Depani decided to make the most of what little light was left and continued on her own, promising to return before nightfall. Lidan looked nervously at the fog, now stained a deep crimson.

'I've been through little swamps and bogs before, this wouldn't be much different, would it?'

Chekry laughed with an unfamiliar bitter tone. 'You know the answer to that.'

'Do you mean Tarin or Critanna?' asked Auran, curious.

'No, just meant little boggy patches and little mires,' he laughed nervously. 'They weren't so bad. Smell wasn't fantastic, but they were alright.'

'Have you been to Critanna or Tarin, Chekry?' asked Auran.

'Never inside them, plenty of times along their fringes, same as Cysgodgors. The Crisiaddwr supplies them all.'

'Are they similar to this?' Auran nodded to the fog.

'In a way, but not on the same scale. You don't want to go in them, in any case. Anyway, why don't you two get a fire started, I'll go and see if I can catch some supper.'

With the marsh itself so close, there wasn't much room to forage for wood to feed a fire. When they eventually got a smoky little blaze to life, it was night, with a bright moon in a cloudless sky. Chekry returned a while later, a plaice in each hand. He looked around, worriedly.

'No Depani yet?'

'She'll be back now, I'm sure,' Auran said.

'Hmm… not like her to be late.'

'Let's just have some food, I'm sure the smell will draw her back.' Auran smiled reassuringly.

Chekry sat with his food untouched, staring into the distance for a sign of Depani's return. Half an hour later and she was still missing. Lidan was on the verge of grabbing a branch from the fire and organising a search party in the dark, when Chekry's lips split apart in a smile of relief.

'You had me worried, you frog!'

'Apologies,' grinned Depani, 'didn't mean to be so long.'

'Have some food, I caught some plaice. Outswam them, you see. Reminded me of you.'

'Aren't you considerate,' she smiled. They ate their fish in less than a minute and lay back on the sandy beach, staring into the marshes.

'It's a shame, really, I was sort of hoping that we'd be able to follow these cliffs all the way around to the Kingdom of the calefs, never have to go into the swamps,' sighed Depani.

'How did it look?'

'The beach ends a few hundred metres up that way, and goes straight into rocky ground, and then there's a big climb to more cliffs. There's only a narrow rocky shelf to walk along, and then it drops off to nothing. A great big gully cuts across the path. I looked for a way to around it, but there was none, besides, from what I could see on the other side, the cliffs were all scree.'

'Any way of crossing it?' asked Auran.

'No chance, it's more than thirty metres wide.'

'What about swimming around it?'

'No, I couldn't see any more beaches anywhere after this one, and from the top of the cliffs I could see the coastline up to a few miles to the east. Chekry and I would be alright, but not the rest of you.'

'Any sign of the Kingdom of the calefs?'

'None. The mist follows the cliffs all the way to the horizon. No, this here is the end of it.'

'What took you so long, anyway?' asked Chekry.

'I just told you! Narrow rocky path, fog, big whopping cliffs. I was being careful! Didn't want to leave you sister-less, did I?'

'Well you shouldn't have gone so far.'

'I had to go far to get a complete report, didn't I? No wonder they call me the better scout.'

'Better scout? That would be the day. We both know I'm Afarn's favourite!'

'Favourite? With your lousy swimming? Who was it who missed that raft with a bunch of Hobbs hiding aboard?'

'That was you!'

'Was it? Well at least I swam quickly enough to double back and warn everyone in time.'

'Only because *I* raised the alarm.'

'Bah, details. I'm the favourite.'

'Are not.'

'I am!'

Smiling to himself as they argued, Lidan made a pillow out of the soft sand and lay down with his back to the fire, staring at the Great Waters in their tranquillity. Beside him, he sensed Auran doing the same. He closed his eyes, safe among friends. It promised to be a peaceful night, with barely a breeze to disturb the waves, and he was soon fast asleep under the canopy of twinkling stars.

Chapter 13

'We can't go through the marsh. Death lies in that fog – can't you feel it?' cried Mostyn, distressed. 'We should salvage whatever driftwood we can find and build a raft to take us across the Great Waters. It's the only sane thing to do!'

'Sane?' exclaimed Widrias. 'Tell me, *Captain,* how will you make a raft large enough to carry all of us to the Kingdom of calefs? How will you survive with no food? No, the intelligent thing to do is to travel through the marshes.'

'I've heard stories of those marshes, Wids, we all have. There's a reason why decent folk don't live there. There are things in there that drive you mad.'

'They might drive you mad, Mostyn, weak as you are, but soldiers of the Council are stronger than petty pirates.'

Mostyn shook his head, not taking the bait. 'I'm saying this for your own good. Cysgodgors Marshes has claimed more lives than you could ever hope to count. I've seen fog similar to this before, far away on the Great Waters, further than any of you've ever been. It seeps through your pores, gets into your mind. Makes you see things. Think things. Lose your wits. But even the mists I witnessed at sea were nothing compared to this… wall of madness. Men far stronger than us have succumbed to mists far friendlier than these.'

'Don't try to frighten us with your ridiculous tales.'

'That's not what I'm doing. Shadows of death stalk all who enter there.'

'With respect, sir,' said Spotal. 'What we could do is to travel east through the marshes until we come to my lands, then proceed with the original plan?'

'No, you heard Depani's report, we're nowhere near the edge. It would take us just as long to travel east until we reach your lands as it would to travel directly to Tarnegrefur. Waste of time.'

Mostyn blinked, bewildered. 'Why do you want to get to Tarnegrefur Mountains? That place is nearly worse than the marshes! I thought you were going to Lleunedd?'

'My reason for visiting the mountains is my own,' Widrias snapped.

'What of the wounded? How will they survive the journey?' asked Mostyn.

'Few of the Council Guard are wounded, and none seriously enough to hinder them,' Widrias waved him away.

'Many of my crew are hurt. They won't survive two days!'

'Then they can stay here and starve. We're going through the marshes, with or without you.'

'You're wounded!'

'Exactly. If I can endure, so can they.'

With a final, withering glance, Widrias limped away to examine the food and fresh water they managed to salvage. One by one, the Council company followed, taking some food, filling their water-skins and standing by the satorr, preparing themselves for the voyage ahead. Mostyn looked at them in disgust. He eventually slinked over. Once again, defeated by Widrias.

'The path through those marshes is the path to death, everyone knows this. Everyone does.'

*

Before entering the marshes, they piled the deceased on the remnants of the *Seascale* and set them alight. Widrias stepped forwards and faced the remnants of the company, the pyre throwing its heat against his back.

'My friends,' he began. 'This bonfire has been lit in remembrance of our fallen companions, those found and those still lost. Although their lives have ended, they will live on in the vast halls of our memories, as strong and kind as they were in life. Keep them in your hearts and their strength and valour will live on through you. I bid you salute them, and wish their ashes be carried away to the fields beyond the clouds. Honour them.'

Spotal drew his sword and held it so the firelight danced along its silver blade. The others followed his example. He kept his gaze fixed on the fire. At the heart of each flame he saw a great man, his polearm a blur, felling all enemies who approached him, holding his

213

honour. Gwahl played a few melancholy notes on his pipe, their haunting tones lingering, providing a voice for their mourning.

Spotal felt a tear trickle down his cheek. Widrias was right, Tanor's memory would stay with him to the end of his days, and his memory would lend to him the strength of the fallen champion.

*

They set off, walking down the hill to the flowing wall of green-tinted fog. Of the fifty Council Guards who set out on the quest, only thirteen remained, the rest claimed by neiad or water. With them strode the nineteen remaining pirates of Mostyn's crew, each of them utterly lost with the destruction of their ship, several of them badly wounded, all of them following Mostyn wherever he went. Each member of the company carried only his weapons, his water-skin and a loose knapsack of food, good for a week's march. If they couldn't find anything suitable to eat by then, which was all too probable, they would starve. At the head of the band was Widrias, his pointed ears standing erect on his head, straining to pick out the slightest sound in the mist.

After a brief march, they came to the edge of the marsh. Tendrils of fog coiled towards them, beckoning them in. Taking a sharp breath, Widrias stepped forward. The change in texture was instant. In the space of a foot the land went from firm ground to oozing mud, clinging to the hairs on his legs. Similar in texture to the roads of Morgenal, only fouler. He curled his lips in disgust, but kept moving forward, his left leg dragging. Resting it wasn't an option. So he limped, bore the pain through gritted teeth. He would carry the limp for the rest of his days.

Behind him, he heard the gasps of the following company as each one experienced the putrid ooze. Narrowing his eyes, he attempted to see through the mist. Hopeless. He could barely see two dozen paces.

'If anyone finds firm ground, a trail of some sort, let me know' he called over his shoulder. 'Might walk properly, then.'

Barely a minute later, he heard a small yelp from behind, followed by a sinister squelch. He turned and pushed back through the bog, crashing through the reeds. Three soldiers stood in a circle, staring dumbfounded at a patch of mud.

'What happened?'

'It's Glorna, sir, he just disappeared – sank through that patch of earth. Right before my eyes, sir, he just went, hardly had time to cry out!'

Widrias grunted. The Cysgodgors Marshes were notorious for claiming the lives of unwary travellers with its hidden pits. Indeed, the offending bog looked as innocuous as any other inch of the marsh, with only the slightest disruption in its covering foam of algae to suggest its deadly appetite. He looked up at the others.

'From now on, you will walk with your swords drawn, tap the earth in front of you before you take a step. I don't want anyone else lost to this treacherous swamp. Will someone please find a patch of firm ground? There are always trails leading through marshes, you just have to look for them!'

He turned sharply and walked away, poking the tip of his scabbard into the ground before committing his foot. He did his best to hide his fear. Glorna was one of the stronger ones, only a bruised shoulder and sprained wrist from the fight. If he could be claimed by the marsh so easily, what hope did a cripple have? They'd barely walked a hundred paces! The further inland they went, the boggier it became. The hungrier it became. In more ways than one.

His leg already hurt. In fact, it hadn't stopped hurting since Gwahl woke him on the beach. Apparently, they reset the bone. Not that he remembered. Certainly, it was swollen, and fiercely sore. Yesterday, Gwahl suggested it might never heal, not on the road, especially not in these conditions. But there was no choice. They had to reach Tarnegrefur. He was hardy, he was resilient. When he was younger, he could run for an entire day without rest. Those days were long gone, but his endurance was still superior to most. The wound would slow him down, but he would not stop.

To his rear was another cry. Fearing another life lost, he turned quickly, only to see Chekry beckoning, jumping up and down. It took a moment to realise its significance. He smiled. You needed firm ground to jump.

He stumbled over and clasped his hands gratefully. The others followed. Their path was found. As the rest of the party gathered round, Pwtrek turned to him.

'It'll be difficult to keep our bearing if we stick to these solid ridges and pathways, do think it wise to run the risk of losing our way for the sake of keeping our boots clean?'

'It is wiser than wading through the bog, running the risk of falling foul of a swamp, my friend,' he replied, glancing at the juggernaut. 'It's not just our boots we need keeping clean. More than a few of us are wounded. I don't want infection spreading through the company if we can avoid it. It's worth the risk.'

Pwtrek frowned, but remained silent, keeping his thoughts to himself.

As Mostyn walked past he shot him a furious glare.

'It's not the bogs you have to worry about,' he whispered. 'It isn't getting lost, or the monsters, or the lack of food or water that will kill you. The mist will see us all off.'

*

Night fell on the swampland, and Lidan collapsed in a tired bundle on a patch of grass, followed by Auran and Spotal. After five hours of walking, Widrias estimated they'd travelled the grand distance of eight miles, give or take.

He yawned. The trail they walked proved harder to follow than expected, with tall clumps of reeds blocking paths, carpets of shrubbery, countless ponds of boggy silt. At this rate it would take them weeks to reach their destination, and weeks they did not have, not unless they found a better path or more supplies.

Spotal stretched beside him, took a sip of water and curled up into a ball, his knees drawn up against his chest. He watched him with a smile before settling down. It wouldn't be his first choice of bedding. The stink of rot and mud made his nauseated, even after a day of it. Shadows of monsters lurked behind every swirl of mist. The chirp and buzz of biting insects. But he was exhausted. The battle was still sharp in his memory. Stinking, sludgy, and slimy as this may be, at least it was steady ground beneath his feet. No waves, no storm. Better here.

It's what he told himself.

Bidding Auran a good night, he closed his eyes. Let it be a peaceful sleep.

*

He lay on his belly on a cold floor of cobbled stone. His tongue lolled. Drool dripped from his chin. His cell was much the same but for the horrific scratch-marks over the walls, outlined with reddish-brown frames. His torn fingernails wept pus, but he couldn't feel it. His eyes were always open, but he saw nothing, madness clouding his vision. His teeth chattered violently with his fitful body, like a puppet in the hands of the freezing cell.

His cell door opened and a chunk of food was tossed inside. Springing up from his daze he tore greedily at his measly meal, not knowing, not caring if what he ate was bread, fruit or meat. A chill at the back of his neck prompted him to look up. Framed in the doorway was the shadowed form of his gaoler, a tankard of ale in one hand and a dulled expression on his face.

He growled and bared his teeth, holding his food close to his breast. He couldn't have it. It was his!

The gaoler laughed drunkenly.

A kick hit him squarely in the stomach. He was sent skidding across the floor. Finally coming to a halt, he fell on all fours. His stomach heaved, and he vomited the few mouthfuls he'd eaten.

He whimpered at the sight of his partially digested meal spreading across the floor. His food. It wasn't fair. Rising, an ethereal screech burst from his burning throat. He charged across the room, but the gaoler stepped outside. The cell door slammed shut. He crashed headlong into the wood and iron, sending him sprawling. Laughter from outside. Belching, the trickle of ale from a casket.

He stumbled back to his food and ate what was left. Still hungry.

He eyed the puddle of vomit on the cell floor. Kneeling, he opened his mouth.

*

Lidan opened his eyes. A hand stifled his mumbles. Spotal crouched over him holding a finger to his lips. He shrugged the hand away, but the calef shushed him.

'Be silent, Lidan. There are troglodytes near.'

He nodded and peered through the mist. Damn their luck. In some morbid way, he wanted to catch a glimpse of the vile monsters of the marsh. The rational part of his mind hoped he never would. There was little doubt which was the stronger desire. He stole a quick glance behind. The rest of the company closed in a tight circle, each one staring into the fog, twitching nervously.

'How many are there?' he whispered.

'Gwahl said thirty at first, now there's more.'

'How many?'

'Fifty.'

'Do they know we're here?'

'If they did we wouldn't be hiding. They'll see us soon.'

'Quiet.' hissed Auran, his hands steadying his axe.

Ears finally clear of sleep's muddle, he heard them. A rustle pierced the fog, first from the right, then the left, then from behind. He turned his head. Where were they? Nothing but shadows and mist. Nothing but marsh.

Beside him, Auran gasped, eyes wide. He followed his gaze through the fog. Just the marsh. Wait. Something new. A new shadow. As he watched, the shadow grew, swelled, circled their camp. The shadow closed in.

'Oh!' exclaimed Spotal.

'What is it?' he asked, heart pounding in his ears.

'You've heard the stories about troglodytes, Lidan, the things they do to their victims?'

'Vaguely, only rumours,' he stared wide-eyed into the mist. Auran and the neiads wouldn't confirm the terrible tales he'd heard as a child. Perhaps Spotal would.

'They're known for their… customary method for disposing their foes,' Spotal breathed. 'You know what it is.'

He tore his eyes away from the pulsating mists, ridden with dancing shadows. Auran's expression confirmed Spotal's warning.

His dark face was unnaturally calm. Lidan nodded. The Southlander clasped him on the shoulder reassuringly.

'Don't let them take you alive.'

Spotal looked around and rose from his crouch. With a flourish, he unsheathed his jian and kissed the hilt. Twirling it around his wrist and adopting a guard, he addressed his companions.

'It seems our slimed swamp-dwellers have found us!' he faced the approaching shadows. They were coming quicker. 'I haven't survived a shipwreck to die here. Neither have you!'

The company drew their weapons and steeled themselves for the imminent battle. Fewer than forty men clustered together. They drew their courage from each other.

Widrias flicked his cloak behind him and lay his sheathed sword on the ground. With a flourish, he discarded the leather binding about the hilt and drew the gleaming blade from its scabbard. It sliced through the fog as he held it before him. His prized greatsword. Had it not been on the eve of battle, Lidan might have admired it for longer. The wide double-edged blade tapered to a diamond point, two parrying hooks set a foot above the hilt. The blade was as tall as Widrias's chest, the pommel reached his temple. Despite its size, he wielded it as easily as Lidan held his sabre. The hilt was just as magnificent as the blade, gold-plated steel with intricate silver inlays. The wonderful cross guard was inlaid with two precious sapphires, cut to the same shape as the steel pommel.

'Stand your ground!' Widrias cried, holding the sword high. 'Don't let them separate you! Hold firm and we will drive their menace away. Stand true in the name of the Council!'

Lidan faced the charging troglodytes with renewed courage. Or was it just adrenaline? Did it matter?

The fog separated. The monsters leapt. Bloated fiends covered in slime, wielding crude flails and blowpipes. They wore no clothes save for a leather kilt around their waists, covered in sludge. Dark eyes gleamed as they leaped and bounded through the bog.

He gripped his sabre and muttered a prayer to the absent winds.

*

Chekry loaded his crossbow. A slow breath as he aimed down the shaft. Exhale and squeeze. The bolt pierced the thick mist and buried into a bloated throat. His target gurgled and fell, only to be trampled by its charging companions. He hurriedly loaded another bolt. Damn thing! Slow. So damn slow. Foot firmly in the cocking stirrup, he heaved the string back to its nut. His sister had no such difficulty. Her smaller, lighter crossbow could be loaded as swiftly as a short-bow, although its range and stopping power suffered for its speed. Shoulder to shoulder, they kept a steady stream going. She concentrated on the closer targets, loading quickly and smoothly. He picked off the ones behind.

Despite their valiant efforts, two couldn't hold off fifty. The few remaining Council archers added their arrows to the neiads' efforts. Not enough, not nearly enough.

He cursed again as the troglodytes came within twenty paces. Throwing down his crossbow, he drew his rapier in a flash. His sister followed suit but kept her loaded crossbow in one hand. They clacked the tips of their blades together for good luck. Two battles in as many days. Bad bloody luck.

Momentum carried the first troglodytes to their deaths. With no time to change course, they ran straight through the needle-tipped blades. Depani kicked the corpse off her rapier and lunged for another. Her target squealed as the blade pierced its flank. Another approached from her left, swinging his flail menacingly, but Chekry was there to slash his neck. A third came behind him and was about to deliver a crushing blow to his unprotected back, but a bolt buried itself between his eyes. Depani lifted her crossbow and winked at her brother, simultaneously parrying a strike to her head.

He grinned, despite the situation. Through thick and thin, she was always there, just as he was for her.

*

Widrias roared as he swung. The blade's arc bit into two troglodytes with one stroke. Blood sprayed his face. He ignored its warmth and kept swinging. Punishing blow after punishing blow. Despite the company's heroic efforts, their numbers were dwindling, forcing them into an ever-tightening circle.

Wielding a greatsword was a battle in itself. It was closer to a polearm than a sword and required more strength and stamina than either. Momentum was key. Sweeping the blade around you in continuous circles, using its weight and counterweight to lift itself off the ground. Wielded properly, it was like a dance. Positioned correctly, on a bridge or walkway, or defending a gate, a single soldier with one of these could hold off an entire army. He was one of the best greatswordmen of his generation. Was.

His leg screamed with each swing. Stability in the core was still there, despite his years and increased paunch, but his stance suffered. The crude splint creaked and groaned, his knees threatened to buckle with every change in direction. Painful sweat stung his eyes. Another troglodyte ventured too close and the blade clipped its jaw, cutting through skin, muscle, tooth and bone. The bloody mess collapsed in a heap. He roared. In pain. In frustration. In exhilaration. He wouldn't last.

Suddenly, they withdrew. He eyed them warily between swings. The troglodytes grinned and lifted their blowpipes. Damned things. He threw himself to the ground, landing heavily on his injured leg. He gasped, but was rewarded by the zip of darts over his head. One of the missiles punctured the throat of another, clad in a heavy pirate-coat. The poor man snatched the dart from his throat, a brief moment of horror on his face. Eyes rolling, he collapsed, frothing at the mouth as uncontrollable spasms wracked his body. Widrias turned away. No helping a dead man.

It would take time to reload their pipes. Time enough to lever back to his feet and engage. Roaring again, he hobbled to the croaking enemy.

Twirling the heavy blade above his head, he slashed and hacked. Sweeping low, he took the legs from beneath one, continued the attack with a vicious downward strike straight through its throbbing gullet. Another launched itself at him, twirling its flail, but the attack was cut short when a chunk of flesh disappeared from its stomach. He recovered from his swing, continuing his dance. The troglodyte touched its exposed innards for a second, an uncomprehending look upon its face before being knocked to the ground by its allies as they leapt on the death-dealing satorr.

Isolated, tiring. A perilous place to be. Fortunately, the poorly-trained troglodytes didn't know how to use their numbers. They clawed and pushed each other, getting in one another's way, leaving him free to engage one or two at a time. It would only last for so long. He was sweating profusely, leg trembling like a leaf. The mud was cloying, stagnating, despite the relative firm ground. Now he was getting hemmed in, the trogs finally using their numbers. He adopted the half-swording technique, one hand held halfway down the blade. Better control, accuracy, and the ability to engage his opponents at closer quarters. He swept the pommel like a polearm in a devastating murder-stroke.

He looked behind. Winds! He'd wandered too far! The bulk of the company were fifteen paces behind, half-obscured in mist. Nothing but shapes and silhouettes maintaining the faintest sign of order in the chaos. If he could battle his way back, there was hope.

As he turned, a club swung. He jerked his head back. Too slow. The gnarled lump of wood clipped his temple, knocking him down. Dazed, he looked up. Leering over him, the troglodyte lifted its club. Damn idiot. Eyes shut, he waited for the end. Despite his pretty speech, this was it. A fool's death.

A second passed. Three seconds. Five. He opened his eyes. Why such a wait?

The troglodyte stared down at the sword tip growing from its chest. The blade withdrew and the trog collapsed, revealing his saviour.

Noswen offered him a hand. He took it gratefully, hauling himself to unsteady feet. She turned and parried a flail, kicking the wielder away and lunging, striking him down. She twirled her falchion and hammered its deadly edge on the head of another, cleaving through flesh and bone. The troglodytes around them shuffled back a few paces, unsure of this new arrival as she slew two more with skilful bladework. They croaked furiously. As one, they leapt forward from the mist. Widrias sighed, gripped his sword, and swung.

*

Widrias and Noswen were five paces away from the rest when Pwtrek reached them, longsword in hand. With one sweep, three troglodytes tumbled to the ground. He positioned himself between the general and the trogs. He'd failed his duty as Widrias' protector on the *Seascale*. It wouldn't happen again.

The enemy retreated, gazing at him with wide eyes. One croaked loudly, like a strangled toad. The sound was repeated by one, then another, and another. Within seconds, they were all croaking, even those already engaged.

What trickery was this? He pushed Widrias and the assassin behind, back to the others. The troglodytes parted. A shadow approached. He took a step back, suddenly afraid.

A massive creature, nearly eight feet tall. Grey skin and a swollen head. In one hand was a rusting trident, in the other a serrated scimitar. A cauldron of a belly, short arms and bowed legs. Its whole body covered in a disgusting yellow crust, secreted from its pores. Wide feet slapped against the ground, webbed toes curling in the mud. He groaned. A golem.

No use avoiding it. Nobody else in the company was capable of facing it. Plenty would out-skill the beast, but skill would only get them so far. He was the only one capable of matching its strength. Tanor might have stood up to it, but now it was up to him.

They circled, taking stock on each other's build, searching for weaknesses to exploit. The battle around them began again, bodies swarming around. Nobody was foolish enough to rush between them.

He made the first move, springing forward, sword aimed at the golem's chest. The golem flicked it away with the tip of its scimitar, lunging with the trident. He knocked the weapon away with his forearm, retreating a few steps. The golem pursued, flicking his blade inches from his face. He snarled, baring his teeth at the monster. Unfazed, it swept its scimitar, striking his flank. He grunted. His pelt spared him, but it was only a searching blow, no real power behind it. Curling his fist, he lashed out, striking the golem's snout. It backed away, snorting.

Spitting a mouthful of blood, it attacked again. Blow after blow came at him with both trident and sword. He parried. Mud and water squelched underfoot, tangling reeds threatened to ensnare his feet. Grey mist swirled.

His sword caught between the prongs of the trident. He pulled. The golem pulled back. Neither able to out-muscle the other. Had his foe been more alert, it might have noticed his unprotected flank and delivered the finishing blow with the scimitar. But golems are dim. It concentrated on untangling the trident, fixated on the task at hand.

He heaved suddenly and the golem lurched forward. An opportunity! He tugged again. This time there was more resistance. His enemy attempted the same. The contest of strength ended as the trident flew from his hand, lost somewhere in the swamp.

Scimitar in both hands, the golem launched a fierce overhead assault. He held his sword firmly, shockwaves running down his arms with each blow. Forced to one knee. Sparks flew as steel struck steel. The golem grimaced, crazed expression amplified by its bloody features.

The strikes weakened as its energy waned. Pwtrek seized the opportunity. Kicking out, he swept the golem's wide feet from beneath it. He jumped up to end it, but a lump of sludge was thrown into his face. He twisted to avoid it and his blade missed, only grazing his foe's shoulder.

Retreating, he wiped the mud away. Eyes were spared, luckily. Glaring at the golem, he searched for a new opening. It was strong, cunning, tough. Tougher than most. It would take something unexpected.

A moment's thought and he shifted his balance. The golem eyed him cautiously. He raised his sword, as if to charge. The golem braced himself for impact, adopting a guard. Their eyes locked. He snarled. The golem growled in response. He threw his sword. It flew end over end, spinning through the air.

Eyes bulging, the golem twisted its body sharply. It raised its scimitar, deflecting the blade. Didn't matter. He didn't expect it to kill it. The weight of the longsword knocked it off-balance.

He pounced, tackling it to the ground. Searching hands found the scimitar, wrestling it from the golem's hands, claws digging into its wrist. At such close quarters, the blade was too long to use. The hilt wasn't. He used it as a club, pummelling his foe's face into a mangled mess, cracking through the hard, clay-like crust. But there was spirit left in golem. Its hand shot out, gripping his neck like a python.

He tore at it, scratching, twisting, and crushing with all his might. Stars erupted. Struggled to retain consciousness. By the four winds, he mustn't black out. Harder. Harder. His claws dug deep. The noose loosened. He tore the hand away.

Now to end it. Opening his mouth, he clamped his powerful jaws around the golem's throat. It struggled between his teeth. Writhed and bucked. Its bloody wrist pounded his shoulder.

His mouth filled with copper. A sickening crunch. His teeth met together. He released. The golem lay still. Panting, spitting out chunks of macerated gullet, he rose to his feet and roared his victory. Strong and deep, the battle ceased at his voice. The troglodytes glanced from juggernaut to fallen golem and fled into the mist.

Chapter 14

When the sun finally rose, saturating the mist with a yellow-grey glow, Lidan saw the full extent of the skirmish. Bodies lay everywhere, most of them squirming in pain as they nursed ugly wounds. Friend and foe alike, united in their suffering. Sobs of agony in his ears. The metallic smell of blood competed with the marsh's stink. He shuddered. Miserable tears did little to reduce the pain of ravaged flesh.

But he was still alive.

Once again, his shield proved invaluable, dented and scratched a hundred times over. His stained brigandine frayed around the edges of its embedded plates. His shoulder ached like a bastard.

He watched Noswen glumly. She seemed unaffected by it all, striding around the battlefield, checking the bodies, silencing the wounded with well-placed thrusts of her blade. More at home among the dead than the living. One by one, the moans, the croaks, the pleads for mercy were silenced. A stillness fell over the marsh. Noswen approached a wounded Council Guard lying in the blood-soaked muck.

She paused for a moment, as if considering her options, before kneeling down and stabbing him smoothly in the chest. As she withdrew the blade, the silence was shattered.

'Traitor!' exploded Pwtrek, bounding towards her.

Lidan recoiled. He'd never seen him look so fierce, so frightening. Even against the golem, it was a look of grim determination he wore, not this mask of distilled hatred.

'You killed him!' his growl rivalled a hydra protecting her nest.

'He was already dead,' she replied, coolly meeting his gaze. 'I did him a favour.'

'A favour to Stolach, maybe, not to us.'

'Look at him. Mangled hand. Stab wounds in the thigh and gut. Look at the blood-loss. No recovering from that.'

'You're no healer, we might have saved him.'

'No. I'm a killer. I know a dead body when I see one.'

'Calm yourself, my friend,' said Widrias, shuffling up to the juggernaut to place a soothing hand on his shoulder. 'What is it?'

'The assassin killed one of our men, sir. Claims it was out of mercy.'

'A mortally wounded soldier was given the gift of a swift death on the battlefield where he fell,' whispered Noswen. 'Surely that's a better fate than leaving him here to bleed to death?'

'We're no fools. We all know where your true loyalties lie!'

'Enough, Pwtrek,' said Gwahl, inspecting the body. He didn't take long to reach his conclusions. 'I'm no surgeon, but I'm the best we have at the moment. This one had no hope. Certainly not here. Noswen did the right thing.'

'This is how it starts,' muttered Pwtrek. 'She'll soon be turning those blades on healthy men, I warn you.'

'Please, Pwtrek, rest. You'll only make your wounds worse if you agitate yourself,' said Gwahl.

'Wouldn't want that, would I?' he grumbled, walking away. 'Otherwise *she'll* give me her mercy.'

Widrias shook his head and sat down on a small hummock, wiping his blade clean with a rag.

'How many are left, Gwahl?'

'Eleven Council Guard, only two pirates,' Gwahl sighed.

'Heavy losses,' said Spotal. He knelt to wash his face and hands on a patch of grass, spitting the filth away into the mist. 'But we still have a few troops left. All is not lost.'

'Don't make light of this situation. We've lost many men on this quest already. Too many. Every death is a defeat. Indeed, *all* is not lost, but *much* is,' said Widrias coldly, eyes blazing.

Spotal bowed his head and murmured an apology, backing away. Widrias watched his retreat with a curled lip, then returned his attention to his blade. As he scrubbed at a particularly tenacious bloodstain, Lidan heard him mutter under his breath to Gwahl.

'You'd think he'd have more sense?'

'He didn't mean it like that.'

'After what happened to him? Damn foolish comment.'

Gwahl shrugged. He saw Lidan eavesdropping and smiled wanly, turning back to the satorr.

'Noswen's actions have raised quite an issue,' said Widrias.

'Pwtrek's always mistrusted her. He'll never accept her,' replied Gwahl, sadly. Lidan glanced at her, sitting alone and out of earshot. Gwahl continued. 'We can only hope neither of them will do anything foolish.'

'True, but that's not what I was alluding to,' Widrias spat on the blade, scrubbing at the stain. 'I was talking about the wounded.'

'I'll do what I can to help them,' Gwahl nodded.

'I don't doubt it. But what if the wound prevents them from marching, or fighting? We can't carry a dead weight with us, the quest is too important to allow such delays.'

'It's difficult,' said Gwahl, rubbing his chin. 'Noswen only ended the life of a mortally wounded soldier. If it's a wound that maims a person but does not kill, what do we do?'

'Our duty demands that we leave them, so as not to slow us down.'

Gwahl paused. 'Remember, you are wounded.'

Widrias scowled, but managed to transform it into a false smile that never reached his eyes. 'You want to leave me behind, do you?'

Gwahl chuckled weakly. 'No, just reminding you how difficult these decisions can be.'

The satorr spat on the blade, scrubbing it aggressively. Lidan wasn't sure if there even was a stain anymore.

'I'm the general of this army, I set the pace to match my own,' Widrias growled. 'If a soldier is wounded badly enough so as not to be able to keep up, we leave them.'

'Here? Alone? That's as good as slipping in the knife,' Gwahl rubbed his chin.

'You're more than welcome to stay with them.'

'I'm asking a question. No need to get defensive,' Gwahl frowned. 'If this is going to be your decision, remember just how difficult it'll be to draw the line, when to leave someone or when to bring them with us.'

Widrias nodded apologetically. 'I know. I'm tired and angry. I know you're trying to help. As hypocritical as it may be, my wounded leg will be the line as to whether we leave someone behind.'

'What about other maiming wounds? If they lose use of a hand and can't fight, what do we do? They'd distract us in battle, be a hindrance. A weak point in the formation.'

'In such a situation, there's nothing we can do. We'll fight in whatever formation gives us the best chance of victory, which depends on the circumstances of the skirmish. If they cannot join the formation effectively, they cannot be allowed to provide a weak link and must be left out.'

'What if they're wounded, but I could potentially heal them to a sufficient degree provided I had a few days to work?'

'That would depend on the situation, wouldn't it?'

'Yes, but would you be willing to lose a few days if it meant saving a life? "Every death is a defeat", as you said.'

Widrias paused. 'Again, it depends on the situation. I don't want to lose anyone else, Gwahl, but we need to win this war and sacrifices must be made.'

Gwahl nodded, accepting the decision, but Lidan couldn't tell whether he agreed with it.

'We'll see how things go.'

Lidan stood and walked away. Conversation over, there was nothing left to eavesdrop on. He walked through the corpses, dragging the bodies of his allies to a designated patch of dry land where a pyre could cremate them. Could've been him. Any one of them could've been him. Praise the four winds it wasn't. He dragged a dead pirate through the mud. Scarred, tattooed face vaguely familiar. The violinist. The one who'd played so happily with Gwahl only a few days ago. A few days. His hands shook. Mere moments were all it took for everything to fall apart. He was so damned lucky.

As he wandered through the dead, his eyes caught on body sprawled face-down among a pile of slain troglodytes. Another pirate. He rolled him over. Horrified, he cried out, stumbling over one of the corpses.

Mostyn's face was torn apart. Flesh hung on by the thinnest threads of skin and muscle. His cheeks were ripped, leaving him with a permanent, grisly grimace, complete with wild, staring, bloodshot eyes. Empty eyes. An ugly gash tore apart his shoulder, so deep he could see gleaming bone beneath. Wounds and welts covered his lower torso, now little more than a field of bloody ridges of raised skin. Grisly as these wounds were, there was worse to come. Chunks of flesh were ripped from his body. From his lower legs to the top of his scalp. All of them circular, ringed by tooth-marks, still wet with saliva.

The others heard his cry. Gwahl reached him first, Spotal and the others close behind.

'What is it? More trogs?'

Struck dumb by the horror of the former captain's fate, he shook his head and gestured to the corpse. Gwahl knelt and gasped. The others pushed forward for a better look. Lidan crawled back, letting them pass to witness the grisly sight.

Even when he was away, the body out of sight, he could still see him. He imagined how he met his end. He shouldn't, but it was impossible not to. Impossible not to imagine himself in the same situation. Separated from the main group. Nothing but mist and monster all around. Battling for his life. Surrounded on all sides. Wounded, growing weaker. The enemy stepping inside his blade, wrenching it from his hand. Defenceless, dragged to the ground. Teeth tearing at your flesh. Slimy tongues lapping up your blood as it pumped from fresh wounds. Cold spit dripping onto your skin.

Mostyn, pirate captain of the Great Waters, dead in the mist and gloom of the Cysgodgors Marshes. Eaten alive by its inhabitants.

*

They placed his body at the top of the pyre. The two remaining crewmates wept bitterly at their loss, their sobs interrupted by sudden roars of uncontrolled fury, challenging any troglodyte to strike them down. None replied. No words were spoken, no eulogies composed, no poems recited. Each whispered their own prayers for the spirits of the fallen to find solace.

They turned away from the flames and followed Widrias, limping into the mist. The flames were lost from sight within three dozen paces. Lidan clenched his fists as they left the battlefield. Everywhere he turned, he saw Mostyn. Each pulse of fog, each clump of grass, they twisted into dislocated limbs and torn stomachs.

Mostyn was right, after all. Death lurked in the mist.

*

Ten days of marching and they were suffering. They managed to survive for so long by eating the food carried by the deceased, but now their supplies were nearly exhausted. Their feet were sore and damp. Some suffered more than others. Gwahl expressed concerns on several occasions that some may fall behind indefinitely. Despite his suggestions for foraging expeditions while the company rested, Widrias refused. Fear of losing someone in the mist and mire was too great. Like startled sheep, they clumped together at rest, taking comfort in the shoulders of their fellows. Gwahl tried to reassure him that he would find them again, but it was no use. They needed their shepherd, lest the wolves have their feast.

As for those wolves, their threat was never quelled. Each unfamiliar sound made them titter and startle, wheeling to face the endless marsh. But the phantoms of the mist were never there. It was always swaying reeds, the ripple of a heron in water, a bubble of gas escaping the thick mud. Paranoia left its mark. Red, sleepless eyes, twitching hands searching for sword-hilts, voices seldom louder than a whisper. The marshes were hungry and their terror was its feast.

At dawn on the eleventh day, after an unappetising meal of dried fruit and a mouthful of water from their water-skins, they set off again, as any other day. He had no idea how far they'd travelled. He had no idea how far they'd strayed. Widrias once hoped to use the sun and stars to navigate, but the mist was too thick. To his credit, the satorr tried putting on a brave face, assuring them against the obvious. It was no good. He was as sure of their doom as anyone else. Perhaps Gwahl was the only one who held on to hope.

They stumbled along, using their weapons for support. Wheezing and groaning like tired old hounds, fighting to keep their eyes open but too afraid to sleep. They barely walked a hundred paces when one of the soldiers trailing at the rear fell, clutching his leg. Gwahl recognised him. He'd been flagging more than the others for a while. One of the ones he'd been keeping an eye on, but was too proud, or foolish, to be examined properly.

The others stopped and stared stupidly as he approached.

His sudden scream made him jump.

Soothing him with gentle croons, Gwahl held his shoulders, denying his attempts at rolling away.

'Where does it hurt?' he asked, softly, gently, trying not to grimace at the smell clinging to him. The smell of rot.

'Leg. North winds save me, my leg.'

'Alright. I'm not quite the north winds, but I'll see what I can do.'

Carefully, he pulled his hands away. The soldier shivered, like a cat in freezing rain. He lifted the filthy trouser hem. It stuck, something keeping it from lifting. The man groaned in barely-contained agony. Gwahl shushed him gently and tried again. No good. Drawing his dirk, he slipped its point beneath the seam and cut it open. It could always be repaired. The smell intensified. The sight, sickening.

During one of the battles, he'd suffered a blow to his calf. It wasn't particularly deep and he must have left it to heal for itself. A mistake. The marshes were dirty, disease-ridden, his trousers caked in mud. Swollen to twice its original size, a dusky tinge from heel to beyond where he could see. Black, blood-filled blisters close to the wound itself. Rotting, decomposed flesh sat in a putrid bed of crusted pus. Despite himself, he retched at the sudden waft of death oozing from the wound. A vile stench of disease and decay. Flies settled on the wound in seconds, drawn by their innate need to feast.

He stepped away, scrubbing his hands furiously with precious water from his water-skin and a few blades of coarse grass. Lidan approached for a closer look. Springing up, he waved him away.

'No, Lidan, go no closer! He's ill.'

The boy stumbled back, dumbly.

Turning to the remaining soldiers, he gestured to their fallen companion. 'Why didn't anyone tell me? I could've kept it clean had I known.'

He was angry. At himself more than the others. He knew he'd been struggling but hadn't bothered checking up on him, assuming that if anything were seriously wrong then the soldier would've asked. Foolish.

They shuffled sheepishly. One, an Islander, eventually answered.

'He didn't want to be killed by the assassin.'

Gwahl sighed. This lunacy again.

'I explained this already. Noswen killed that soldier because he was already dead. She eased his suffering!'

'But after that, you said if we were too badly wounded we'd be left behind. Simef didn't want to be left behind.'

'And now look what's happened! He didn't clean it. The wound turned foul. It's a marvel he survived this long.'

'Is there anything we can do?' asked Widrias.

'Nothing now,' he spat. 'The leg's lost. Chances are, the infection's already spread. He should be put out of his misery.'

They glanced at Noswen, who dutifully drew her dirk. He shook his head, stopping her in her tracks.

'I'll do it.'

'Just like that?' exclaimed Pwtrek. 'No discussion, no consideration? Decision made in a split second.'

'Do you think he can keep up with us?' he asked. 'Give it a few hours and half his leg will fall off.'

'We could light a fire, cut away the rot?'

'Look at him!' Gwahl snapped, pointing to the man, trembling on the ground. 'Look at his leg. Where do you suppose the infection ends? Up to his hip, no doubt, probably beyond that. He'll die of blood-loss or shock if we tried it. And in these environments? Another infection will surely follow. You're not thinking clearly, Pwtrek!'

'I can carry him.'

'You'll do no such thing. I don't want anyone going near him, lest they contract an infection as well.'

'There's nothing we can do, Pwtrek,' said Widrias, gently. 'Simef has done well to reach this far, now it's time for him to rest.'

Pwtrek turned back to Gwahl, shoulders sagging. 'Make it quick for him.'

'It'll be a relief from his suffering,' he nodded, reassuringly.

With a grimace, he returned to Simef to do his duty. He didn't struggle.

In silence, he half dragged, half rolled the stinking carcass away from the others and into a suitable peat bog. With care, he pushed the body as far into the mire as he could. He paused briefly to watch Simef be slowly engulfed, leaving no trace.

Returning to the others, he approached Widrias.

'I'm sorry I didn't give him the proper death-rites. There's no time for ceremony right now,' when Widrias didn't reply, he took a breath, and continued. 'I'd also like to take another look at your leg. In fact, I should inspect everyone's injuries. I underestimated the marsh. I won't do it again.'

Widrias nodded, and repeated the request to the others. To his relief, his leg was clean and healing well, albeit slower than he would've liked. Not unexpected. Lack of rest and proper nutrition was likely the cause. He examined the others, paying special attention to Pwtrek, whose thick hair acted as a sponge in the mud, hiding his injuries. Fortunately, neither the juggernaut nor anyone else showed any sign of infection. Fatigue and hunger, but no infection. Of course, even if they were infected up to their ears, in their current disorientated state, he doubted they'd have the sense to tell him. They might not even notice their bodies rotting away with each step. Even if they did, fear of being left behind would keep their tongues quiet.

*

Lidan stumbled. One foot in front of the other. Walking on a cloud. In the sky. He was smoke. Immaterial. Ephemeral. Floating through the reeds on gossamer wings.

The mist pulsed.

He was trawling through the mud, wading through bogs and mires. Clothes saturated with filth dragged him down. Heavy as a rock. Like clay, squeezing through the fingers of a potter. Moulded tall, thin, squashed back down to a lump.

The mist pulsed.

Snapped back to reality. The line of the company stretched ahead. He dragged heavy feet. Sharp grass against his arms, against his shins. Biting flies on the exposed skin of his head and neck. Itching. Burning.

Burning flesh. The stink of it in his nostrils. Raging furnaces and smoking brands. Dry skin shrivelling. Drunken laughter booming.

Not real. Just a memory. A nightmare. But he wasn't asleep.

The mist pulsed.

Shadows in the corner of his eyes. Flails swinging. Blowpipes shooting. Mostyn's corpse reached out to him, half his arm chewed away. Trogs lurked behind, the puppeteers to Mostyn's marionette. He whimpered. Found Auran ahead of him. Hid behind his back. Peeking around, Mostyn was gone. Auran shoved him away with a growl.

He turned. Sea-neiads sprang at him, lightning in their hands. The ground turned and rolled with the storm, trying to throw him off his feet. He gripped a small bush, sharp branches digging into his palms. Another shadow sprang, gaping mouth full of rows of sharp fangs. Good for tearing flesh. Ripping it from his bones. Better than any butcher's cleaver. He ducked behind the bush. Thorns dug in. Mostyn was there again, groaning, weeping. Burning brands into his hands. Drunken laughter boomed. Croaks all around. Gleaming eyes from dark shadows. Grey eyes.

The mist pulsed.

*

On the fourteenth day, they were almost immobile. Despite Gwahl's words of encouragement, despite his goading, his compliments, they crawled at a snail's pace. Even Pwtrek, despite his strength and stamina, now reduced to a shambling mess, walking with eyes half-closed, murmuring incoherently.

'Come with me, my friend,' said Gwahl, taking the juggernaut's hand and leading him away from an especially boggy patch of ground. 'We'll soon be out of this mess, you'll see.'

The juggernaut made no reply. At least none he could understand, letting the daemon guide him back to solid ground.

Just as Pwtrek was made safe, he saw a soldier stumble and fall face-first into a puddle of stagnant water. Cursing, he hauled him to his feet. He looked alright. Apparently didn't even realise he'd fallen. Shaking his head, he whispered to him to keep going, to hold on to hope. The man just stared ahead, dumb as the others.

Gwahl checked his pulse. There it was, faint and fluttering. Unstoppering the soldier's water-skin, he tipped it to his lips. Empty. Of course it was. He clicked his tongue against his palate and gave him a swig of his own rapidly-dwindling water. As much as it pained him, he only allowed him a few sips, otherwise there'd be none left for him. An unpopular decision. The man growled when the skin was taken away. He greedily tried to snatch it back, but Gwahl was too swift and caught his hand.

'You can have more later. For now, you must keep walking.'

He looked around. Out of everyone, Noswen and Spotal fared best. Although they were in no particular danger themselves, they lacked the energy to help anyone else and kept to the head of the company, picking the path through the marsh. Behind them were the bulk of the survivors. A shuffling group of degenerates, shadows of their former selves as they stumbled through the mists, like elders suffering from the trembling-sickness. Pathetic. Stumbling steps and wide-eyed stares into the mist, searching for the fears of their tortured imagination. Behind these were the stragglers. Two guards, Pwtrek, Widrias, and Lidan. The worst. Although the others had grown slow and stupid, these stragglers looked close to death.

A splash from ahead. By Enadir's grace, who now?

Widrias. Why him? Stumbled headfirst into boggy ground. The satorr did nothing as the mud slowly crept up over his back, his neck, around his chin. All he did was stare. As if waiting for Cysgodgors to take its deadly toll on the fools who dared brave its path.

Snarling, he rushed to his aid. He pushed past the others, staring ahead in dumb horror. Into the bog. He trod lightly, stepping forwards with his back foot before the front foot found solid ground, swimming more than walking. By Enadir, he'd wandered far. Eight feet of peat still separated him from the satorr. Falling onto his hands and knees to distribute his weight, he made his way to his companion, pushing through the mud. Eventually, he reached him, just as the mud reached the base of his nose.

Straining against the pull of the mud, he managed to heave Widrias onto his chest. He lay still for a few seconds, panting. Now to return. The most important thing was to keep as flat and still as possible while still manoeuvring them back to solid ground. Easier said than done. Dragging someone through water to dry land without letting them drown was difficult enough, but fighting against the vacuum of the swamp was next to impossible. But he would try. For all he was worth.

How many battles had he fought and lived? How many foes defeated? How many friends saved? Too many to remember. This was just another battle, another foe, another friend to save, just like countless others. Groaning, he slowly dragged them to safety. Whenever he could, he grabbed hold of reeds, sticks, anything to help propel them to the precious safety of firm ground.

Slowly, he dragged them to safety.

Enadir curse the swamp. The battle was already lost. Minutes of fighting and they'd barely moved three feet. Too slow. Too heavy. Too late. In desperation, he screamed for Noswen and Spotal. Either they didn't care or the mist swallowed his voice. They didn't come. Straining his neck, he saw the others had all left as well. Probably frightened away. He was alone.

Heart crashing against his chest, ears ringing with his pulse, he accepted the ugly reality. Defeat. Widrias was lost. It was all he could do now to get himself back to land. At least then he might lead the rest of these poor, lost fools to some semblance of safety.

'I'm sorry,' he whispered. He slowly released his hold.

Widrias looked at him. He saw understanding in his eyes. A brief moment of clarity. No anger, no contempt. Acceptance.

Frustration built again. If only there were one other whose mind was not warped by the marshes, one more person to help. But no, he was the one remaining with his wits intact. Damn them all. Damn Spotal and Noswen for ignoring his calls. Damn the others for being too weak to resist the nightmares of the mists. Damn himself for his weakness.

The mud rose up around Widrias's chin. He screamed. The mist recoiled momentarily as a heavy gust blew through the marsh. Let the trogs hear. Let them come. He needed something to destroy.

'Daemon!'

Jerking his head around, he saw them. The two remaining pirates stood there, excited looks in their eyes. Perhaps he was not so alone.

'You're in a bit of a pickle, daemon. Does old Wids require our assistance?'

'Get in here now before I lose him!'

The largest, a hulking Hobb by the looks of his tattoos, took off his greatcoat and handed it to his companion, a leaner, wirier hanex. The Hobb strode into the mud much as Gwahl did, spreading his weight. Minimal movements. Experience in the swamp. All he could do was wait and keep Widrias's head above the silt.

Finally, he reached them. Together, man and daemon edged their way back to the hanex. Eventually they were close enough for the pirate to toss them the Hobb's coat and drag them the remaining few feet to dry land.

Panting, Gwahl lay on all fours, regaining his breath. Few times in his life had he ever been so grateful to feel firm land beneath his feet. He turned to Widrias. By Enadir's grace, he was alright. Aside from the thick coat of stinking slime, the satorr seemed quite well for his ordeal. He looked up at the hanex and nodded.

'My thanks. I was ready to leave him,' he paused. 'Where have you both been? I could have used your aid shepherding the rest of these lambs.'

The hanex shrugged. 'Keeping to ourselves. Didn't want to disturb the great General Widrias and all of his brave soldiers of the Council on their secret mission.'

Gwahl narrowed his eyes. 'So why now?'

'We heard you yell,' he replied, offering his hand.

The Hobb growled and patted the hilt of his cutlass remorsefully. The hanex nodded in agreement.

'Truthfully, we hoped you were being attacked by trogs and felt a bit left out. Since there aren't any, old Fedza and I will be on our way.'

'No, you won't,' Gwahl held up a hand to stop them. 'I need you. I can't get through these swamps on my own, not with this lot in such a condition. You're going to stay and help.'

'What if we don't want to?'

'I'll kill you both. You know who I am.'

The hanex sneered, but Gwahl could tell he was afraid, as was Fedza, shifting nervously, wringing his hands. Raising an eyebrow, he waited for their reply.

'What do you need us to do?' the hanex growled.

He smiled. 'First of all, you can help me gather them all up into one group, before they all end up like Widrias. Then, you can help me guide them through this place until we find a suitable spot to set up camp for a while.'

'What'll you do when you set up camp?'

'I'll make them better. It will take time, but I can manage.'

'So, we can leave once you find this campsite?'

Gwahl paused. 'Once we find it, you can go to die in whatever way seems best to you.'

The hanex smiled. 'Excellent. Probably locked in battle with a filthy trog.'

Gwahl snorted. 'He's Fedza, what's your name?'

'Sanbeq Naderr, bosun of the fine vessel formerly known as the *Seascale*.'

Gwahl nodded. 'Good, it's a pleasure. Now help me gather them.'

*

Two days after their initial meeting, Gwahl was beginning to like Sanbeq. He was insolent, irritating, and unnecessarily aggressive at times, but obedient. Years of servitude made it a habit for him,

239

albeit with a good deal of cursing and complaining. Fedza never spoke. Gwahl wasn't sure whether he was dumb. It didn't matter. The Hobb was as good as Sanbeq at guiding their addled companions through the mist.

After rescuing Widrias, he confronted Noswen and Spotal. The calef shrugged miserably.

'What could we do, Gwahl? I've barely got the strength to walk on my own, let alone swim into the swamp to save an armoured satorr.'

'You could've thrown me your cloak, tied your belts together to make a chain, anything! You abandoned me, Spotal, you too, Noswen. I thought you were better than that.'

'I'm sorry, Gwahl,' said Noswen, head bowed. 'I'm ashamed. As Spotal said, I'm so tired. It's all we can do to keep each other going.'

'The fact that you're both so far ahead of the others, the fact that we're even having this conversation, shows to me you're both well enough to help. I expect you to do so.'

'I won't be able to save anyone who strays into the swamp,' Spotal said, rubbing his eyes.

'I don't need you for that. I need you to help me steer them along, stop them from falling into the damned swamp in the first place. The fact that two pirates were more prepared to help me than you two…'

He left them to dwell on his words. Had he gone too far? No. They deserved to hear it. No point softening the blow. At times like these, you needed a strong hand. It achieved the right result, in any case. They dutifully remained with the rest of the party, gently coaxing anyone who strayed too close to the bog back to firm ground.

Finding a suitable place to set up camp proved as difficult as anticipated. They needed somewhere sheltered, large enough for them all to sleep comfortably, but still easily defensible. Perhaps he was asking for too much? So far, they hadn't found anywhere suitable. Endless long, thin pathways weaving their way between bog and mire. A constant, infinite maze. Even these would betray them, leading them to dead ends or dropping away suddenly into lakes of slime. All the while, his friends deteriorated. A steady descent into madness.

He was forced to tie them together by the belts with torn pieces of cloth to make sure nobody wandered. This brought its own problems, slowing them down and setting up a domino effect if one stumbled, leaving a tangled heap of groaning, complaining fools. It made Sanbeq laugh, but the hanex' sniggers soon died with his glowering stare.

'We need fresh water,' said Spotal, the first time he'd approached Gwahl since his tirade. 'My brain's getting sluggish and heavy. These ones must be dry as a desert.'

He nodded. 'I have a trick to get clean water, but I need a good campsite before I can do it.'

'What constitutes this "good campsite"?'

He explained the desired features to Spotal's sceptical expression, chewing his cheek in thought.

'Forgive me for saying, but I doubt we'll find anywhere perfect. The best you can probably hope for is a tight cluster of hummocks with some firm ground in between. I'll keep an eye out.'

'You never know, we might just find somewhere. We could use some luck.'

Spotal nodded and walked away, before turning, nervously rubbing the amulet about his neck.

'Gwahl. I never apologised. I wanted to let you know I'm truly sorry, and ashamed, for neglecting my duties. I won't let you down again.'

He smiled. 'I know, Spotal, I'm sorry too. I was tired and frustrated. I know it's difficult when you're so exhausted.'

Spotal shook his head. 'No, it's no excuse. As an officer you must always put the interests of your men before your own, otherwise you're nothing more than a slavedriver cracking a whip. I should've done better.'

Spotal trotted away to lend a steady hand to Lidan as he stumbled. Gwahl nodded. A good friend.

His ears pricked. Someone approached from behind. He turned sharply. Sanbeq. Crouching, head low, legs bowed, as if ready to pounce. Raising a disapproving eyebrow, he stopped and faced the pirate.

'What do you think you're doing? You're to keep an eye out for them, not stalk me like a snake.'

The hanex straightened, shrugging. 'I wanted to see what it took to sneak up on you.'

'More than what you just exhibited.'

'Clearly. My creeping skills are nothing compared to the trogs.'

He frowned. 'What do you mean?'

Sanbeq motioned for Gwahl to follow him down the line to Pwtrek, the last in their column. He groaned. Pwtrek wasn't supposed to be the last. There used to be two others behind him, a man and a satorr, but both Council Guards were gone. A sheared piece of cloth dangling from the back of Pwtrek's belt was their only remnant. He inspected the frayed ends. Cut with a crude blade.

He clasped Pwtrek's hand. 'Pwtrek, what happened to the two who were behind you? Where have they gone?'

The juggernaut made no reply, but continued to shamble ever onwards.

'Did they cut themselves loose? Did someone else cut them loose?' he paused. 'Did you?'

Still not reply. There wasn't even an acknowledgement of his presence.

'I wouldn't bother, you'll get no sense out of this lot, the fog's gone to their heads, filled their empty brains with its whispers.'

'Be silent,' he snapped. 'If you have nothing useful to say then hold your tongue.'

'I do have something useful to say, if only you'd ask nicely.'

When the hanex saw his face, he quickly dropped his brazen attitude and gestured back over his shoulder.

'It can't have happened too long ago. I've been walking around the back for a while and only just noticed they've gone. It wasn't your friend who cut them off and they definitely didn't cut themselves away. They got snatched by some trogs, sure as the sea's grey.'

Gwahl cursed and spat. He peered behind them. The fog danced and glimmered. Taunting.

'We need to find them. If they get away then they'll only tell others we're here, then we'll really have something to worry about.'

Sanbeq smiled like a wolf. 'Exactly what I wanted to hear. I'll get Fedza, you go tell your calef and assassin to look after these idiots and we can go hunting.'

He nodded. Perhaps he should remind the pirate who was giving the orders? No point. Wouldn't change anything, and no point stirring up any animosity. He ran back to his companions.

'Let us come with you,' said Spotal. 'We're better trackers.'

'You're also better fighters and you actually care about these men. Those two pirates wouldn't protect our friends if attacked. I need you here.'

'How will you find us after? Night will fall in a few hours and you don't know how far they've gone.'

'They can't have gone too far. Besides, at our pace, I'd be surprised if you get another kilometre out of this lot before sundown.'

Spotal curled his lip. 'I'd be surprised if we made it that far in a week. Good luck, Gwahl, make sure you catch them.'

He nodded. Sanbeq and Fedza were waiting for him, cutlasses drawn in anticipation. He shook his head at them.

'Put them away for now. The time for blades will come.'

Sanbeq ignored him and clipped the head from a cattail. Gwahl sensed his stares as he scanned the trampled path that lay in their wake.

'Why are you bothering tracking from here? We know we lost them back there.'

'I'm committing to memory what *our* tracks look like, so if I see any changes, we'll know something disturbed them. That'll give us a good idea of where the troglodytes ambushed.'

It didn't take long to memorise. He'd tracked often enough to know what to look for.

'Very well, let's go. Keep behind me at all times, I don't want you disturbing the trail.'

Retracing their steps through the bog, the mist pulsated around them, shuddering and shimmering in what was, at times, a beautiful whirl. Memorising their footsteps as he had, there was little need to crawl along the trail at a snail's pace, searching for any signs of change. They ran, eyes fixed on the ground, the two pirates following a few paces behind.

'Try to enjoy yourself, daemon, we get to kill monsters today.'

He curled his lip. 'Be silent, we're not doing this for sport.'

'I'll find enjoyment wherever I can. Wids led us to the destruction of everything I had, and the trogs destroyed what remained. I'll do what I can to take revenge, and you can believe me when I say I'll enjoy every second. Now you can see Cysgodgors destroying your friends. Let your discipline go, take pleasure in vengeance.'

'Discipline will help me save my friends and overcome this enemy. Your brazen, callous way of dealing with your grief will ultimately end in disaster.'

'Mostyn warned you against coming through this place,' said Sanbeq, panting slightly. 'Now look where you are.'

'It was the general's decision.'

'It was the wrong decision, daemon, and you know it.'

'No. Necessity drove us in, and it will pull us through to the other side, no matter how strongly the current flows against us.'

His words felt hollow, but he masked it. They mustn't know his doubts.

'Necessity doesn't seem to be doing much good for you right now. You're all crumbling faster than an old mussel shell under an iron boot.'

He snorted disdainfully, but couldn't think of a retort. The smug hanex was right, but he'd never admit it.

'I must say,' he changed the subject. 'I'm surprised at how well you two are faring in these conditions. I'd have expected you to fall sooner than the Council Guard.'

Both man and hanex laughed loudly, drawing another glare as he tried to quell their merriment.

'Do you want to call every golem in the marsh? Be silent,' he seethed.

'I thought that was the idea? To get to the ones who spirited away your soldiers?'

'To those ones, yes, not every damned trog in Cysgodgors!'

After spluttering out their final chuckles, they eventually composed themselves. To his relief, no enemies leapt out of the mist. Yet.

'Your soldiers may have been trained for battles, but we've been through worse,' Sanbeq eventually said.

'Mostyn mentioned encountering a similar fog.'

'Not just once, several times. None as thick or malicious as this, obviously, but we've endured them nonetheless. Several crewmen ran off deck into the sea as they were driven mad by visions, others had to be killed before they hurt too many of us. I remember one on a particularly disastrous voyage who hacked off both his feet with a hatchet. He screamed afterwards they were crabs, consuming his limbs. Another time our quartermaster took a boat hook and used it to bugg-'

'There!' Gwahl cut across Sanbeq, pointing to the ground before them. To his experienced eye, the change in the features of the trail was as clear as day. From the constant, though slightly haphazard, trail of boots trudging through the mud to a churned mass of slime and broken-down reeds. Holding up his hand to halt the pirates in their tracks, he knelt down and inspected the mud, lightly running a finger over the raised ridges in the ground. Three troglodytes. Maybe four. Judging from the direction of the displaced mud, the cannibals came from all sides and fled to the right.

Standing, he relayed the information to his two companions, who nodded and fell in line behind him as he ventured into the swamp. Now they knew *where* their companions were attacked, they had the far more difficult task of tracking the troglodytes through the chaotic sludge of the mire. Troglodytes travelled in mighty leaps, sometimes jumping as far as twelve to fifteen feet with each bound. This could move quickly, avoiding large boggy areas in ways he could not. But they'd also be hindered by their captives. Hopefully, they wouldn't have far to search before coming across their adversaries.

He did his best to avoid the larger bogs, sticking to the hummocks and reed beds, but at times it was necessary to wade through the sludge so as not to lose sight of the trail. At these times they would go one-by-one, with the two who were not in the mud standing at the ready with the pirate longcoats. Fortunately, they didn't get caught in the pull of the marsh. For now.

'So, what are you going to do about water?' asked Sanbeq as he gestured to a stagnant pool.

'I have a trick to clean undrinkable water. It should work, even for this algae-ridden swamp-filth.'

'Let me guess; boiling it and collecting the steam?'

Gwahl nodded, only mildly surprised that the hanex knew. 'That's right. It isn't efficient but I have to try.'

'It works quite nicely with sea-water, if you don't mind cleaning your bowl of salt crystals, that is.'

'You've had to do it before?'

'Plenty of times to know the water tastes odd, especially when it's served warm. But we only ever had to drink it for a few days at a time, by then Mostyn would've chased down a raincloud and we'd cover the deck in barrels to collect pure rainwater.'

'What if it was a storm? Would the waves not fill the barrels instead?'

'He never sailed into a storm, he sailed into rain. Our captain was a wise seafarer, he knew all the tricks in the book. Never had a completely unsuccessful journey under his command.'

'I mean no disrespect to Mostyn when I say I doubt that.'

'It's true! Maybe we didn't return with exactly what we wanted, sometimes lost good men, but we always returned with *something* to make the trip worthwhile…'

He raised an eyebrow as the bosun's voice trailed off in thought. 'Realised that's not true, have you?'

'Only once.'

'Once,' he chuckled. 'Mostyn had a fine reputation, but not that fine, Sanbeq. What was this one journey that ended in disaster?'

'Only one,' repeated Sanbeq softly. 'I'd almost forgotten about it until now. This mist, the lack of water, the lack of food…you. Nothing compared to that one journey where everything went bad.

'Four years ago, the captain came to us with a mission set by Baron Pesk to the Jagged Isles, in search of some artefact hidden under a fortified island. The baron paid well, and we set off. We fought through the fort, or temple, defended by a handful of knights in polished armour with fiery weapons. We retrieved the artefact and bought it back to Morgenal. Mostyn took me with him, along with the others, when we presented the artefact to the baron. She wasn't alone either. Along with her bodyguards was another person, waiting behind in the shadows. A daemon. He looked like you, but nothing like you at the same time. I don't know how else to describe him.

'The artefact was in a sealed container. We didn't know what it was. The carvings on the outside were unfamiliar to us, but Old Keli, our Mate, was adamant they were old giant runes. Anyway, the baron handed the container to the daemon and he broke it open with one twist of his hands, as if it were made of paper. Inside was a tablet made of black jet, covered in funny runes.'

Gwahl nearly stumbled. Enadir's grace. He glanced at the hanex, but Sanbeq didn't notice, too absorbed in telling his tale.

'The daemon got all excited and started asking Mostyn a load of questions about where it'd been found. We could all tell it was something important, but then again something truly valuable would've been better guarded, as opposed to this thing in its puny, weakly-garrisoned fort.

'The baron discussed something with the daemon, and they gave us another mission. Of course, we hadn't received our payment for this one yet and Captain Mostyn wasn't particularly happy about that, but the baron assured us double pay for this mission, plus triple pay for this next one. With those kinds of numbers, we'd be fools to refuse.

'Three weeks later, we were all ready to go. Just as we were pulling up the gangplanks, the daemon came running down the wharf and jumped onto the *Seascale*. Apparently, that was one of the conditions of the voyage, that he would be there to help lead us to our next destination.'

'Where were you going?' asked Gwahl, quietly, knowing the answer.

'Apparently, there were more of those plates on your home. Daemon Isle.'

He exhaled slowly. 'What was the daemon's name?'

'I don't remember. It started with a P, maybe Palan?'

'Paron.'

'Yes, maybe, I don't remember. You knew a Paron?'

'I did, and I know he died at sea. I didn't realise it was aboard the *Seascale*.'

'Not that it was our fault! He jumped aboard, strode up to the captain, and started ordering him about, telling him how he would have no hope of finding the isle without him. The captain didn't take kindly to the insults, but we were getting paid well, so we all bit our tongues and let the daemon assume navigation duties.

'The fool led us to our doom. For weeks we sailed west. Months. Always west, like an arrow, through storms and sandbanks, past unknown islands covered in strange creatures, through mists that rival these, battling stronger currents than we ever had a right to. Eventually, we found what would ultimately end us. A monstrously strong current, bludgeoning its way east through the Great Waters. The daemon seemed pleased to have found it and assured us that at its other end lay the Isle. By now our food had all but run out, so had our water, and our patience. Mostyn told him it was impossible to fight a current that strong, that we would have to find a way around it, but your kinsman would not listen, insisting that such currents surrounded the island on all sides.'

'There are worse things than mere currents surrounding our island,' said Gwahl as he inspected a reed bed for tracks. He nodded approvingly when he found the crushed plants and displaced mud pointing in the direction the trogs' flight.

'That's what he said too. With no other option, we followed his directions and fought the sea. Each time we sailed in we were thrown back, weaker and wearier than before, losing lives with each attempt, but still the accursed daemon pointed west. The final time we sailed into the current, the daemon stood on the prow, like a living figurehead, as we all strained our oars, begging the mast not to split under the strain of the howling winds. We made it further than ever before, but the current only grew stronger, the weather turned foul with hailstones as big as pebbles hammering the deck. Then the wave appeared.

'Forget that one with the neiads. This one was bigger. Easily eighty feet tall, it rushed towards us like a wall of turquoise steel. We waited for it to hit us, nothing else we could do. I pissed myself that day. Wasn't the only one, either. When you see the waters turn on you like that, nobody keeps their cool. But the daemon stood up. I saw him hold the black tablet in front of him. I didn't even know he brought it with him. I don't know what happened next, but one of the others said a light burst from the tablet and shot into the wave, evaporating it into a blinding cloud of mist. I don't know about the light, but I do know the mist is true, and the wave never hit us. I also know the daemon was screaming as he was swallowed in a ball of fire.

'Nobody tried to help him. We were all too afraid. Eventually he jumped into the raging sea, still screaming. For our part, the current spat us back out to calmer waters and we returned to Morgenal, defeated. Over half our men died on that voyage because of that daemon's absurd requests. I don't know whether your Isle exists, but I do know it's impossible to reach it by that road.'

'What happened to the Drac-' he caught himself, '–the – the black tablet?'

'We wanted nothing to do with your daemon magic. At first, we thought it was lost in the sea, but we later found it stuck in the bulwark next to our figurehead. I wanted to throw it away, but Mostyn kept it. A good thing, too, because Baron Pesk wouldn't give us any money at first, she was upset about the daemon dying, but Mostyn whipped out the tablet and gave it to her in exchange for full repairs for the *Seascale*, compensation for the lost souls, and money to hire a new crew. Eventually we walked away from those two missions with no profit, and much pain.'

'The baron still has it?'

'I don't know, she might still have it, she might've sold it. Makes no difference to me.'

'Do you have any idea what it was?'

'Some daemon artefact, nothing that good people should interfere with.'

Gwahl smiled, despite himself. 'It is not daemonic, bosun, but you're right to say that it shouldn't be interfered with.'

'Well anyway, that was the one voyage that was disastrous. Apart from this one. Come to think of it, both voyages where things went bad included a daemon. I think your kind are bad luck.'

'So I'm told.'

Gwahl stopped suddenly. He held up a hand for silence, gazing ahead into the swirling mists.

'Bad luck on voyages at sea, maybe, but not in hunting,' he whispered. 'Heard a croak from ahead, where the tracks lead. I reckon we've found them.'

They proceeded with caution, doing their best to remain silent. In fairness, the pirates were stealthy enough, only squelching into the mire a few times. Gwahl could sense their excitement. Their fast, shallow breathing, their constant fidgeting, the awful sound of their grinding teeth. For his part, he was calm as ever and moved forward with silent feet, easing apart reedbeds and sliding in between cattails. Another croak sounded, closer this time. He glanced back to the pirates. Both nodded in unison, acknowledging the sound.

He continued, keeping his eyes sharp, ignoring the phantom shapes of the fog and concentrating on true, physical things. Seconds later, hunched figures materialised before him out of the grey wall. He drew his dirk. Behind him came the low swoosh of drawn cutlasses. Without needing any orders, Fedza and Sanbeq spread out from behind to surround the troglodytes. They converged.

Closer, he saw them. Four, clustered around two fallen bodies. No surprise. He knew the soldiers were dead as soon as they went missing, their task was killing the four. Glancing to both srides, he saw the pirates were quickly approaching their opponents, hungry for blood. Had this been a mission requiring stealth and guile to stalk an able soldier, he would've been concerned about their tunnel-visioned approach, but the trogs had other things on their minds.

It was over in a matter of seconds. Sanbeq jumped forward and hacked through the neck of one, Fedza disembowelled the second and viciously fell on the third, slicing him apart. Gwahl took care of the fourth, grabbing her around the shoulders and sliding his blade between her skull and first vertebra. She shuddered in his grasp, and he eased her to the ground.

Looking up at the others, it was disappointing to see them still hacking at the carcasses. Eyes wild, teeth bared, spittle foaming at the corners of their mouths. Animals. He waited for them to satisfy their frustration. Once both were panting and dripping with sweat, he quickly inspected the fallen Council Guard. Long dead. Cut throats, half-chewed limbs, empty eyes.

Shrugging, he dragged all six corpses into the nearest peat bog and pushed them in. Fedza and Sanbeq didn't help. They sat dull-eyed, swords still drawn, blood crusting on their blades and clothes. Like an addict after ingesting that first dose of Azag syrup. Vengeance was a far deadlier drug.

Chapter 15

'Dead?'

Spotal sat with Noswen, a short distance away from the main group. During Gwahl's absence, they'd led the group to a decent campsite, almost exactly as Spotal described. A loose ring of grassy hummocks, six in total, with a depression in between half-filled with reeds. The ground wasn't as dry as Gwahl would have liked and neither were the grassy mounds tightly clustered enough to create the natural wall he'd hoped for, but it was better than camping out in the open, and just about dry enough to stay for a few days.

'Did you expect anything else?' the daemon sat next to his friends, suddenly tired.

'No,' admitted the calef. 'Did you at least kill their captors?'

'Our pirate friends saw to that.'

'Slaughtered them, did they?'

'You should've seen them. Very angry.'

'No discipline,' muttered Noswen.

'Can't expect much more from thieves,' Spotal shook his head.

'Honestly, I'm not too concerned about their methods right now, as long as they do their duty,' said Gwahl.

'For now,' agreed Spotal. 'In time, their methods might lead to difficulties. Do they intend to stay for long?'

'I don't know,' admitted Gwahl, wearily. 'I didn't ask. I think it's good to keep them around, to help us guard our lost lambs,' he gestured to their disorientated companions, milling about the reed-bed in a daze. Eventually they all sat, one by one, slumping heavily onto their rears. He shook his head. The dull-eyed soldiers were as sorry a site as children with minds of rot, wandering the slums of Morgenal.

'How will you heal them?' asked Spotal, following his gaze.

'Slowly, with water and fire, I'll drive the fog out of their heads.'

'What will we do for food?'

'There's plenty of food to be found here, you only have to know where to look. While we were travelling, I didn't have time to forage, but now we have a campsite, I can provide for us.'

'Not if you're healing the others,' said Noswen. 'You won't have time. It would be best if you showed me and Spotal how and where to find this food.'

Gwahl nodded. 'You're right, tomorrow I'll show you how to catch frogs and herons, what parts of bulrushes and water chestnuts are edible, where to find dandelions and watercress. The most important thing right now is clean water. We need wood for a fire.'

'There are shrubs everywhere, we can use them,' Noswen grimaced.

'They'll burn with much smoke and little heat, but I suppose we have no other option,' said Gwahl.

'What will we use to hold the water?' asked Spotal.

'Pwtrek's plate armour, helmets, shields, anything we have.'

Noswen stood and walked away into the swamp, calling over her shoulder. 'I'll get us started with as many shrubs as I can find. We better get this fire going before sundown.'

*

Upon drinking that first mouthful of hot water, his spirits lifted. It tasted metallic, but clean, which was most important. His contraption for collecting clean water consisted of their fire, as smoky as Noswen promised, with three helmets filled with unclean water hanging from a spit over the flames. Above the helmets was Lidan's shield, with the steel-plated surface facing the water-filled helmets at an angle. As the water boiled, the steam rose, condensed on the shield, and ran down its surface to drip onto Pwtrek's steel cuirasses, both of which were somewhat spoon-shaped, and served a previously-unknown secondary function to collect the clean water. The water in the helmets would often need replacing, and the helmets required cleaning of the muck left behind, so they were kept busy making trips back and forth to the nearest stagnant pool to collect new water to be boiled.

After that first beautiful sip of water, he gave some to Spotal and Noswen, then Sanbeq and Fedza, followed by the rest of their company. It was a small challenge to ration the water between their incapacitated friends. In their sorry states, they clung to him as he fed them, clawing at the water in desperate greed.

'Easy, my friend,' he soothed Lidan, easing Pwtrek's poleyn from his lips. 'There'll be none left for everyone else.'

Lidan whimpered like a child and snatched at the poleyn, but Gwahl was too quick and swerved out of the way. He approached his next patient, Widrias. As with the others, their commander had an expressionless face, limp limbs, red eyes from sleepless nights. As always, Gwahl saved him for last. He needed time to fully inspect the leg.

As expected, it was inflamed, angry, crusted in old pus. Fortunately, the tissue was still alive, lacking the duskiness of necrosis. Just a localised infection. For now. It wouldn't take much for it to go the same way as Simef. He washed the area of filth with boiled rags and made a small incision into the leg. Stinking pus oozed. With gritted teeth, he massaged the leg, drawing the infection from the tissues in pulsations of foul fluid. Once done, he wrapped the leg back up in a loose linen bandage and propped it up on a small branch to keep it from the mud. Not once during the whole procedure did the satorr shout out or resist in any way.

Gwahl sat back and scrubbed his hands clean, just as Spotal approached him with handfuls of bulrushes.

'So how do we eat these?'

'You don't,' smiled Gwahl. 'The parts you eat are the rhizomes, the bits you left in the ground. These are no good.'

The calef huffed and threw away the useless harvest of inedible plants.

'I did wonder, I must admit.'

'We'll be here for long enough for you to be a master swamp forager.'

'Hopefully not too much of a master. How long do you think it'll take?'

'No longer than a week.'

'Not too bad. Unless we're found before then.'

'That's my one concern,' he admitted.

'There's not much we can do about that. We need a place to stay otherwise we'll never get through this.'

'I know, we'll just have to remain vigilant.'

'What will we do for food when we reach Tarnegrefur?'

Gwahl grimaced and clicked his tongue against his palate. 'It'll be difficult. There should be some goats, moose, and other mountain animals to hunt, but they aren't exactly teeming with life. We'll have to stock up on what we can from the swamp.'

Spotal rubbed his eyes and exhaled sharply between gritted teeth. 'Who'd have thought such a simple-sounding journey would develop into such a challenge?'

'I've been on far simpler-sounding journeys, all of which turned out far more challenging than this one.'

He yelped as Spotal flicked mud at his face.

'You always do that. Mention some grand old adventure once upon a time, which without fail was more challenging than our current one!'

'One of the advantages of being a seasoned old grump,' he winked.

The calef scratched behind his ear with a claw. 'Well, it's irritating. I don't want to hear about how your other quests were so much bleaker than this one. Let me wallow in my misery.'

Gwahl chuckled. 'In years to come, you can do exactly the same when some young calef complains about a trip down the river.'

'I look forward to it. I'll have the same smug grin that *you* have as well!'

*

'That hurts!' exclaimed Widrias as Gwahl gently cleaned his wound, now a daily routine in the festering swamp.

'I know, but pain is better than numbness.'

'Perhaps for the healer, not so much for the patient.'

'Pain shows it's still alive and healing. If I didn't do this, then think of how awful the numbness of an amputated limb would be.'

'I knew an old veteran once,' said Spotal, crouched over a shield filled with ground bulrush rhizomes. 'He'd lost his left leg in battle, but said he could still feel the leg and wiggle his toes.'

'The mind is mysterious, it can play tricks on your body after trauma. Think about how on a battlefield you could be gravely wounded but fight on and it's only after the combat is settled that you feel pain.'

'Battlefield anaesthesia,' nodded Widrias. 'Designed by the body so that immediate action can be taken to avoid further damage. A part of the fight-or-flight reaction, where pain would be a hindrance in the situation. I know some physiology. Or I did, before all this.'

Gwahl nodded. His friends were finally coming out of the fog. 'Then put that knowledge to good use and rest your leg. The more you rest it, the sooner we'll be able to get moving.'

'I can put my weight on it now.'

'Good, but I'd rather wait a little longer, just to be sure.'

He stood and surveyed their camp. For four days they'd squatted in the same place, slowly filling their water-skins with the collected water, tending their fire and living off the swamp. Auran proved an excellent forager, to the extent Gwahl suggested he drop all other duties and concentrate solely on gathering food for them. He was more than happy to accept the responsibility.

Spotal on the other hand, while being a capable forager, clearly disliked the process. Instead, he gave him the duty of preparing food. For some reason, the calef took to it with great enthusiasm and spent much of his day cleaning their harvests, boiling, and preparing meals for his companions. When Gwahl showed him how to grind down the bulrush rhizomes into a sweetish flour to make small flatcakes, Spotal excitedly began throwing more and more ingredients into the mix. Chopped water chestnuts, watercress, dandelion roots, all went in, and the resulting flatcakes were not only nutritious and tasty, but ideal for storing for long journeys. As more and more of their companions recovered from their dazed states, they joined him in his culinary crusade. Such as it was, the newly-appointed cooks, with Spotal at their head, were churning out masses of flatcakes for them to carry with them through the swamps and – hopefully – to Tarnegrefur.

Reluctant to join them in their preparations for the journey were Sanbeq and Fedza, both of whom grew increasingly restless and agitated. Like any other addiction, it seemed their indulgence of bloody violence had awoken a hunger for more. To keep them from running off into the swamp on an avenging hunt, he gave them the duty of patrolling the perimeters of their camp. Noswen went with them. He hoped their fear of the assassin would overcome their thirst for violence. So far, it worked, but it wouldn't last.

'How much longer is "a little longer"?' asked Widrias.

'Two more days,' said Gwahl, plucking the number out the air. 'You'll thank me for it before the end.'

'I will not die in this swamp, Gwahl,' he hissed. 'If I must go, it'll be on the battlefield, fighting to my last.'

'Then you must rest.'

'We are wasting time.'

'You set the pace, sir, and you need more time.'

With that, he left the satorr and sat next to Lidan, who was helping Spotal grind rhizomes into a soft mush. The boy handed him a few water chestnuts to cut up and add to the mix. Gwahl smiled gratefully and lost himself in the task of cooking.

*

Two days later and it was time to leave. To Gwahl's regret, one of the soldiers, a man called Stemen, proved too lost. Despite efforts to restrain him, he wandered off into the swamp one night and was never seen again. He hoped it was a bog that claimed him.

All things considered, they were doing well, but it was high time to leave. What was initially a welcome respite was now a nidus of frustration. A tense atmosphere of forced restraint permeated the hummocks, exposed by glowering stares and sullen murmurs. By the end, the pirates seemed almost pleasant company.

Yes, he was more than glad to be on their way again.

Widrias stood some way away from them, leaning heavily on his scabbard. He glanced at him.

'Ready?'

Gwahl looked at their companions, gathering their belongings and shouldering packs. 'In a few minutes.'

'Good, we've lingered for long enough.'

'Your leg is much better now, is it not?' he asked, sweetly.

Widrias gently rocked on his feet to put more and more weight on his left. 'It is better. I don't know for how long it'll hold up.'

'For long enough, I'm sure. If you feel it troubles you at any point, let me know straight away.'

'So you can force us to stop again and fuss over me? Unlikely. We've wasted too much time already. One thing we don't want is to be caught in the Tarnegrefur Mountains in winter.'

Gwahl snorted. 'Winter is still some time away.'

'How do you know? I've completely lost track of time here, we might have been here for an entire season for all I know.'

'It isn't winter, not yet. Autumn is certainly upon us, but we won't be caught on the mountains to be frozen.'

'Autumn will make those peaks cold enough. We might yet freeze, Gwahl.'

'We will not.'

'I hope you're right,' the satorr's head dropped. 'We cannot fail, Gwahl, the Council is depending on us.'

'I know.'

With that, Widrias turned to address what remained of their company.

'Soldiers of the Council, it's time we once again do battle with the marshes. Keep together, watch your feet, and we'll have nothing to fear. We've seen the worst this swamp has to throw at us, and we remain. Tarnegrefur awaits us!.'

*

They soon came to realise that they had everything to fear.

Stemen had not been claimed by a bog, as Gwahl hoped. He couldn't know for sure his exact fate, but there were plenty of possibilities. Perhaps he'd got stuck in a mire and floundered until a trog happened upon him, perhaps he stumbled into a golem's lair, perhaps the trogs knew where they were all along and were just biding their time. Either way, it didn't matter much

Spotal heard them first. Ears flattened in fear as he reported it to Gwahl. He heard it soon after. A faint croaking and clamouring in the distance. Widrias paled at the news. A new wave of panic rippled through the company. They ran. Gwahl and Auran stayed behind to conceal their tracks as best they could.

It was practically impossible to cover them. The mud was too thick, the moss too delicate, and the passing of forty-odd running boots was engraved into the ground like a message on a stone tablet. Nevertheless, they did their best, creating false trails into the swamp, bending bulrushes back into place, confusing the tracks in the slime.

It wasn't enough.

Snatches of the approaching hunters floated through the mist. First distant, now less so. Brief, beautiful periods of silence filled them with cruel hope, only to be shattered by the harsh sound of their pursuers.

It was darkening when they caught up again with the rest of their party, panting and stinking with sweat and fear. He shook his head at Widrias.

'They still approach. There's little we can do to throw them off our trail.'

'Damn them, by the four winds!' Widrias snarled. 'How many?'

'I'd rather not find out.'

'We'll have to find out, we've been running blind all day, for all I know we could have been running south!'

'I'll find north for us.'

'How?' snapped Widrias.

'Call it my daemonic intuition.'

He walked a few paces away. Now for some theatrics. Deia would disapprove of the show, but Deia disapproved of much and it never stopped him before.

Dipped his hands into the filthy water, he stood still, palms outwards. He turned around in a slow circle, mouth open. It would look strange to the others, spinning around, tasting the air, fingers twitching. But that was the point. Adds to the mystery. He wouldn't explain himself. Deia's warnings were for their own protection. These pointless theatrics were just sleight of hand. They could never know the truth. Just let them trust him without an explanation. Let them revel in the mythos of his race.

A familiar sensation at his fingertips, on his lips. Not that he was surprised. He always knew where it was. As much a part of him as his beating heart. His soul. His everything.

He returned to Widrias and motioned over his shoulder. 'North is that way.'

Widrias raised his eyebrows. 'How do you know?'

'I just know.'

Widrias shook his head. Not good enough. Disappointing. Apparently a small explanation was needed. Deia wouldn't have to know.

'I could feel the west wind blowing from my left when I faced that way, so that must be north.'

'You could feel the west wind,' Widrias looked more sceptical than ever, lip curling.

'Yes. I could feel it, taste it, generally I could sense it. It carries with it the warmth of the black desert and decomposing leaves of the Dailas Forest. Trust me.'

The satorr stared at him for a moment. He held his gaze. It was all the information he was willing to give. Even that was too much.

'It's worth a try,' spat Widrias, bitterly. 'Mark it with something and we'll follow it in the morning. From now on you lead us, someone else can join Auran covering our tracks.'

*

The next few days were arduous, but he didn't give up. Every day Widrias pushed them harder, forcing them to run on through the mud, the reeds, the stench, sticking to the maddeningly winding paths around the bogs and pools. Maintaining their heading was increasingly difficult. All the while was the constant threat of the troglodytes, with only a few false trails and ill-concealed tracks protecting them from their hunger.

A difficult few days.

Each night, Widrias would congratulate them, but surviving one more day wasn't enough to lift their spirits. Fear still stalked their shadows, causing each unfamiliar sound to turn into the croak of a troglodyte, each small bush shrouded in fog to turn into a crouching golem, each drip and plop of mud to turn into a stream of blood.

Gwahl fretted about Auran and Lidan, clearing their trail at the rear of the column, willing them to remain two steps ahead of the troglodytes. Each night, a rush of relief met their return. Each morning brought a new wave of concern.

Slowly, the mist snared them again. It started with the justified anxiety of the pursuing trogs, but slowly progressed to a dangerous paranoia. They fidgeted, eyes wide, shoulders hunched. It took time to settle down in the night and morning saw them jump up as the dimmest rays of light penetrated the fog, desperate to be running again. Admittedly, it meant they were making good time, but it was exhausting, even for him. Adrenaline would only carry them so far.

As the days passed, people started disappearing. Consumed by swamp and mist, they never found out what happened to them. The disappearances fuelled the fear. Whispers circulated that the trogs took them in the night. For all he knew, it could be true.

*

At one point, they passed an unusual thing. A thick log placed deeply and securely in the marsh, freshly hewn and polished. Ten paces further on was another, each standing a few feet above the marsh. He leaned against it as his companions ran by.

Unusual things. Not placed by trogs, that's for sure. There were a few odd folk who chose to dwell in the marshes on their own accord, surviving much as they had on the frogs and bulrushes, but this wasn't their style. A shift in the mist revealed another two, parallel to these. Then another two beyond them.

He frowned and ran his hands over the log. Strange things. Monuments to some new deity? Perhaps. Corusul would be worried if he knew, if he were still alive.

Another breath of wind from the west made his ears prick. Bellowed orders, clanging tools. Something organised. He chewed his lip. What?

The final Council Guard passed. No point dwelling on the mystery. With luck, the pursuing trogs would be just as baffled by them as he was. It might make them pause for a second.

Then again, with fresh meat on the menu, it probably won't.

*

A week after passing the forgotten mystery, Gwahl heard Chekry cry out. His heart skipped. His hand instinctively found his dirk, baring his teeth in anticipation for battle. The neiad stood tall, mouth open, pointing over his shoulder.

He spun, ducking low to avoid the strike of anyone who stood behind him. Nobody there. Just a thinning mist and the putrid marsh, stretching for miles around.

A thinning mist?

He smiled.

But the sprawling landscape of bullrushes, reeds, peat bogs, crooked hills, and crippled trees was not what Chekry pointed at. A line of mountains, peaks lost in banks of cloud and covered in snow. They stretched for miles across the lands as a jagged set of teeth, the snow stained crimson in the rising sun like crusted blood.

The sight did wonders. Fears were forgotten as this symbol of hope lifted hearts and souls, filling them with a sense of victory. Widrias practically bounded away, as much as his leg would let him. They were still days away, but at least they could see their goal, and that was enough.

With the unfamiliar warmth of joy, they began the final leg of their journey through the dreaded, blighted, cursed, Cysgodgors Marshes.

Chapter 16

Lidan craned his neck, trying his best to see the peak. At the base of these towering giants, he finally understood their reputation. A kilometre behind, the ground turned from the vile, spongy earth of the marsh to firm, hard rock. Even the mist was left behind, spitting them from its foul prison like a youngster spitting a cherry-stone. Briefly glancing over his shoulder, he vowed to never return. He'd rather face his old gaol than be thrust back into the marsh.

Such an opinion was not universal. Fedza and Sanbeq left them yesterday. They told Noswen first, with whom they'd developed a curious companionship. Whatever her reaction may have been, it couldn't have compared to Widrias.

'Abandoning us?' he seethed.

'The mountains are no place for sailors. We'll stay, kill more trogs.'

'If you leave, then you leave without supplies. Give us all your food,' he held out his hand, expectantly.

'We won't need supplies. We won't be there long enough to starve,' sneered Sanbeq.

'You go there to die?'

'We died when the *Seascale* died, when Mostyn died, when the rest of our crew died. All that's left is revenge.'

Widrias snorted. Sanbeq stepped forward and pointed threateningly at the satorr. Pwtrek jumped menacingly behind him.

'You deserve to die, Wids,' he snarled, ignoring Pwtrek. 'You caused all this. We should kill you… but no. Fedza and I'll satisfy ourselves with trogs. We'll sleep easy with the blissful knowledge that the mountains will kill you.'

'You are fools.'

'As are you.'

With a final, chilling look at them, the two pirates dropped their packs, picked up their weapons, and jogged back to the swamp. They kept their water-skins.

At first, he expected them to return. Now they were at the foot of the mountains with no sign of them, he accepted their departure. Only Gwahl seemed saddened to see them leave, the others were either angry, like Widrias, or indifferent. He had no idea how Noswen felt. Personally, he was of the latter kind, although he hoped the two found what they were looking for in those swamps. Vengeance was a familiar goal, after all. Whether or not they would satisfy their urge was a different question.

Tarnegrefur. The mountains stood before them, the final barrier to the Serpent Key. So tall their tips were lost in the sky, so strong the wind was crushed when it came into contact with their slopes. They were the polar opposite of the marshes, yet the same in many ways. Both were unforgiving, merciless, deadly.

Staring in awe at their majesty, he realised the enormity of their task. Finding a key in these monoliths would be like searching for a single fallen leaf in an autumn forest. Pwtrek was right to have doubts. If the king's hordes couldn't find the artefact, what hope did they have, a company of fewer than twenty? It was foolish to even attempt such a feat.

He was about to voice such opinions when Widrias ordered them on, striking a path to the nearest mountain, leaning ever so slightly on his injured leg. Lidan grimaced and fell in line behind Noswen. When they reached the foot of the mountain, they began their steady ascent. Although the slopes were built of solid rock, there were enough ledges and handhold to grab, making the journey no more difficult than climbing a staircase. A long, cold staircase.

After an hour of climbing, Widrias called them to rest. Lidan sat on his hunches with a sigh. He made the mistake, the cardinal rule when climbing great heights, of looking down. Muffling a cry of surprise with his hand, he caught hold of a nearby ledge. As he teetered, the wind caught him, threatening to drag him over. He would fall to his death. Three hundred feet and then nothing. Another gust of wind flew swiftly and cruelly up the slope, this time throwing him back onto the ledge. Arms shaking, he picked himself up and hugged the side of the mountain. He looked over to Gwahl, chewing a flatcake.

'Is the wind always so eager to try to pull you down?' he asked voice trembling.

'Yes,' said Gwahl. 'You should never stray to the edges for too long, and never stand up tall. Keep low and it makes it more difficult for the wind to get a good grip on you. Believe me, these mountains are treacherous.'

'You've been here before?'

'I've been most places. I've used these mountains as an, admittedly, rather elaborate hiding place. These slopes saved my life more times than I care to remember. Saying that, they've tried to claim it just as often. We have a mutual respect for each other, these mountains and I. Take care around the ledges, Lidan, the wind can turn more quickly up here than anywhere else in Nefarwy. A dangerous place.'

'More dangerous than the marshes?'

'Undoubtedly. You see up there, the highest tips of the mountain, where the snow takes hold? No sounds can be heard, nobody will hear you fall, or scream, or the malevolent laugh of the wind as you plummet to your death. The marshes may be frightening, these mountains are terror.'

Widrias's call to climb brought a surge of relief, an excuse to end the conversation. He'd rather not know how lethal the mountains could be. At times like these, ignorance was bliss.

Two hours later, they hit the first of the snow. It settled deeply on the ledges, making the slopes slippery and treacherous. It soaked his clothes and clung to his hair. The sparse winter clothing that survived the journey so far wasn't enough to keep the chill away. He winced as his fingers felt the icy bite, grimacing as it fell down the back of his shirt.

Carelessly, he shifted his weight onto his right foot, without assessing the foothold first. The veneer of black ice was smooth as glass. His foot slipped off as soon as he transferred his weight. It was only his quick reflexes that saved him from plummeting to his untimely demise. Exhaling shakily to calm his thundering heart, he looked for the others. Auran caught his eye and shook his head in a silent warning to take more care.

As if making the climb more treacherous weren't enough, the snow wore their patience thin. He, along with everyone else, grew shorter and sharper with each other, snapping back and forth like wild dogs. Whenever someone fell behind or needed help, they grew haughty, irate, petty. Most times, it was him and Auran who bore the brunt of their irritation. Unused to the altitude and freezing temperature, they were always the last ones to reach a rest stop and Widrias would cruelly only allow them a few minutes' rest before setting off again.

After this happened for the fifth time in the space of an hour, he snapped. Enough was enough. He was as tired as everyone else, what right did Widrias have to punish him for his inexperience? He wouldn't admit it aloud, but there was more than a drop of pride involved. The satorr had a wounded leg, but still endured where he faltered.

Mere moments after he and Auran dragged themselves onto the ledge where the others rested, Widrias gave the order to move. Pent-up frustration burst forth. He stood his ground and faced the satorr, urging his teeth to cease their chattering, lest he look a fool.

'No, sir. We need more rest.'

Widrias started in surprise. 'What?'

'Auran and I, we only just made it up here. I'm telling you now we need more rest to regain our strength.'

His ears burned from a mixture of freezing wind and fierce embarrassment. They were all staring at him, eyebrows raised, lips curling in amusement as they waited for the general's response.

'But we must keep moving, Lidan. Surely you can see that to linger here in the cold would be our undoing? You wouldn't wish us to suffer now, would you?'

'Sir, I cannot help but think you're punishing us for something we can't control.'

'How am I punishing you?' asked the satorr, his tone harsh.

'We've had next to no experience travelling in this climate. It's difficult to keep up.'

'Can't keep up with me? The one with a mangled leg?' he laughed, bitterly.

'We've never been anywhere like this before, it's completely new to us,' he insisted.

'Are you implying we aren't struggling too?' snarled Chekry.

'No, but you're more used to it than us, so you know how to deal with it better,' replied Auran, shivering violently.

'It seems to me like you two are being lazy!' shouted Depani, jumping to her brother's defence. 'If we can climb, so can you!'

'Perhaps we should leave you behind,' muttered one of the Council Guard, Ghankul, in an off-hand comment.

The others turned to stare at him. Lidan shook his head slowly, all traces of anger replaced by shock. He probably didn't mean it, he probably said it without thinking, perhaps he didn't even realise he was saying it aloud. But the fact he could even have such a thought was crushing. Ghankul flushed, surprised by his own callousness.

'How could you say that?' he asked, trying to catch his eye. 'We're as much a part of this quest as you are. All we ask is you slow the pace a little! Don't punish us like this.'

'Back to the punishing, eh, Lidan?' cried Widrias, 'Why are you so sure that we have something against you? Why are you so certain that everybody here is your enemy? All we're trying to do is reach the summit by sundown. To do that, we're going to have to keep up a good pace, and you, my friend, are holding us back!'

'Would you stop bickering?' Pwtrek roared, rising to his full height. 'I am ashamed, truly ashamed to call you my companions when you act like pathetic infants. General, all they ask is you wait for a few minutes longer at each rest stop for them to catch their breath. It isn't such an unreasonable suggestion. Besides, within fifty feet the ground levels out considerably. We can walk along it, and the climbing will be over. We can rest there for a while. When we can calm down and grab a bite to eat, we can sort out any squabbles, agreed?'

'Pwtrek is right,' said Gwahl. 'I also have a suggestion to make, if you would permit me?' he glanced at Widrias, humbled, who nodded for him to continue. 'Why don't Lidan and Auran go first, so they can set the pace? That way, nobody gets left behind. The untrained have a hard time up here, but they didn't mean to imply the rest of you aren't suffering. These mountains take a considerable toll. This is but one of the obstacles we shall face.'

Uncomfortable apologies were exchanged and they rested for another five minutes before Lidan and Auran set off again, this time knowing they would dictate when to stop and for how long. In this fashion, the remaining fifty feet were easier, and despite the few frustrated huffs at the slower pace, they made it without much difficulty. It was, as Pwtrek promised, much more even along this part of the mountain, and indeed on each adjacent mountain. It was almost as if the initial climb was a wall, and this was the garden concealed behind, where only the most insistent of thieves would reach. The gentle slope rose up steadily and was lost in the clouds about two hundred feet away. But the peaks weren't their destination. The plateau was hidden somewhere here, and on the plateau, the key.

The continued along the gentle slope until they came across a low overhang, sturdy enough to camp under. Collapsing on the cold rock, they lay where they fell, regaining their breath and shivering against the cold.

His eyelids grew heavy. He was exhausted. When he was young, he could never sleep while cold. Today, for some reason, it didn't bother him. He could rest. In fact, the rock felt as comfortable as a feather bed. Sinking into its folds, he drifted closer and closer to sleep.

Shaken awake. He jumped, but Noswen had already moved on to Auran.

'Stay awake,' Gwahl called from the entrance. 'The cold will kill you if you fall asleep without the proper protection! Everyone up, for Enadir's sake!'

One by one, the rest of the party awoke from their near-slumber and set about preparing suitable places to sleep, eat and discuss their options. Pwtrek shovelled walls of snow around the edges of the overhang to create an artificial cave, for shelter from the wind. They sat in a circle for Widrias's briefing.

'Well done today. We've accomplished a mighty task reaching this far. I know it's been difficult, but I'm proud of you. All of you.'

Lidan smiled. After their disagreement, he was worried he'd fallen out of favour. Widrias caught his eye and nodded, briefly. He nodded back, relieved he was wrong.

'Now,' continued the satorr, 'we're nearing our goal. Somewhere in these mountains lies the plateau where Stolach murdered a company of dreyads in his search for the Serpent Key. I'm not going to lie, it'll be difficult. The king's armies couldn't find it after three days and nights of solid searching. We will succeed – we must succeed – where he failed.

'Tomorrow, we'll head deeper into the mountains. Then, once we find a suitable base, five pairs will set out in different directions and search for the plateau. Once you find it, remember where it is and return to the base. Nobody is to be away for more than four hours. That means a maximum of two hours searching the mountains, then two hours to make your way back. Your own safety depends on you following this rule. I have no wish for any of you to freeze to death. The rest of us will wait where we are and guard our camp.

'The day after tomorrow we'll all go to the plateau and set up camp. Then we can search it until we find the key. Depani, how do our supplies look?'

Depani crawled over to their knapsacks and rooted through them, teeth chattering.

'Maybe enough for about four weeks? But only if we're careful.'

Widrias chewed his bottom lip. 'That might give us about a week to search up here, then three weeks to get to the Kingdom of calefs. We have less time than I initially thought... It matters not! We'll find the plateau by tomorrow and will have the key by the end of the week! Now, everybody get some food and have some rest. Two men on watch, wake another two in three hours to take over, I don't care who.'

*

As it turned out, nobody found the plateau the next day, or even the day after that. Despite searching for longer with each new dawn, it seemed it would never be found. Every day, they set out, marching ever deeper into the heart of Tarnegrefur for the first few

269

hours, choosing a campsite, and setting out on their scouting missions from there. A fruitless search.

Just like in Morgenal, he wasn't trusted to go out on a scouting mission. This time, however, he didn't mind. It meant he could stay in camp, make it ready for nightfall, and concentrate on keeping warm.

Fruitless until, late on the third day, when all other scouting parties had returned, Depani and Jeret, a Council Guard, came bounding across the ice and snow to the camp.

Widrias stormed over, furious. Over six hours late, they'd very nearly given up on them. Convincing Chekry to stay put had taken a combined effort from them all. He'd been ranting at the others, apparently preparing to unleash his anger when their jubilant cries echoed across the snow.

'We've found it! It's here!'

Lidan brightened. Could it be?

Depani skidded to a halt and saluted the general, beaming.

'We found it, sir, Jeret and I found it.'

'Where? How far?'

'Wouldn't it be better to have this discussion inside?' Gwahl said, stepping out from the overhang of their latest camp.

'Yes, certainly, get out of the cold,' nodded Widrias, ushering them inside, eager to hear their report.

It was crowded beneath the overhang, and far warmer than outside thanks to Pwtrek's experienced construction. It was one of Lidan's little victories over the last few days. While the scouts were away, the juggernaut taught him the basics of building snow caves. The snowy walls acted as natural insulation, trapping the heat of the cave. The rest of their companions lounged about, resting, eating, maintaining their equipment. When Depani entered, all activity ceased, apart from Chekry.

'Idiot!' he shouted, rushing to his sister, bent double to avoid knocking his head on the low ceiling.

'Can't call the neiad of the hour an idiot,' she chuckled, grabbing her brother in a headlock.

'Surprised you know what an hour is, because you're over six of them late,' he wriggled free from her grip and tackled her to the ground, nearly crushing Auran's pack as they wrestled.

'Alright, alright, I give up,' Depani laughed.

'Admit you're an idiot?'

'Yes!'

'And I'm the better fighter?'

'Fat chance, I've been scouting for six hours longer than you.'

'Your own fault for being an idiot.'

'Your fault for being so fat. Never going to out-wrestle a whale, am I?'

'Enough now,' smiled Widrias, sitting down beside them. 'You'll have time to argue later. Now, where's the plateau, Depani? Is it far?'

'It's some distance away, east by northeast,' she brushed stray snowflakes from her coat. 'Jeret and I crossed eight peaks before we found it. The route itself is fairly easy, there are patches of deep snow that we should avoid, and I nearly lost my footing at one point where the wind is channelled between two walls, but apart from that, not too bad.'

'How long will it take us?'

'It took us around six hours to reach it, but only four and a half on our return journey once we knew what routes to avoid. Saying that, we set a good pace and had little to carry. If I had to guess…I'd estimate we reach it within five hours, perhaps a little more?'

'Ah, it's so close,' sighed Widrias. 'What did the plateau look like? Did you see anyone?'

'Not another soul. It's wide and flat, as if someone took a whopping big axe and cut the top half off a mountain, leaving its stump. Like a big empty lake. We didn't stay for long. We knew we were running late, so I can't give too much detail.'

'Don't worry, you've both done well. We'll have it soon!'

Pwtrek snorted quietly, but not so quiet that Lidan, didn't hear. He smiled. So stubborn! Nothing would change his mind about it, he probably wouldn't even believe in it if he held it in his own hands. Unless it was all a grumpy act to hide his hopes.

'I think that you secretly *do* believe in the key, Pwtrek.'.

Pwtrek laughed softly. 'You're not far from the truth. I dearly want to believe in it. If, by some miracle it does exist, it makes this war so much easier to win. But realistically, the chances of it existing, or finding it if it does exist, are tiny. It's easier to prepare for the worst, but desperately hope for the best.'

'I'd never put you down as a pessimist,' commented Gwahl, sitting on a rock beside them.

'How did the king lose the key on the plateau? If he had an army searching for it how come he didn't find it?' Lidan asked it quietly, so that only the other two would hear.

As Pwtrek growled his agreement. Gwahl replied. 'That's because the king is a unique character. He's cunning, ruthless, and undeniably intelligent, he's skilful and strong and brave. But he's also impatient. He overlooks obvious things. He only sees what he wants to see. That's why he didn't find it. He can be deceived, especially if a doubt is already in his mind. There are a few secrets that Stolach will forever remain unaware of.'

'I saw the king once,' he said. 'He didn't strike me as the kind who would fall for a lie. He just looks straight through you.'

'That may be because you're too honest, Lidan,' chuckled Gwahl. 'No, I know of one definite creature who could lie to him, who could manipulate and deceive him.'

'Who?' asked Pwtrek, curiously.

'Come on, Pwtrek, you know. The king's old teacher, the old sage from his past. I met him once, after he'd left the king's service.'

'You met him?' gasped Pwtrek. 'You are full of surprises, Gwahl! Tell me, what deceptions did he pull on Stolach?'

'Trivial things, Pwtrek, little lies that gave him power and wealth, sometimes security. By concealing certain facts, he ensured that when Stolach grew tired of his teachings then he would be able to survive and evade his wrath. They didn't trust each other, by the end.'

'Is he still alive?' asked Pwtrek. 'He could have valuable information about the king?'

'No, he died years ago. He was very old and tired, wearied by his wanderings through Dailas. I last saw him in a cave, lying on a stone ledge, waiting for death. He spoke to me as a kind of confession. When our conversation was finished, he invited me to stay the night, in the morning he was gone.'

'What did he look like?'

Lidan jumped. Noswen perched next to him. He never realised she was there, lurking in the shadows.

'Don't you know?' growled Pwtrek. 'I'd have thought that as Stolach's favourite pet, you'd have seen him plenty of times.'

'Never,' she hissed. 'I always assumed he was little more than a story, some ghoul created to frighten people; a mysterious old man with great knowledge of everyone and everything, waiting to rule the world.'

'You expect us to believe that?'

'The truth is the truth, Pwtrek, whether you believe it or not. Contrary to what you seem to think, I didn't spend all my waking hours with the king. In fact, I was hardly ever in his presence.'

'Too busy murdering?'

'Enough, Pwtrek,' warned Gwahl. 'No need to fight. Noswen, the sage was real.'

'Still doesn't explain why Stolach didn't find the key,' said Lidan, returning to his original question.

'I told you, he is impatient and overlooks things, that's why.'

'But not everyone in his army was impatient and overlooked things, surely someone would have seen it in the three days they were there? Besides, if it's as featureless as Depani said, there can't be that many places to hide it?'

'What if it's already been found by the twelve who remained?' Pwtrek rubbed his chin. 'How would we know?'

'If it was found I can assure you we'd have found out by now,' said Gwahl. 'As for why it has remained hidden for the past sixteen years, despite so many people searching? Don't know. They weren't looking hard enough, or didn't know what they searched for.'

'So what will we do differently?' Pwtrek grunted.

'A fresh set of eyes. Experience. Noswen's seen several keys in the past, she knows what to look for. As do I.'

'A weak argument,' said Pwtrek, smiling. 'You're suffering from a desperate hope that this key exists, nothing more.'

'No, I know it exists…' his voice trailed off.

Pwtrek's smile turned into a deep frown, burrowing his eyes beneath his heavy brows.

'Have you never considered these questions? Surely you must have been suspicious that it wasn't found after so long? On that note, why have you never looked for it yourself?'

Gwahl opened his mouth to reply, but said nothing, and fell into silence. He had an unusual expression on his face which Lidan couldn't identify. Was it irritation? Anxiety? Stubbornness? Or was it something worse, something so awful that he would never admit it. Was it realisation?

Whatever it was, it was unsettling. He glanced at Pwtrek, who looked equally concerned. Perhaps he'd been expecting, hoping, for a good answer from the daemon and now that none was forthcoming, he regretted asking the question. The conversation promptly ended. A brooding silence remained.

Chapter 17

He shivered as he trudged through the trench dug by Pwtrek. The juggernaut was acting as a plough for the rest of the company, battering his way through the deep snow to clear a path for his companions. Lidan could hardly see above the snowy walls. He shuddered to think how difficult it would've been for them to journey through the snow without his aid. Worse still, they were still on the first mountain of the day. Apparently it snowed heavily during the night and after twenty minutes of Pwtrek's steady work, they'd barely travelled more than five hundred metres.

One advantage of the slow pace was the fact that he was no longer hampering the rest of the company. The trench also offered them at least some protection from the biting winds. Ever since that first ascent, he'd grown fearful of the wind, its fickle nature, its malicious intent.

They travelled in silence, each concentrating on securing steady footing before transferring their weight. Those at the back had it worst. With the passing of so many boots, the ground was flattened and compressed, until it was as slippery as a sheet of thin ice over marble.

Again, he shivered, clenching his jaw to stop his teeth from chattering. He crossed his arms before his chest and drew his brigandine tighter around his body. Never before in his life had he felt so cold. If it weren't for the trench's walls, the chill of the wind would surely freeze his blood, lock his limbs, and tear them from his body even as he walked.

He stumbled and fell heavily on the ground, scratching his cheek on a jagged shard of ice. He cried out and sat on his hunches, nursing his cheek. Auran was quickly beside him, helping him up off the floor, brushing snow from his clothes.

'On your feet, Lidan,' he said. 'Brush off all the snow from your body, good boy. I don't like it here either.'

'Sorry, didn't mean to fall.'

'Nonsense. We're sticking together, alright? We have to.'

He nudged him on and quickly caught up with the others.

*

After five hours of walking, the company reached the fifth mountain. It was the highest peak yet, climbing a good twenty metres higher than the previous four and was much colder for it. As Depani warned, the incline was fairly gradual and easy-going, but the snow was deep. Even Pwtrek was too short to reach to bottom of some snow-drifts. Fortunately, there were always other routes. On their way down from the peak, it began to snow again. At first, it fell lightly, a mere sprinkling of powder. As the hours trickled by, the shower grew heavier and heavier, until the air was filled in a blinding flurry.

He raised his arm to shield his eyes from the onslaught of the cold, shaking his head to dislodge the settling flakes, but they were soon replaced by more. Soon, their heads were helmeted by a cap of snow, like the foamy head of a tankard of ale. It clung to their shirts, their trousers, their jackets, settled in the rings of their chainmail and on the plates of their brigandines, covered their weapons in frost. Soon, they were perfectly camouflaged with the surrounding terrain. Walking snowmen in the mountains, like the bedtime stories his mother used to tell.

At first, he found it funny, but his amusement was short-lived. With the blinding flurry saturating the sky, it was difficult to look around and now they were camouflaged, he was losing the others. A shallow pass provided a brief respite, but when he emerged on the other side, Pwtrek's trench was gone.

Directionless, he wandered aimlessly. He called out to them, screaming their names above the wind. Turning, he wandered the slope, panic setting in. Up here, alone in snow and ice, he would die. An ignoble end to his journey.

'Lidan!'

It came from his left. He didn't recognise the voice, it was too muffled by the snow.

'Here!' he cried, desperately, 'I'm here!'

'Lidan!'

'Here! Please! By the north winds, please!'

'…Find you!'

It sounded further away.

'No! Here! Come back!'

He scampered away, to where he thought the voice was coming, but the wind distorted the voices, threw them away, only to bring them back from a different direction.

'Help me, please! I'm here!'

No answer. There was nothing around him, only grey and white. He stumbled on, crying out with each step, begging them to find him. He tried making it back to the pass. No use. He could hardly see four paces in front of him. The calls stopped coming. Now there was only the whistling cackle of the wind, tearing through the mountain.

He tripped and fell heavily into the snow. It stung his cheek. He would have wept had he not been too afraid of the tears freezing his eyes shut. All sense of direction lost, he forced himself to his feet and wandered on.

'Lidan!'

'Yes! Please help me! I'm here!'

'...are you? Coming to…where you…'

'What? I can't hear!'

Silence.

'I'm here!' he bellowed, as loud as he could. His throat hurt from shouting. He waited for their reply. The wind buffeted him where he stood, trying to knock him over. Growling, he stood firm.

'Lidan!'

Louder than even before, from straight ahead. Sobbing with relief, he ran, falling through the thigh-high snow to reach the voice.

Out of the white, a black shadow materialised.

'Pwtrek!' he cried.

It wasn't him. A cliff of black rock, nothing more, against which the wind threw the voices of his companions, bouncing them back to confuse him, trick him, beat him. Defeated, he sank to the ground, enveloped in snow. Lost.

'Lidan!'

He ignored the call. The wind would gain no more joy from his sorrow. Crueller than any troglodyte, golem, or goblin, an enemy impossible to defeat. He could try to dig a snow-cave, somewhere to wait until the storm passed by, but was too inexperienced. Pwtrek's lessons had been too brief. Built incorrectly and it might collapse. He'd suffocate. Then again, if he didn't, he would freeze. Suffocation or freezing? He'd heard tales that suffocation was painful. Apparently freezing was just like going to sleep. He sniffed, he was quite tired, after all.

He prayed one final time to the north winds to save him. No response. He didn't expect any. Just the silence of the snowstorm.

He closed his eyes. Suddenly, the snow was no longer harsh on his cheek. There was no sharpness, no bite. As soft as a feather bed, he nestled deeper. On the bright side, he was as far away from his old dungeon as he could possibly be.

Above, the wind turned and stilled, only for a second. Within that second, came a voice.

'Lidan!'

He stirred.

'Lidan! Where are you?'

He groaned. The snow was losing its softness, growing harder, hotter, burning his skin.

'By the bane of the giants, Lidan.'

Hard hands were thrust beneath his arms, hauling him to his feet. He blinked.

'Gwahl?'

'Come with us, we need to get to the others,' shouted Gwahl. Noswen and Auran stood behind him, the former seemingly-unaffected by the snow, the latter shivering uncontrollably.

'You found me.'

'Of course I did,' Gwahl smiled.

'I got so lost.'

'You're not the only one. Storm blew us all apart, but we're all back now, now I've got you.'

With Gwahl's hand firmly around his waist, he clung to his friend's shoulders, too afraid to let go. He didn't know where the daemon was taking him, the snow was still falling too heavily for him to see. It didn't matter. He'd been found. He was safe.

Somehow, Gwahl guided him back to the others, clustered around a rock, sheltered somewhat from the snow. Everyone else was there. Pwtrek embraced them both. Lidan tried to untangle himself from the juggernaut's iron grip, but Pwtrek held him tighter.

'Don't, I'm warming you up. Must be half-frozen.'

'Found him lying in the snow,' mumbled Gwahl, voice muffled.

'Bloody storm. Bloody mountains.'

Sensation gradually trickled back into his limbs, bringing unwelcome pins and needles as his blood worked its way through his extremities. He shivered and Pwtrek finally released him.

'Have some food, get your strength back. Everyone,' Pwtrek ordered.

Nobody argued. Even Widrias sat down and dutifully ate a flatcake. Once they'd finished their meal, Widrias addressed them.

'That can't happen again. Six of us lost within a few minutes, it's a miracle we all survived. We'll tie ourselves together again, like we did in the marshes.'

Lidan bound himself between Auran and Jeret. Once satisfied they were all secured to the line, they continued marching.

As if by some cruel joke, after twenty minutes of walking, heads bowed against the wind and snow, the sky cleared. As quickly as it came, the storm ended, as if the mountains, seeing their rope, had grown bored of its cruel game. Even so, they kept themselves linked, in case Tarnegrefur decided to throw another storm their way.

In the confusion, they'd veered slightly off course. With less than an hour left of daylight, they reached it.

He ate another flatcake, looking down at the plateau from their camp on a neighbouring slope. Widrias decided not to begin their search until dawn. Cold, tired, and shaken as they were following the fierce storm, nobody complained. Besides, as Depani pointed out, searching an unknown plateau in the dark wasn't particularly safe, with all the hidden crevasses and gorges that one could fall into.

He finished his flatcake. Perhaps he should have another? He was still hungry, after all, and needed the energy to stay warm. Then again, they were supposed to ration them. He shivered and took out another. No point keeping rations for when you're already frozen.

'Why don't we light a fire?'

Auran looked at him, surprised, and shook his head. Spotal leaned over.

'Where would we find wood, my friend? Even if we had wood we wouldn't light it, who knows what enemies may be on these mountains? We wouldn't want to give away our position.'

'Then shouldn't we find a better cave to sleep under?'

Their overhang was shallow, and although Pwtrek did his best to pile up walls of snow to keep the wind at bay, it was by far their poorest shelter to date.

'We'll just have to lie close together, I'm afraid. Keep warm with body heat.'

He nodded. It made sense. Besides, it was far too late to look for a better shelter now. Not that they needed much room. Of the company who set out, only three Council Guard remained, Ghankul, Jeret, and Kres. The others, and Tanor, claimed by sea, swamp, and mountain. If an army of any real strength waited for them down there, they'd be crushed.

Gwahl wasn't with them. Neither was Widrias. They were somewhere outside, discussing what to do tomorrow. Curious, he went to find them. They were sitting together a few paces away, downhill. He approached quietly and they didn't notice him. As he neared, he caught a few snippets of conversation.

'...caves... don't know if it's... might be some difficulty getting past... warn you, there are many... the key, our hopes of victory without it... more cunning than... lie... lured to danger on these mountains... heed my words, general, there are hideous... met a territorial tro-'

Gwahl stopped suddenly when he saw him. He smiled and Widrias beckoned him over. He sat down and wrapped his arms around his legs, holding his knees against his chin.

'Tomorrow will be the beginning of the end, Lidan,' said the satorr. 'We'll finally find the key and return to the Council with our weapon.'

'It might take more than a day. Besides, we don't know who or what may be guarding the plateau,' muttered Gwahl.

Widrias shot him an annoyed look. 'Please, Gwahl, have some optimism. Are you looking forward to returning to Dailas?' he asked Lidan.

He nodded. 'I look forward to returning anywhere, as long as it's far from here.'

Widrias chuckled. 'The sooner we find the key, the sooner we'll be back in our forest. Don't worry, we'll find it soon enough. Everything will be fine.'

Lidan nodded and closed his eyes, nearly missing the disapproving glance Gwahl aimed at the general, and Widrias's arrogant dismissal of it.

'Come Lidan, general,' he said. 'Let's get back to the others before we freeze.'

*

The freezing cold of the mountain was replaced by the blistering heat of a forge. Strapped to a chair facing the raging inferno, he shut his eyes against the glare. Compared to the cold and damp of his cell, the heat was incredible. It was small for a forge, big enough perhaps for one blacksmith and his assistant, no more. Nothing compared to the enormous forges found in the first level, where armourers and sword-smiths toiled night and day to feed the king's machine of war. Then again, this forge wasn't meant for that.

His face dried and crackled as the heat shrivelled his skin. He opened his mouth to scream but as soon as he did, his throat was dried by the heat. All he could manage was a croak. He wanted to cry, but his eyes were too dry to spare the water. After ten minutes of sitting before the furnace, his gaoler closed the opening to the furnace, cutting off the river of heat.

A bucket of freezing water was thrown over him. The chill was just as painful. He gasped, breath knocked out. The gaoler laughed at his discomfort and dragged him to a wall, where he shackled him to the stone. He dangled, watching the gaoler select his tools. From the far wall hung an assortment of utilities; sickles, screws, spikes, pliers. Each one different in appearance and purpose, all used for the same intent.

Grinning evilly, he approached, a pair of iron tongs in hand. Leaning down, he took his foot, and placed one of his toes between the cold iron jaws. Months ago, Lidan might have fought him, but now all he could so was wait for it to begin and pray for its end. The fat man threw his entire weight onto the tools, crushing Lidan's toe between its iron teeth. Blood spurted. Lidan gasped. Breathing through the pain was hard, but he managed. By now, he'd been through it often enough to manage. Another gasp as another toe was crushed. His gaoler sighed with pleasure as his clothes were sprayed with blood and turned back to the wall to select another of his twisted toys.

He selected a thin iron sickle, its serrated edge glinting in the candlelight. Chuckling quietly to himself he grabbed his leg and slowly opened his calves, smiling as he swept through the layers of skin. Next, he set to work on his chest, running the blade along each rib, peeling the skin away to reveal the glistening bone beneath.

Lidan coughed, shaking. The gaoler was skilled. Each cut was deep enough to wound, to burn, to consume his body with pain, but never enough to kill. That was one consolation. He knew he'd never die at this torturer's hands. If you could call it a consolation. His skin was in tatters, his ribs bare, his blood pooling in a miserable puddle at his feet. He coughed again, the movement of his ribs on flayed skin agonizing. No, it was no consolation.

The gaoler turned to the wall, his hands resting on the handle of his favourite toy.

He looked at his gaoler, his torturer, with weak eyes. He no longer had the strength to glare his hatred. All sense of spirit slowly bled from him with each session. The gaoler returned, spiked, spring-loaded device in hand.

He took his dirty foot. He placed it on the device with a smug grin. A tug on a latch and the spring snapped shut, spiked jaws closing around his foot.

His eyes bulged. He opened his mouth wide to gulp in as much air as he could. The pain was too much. Silent, he hung, chest and eyes bulging. Pain washed over him. Finally, he drew a long, ragged breath. His head fell, bordering on unconsciousness.

The cruel, fat torturer laughed and prised apart the blocks. He had difficulty. The device was slippery with blood, difficult to get a secure grip. Finally, he was able to reset the device and tear Lidan's foot from the nails. The gaoler held up the mangled appendage with a bemused look on his face, as if surprised by the damage.

Lidan was dimly aware of a young satorr, newly-appeared and whispering something in the torturer's ear. At first, he snarled, but after the satorr whispered something else the snarl warped into an evil chuckle. He dismissed the satorr and lifted a second bucket of water. Snapped back awake, his breath caught again. Freezing water ran down his body, collecting blood in scarlet rivulets.

He weakly licked some of the water from his lips, releasing the breath in a groan. Torn away from the soothing peace and darkness of unconsciousness. Thrust back into the screaming pain of the waking world, he wailed.

The gaoler leaned forward and whispered into his ear, his words floating through the fog of pain.

'Enough for now, boy. Body is broken enough for this cycle. We'll meet again, when you're nice and fresh.'

He groaned as he was unshackled, supported by his hated torturer. The gaoler half-carried, half-dragged him across the room to a door, his mutilated feet bumping over the stones, bruised, bloodied, and broken.

The door slammed shut, the noise ringing in his ears.

*

He woke on the mountainside, squashed between Spotal and Chekry. Rubbing his eyes with his fists, he thought about his dream, reliving each detail of the horror story that unfolded whenever he slept. Some nights would pass peacefully, others would be torture as he was thrust back to Crastalan. As long as they were only dreams of his imprisonment, or torture, he could endure them. As long as he didn't remember what caused it all. As long as he didn't think of Zile.

Jaw clenched, he promised that one day that hated face would look at him in fear and beg for mercy before he ended the fat torturer's cursed life. He imagined a hundred ways to maim him, before granting him the mercy of his sword.

He shook himself, suddenly ashamed of the pleasure he found in these cruel fantasies. This journey had changed him, there was no doubt about that, but had he changed too much to return to his old life once it was over? Originally, his plan was to help end Stolach's reign, have revenge on the ones who'd made him suffer, and then start a new life in peace. But was that future still there for him? Was he still able to have a peaceful life? Racking his brains, he searched for the name of the hanex he'd killed in the cave with Gwahl, so long ago.

'Dirdin,' he finally whispered. Pent-up tension drained away. As long as he held on to that name, as long as he remembered the face of every goblin, hanex, neiad, and troglodyte he killed, a peaceful future was still possible. He wouldn't become a cold, uncaring killer like the others.

Sitting up properly, he yelped as a gust of wind stabbed through his clothes and wrapped his arms around his body. Around him, his companions slowly stirred into wakefulness, aroused by his cry. Before long everyone was up and stamping their boots in the snow, desperately trying to keep warm in the chill morning.

After a brief breakfast of flatcakes washed down with melted snow, Widrias gathered the party.

'My friends, today we begin our search. The end of the tyranny of the king is in sight. We need only find it and victory shall be assured. Depani said the plateau is deserted, but we know for a fact that Stolach left a dozen soldiers to guard it. Whether they still live I don't know, but we must be on our guard. Now, let us end this.'

He turned on his heel and strode down the mountainside, heading directly to the plateau. One by one, they followed, Gwahl taking the rear.

Lidan stole a quick glance behind. Instead of looking at the plateau, like everyone else, Gwahl watched the surrounding slopes. He frowned. Unusual. He expected him to be as eager as anyone else to find the key, not worry over the surrounding terrain. Perhaps he was watching out for rockfalls or avalanches? Then again, something about the way he circled was unusual. It wasn't the terrain he was looking at, it was something else.

There was a look on his face he'd seldom seen, so rare it took him a while to realise what it was. More than concern, more than worry. Fear.

As he stumbled down the slope, concentrating on his footing, his thoughts wandered back to the broken conversation he'd heard during the night. Gwahl was warning the general of something, something to fear in these mountains, but what? And why should Widrias dismiss it?

*

Half an hour later, they were huddled together on one side of the plateau, staring in silence. It was a marvel. Amid all the giants of the Tarnegrefur Mountains, here was a single flat plateau. It was riddled with crevasses and crannies, not wide enough to fall through, but just big enough to catch an unsuspecting foot, to twist or break an ankle. The rock itself was black, soaking up the sun like a sponge, melting all but the faintest scattering of powder snow. Its warmth was a welcome respite from the freezing mountain. Of course, with such a featureless plateau, there was no shelter from the wind, which howled as it worked its way through the cracks in the stone. He'd never imagined such a place existed.

Gathering his wits, Widrias addressed them. 'Fan out, search the plateau for any sign of life. We must first make sure we're not to be disturbed during our search. Once we've established our safety, we can find a suitable place to set up a camp for the rest of our stay here.'

They nodded and spread out across the plateau, searching for old campsites or the remains of old dwellings. Lidan was on one side of the plateau. If he faced the centre, he could pick out Chekry on the far side. He waved and the neiad waved back. The plateau was flatter than a pane of polished glass. If anyone were here, they'd know about it.

He continued his search, mainly concentrating on the surrounding mountains. A dark spot on one of the surrounding slopes caught his eye. He narrowed his eyes and walked closer. Yes, there it was. A cave on the slope. A chill ran down his spine. He called to Widrias.

The satorr bounded over and leaned close.

'What is it, Lidan, what do you see?'

Lidan stayed still, keeping his eyes trained on the cave. 'You see that cave up there?' Widrias nodded. 'It could be a campsite of some sort?'

Widrias nodded and signalled the others over.

'Lidan found a cave. I don't know if there's anything in there, but it's worth checking. Besides, it would make an ideal campsite for *us* if it is empty. We'll split into four groups of three. One group stays on the plateau, another guards the entrance to the cave, the others go inside, taking flanking positions of each side. Gwahl, you stay here with Jeret and Kres,' he nodded to two of the Guard. 'Auran will guard the entrance with Chekry and Depani. I'll take the left flank with Spotal and Lidan. Noswen, Pwtrek and Ghankul' he nodded to the remaining Council Guard, 'will take the right flank. On my command, move!'

*

The four groups split apart and headed their own directions, to fulfil their orders. Gwahl kicked at a rock. Excluded! Like a child! Kres and Jeret backed away, wary of his anger. He rolled his eyes and watched the mountains. This was not the only cave. There were dozens more. Unusual to have so many. Some must be unnatural. He hoped he was wrong. He thought back to his conversation with Widrias last night. With luck, the satorr might have listened to some of his warnings. Then again, the fact he was marching straight into a cave suggested otherwise.

As he watched the others clamber up the slopes to the cave, he recalled his conversation with Pwtrek and Lidan, the questions asked that he could not answer. Pieces of a puzzle he didn't know existed were falling into place, forming a picture before his eyes, one that looked all too similar to a tragically, horrifically, empty plateau.

He hoped he was wrong.

*

Lidan jogged behind Widrias to the left of the tunnel, breathing lightly as his boots crunched through the snow. He skidded to a halt as they reached the entrance. Noswen led the party on the other side. Auran crouched before the entrance with the neiads, hidden by a snowdrift. Widrias nodded once to Noswen and the two groups ran into the cave.

The cave turned into a tunnel, twelve paces wide, high enough for Pwtrek to stand at his full height.

Someone was here.

Burnt out torches littered the ground, scraps of cloth, footprints, discarded weapons. It stretched back for some distance, dipping up and down a few times and taking a couple of sharp turns. Side tunnels branched off, but they stuck to the main passage. Soon, the light from the entrance was left behind but they weren't left in darkness. A faint glimmer shone in the dark. Torchlight.

He followed the satorr forward, heart in his throat, Spotal close behind. Noswen, Pwtrek and Ghankul could be seen on the other side. They approached the light.

*

Auran peered into the darkness, gripping his battleaxe tightly. Something was wrong. Chekry and Depani shared the sentiment. They were uncharacteristically grim and silent, their hands cradling their crossbows in white-knuckled agitation.

He saw something move in the darkness. A shadow against the dark. He growled a warning to the neiads. They nodded. They'd seen it too. He stepped forward into the cave, the twins covering him with their crossbows. He took a tentative step inside, then another. He forced himself to relax. A pulled muscle up here would be disastrous. A bead of sweat trickled down his forehead.

He froze. Someone was close by, not five paces away. Something skulking in the darkness. He breathed slowly and deeply, preparing for the inevitable clash. Shifting his weight to his front foot, he raised his battleaxe a fraction. He strained his eyes and ears in the dark, making his final judgements.

Roaring, he sprang forward, swinging his axe in a precise, clean, controlled swipe to his right. He was rewarded with a cry, followed by an impact. Vibrations reverberated up his arm as his weapon met flesh. No time to pause to assess the damage. He dropped to one knee and rolled back to the safety of the sunshine outside. As he rolled, something passed within a hair's breadth of his back. Two musical twangs of the twins' crossbows sang as they fired their quarrels into the darkness.

Recovering from his roll, he stared into the darkness. Two puddles of blood spread from the cave. He sniffed and nodded to the twins. They retreated a few steps back from the cave, reloading their weapons. They didn't wait for long. Two men clad in the scale mail and surcoats rushed from the cave. The neiads bolts thudded harmlessly into their raised shields. The first was cut down by the Chekry's swift blade. The second barely had time to raise his sword before battleaxe and rapier tore into him. Three more jumped out when the two fell.

Auran smiled grimly and held his axe high. Past wounds would never be forgotten and he would someday have retribution, but for now, these pawns would do.

*

Sounds of battle echoed down the tunnel. He froze and turned, searching the blackness for the source of the clash. Spotal nudged him forward.

'It's coming from the entrance. Seems like we've been lured into a trap,' he whispered.

Lidan nodded and trotted after Widrias, anxious not to be left alone.

They came to a sharp corner around which the source of the light shone fiercely. Widrias called them to a halt and signalled Noswen to move on his signal. The six tensed their muscles. They held their blades high. They charged.

Around the corner and into a small cavern, illuminated by flickering torches from iron brackets hammered into the dark stone. Barely twelve metres wide, the ragged, uneven walls suggested it had been artificially expanded some time ago. The ceiling was uneven, dipping and rising like the tide. On the floor were woven mats and mank, woollen blankets, old weapons and armour, ragged clothes, rotting food and discarded water-skins. A dozen and a half soldiers hurriedly prepared themselves for battle, strapping on sword-belts and throwing on scale armour. They froze when they saw them rush in, weapons at the ready. But only for a moment. With a swiftness born of hours of training, they unsheathed their swords and counter-charged.

Lidan dove under a sweeping sword, rolled over his shoulder, and sprang up behind his enemy, raising his shield behind his back to block the strike of another. It almost felt natural. Two battles and he felt like he was finally getting to grips with it.

The sword clacked off his shield, throwing him forward. He took advantage of the momentum and lunged at the throat of the soldier in front. Before his blade met its target, his enemy lifted his shield and his sabre glanced off the tapered wood.

He barely had time to recover before both soldiers struck as one, their twin blades cutting towards him. He desperately swivelled his body around, crashing into a third enemy and sending him sprawling. Despite his acrobatic efforts, the tip of one sword still scraped across his brigandine, leaving a deep furrow in the leather.

He turned again to face his enemies, shield covering his body and sabre jutting from the top. The men he faced sneered at one another and approached cautiously, levelling their swords and kite shields. Emblazoned on them was the king's manticore. That sigil, fluttering from every flagpole in Crastalan, on the shields of all those soldiers who abused him. On the breast of the man who sent him to the dungeons, who mutilated Zile. As much a symbol of pain and suffering as it was the king's heraldry.

Hatred washed over him anew. He grunted and crouched behind his shield, his anger giving him strength. He feinted to the left then turned his wrist to bring his sabre sweeping low and fast towards the opponent to his right. He expected to feel the bite of steel into flesh, to cut into the thigh, just beneath the hauberk. Such a wound would incapacitate his foe, let him concentrate on the other. But no. His sword recoiled off the shield, bouncing back, throwing him off balance. He stepped back to regain his footing. The sound his sword made was ugly, a dull clang that echoed around the cave, resounding from the cold stone walls. His heart hammered away in his chest like a possessed blacksmith. That should have worked. It would have worked against the trogs. Evidently, these were trained veterans, not prone to falling for such cheap tricks.

They continued their advance, hitting him forcefully with their shields, knocking him back. In his retreat, he tripped over the fallen bodies of others, stumbled on the clothes and blankets strewn across the floor, slipped on rotting food. They were too strong for him. He tried retaliating, but their shields were too tall, too broad, always there to meet his blade.

He retreated further and further, nearly backed against the wall. Pushing back with his shield, he tried muscling them away. Too strong again. His feet skidded back on the rock. They weren't bothering with their swords. Didn't need to. If they got him pinned against the wall, they'd have plenty of time to skewer him.

Out of his depth, yet again. Nothing he could do. Looking to escape, he darted to the left. They side-stepped with him, blocking the way. He stabbed from above, below, left, right. He feinted, ducked, barged forward. No good. They kept coming. A boy against men.

Ghankul crashed into the flank of one of his assailants, knocking him off his feet. Suddenly free of their bullying, Lidan took advantage of the momentary distraction to start hacking. His foe's upraised sword clashed against his own, shield knocked aside by Ghankul's charge. Steel grating on steel, he bludgeoned away. Roaring. Spitting. Growling in each other's face. By some chance, he disarmed his enemy with a savage cut, throwing the sword across the room. The tide turned, the momentum shifted, and now he was the bully, battering away with his shield. The soldier was slowly forced to retreat, panting as he desperately fended off his attacks.

Finally, he knocked the shield wide enough to stab with all his might. It didn't penetrate the mail hauberk, but he knocked him to the floor. As he fell, his head jerked back, exposing his neck. On instinct, he cut. The sabre bit. The throat opened.

Shaking with adrenaline, he turned. Ghankul was battling two others. Taking a breath to compose himself, he sprang forward to attack from behind. One fell immediately as Ghankul's axe smashed into his thigh, nearly taking the leg off. Lidan's clumsy attack was enough of a distraction to give Ghankul the opening he needed to sink his axe halfway through the other's neck.

Lidan panted. Still a lucky bastard.

He nodded to his brother-in-arms, who patted him on the arm and engaged another. He was about to help him when a satorr stepped up. Formidably-armed, with full plate armour complete with a gilded trim. The king's golden insignia shone form the centre of the breastplate.

He raised his shield and stared at his opponent over the rim. Come on then. The satorr was powerfully built. Six feet tall with broad shoulders and long, curving horns like a ram. He held a fearsome poleaxe in gauntleted hands. His expression was ugly, arrogant, with an upturned lip and narrowed eyes.

The satorr struck first, swinging the poleaxe with frightening speed. He barely had time to lift his shield to intercept the strike. Once again, he was knocked back. Recovering quickly, he dropped his shield-arm to see his opponent. Mistake. He lifted it again, just in time to intercept the other end of the poleaxe, its long spike rushing towards his chest. The weapon glanced off the tapered edge of his shield, whistling harmlessly over his shoulder.

Jumping forward, he swung his sword, desperate to get within striking distance. The satorr spun his weapon, parrying his sword with the shaft. Blade askew, the satorr followed up with another swing. The shaft caught his jaw and sent him flying. He landed in a heap, dazed.

The satorr approached victoriously, smiling as he twirled his poleaxe around his body. Suddenly Ghankul jumped before him, swinging his axe. The weapon swept past the satorr's poleaxe and smashed against his breastplate, but failed to pierce it. The satorr growled and kicked Ghankul in the fork of the legs, before hitting out with the butt of his poleaxe. It struck him across the cheek, spinning him around to face Lidan. Their eyes met for a second. The spiked butt of the poleaxe smashed through his chest, exploding in a mist of blood and gore and shattered bone.

His eye rolled up into his skull as the satorr lifted the weapon, the squirming body stuck on the end. Thick blood ran down the shaft of the weapon and dripped over the satorr's hands, falling to the ground in a puddle. The satorr swung his weapon swiftly, dislodging the body at its end and sending it flying across the cavern. Ghankul crashed against a wall and slithered to the ground. His chest heaved as he coughed. Blood spluttered from his mouth. He lay still.

Lidan looked at the corpse in horror. He staggered to his feet, head spinning. Stumbled a few paces towards the satorr. Nearly collapsed. Spotal was beside him, arms around his shoulder.

'Rest, Lidan. Noswen and I will handle him.'

The calef and the hanex circled the satorr, their relaxed bodies contrasting the tense frame of their foe. Their enemy pounced, swinging his poleaxe at Spotal, but the calef rocked backwards on his foot. The poleaxe passed within an inch of his chest. At that exact moment, Noswen lunged and slashed her falchion down to the satorr's shoulder. The blade couldn't cut through the formidable armour, but it knocked him off-balance. He stumbled clumsily.

Spotal swung his jian in a swift, precise strike. It cut a deep gash in the satorr's cheek. Their enemy gasped and swung his weapon wildly. The strike was flailing and clumsy, easily evaded. Spotal followed up his attack with a sharp stab to the satorr's ankle, extracting a shrill yelp. Noswen sprang forward and cut cleanly through his forearm, just where his steel gauntlets ended.

The satorr screeched and swung his poleaxe one-handed. She ducked and spun on her heel, her falchion sweeping across the satorr's chest, biting deep into the breastplate, scratching through the king's insignia.

Spotal stepped forward. He paused for a moment and thrust. His aim was true. The blade slid cleanly between the enemy's pauldron and breastplate, sinking deep into his chest. The satorr gasped as the blade withdrew, staring at Spotal in horror. They stepped back. He fell to the ground with a clatter, Ghankul avenged.

Noswen helped Lidan to his feet. He looked around groggily. Only one soldier remained, leaning against the rocky wall, panting. His sparse armour was stained with blood and grime. Seeping wounds covered his body. He wiped his mouth with his hand to clear the blood and lifted his heavy sword. Widrias walked towards him, gore-encrusted greatsword gripped in both hands. The soldier attempted to swing his weapon, but the effort was too much for his wounded body. He collapsed to the cavern floor. Widrias wiped the blade of his weapon with the hem of his cloak and returned it to its scabbard. Kneeling next to the collapsed soldier, he gathered a dagger from the floor and placed it against his breast.

'It isn't here,' spluttered the fallen soldier, his gurgling voice echoing throughout the cavern.

Widrias paused, the dagger resting on his chest. 'What?'

The soldier laughed. It was a hideous, choking sound. He spluttered and coughed, spitting the blood collecting at the back of his throat.

'What you're here for. The fabled "serpent key" isn't here, it isn't anywhere.'

'What do you mean?' asked Widrias, dagger hovering.

'Your journey's all for nothing. There is no key.'

'Your lies are pathetic.'

'No lies,' the soldier chuckled.

'No? Why else would you be here if not for the key?'

'For you. We 'e here for you, fool.'

Pwtrek stepped up next to the general and snarled into the soldier's face. 'Explain yourself fully, you wretch!'

*

Auran wrenched his axe from the soldier's flank. He looked around and sniffed. Seven dead soldiers were strewn across the mountainside, their warm blood slowly freezing in the cold. The battle was fast and furious. He'd been fortunate yet again not to suffer any wounds. Depani was equally fortunate. Chekry now bore a roguish scar across one cheek.

Their skirmish had not gone unnoticed by Gwahl, who sat with Kres and Jeret a few dozen paces away, near enough to the entrance to the tunnel to intervene in any other battles, close enough to the plateau to keep sentry.

293

He approached another fallen soldier. This one was only wounded, blood pouring from his thigh. He'd die eventually, but slowly. Deserved a quick end.

Something burst from the cave and slammed into him, knocking him down. Crying out in surprise, he swung his gauntleted fist. Missed. His assailant, a tall satorr, ignored him. He tore across the mountainside, a tinderbox cradled in his arms.

Chekry lifted his crossbow and shot at the speedy satorr. Missed, the quarrel thudding into the snow by the creature's cloven feet. The satorr squawked in surprise and sped up. Depani shot as well, but her crossbow lacked the range and the bolt fell short.

Cursing their ill fortune, they pursued.

'Where do you think he's going?' panted Auran, struggling to keep up with the two.

'Nowhere,' replied Depani. 'He's just a fool trying to live a little longer – we'll teach him the price of cowardice!'

Auran watched the satorr carefully. 'No, if he were running for safety he'd be scrambling all over the place, ducking behind cover and such. This one's heading somewhere specific.'

'You reckon?'

'We can't let him reach it!'

'Aye,' muttered Chekry, kneeling as he aimed another quarrel. He squeezed the trigger and sent the missile flying. This time, his aim was true. It pierced the creature's shoulder, making him stumble. Chekry chuckled and winked at Auran. His smile faltered, turned into a growl. The determined satorr was back on his feet, still running.

Suddenly the satorr collapsed to the ground next to a boulder and began striking the flint to steel. Sparks littered the snow around him. Auran observed carefully. Sun above! That's what he was up to! He grabbed Chekry's arm.

'Shoot him! Before he succeeds!' he turned and ran back to the cave.

*

'Succeeds in what?' called Depani after him.

He didn't answer. Shrugging, she returned her attention to her brother. Calmly, he aimed his weapon for the third time. As the

294

neiad's finger touched the trigger, a massive burst of flame erupted before the satorr. A beacon, not a boulder. A spark had taken to the pitch-soaked wood.

Chekry lowered his weapon and looked at the bonfire in wonder. But the satorr wasn't finished. He staggered around the pyre and found a horn. Putting it to his lips, he blew.

Depani winced at the sound. A wailing, booming call of a war-horn. She turned to her brother, desperately. Chekry lifted his crossbow to his shoulder and shot. The horn was silenced and the satorr finally slumped face-first into the flames.

The neiad nudged his sister. 'Should we try to put that out?'

'No point – it's too big already. Besides, it's too late,' she pointed to the surrounding mountains. A few seconds later, another beacon was lit, and another. Soon enough, half the mountains around the plateau had a spot of blazing orange against the white snow. Far to the west, another peak burst into flames.

She shared another glance with her brother and tore down the mountainside after Auran.

*

He skidded to a halt before the tunnel entrance and ran inside. Suddenly, someone grabbed his forearm. Auran turned to fight, but saw Gwahl's face in the darkness.

'Auran, tell them to get back out here! More soldiers are coming.'

He brushed the hand away. 'I know, Gwahl, we need to get away.'

He jogged along the winding path, stumbling against unseen rocks and loose pebbles. He ignored the side tunnels. They wouldn't have gone down there. Soon, the white light of the entrance was replaced by the golden light of the cavern. He heard Widrias's voice and sprinted inside, axe held at the ready.

He looked around and lowered his axe, quickly taking stock of his surroundings. Dead soldiers, breathing companions. Ghankul was dead, but the others were safe. Grim-faced, he approached Widrias, kneeling over a fallen enemy, Pwtrek at his side.

'Explain yourself fully, you wretch!' snarled Pwtrek.

He crouched next to Widrias and whispered in his ear. 'Sir, a soldier evaded our guard at the entrance and managed to light a beacon. Several others are lit around the mountains. More are coming.'

The fallen soldier chuckled and murmured. 'As I said, we're here for you. There is no key.'

'Tell Lidan, Spotal and Noswen to leave the cave. Get ready to run. Go with them,' Widrias waved him away and turned his attention back to the soldier.

Auran paused. 'What did he say?'

'Nothing, just go, Auran, take the others. I'll follow shortly.'

'Did he say there was no–'

'Enough! I gave an order, follow it.'

He lingered for a moment, but the look in Widrias's eyes was enough. He signalled the others. One final glance over his shoulder at Widrias and they were back in the tunnel.

*

'Now, where is the key?'

'I told you.'

'No, you lied.'

He coughed again, his breath ragged. Widrias seethed. The man was dying. Time was running short.

'Stolach came and searched. Everyone knows this. Why else if not for the key?'

'To set the scene.'

'And leave you here to rot?'

'To wait for whoever came.'

'You believe this? How can you be so sure there is no key? Why would Stolach give a lowly soldier such as you this information?'

'He wouldn't. He told his juggernaut, who told our captain when he left us here to wait. Our captain told us. We were simply here to wait.'

'Why tell me this?'

'To see your face, the great Widrias, beaten by me, a lowly soldier,' he cackled again. More blood dribbled down his chin.

Widrias snarled. He grabbed the soldier's wrist. With a steady hand, he lifted the dagger and slipped the blade beneath a fingernail. The soldier's scream was chilling. It didn't deter him. He needed the truth, to coax it through pain. If this is what was required, then so be it. One by one, he desecrated the soldier's fingers.

'You're lying! Tell me where the key is! You can't have been here for so long and not found it! Give it to me!'

'There is no key,' he wept, only to scream louder as another two fingernails were lost in quick succession. The soldier heaved and vomited, the liquid containing as much blood as it did bile.

'Give it to me!' he roared, slipping the blade beneath another nail. 'Give me the key and the pain will stop! Give me the key!'

'I swear, there is no key! Please, there is no key!' he screeched, amid his sobs. His body shook uncontrollably, his limbs flailed and his head tossed.

He lifted the knife and plunged it deep into a kneecap, screaming at the tortured soldier.

'Give it to me!'

The soldier's head crashed against the rock, time and time again. Finally, his shaking stopped, and he lay there, breathing lightly, a trickle of blood dripping from his ear. His eyelids fluttered.

'There is no key,' he whispered, before closing his eyes a final time.

Widrias stared at him, shoulders slumped. He let the bloodied dagger clatter to the floor by his feet.

'They were here to wait,' murmured Pwtrek from behind.

'To wait for us,' he whispered. He turned and looked at him. 'Pwtrek, we need to get out of here. The very foundation upon which this quest was built is a fabrication. A lie. I've led us here for nothing!'

'He may have been lying, sir, trying to get in one last dig before he died? It might be here.'

'It isn't. I tortured him. Winds! I tortured the man. What are we doing?'

'Might have been trained to withstand torture? It could still be here.'

'You know it isn't. Come, we must leave here, now.'
'We could search for a little while?'
'You heard Auran, there are more coming, we need to go.'
'Just a few minutes?'
'No! I won't waste any more time. I've been a fool. Taken in by a story. I won't make that mistake again.'
'Very well, sir.'
'And make haste, Pwtrek, we need not linger on these mountains any longer.'

Chapter 18

Gwahl shifted on his feet. Harsh war-horns sang their chilling music. Getting louder. The snow on the mountainsides shifted under the drumming beat of marching boots. He chewed his lip and scanned the plateau for approaching enemies. They'd be here soon.

Chekry's teeth chattered. Whether from cold or fear, he couldn't tell. Probably both. The neiad fumbled when loading his crossbow, dropping a quarrel into the snow. Gwahl reached down and picked it up, before taking the arbalest from the neiad and loading it for him. He handed it back with a weak smile.

'Have courage, my friend, as soon as Widrias returns we'll be away.'

'It's a whole damned army, Gwahl, just listen to them. We're done if they catch us.'

'On the contrary. We are few, they are many. We can hide in places where armies cannot, we can camp in places with less food available, or shelter in more inhospitable areas. If we run, we'll evade them for many days, maybe weeks!'

'I thought there were only twelve up here?'

He didn't answer, his fingers twitching nervously. If he'd been misled about the number of soldiers…

'Why can't the general hurry up…?' moaned the neiad, stamping his feet in agitation. 'I just want to leave!'

Gwahl was about to reply when the horns sounded again, this time louder. One of the men took out a small brass spyglass from his pocket and peered through it. He yelped in surprise. Gwahl reached over and took the spyglass.

He squinted through the scope. His breath caught. On the far side of the plateau, an army gathered. It was big. Bigger than he'd anticipated. By quick estimation, there were maybe two hundred, marching under the pale blue banner of the King. He shut the spyglass with a snap and tossed it to the guard. Time to go.

Glancing at the tunnel, he grumbled impatiently. What was keeping them? Running over, he peered into the darkness, willing

Auran to return. He didn't wait long. Auran came running out of the tunnel half a minute later with Lidan, Spotal and Noswen in tow. He grabbed Spotal by the forearm.

'Where are the others?'

'They'll be coming soon enough – the general's just questioning a soldier.'

Gwahl grit his teeth in frustration and paced outside. Every so often, he glanced over the plateau. The newly-assembled army was closing the gap. The rest of the company clustered around the tunnel entrance, staring nervously at the approaching foe. Their fear set him on edge.

'By the bane of the giants, instead of quaking in your boots why don't you plan a route away from here?' he snapped. 'Spotal, why don't you take charge?'

The calef nodded and sent the others away to scout out any suitable paths. Gwahl ignored them, returning his attention to the tunnel entrance, afraid of what would emerge. He waited ten seconds. Another ten. Grumbling again, he entered the tunnel. Damn the general. Auran would have told him there was an army approaching, now was not the time to indulge in questioning. If he had to drag him out, he would.

Two steps into the darkness and he came face to face with Widrias, who brushed him aside in a hurry. Pwtrek followed immediately after, ushering him out.

Once in the open, Widrias took one look at the approaching force and shook his head. He looked like he might collapse. Gwahl jumped up to steady him. With a gentle hand around his shoulder, he steered him away from the plateau.

'Not right now, my friend,' he whispered. 'You must stand strong in front of your men. Give them the order to move away from the plateau, we can return in a few days' time.'

Widrias moaned and shook him free, collapsing heavily against a rock. He looked questioningly at Pwtrek.

'I was right, my friend,' said the juggernaut sombrely. 'The key was a myth, a lie devised by Stolach. Bait for his trap.'

His heart skipped. He turned slowly to the desolate plateau, empty save for snow and soldiers. With a dry mouth, he turned back to his friend.

'What do you mean?' he whispered.

'The key doesn't exist. It was just a story.'

He shook his head. 'That can't be true… I was … I saw … He *said…*'

'Whatever you heard was a lie, my friend, one of the soldiers told us.'

'He's lying to protect the key!' even as he spoke the words he knew they were false.

'No,' the juggernaut replied. 'Widrias tortured him, not that it would have made a difference. He believed what he said. Accept it, Gwahl, this was all a folly.'

He couldn't think of a reply. Bitter memories sprang to mind of a time gone by. Tears welled the curtain of deception was lifted. Realisation that danced behind it for sixteen years finally came to the light. They were here for nothing. Brave soldiers dead for nothing. Precious weeks wasted for nothing. Their greatest hope of overthrowing Stolach was lost, worse, it had never existed. No great weapon to aid them. Nothing.

Rage and despair were unmatched, save for the more terrible feelings of betrayal, of insult, of crushing guilt. Worse still, in his heart, he knew this would happen. There was a reason why he never came here before, a reason why he always found an excuse not to come. He knew it was a dream. The excitement, hope, and vitality that Widrias poured into the tale had swept him up in its promise. He should have never told him about it. No. That was unfair. It wasn't the general's fault for believing the tale; it was his own for not listening to his gut, for ignoring the signs. It was his fault.

He steeled himself, forced his anguish deep down where it could be forgotten. At least for the time being. He looked up to Pwtrek and nodded. The juggernaut quickly hid a suspicious frown and nodded back, before returning to Widrias and gently lifting him to his feet.

With a painful knot in his stomach, he trotted over to Spotal.

'Time to go, Spotal. We're all ready now.'

Spotal nodded and pointed the best path from the plateau. He nodded. Rocky, narrow, and a steady incline. Perfect. He called them over, just as another horn called its challenge.

'That's our signal to leave,' he forced a smile. It wasn't returned. Now was not the time for humour.

Motioning them forward, they ran, Spotal at the lead. Noswen followed close behind, then the twins, the two guards, Auran and Lidan came next, both breathing heavily. At the rear was Pwtrek, his arm around Widrias.

He fell in behind them, walking backwards, keeping an eye on their pursuers. They had a long night ahead.

*

They fled through the mountains for hours. No matter how far they travelled or for how long Gwahl pushed them, the pounding of marching boots and the howling of war-horns snapped at their heels. They ran on into the night, with Spotal and Gwahl leading them ever eastward towards the Kingdom of calefs. If they reached it, it might provide sanctuary. It was a big ask.

Lidan's breath came in a fine mist as his boots crunched through the snow, following the distant form of Auran. One advantage of running so high was that it didn't ever go truly dark, so he could always see where he was running, his path illuminated by the shining moon and stars. His flank ached with a stitch. Soon, he'd be forced to pause for rest.

As if to intentionally disprove his point, Gwahl came jogging down the line, pausing to exchange a few words with each member of the company before moving on to the next. His endurance was unnatural. By now, the daemon had probably run twice the distance of everyone else with his constant back-tracking to see how everybody was, yet he hardly showed the slightest signs of fatigue.

He smiled as Gwahl finished speaking to Auran and jogged down to him, turning sharply on his heel to run beside him.

'How are you, my friend?'

'Fine' he grunted. 'A bit of a stitch.'

'Don't worry, we'll be stopping for the night in a few minutes. I think we've out-paced them for a while yet.'

'I feel so slow.'

'Because you are. We all are. It's the thin air. Take comfort in the fact that our pursuers will be equally slow.'

He nodded, 'You know, this wasn't exactly what I had in mind when I decided to join the Council – running up a mountain in thin air in the dead of night isn't quite the quest that I'd hoped for.'

'It's not what any of us expected,' muttered Gwahl. 'But here we are, and we must weather this new challenge or face our deaths.'

His reply was cut short when the ringing wail of a war-horn sounded in the distance. As one, their heads snapped around, but all they could see was Pwtrek carrying Widrias, fifty paces behind.

He glanced at Gwahl. 'What's wrong with the general? Was he wounded?'

'You might say that. I'll explain it all once we make camp,' he paused. 'Unfortunately, I fear we may have to keep running for some time. That horn sounded quite close.'

He sighed. More running. 'Did you try to warn the general about the army? Last night before we went onto the plateau I overheard snatches of your conversation. Sounded like you were trying to warn him.'

Gwahl smiled, despite the situation. 'You're quite the eavesdropper, aren't you? I was warning him of something, but not the army. I had no idea they were here. There were only supposed to be twelve.'

'What else would you have to warn him about?'

'I'll tell you all when we make camp.'

'When will that be?'

'I don't know, my friend. As I said, it probably won't be for a while. We need to put more distance between us.'

The daemon clasped him on the shoulder and jogged back to Pwtrek, leaving him to run on in contemplative silence.

*

Not until the first light of dawn did they rest, the red sun staining the snow a fiery orange. Like the bloodstained teeth of a fierce wolf, the mountain peaks surrounded them, jagged and terrifying against the crisp morning air. The imposing beauty of their surroundings was lost upon him, the colourful slopes simply a challenge to overcome, not a sight to enjoy. Huddled under a rocky overhang, bunched up together for warmth, he waited for sleep or for the order to start running again, whichever came first.

He closed his eyes and waited to drift off, but as is often the case after physical strain, he was too tired to asleep. All he could manage was an empty stare into space, fully aware of his surroundings, but not taking particular notice of anything.

His waking-sleep was disturbed as Gwahl called them to attention. There were groans all around as they prepared to start running again, but the daemon signalled to keep sitting.

'No, you may rest for a while yet,' he said. 'I'll just explain our current situation, based on the information Widrias extracted from the soldier and from what I've surmised.

'You know why we're here. Stolach, the dreyads, the key, twelve soldiers… obviously, he left a few more than anticipated.'

No chuckles. Only hard stares. Unfazed, Gwahl continued.

'What the general learned from the soldier…' he paused, wringing his hands. 'This was a little more than a rumour devised by the king himself, purposefully released to his enemies.'

He frowned. Surely not? Suddenly awake, more so than he'd been for hours. The others stirred as he did. Exchanging dark looks. Gwahl continued.

'He left an army. Why? Not to search for the key. He knew it… doesn't exist. A spider at the centre of the web of lies.'

Heart pounding, palms sweating. His brigandine felt suddenly too tight. Suffocating. He struggled to unclench his jaw. A lie?

Gwahl shook his head. 'His enemies would be lured to the plateau by this story of a key that opened a secret passage into his castle, and as they searched the plateau the beacons would be lit and the army would march. Who knows how many others have already fallen foul of the trap? We've been deceived. A lie so blatant and outlandish we thought it had to be true. The key to his downfall. I'm sorry.'

He sat down, dejected. Lidan stared at him dumbly. Deceived. All of this for nothing? The silence stretched for what felt like hours.

Spotal frowned. 'How do we know that? Surely the soldier was lying in a last-ditch effort to protect the key?'

'No, Spotal. The more I think about it the clearer it gets. Of course there's no key. If there were, Stolach wouldn't have left the plateau until he found it. As impatient as he might be, he knows better than to expose himself in such a way. We were stupid coming here. So pathetically stupid not to have seen through him.'

'So, the key never existed,' scowled Auran. 'Tanor, close to fifty Council Guard, and an entire crew of sailors died for nothing.'

The silence returned.

Pwtrek scowled at Noswen. 'You claim you didn't know?'

'I had no idea,' she said, tonelessly.

Chekry scowled. 'What about your business with the lion key? Did that not exist either?'

She sighed. 'There *were* keys to the fortress, but evidently this final key was a myth. I agree with Gwahl, the keys I helped gather were all to open various gates around the citadel, not hidden tunnels. Real gates that just led to the other side of a wall.'

'I thought all the keys were for hidden passageways?' growled Pwtrek.

'No, only this final one.'

'Well this gets worse and worse,' exclaimed Depani.

'How could anyone believe such a ludicrous...' Auran shook his head, words lost in a mumble.

'Had you given this information to us we may have re-thought this entire mission!' cried Pwtrek.

'She told Widrias and the other high chancellors,' said Gwahl. 'I knew already, but the Council decided to send us here regardless. The fact that others knew wouldn't have made a difference.'

'Would've made a difference to me. You purposefully deceived us,' Chekry pointed at Gwahl.

'Despite knowing the other keys were just for gates, you still believed there was a secret passageway?' Pwtrek sneered at him.

'I had my reasons to believe.'

'Because you met this sage once? Come on. From the sounds of it he was old and tired. He was probably in on the lie, protecting his protégé one last time. You're supposed to be the best of us, Gwahl!'

'Yes, because I was there with him! I heard him say it. There are things you don't understand. At the time, having a key to unlock a passageway didn't seem so unreasonable,' Gwahl closed his eyes, ashamed.

'You believed because you wanted to,' Pwtrek shook his head. 'And damn well killed us for it.'

'If the king devised this myth why did he come here in the first place?' asked Lidan.

'Two possible reasons,' replied Gwahl, quietly. 'Either he knew all of this and planned this elaborate trap for some time, or he only found out after he caught up with the dreyads and they told him there was no key.'

'Which leads to another question,' said Auran. 'Why were the dreyads running away from the king if not to protect a treasure?'

'Wouldn't you run if you heard that the king was looking for you, intent on killing you? They were doomed the moment he devised this plan, it's only bad luck on their part that they were the ones he chose to pursue,' Gwahl opened his eyes and looked at them. 'The key doesn't exist. I've allowed us to be taken in by a dream. We should return to the Council as soon as possible to devise a new strategy.'

'That's enough, Gwahl,' said Widrias. He'd been lying on his back a few paces away from the group. 'I thank you for assuming command while I was incapacitated, but now I shall take back my position.'

He crawled over to them and sat between Spotal and Chekry. He'd never seen the satorr look so haggard. Dark bags under his wild eyes, grey skin, slumped shoulders. He did his best to look strong, but failed. Lidan's eyes met Gwahl's for a second. The daemon thought the same.

'Now, I see you've been leading us east to your kingdom, Spotal?' the calef nodded and Widrias continued. 'I agree, this is the best course of action. Once we reach the kingdom of the calefs we shall travel south to Muranath Castle to seek advice from King Lleunedd and General Teig. We can possibly borrow one of their ships and return to Dailas as soon as we can.

'We must travel swiftly, lest these animals at our heels drag us to our deaths. Know this, my friends, it is not we who have failed, it is Stolach. As long as one of us survives, his ploy has failed, for his trap will be revealed to the world. Keep running, keep sharp and we will win this fight.'

'Might I point something out?' asked Auran, before continuing at the general's nod. 'Gwahl said that army has been here for *sixteen years*? How did they survive for so long up here? Where did they get their food? There's nowhere to farm around here, and there's no way they could have had enough provisions to last such a long time.'

'They had a way of bringing supplies up here, what's your point?'

'*They had a way of bringing supplies here*! You said it yourself. There must be some pathway off the plateau and down to the Dailas, bypassing the marshes. Why don't we find that route and follow it? That way we can return to the Council straight away, without needing to go to Lleunedd.'

'With all due respect, Auran, I believe we could use the advice of Teig and Lleunedd,' said Spotal.

'It would mean taking a long time to get back to the Council,' murmured Chekry, chewing his cheek in thought. 'Auran's right. The path from the plateau must be an easy one to allow food carts to get to and from Dailas, so the journey would be far easier than our search for the place.'

'How much time do you think we have?' asked Widrias. As if in reply, the droning wail of the enemy's horns echoed around them. The satorr pointed behind. 'You hear them coming? Do you want us to turn back to the plateau and risk getting caught by the army? We'll be caught and killed. There's no easy way out. My decision is made, we've had enough time for rest. Spotal, you lead the way to your kingdom.'

'Sir!' cried Spotal happily. Only Lidan saw Widrias's face fall after his speech, his eyes fill with tears, hastily blinked back before anybody noticed.

They set off again through the mountains, the sun casting a golden glow on the snow. Still early. They had a full day ahead.

*

After running for so long, he realised he could almost sleep on the go, slipping into a steady rhythm of jogging, breathing and pumping his arms. He was only dimly aware of direction, which was enough when all he had to do was follow Auran.

It was well over three hours since they'd last heard the crow of the king's war-horn. Widrias was confident they were safe. Still, Lidan recalled Gwahl's warnings to Widrias. Would he ever find out what he was warning the general about? Probably not. The daemon loved his secrets.

A cry from behind. Gwahl, who'd been following up the rear, sprinted up. The daemon nudged him as he passed.

'Faster. They're here!'

He needed no second bidding and tore up the mountainside, too scared to look back and risk losing his footing. He passed Auran.

'Run, Auran! They're here!'

Without questioning him, he responded, sprinting beside him. All of a sudden, Gwahl shot past, tearing up the column to warn Widrias and Spotal.

The general's hand shook violently, but he steadied it by gripping the hilt of his sword.

'On the double! Go!' He turned to Gwahl. 'How many are there?'

'A mere fraction of the true force, twenty at the most – scouts sent to hinder and slow us down.'

'Scouts? Are they…?'

Gwahl nodded to the unasked question. 'Grey dreyads.'

Widrias cursed and spat. 'Do you think we could hold them off for a while?'

'If you please, sir, we shouldn't try. It'll only slow us down and tire us further.'

'For the love of the four winds what should we do? We can't all out-run dreyads, and I shan't abandon anyone else, but we can't fight them either! What do you propose we do? Hide?'

'Yes. We should find a cave or something and lay low, cover our tracks and pray they don't find us.'

Pwtrek stepped up behind him. 'Sir, I don't like the idea of hiding, but Gwahl's right, we mustn't expend any energy with needless fighting.'

'Fine,' grumbled the satorr. 'Keep a look-out for any suitable places, Gwahl and Spotal can take up the rear again and cover our tracks. I will not suffer yet another defeat. We *will* survive this challenge.'

They set off again in a tight formation, the daemon and the calef running a few paces behind, covering their tracks with snow. Suddenly Auran stopped running and stared up the slope. Lidan followed his gaze, and sighed. Here was the end of it.

On the slope were the dreyads, staring down at them with drawn weapons. The two companies faced each other for a few moments. The dreyads descended.

'We did our best,' proclaimed Widrias. 'We'll face them as soldiers, and show them how free creatures fight.'

They formed a line facing the oncoming foe, outnumbered and exhausted.

Lidan stood still in the snow, sweating as their enemies rushed against them. He gripped his sabre and shield with white knuckles. Despite his efforts, his hands still shook. His right flank was protected by Auran, his battleaxe held ready. Somehow, the Southlander seemed calm, composed, at ease. Spotal was the same, his sword resting against his shoulder. Between these two, he'd be alright. It's what he told himself.

The dreyads shot as they ran. Arrows zipped around them. Shield raised, he protected himself. An arrow clattered against it, landing at his feet. Another glanced off and disappeared somewhere behind. To his left, Spotal ducked low as the missiles sped through the air, one even clipping the calef's torso, but his white brigandine spared him from any harm.

They were on them, hacking and growling. Nobody roared any battle-cries. All he heard was the clash of metal on metal, the grunts of fighters, the occasional thud as blade tasted flesh.

Parrying an attack with his sabre, he lashed out with his shield, catching the dreyad on the jaw, knocking him to the ground. He was about to finish him off when an arrow flew. He lifted his shield and backed away, giving his opponent time to recover.

The dreyad charged, dodged under his sabre, and snaked his blade past his shield. The edge glanced harmlessly off his brigandine. He knocked it away with his shield and countered. The dreyad evaded his swings and lunged. Stepping aside, he twirled his sword in a circle, sending him clattering past.

He advanced. Press your victory. The dreyad was off-balance, open for attack. He raised his sword to strike, but his eyes caught on an another. Bow drawn, a dreyad at the rear turned to him. Swerving away, he brought up his shield. Too late. the arrow flew true and struck his shoulder. The brigandine took the brunt, but it hit hard enough for his arm to seize. His hand spasmed, his fingers opened. His shield fell with a thump in the snow. The arrowhead hadn't pierced his skin, but it was there, hampering his movement. Gripping the shaft, he tore it out. He was out in the open. Exposed. No shield. The dreyad was there again, drawing his bow. He sighted down the shaft and released.

His gut seized as the arrow struck. He dropped to his knees with a whimper. Footsteps behind. He couldn't see who. His head exploded in a crescendo of pain and he dropped to the glistening snow, swallowed by sparkling darkness.

End of part 1

A Key to a Throne

A Key to a Throne

Part 2 – Lands of Darkness

314

Interlude: The Lost Key
Sixteen Years Earlier

Irritated, he brushed the gathering snowflakes from his eyelashes. It would not do to be blinded in battle. The steel of his breastplate was cold enough for thin crystals of frost to gather at its edges, glittering in the sun like the sea in moonlight. Not that he felt it. His gambeson was warm and thick, his glacier-blue cloak soft, sheltering him from the howling wind.

Such wind! Seldom had he faced such fierce gales, channelled and concentrated between the steep slopes to batter the plateau, shrieking a banshee as it found its way through crevices and gullies. It carried the flurries of snow high and low, swirling in a thousand directions to sting his eyes.

He blinked the snow away again. The rock of the plateau was dark, ominously so against the bright snow, surrounded by grey slopes of ice and stone. Before nightfall, the white would turn crimson and the dreyads would be still.

Not that they looked particularly lively right now. He narrowed his eyes. There they were, clustered together in a little band, hooded cloaks over their heads to battle the wind. An attempt as futile as their imminent challenge. When thirty faced three hundred, there was no battle, no skirmish. Only slaughter. He almost felt sorry for them. Almost.

Nodding in their direction, he turned to his second.

'So, here we are at last. The final stage.'

The juggernaut nodded vigorously. His heavy frame rippled with strength, but he still flinched at his master's voice. The familiar ugly scar distorted his features, made worse when he spoke.

'Indeed, sire.'

'Let's not waste any time, you know what to do. We need one alive.'

Tomon's roar shook the mountains, bouncing from slope to slope, echoing between the rocks, resonating from tallest peak to deepest valley. The horde at their backs answered with their own cries. He smiled. Enough to set his heart pounding, Enadir herself only knew how the dreyads must feel. Tomon's roar tailed off to a throaty gurgle, spittle foaming at the corners of his mouth. Ugly, fierce, loyal. An ideal ally in battle.

He took the first steps forward, Tomon close behind.

He drew his sword.

They charged.

His boots thudded against the plateau. His soldiers followed. A reverberation as loud as an earthquake.

Halfway across. They roared their battle-cries again.

Around him, men lowered spears, lifted axes, and pointed blades at the enemy.

He was at the front. Lips drawn back in a vicious snarl as he bore down on them, standing so defiantly before him.

He could taste it. His victory. So much planning. Such cunning and guile. It had all led to this encounter. He had to play his part. Victory awaited. He would not fail.

The horde nearly swallowed the dreyads. There was no grace in the fight. No splendour. It was a fight to the death. You'd spit, you'd claw, you'd give no quarter.

He was in the middle of it. Magnificent sword singing, cutting down all foes before him. One stepped up and swung her axe at his chest. He deflected it and spilled her innards on the floor with a swift cut. Another managed to snake his blade past his sword, but it clacked harmlessly against the breastplate. Hawking foully, he spat in the dreyad's face. As he wiped the bile from his eyes, he disembowelled him with a deft flick of the wrist. Sloppy, letting his guard down like that.

No more immediate foes. He surveyed the battlefield. Barely a minute passed since the two forces met, yet only a handful of the foe still stood. Even as he looked, more fell. A bloodbath. His eyes caught on one of the last. Strong and tall, this dreyad stood over two dead men. Bleeding and wounded as he was, he fought on, snarling like a lynx at anyone brave enough to engage. He smiled. This one would do nicely.

He approached. The ranks of soldiers parted. The dreyad glared with poisonous eyes. He laughed as his adversary swung his sword, catching the blade in the crook of his arm. A sharp twist of the torso and he tore the weapon from his hands. Disarmed, the dreyad stumbled and fell to one knee, finally feeling the weight of his wounds. Mercilessly, he kicked his opponent to the ground, savouring the grunt of pain. Leaning over, he grabbed his gambeson and hauled him back to his feet.

'Where is it?' he snarled, injecting the words with as much venom as he could muster.

'Where is what?' the dreyad gasped.

'The key, fool! Give it to me or prepare for a painful end.'

'You have all the ke-' the dreyad stared in confusion.

'Tell me where it is!'

'I – I don't kno-'

He punched him forcefully in the stomach, doubling him over in pain. He turned to Tomon.

'Take this filth to my pavilion. I'll question him further inside.'

His soldiers parted before him like minnow to a shark. He crossed the plateau to the hastily-erected tent on the opposite side. Tomon followed, the winded dreyad thrown unceremoniously over one shoulder.

They entered his pavilion, filled with servants hurriedly setting down fur-draped chairs. He dismissed them with a wave of his hand. Tomon threw the dreyad to the floor at his feet. He didn't even look him, stepping over him as he approached his companion.

'How did I perform, Tomon? Convincing?'

'Of course, sir, the soldiers had no reason to suspect.'

'Nevertheless, it would certainly add to the realism of my drama if a few screams...' he trailed off, suggestively.

Tomon nodded. He approached the dreyad, struggling to his unsteady feet. The juggernaut gripped his thin arm with both hands. Without blinking, he moved his hands in opposite directions, shattering bones. Screaming, as promised.

He motioned for him to continue. Now for his own screams. Not of pain, but rage. Questions. Ones to which he neither expected nor needed answers.

From outside the pavilion the soldiers would cringe as they heard the dreyad's pleads. His sobs and screams as another bone was broken, another tooth snapped, another strip of skin dissected. He made sure his own screeches drowned out the dreyad's.

'Give me the key! Tell me where! The key!'

A quarter of an hour after the torture commenced, the dreyad fell limp in Tomon's hands. The juggernaut looked questioningly at him. Stolach sighed and shrugged. Didn't last long.

'I do believe that was convincing enough,' he said, drinking from a goblet of wine to soothe his throat. 'He performed admirably. Almost as if he knew what we needed.'

'So, what now?' asked Tomon.

'Now, you'll go outside and tell the troops that despite our efforts we couldn't glean any information out of the prisoner. Tell them the key is lost. Order them to search the plateau for three days and three nights.'

'What then?'

'Don't interrupt,' he snapped. 'This next part is vital. After said days and nights, you will proclaim the key lost and move the army away from this plateau, but leave a battalion to guard it. A few hundred should suffice. Then we return to Crastalan. The trap is set.'

'Very well, sir,' Tomon saluted as he departed, dragging the dreyad's corpse behind.

*

A fortnight later, he was in his carriage. The Dailas Forest bounced by his window. He smiled. The Midlands were his. After battling for so long and sacrificing so many men he had at last secured his grip on the country. He'd conquered the land and could now reap the rewards.

He caught himself. Not for rewards. He recalled the words of his teacher, sitting quietly opposite. He was not king for gold and riches. He was king because he was strong. Like everyone else, he'd suffered in the anarchy scouring the lands before his rise to power.

318

Now was his chance to secure safety, to ensure the inhabitants of his kingdom would never again feel too fearful to venture from their homes. He had an idea, a goal to build the perfect land.

It wasn't easy. Several times, he'd nearly given up. Without his wise old mentor he might have. Without him, he'd probably be dead, killed in some idiotic scrap with a bandit or Desired Hobb. He studied his teacher's face, smiling at the grumpy expression. There were few people in the world who could look quite so irritated.

His smile faltered. The thought slowly growing in the depths of his mind surfaced once again. The very thought that spurned this journey, this ploy. Like a deadly cancer, it grew over the past few months. There was no hiding from it, no starving it of attention.

He didn't trust him anymore.

He disapproved of some of the means by which he'd secured the keys, but was this not his idea? *He* gave him the means to conquer the lands, therefore *he* should be proud of his pupil. But no. Out of the corner of his eye, he caught the disapproving looks. The judgement. The betrayal of his true feelings. Disappointment. No, disappointment was too soft. He resented him, and resentment would lead to hate, and hate to open opposition.

So he played his games, carefully setting the pieces to protect himself should anything happen. This was the latest in a string of schemes set to catch his enemies. It was elaborate, far more elaborate than most of his others, but that would only make it more satisfying. To catch a rat in a convoluted trap would be the final diamond in his crown. Besides, he wouldn't be missed. Stolach confided more in Tomon than this old sage. The juggernaut may not be half as intelligent as this ancient, but he was a hundred times more loyal.

He recalled the final part of his charade and cleared this throat.

'It's a real shame the key is still lost in the mountains,' he sighed.

'What?' asked his teacher suddenly, shooting him a sharp stare. 'I thought you had it?'

'Alas!' he cried. 'The dreyads hid it too well. I had to leave the plateau after three nights of searching. It remains to be found.'

He studied him for a moment. 'You should have left someone to keep looking.'

'That's what I did! I left a dozen men.'

'Twelve soldiers won't be enough.'

'But who else would go up there? What reason would anybody have to go up to those mountains, to the plateau?'

'To find the key!' he cried. 'If any of your enemies get wind of this then all the work we did will be for nothing.'

'Believe me, my friend, if my entire army couldn't find this key after three days and nights, then what hope does anyone else have?'

'A waste,' he shook his head bitterly. 'All that work, thrown away. Everything you did to the calefs.'

He didn't have to feign his irritation. 'It was necessary.'

'No. I *told* you. Sending your assassins… You're honing the axe for your own neck.'

'They would have never given me the key.'

'They didn't need to. It could have been a sign of trust between the two of you, peace and prosperity between your kingdoms. That's why we did this, to drag the land out of the mud, return it to past glories, not spark petty wars between dynasties.'

'There could be no peace while they held a key to my fort.'

'Trust, Stolach, trust. You cannot rule without allies. Peace won't exist without it.'

'I don't trust them. How could I? I don't need them, anyway.'

'No? You think you'll maintain a peaceful land while making enemies for no need? It won't end well.'

'You think they'd dare attack? They don't have the gall.'

'No, they have no reason to attack, but they won't aid you should a new enemy arise.'

'With my fortress secure, I won't need their aid.'

He shook his head. 'The Serpent Key leaves a chink in the armour.'

'I told you, it's lost.'

He sighed deeply. There was a silence for a few seconds.

'Let me see the passageway, let me see its secrets. The hidden tunnels within the Rhetta Mountains are well known to me, if you let me see the ones in Crastalan then I can aid you in setting up defences, I can tell you the risks of leaving it unlocked. Given time, perhaps I could find a way of fashioning a replica?'

'No, my friend, nobody is to approach it,' Stolach reassured.

'Leaving the key unfound in an invitation to your enemies.'

'Not unfound, lost. It's gone, and the tunnels cannot be opened without that key, I'm perfectly safe.'

'If the tunnels of Crastalan are anything like the ones I knew in the north, as long as the key is hidden, you are not safe.'

'But as you said, you only know the ones in the Rhetta Mountains, not the ones in Crastalan. They may be different.'

'I know enough. Be wary. You're leaving the door open for your foes.'

'A handful of daemons are left who know about the tunnels. Fewer still know about the key. I have no quarrel with old Deia. I'll be safe. Sleep easily, my friend, I know I will.'

The old sage grumbled moodily and looked out the window. Stolach studied his face for a long time, noting the slight twitches in his cheeks, the shifting eyes. Tell-tale signs of planning and plotting.

He settled back into his chair, letting the carriage rock him to a gentle sleep. His plan was complete. All that was left to do was wait. Once they'd returned to the fortress, he would toast the success this ingenious scheme to draw out treachery and unmask any resistance once and for all.

Chapter 19

Crastalan. At the centre of the city was the tower, pointing accusingly at the searing sun above. Its twenty storeys held many rooms, from cloakrooms to grand bedchambers reserved for the lords and ladies of the city. Few had ever stepped foot inside this monolith, its secrets guarded from the outside world, left for the speculation and imagination of the masses.

The seventeenth, eighteenth and nineteenth storeys had been converted into a massive library, its walls lined with groaning shelves under the weight of thousands of tomes, scrolls, plaques and inscriptions, as well as other mysterious artefacts from ages past. Windows were scarce, candles provided the majority of the light, casting long, flickering shadows in the golden glow. Grizzled old scholars in robes scurried about on ladders and across walkways, carrying armfuls of tomes. A wealth of knowledge. Literature, history, alchemy, the supernatural. A collection unrivalled save for the library in the mountains. On the lowest level were long, rectangular tables stretching the length of the room. The scholars sat at them, scratching away at parchments with owl-feather quills, making notes for their king.

Stolach sat at the end of a table, a flickering candle next to him as he scoured the tome. Manticore-skin cover, gossamer-thin parchment pages held together with a shining silver spine, it was a fragile thing. Fragile enough to demand linen gloves when handled. He didn't mind. A small sacrifice for the knowledge it held. 'A study on the flora of the East'. Dull reading for most. Not for him.

He flicked a stray strand of hair from his eyes and over his ear. It was cold in here. Not damp, just the same bitterness as the desert at night. His heavy cloak spared him the worst of it, spilling across the floor behind him like an overturned goblet of wine.

Tomon burst into the library, shattering the silence. The oaf threw aside the scholars standing in his way, searching wildly, possessed. He spun furiously in the middle of the room, narrowed eyes peering into the dark corners. Stolach didn't look up from his book. He would find him eventually. His charcoal skin always kept him in a half-shadow, useful at times, a bore at others. Finally, the juggernaut spotted him and stomped over.

'A library is a place of study, learning and *silence*,' he hissed.

'My apologies, sir,' Tomon saluted, 'but I have urgent news from Tarnegrefur.'

Stolach frowned. A triviality, no doubt. A small village in the foothills with urgent concerns about a non-existent problem. Hardly worth the disturbance. He glanced at the juggernaut, about to voice his misgivings. A memory sparked in the recesses of his mind. Tarnegrefur.

It was years since he'd given any thought to what lay at the heart of the mountains. From Tomon's tone, there were developments. He nodded carefully, delicately shutting the tome and sliding it across the table to the pile of discarded books to his side.

'Take those and put them back to their homes and come to the throne-room.'

Pushing his chair back, he left the library. Tomon scrambled behind him to return the books, settling on dumping the responsibility on a scholar.

He descended fifteen flights of stairs to the second level, built into a single great hall. The throne room. Vast and circular, its high roof supported by thick marble pillars, their bases lined with silver. It was one of the few rooms in the entire city not made of granite, built instead of smooth, polished, dark blue marble, laced with thin lines of jade green forming intricate patterns in the stone. Its high ceilings, originally built to house giants, towered above their heads, intricately crafted by master stonemasons following the designs of ingenious architects into a mesmerising sea of arches and alcoves. One could lose themselves for hours staring at that ceiling, with its statues and gargoyles clinging imposingly to the roof, staring down at all that took place beneath. Who knows what wonders those stone sentinels had seen? Centuries of courts and hearings and audiences with lord and king alike, from today's fonex to yesterday's giants and daemons. It was staggering that they remained, after all these years, as perfectly and intricately grotesque as ever. Twelve long windows circled the room, each sill eight feet from the ground, far too high for any living race to see above, another reminder that they lived in the great halls of a greater race. A white carpet ran from the vast double doors leading from the staircase at one side to the great throne on the other. Said throne was large and imposing, worthy to seat the king of Enadir. The throne of Pimen Jestel, last king of the giants, was long gone. Stolach had ordered this new one to be carved out of a solid block of white marble, studded with a hundred diamonds and sapphires in golden clasps. There were no fabric cushions or armrests. It was a throne of power and leadership, not pomp and comfort.

Stolach sat on the floor with his back to the throne, waiting for Tomon's approach. The juggernaut stopped three paces away and cleared his throat.

'My king,' Tomon began. 'Our scouts have reported a great deal of activity in the Midlands. I don't know how it's only just coming to our attention. Information concerning the Council and Tarnegrefur,' he paused, waiting for a response, but Stolach was still. Tomon continued. 'I shall tell you what has happened in chronological order, to the best of my knowledge.

'A few months ago, the Council sent out a small company from their base in Dailas to Morgenal. We learned recently that this army included many figures of interest, including Captain Spotal, the traitor Noswen, Pwtrek the juggernaut and most importantly, the great General Widrias. It's possible there were others, but unconfirmed.'

Stolach narrowed his eyes. Big names, but not the one he looked for.

Tomon continued. 'As I said, they travelled to Morgenal and acquired a ship with the pirate Captain Mostyn. Scouts report our sea-neiad allies sent a ship out to intercept them, but they never returned. We assume they reached calefin waters and were escorted to Lleunedd. We still don't know why. On his deathbed, the king may have sent for his allies, maybe they wanted Noswen's advice on the poison. It's all just speculation.

'Six days ago, the beacons of Tarnegrefur were lit. When our Northland scouts saw them, they immediately sent the message back to us, sparing no time for rest or food, passing the message along in a magnificent display of communication,' the juggernaut couldn't keep the pride out of his voice. Stolach tapped his fingers impatiently.

'We just received the message half an hour ago, and came to inform you immediately of this news.'

Stolach rose and stretched, pacing around his throne. In all the years since he'd first planted the trap in the mountains, he'd almost forgotten about it. For the first few days, he was hardly able to sleep with excitement, so proud to finally trick his old teacher. As days passed to weeks, and weeks to months, and months to sixteen long years, that excitement had all but died. So many other masterful schemes replaced that one, so many more important ones than this little trick. He'd all but given up hope it would ever work. He'd cast it aside, forgotten the troops stationed there, their supply carts nothing but a footnote at the bottom of the breakdown for his northern armies. But some part of him held on to the ruse. A part of him wouldn't let him recall the troops, abandon the plateau, use them to reinforce other fronts. Some part of him kept faithful to his cunning. Time, apparently, was all it took to come to fruition. Patience was to be rewarded.

'So, someone has been to the plateau and my fine army has been alerted of their presence. The Council company, the voyage east across the sea. It probably was the great Widrias who stumbled across the plateau. Hah! A fine bonus for us that the satorr has gone to his doom, although he is not the true prize. Do you know if *he* was with them?'

'I don't know, sir. He must be dead by now. He was ancient when he left us. He couldn't have survived for long after being cast out.'

'Nevertheless, I won't consider myself victorious until his head rests on my table. Let's hope the trap is sufficient to destroy their company. How many were there?'

'Sixty, give or take. But there's also Mostyn's crew to account for, plus reinforcements from Lleunedd, if they approached him.

'It's unlikely Lleunedd could spare many to aid them. They have their hands full dealing with troglodytes. They need all the troops they have to defend their borders,' he chuckled. 'Teig will certainly need all the soldiers she can muster soon enough. Our plateau battalion should be enough.'

'Indeed, sir.'

'How goes the road?' he changed subject.

'Built and ready for use, sir, they finished setting the foundations to the walkway months ago. Finished the walkway a few weeks later.'

'Excellent, make sure the workers are paid fairly, they've done well. Finally, we have a way of linking the Midlands and Eastlands...'

'Yes, sir, when shall we start sending troops?'

'As soon as we can. First we need the woodsmen. I just need to finish my notes and I'll send them over to Strikk.'

'You've done it?' Tomon smiled.

'I was making the final notes when you disturbed me. I just need to dispense the information. I'll let you know when they're ready to go.'

'Very well, sir.'

'I need to return to the library, villages in the north are unhappy about their higher tax rates. With so many hydras devouring the troops I send to protect them, what more can they expect?'

'What will you do, sir?'

'Keep raising the taxes to a level that covers the cost of their protection, I have my own soldiers to think about as well, the ones who risk their lives to protect these villages. They deserve payment for their services. I have many books but few that deal with hydras, and fewer still in any depth. I need information.'

'As they say, sir, knowledge is power.'

'Courage is power. Intelligence is power. The ability to manipulate fear is power. Knowledge is a boon, an asset to be exploited by those with power. It only gives information. Power is hard to come by, you must fight and struggle and wrestle with the world to obtain it, and guard it jealously to retain it...' he paused and turned back to the juggernaut.

'Speaking of which, I have a something to show you. A little curiosity'

'Oh?'

'Somewhere...' he searched his cloak pockets. 'Ah! Here.'

He held the little pouch up by the drawstrings. Tomon sniffed, unimpressed by the shabby leather package. How things would change.

'What's in it?'

'Gogofaint gave it to me. Apparently it's some sort of alchemy. Strange for a daemon to meddle with it. No records of it anywhere in the library, I've searched for long enough. I'll keep looking, just in case something comes up.'

'Is it dangerous?'

'Yes. At least, if we had more of it.'

'What is it?'

'See here,' he stopped and untied the pouch. Kneeling to the floor, he poured a pinch of its contents to the marble floor. A small pile of grey powder, glittering in the torchlight from the thousand tiny crystals hidden in its grains.

'Charcoal?'

'In part. Hand me a candle.'

He wandered off to an alcove and returned with the requested light.

'Now, stand back.'

Holding the candle at arm's length, as far away from the flame as possible, he lowered it to the powder. When Gogofaint first demonstrated it to him, he'd jumped in his seat, clapping his hands like a child before a conjurer. How would Tomon react?

The flame was a few millimetres from the powder when it flashed, igniting in a sharp crack and a burst of flame. Tomon sprang back with a cry, blinking furiously.

Smiling, he withdrew his hand and shook away the debris. It would smell of rotting eggs for hours, but it was worth it.

'Magic! How?'

'The fire sleeps in the powder, all it needs is a spark to jump out.'

Tomon rubbed his chin thoughtfully. 'It would be useful in battle. To shock our enemies, blind them, stun them...'

'A thousand uses.'

'We have more?'

He shook his head. 'The daemon gave me this pouch, it's all he had. Charcoal is one part, but there are others, parts we do not have here.'

'Can we get them?'

He shrugged. 'Potentially. One part is from the Burning Eye, it's where he got it. The other is rarer. The daemon only had a small vial, all of which was used to make the contents of this purse. Came from an alchemist. A calef.'

Tomon nodded knowingly. 'And we happen to have an army ready to go there.'

'It might aid us. Then again, it might not. As I said, it's daemon lore. The fact we have no record of it worries me. It might be dangerous.'

'But powerful. I think it's worth considering.'

'Leave such considerations to me. As entertaining as it may be, it comes from an untrustworthy race, and is secret enough to be kept from history. We must treat it with caution.'

He stood and continued to the stairwell.

'Now, make yourself useful, Tomon, there has been a sharp rise in bands of rogues and bandits these past few months, a third party, if you will, in the battle between us and the Council. They're making my people uneasy. I need you and the rest of my war council to start planning an offensive to destroy them...'

His voice trailed away as he climbed the stairs back to the library. Tomon trailed behind, leaving the grand throne-room at the heart of the city cold and empty.

Chapter 20

In one of the infirmaries in the third level of the city, a boy stirred. His left foot was swathed in bandages. His wounds were skilfully sutured. He lay on a cold rock slab in a vast room, filled with other beds. Most were occupied. Three beds to his left was a Southlander, lying completely still as healers scurried around him, tenderly dabbing cloths soaked in medicine on the ragged stumps where his legs once were. Four beds to his right was a hanex, wailing as healers staunched the gaping wound in the small of her back with bandages. Amid the screaming and pitiful whimpering of the infirmary, nobody noticed him stir.

Lidan's eyes fluttered. He opened them slowly, gazing at the high ceiling. Awake again. Cautiously, he flexed his limbs, testing their strength. He winced as he braced his legs, pain sparking from his knees and toes, but he could still move them. Now to orientate himself. An infirmary. A neiad occupied the bench beside him, chest torn open. Healers carefully operated on his vital organs. Stifling a cry, he turned back to the ceiling and closed his eyes. He couldn't close his ears.

They didn't operate for long. A curse, a splatter, a clatter of discarded tools. Something heavy fell to the floor and was dragged away. Shifting his head ever so slightly to the left, he saw an empty bed and a trail of blood leading to the door. Slowly, he edged his way to the side and slipped off. It was surprisingly high. He fell heavily on his narrow chest, winded. Gasping, he crawled behind the stone slab and leaned against the wall, out of sight. A chance to escape.

*

Spotal held his jian firmly, point high. He circled his foe. The dreyad spat in his face and lunged. He knocked the point aside and delivered a glancing blow to the dreyad's left shoulder. Off balance, the dreyad fell hard on the snow. He didn't look down as he thrust beneath the dreyad's scapula, forcing his jian through cloth, skin, lung, and out the other side. A few painful shudders and the dreyad was still. He hardly noticed. His attention was elsewhere.

A body lay face-down upon the mountainside. A leather brigandine, sabre and shield lying on the snow beside him. A dreyad stood above, holding a cudgel.

Yelping in horror, he barged his way through the throng. The dreyad saw him coming. Snarling, he took an awkward swing with the cudgel, but he deflected it with his jian, parried the follow-up, and drove it into his enemy's throat.

Kneeling, he rolled Lidan over. The arrow jutted from his stomach like a flagpole. The red snow marked where he'd fallen. Choking back a scream, he scanned the battlefield, searching for archers hanging around the fringes. There. Kneeling behind a cluster of boulders, the long shafts of their arrows giving them away.

With a curse on his lips, he charged. Gaining a foothold on a smaller rock, he leapt over them, swinging his sword in a blurring circle. Its tip trailed blood through the cold, thin air as it bit deep. Again, and again, his arm jarred with the impacts.

Enough. Discipline. Bloodlust controlled, he ceased his swings. Three lay dead at his feet, barely distinguishable as dreyads after the bite of his vengeance.

He left the carcasses and returned to the battle. Only a handful remained. Auran's battleaxe smashed through the collarbone of one, Gwahl's dirk punctured another's chest, while Depani ran another through with her rapier. The remainder fled, stumbling over each other in their haste.

He rushed over to Gwahl.

'Lidan,' he whispered, but couldn't finish the sentence.

Gwahl's face softened. Scanning the snow, littered with bodies, he searched for their friend. Spotal pointed over his shoulder and Gwahl followed his hand, kneeling by Lidan's side.

He didn't follow. Collapsing into the hard-packed snow, he watched Auran walk over to the slumped bodies of Jeret and Kres, stretch out his hand, and close their eyelids. War horns sounded in the distance, approaching. They were hunted deer, pursued by a ravenous pack of howling wolves, snapping at their heels. Their army gone, along with two friends, how long would it be until they joined them?

Another campaign lost. He would surely be forgotten.

A few paces away, Gwahl rested light fingers on Lidan's chest, his cheek close to his mouth. Suddenly, he smiled and nodded to the rise and fall of his hand. A nod to Spotal. He sighed with relief.

It was short-lived. Alive, perhaps, but still in a perilous situation. Losing blood at high altitude, at risk of exposure, with an army in pursuit. He needed warmth, water, and rest. None of which were easily-found in these climates.

He approached Widrias, breathing heavily, leaning awkwardly on his leg.

'It's Lidan. Gwahl's with him. Wounded, but alive.'

'Show me,' Widrias grunted.

They skipped over to the daemon, who glanced up from tending their friend.

'He's alive. Wounded, but I should be able to patch him up.'

'Good. How long?' Widrias frowned.

'It'll take time,' Gwahl shook his head.

'How much?'

A shrug. 'Can't tell, I need to examine him properly. We need to get away from here, stick to our original plan and find a place to hide until they pass by. He needs rest, and he can't have that if we're running.'

'That's all very well, Gwahl,' growled Widrias, 'but who will carry him? We're all tired. This skirmish didn't help. It pains me to say it, but he'll be an unnecessary burden.'

'Leave him?' asked Spotal, appalled.

'We can't risk losing anyone else to fatigue.'

'No!' Spotal cried. It wasn't right.

'The quest is lost, Spotal, we are defeated. Now, our objective is survival and minimising our losses,' he sighed heavily.

'But leaving Lidan? Gwahl said he can patch him up.'

'With time, which we don't have.'

'If I can heal him, so can they,' said Gwahl.

Widrias shook his head. 'So?'

'They might take him prisoner, revive him enough for questioning…?' Gwahl raised his brows.

Widrias paused. 'He doesn't know enough to be useful to them.'

'That we know of, who knows what he picked up back at the Council? Would you risk it? Would you condemn him to death and torture?'

'I warned you back in the marshes, if anyone is wounded too badly to keep up–'

'I'll carry him,' Spotal interrupted. 'He's nothing but skin and bones anyway, I'll have to leave his shield and sabre, of course...'

'At this altitude? You wouldn't make it half a mile. You're not dying as well.'

He glowered at the satorr. This was not leadership. It wasn't honourable. Abandoning the boy to be captured, as Gwahl said. It wasn't Widrias's fault, of course. He was wounded, in more ways than one, but it didn't mean they had to accept his poor decisions because of it. For all his promises of carrying him, he knew how impractical it would be. Skin and bones he may be, but carrying a body was taxing. He might be able to stay ahead of the main army, but the dreyads? It didn't matter. If it meant protecting his friend, he would gladly face them a hundred times over.

'I'm from the Northlands,' growled Pwtrek. 'These climates are nothing to me. I shall carry him.'

Widrias scowled and rubbed his chin. He nodded. Spotal grinned at his friends. Praise the four winds. Gwahl caught his eye, a smirk threatening the corners of his mouth, before turning to the general with a blank expression.

'We should go. Those horns sounded close.'

Widrias nodded again.

'Onwards!' he bellowed, before turning back to Gwahl. 'I'll lead the way. You stay at the back and wipe our tracks. Understood?'

The smirk still threatened. The daemon nodded. Widrias looked him up and down, as if in distaste, and limped away. Spotal glanced at his friend and raised his eyebrows. The satorr's tone was surprisingly spiteful.

'Everything alright?'

'Fine, he's just taken the whole business with the key to heart.'

'I can tell.'

Gwahl shrugged. 'I've had my fair share of grumpy leaders, nothing I'm not used to.'

'You think Lidan will be alright?'

'As I said to Widrias, it's difficult to say until I examine him properly, but yes, I think he should heal, provided he's given the time to do so.'

He nodded, smiling. Gwahl urged him after the others, glancing over his shoulder. He followed his gaze down the mountain. Time, as the daemon said, was of the essence.

*

They ran for miles. Breath steamed before their noses as their boots pounded the mountainside. The jagged slopes forced them to run along the connecting peaks, where the air was thin and the wind as sharp as knives.

Finally, by nothing more than chance, they spotted a cave. Hidden beyond a cluster of rocks, nestled at the bottom of a valley. It was perfect for their purpose. They made the perilous descent, avoiding the snowdrifts and icy sheets. Following up at the rear, Gwahl had the easiest task as the route was already planned. Widrias had the worst, made all the more difficult by his leg. An unexpected patch of ice caught the satorr unawares, taking his legs from beneath him. Pwtrek was by his side in an instant, helping him up, supporting him, despite Lidan's added weight on his shoulder. Gwahl shook his head. The juggernaut's loyalty was matched only by his resilience.

At last, they overcame the harsh terrain and faced the cave's mouth, their laboured breathing echoing against the black walls. Chekry stepped forward to explore the cave, but Gwahl waved him back. The mountains were unsafe. By the bane of the giants, he was sure of it. Not because of soldiers, fabled keys, or even the terrain. Foul creatures existed in the depths of the wilderness, ones too terrible to face. If anyone were to put themselves in harm's way exploring, it would be him.

Fortunately, this cave was shallow, barely stretching back twenty paces, with no sharp turns or crevices obscured in shadow. They were alone.

Relaxing, he returned to the mouth and gave the all-clear. Sighing with relief, they filed in after him and collapsed on the floor. Nestled as it was among the rocks, there was hardly any snow in the depths of the cave, and although the rocks were ice-cold to touch, they were dry, or as dry as he could hope for.

Settling down to one knee, Pwtrek eased Lidan from his shoulder and set him down on a discarded cloak that Auran plundered from a dreyad's corpse. A second cloak was draped over him as a thin blanket. Shooing the others away, Gwahl knelt by his side. They shuffled away to prepare their new campsite. He watched them for a second before turning his attention back to the matter at hand.

In the absence of fire, cleaning the wound would be difficult, even with the medicine pouches he'd carried since the shipwreck. Improvisation and compromise would be necessary.

Slowly, carefully, he removed the brigandine, undoing the buckles, easing the armour away. The underlying shirt was covered in blood. He cut it away, revealing Lidan's thin torso. His lacing scars were a grim reminder of his ordeals. Gwahl ignored them, they were unimportant. Two fresh, open wounds stared at him like grisly eyes. The wound in his shoulder was superficial, barely a centimetre deep, easily fixed with a needle and thread. His stomach seemed worse. By some ill-luck, the arrowhead had struck him cleanly between two of the plates of his brigandine. Fortunately, the toughened leather spared some of the force of the arrow. Its iron head was barely buried an inch into his stomach, snapped off at the base.

Gripping the head with one hand, supporting the stomach with the other, he teased it free. Blood oozed. He staunched the wound with a piece of lint. A minute of sustained pressure. He removed the lint and examined the wound again. First, the smell. Only dried blood, none of the distinct malodour of a perforated bowel. He dabbed again, stretching the wound to see its base. Dabbed again. No spurting, no active pooling, just a generalised ooze. No extension beyond the deepest layer of muscle. The boy's lean, hard midriff took the entirety of the wound, his internal organs spared. Lucky fool.

Lidan stirred against his touch, eyes flickering. He placed his hand on his forehead and shushed him gently, as if comforting a sick

334

child. He slowly relaxed, enough for him to continue. A length of waxed string and a fishbone needle to suture the wounds. Only a few soft moans, nothing more. He dressed the wound with more pledgets and linen bandage.

Rolling him over, he inspected the back of his skull. He took care, softly palpating the wound, searching for the raised edges of broken bone. It was intact. An ugly laceration needed more suturing. Whether there was any internal damage, only time would tell. He'd seen men in similar situations lose consciousness of the battlefield and recover a few minutes later, seemingly well. Their convulsions and eventual death hours later were stark reminders of the perils of such injuries.

Leaning back on his haunches, he sighed, admiring his handiwork. He was no surgeon. Situations like these, like Widrias' leg, were exactly why he needed to keep on top of the practice. It was crude, untidy, and the wounds would undoubtedly scar, but it would do. Now, he could only hope the brain was intact and infection wouldn't eat the wounds alive.

He cocked his head. He had an audience.

'How does it look?'

'See for yourself,' he replied.

Pwtrek leaned forward and pulled the blanket aside. After a few seconds, he gently placed it back.

'Looks decent,' said Pwtrek.

'It'll do.'

'Were the wounds deep?'

'No, nothing too serious. They looked a lot worse than they were.'

'That's good,' Pwtrek nodded.

While he'd been working, the others had pushed as much snow as they could to the mouth of the cave, building up a snowy wall to obscure it further. With luck, they would remain undetected. Widrias oversaw the building of the wall, rubbing his leg as he watched them.

'I'll take care of him, don't worry,' said Pwtrek, still looking at Lidan.

'Thank you,' he smiled. He nodded to Widrias. 'Watch over him as well. He's taken our failure with a heavy heart. It's affecting him.'

'I know, I've always watched out for him. I won't stop now.'

He nodded and cleared his throat.

'One more thing.'

'What?'

He scratched behind his ear. Widrias may have discarded his warnings, but Pwtrek wouldn't. Not in these matters. 'Watch out for the Horrors of the Mountain.'

Pwtrek stared at him, his features suddenly dark. 'They're extinct, Gwahl, they died long ago, before I was born.'

'No. They live to this day, skulking in the dark, preying on whatever meat Enadir sees fit to provide them with.'

'Why?'

'Why what?'

'Why are you scared of them? Surely we've had enough myths on this quest already?'

'It's no myth, Pwtrek.'

'A bedtime story to scare children.'

'The night before we found the plateau. I found a boulder with three gouges cut into it. Claw-marks. I've been keeping an eye out. It wasn't the only one. No other creature can cut stone like that.'

'Doesn't prove anything.'

'There aren't any animals,' he pressed, urgently. 'No mountain-hares, no lynxes, eagles, goats, not even rodents. What could have scared them away?'

'The garrison on the plateau might have hunted them?'

'No. They couldn't have hunted every single animal in the area. They've been scared away. By the Horrors. I tried to warn Widrias but he wouldn't listen. I beg you, listen to me now so you might be prepared.'

'We must tell the others. If you're worried they're still alive, everyone deserves to know.'

'No. Widrias ordered me not to tell anyone. If I were to go against his orders, it would undermine his command. By the bane of the giants, we need a strong leader, or at least someone who plays that part. Tell no-one.'

'So why tell me?'

'You're used to these climates. You and Noswen. You're likeliest to recognise any abnormalities in the terrain, any signs of something…wrong.'

Pwtrek looked doubtful, but said nothing. Eventually, he nodded, and turned to help the others.

Gwahl rubbed his chin. Hopefully, he was wrong. But how likely was that?

*

It became apparent the wind lied about the closeness of the pursuit. It was several hours later that the army passed them by. The tramp and stamp of boot on crushed ice and packed snow sounded their arrival and departure.

Spotal peered over the snowdrift at the enemy. Scouts fanned out in an ark either side to the main column, stooping low to the ground as they searched for tracks that might lead them to their quarry.

He held his breath as a dreyad passed within forty paces of their hideout. Ducking low against the snow, he watched, scarcely daring to blink. The scout knelt to the ground, tracing a finger across the snow. A sharp turn of the head and he stared intently at the surrounding mountains, to their right. He stepped forward. A few paces too close.

His hair stood on ends. He wasn't concealed well enough, his crown was visible, but he daren't move. A movement might catch the eye and the scout was too close to risk it.

Another few paces. He was close enough to see the fine scar on his cheek. Or was it just the natural texture of his bark-like skin? His belt buckle was carefully shaped like an acorn, quite beautiful. His arrows were fletched with owl feathers. The arm guard was on his right hand. A left-hander. Many swordsmen disliked fighting left-handers, it demanded a change in stance they found unfamiliar. Not him. He kept the same guard. Why change his approach to suit his enemy? True, it would open him up to an attack, but his enemy would be similarly exposed.

Another few paces. A hand crept up to the quiver, fingering an arrow.

His hand slipped beneath his stomach, searching for his hilt.

A final step. A pause. Narrowed eyes.

The hand dropped from the quiver. Straightening, the dreyad turned and walked away, following his companions along the mountain ridge. By the grace of the north winds, they remained undetected.

He released the held breath into his hand to hide the treacherous mist and slithered back to the safety of the cave.

The twins were sleeping by the entrance, Pwtrek next to them, his barrel chest rising and falling steadily. Gwahl sat on a rock with his chin in his hand, deep in thought. Auran lay staring at the ceiling. Noswen slept with her back upright against the wall, her hand on her falchion. The general sat beside her, watching him. At the back of the cave Lidan twitched in his sleep.

Stepping over the huddled neiads he bent to Widrias.

'A scout just passed us, I doubt they'll double back to re-check every pace. I think we'll be safe for a while.'

'Is the main force still outside?' shivered the satorr.

'Still walking past. They've formed a thin column, only three wide, stretching back for quite some distance.'

'Moving quickly?'

'Slower than expected. Perhaps they're tiring?'

'Perhaps, but that only means that they'll be doubling back soon to return to the plateau. It doesn't matter, we can stay here for a while and wait for Lidan to heal.'

'If I may,' whispered Gwahl. 'I wouldn't want to stay in any one place for too long. It only increases the risk of someone stumbling on us. We can keep making small gains towards our destination as well.'

'No, we won't last long wandering about in the cold. We can stay here for as long as we need,' Widrias shook his head.

'Our small company can avoid their slow army easily enough. Besides, as much as moving him may affect the healing, infection would make it worse,' said Gwahl.

'Infection?' said Widrias.

'Aye. Crowded together in here as we are, stagnating air, difficult to maintain simple hygiene practices… infection is only ever one contaminant away. Besides, who knows what we've brought with us from Cysgodgors?'

Widrias growled. 'We shall leave it until the very last moment before we move away from safety. I don't want to be caught in that cold for longer than we need to.'

Spotal frowned. It sounded suspiciously like the desire to stay put for a while. As Gwahl said, if they moved every few days at least it was progress.

'With respect, sir, shouldn't we try to reach my Kingdom sooner rather than later?'

'Yes. But we need this rest. I set the pace, not you,' said Widrias.

There was that spiteful tone again. He should leave him alone, let him calm down. It's what he should do. Should.

'But our supplies,' he continued. 'We need to eat more in these climates just to maintain bodily function. Won't we run out?'

'Why do you all constantly question me?' hissed the satorr. 'Am I not good enough for you? Do you want me to step down as leader?'

He flinched. This was unexpected.

'I – I apologise, sir, I didn't mean to imply anything.'

'"I didn't mean to" why don't you think before opening your mouth?'

'Sir, please, I never meant to-'

'Don't waste your breath, Spotal. I hardly care about what you think. I don't blame Lleunedd for discarding you from his council.'

He blinked. His jaw tightened, pressing his teeth together until he was sure they'd shatter. Opening his mouth, he searched for an appropriate response. There was none. With a grim expression, he turned away. Once at the cave mouth, he sat and stared at the sky through the narrow window between rock and snow. He idly played with the talisman on the thong about his neck. A nervous habit, a close friend once told him. From behind, he heard Widrias snort, followed by a rustle as he lay down to sleep. He should have left him alone.

A touch to his shoulder made him jump. He hid the talisman again beneath his brigandine.

'Pay no heed, Spotal. He's sour with loss, he didn't mean it,' said Gwahl.

He shrugged. The insult was as wounding as it was unexpected. Difficult to brush away. But then, truths were always more difficult to ignore than petty lies.

'If it's any comfort, I agree with you,' said Auran, crawling up next to them. 'We've not had a chance to wash properly, our clothes are undoubtedly crawling with disease. The sooner we get off these mountains, the better. As ever, your advice was sound.'

'As ever,' agreed Gwahl. 'I know better than to ignore the advice of a soldier of your calibre.'

'My calibre?' he whispered. 'The lowest possible.'

'Don't say that,' frowned Gwahl.

'It's true.'

'You're being dramatic,' said Gwahl.

'No,' he shook his head. 'No, he's right. You know full well why I'm here, instead of defending my country's borders. You know I failed my duties to Lleunedd. You know what kind of soldier I am.'

'I do, a fine one.'

'Aye,' agreed Auran. 'Don't let your past haunt you, whatever it may be.'

'Well I have real regrets. Real consequences to my mistakes. Things you wouldn't understand. Losses beyond you.'

Auran sighed but didn't reply. Gwahl tutted lightly, as if scolding a child with a tantrum.

'We are all subject to the torture of memory. Don't pick on Auran, my friend, it is out of your character. You should all get some sleep, there's little else to do around here.'

*

He stirred and opened his eyes. His head ached, his stomach stabbed, and a rock dug into his back. Everything was blurred, distorted, in shadow. One of the shadows shimmered, warping into a silhouette, reaching out.

He recoiled, twisting to avoid the touch. The pain in his stomach flared, shot through his core. His head felt like it would split open, searing, throbbing, burning pain. Groaning, he lay still, willing the agony to end. A familiar voice pierced the mist of pain.

'Lie still, my friend, you're safe.'

'It hurts,' he moaned, flinching as a cool hand rested on his forehead.

'Yes, you've been wounded. No! No, lie back,' his attempt to sit up was cut short by a firm push. 'The best thing for you to do is sleep. I'll fill you in on what happened later.'

'I have a headache.'

'Drink this.'

A helmet of melted snow was handed to him, wonderfully crisp and fresh. He lapped it up gratefully, soothing a parched throat. Thirst sated, he lay back down.

*

He woke again. His head felt clear. As much a blessing as a curse, with the intensified awareness of the ache in his gut. In a vain attempt to ease the gnaw, he rolled into a ball. No use. The movement only exacerbated his discomfort. Panting from the effort, he lay still.

Gradually, the tenderness drained away and he was able to take stock of his surroundings. A cave, blocked by a snowdrift, filled with dark rocks, each one emitting steam at regular intervals.

One of the rocks moved and stood. A cool hand rested on his forehead. He relaxed.

'Good, you're awake.'

'How long until I'm better?'

Gwahl shrugged. 'Who knows? Your wounds aren't too serious, you should be fit to travel within a few days. Until then, you need rest. Don't move, now, be still. Still, Lidan! Let me work.'

He did as he was told and watched his friend re-dress the wound in his gut. The sight of the bloody mess made his head spin.

Thankfully, it was over soon enough and a fresh bandage was secured.

'Did everyone survive the skirmish?'

Gwahl's face dropped. 'Jeret and Kres died. You were wounded, as you know, but everyone else made it with nothing but minor injuries.'

'Where are we?'

'Still on the mountains. Be sure to thank Pwtrek, he carried you here from where you lay.'

'The army?'

'Passed us four days ago. You've been in and out of consciousness.'

'I don't remember,' he shook his head. It made it spin so he stopped. 'Are we safe?'

He grimaced. 'Probably, for now. They must have returned to the plateau by another route. We must take care as we proceed, I doubt they'd let us go so easily.'

'Easily?'

'Relatively,' he smiled.

He smiled back. 'I suppose this whole ordeal's been relatively easy for you?'

'What makes you think that?'

'The elders from Weaverlodge used to tell stories about daemons,' he watched him carefully. 'Your adventures were always so grand, things like this must be so... ordinary.'

'I'm sorry to disappoint you, but this is as unique as any other quest. Far from mundane, far from easy,' Gwahl chuckled.

'Do you have any stories?' he asked, after a pause.

'Plenty.'

'Would you tell one? I'd like to hear about a daemon adventure from your own perspective, see how it compares to the tales I've been told.'

'Any in particular?'

'How about your home? A story of your home would be good?'

He waited for an answer, but there was only silence. Turning, careful not to twist his torso too much, he examined the daemon's face. A thoughtful expression, as if carefully selecting a single account from a vast library of tales.

'It doesn't matter if not, it can be something else?' he suggested, eager to have it out.

Gwahl shrugged and smiled faintly. 'I am from a forgotten island, beyond the borders of any of your maps. When young, I began wandering and sailed across the Great Waters to distant lands. I was born and now I travel, one day I will die.'

He blinked. Possibly the worst story he'd ever heard, made worse by the anticipation.

'Come on…' he began.

'A typically vague answer,' breathed Spotal from nearby. He shuffled over to them and sat by their side. Auran followed.

'All your adventures, yet you'll only give a few meagre sentences?' said Spotal.

'You asked for a story, there's the entire story of my life!' Gwahl smiled, teasing them.

'Trust me, Lidan, I've known that daemon for longer than I care to admit, and his life is still a mystery,' sighed Spotal.

'It doesn't have to be a massive, sweeping adventure? How about one from before this war?' he suggested.

The smile faltered for a moment, before flashing again, but perhaps more thinly.

'He's too stubborn,' Spotal sighed. 'Too preoccupied with keeping this mysterious allure. The illusion would be lost if we knew all about him.'

'What about you, then?' he turned to the calef. 'Do you have any stories? How did you come to join the Council?'

'Oh,' Spotal frowned, and shook his head. 'A sad and pathetic tale, hardly worth listening to.'

'I'd like to know?' he asked.

'I might not want to tell it,' said Spotal.

'Yet you judge Gwahl for being secretive?'

A moment's hesitation, and the calef shrugged. 'I'll tell you mine if you tell me yours?'

Now Lidan fell silent. 'I'd rather not.'

'No?' asked Spotal.

'No,' he shook his head. Their judgement would be too damning. He refused to endure his friends' withering, scathing looks at the revelation of his past failings. He refused to recount the tale, even to himself. To recount his loss… and Zile.

'Well I'm in the mood for a story,' grumbled Auran.

'I'm afraid it's a bartering system we have in this corner of the cave,' smiled Gwahl.

'A story for a story it is, then, although it's hardly an interesting one,' Auran shrugged.

'Oh, I'm sure Lidan will be the judge of that.'

Chapter 21

'My home is in the Southlands, as you know,' Auran began. 'I lived in a town to the north-west of our country, close to the Werlit River, on the east bank. Quite far from Maralen.'

'Maralen?' asked Lidan.

Auran nodded. 'Yes! Capital of the Southlands. Our jewel, built of marble and glass and gold and silver. It would catch the rays of the rising and setting sun and light the way for returning sailors. It was beautiful.'

'I've been there a few times,' smiled Gwahl. 'Truly one of the most beautiful cities ever built.'

'It was glorious. As I said, my home is a town many miles away from it, across the vast Werlit. It wasn't a large, fewer than thirty buildings, but we owned a lot of land where we farmed crops and kept our livestock. We were all farmers, craftsmen and guards to our homes. Although our lives were simple in comparison to some, they were far from easy. Early rise and late to sleep, caring for our land and protecting our fields from the terrors of the Daiwen Jungle, which lay only a few miles away. Of course, the grasslands where we lived held their own dangers, from wild animals that preyed on our livestock to the thieving nomads of the plains. Beyond the grasslands were the great deserts, which had their own perils... Nevertheless, it was a good, honest life, to work the land with the sun warming your back. The only life I ever wanted.

'The people of my home were kind and true, we would obey the commands of our wise elders, and through them the commands of our lord in Maralen. There was a daemon in our village as well, Gwahl, I'm not sure if I told you before?'

'You didn't!' exclaimed Gwahl. 'Do you recall his name, or what he looked like?'

'Of course. His name was Dwerel, he looked quite similar to you, only older.'

Gwahl sat back, smiling. 'Dwerel,' he repeated. 'I've not seen him for a long time... I knew he was in the Southlands, but never guessed he was in your village. He carried a gnarled willow stick, with a large blue tourmaline crystal on its head, yes?'

'That's him! How did you know him?'

'There are few daemons left, we are all generally aware of each other. Please, continue with your tale.'

'Of course. Dwerel was one of our elders, but he spent much of his time away. Sometimes in Maralen with our lord, or deep in the jungle, up to our sacred Setarack Temple. We didn't mind though, we valued the time he spent with us and when he was away we'd just get on with our lives. I was just about to start a family, My wife was expecting and everything was going well for us.

'As all stories of peace and prosperity go, our lives were set to change radically. King Stolach decided to expand his kingdom across the Great Waters. His first port of call was Sea Neiad Island, the inhabitants of which were only too ready to sell their ships to his cause. Many men from across the land were called from their homes to serve in the army of our lord and battle the neiads in great naval clashes near our borders. For a long time, our forces were able to repel these attacks, and after a while they ceased altogether.

'Initially, we thought they abandoned the fight, that the king realised he would never manage to conquer us. After weeks of waiting for another assault which never came, we were decommissioned and sent back to our homes.

'We later learned that Stolach instead gathered his forces for a vast invasion of the Jagged Isles, and after a whole summer of war, conquered more than half of the islands. Nobody heard anything of this invasion until too late. The neiads saw to that. Intercepting any ships trying to get into those islands, or any poor fools brave enough to attempt escape. Anyway, the point is he conquered the lands and has forged alliances with the various lords of the islands. In return, he left their homes relatively intact. He now had massive resources of new soldiers to call upon.

'With these new forces, Stolach restarted his quest to conquer the Southlands. Unprepared, our lord had barely enough time to prepare a counter-attack with our own navy to stall this massive fleet. I was away hunting in Daiwen with my companions when the messengers came from Maralen requesting us to re-enlist. We were not there when our navy was swept aside like dry leaves in an autumn storm. We were not there to defend our beaches and farmlands as Stolach's army swept across our land. They sailed their ships up the Werlit River and his troops ransacked my village and slaughtered everyone, including the women, the children,' Auran closed his eyes, 'my Arined.

'When we returned from the jungle, we were greeted with the sight of our town burnt to the ground, our families left to rot, and one of the king's standards planted in the ashes. My companions and I set fire to our loved ones, left the village, and headed for Maralen. It took time, as we had to avoid the campsites of the invading forces. When we finally reached our golden city, it was destroyed. Completely destroyed. The Light of the Southlands had been extinguished, as had our hopes of driving away Stolach's armies.

'So, we left, and turned back to the Daiwen Jungle, where we planned to survive for as long as we could, possibly fighting a guerrilla war against Stolach's army. In our hearts, we knew it was futile. We spent a week in the jungle, hiding and surviving as the king's army penetrated the jungle to destroy the few villages beneath the trees. Everywhere we went, we heard yet more screams as men and women were slain in his name. It seems as though our lord made it clear that we would never submit to his rule, so Stolach decided not to show us the same mercy he showed the inhabitants of the Jagged Isles. In fact, he cared so little about us, he returned to Crastalan after Maralen fell, leaving General Hanem Kreherr in charge of the invasion.'

Spotal, shook his head. 'That maniac.'

'Yes,' continued Auran, 'he doesn't understand mercy, only cruelty. One by one, our villages fell, and the jungle grew silent. Animals grew fat as they feasted on the flesh of the slain. Even after the last village fell, the soldiers remained in the jungle. At first, we couldn't understand what they were searching for, before realising Hanem's greed could not be satisfied by the bounty of gold and precious stones in Maralen alone. He searched for Setarack Temple, to ransack it and plunder it of its treasures. None of us had ever been there before ourselves, but we had a general idea of where it lay from what Dwerel told us. Without much optimism, we set off to warn the few men who lived there of the approaching danger. Took us weeks to find it. By now, Stolach controlled just about the whole civilized country.'

'The Setarack Temple?' asked Lidan, curiously. 'I've heard of it before but never understood what it was?'

'The holy temple of the Southlands, the place where the blessings of the Sun fall greatest.'

'The sun?' Lidan remarked, surprised. In all his life, he'd only ever heard of worship to the winds, the winds that brought life and hope to the world, or so they said.

'Yes,. The giver of light and warmth to us. It gives its energy to the plants of the world, which give energy to animals, which give energy to us. It's the giver of life. Though it may seem strange to you, my friend, the way most of the inhabitants of Nefarwy worship the winds puzzles us,' he held up his hand when Lidan opened his mouth to reply. 'It matters not who or what we pray to, the messages and morals behind each prayer are identical. I have no taste for discussing this topic right now. Where was I?'

'Trying to find the Temple.'

'Of course, thank you,. When we finally found the temple amid the jungle's mountain slopes, to our joy we discovered our lord managed to escape Maralen with threescore soldiers, and Dwerel led them to this haven. Here they intended on remaining until they could think of a new plan of action. In the end, our lord bravely decided to remain in the temple with a score of soldiers and all the temple sages. The rest of us were to cross the Great Waters to find the Council.

'Dwerel led us across the mountains and through the jungle, across the vast grasslands and to the northernmost point of the Southlands. There, we attacked a small garrison of soldiers who were guarding a tiny merchant vessel, and stole the ship. However, with so many soldiers across the land we knew more troops would soon be after us. Dwerel got off the ship and started scuppering the two other vessels in the small harbour. We turned back to get him, but he ordered us to go on, that it would be foolish to return for him. The last I saw him he was standing strong against dozens of the king's troops. We did not see his fate,' he paused momentarily and glanced at Gwahl, but he said nothing.

'We sailed north and said farewell to our home. My friends, Piknex, Drei, Ken-ijj, Laparn, and the rest of us, numbering only a few over forty. All that remained of our Southland army. When the Kingdom of the calefs came into sight, so did two calefin warships come to greet us. We managed to convince them that we were not there to invade, rather to escape, and they guided us to a safe place to disembark in the Midlands. We left the ship where it was and travelled through Dailas Forest until the Council Guard found us. That's how I came to be here.'

'I thought you said it wasn't very interesting,' said Lidan, softly.

'I don't find it that interesting,' replied Auran, 'only painful.'

'Of course. Is that why you're here, then? For revenge for what Stolach did?'

'Partly for revenge, partly because the life I knew is lost forever, partly because my lord sent me, mostly because Stolach's greed must be stopped..'

'What about Hanem?' asked Spotal. 'Will you hunt him down?'

'One day, perhaps, but not until Enadir is rid of Stolach. He's the main priority. Personal vendettas can wait.'

'It's hardly personal. A man like him deserves to die.'

'Probably, but right now our task is Stolach. Who knows how long this will take? I would like to kill Hanem, I admit, but now we must all focus on the task at hand.'

'But don't you hate him for what he's done to you?' asked Lidan.

'Of course I hate him,' said Auran, 'but I won't let that hatred cloud my actions. I believe that one must keep a cool, level head in battle. If you give yourself over to hatred then your vision becomes like a tunnel, as you see nothing else around you apart from the thing you loathe, which is dangerous. Imagine if you were fighting and you saw your enemy across the field, but to your right your friend was hard pressed against another foe, in dire need of help. If you completely gave yourself to your rage, then what would happen? You would see only your enemy and attack him, and your friend would die. That's how I see it, anyway. One day I will meet Hanem and I hope I'll be strong enough to push down my hatred and fight the battle around me.'

Lidan chewed his lip. What Auran said might apply to Auran, but to him? No. His hatred gave him strength. Strength necessary to overcome his foes. Besides, Auran spoke of hating a single individual, his own hatred was directed towards any who served Stolach.

No, that was a lie. There was one. Grey eyes.

Another thought struck and he turned to Gwahl.

'What will we do, Gwahl, after we've won? Auran just said that after Stolach's gone people like Hanem will still be around, what will we do about them?'

Gwahl didn't say anything for a while, slowly tracing patterns in the dust at his feet. Finally, he replied.

'We'll have to do what's necessary. Once Stolach is eliminated, most of his armies will surrender. There will be a few, however, who will not, and we'll have to fight them.'

'So this mission is just the first step? And we have an entire race to run ahead of us?'

'Not at all. The first steps were taken a very long time ago, we are well into the race now, as you put it. True, we have a lot left to do, but it isn't an impossible task.'

They were silent for a while before Auran looked up again.

'A barter, you said, now it's your turn for a story.'

Gwahl rubbed his chin dramatically.

'Excluding any stories about me, what would you like?'

'You must have lots of stories about these Northlands?' Lidan asked.

'We're not in the Northlands,' chuckled Gwahl. 'You'd know if we were in the Northlands. As for stories, I can tell you an exciting story about a courageous calef, if you like? A swordsman like the world has never seen before!'

'He doesn't need to hear my life story,' said Spotal with a wink.

'A calef whose skills far exceed your own, I'm afraid!' Gwahl smiled as Spotal clamped his hand over his chest in feigned insult. 'It's a tale that's passed into folklore by now, but I can give you its true, unflinching account.'

'Now I'm excited,' said Auran, shifting around to find a more comfortable position.

'Our story is set many centuries ago, during the time of the Cataclysmic War, when the cockatrice fought with the giants for Nefarwy. Our hero is the calef, Casset Ffersiil, known as Casset the Dancer-'

'The Battle of Burning Snow!' exclaimed Spotal. 'I adore this tale, my mother used to tell it to me when I was young.'

Gwahl frowned at the calef. 'Yes, the Battle of the Burning Snow. Now if you'd let me...

'Let me set the scene...the war between the giants and cockatrice has been ongoing for three years already, eight if you count the destruction of Alnaitack, and the land is already ravaged and scarred by countless battles. The inhabitants of Nefarwy fight tenaciously beside their ruling giants, but the cockatrice are many, their numbers bolstered by the monsters of the lands. You see, Lidan, the cockatrice were a race unlike any other. They were intelligent and sentient, but monsters at the same time, not unlike the dragons of old. Their main skill was of languages, for they could twist their tongues to communicate with all living things, from hydras to horses, giants to troglodytes, all creatures in Enadir could understand and be understood by them. It was because of this talent that the monsters of the land joined them and fought as armies against the giants. Of course, it was not only monsters who joined. A large number of men, satorrs, dreyads, juggernauts, goblins, even a few treacherous giants also listened to their sibilant hisses. But of all our races, it was the troglodytes who most listened to these serpents.

'Anyway, back to our story. The cockatrice were fierce and difficult to fight, as to hold their stare for too long would drive a strong man mad, and that's without considering their razor-sharp talons, serrated beaks, and whipping tails.'

'What did they look like?' he cut across. 'Were they serpents or birds or what?'

'A mixture of both. Long serpentine bodies with two large feathered wings and two short legs like a bird. Their feet ended in vicious talons, and their feathered heads were covered in horns. Their beaks were like scythes, capable of disembowelling a man with the softest touch. Finally, the tips of their long tails had a long bony blade, which they would lash at their enemies like a sword. Most grew to twenty feet long, seven feet tall when standing, but the largest one I ever saw was easily over fifteen feet tall.'

'You've *seen* a cockatrice?' asked Spotal, mouth open.

'I am old, Spotal, I've seen many things. Go to Rhetta Mountains one day, the library has a few intact skeletons for you to ogle at if you wish. As I was saying, the war was well underway, and far away to the north, in the midst of the Rhetta Mountains, was the stronghold of Mount Stohn. A former seat for the kings, shared with Crastalan. However, the last king, Ukrid Aggalusik, had been slain two years earlier after ruling for only a matter of weeks. For the next decade, including the Battle of the Burning Snow, the lands were ruled by Deia the daemon, as steward.

'Deia was at Mount Stohn with a great army when he was informed of a horde of enemies fast approaching, ignoring all other armies and settlements as they headed directly to the citadel. He sent urgent appeals for help to his allies, but was unsure whether they would reach them in time. In a fortnight, the cockatrice were battering against the doors of the stronghold. Despite the valiant attempts of the countless soldiers under Deia's command, the enemy were too many and the stronghold was breached.

'Mount Stohn is a hollowed-out mountain, and at the time was the most heavily defended place in the entire land, but the enemy were so many that even these ancient, formidable defences could not hold out. Slowly but surely, over the next three weeks, our forces were driven out of the lower levels. Can you imagine the horror of fighting in that mountains? The halls ringing with the screams of the dead and dying, the shrieks of monsters, the wretched, frantic babbling of maddened men. All the while desperately trying to make your supplies last, fearing your turn at the front line to do battle with the cruel cockatrice and their thralls. At the beginning, a large battle was fought in complete darkness in an attempt to avoid the gaze of the monsters, but the sheer slaughter that resulted was proof of such folly. These soldiers did not have the skill to fight blind and their punishment was ultimate. I don't know who thought of such a foolish plan, but surely they was among the first to meet their bloody end.

'Things were looking dire for Deia and his army, retreating day by day, level by level. But help finally arrived. From the west came a massive fleet of ships, their decks heaving under the weight of hundreds of thousands of soldiers. Giants, calefs, daemons, minotorrs, men, hanex... all had come to lift the siege. At their head was Hakkalai the minotorr, who had gathered together this relief force to save the steward.

'With a cry that echoed for miles, the leader of the cockatrice, Sunstrike, ordered his forces to split in two, one half continuing the attack on the stronghold while the other faced the relief force. From the prow of his ship, Hakkalai saw the enemy form up on the shore, preparing themselves for the imminent clash, and he gave the order to fire the fleet's war machines.

'As great boulders and mighty arrows flew from the sea towards the cockatrice and their minions, the cursed serpents took to the skies as a dark cloud and dive-bombed the ships, destroying as many of the war machines as they could. Desperately, Hakkalai and his captains attempted to manoeuvre their ships into a defensive formation, but the war was still young and nobody had yet enough experience to devise any truly effective battle formations to counter the aerial threats of the cockatrice. The losses Hakkalai suffered were heavy, but the sea was also littered with the floating carcasses of felled enemies.

'Knowing full well the main battle lay within the fortress itself, the minotorr ordered his armies to the shore in their longboats, as the war machines and archers did what they could to cover them. Now the bodies of dead giants, calefs, men, and hanex joined the cockatrice on the waves as they were plucked from the longboats by the ones who'd made it through the barrage of missiles. But for every soldier taken screaming into the sky, thirty more made it to land, forming ranks to meet the waiting enemy.

'The melee on the beach was fierce. The first wave of the relief force were cut apart nearly as soon as they stepped foot on the freezing sands. All of them apart from Casset the Dancer. This sword-master was named after the elegance and fluidity of his fighting. A sweeping, gliding movement that saw him spin past the blades of his foes and kill them before they knew what happened. His sword would flash like lightning and cut down countless enemies in minutes. He was so confident in his abilities he wore no armour, only loose-fitting silk garments as smooth and free-flowing as his fighting style.'

'Arrogant,' muttered Auran.

'No,' said Spotal, 'a master with the blade.'

'A performer,' continued Gwahl. 'A calef who knew how to inspire his companions and urge them ever on to victory. When the rest of the first wave were hacked apart as they stumbled through the freezing waves and on the sludgy sand, he danced into the heart of the enemy and tore a hole through their phalanx. Fountains of blood exploded around him, but his white silks remained pristine as he weaved through the lines, delivering a swift death to those foolish enough to cross his blade. His dance of death spurned Hakkalai's forces on, and the second wave of soldiers landed on the beach, then the third, and fourth, and fifth. Eventually the relief force was pushing back the enemy, Casset at their head, and the army of the cockatrice found themselves caught between Mount Stohn and the liberating swords of the relief force.

'The winged serpents themselves soon gave up harrying the war machines of the ships and swept into the flanks and rear of the relief force, but that did little to stem the tide.

'It was when Hakkalai's army was within fifty feet of Mount Stohn's cumbersome outer gate that Sunstrike descended from the skies and landed before Casset. He fixed his gaze on the calef and challenged him to a duel. Single combat to the death. Casset knew the risks of such a duel, as Sunstrike had a reputation of being a cunning and competent fighter. Sunstrike also had a particularly potent gaze, even for a cockatrice, and several mighty warriors were already broken after engaging in single combat with him.

'But the calef was a proud soldier and the idea of walking out of this duel as victor was all too appealing, so he gave an eloquent bow and accepted the challenge. It was at this moment he did something truly incredible, he gripped the hem of his silk cloak, ripped off a length, and tied it around his eyes to blindfold himself.'

'No, he didn't!' objected Spotal. 'He blindfolded himself with a ribbon his love gave him!'

'A romanticized version of the true tale. Casset's only love was war, his only pleasure the kiss of battle. I can tell you with confidence, he tore the hem of his silk cloak as a blindfold. Anyway, when Sunstrike saw what the calef had done, his feathers bristled with fury, for there were few things he enjoyed more than seeing courageous heroes crumble to broken, pathetic shells after looking into his hellish eyes for too long. With a cry of rage, he swept his tail at the calef in a whiplash that would have cut an oak in two.

'Casset pirouetted out of the way, and the duel began. They danced this deadly dance for an age, the calef relying on his other senses to guide him as he felt his way towards the cockatrice, the lighting in his hand glimmering as it parried the serpent's claws. Round and round the champions went, probing each other in search of weaknesses and retreating when none were to be found. Eventually, Sunstrike grew tired and flew up high, his intent to dive-bomb the calef and end him. Casset felt the winds change and once again skipped clear of his enemy, lunging with his sword as he landed. The blade slipped through Sunstrike's breast like a hot knife through butter. The serpent fell to the ground with a crash.

'Casset tore off his blindfold and strode up to the dying cockatrice, looked him dead in the eye, and whispered these words-'

'"Nefarwy will soon be purged of your filth. Look at your conqueror and shiver, for you and your people have brought upon yourselves the doom of your kind."' Spotal recited the thords with a smile.

'Sunstrike shuddered with his final breath and Casset looked away, a tear on his cheek. Soon after, the rest of the army was broken and driven away, out of Mount Stohn. Deia thanked Hakkalai and his captains dearly, and to Casset he gave a great gift; a dragon scale. The daemon related to the calef how centuries ago, the dragons drove the cockatrice out of Nefarwy, and believed that Casset would help them do the same again. The calef wore that dragon scale on his breast from that day on, and was greatly feared by the cockatrice.

'They cleared the battlefield of the dead and made an enormous funeral pyre, with the body of Sunstrike buried at its heart. There were so many carcasses that when it was finally set alight, the inferno was hot enough to burn the earth beneath the snow, hence the name of the battle.'

Lidan nodded his head approvingly. 'Casset must have been a great warrior. Did he defeat the cockatrice in the end?'

Gwahl shifted. 'Not exactly, the cockatrice were eventually defeated, sixty-four years later, but Casset died in battle twenty years before the final cockatrice was killed. He was burned alive by boiling tar and quicklime, poured over him from the skies.'

'How did he not lose his mind after looking into Sunstrike's eyes at the end?' asked Auran.

'The power of their stare was lost after death, and Sunstrike was dying, so Casset would not have lost his mind by meeting his gaze in his last moments. But he *was* still affected, as Sunstrike's eyes still reflected the darkness of the world. He was a much grimmer calef from that day onwards, forever haunted by those visions. Of course, some say that this made him an even greater warrior, as he fought in vain to clear the world of the doom he witnessed in the eyes of his fallen enemy.'

'What kind of things did he see in Sunstrike's eyes?' asked Lidan in a whisper.

'Who knows? There are preserved cockatrice eyes to be found around the world, but there is nothing to be seen in those pickled old things, anyone who says otherwise is just trying to sell you something. The serpents are dead, and Enadir is a better place without them.

'But I believe that's enough story-telling for now, we should get some sleep. I trust we have many long days ahead of us, and sleep is needed for them all.'

*

The following morning, Widrias agreed to move camp.

'Too close to the plateau, here,' he announced, gruffly. 'Easy for them to stumble on us.'

Lacking the strength to walk, Lidan was strapped to Pwtrek's back like a newborn. At first, he flushed at the indignity. It was shameful to be carried in such a way when his companions trudged along in the snow. Several times, he struggled against the bonds, trying in vain to wriggle free. Each time, Pwtrek shrugged his shoulders roughly, silencing his efforts. Eventually, the wind picked up, his limbs grew cold, and he buried his face into the depths of the juggernaut's mane, too cold to remember any pride.

As darkness approached, they searched for a suitable camp, one where Lidan could recover. Another shallow cave with a rocky overhang made a suitable site. They rested, relieved to be nearer the end of their journey. Albeit not by much.

Gwahl redressed his wounds.

'Healing quite well,' he nodded. 'But needs more time. Always more time. You're not too cold?'

He shook his head. A lie. The moment Pwtrek loosened the bonds and eased him from his back, he longed for the warmth of his coarse pelt. He wore every item of spare clothing in his pack, wrapped in enough cloaks to dress a family of farmers, but the chill still found its way in.

'Sure? I can see you shivering.'

He nodded, forcing his body still, clenching his teeth to stop his jaw. It was no use, and he nestled his face into his chest, hiding beneath the cloaks.

'Come, sit next to me. Have you heard of the black birds of the north? No? Quite different to the blackbirds of the forest. These are unique, mighty fishermen, whose wings are developed to fly beneath the waves. In winter, when the sun goes missing for months, these birds gather together to survive, huddling next to one another to share body heat.'

'I'll sit next to Pwtrek,' he chattered.

Gwahl smiled and gently led him to the cave wall. The others joined them, and they were soon lined up, shivering next to one another as they shared food and drink.

He pressed against Pwtrek, whose arms were long enough to wrap around both him and Gwahl. From the juggernaut's opposite side, he heard Spotal's hushed conversation with Widrias.

'Imhara Pass would give us an easy route from the mountains. Rock will turn to grass, and we'll be in my kingdom,' his sword scratched as he drew a crude map of the land in the snow.

'Imhara Pass will take us too far east,' replied Widrias, thoughtfully. 'I doubt our supplies will last that long.'

'If we're careful we'll make it.'

'You're being far too optimistic.'

'It's the best way off these peaks. Unless you'd prefer a steep climb down the cliffs…?' his voiced tailed off. Lidan imagined his eyes lingering on Widrias's injured leg.

'If we aimed for Imhara, we'd be travelling for at least a week with no food. In these climates, that's death. We must leave before it.'

'Precarious slopes border the mountains. The ones lining the pass are gentler. We use the pass as a place to ascend Tarnegrefur all the time. It's safer.'

'Only if we reach it in good health. Which we won't. Where do the marshes meet with your lands?'

'Only in the south. In the north we have the brambles.'

'Of course. Where do they end?'

'A few miles west of the Atrael.'

'And we can climb down there?'

A pause, 'Potentially, yes. But Imhara is best.'

'Not for our purposes. How far is the Atrael from here?'

'I don't know where "here" is, sir.'

'Guess. Surely you have some idea of where we are and how far we've travelled since arriving?'

Another pause and Spotal exhaled heavily, 'Its sources are many, deep in the mountains, twisting and turning a thousand times, heading east for many miles before cutting south.'

'How will we recognise it as the Atrael and not just another mountain spring?' asked Pwtrek, turning to their conversation.

'That's easy. Atrael follows its path along a riverbed containing a certain naturally-occurring compound that turns its waters a golden yellow. It's this compound that makes my country so fertile and bountiful. The water from the spring will therefore be slightly golden, will taste sweet and leave you feeling replenished and full. Other, ordinary, mountain springs will just have ordinary crisp water.'

'Excellent!' exclaimed Widrias, 'Well done, captain, we'll look out for it.'

'Just don't drink too much of it. If you wish to fill your water-skins with it, remember to dilute it with ordinary water. The compound, though excellent for plants, is irritating to your bowels and kidneys in large quantities..'

'Thank you, captain. Once Gwahl determines Lidan to be well enough to travel again, we'll be away! Hopefully his strength will hold true. Come, my friends, let's sleep.'

Lidan leaned back, turning his face to Pwtrek. His fingers traced patterns on the smooth rock against his back. Every once in a while, they caught in deep cuts in the rock, made at regular intervals, but he paid no attention to the gouges and was soon asleep.

*

Three days later, they set off again. Finally, he was able to walk, albeit slowly. Despite his protests, he was once again strapped to Pwtrek's back to save his energy for recovery. A stern look from Widrias was enough to silence his complaints. With a sour expression, he let himself be carried.

They made good headway for the first few days, travelling great distances in the forgivingly mild weather. Of course, it was still cold, cold enough for him to be grateful once again for Pwtrek's mane. From what he could see, the mountain ridges were relatively

359

flat, with only a handful of steep slopes to navigate. Even Widrias was able to tolerate the route without too much difficulty.

It was, as always, thanks to Gwahl. The cunning daemon scouted ahead, finding the safest path, consulting with Spotal to make sure their heading remained true. He ran to and fro, sometimes as far as a mile ahead, avoiding crevasses and snowdrifts, seeking the safest paths through the ice. Sometimes he walked by their side, encouraging them on, updating them on the road ahead. By night, he kept watch as often as any other, despite the hours of running by day.

On the fourth day, the wind turned. Gone were the light breezes that teased them for the majority of their journey, replaced with a violent, bludgeoning gale. Each gust was a hammer blow, a smith's strike on the anvil, crushing their ribs, snatching their breath away. Gwahl did his best to steer their path to shelter, heading from the peaks to the valleys. But here the slopes channelled the wind even more and they were forced back up. Now, the wind pushed them horizontally in its malicious attempt to cast them from the sheer slopes, to shatter their bones on the jagged rocks below.

Gwahl stopped scouting. As if this next challenge were the final obstacle to exhaust his resolve, he trailed at the rear of their company. He tried twisting around Pwtrek's back to look at him, but the bonds were too tight and the wind too cold to expose his cheeks for long.

As if the ferocity of the wind were not enough, it started playing tricks. Dropping as suddenly as it blew, changing directions, first from the east, then the west, wavering in its power. Had it been a constant force, they might have been able to lean into it, to keep their feet. Now, any attempts at balance were in vain. They tripped, fell, struggled to their feet, only to be battered to their knees once again.

But even so, they fought on. With no shelter available, what choice did they have but to carry on, on their feet, knees, scrambling on their numb hands.

It snowed.

At first, nothing more than a light dusting, irritating and sharp in the swirling wind, but nothing to add to their discomfort. That soon changed. It fell heavier as the winds brought the grey clouds overhead. The flakes grew in size, swollen clusters of frost pummelling their bowed heads. They were halted.

Beneath him, he heard Pwtrek growl. He was the only one still on his feet, the others all brought to their knees. Even Noswen, born in the Northlands, was still, her arm around Spotal's shoulders. Pwtrek dug his heels into the snow, his hands resting on the slope, and clawed his way forward. Even on his back, he could feel the strength in his legs, standing like a living monolith in defiance to the wind.

He curled into a ball. The wind cold enough to burn. He daren't open his eyes, lest the ice blind him. Not that he needed to, there was only one person who Pwtrek would battle so hard to reach.

'Sir,' he rumbled, finally reaching the satorr.

'We can't go on,' he roared back, fighting to be heard. 'My leg is too much of a burden. I'm spent.'

'The others too. Shelter!'

'There is none.'

'We make our own.'

'Go.'

Pwtrek turned and clawed his way back to Gwahl.

'Snow caves. Or we die.'

'I'll ask Noswen to help,' the daemon shouted back.

Pwtrek grumbled, and stumbled a little way further down the slope to where the snow was dense. Nestled as he was between his shoulder blades, Lidan couldn't see what was going on, but from the motion of his arms, he guessed he was digging.

Finally, at a lull in the wind, he opened his eyes. Noswen and Gwahl were buried up to their waist hacking away at the packed snow with their weapons. He shut them again as a flurry blew into his face. When it died, he looked again and saw the others had joined the two digging in the snow.

Pwtrek suddenly moved forward, untying the bonds, practically throwing him into the cave. Instantly, the sound of the wind was cut off, as if he'd been plunged underwater. Widrias joined him, and the cave was plunged into darkness.

'Keep as dry as possible,' rumbled Pwtrek. 'Now we wait.'

Chapter 22

He shivered. To his surprise, there was enough light to see dim shadows in their claustrophobic cave. At some point during his sleep, someone, presumably Pwtrek, dug an air-hole in the roof of the cave; their only source of light. Not that it was enough to illuminate the cave completely, but enough to pick out vague shapes.

Sitting up on his haunches, he waited for his eyes to adjust and drew his cloaks tighter. They'd all lost weight on this journey, even Pwtrek was noticeably slimmer. He should know. He wondered how he must look. Undoubtedly, he'd be gauntest on account of his wounds. The pain was less, thank the north winds, but still present. He lied to Gwahl, Widrias, and Pwtrek, claiming each day the wound felt as good as new. But then, he'd always been a poor liar. They knew the truth. As Gwahl reminded him each night, it wouldn't be until they reached level ground before his health was returned.

Sniffing, we wiped a string of slime from his nostrils and crawled on his hands and knees to explore. Long and narrow, it was more of a tunnel than a cave, and he headed to where he presumed the entrance to be. The light from the air-hole suggested the weather was fair once more, or so he hoped.

His hand brushed against the hem of a cloak. Stretching, he explored further. He found a foot, no, a cloven hoof. Embarrassed, he jumped back and hit his head against the roof, showering snow down the back of his neck.

Yelping, he wriggled about, dislodging more from the walls.

'Quiet, Lidan, go back to sleep,' warned Widrias, tiredly. 'Your games can wait until morning.'

'Apologies, sir,' he chattered, 'but I think it might be morning. See the sun?'

'Yes. Good.'

A rustle as the satorr stirred to change position. A shadow passed before his eyes as he crawled past, heading to the cave entrance, groaning wearily. Something dragged behind him. At first, he assumed it was the General's sword, but no, that was in its scabbard on the opposite wall, he could see the glint of its steel fastenings. It was his leg, twisted awkwardly to avoid placing any weight on it. Widrias stopped where he was and pushed at the cave entrance, muttering under his breath.

He watched him curiously. Was he trying to push through the snowy wall on his own? For that matter, where was Pwtrek? Searching the cave, he couldn't find any other shadows in the gloom. With a start, he turned back to Widrias, and his eyes opened wide.

It was Pwtrek's sleeping form that Widrias pushed. He sat with his back to their cave entrance, filling the opening to act as a living insulation to them. Startled, he crawled over as quickly as he could and squeezed next to Widrias to shake Pwtrek from his slumber. Falling asleep while exposed to these elements was dangerous. Even for a juggernaut.

Panic gripped him when he remained asleep. He could see it now, being forced to leave his frozen, rigid corpse behind, to be picked clean by what scavengers survived up here. After everything he'd done for them, they wouldn't even be able to get him home, or give him a proper goodbye.

But no, there was the faintest movement, a flicker of the eyelids. He stirred, opened his eyes, and yawned.

Lidan sat back, heart pounding. Widrias frowned at him.

'You alright?' he asked, gruffly.

'Yes, I was worried about...' he gestured to Pwtrek, who stretched his arms out in front of him and rolled his neck.

Widrias snorted. 'He's fine. No juggernaut has ever died of cold.'

'Not strictly true,' yawned Pwtrek, again. 'We're not immune to the cold, we just know how to survive it.'

'Sorry,' he apologised, meekly. 'You just weren't responding and... I don't know.'

'Don't be sorry! No harm done. Let's get out of here.'

The juggernaut brought his knees up to his chest and pushed back, forcing his way out to the slopes.

Blinded by the sudden explosion of light, he shut his eyes. A faint breeze tugged at the hem of his cloak, breathing fresh mountain air into the stuffy cave. He shivered again. The sky may have cleared. The wind may be gentle, but it was still cold, colder than anything he'd ever experienced.

But there was no use staying in the cave. Gritting his teeth, he crawled out, following Widrias's example. The satorr stood, slung his sword over his shoulder, and walked a few paces uphill, surveying the blizzard's aftermath.

Pwtrek stood and turned. To his surprise, he saw the juggernaut's back was covered in a shell of snow and ice. As he watched, he flexed, and there was a loud crack as his powerful shoulders shattered the ice, to fall in enormous slabs to the snow. He caught Lidan's eye and winked.

'Wouldn't advise you trying that. I was born in snow and ice, they'd never kill me.'

'I thought that wasn't strictly true,' he quoted, smiling.

Pwtrek laughed. 'Well, we'll keep that between you and me.'

'How did you do it?' he played with one of the slabs with his foot. Nearly an inch thick, curved like a bowl, formidable as a plate of armour. 'All this ice, and your back to the blizzard…'

'It's a trick we juggernauts use. Our pelts act as insulation for us, as you know, but we can also soak the hair and let it freeze over as a sheet of ice, which becomes a second layer of insulation. It keeps us warm. We use it often during winter in the Northlands. Manticores do it too.'

'Can hanex do it as well?' he asked, thinking about Noswen.

'No. Only us.'

'But hanex are native to the Northlands as well?'

'If anyone else tried it, they would freeze,' he said, firmly. 'Speaking of which, you're shivering. Get your cloak on properly and climb on my back. I'll keep you warm.'

Too cold to argue, he did as he was told, gently rocked back and forth as the juggernaut ploughed through the snow to find the others. Soon, everyone was outside, stamping their feet and rubbing their hands.

'At least the sun's out,' muttered Chekry, wryly.

'We'll be warm enough within a few hours of marching,' reassured Widrias, his overconfident tone betraying the falseness at its heart.

'Don't know about the rest of you, but my pack's starting to feel a bit light,' said Depani, lifting the offending pack with one hand to demonstrate.

'Fat pig,' smiled her brother, before turning serious. 'She's right, though. I hardly have enough for a week.'

'If we set a good pace, we'll find the river,' said Widrias, firmly.

'If anyone sees an animal, let me know,' said Depani, shouldering her pack and hefting her crossbow. 'I'll put meat on the menu tonight.'

'Good luck with that,' Gwahl rolled his eyes.

'Luck's got nothing to do with it. One shot, any hare or goat will be ours.'

'Let's keep our fingers crossed. Come,' Widrias urged them on.

Tired, cold, with limbs stiffer than iron bars, they set off again. The rhythmic pacing soon made his eyes heavy, and he drifted to sleep.

*

Panting, he leaned against the stone wall. He bit his cheeks, desperately restraining a scream. The burning in his lower limbs and chest flared, quietened, and rose up again. The pain subsided. He exhaled, sweat trickling down his temple. He shifted his weight and his leg throbbed. Nothing too bad. Sore, but bearable. If he braced himself, tucked in his stomach, locked his legs, he should be fine. He could move. But where?

Nervous, he looked around to gather his bearings. The infirmary was large, twenty slabs of rock lining each wall. Hardly a third of them were occupied by patients. He could still hear the hanex to his right weeping as the healers worked on her wounded back.

His bed was near the centre of the ward. Inconvenient. Both exits were at opposite ends of the infirmary. He had a long way to drag himself before getting out. But what was he to do once he was out? Injured as he was, he couldn't out-run anybody outside, and any guards would simply take him back to the cells. That would not do. He'd be damned if they tried taking him back. Even if it meant death, he would not go back.

Licking his dried lips, he crawled to his left. At least this way, his stronger right side would be facing the open. If anyone tried stopping him, he wouldn't be able to put up much of a fight, but he felt better for it in any case. He dragged his worn, wounded body from one bed to the next, resting behind each one.

The hushed whispers of the healers filled the silence with their echoes. One by one, the moans and wails died down. Others would take their place, then the whispers would intensify, and the moans would cease, and the cycle would repeat.

The Southlander was next. His healers were at the other end, tending his bloody stumps. He could make it along the wall unseen. Heart in mouth, he crawled forward.

An inch. Another. His foot scraped lightly against the stone. It hardly made a sound, but in the heart of such imposing silence, it may as well have been the clash of shattered glass. Choking, he retreated, nearly slipping over his scrambling elbows.

Nobody investigated. Mouth as dry as a forgotten well, he peered around the bed. The healers were too preoccupied with the patient and paid no attention to him. At least, not for now.

He breathed deeply. Calm, keep calm. He started forward again. Inch by inch, he slithered along like a misshapen lizard, keeping one eye on the healers.

No! Disaster. One of them came around the end of the bed, to the Southlander's side, for better access to one of the wounds.

His heart pounded like a drummer boy at the eve of his first battle. It was so loud. He was sure the healer would hear it.

He was so close. If he reached out, he could have grabbed his leg. If he turned his head only slightly, he'd be seen. If he dropped a knife, or a suture, or a bandage, and knelt to pick it up, he'd be caught. If he moved, the motion would draw the eye, and he'd be caught. Like a mouse in an open field, gazing at the circling owl above. Five seconds passed. Ten. Should he move back? Should he move forward? If he stayed here, it was only a matter of time before someone turned. There was nowhere to go. Nothing to do. Nothing but pray for mercy.

A blessing. The wretched patient let out a final rasping snarl and died. More healers clustered around the sides, but their attention was on the corpse. He may as well have been part of the wall. Without a word, the body was taken away, taking the healers with it. As soon as they were out of sight, he scrambled forward and was safe behind the bed.

As he lay panting, more exhausted than he'd ever been in his life, his prayers were answered. A small door set in the wall behind the next bed. He sat frozen, hardly daring to believe. Was it a trap? Was it safe to enter? Or would it be thrown open at any moment, to reveal the gaoler, laughing as he dragged him by the neck to the shackles. But it remained closed. For an entire minute, he did nothing but watch it, ears straining for the sound of approaching footsteps. None came. In that case, it must be locked. There was no way he'd be gifted a way out. It was too improbable, too merciful. And yet...

He glanced around. The coast was still clear, the healers flocking to the latest agonised wail at the far side of the room. He crawled to the next bed, faster than before. His wounds sparked but he ignored it. Adrenaline took over, muting the pain with its excited tremor. Safe again, he sat with his back against the bed, facing the door.

To his right, he heard a ragged chuckle. A grizzled old man, half his face a mess of stitches, like the reverse side of a grisly tapestry. A disgusting grey and yellow tongue lolled out of his mouth as he laughed, grey bits of spittle shooting out. A single, crazed eye stared at him. He slowly lifted a finger to his pursed lips and winked. He motioned to the door with the same gnarled, arthritic finger.

Too terrified to turn away, he held his gaze. This senile worm would give him away, chuckling and pointing as he was. Desperate, he shook his head, hoping it would shut him up. It didn't. If anything, it made it worse as another rasping chuckle gurgled forth from his scrawny, twisted neck.

Exactly as he feared, a healer came. Drawn to the sound of the sickly madman, he came around the bed to stand between them, placing a vial of cloudy medicine to his lips. At first, the man resisted, turning his head away, but the healer pinched his nose shut and poured the tincture down his throat when he gasped for breath. Coughing and spluttering, the madman yelled incomprehensively at the healer, who turned away without a word.

A minute later and he was still yelling. Flailing his scrawny arms and kicking his legs in feeble protest, he voiced his stubborn defiance to the medicine. Two healers soon returned and restrained him with firm hands. It only distressed the man further and his protests rose an octave higher.

One of the healers barked a sharp command and they marched away from the bed.

Still in the same position as before, he stared in horror at the now-empty bed. Another close call. He dared a glance around the bed and saw the healers drag the grizzled wretch away by the armpits. The poor fool dribbled and spat, smiled one last time, and was lost from sight.

Disturbed, he turned back to the door. It would be locked. It must be.

He reached up to the latch. Turned his wrist.

A click. He gasped. The door swung open on its hinges.

Pitching forward, he rolled inside, kicking it closed behind, and was once again shut in darkness.

*

In darkness, he woke. A moment of panic – he was still in the dream! But no, warm cloaks around his shoulders, a sabre at his side, a biting chill in the air. He relaxed. He must have slept all day. Presumably, this was their latest campsite, another shallow cave. In contrast to the other campsites, this one wasn't buried in snow. True, there was still a good few inches around the mouth, but nowhere near the amount they'd fought through before.

Feeling surprisingly fresh and replenished, he rose and walked to Spotal. The calef sat on a boulder outside as sentry. He smiled as he approached, shifting aside to make room for him on the rock. He sat down and peered into the darkness. Playing with the thin blanket on snow by their feet, he turned his face upwards. Nothing. No stars, no moon, no navy night sky. Only darkness. Dark clouds full of snow must be gathering above. And yet it was significantly less cold than yesterday.

'It's quite warm,' he said.

'You think so? I'm still cold enough.'

'Well, not warm,' he admitted, 'but the cold isn't quite as cruel.'

'Well it wouldn't be, would it? We're on the lower slopes tonight, to avoid getting caught up in any more blizzards.'

'Did we find the river then?'

'Hah! No, not yet, I'm afraid. If we had I don't think that we'd have stopped for the night, we probably would've followed it as far as we could in the darkness.'

'How far down the mountain have we come?'

'A hundred and fifty metres or so, on the sheltered side of the ridge, so no wind will reach us tonight, provided it doesn't completely turn direction.'

'Will it be difficult to get back up to the ridge?' he asked, dreading the morning's climb.

'Not too difficult, it's a bit steep at times but we should be fine.'

They fell silent. The darkness was surprisingly peaceful, as if the whole world were asleep. In their shelter, there wasn't even any wind to break the silence. Even if there were, the few inches of snow was more than enough insulation to gobble up its howls before it became too loud. He saw something stir in the sky and the promised powder snow danced its way to the slopes. With the silence, darkness, the falling snow and comparative warmth, it was surprisingly pleasant. A smile crept up his lips, surprising him with its unannounced arrival. Faced with such a tranquil setting, he almost forgot where they were, what was at stake. But it didn't last. A day of sleep left his stomach empty, and it reminded him with a sudden grumble.

Placing his hand about his midriff, he reached for his pack.

'Do you think we'll find the river before it's too late?'

He took out a flatcake, one of the few he had left, and broke it in half. Spotal shook his head at the offered half in polite refusal. He smiled thinly.

'Yes, my friend, I do.'

He nodded, chewing on the stale, tasteless rations, and turned back to watch the dark.

'Gwahl's afraid of something.'

From the corner of his eye, he saw Spotal twitch. He glanced at him, meeting his serious gaze.

'What?'

He shrugged, with false nonchalance.

'He's afraid of something in the mountains, I overheard a snatch of his conversation with Widrias, before the plateau.'

'Perhaps it was just about the soldiers?'

'Maybe,' he mumbled. 'But maybe something else?'

'If there were any danger he would've told us about it,' he said, rather unconvincingly. 'Go and get some sleep, Lidan.'

'I've slept all day. I can keep watch if you want?'

'We have difficult days ahead of us, get all the sleep you can.'

He grunted and rose from the boulder, leaving the calef to his thoughts.

*

The following days, Widrias led them back up to the ridge. Their path rose and fell with each new mountain, their eyes ever cast down to the lower, rockier slopes in the attempt to catch a glimpse of a stream or brook.

Several times, someone spotted the glint of water in the distance, but it was never one of the sources of the Atrael River. These springs were always crystal clear and fresh, good for little else but filling their skins.

Finally, after another three days of fruitless search, Chekry returned from his scout, a faint smile on his face.

'General. I spotted another stream. Water appeared slightly discoloured, it might be it.'

'Where?'

He pointed. Spotal stepped up and shielded his eyes.

'Could be the one. Difficult to say from this far. Let's take a closer look.'

Chekry led them along the ridge, Spotal by his side, eager to investigate. From his elevated vantage point on Pwtrek's back, Lidan spotted the stream a few seconds before the others. At first glance, it wasn't anything particularly spectacular. It had the same fresh, honest beauty as any other spring, bouncing enthusiastically down the slopes, flicking up droplets of fresh water as it struck the rocks in its path. But there was nothing to distinguish it from the others. His heart sank. It would be best if the majority stayed up here and left Spotal to investigate the stream.

Widrias evidently felt the same, and called the rest of them to a halt, allowing the calef and the neiad to investigate alone.

Lidan watched them make their careful descent, skipping down the slope, more often than not with both hands steadying themselves against the rock. Eventually, they reached it, thirty strides away, bubbling from its unseen source to coil around the mountain like a bouncing, sprightly snake.

They watched Spotal kneel next to the water, make a bowl with his hands, inspect its colour, and take a sip. They all waited for him to rise, shake his head, and return. It's what they expected. It's what they'd grown used to. Auran went so far as to take another step along the ridge, pre-empting another failure. Only one step. Despite the resigned acceptance of failure, they couldn't completely eliminate hope.

His eyes widened. Spotal rose, but instead of the slow, tired rise of defeat, he practically jumped to his feet. Chekry whooped happily. Depani answered with her own victory-cries.

Needing no further invitation, they stumbled down the slope to join them. Spotal smiled and nodded to Widrias. The satorr knelt awkwardly, cupped his hands, and took a small mouthful. Lidan watched him, fascinated, as he swallowed, stood, and shivered. It was not a shiver of cold. He had enough experience of such shivers by now to recognise its character. Instead, this was a shiver of delight, like a child eating a pastry.

'The Atrael River,' he proclaimed. 'Our golden path from these mountains. Come, brave soldiers, the kingdom of the calefs awaits.'

He turned and followed the stream down the mountain, tinkling merrily as it led the remnants of the company from their misery.

Pwtrek dipped his water-skin into the stream and passed it over his shoulder to him. He took an apprehensive swig and blinked in surprise at its sweetness. As soon as it settled in his stomach, it felt as though an enormous weight was lifted from his shoulders. His arms and legs felt inexplicably strong, his back felt straight, and the straps binding him to Pwtrek's back were suddenly so confining. He squirmed, desperate to break free, to march once again along his companions.

Pwtrek grunted in irritation and shrugged his shoulders roughly.

'Sit still, Lidan. You're still not strong enough to walk down these slopes on your own. Your wriggling is setting me off balance. The mountain's still treacherous and the ground still slick with snow and ice, not that you'd know from up there. Keep this up, and you'll send us both tumbling to our deaths.'

He ceased his struggling and huffed moodily, 'I'm sorry, Pwtrek, but it's so frustrating being so hopeless. The river gave me strength to walk, I can feel it in my limbs.'

'Keep your frustration to yourself, little one, once we get down past the snow you might, *might*, be able to walk on your own. Until then, try not to make me lose my balance...'

Pausing the readjust the twisted straps, Pwtrek leant on his spear and followed the party down the mountain. It gave Lidan the opportunity to admire the Atrael. Now he was close enough to it, he could finally see its colour. Far from being the river of bright yellow he'd initially expected, its waters were as clear as any other, but there was a slight golden hue. Most obvious where the river flicked up its waters as they broke against the sharp meanders or heavy boulders of its bed, the spray holding a distinct gilded edge.

Much to his disappointment, and the disappointment of everyone else, the stream had a frustrating course. Often running all the way around a mountain to form a near perfect circle, before finally cutting down again to continue its winding route down the slope. They didn't dare risk taking any shortcuts, just in case they lost it. That being said, it often proved troublesome enough to follow without the complications of shortcuts. On several occasions, the water flowed into underground channels, seemingly lost, before reappearing two dozen yards down the mountain. However, each time it reappeared from the various crevices and fissures, it flowed stronger, the streambed wider and deeper, indicating the convergence of several streams beneath the surface. By sundown, they left the worst of the snowy slopes behind, and the stream was at least a metre wide, running swift and strong.

As they camped beneath a rocky overhang a few yards away from the streambed, Chekry observed the path of the stream, and frowned.

'Tell me, Spotal,' he said, 'why does it meander so often so close to its source? Its course is more similar to a river near its estuary than a lively young stream.'

'I have no idea,' admitted Spotal, honestly. 'The Atrael and its various brooks and creeks are unlike any other waterways that I know of.'

'It irritates me,' snorted Chekry, jokingly. 'It should be running in a nearly straight line right now, not twisting and coiling around like a snake...' he trailed away, before continuing, waving his finger in caution. 'Take it from a neiad, this river is odd. Not just its course or the composition of its water. There's something inherently different about it. I don't feel any connection to it.'

'Why is that odd?' asked Lidan.

'Neiads have a natural affinity for the waterways of Enadir,' said Gwahl, 'just like the dreyads and satorrs are considered the spirits of the woods, the neiads are spirits of the rivers, lakes, and seas.'

'Therefore, when we feel no connection to a river, it is not an ordinary river,' said Chekry.

'What does that mean? Is it dangerous?' he asked, suddenly conscious of how much he'd drank from a river deemed 'odd' by a neiad.

'No, it just means it's different, it doesn't belong to us, that our race has no place in its waters.'

'Not particularly surprising.' muttered Gwahl.

'Why so?' asked Depani.

'It belongs to the calefs.'

'What does that mean?' asked Lidan. 'How can a river *belong* to a particular race?'

'Not much to it, really,' yawned Pwtrek, lying nearby with his eyes closed. 'Do you remember how I told you briefly of Enadir's ancient history? Of the war between the giants and cockatrices? After the war, the calefs took the Eastlands as their own, renamed it the Kingdom of the calefs, and have remained there ever since. Now, as Enadir herself is alive, she listens and responds to those who inhabit her, and changes her face depending on what creatures live in the various parts of her land, provided they have resided there for long enough. The minotorrs have lived in the Mountains of Iadden since the last cockatrice was slain, the calefs in their Kingdom, and the daemons lived somewhere across the sea. Seeing as each of these races remained in those lands for so long, Enadir has changed her face in those lands to reflect the inhabitants. If you went to Iadden, the rocks are sharp and strong, the trees deep-rooted and gnarled, the climate as hard and cold as the minotorrs who live there. The "forgotten island" of the daemons, I assume, reflects its own inhabitants in the same way...' Pwtrek paused, glancing at Gwahl for confirmation, who nodded slowly. Pwtrek nodded, as if pleased with himself. 'Similarly, the Kingdom of the calefs is as mysterious and mystical as its inhabitants, with the trees of its woods as slender and elegant as its inhabitants, and – evidently – the Atrael River following an unusual course as it suits the calefs in some way. So, as Gwahl said, it's not that surprising that neiads don't feel a connection to it, because the river is, essentially, a calefin river.'

Chekry pulled a face, clearly sceptical about a calefin river, but said nothing.

'Well whatever the reason for its oddity, it's frustrating how it forces us to travel the entire circumference of each mountain before descending!'

Lidan nodded in agreement. 'Speaking of which, how far down do you think we've come today? The snow is all but gone and the mountain peaks are beyond the clouds now, so we must be close to the foot of the mountains?'

Spotal laughed. 'Not really, although the snow is mostly gone, that's mainly because my homeland has a warmer climate than the Midlands. The river will run east for a long time before it begins its true descent. The journey is far from over.'

'Do you think we're still above Cysgodgors? Or have we left it behind?' asked Chekry.

'Almost certainly. If we were to attempt to head directly south now and somehow scale the slopes of the southernmost mountains, we'd find ourselves in the brambles,' said Spotal.

'And that's not a particularly pleasant place, I assume,' muttered Lidan, recalling overheard conversations.

'Covered in a sea of brambles with poisoned thorns, so not particularly pleasant at all. Saying that, it provides a fantastic natural barrier between our land and the northern marshes, so we're grateful for it.'

'What protects your southern borders from Cysgodgors?'

'The Atrael, mostly,' he threw a pebble into the stream. 'The troglodytes have no love for this river. They find it difficult to swim over, and the flimsy rafts they build to ferry themselves over to our lands are easily destroyed by our own battle barges.'

'So, they don't pose much of a threat?' asked Lidan.

'I wouldn't go that far. Although their attacks are repelled without too many complications, we are few and they are many, and there is a great stretch of river to defend. We must be constantly on our guard. It becomes tiresome.'

'You said in your report back in the Council that the troglodytes' attacks are becoming more frequent,' remarked Pwtrek.

'They are, which is why we find ourselves in troublesome times.'

*

True to Spotal's word, it was three more days of hiking before he saw clear skies. Framed by two steep slopes, its brilliant blue more welcoming than a flame to frozen fingers. Spotal whooped, skipped, and jumped for joy, drawing a smile even to Widrias's stern lips. Lidan laughed. The river finally led them to safer lands and he marched along the riverbank, chin high and shoulders back. Gone was the gnaw in his belly, the ache in his knees, the burning in his thighs, replaced by a bubbling, tumbling enthusiasm.

It was early evening by the time he stood at the edge of a cliff, watching the Atrael cascade over the edge in a golden mist. He'd seen plenty of waterfalls before. Small brooks gargling joyfully as they tumbled down slick rocks, to merry rivers gushing over shallow cliffs. None compared to this.

The golden water was practically thrown off the precipice, spitting out as a great, foaming column before falling to an enormous plunge pool. After this, the churned, silt-ridden water pushed its way through the foothills as a powerful, glittering river, meandering to and fro to the distant horizon.

His awe gave way to concern. If this were to be their path off the mountains, they'd certainly picked a difficult one. True, the cliff face was rough, riddled with a thousand ledges and handholds, but it was slippery. Spray and foam from the waterfall made it as slick as old ice, and the thirty-metre fall to hard earth would be lethal. Caution was the name of the descent.

Another wary look over the precipice. He rolled his shoulder. If anyone asked, he'd insist he was well, but he knew in himself the extent of his injuries. He glanced at Widrias, but the satorr was looking at Gwahl, gently tapping his leg. They all suffered injuries, perhaps his and Widrias' were most serious, but if everyone else could make it, then so could he. Pwtrek would offer to carry them down, perhaps at the same time, but he wasn't strong enough for it. Carrying him for so long had drained much of his strength, he could see it from the way his shoulders sagged at the end of each day, how his breath came quicker. No, any noble offer from the juggernaut would be refused. He would brave the cliff alone.

'We need to scale the cliffs behind the waterfall,' said Spotal. 'If we climb down a little bit, find a suitable path, we can get down the other side.'

'Why not stay on this side? Cross the water further downstream?' asked Auran.

'There aren't any fjords, and the current is too swift for us to swim across. It's better to cross here, before the brambles give way to the marshes.'

'We could try?' suggested Depani.

'It would take a long time for you to ferry us all over…' Spotal trailed off, looking to Widrias for guidance.

'I'd rather not get wet,' he said, after a while.

'It's a difficult climb behind the waterfall,' warned Gwahl, looking pointedly at the satorr's leg.

'It's a difficult climb either way. If I have to make it anyway, I may as well do it without worrying about the inevitable plunge through the river to follow.'

Lidan turned away from the waterfall and looked west. Sure enough, across a relatively featureless flatland plain was the forest of thorns. Its dark green blur stretched for miles to the west, before ending in swirling tendrils of mist, marking the onset of the marshes. So close, and yet it felt like an age ago they struggled through its mires.

Noswen lay a hand on his shoulder and gently pushed him out the way. Wordlessly, he stepped away and she leaned over the edge to survey the climb. Gwahl stepped up next to him.

'Our best climber,' he remarked. 'I trust her to pick the best route for us.'

'Safest route,' corrected Noswen, over her shoulder. 'Not best.'

'Surely safest is best?'

'No, safest may be longest. Do you have the stamina in your forearms for a long climb? I doubt it. Can you hold on to wet rock for prolonged periods? Lots to consider.'

'I leave it in your expertise,' Gwahl shrugged.

He watched her for a few moments, hunched at the precipice like a crow. It took her a few moments before she stood, stretched, and blew on her fingers to warm them up. She glanced down, unshouldered her pack, unbuckled her sword, and threw both to the eastern riverbank. Meeting his eyes one final time, her gaze as cold and empty as ever, she lowered herself over the edge.

Eager to watch, he shuffled over and peered over the edge.

Now someone was scaling the rock, he could truly appreciate its challenge. Previously unseen moss and other lichen clothed the mountainside in a slippery jacket, forcing the hanex to cling to the rock with an iron grip. Her calloused fingers hooked into crevices and crannies, securing her to its face. She was motionless for a few agonising seconds, acclimatising herself to the climb, before beginning her descent.

Gently, she lifted her foot and searched for a hold. Next came her hand, her other foot, her second hand, and then the first foot again. Her movements were smooth, fluid, like water trickling down a gentle slope. There was no jerking, no faltering, no confusion. Her route was set, outlined as clearly as a stairway, although invisible to Lidan.

Five metres down, she turned and angled towards the water. There was an awful moment when she tested the weight of the water with a hand and nearly lost her footing. A collective sigh of relief rose from his companions when her scrambling toes found a hold to sink into.

At the very edge of the water, she stretched her hand again, inching across as slow as poured treacle.

Then she was gone. Behind the waterfall, or dragged to the churning plunge pool below, he couldn't possibly tell. A minute passed. He shifted nervously. Still no sign of her.

Catching Gwahl's eye, he gazed at him pleadingly. The daemon raised a reassuring hand.

'She'll be fine.'

Another minute. He searched the Atrael for any sign of her broken, battered body. There was none. The waterfall had swallowed her up completely, devoured from the face of Enadir.

Another minute. The others exchanged wary looks. Even Widrias rubbed his beard nervously. Nobody said anything. It didn't seem appropriate. Pwtrek looked back upstream, as if searching for anywhere they might be able to cross instead of climbing behind the waterfall. He turned away a few moments later, frowning in disappointment.

Five minutes. He sat, dangling his legs over the edge. Perhaps it would be better to brave the currents of the river after all.

Ten minutes.

'Told you.'

Gwahl pointed, a smug smile on his lips. There she was, collecting her sword and pack from the riverbank, turning to wave a greeting.

He blew out his cheeks and giggled nervously.

'Who's going next?'

'Me,' Spotal pushed forward to the cliff. 'Can't wait to get home,' he winked at him.

He smiled. 'Good luck.'

'Noswen will guide you once you reach the water,' said Gwahl, stepping up. 'Keep looking down and watch out for her instructions. You might not be able to hear her over the roar of the water, so watch her signals. We'll tie this rope around your waist. If you fall, it might spare you some of the force, but you'll still swing. In fact, you might be able to abseil a little on this side. Obviously not all the way, don't have nearly enough rope for that. Once you're safe behind the waterfall, just slip out the loop and do what Noswen says. Any questions? Alright. Ready?'

Spotal nodded and Gwahl slipped a simple noose around his chest. The calef grinned weakly and disappeared over the edge. Chekry, Lidan, and Auran took his weight, while Gwahl instructed them on how much rope to give.

From his current position, he couldn't watch Spotal's descent. A sharp jolt marked Spotal's passing behind the waterfall. A few seconds later, the rope became weightless. He scrambled to the precipice again, but Gwahl steadied him with a hand to his shoulder.

'Careful, now. He made it safely behind the water. It'll take a while for him to make it to the other side, so don't start worrying, now.'

Half an hour later, a cry sounded his safe arrival at Noswen's side. Lidan sighed with relief. Knowing Noswen could complete the climb was one thing, but given the hanex's reputation for superhuman feats, following her footsteps gave no guarantee of success. That Spotal made it was proof the climb was possible.

By the time night fell, Chekry, Depani, and Widrias joined the other two at the base of the waterfall. The rest waited until the morning, reluctant to climb in the darkness. It was a peaceful night, with barely a breeze to curl their hair. Completely different to the morning. Rainclouds appeared, having crept up on them during the early hours, lurking over the mountains.

Wind and drizzle made the climb precarious. Seeing the treacherous conditions, Gwahl ventured first. From the way he swung on the rope, the wind was fierce on the cliff face, twisting him like a vine around a trunk. The rain didn't help. The rope was slick between Lidan's fingers, difficult to control, slipping too far. Gwahl did his best, clinging to the rock by his fingertips, flailing his legs, grunting harshly as he continued his descent. Eventually, he made it to the waterfall and the rope fell slack again.

Twenty minutes later, the daemon jumped to the opposite bank of the plunge pool.

Pwtrek went next. The juggernaut's strength, though waned, allowed him to make the descent quickly and confidently. Fortunate, really, as he and Auran were far from stocky enough to take his weight should he fall.

Within a few short minutes, the juggernaut disappeared behind the waterfall, leaving him and Auran on the cliff.

They waited for Pwtrek to reappear, as the others had, silently wondering who'd be next. He supposed it was the polite thing to offer to go last, but the promise of finally breaking free of the mountains was too tempting. Hopefully, Auran would offer.

But something was distracting the Southlander. A frown furrowed his brow, and his jaws clenched anxiously. He followed his stare and saw Chekry and Depani below, beckoning them down frantically. He could see their mouths move, but their voices were too small to be heard above the foam. Nevertheless, their intention was clear. But there was still no sign of Pwtrek?

'You go, Lidan.'

Relief flooded his body.

'You're sure?'

'Yes, we must be in a hurry. I can imagine why.'

'What do you mean?'

Auran turned, and peered suspiciously at the surrounding slopes.

'I heard something last night. Heard it again this morning. A growl, or snarl, or something. Something echoing through the mountains.'

'A bear?'

'Unlikely.'

'The army?'

A grimace, and a shake of the head in disagreement.

'Some beast, I'd imagine. Drawn to the sound of the water, or our scent,' he glanced at him. 'Go, Lidan. Must be a reason why they want to hurry us along. I'm only putting two and two together'

Suddenly afraid, he stepped to the edge and swung his legs over the edge. Hoping for a refusal, he glanced at Auran one last time.

'Are you sure? Maybe you should go first. I'll probably take more time than you.'

'I said go. You threw your sword and shield down earlier, didn't you? How would you defend yourself if something was stalking us? Go on, now, no more of this.'

He turned his back to him again and faced the cliffs. Sensing the decision was already made, Lidan secured the rope about his waist and lowered himself over the edge.

The first few feet were easy enough, as his hands were still secured against the cliff edge. Once beyond the precipice, however, things became more difficult. He searched frantically for a secure hold, his hands clawing out loose rocks and handfuls of dirt, sending them tumbling to the ground, so far below.

He found purchase and clung on. His foot searched for a ledge to hold his weight, but found nothing. Alarmed, he looked down. Mistake. He should've remembered from that initial climb up the mountains. A dizzying nausea overcame his senses. If he fell, he would die. Hopefully, it would be instantaneous. Lying at the foot of the mountain in a broken, bleeding body, waiting for his shattered ribs to slowly suffocate him…

The freezing spray brought him back to his senses. He tugged the rope about his waist experimentally. A comforting tug back from Auran took his weight for a moment. He'd be alright. Auran was more than strong enough to take his weight, small as he was. This part should be easy enough, especially if he trusted his companion.

Breathing heavily, he continued his descent. He longed for dry rock without this slimy moss, for a bag of chalk to dry his sweaty hands, for a respite from the blinding spray of water. Twice, he stumbled. Neither were serious falls, but were more than enough to set his heart pounding like a stampede.

He scaled the cliff until he was a good ten feet below the edge, the waterfall cascading down beside him in a torrent. He moved to his right carefully, inching his way across. The rocks were wetter, like polished glass. Nearly a minute at a time was wasted searching for a secure hold. Soon, he would face the greatest challenge, getting behind the waterfall.

Drenched to the bone, he gripped the rock with his left hand. Bracing his feet, flattening his body, and stretching his right hand, he explored the rock immediately behind the falls. Initially, his hand was too far from the cliff, and gallons of water pounded down, nearly ripping him from his position.

Startled, he returned the hand to safety and pressed his face against the cliff, breathing rapidly, composing himself, preparing for a second attempt.

This time, he stretched his arm slowly, sliding it against the cliff face until he found what he was looking for; a deep crevice. His fingers latched on, and held. Stifling a laugh, he stretched his right foot.

Exploding from behind the water came a hand. Big as a shovel, it grabbed his arm.

Auran's warnings of mysterious growls, Gwahl's apparent fears, both were suddenly all too real.

The hand pulled him hard, yanking him away from the rock. He screamed, or would have, had half a pint of water not rushed into his mouth. His hands clutched and clawed, to no avail. His feet cut loose, and he was off the cliff. Only the rope and the grasping hand kept him suspended in mid-air.

Slowly, the hand pulled him through the waterfall, dragging him beyond the powerful sheet of water.

He thought to tug on the rope, to beg Auran to pull him up, but fought the temptation. It was likelier for Auran to be similarly pulled to his death. With a painful shrug against the weight of the water, he managed to wriggle free of the rope, with only the ensnared arm still caught in its loop.

He was pulled inside, his entire body immersed in water. He pressed his face into the nooks and fissures behind the curtain of water, struggling to draw breath. The water was cold, enough to make his teeth chatter.

Finally, after what felt an age, the water fell behind and he faced his captor.

'Why are you still here?' he spluttered.

'Helping you,' growled Pwtrek, his muscles bulging alarmingly as he clung to the rock, his long claws wedged tightly into deep crevices.

'You've been here this long?'

'You'd have never made it alone.'

'Come with me now, you can't hold on forever!'

'Need to wait for Auran. Way down is easier. A few metres over and you'll see Gwahl and Noswen. They'll guide you the rest of the way.'

He nodded, too anxious to argue.

As promised, half a dozen handholds later, and the Throne daemon and hanex were there, shouting encouragement and gesturing to the next ledge or crevice. In all fairness, now behind the waterfall, the climb down was far easier. Although still assailed by spray and the occasional slap of water against his back, he made it across the plunge pool.

Swirling and churning violently with the crushing weight of the falling water, he shuddered. Should he fall, he'd be bludgeoned to death in the violence. He flicked a droplet of water from his nose and continued scaling the cliff.

Thanks to the erosive pool, the cliffs around the basin were far wider than the column of water supplying it, and he was soon free of all but the faintest shower.

He was nearly at the bank when a crack echoed from above, followed by an agonised grunt. Out the corner of his eye, a shadow fell, tumbling through the mist.

He turned at the same time Pwtrek hit the water. Gasping, he watched his friend disappear beneath the foam. For a second, he was transfixed, paralysed, turned to ice. Eventually, he managed to break free and turned back to Gwahl and Noswen.

The daemon was pale, his eyes avoiding the pool, fixed on Lidan. Noswen was staring into the water, her expression unreadable. Gwahl urged him on again. He forced his limbs to obey, climbing the final few feet to the bank.

Gwahl grabbed his hand and pulled him to safety. Noswen helped, her hands firm on his shoulder. As soon as his feet were on firm ground, he turned on his heel, gazing into the white water. There was no sign of him.

Depani eventually wandered over and clasped his shoulder encouragingly. He remained silent. What could he say? Nothing. Pwtrek had fallen. There was no way he could survive that. If the water was powerful enough to erode rock, what chance did a living being of flesh and bone have?

'Pwtrek fell,' he croaked, finally.

He wandered a little further down the bank and sat down hard. The grass was lush and full, longer and broader than in the Midlands. More than that, it was denser, thicker, supporting his weight like a deep cushion in a neat cradle of cool green. Presumably because of the Atrael. He was sure Spotal mentioned something about it being the source of his country's bounty. A bringer of life. And yet so cruel.

Coming back from his daydream, he saw Spotal at the riverbank, pleading with the neiads. They ignored him, stripping down to their breeches, casting their weapons and armour aside.

'You can't!' begged the calef. 'The odds are stacked against him. It's too dangerous to go in there. We could end up losing all three of you.'

The twins pushed him aside. They nodded to Widrias, his face unreadable, and dove into the white water.

He waited with the others, his eyes never leaving the foaming surface. Pwtrek had grown to be a dear friend, if he were lost... he couldn't finish the thought. Even imagining it was too painful. He glanced quickly at Widrias, who still wore his emotionless mask. How long would it last? If Pwtrek didn't...

He shook himself. Pwtrek would surface soon, none the worse for his ordeal, and would laugh at his clumsiness later. He would. Of course he would.

Chapter 23

Oblivious to the drama below, Auran gripped his battleaxe tightly, struggling to still his shaking limbs. All around were hideous, horrific sounds, terrible enough to freeze heart and mind. Soft moans carried by the wind, the prattle of dislodged stones on rocky slopes, strange snarls, stranger growls. In the white landscape of his thoughts, he struggled for an explanation. Wolves? Bears? Lynxes, elk, mountain cattle, goats? All suspiciously absent. Gone without a trace. Not that he expected to suddenly stumble on a mountain goat. But to disappear with no tracks, with no dens or nests, not even any old droppings. Could they be returning now? Converging all at once?

Of course not. Whatever killed or frightened the animals away had done so for good. Something about Gwahl's behaviour suggested he knew. Perhaps the daemon thought he'd concealed his suspicious behaviour from the others, perhaps he had, but not from him. Keeping a late watch, glancing nervously over his shoulder, concealing their tracks with far more care and attention than was necessary. All little things he'd noticed. When you hunted in the Daiwen Jungle, you learned to notice the little things.

But these, they were alien sounds. Unrecognisable. Closing his eyes, he listed the creatures he feared Gwahl was looking out for. Creatures from his homeland and their tell-tale signs. The manticore was large and fierce and a proficient hunter, but the flapping of its leathery wings and its trumpeting roar would have been heard long ago. Hydras were surely too large, and he'd never heard of any in Tarnegrefur. It was unlikely to be chimerae, whose shed skin would be abundant if they inhabited any cave within a ten-mile radius. The same applied to the cerastes, besides, they dwelt in sand, not snow. A crocotta, perhaps? It would explain the absence of wolves, but again, it was a monster of warmer climates than these.

Nothing he could think of fit the approaching threat. He cursed these unfamiliar lands with their unfamiliar inhabitants. All he knew was what was told to him, not what he discovered himself.

A deep growl brought him back to reality. It was close. From behind the cluster of rocks twenty metres to his left. He spun quickly and stared hard. Whatever lay behind the boulders was hidden in the deep shadow of an overhang. Easily large enough to hide a cockatrice. But it couldn't possibly be one of those...

Maybe a gryphon? Supposedly confined to the Far Eastlands nowadays, one might have flown to the mountains? It seemed feasible. After all, legends told of giants riding these mighty creatures as one might ride a horse today. But there hadn't been any reports of gryphons for centuries, at least not in the Southlands. He should ask Gwahl.

A minute trickled by. Was that a movement in the shadows? Or was it just the wind playing with the snow? A silhouette against the dark stone, or just his frightened eyes searching for a reason.

Swallowing, he edged back to the precipice.

Sooner or later, one of them would make a move. Would it be better to stand his ground and fight the unknown, or turn on his heel to follow the others? Probably the latter. Hunter he may once have been, but he was under no illusion that one man might slay a monster alone. It required a team to fell hydras, manticores, cerastes. There was nothing to gain from staying.

But what if it waited for him to turn his back? Those moments of stillness as he clambered clumsily over the edge. A few seconds was ample time for an animal to close the short distance between the rocks and his thundering heart.

He would have to be quicker, then. Keeping one eye on the overhang, he tied the rope around a boulder and stepped into the loop.

He flung his axe to the opposite bank far below, took hold of the rope, and shuffled to the edge.

Now that was definitely a movement. A limb, or a tail, or an elongated neck. Something slinked forward. Curious as he may have been to find out what it was, caution urged him off the cliff.

Stepping back into thin air, the ground fell away beneath his flailing foot, and the edge rushed up to meet his waiting hands. Abseiling wasn't an option. He could only climb.

Did something wail from above? Or was it just the wind? Was that a claw picking at the fibres of the rope, or just the natural friction against jagged stone?

He hoped never to find out. With an efficiency born of fear, he reached the falls almost as quickly as Noswen, and plunged through the ice-cold sheet.

Had he not been gasping from the freezing water, he might have sighed with relief. Behind the waterfall, he was safe, and slipped from the rope before whatever was above could drag him back by it. Shielded by the Atrael, he made his way around the cavern. On the far bank was Gwahl, pointing out the best route across. Fighting to still his racing heart, pumping hard enough to be felt even in his fingertips, he made the journey.

Reaching the bank, he collapsed and kissed the earth. Even here, in this foreign land, the Sun blessed his life. Possibly because the mountains were so high, closer to the giver of light itself. It was a comforting thought.

Rising, he smiled his thanks, but the daemon was gone, running to join the others clustered about the riverbank. Something was amiss. Pwtrek and the neiads were absent, while the others peered intently into the foaming water.

Approaching the party, he touched Lidan on the shoulder, making him jump.

'What's wrong?'

'Pwtrek fell, on the way down' he stammered.

Unfortunate. Highly so. If the fall didn't kill him, the water probably would. Even a mountain of a juggernaut was as fragile as an autumn leaf in the face of those pounding waters.

He joined the others at the bank to search the glittering waters for any sign of their friends. Clean and fresh as it was, its depth and yellow hue obscured the riverbed. There could have been an entire army of neiads waiting down there and he would never have known.

Shortly, Widrias commanded them to spread out along the bank. Obediently, he trotted ahead a few paces. Of course, he really didn't see much use. The current was powerful and the river deep, and it was many minutes since Pwtrek fell. In all likelihood, the juggernaut was drowned. From the expressions of the others, it seemed they knew as much. Lidan looked panicked, desperately gazing across the water in his childlike confusion. Spotal dragged his feet miserably, looking away from the river more often than not. Widrias stood stone-faced, his bulging masseters betraying his apprehension. Gwahl and Noswen were too far ahead for him to see their faces.

A movement on the far bank caught his eye. Even here, at the very foot of the mountains, countless leagues away from the sea, the river was easily twenty metres wide. Some forty paces ahead of him, one of the neiads, too far away to tell which one, clung to a rock jutting from the bank. He glanced behind his shoulder and shook his head at Widrias before diving back underwater.

He bit his cheek. Even if they found the body, what then? Could they spare the time to dig a grave large enough to bury him? His sodden body certainly wouldn't take light on a funeral pyre. That left returning the body to the river the only option, making it pointless to retrieve in the first place. But were they cold enough to abandon their friend's body? He hoped not.

Not thirty seconds after seeing the first neiad, Noswen gave a shout from far ahead.

Heart in mouth, he ran with the others. She stood at the inside bend of a meander, waist-deep in the river. The water was gentler here, depositing its loads, from the numerous boulders and small pebbles that clacked underfoot, to blocks of ice large enough to survive the pounding waterfall. This was the Atrael's first meander of any significance beyond the waterfall. Of course this would be where they found the body.

He was third to reach her, after Gwahl and Spotal. Grunting with effort, they struggled with a massive sodden heap. Splashing into the cold, he slipped his arms under Pwtrek's arm and heaved with the others. Eventually, they managed to drag him to dry land. Noswen supported the juggernaut's head, keeping it above the water. Noble as the gesture may have been, it was surely too late. A dead weight in their hands.

Chekry and Depani were the next to arrive, shooting out the river like otters. Joining them, they half-dragged, half-carried the waterlogged heap. Widrias arrived last, his arm slung around Lidan's shoulder in support.

He blew like the bellows, struggling with the others. So heavy! The plate armour on his legs sank to the riverbed. His thick fur soaked up water like a sponge. Even his one arm, thick as a tree trunk, was heavy enough for his back to ache with the strain.

Finally, the water was barely licking his ankles and he let go. Pwtrek fell with a slap into the shallows. Sighing in exhaustion, he leaned back, hands on hips, breathing through his teeth.

Noswen was first to move. Tilting Pwtrek's head back, she pinched his nostrils closed, pressed her mouth against Pwtrek's and exhaled hard. She tried again, and sat back, shaking her head.

'Can't inflate his lungs. There's something blocking his throat.'

Scrambling around his body, she planted her hands on his chest. Grunting with effort, she pushed as hard as she could. They watched her struggle for a second. It wasn't working. Pwtrek was too large, she wasn't strong enough. Chekry pushed her aside, and used his bulk to compress the chest.

He chewed his lip, watching the neiad work. Noswen lingered by, rubbing her chin.

Depani gently pushed her aside to mimic her attempts at inflating the lungs.

Still nothing.

But there! A twitch. A spasm. Pwtrek jerked, rolled over, and vomited. A glob of dank weeds, silt, and stinking bile poured from his gaping mouth.

Never before had vomit smelled so sweet.

Pwtrek twisted, pushing himself up, coughing aggressively.

Auran smiled weakly. He might have laughed were his heart not still racing in panic. Miserable and water-logged as this soaking, sodden mess may be, at least he was alive.

The juggernaut rose shakily to his feet, blinking rapidly. He smiled wanly and stepped forward, but nearly collapsed. Noswen jumped forward to steady him. Pwtrek shrugged her away with a growl.

'Stay away, you.'

Noswen said nothing, her mask secure, and stepped back. Pwtrek motioned Chekry to support him. The neiad helped him shuffle away from the river. Auran and the others trailed behind. A few feet clear of the water, Pwtrek sat down hard and coughed.

'Thank you, Chekry, Depani,' he spluttered. 'I would have died if it weren't for you.'

'No need to thank us,' smiled the neiad. 'We only did what any friend would do.'

'Besides, it was Noswen who found you and initially tried to revive you,' added Spotal.

Pwtrek coughed again. 'Well my thanks to you too, Noswen,' he muttered.

She nodded.

An awkward silence followed. Pwtrek sat with his arms around his elbows, frowning like an enraged boar. Gwahl fussed over him for a while, but was promptly brushed away by the juggernaut. Exhausted by their brush with death, Widrias signalled them to rest, to wait until Pwtrek was well enough to travel. Sensible, really, the general looked nearly as worn with worry as Pwtrek himself.

He breathed deeply. Compared to the thin air of Tarnegrefur, down here it was wonderfully heavy and full. Already, he could catch his breath that much sooner than in those snowy peaks. Downstream, tall green grass and sloping hills stretched to the horizon while the river twisted and turned as it wove its way through the land. Although the perils of the mountains proper lay behind, they were still well above sea level, and to the east and south the ground dropped away gradually to give way to the Eastlands; the Kingdom of the calefs. Beyond the far bank, perhaps two miles away, were the bramble plains. Even from here, he could make out the dark line of the shrubs on the horizon. Poisoned, Spotal named them, a place of little worth. He disagreed. Brambles bore fruit, and as they'd been reminded in the marshes and mountains, food was life. He said as much to the calef.

'They do bear fruit,' he admitted, 'but it's not one species of shrub that makes up that forest. Several different strains of bramble grow on those plains, all of which bear vicious thorns. Some are wide and long as daggers, others needle-fine, better to slip through chainmail and prick the skin. All secrete a potent toxin from their tips, but not the same toxin. No antidote is the same for any two plants. To travel safely through, you'd need a hundred doses of a hundred different medicines, and know which ones to use for which plant. An incredibly dangerous place to dwell.

'As I said,' he continued, smiling sadly, 'the plants bear fruit, each one plump and ripe and bursting with sweet juice, but most of these fruits would kill you if you were to consume them, as many contain the same toxin as the thorns.'

'Many,' he repeated, 'but not all?'

'Not all. There are one or two safe enough to eat. Not that you'd be able to harvest them. The risk of impaling yourself on a thorn is too great. It's not worth it.'

'But you *could*,' he insisted.

'Why do you ask?' grumbled Widrias. 'Our path does not lead that way.'

'Well yes you *could*, of course,' said Spotal, with a shrug, 'but I can't see why you'd want to. It's difficult to differentiate between the safe and the dangerous brambles, you'd be constantly imprisoned in a cage of poisoned daggers, and even some of the non-lethal fruit could leave you with a rotten gut. It's not something that I would advise. There's a reason we don't farm the brambles. Why?'

He shrugged. 'Supplies.'

'I wouldn't go looking there,' snorted Spotal. 'As I said, the risk is too great. There'll be plenty of opportunity for finding food later on. We won't go hungry in my country, I guarantee it.'

'There are fish in the river, you know,' said Depani. 'Perhaps we could catch some and have proper food?'

'Good idea,' coughed Pwtrek, clearing his throat. 'I've had enough of these ridiculous flatcakes,' he gestured towards his pack. 'One cannot live on them alone. I need meat. I waste away from lack of prey in my belly.'

He had to agree. Although the flatcakes had sustained them for so long, by now they tasted foul in his mouth, and the energy they provided felt empty. He longed for the smell of an animal roasting over a fire. The crisping of the skin, the sizzle of fat, the crack of bones as you bit down. Besides, the flatcakes were nearly all gone, and it wouldn't be wise for them to eat them all in a land of such supposed plenty.

'Once we clear the foothills there'll be plenty to hunt,' smiled Spotal. 'The forests are full of deer and boar, the plains teeming with wild horses and bison, birds everywhere. You'll have your fill when we get there, my friend. In fact, you'll wonder how you ever lived in the Northlands or Midlands with such a bountiful country on your doorstep. Fish isn't exactly what I had in mind.'

'For lack of any bison, I think the fish will do for now,' Depani grinned, and dived into the water with her brother.

They surfaced moments later, each with a large, struggling barbel in their hands. A sharp knock between the eyes stunned them, ready for slaughter. As they bled the fish, they cupped some of the blood in their hands and drank.

He nodded respectfully. The old hunting ritual was seldom seen nowadays. A way of ensuring the prey's strength lived on. From the look on young Lidan's face, he was clearly unfamiliar with such traditions. He smiled at the youngster's wide-eyed gaze at their bloodstained mouths.

There were trees scattered around the foothills, mostly pine and fir, but Spotal wouldn't let them cut them down for a fire, not even to roast the fish.

'They've stood here for decades, centuries even! Who are you to end their lives so prematurely? And no, don't even think of cutting down a sapling.'

'We won't fell the whole tree!' Pwtrek argued. 'Only a few branches from the lower limbs.'

Spotal wasn't swayed. 'A woodcutter is an honourable, complex vocation. In our culture, it takes longer to master its craft than to become a soldier, even. I would never dream of laying a blade to a living tree. I lack the proper skill.'

'Luckily, we do,' said Chekry.

'Not here you don't,' he raised a finger. 'You don't touch them. Not while they live.'

'What about fallen branches?' suggested Lidan, recovered from his horror at the neiad's hunt.

'Fallen branches are fine. As long as they're already dead, they're fine for firewood.'

The neiads grumbled in agreement and wandered off to gather the required fuel for a fire. Truthfully, Auran was glad. His was the only axe. It would have been up to him to act as woodcutter, and his battleaxe was made for flesh and steel, not bark and sap.

A merry blaze in the tranquil valleys, roasted fish falling apart in their mouths, safe company among friends. He gazed at the sky, soft clouds and silent stars. So peaceful. It almost seemed artificial after what they'd been through. Best enjoy it while they could. Safe in the Kingdom of the calefs.

*

Lidan panted in the darkness. Blacker than pitch, it made him dizzy, disorientated. His only sense of direction came from the cold wooden door against his back. He waited for his vision to adjust, his eyes wide open as he searched for the faintest glimmer of light. Finally, the faint grey outlines of his surroundings came into view. A storeroom. Filled with barrels, with a cold stone floor and a low ceiling of dark wooden beams. An empty hearth occupied one corner, but the absence of any ash or the smell of smoke betrayed its disuse. The room was small, and the darkness made it claustrophobic. The barrels, large and imposing as they were, pressed against his flanks. They would crush him if he stayed. They would hold him captive, to be discovered by his gaoler, taken back to the cell.

Move on. Through the trembling, the pain, the exhaustion. He had to move on.

Mustering his strength, he heaved himself to his feet, leaning heavily against the wall. His knees nearly gave way, his toes burned, his head spun. But he was standing. Once his head cleared, he peered around the room again. There it was. Another door to his right, behind the bulky barrels.

Licking his cracked lips, he attempted a step. His leg buckled and he stumbled against a barrel with a strangled sob. If he couldn't walk then there was no hope for him, he'd be dragged back to his torture chamber.

Trembles ran through his body. No. Never again. Grunting, he was back on his feet. The barrel's rim provided the necessary purchase to pull himself around, taking the weight off his wounded legs. Finally, he made it to the other door and tried the latch. Mercifully, it was unlocked and opened into a long passage, stretching away to both sides, lit ever so faintly by small candles set in sconces in the wall.

The light troubled him. It showed this passage was in use by the healers. In such an empty corridor he'd be found. But what choice did he have? Behind was the certainty of capture, ahead was a possibility of freedom.

Before leaving the storeroom, he lifted the lid from a barrel and stuck his hand inside. Full of apples. Close to weeping, he fell on the fruit with a ravenous hunger, wolfing them down, core and all, sobbing his thanks to the northern wind for such a gift. Juice dribbled down his chin as he feasted. None of the apples were the choicest. Soft and mushy, mostly bruised with waxy skin, but today, they tasted of sweet, sweet life. He couldn't remember the last time anything was so delicious.

Five apples later, his stomach was full. Another two he kept in his threadbare shirt for later. He opened the door a crack and glanced through. The coast was clear. He slid into the passage.

It was cold. The stone floor pinched his bare feet as he dragged himself along the wall. His bony fingers grasped for handholds in the rough granite walls. When he passed the first sconce, he shut his eyes tight so as not to be blinded by the light of the candle. Behind it, hidden in a shadowed archway, was another door.

He twitched. On closer examination, each candle's pool of light concealed a similar stone archway, the shadows offset by the flickering tapers.

The twitch developed into an uncontrollable tremor. The passageway was a long, stretching away into the darkness. Which door to take? The way out could be this first door, the last, or any one in between. It was perfectly possible that none led to salvation. He'd be trapped in this labyrinth until death.

Panic set in. It couldn't be this first one. Too easy. Soldiers lay behind, or another storeroom, or a stairway to some filthy, dank cellar. No, the way out was further on, he knew it.

Shaking, he heaved his tired, weak body from archway to archway. He ignored the second, and third, and each one that came after. He dragged himself until his arms were aching, the bandages around his feet were ragged, and his knees were grazed and bruised. Still he dragged himself on. None were safe.

On and on, inch by inch. Crawling on his hands and knees. His bandages tore. A trail of blood left behind, like a gruesome snail. At any moment, a healer would pad down the corridor to take him away. Too slow, leaving a path as clear as day. Capture was inevitable.

Panting, he scrambled on, crawling and crawling until his hands and elbows bled with his knees and feet. Nearing exhaustion, he collapsed. His cheek was sticky with tears against the floor. It was too difficult. No matter how far he pulled his weary body, there was no end, no promise of reaching fresh air. Rubbing his hands, his calloused fingers traced the old, familiar scars on his skin. New ones would soon replace these, as surely as the sun rose.

He paused. Old scars. All old. No grazes, no lacerations, no abrasions. A scone was a few feet away, its light barely enough to reach him, but even in the flickering gloom, he could see his hands. Bloodstained. But whole.

Stomach churning, he looked to the floor and sobbed. The foul trail of blood stretched ahead and behind. Old blood ahead, new blood behind.

There was no end, no beginning. An infinite circle.

Curling into a ball, he wept.

*

Gwahl kicked him awake. He jumped, startled, and breathed. Just a dream. With a groan, he stretched the stiffness from his sleeping joints. It was not yet dawn, with a fine dew gracing the sweeping blades of grass. Shivering, he stamped his clumsy feet, banishing the pins and needles. The others were already gathered. Fishing in his pack for a stale flatcake, he stuffed it into his mouth, washing it down with a swig of water.

Spotal smiled as he approached.

'Still happy to walk?'

'Definitely!' he enthused. He was part of the company once again, instead of shackled to Pwtrek like little more than living baggage.

'I'll be here if you need,' said Pwtrek, clasping his shoulder.

He smiled back. The northern winds themselves couldn't have convinced him to accept the offer.

'Sun's up,' muttered Depani, blinking wearily.

As promised, the golden rays chased away the shadows, and Widrias addressed them.

The satorr leaned on his greatsword, his weight on his right leg. Despite Gwahl's efforts, the general's leg was clearly deteriorating. It was something he tried to keep from them, put on a brave face so as not to seem weak or vulnerable, but it was painfully obvious. If Lidan could see it, after knowing Widrias for such a short time, surely everyone else knew as well. Of course, the satorr wasn't the only one wounded and weakened. Pwtrek was looking suitably haggard after his ordeal, and he himself was nowhere near his full strength. None of them would admit it.

'We had a day of rest yesterday, a day to recover, a reward for finally leaving Tarnegrefur,' began Widrias. 'But yesterday is gone. Today we march south, and we march hard. It will be a long day, but we must reach Muranath. Spotal,' he turned to the calef, 'how far is the journey?'

Spotal rubbed his chin. 'Muranath is at the southernmost point of my country. Hundreds of miles away. It'll take us weeks.'

Widrias nodded. 'We have quite the march to look forward to. What direction? You are our guide.'

'South!' laughed Spotal. 'No, it's probably easier to follow the course of the Atrael for the time being, maybe for the first couple of days, then cut directly south. The river follows a southwest course, you see.'

'Is it safe to remain so close to the riverbank? There won't be any predators?' asked Auran.

'There shouldn't be, I don't think. Maybe we should walk a half mile away from the river, though, just in case. We'd be close enough to the water to keep to its course, but far enough away to evade any animals unsuitable to hunt.'

'What predators?' he asked again.

'Up here, there are bears, cougars, lynxes, maybe the odd pack of wolves from the Far Eastlands. Further south there are fewer predators. The most dangerous animals are the ones we'll be hunting. Stags and boars and such.'

'We shouldn't expend too much energy hunting,' said Widrias, 'remember our goal here is to head south, not to chase game.'

'No, but we'll need the food, and we shouldn't pass on the opportunity should it present itself.'

'Very well,' sighed Widrias, 'when we reach the grasslands you can hunt. For now, we march south, I'll lead. Noswen, you scout ahead, report back every two hours.'

He turned and walked away, sheathing his sword. Lidan followed with the others. Noswen jogged past them, lost from sight within minutes.

The march was easy enough, sloping hills covered with thick grass, trickling brooks, sparse forests. The odd rocky cliff or game trail broke up the monotony of the road. Not that Widrias permitted any of them to follow said trails. Two hours passed quickly and Noswen returned for her report. She had nothing of consequence to say and promptly raced away again.

However much he enjoyed being allowed to walk again, he soon tired. His breath came in snatched gasps and he stumbled on his sluggish feet. Gwahl noticed and offered to carry his pack. He initially refused, his pride refusing the aid. But when he stumbled again, Gwahl took away his shield, ignoring his protests.

'There's no point exhausting yourself. Besides, I'm not carrying your pack, just your shield.'

He thanked him. Despite his initial reservations, it was a heavy burden.

'How is the river so wide already? It must have doubled in width since the waterfall.'

Spotal answered. 'There are underground tributaries feeding it. A few might be beneath us right now. Countless ones beneath the bramble plains, which is why they grow so large and wild. It's also why there are such large fish so far upstream. Normally we wouldn't see fish like the ones Chekry and Depani caught until way downstream.'

'Interesting,' he nodded.

Spotal continued, enthusiastically. 'Yes! What's more, all the underground tributaries form an intricate network beneath our feet. There are many hidden, subterranean caves and lakes in which fish can thrive. Occasionally, they venture into the main flow of water, where our fishermen catch them.'

'I see,' he smiled, losing interest.

'There are thousands of caves and tunnels throughout these foothills, some twisting and turning to the heart of Tarnegrefur. There was an explorer once, tried mapping out the tunnels. Never returned. Might have drowned, or got trapped, or just wandered until he died of exhaustion. There was a story in my old river patrol regiment, a soldier found a satchel on the riverbank. Belonged to the explorer. Washed all the way from one of the underground streams to the estuary.'

'Scary,' he agreed.

'Of course, the subterranean labyrinth helps us. With all those lakes, enclosed so far underground in steady climates, the fish have plenty of areas to use as spawning pools. Mixed with all the nutrients from the Atrael, there rivers are always plentiful. But yes, it's much wider down here thanks to the streams, both underground and overground,' he gestured to a rivulet they'd just crossed.

He smiled and nodded. Spotal's love for his country was endearing, but another conversation about the wonder of the river hardly held his interest. Spotal sensed his awkwardness and smiled apologetically.

'Sorry, it's been a while.'

'I know.'

As they walked the miles, the party stretched out, drifting further and further apart. The fittest, healthiest took to the front, overtaking Widrias, and the injured lagged behind. Lidan was among the last.

Far in front of him were Gwahl and Spotal, two distant figures walking together, with Auran close behind. It seemed the Southlander's struggles were limited to cold mountains. He didn't know where Chekry and Depani were, but from overheard snatches of conversation, assumed they were swimming ahead in the Atrael.

Widrias was, by now, some distance behind Lidan. Hobbling along, leaning heavily on Pwtrek's arm, they dragged their weary feet through the lush grass. He felt sorry for them both. Being the last man in the column was awful, seeing everyone else stretching further and further away while your strength flagged with each step. As irrational as it may be, you couldn't help but feel you were holding the others back. The kind thing would be to drop back, to walk with him, keep him company. But then again, he wanted to keep up with the others, to show them he was strong enough to be at their side. So, to his shame, he kept his pace.

Surprisingly, the sun was already hanging low. Most of the day gone, lost in the miles of their footsteps without him even noticing. As beautiful as the country may have been, it was lost by the third mile of mostly-unchanging terrain. With such monotony, time passed in its bizarre method, simultaneously crawling along and passing in the blink of an eye. Turning, Tarnegrefur's peaks still towered above them menacingly. He couldn't guess how many miles they'd walked, but those mountains still seemed as close as ever. Or was that just because of the failing light?

Sniffing, he turned away and kept walking. A short climb to the crest of another hill, then the descent down its gentle slope. His shins twinged. They'd been aching since noon. Pausing in the long shadow of a young pine, he took a breath. With the sun so low in the sky, its rays were blinding, and he was glad of the shade, however momentarily.

Such pines were everywhere. He thought there were a lot at the foot of the mountains, but down here, you could scarcely walk fifty paces before coming to another.

There were animals too. Hares fleeing before them, squirrels chattering in their trees, birds flying ahead, even an angry pine marten snarling from a collapsed tree. He considered hunting a few, but had no bow, and didn't fancy his chances with his knife. Besides, he was too tired and inexperienced for such antics. Best leave it to the others.

Noswen appeared and jogged past. In a quiet voice, she mentioned something about the others resting ahead, but was gone before he could question her further. He huffed and trudged on as the hanex trotted back to the general.

When he reached the others, ten minutes later, they were camped in a small depression in the ground, filled with mossy rocks. A little blaze crackled, carefully tended by Auran. Water dripped from the neiads' clothes, two more dead fish by their sides. As homely a sight as he could ask for.

He collapsed into the grass with a sigh and rested his head against a soft mossy cushion. Gwahl prodded him.

'Are the others far behind?'

'Not too far,' he replied. 'I think Widrias and Pwtrek are about another quarter of a mile behind me.'

'Shouldn't be too long, then,' the daemon rose to help the neiads prepare the fish.

The others arrived within a few minutes. Although Noswen was barely out of breath, the other two panted like dogs. They sat down hard on the ground and took long gulps from their water-skins.

While his sister was away, refilling their water-skins, Chekry spit the fish and set them carefully over the fire. For the second night in a row, the delicious smell of roasting fish washed over their campsite, and Lidan was content. Once Depani returned, they cut the fish into equal portions and shared it out. The skin was crisp and the flesh was flaky, and he nearly burned his mouth in his eagerness to wolf down his supper.

Spotal unsheathed his jian. Out of his pack, he took a small, stained cloth. He rummaged in his pack for a few more seconds, before hissing and turning to Noswen.

'Could I please steal some wax? I think I've used all mine up.'

She nodded and tossed him a small pot from a pouch at her belt. Lidan watched carefully as he wiped down his dry blade, scraped up a small globule of the wax, and polished it to a faint sheen. He'd seen the Council soldiers polish their swords similarly, although never bothered with it. Didn't need to look good for a sword to be useful.

'How often do you do that?' he asked.

'When you're not using the sword, perhaps once every four or five weeks, but these days I've been polishing it far more frequently. You need to clean it after every use, otherwise it'll rust.'

Gwahl smirked when he looked at him. 'You haven't been cleaning your blade, have you, my friend? You should probably see to it.'

He flushed. He hadn't even thought of cleaning it out of necessity. It was the same one he'd carried since Crastalan. Through battles, rain, sea, mud and snow. The last time he'd drawn it was way back in their scuffle against the dreyads. Who knew what the blade looked like now? Holding his breath, he drew his sabre and inspected it in the firelight as his friends watched. Sitting back, he sighed in relief. No signs of rust.

Noswen reached over and plucked it from his lap. Within a few seconds, she snorted and rolled her eyes, passing it to Spotal. The calef beckoned Lidan closer.

'See here?' Spotal pointed to the forte, right next to the hilt. 'The slight discolouration? It's easy to miss in the firelight, but look at the texture of the metal. Rough, ugly, dry as a bone. In fact, the whole blade is completely dry. Ah! Look, Lidan, another spot of rust here,' he pointed further up the blade. 'A cluster of very small flakes. Here as well, at the tip. Rust all around. No, leave it with me, I'll polish it this time, but you need to take better care.'

'Perhaps you should let it rust,' said Gwahl. 'Then he'll have to get a better one.'

Spotal smiled, 'Perhaps. But I won't, don't worry, my friend, I'll save it for you.'

Chapter 24

Gwahl paused for breath at the crest. He scanned the gentle valley below. The hill was part of an encircling ring around a deep, lush basin, half a mile in diameter, a small forest at its heart. Pines, probably, it was mostly pines around these parts. He only gave them a passing glance.

A young deer snuffled at the grass, three hundred paces away. This was the best prey he'd found. After following the tracks for hours, he was nearly close enough to close in.

They were a week's march from the waterfall, finally free of the foothills, although the tips of Tarnegrefur were still visible on the horizon, far behind. Widrias promised a hard march, and that's exactly what they endured. Crossing leagues each day, pausing rarely and sleeping heavily come nightfall. Most nights they ate fish. This was the first time Widrias had allowed them to hunt for meat.

He glanced to the crest of the hill immediately to his right, where Spotal hid. A raised hand acknowledged him and he turned back to the game. Fortunately, the steady breeze came from the south, keeping the animal upwind.

At his side was the short spear he'd carved the night before. It was a crude weapon, slightly contoured in places and of varying thickness along its length, but made by his own hands. It would serve him adequately. Running his fingers up and down the wood, he flicked the fire-hardened tip, satisfied it was sharp enough to pierce the hide. Provided, of course, his aim was true.

It was only he, Spotal, and Noswen enjoying this particular hunt. Auran initially offered to help, but he told him to stay. It would be easier to find good prey with three hunters who knew the lands, as opposed to having an additional pair of alien hands hampering them. Auran didn't mind, and was with the others a few miles behind them, slowly following their tracks. The Southlander was an able hunter, judging from his stories. It was with more than a ghost of regret he was left behind. Perhaps one day the opportunity would arise to hunt game together.

Lidan asked to come too, his curiosity and ambition ever driving him to seek new thrills. He smiled. Such a brave boy. Pray to Enadir this quest wouldn't be his death. After all, it was he who recruited him to the Council, his fate was his responsibility. Especially as the quest took increasingly dangerous turns. Exactly why he'd bought him along, he didn't know. Surely the last time would have been a lesson? But no, the temptation was always there, to guide, to teach, to steer a young mind to greatness. If they survived.

He shuddered. Lessons learned, both for him and his followers. In time, he might teach him the skills to track, but not today. Tomorrow, or one of future's many tomorrows. Besides, Lidan wasn't up to his full strength, and a hunt with Noswen and Spotal would exhaust him completely.

The hanex was crouching behind a boulder between him and Spotal. She looked at him questioningly. He nodded and gave the signal to advance.

They needed to get close for an accurate throw. It was a shame they had no archers. The neiads were efficient with their crossbows, but inexperienced in hunting game, and neither he, Spotal, nor Noswen were confident enough in their skills with a crossbow to borrow one. Well, Noswen probably was, but she was reluctant to ask to borrow their weapons. Instead, they relied on the strength of their throws. Of course, this meant getting dangerously close, at least ten metres, to maximise accuracy.

Creeping forward, he kept his eyes on the deer, taking care to place his feet securely and quietly. Keeping as low as possible, they slinked as cautiously as a pack of wolves. The grass was long, its blades reaching their hips, parting to their advance.

All three were proficient, silent, deadly. They slid down the slopes to the valley, where he and Spotal circled wide to surround the deer, to trap it between them. If they were lucky, such precautions would be unnecessary and the hunt would end with only one throw. Noswen would have the first spear, him next, and finally Spotal, should the other two miss their mark.

It took a long time to get into position, especially for Spotal, whose circular route took him upwind. To counter, he saw him rub dirt into his groin and armpits, to mask his scent as best he could.

Oblivious to her approaching doom, the deer strolled nonchalantly through the grass, chewing at the softer blades. Presumably she'd been driven away from her herd by something, or perhaps her mother was killed by a predator or another hunter. In any case, she was alone, but seemed content enough in her solitude. After all, the valley's entire bounty was there for the taking. She would not want for anything, save perhaps some company.

She bolted upright, ears flared, eyes wide. Her nostrils twitched. Gwahl froze, his foot hovering an inch above the ground. But her eyes were not on him, but to the south, to Spotal. Evidently, the dirt was not enough.

Painful seconds trickled by, both hunter and hunted frozen, waiting for the other to make a move. Spotal was still hidden, but for how long?

Their luck changed as swiftly as the wind. An unpredictable western gust picked up, blowing hard against the southern breeze, confusing the air. It made him shiver, but at least Spotal's scent was hidden for the time being.

The deer, however, disliked the curious weather. Any hope of her returning to graze was lost. Her chestnut eyes flicked cautiously across the valley, struggling to find the danger. He saw the rapid rise and fall of her anxious chest. It was now or never. Now she'd sensed danger, the valley, despite its hoard of food and shelter, was a threat. She would flee, spring away on her long legs, half a mile away within a minute, taking their dinner with her.

He was tired of fish.

Cooing lightly, he mimicked a woodpigeon, to draw her attention. She whipped her head around. Spotal and Noswen heard his signal and flitted across the valley, closing the distance.

The hanex threw first, as planned. The deer heard her grunt, but too late. It flew straight and true and took the animal in her flank, just behind the foreleg. She gave a painful whine and tried to flee, but the shaft hindered her flight. She fell.

Gwahl rushed over, drawing his dirk. He eased her passing and she was still.

Exhaling forcefully, he chuckled.

'For a moment there I thought we'd lose her.'

'Never any doubt,' smiled Noswen.

'It was when she caught my scent, I was sure she'd bolt,' agreed Spotal. 'Lucky the wind picked up, been looking forward to some real meat.'

'Lucky indeed,' he smiled. 'We should get to butchering the carcass. Could you please collect some firewood? I'll carry the deer to the forest, we may as well camp there tonight. If she was here, I doubt there's any danger.'

'Should we let the others know?' asked Noswen.

Spotal nodded. 'Probably best if we do. It'll take a while to get everything ready. I wouldn't be surprised if it's dark by the time we're done. It's easier if we set up camp here. Do you want me to go?'

'No, I'll go, you help Gwahl. I'm quicker.'

He chuckled at Spotal's raised eyebrows. Noswen flicked her eyebrows jokingly.

'Can't argue with her,' he smiled.

'Course I can! I'd be wrong, of course, but I could still argue my case,' Spotal grinned.

'I'll be back soon.'

'Before you go,' he motioned to the deer, 'your share of her strength.'

Noswen nodded and knelt by the carcass. She pressed her lips to the wound in the deer's chest, and gathered a mouthful of blood. She swallowed.

'Your heart runs with mine,' she recited.

He nodded, satisfied. She left, jogging back the way they'd come.

Nodding at Spotal to gather the requested firewood, he heaved the carcass over his shoulder, knees buckling momentarily under the dead weight. Young and healthy, she would feed them for many days.

Spotal ran ahead to find and prepare an appropriate campsite. He followed at a slower pace, taking care to keep the wounds as high as possible to prevent any undue loss of her precious blood. When he reached the shelter of the trees, the calef was hunched on his knees, tending a fire. A wisp of smoke marked his success and he swiftly added twigs, dried pine needles, and sap-encrusted bark.

He shrugged the deer from his shoulder. Now for the messy part. First, he carefully drained as much blood as he could, collecting it in his and Spotal's water-skins.

'Your heart runs with mine,' they intoned, gulping down the warm fluid.

It settled heavily in his stomach, its rich taste overpowering. He persevered and drained his skin, wiping his mouth with the back of his hand. Closing his eyes, he breathed deeply, savouring the strength, the life. It was good. A bit sticky, he knew it coated his teeth, but after a few licks, they'd be clean again, free of the coppery film. As big as his water-skin may be, two were not enough to hold all her blood.

Kneeling again, he refilled it. Some was lost to the ground, or over his hands, but that was unavoidable. He licked his fingers clean and turned to take Spotal's, to refill it.

The calef looked unwell. He'd barely drank half his share and was breathing heavily, staring at the bulging skin disgustedly.

'Not done this for a while,' he smiled weakly. 'Certainly not a whole deer between two.'

'We won't have to eat much tonight after this.'

'Don't think I could stomach it if I wanted to,' he shuddered, lifting the skin to his mouth once more. One small sip and he nearly retched.

'It's alright,' he said, taking the skin from the calef's trembling hand.

'I'm sorry. We don't do it like this anymore.'

'No?' he blinked.

'Not really. Hardly anyone shares the strength nowadays. The neiads still do, for the most part, and some fonex, but that's about it. Everyone else has either forgotten the tradition or only have a token mouthful. Even the minotorrs have abandoned it, from what I understand.'

He shook his head. 'It's more than tradition. It's gratitude, respect. We honour the hunt. It is as it has always been, since before even the time of the giants.'

'Times move on, Gwahl. I do my best for the most part, but my stomach's too weak for these old beliefs.'

He shrugged. 'Well, if you won't have it, pass it here.'

Turning his friend's skin to his lips, he drained it in one, followed by the rest of his. He loosened his belt to ease his bulging stomach. The blood sloshed about whenever he moved. At least there'd be no need for food.

Spotal's complexion had a concerning green tint, so he sent him away to gather more firewood. The calef jumped at the excuse and disappeared. He pretended not to hear him vomit as he continued to prepare the carcass. If his stomach was this weak with the blood of a deer, imagine the effect the foul-smelling blood of a wyvern or cerastes would have! He smiled at the thought and shook his head.

The task of butchering the deer was far from done. He began by skinning the carcass, neatly slicing the hide from the underlying muscle. Tiny lumps of fat clung to the inside of the hide, but he left them for Spotal to remove.

Next, he strung together a few suitable branches to make a rack and set about carving thin slices of meat from the carcass. After feeding the fire to his satisfaction, he added an armful of damp, green branches and grasses, and was rewarded by a plume of white smoke. Setting the meat-laden rack immediately downwind, it would hopefully dry and smoke the meat well enough to keep for travelling. The rest they could eat tonight or tomorrow morning.

'Looks good,' he nodded to Spotal, admiring the hide, scraped clean of all traces of fat and flesh.

'Pretty, isn't it?'

'No tears, no rips, and a good start on removing the grain. You've done yourself proud.'

'Shame we don't have time to tan it properly.'

'I'm sure we'll find time? It'll take a few days but we may as well use it for an extra blanket or jacket?'

'If you fancy preparing the brains to tan it?'

'Why not? It'll be a project for you. Keep you busy at night. Show Lidan, he'll appreciate something like this. Get him to help you and he'll feel important.'

Spotal chuckled. 'I suppose it would save me a lot of work if I had his help.'

'Just don't be unkind. Don't make him mash up the brains if he doesn't want to. I don't know whether he'd be able to stomach it.'

'I wouldn't! It's going to smell like a bear's den within a few hours if I don't wash it.'

'Just do it tomorrow when we head back to the Atrael. Come on, help me roast the rest.'

Skewering the remainder of the carcass, they set it over a second fire. The heart, liver, and kidneys were placed on a flat stone over the flames. These rich organs would provide the bulk of their meal tonight, the rest of the roasting meat could be for tomorrow morning. The entrails, stomach, and other offal were thrown away some distance from the camp, for the crows. By the time they were done, the sun was well on its way over the hill.

'A lot of meat,' sniffed Spotal.

'We'll see most of it off. All of it, probably.'

'Shall we keep the bones? I don't have any use for them, but they might come in handy?'

He rubbed his chin. He missed this ritual. The hunt, the cleaning of the kill, using all the parts of the animal, spending the following days preparing the carcass. Meat for nourishment, the hide for clothing, sinew for string, the stomach or bladder for a water-skin, the bones for tools. There was a peace to it, a completeness, an order, a balance. The honesty of a well-deserved kill and the respect to the life given to sustain his own. Simplicity, reminiscent of a time before wars and thrones. Or was that just the gilded view of hindsight? Was it not always like this, stealing brief moments of order in a world of chaos? Would it be forever?

'We'll see if any of the others want them. I won't have the time to make anything of them.'

'Take them with you?' Spotal suggested.

'Don't feel like carrying them.'

'Lidan might be curious how to carve a bone into a knife or spearhead?'

'Then he will remain curious,' he snorted. 'Tanning the hide is curiosity enough from one hunt.'

Spotal shrugged and turned back to tend the meat. The sizzle of fat pattering into the blazing logs was as comforting as the warmth of the flames. He sniffed and strolled back to the clearing to wipe his bloody hands on the cool grass. Perhaps he should keep a bone to carve into an awl, or simple knife, something to busy Lidan's mind on this journey. But suddenly he had no desire to tutor anyone. As enjoyable as the hunt was, now it was over, and he wouldn't have the time to utilise the carcass to its fullest. Even that brief moment of balance was gone, wrenched from his hands by their need to move on.

Glancing at the sun, perilously close to the hilltops, he sniffed. The others had better reach them soon, or the final strides of the day's march would be lit by starlight. Hands clean, he returned to Spotal, pausing to check on the smoking meat.

'Whoever's on watch will have to keep an eye on the smoker,' he muttered.

Spotal nodded. Stretching, he yawned loudly.

'Winds! Forgot how exhausting hunting can be,' Spotal poked idly at the roasting meat. 'I feel so drained. All I want is to sleep.'

'I'm tired too,' he breathed, softly. Spotal glanced at him. 'It's been a long slog,' he explained, hurriedly. 'Why don't you eat some liver and sleep? I'll tend the roast. See you in the morning.'

'I have no taste for liver right now. I can still taste the blood.'

He chuckled. 'Then have some of this,' he leaned forward to slice a chunk of meat from the spit, but Spotal held him back with a hand on his shoulder.

'No, I'm just not hungry right now.'

'You need to eat, especially if you're that tired. You've not had a chance to eat anything properly today, you'll only get worse if you abstain.'

'You've not eaten either.'

'I drank a lot of blood,' he cut off a sizeable chunk of sizzling meat.

'Good point,' the calef's lip turned in disgust, and took the offered meat. He sat back against a tree trunk, chewing slowly, one hand resting across his chest, playing with his amulet. Gwahl felt his eyes on him and waited for the unspoken question, whatever it might be.

'Lidan said something strange to me on the mountains.'

'Oh?' he asked. What trouble had the boy stirred up now?

'Mmh. Said you were afraid of something.'

'Afraid?'

'Yes. Why would he say that?'

He stopped poking the meat and turned to him. There was hurt in his eyes, almost betrayal, an accusation of dishonesty. It was true, he'd kept his fears from him, but only to keep it from spreading, to isolate its corruption within him alone.

'He might have overheard a conversation with Widrias.'

'So, you were afraid.'

'I didn't want my... apprehensions to spread, potentially misplaced as they were.'

'What were you afraid of?'

'Just... something we might have found on the mountains.'

'Like a lie about the serpent key?'

He flinched. 'No, well, yes, I suppose I always was... but no, something else.'

'What?'

'It doesn't matter, nothing came of it.'

'What?'

He sighed. Spotal was irritatingly stubborn at times. Besides, and admission of this fear might avoid a more uncomfortable conversation about the damned key.

'Horrors.'

Spotal narrowed his eyes. 'Horrors?'

'Indeed.'

'They're–'

'Not extinct,' he interrupted. 'I'm certain of it. They lie in the shadows of those icy peaks, lurking and waiting. I'm afraid of them, Spotal. I tried to warn Widrias, but he waved away my fears. As it happens, he was right, so it doesn't matter.'

'No? You should have told one of us, Gwahl. What if you were right and they really were out there?'

'Why does it matter? Nothing happened, nobody was harmed, Widrias was right.'

'If you're afraid of something, you of all people, I want to know. How many things frighten you? A short list, I'm sure. We had a right to know if we were in danger.'

He held up his hands defensively. 'Alright, I'm sorry, next time I'll tell you.'

Spotal shook his head. 'We both know you won't. You keep everything inside, never let anyone in.'

He shook his head. 'What do you want me to say, Spotal? I didn't want anyone to panic because of my empty fears. Widrias ordered me not to tell anyone and I couldn't undermine him, could I? Besides, both people I told dismissed those concerns as soon as I voiced them. I saw no benefit in telling anyone else and causing undue worry.'

'Both people? I thought you only told Widrias?'

'Pwtrek as well. He was always at the rear, so he'd be the first to fall foul of their claws, but he was sceptical.'

Spotal snorted mirthlessly. 'Come on, Gwahl, you know you should've told me. I'm your friend, more of a friend to you than Pwtrek, yet I hardly know anything about you. No, don't give me a life-story, now is not the time. I just want you to let me know from now on whenever you have concerns. Things that frighten you are things that should frighten us all. Please, tell me next time.'

He sighed, and nodded.

It was true, he kept things to himself, but it was always his way. Why should he burden these young beings with his ancient troubles? They could never grasp the depths and complexities of his feelings. How could they? A child would never understand the burdens carried by a grandparent. It was only in fellow daemons he could confide, only they could truly empathise. But no, that way lay more pain, more loss. Better to spend his life with the fleeting existence of the men, calefs, fonex, and all the others, than to endure the painful memories of his kin. Or was it? Spotal was hurt by his privacy, which hurt him. At least with another daemon, there would be no secrets, only understanding. He smiled weakly. No, there were always secrets. Ones even too shameful to share with his own people.

But then, what use were such secrets to these people? That's not what Spotal asked for, only for the small concerns that affected him and his companions.

'You're right, next time anything gives me cause for concern, I won't hide it from you. You're my friend, and you have a right to know when I'm afraid for your safety.'

'I'm afraid, Gwahl,' whispered the calef, suddenly. He drew his knees up against his chest and closed his eyes. 'I'm afraid of what will greet me when we reach Muranath. Will Lleunedd scold me and strip me of my title? Exile me from these lands for our failed quest? It doesn't seem fair. I hope he gives me another chance.'

'He will.'

'My position as ambassador for my people is not yet done,' he continued, ignoring him. 'Not until Stolach is defeated or I am slain.'

'He won't exile you,' he said, as comfortingly as he could. 'Lleunedd is wise and will understand this mission has been but a single task in your new position. He might not welcome you back into his forces straight away, not until you accomplish something he deems worthy, but he will not exile you.'

'You sound so sure I can almost believe you, but not quite. This hopeless venture has cost us so much already. Winds! I regret ever coming. I wish I stayed with the Council army, training them, spending time with my men, not trudging across endless leagues after a dream.'

'You and me both, Spotal. We can't help it now, though, all we can do is learn from it and reach the next stage of our journey.'

'Have you considered what will happen when we do eventually get back to Dailas? The high chancellors pinned their hopes on this mission, which we failed. How can we hope to win after this?'

He poked at the meat and a dribble of fat spurted out to drop sizzling into the flames.

'The chancellors almost certainly have another plan of sorts. In fact, I doubt they put any real hope on this mission.'

'Why not?'

'Because Widrias was the only chancellor to truly believe in the serpent key with any kind of conviction, the rest simply saw it as a fairy tale.'

'You're sure?'

'Almost certainly. Why else would a chancellor come with us? Why else would we take so few men? The others probably foresaw this venture as a fool's errand, which is why they didn't march the entire Council army over to the mountains. The general probably came in order to prove to the others that he was right to believe the tale and they didn't stop him. No, this was a wild throw of the dice, an unlikely chance they decided was worth taking, if only to appease Widrias.'

'So all that about splitting up the chancellors for their safety was a lie?'

He shrugged. 'In part, probably. Perhaps they just capitalised on the opportunity.'

'I see… that's good. So when we're back, they'll have another front to strike at Stolach?'

'Their hopes weren't pinned on us, but I don't know how well-thought-out their alternative may be. Aside for an outright assault on Crastalan, I heard no whispers of any real plan of attack.'

'Let's hope it doesn't come to that,' murmured Spotal. 'So, the other chancellors sent us away knowing full well that there was no key. That makes me feel so needed. It's ironic that Lleunedd sent me away to the Council to be rid of me, only for them to consider me unhelpful enough to immediately send me away,' he shook his head. 'My reputation precedes me.'

'Not true, Spotal. You're in fine company. Tanor, Noswen, Pwtrek. All of them valuable to the Council, in all likelihood sent to protect Widrias and keep him from harm should things turn foul. Remember our original plan was to reach Muranath by sea, they probably hoped you'd be able to convince Lleunedd or Teig to give us an escort up to Tarnegrefur. Everybody who sat at that crescent table had a reason to be sent here.'

'Maybe, I hope you're right, Gwahl.'

'I'm sure I am,' he smiled reassuringly.

What he said may have been speculation, but he was confident it was true. He'd had enough time to contemplate its truth since the plateau. It was only Widrias who believed in the key. The other chancellors just went along with it to silence him. It wasn't fair on Spotal to suffer this needless defeat, burdened with failure as he was.

Further conversation was halted as Chekry and Depani bounced into the camp and collapsed exhaustedly next to Spotal. Auran followed soon after with Lidan, and lastly came Noswen, Widrias, and Pwtrek.

The satorr nodded to Gwahl and Spotal and settled down with his back to a tree, groaning as he did so. He turned to the daemon.

'Gwahl, your hunt has taken us some distance from the river. I thought it was agreed we would stick to its course, to reach Muranath as soon as possible? I warned you not to turn this march into a hunting holiday, yet that seems to be what you're doing.'

'My apologies, General, next time I shall ask the deer to keep to our path, so as not to lead us astray.'

A few weary chuckles met his sarcasm, but the satorr was not amused.

'It's no laughing matter, Gwahl, we need to get to Lleunedd as soon as we can, and this detour has cost us valuable time.'

Spotal rolled his eyes and spoke up in his defence. 'If you please, sir, I know this valley, the Atrael is only a few miles west, an hour's march at most. If we take a gradual southwest path from here, we'll be back on track without losing any real time. We've actually been incredibly fortunate the deer stayed so close to the river.'

'Nevertheless, if ever you do decide to hunt miles away, make sure you carry the game back to us and don't summon us to you. Saying that, I am grateful.'

Gwahl nodded and turned away, serving fresh venison to his companions.

*

Sunrise was greeted with groans as the party rose, ate, and hoisted their packs over their shoulders. Gwahl's stomach grumbled unhappily. Consuming such rich meat after living off rustic flatcakes for so long disagreed with him. He swallowed hard, took a swig from the water-skin Lidan handed him, his own being empty of all but crusted blood, and joined the march out of the valley, heading due south.

The day passed slowly, dark rainclouds gathering on the horizon, promising showers to come. Midday came and went, and the wind steadily rose, until it was blowing hard in his face, forcing him to narrow his eyes and clutch his cloak around him for warmth.

Out of nowhere, a familiar smell hit him. He glanced at Noswen, ten paces behind. She had her nose turned upwards. Spotal was the same. Ash and smoke. Not the clean, comforting smell of a campfire or roasting meat, but acrid, pungent. Widrias called them to a halt and limped up, frowning.

'You all smell it,' he said in a raised voice, to be heard above the wind. 'It may be a few miles ahead of us yet, with the wind carrying the scent. I can't see any smoke, but again we probably have the wind to thank for that. Be on your guard, any calefs who recognise us won't harm us, but dressed as we are and carrying our arms, they might think us enemies.'

As predicted, the source of the stench was nowhere near, and they marched for nearly four miles before they finally saw the faint tendrils of smoke rising to the sky, only to be blown away and carried across the country to their nostrils. The source of the fire was, as yet, invisible to them, hidden from view by a small wood.

Accepting the cover Enadir gifted them, they approached through the trees. It was not a wild wood. The trees were too widely-spaced, with no fallen boughs or storm-felled trunks blocking their path. It was well-maintained, tidy, with new saplings at the border of neat clearings. Whoever lived nearby took good care of it. But it was difficult to appreciate the level of cultivation when his senses were otherwise bludgeoned by the overwhelming stench of smoke, ash, and something altogether more unpleasant.

It would have to be a large blaze for them to smell it above the natural odours of the forest. What reason would the calefs have to build such a blaze? It was wrong. Unsettled, he continued through the pristine little wood, his hand clasped about his blade.

The answer was revealed as soon as they emerged from the cover of the trees.

Before him was a beautiful village. Neat houses, slender buildings, paved stone roads. All the roofs were made of straw or dark green slate, the walls of wood and white clay. Everything was charred and blackened, the air hazy with smoke, the ground stained brown with old blood.

He stepped forward wordlessly. What could he say in the face of such destruction? Spotal gasped and sprinted past him into the village, jian drawn. Widrias shouted at him to come back, but the calef paid no heed, disappearing between the houses. Auran started after him, but the Widrias pulled him back roughly.

'No, Auran. It could be dangerous. Caution.'

'Danger indeed, and Spotal's gone running straight in!' Auran hissed, pulling himself free.

'So we'll follow, but in an organised manner, carefully. You, Noswen and Gwahl go in first, then the neiads, they can cover you should anyone attack. I'll follow next with Lidan. Pwtrek takes the rear. Draw your weapons, tread carefully. Go!'

They moved as a tight unit, padding down the streets between buildings, searching for any sign of life. There was none. Everything was black and dead. Not a single weed, not a single stray animal survived the ordeal. Slumped along the sides of the road were calefs, bodies hewn and hacked apart as they fled the madness.

Before long they reached the village square and there was Spotal, kneeling amongst his slain kin, sword sheathed, clutching something in his hands. He looked up as they approached, and Gwahl saw the redness of his eyes, though whether he'd been weeping with anger or sorrow, it was impossible to say.

Spotal nodded at their weapons. 'Put them away,' he croaked. 'Nobody's here. The village is dead.'

'What happened?' asked Lidan quietly, looking around him in a mixture of horror and disgust. 'Who?'

Spotal trembled and lifted his hands, showing them what he held. A torn tunic with a golden manticore.

'I took this off a body, the only enemy in this whole town. Over a hundred dead calefs, only one dead soldier. So many of my kin, but only one enemy is dead to atone for them. Stolach will pay for this. He will burn for this!'

Gwahl stepped over and put his arm around him. Spotal resisted for a moment, then clutched him tight and sobbed into his shoulder. The others stood by solemnly as they waited for the calef to purge his heart of grief. It took time, but eventually Spotal's sobs ceased. He stood, jaw clenched.

'What should we do?' asked Widrias, referring to the bodies.

Spotal twitched. 'We must burn them properly, to put them to rest. If we place them all in the village centre, we can make a funeral pyre and set their souls free.'

'Very well. Leave nobody behind, save for Stolach's soldier. He can rot in the sun.'

It took them the afternoon to collect all the calefs. A miserable task. Gwahl did his best to be gentle with the carcasses, to preserve them, but often they were so horribly mutilated that they fell apart in his hands. Acid from his stomach burned his throat as he found the beheaded bodies of four children, slumped together in a line, executed one by one. He could only imagine the terror that the fourth child felt, hearing her friends die, awaiting her own turn. He couldn't look at their faces, but carried their heads by his side to the village square, where he placed them carefully next to their resting bodies. He didn't show Spotal.

The next horror he found made him gag. Cradled in Noswen's hands was a young calef, terror etched on her pale face, blood covering her swollen stomach. The hanex tried to say something to Gwahl, but no words could describe such a monstrous deed.

Each new discovery, each murdered innocent, set his heart pounding. There could be no reason for such a deed. No justification.

Eventually all the bodies were recovered. Spotal lit a torch and threw it on them. Gwahl waited with his friend as he watched the fires consume his kin. Before long the heat of the inferno became unbearable and they left to join the others outside the village. Spotal didn't say anything, but Gwahl knew he was grateful for his company.

It was dark by now, made darker still by the thick smoke. The air was so filled with the rancid reek of burning flesh, they had to walk some distance upwind of the village to escape its foul stench. Eventually, Widrias called them to make camp around a cluster of tall stones.

Spotal hadn't said anything since leaving the village. Hardly anyone spoke. A brooding silence hung over them as they chewed slowly on smoked deer meat. Gwahl noticed Lidan start to shift beside him. He was desperate to ask something. Just let it be gentle, for Spotal's sake. Before long, he broke the silence.

'Why are Stolach's soldiers here?' asked Lidan.

'Why isn't the question,' replied Pwtrek in a weary grumble. 'What I'd like to know is how?'

'By sea, perhaps?' suggested Auran. 'Maybe they attacked from the south and are advancing north with their armies, burning villages as they go.'

'They can't have come by sea,' said Spotal, breaking his silence. 'The calefin fleet is far too strong for them to defeat in a naval battle. They would also have to take Muranath before planning any kind of campaign northwards, and that city can hold out for months. They didn't come from the south.'

'So, the north? It's possible they attacked from there, moving troops around Tarnegrefur?'

Gwahl shook his head. 'Unlikely. Had they come from the north then they would either have to fight through Imhara, which is heavily defended, or, as you said, circle around the mountains, which would take months. We would have heard tale of such a campaign if it were true. We would also have found evidence of an army passing before us. Campfires, scattered prey, churned up ground. We saw no such thing on the way down.'

'So where? The northwest border is impenetrable, the southwest border heavily defended, the east impassable.'

'Why is the east impassable?' asked Lidan.

Gwahl blinked, once again startled by how little the young one knew of Nefarwy. 'The Far Eastlands are too wild and dangerous for any attack to have come from there. The eastern coast of the Kingdom of the calefs is also out of the question. The calefin fleet is too strong. No ships could have landed on the coast. Even if, by some miracle, they did manage to slip past the calef navy, it would take months to make it all the way over here. It doesn't add up.'

'Then they appeared out of nowhere,' grumbled Depani, sullenly.

'It seems so,' frowned Widrias. 'Right now, however, I am slightly less concerned with where they came from as to how many are here.'

'A great number, I would think,' said Auran, nodding. 'To have killed so many people with only one casualty, they must have had enough soldiers to completely overwhelm the villagers, gang up on them, cut them down in groups.'

'We're assuming there's an invasion here,' warned Chekry. 'Is it at all possible that this is but a single army of a hundred or so men? Maybe they're the soldiers from the plateau chasing after us all this time?'

'I don't think so. The army in the mountains had dreyads, they would've found us by now, especially with us keeping so close to the river. It's not the army from the plateau,' Widrias paused. 'You're right, however, to say that we mustn't assume this to be a large invasion force. Maybe it is a small army working alone, trying to spread discord and panic.'

'Why would Stolach send a small army?' asked Gwahl. 'If he's found a way into the Kingdom unseen, surely he would invade as soon as possible? To ravage and plunder, make the lands his own. I can't see him passing on such an opportunity.'

'I think it all boils down to how they got here,' said Spotal. 'If we find their path into the land, we can estimate how large an army would have been able to travel along that path. That's why we need to find out how they got here.'

Widrias brooded for a moment. 'Perhaps you're right. But this new development doesn't change our goal. In fact, it gives us even more incentive to reach Muranath as soon as we can, so we can warn the king of the dangers roaming his lands. We must proceed with caution. I will not have us stumble on an army of Stolach's soldiers unawares. Remember that we are few and not up to our full strength. We must keep away from confrontations. Tomorrow we march hard, fast, and carefully. Everyone get some sleep. Lidan and Spotal can take first watch, we set out at dawn.'

Chapter 25

The infinite corridor stretched away before him. He couldn't tell whether he'd been asleep for seconds or hours. The dampness on his cheeks from fresh tears suggested it hadn't been long.

He sniffed and ate his two apples, still tucked away in the folds of his shirt. His bandages were frayed but the bleeding had stopped. He traced his fingers across the scars on his knees and heels. By some miracle they were still closed. The blood on the floor was from the grazes and blisters he worked into his skin by crawling.

Coughing faintly, he looked to the door in the arch. It was as good a door as any. Maybe this one would lead him to the outside world, to freedom.

It didn't. It only led to another short passageway, this one straight, with only two doors at the other end. He eased open the first. Stairs leading down into darkness. The second was another storeroom, similar enough to the first room he'd found himself in, filled with sacks of grain and oats. He dragged himself inside and closed the door with a creak. He held his breath. Someone must have heard. Betrayed by un-oiled hinges. Seconds passed with no disturbance. He released the breath. Deserted. Praise the north winds.

Dragging himself inside, he made for the discarded sacks at the back, beyond the rows of crates. A makeshift bed. Tucked in the burlap, he'd be invisible. A safe resting place, at last. He was so tired.

Past the first row of boxes.

He yelped.

A pair of sandals, jutting from beneath a brown wool robe. He raised his head, tears filling his eyes. Discovered.

A man. Bald head and round cheeks. Close-set blue eyes and a large gut that spilled over his cord belt. He lifted Lidan by his armpits to his feet. He neither had the strength nor the will to resist. He was found, he had failed, he was doomed.

The man set him down on one of the boxes, propping his back against the wall so he wouldn't fall.

Tears poured from his burning eyes, blurring his vision. His captor reached into a box and pulled something out. A chubby hand forced it into his mouth, between his teeth.

'Chew,' the man commanded, in a deep voice. 'You need to eat or you'll never recover.'

He did as he was told. Not because he wanted to, but for the possible punishment if he disobeyed. It was a piece of dried meat. Strong and smoky. It made his jaw ache, the salt left his mouth dry. The man anticipated it and handed him a skin of water.

He gulped it down. Do as you're told or be punished.

His eyelids drooped as a sudden weariness descended upon him. He whimpered. Drugged. As if captivity weren't humiliation enough. His apparent saviour loomed over him. His head was too heavy, his neck couldn't support its weight. He fell into soft hands. Darkness.

*

He woke with a jump and saw red skies. It was time to march again. The smoked deer meat reminded him of the dream, the memory. Shaking his head, he collected his possessions and waited for Widrias to give the order.

He and Gwahl were the first ones ready. Widrias saw them standing to one side, waiting to leave. He called them over.

'Seeing as you're both up, you can scout ahead. Look for signs of the army, but be discreet. Report back after midday.'

Gwahl nodded and jogged away. Lidan followed. When they were out of earshot of the others, he asked Gwahl if Spotal knew any of the calefs in the village. Gwahl shook his head.

'Unlikely.'

'So why was he so upset?'

'They were his kin, Lidan. He didn't need to know anyone.'

'People in the Midlands are killed every day, none of us weep about it.'

'Maybe, but the Midlands are in the midst of a war, its inhabitants desensitized to the tragedy of innocent lives lost. The calefs didn't expect their villages to be ransacked. They thought their borders safe.'

Lidan nodded. The brutality of it, the savagery… after Crastalan's horrors, he thought he'd be too hardened to baulk at violence. But at every stage of the journey so far, he'd been repeatedly disgusted and amazed by people's capacity for cruelty.

'I meant to ask sooner,' said Gwahl, 'how's your wound?'

'Well,' he replied happily. 'Just a small scar now. It isn't painful.'

'And your head?' asked Gwahl.

'Fine.'

'No memory loss, no loss of sensation, moving all four limbs normally?'

'All good,' he laughed.

'Good,' Gwahl nodded. 'You gave me quite the fright when I first saw you, head all bloodied.'

'I was frightened too,' he admitted. 'But it doesn't matter. All better, thanks to you!'

'It does matter. Remember how it happened so it doesn't happen again. How did you get walloped on the back of the head with such a big shield?'

'He came from behind!'

'And you got shot. Twice.'

'I wasn't expecting it.'

Gwahl laughed. 'Well here's a lesson for you; enemy archers have a habit of shooting at us!'

'That's not what I meant,' he smiled. 'I was fighting another dreyad. I was preoccupied. I left myself open when I moved in and the arrow found me. Then the other guy hit me on my head.'

'You might want to ask Spotal for more lessons on how to maintain your defences even while attacking. Perhaps a helmet too,' he cuffed him lightly around the head.

'Why can't you tell me?' he asked.

'I'm not as good as him, and I fight with a dirk, not a sword. Oh yes, I know the theory behind sword-play, but am unused to its practical application. Just ask the calef.'

'I probably won't ask him right now.'

'No, obviously not, but soon.'

They arrived at the riverbank and followed it south at an easy pace, jogging lightly so as not to lose their breath. They hadn't run for half an hour before Gwahl stopped him, lips pursed, eyes narrowed as he peered downriver. He followed his gaze. There was a faint, blurred line on the horizon.

'What is it?' he asked.

'I think I know... We must be careful from now on,' Gwahl beckoned him on, ran forward a few paces, and halted abruptly. 'Actually, let's cut southeast. I think we may find something.'

He didn't ask what. He doubted Gwahl would tell him, with his love of secrets.

They ran for the best part of an hour over sloping hills, fallen trees, and moss-covered rocks, until they came across what Gwahl was looking for. Churned, muddied soil left in the wake of a marching army. Gwahl examined it carefully.

'Pretty big force,' he said. 'A hundred men, give or take. Can you tell which way they were heading?'

He shrugged his shoulders and guessed. 'North?'

'Exactly. Well done. See the grooves in the mud? Definitely headed north, back the way we came. If you line up where they came from to where they were going...' he paused, thinking. 'This could well be the ones who ransacked the village. In fact, it almost certainly is. The trail is more than a few days old, judging by how rounded the tracks are.'

'Well at least it means Widrias and the rest aren't headed straight for them.'

'Indeed,' nodded the daemon. 'It also explains why we never came close to any soldiers. All mounted. A cavalry force. You can see the imprints of their hooves. They'll be moving quickly. But how did they get here?'

He waited for him to continue, but the daemon said nothing, lost in thought.

'What should we do now? Report back? It's not midday yet.'

'No, we'll press on, follow this trail south to its origin. Although I think I know where it is now.'

'Where?'

'That dark line on the horizon we saw at the riverbank. It was probably another army.'

He said nothing, suddenly afraid. He'd seen the destruction a single army could cause. A second only meant more death.

'Should we keep some distance from this trail? If another army comes up, especially cavalry, then we'll be caught in seconds!'

'We need to follow it,' said Gwahl. 'I don't think it's very likely we run into another force. Why would they head north? There's nothing there. If I were invading the Kingdom of the calefs, I'd send the majority of my forces south, to plunder the more bountiful lands and take Muranath...' the daemon looked at him. It was a worried look, one he was sure was mirrored in his own features. 'Come on. We need to find where they came from.'

They ran for about an hour, keeping low, saying nothing, straining their senses to detect any sign of an approaching foe. Fortunately for them, no soldiers followed their trail and their journey was easy, if not nerve-racking.

Finally, they heard the trumpeting of horns and the pounding of boots and hooves on soft mud. Gwahl signalled for added caution. Dreyad scouts could be nearby. If they were, he didn't see any. They edged nearer and nearer to the sounds of a marching army. Finally, when they crawled to the crest of a hill, all was revealed.

The Atrael was a few hundred metres to the west, and beyond that was a great grassland plain a mile or so wide, with the tangled blur of the bramble plains to the west of that. Cutting across all three stretches of land and piercing the land of the calefs, a kilometre south of their hill, was a huge snaking army. Countless soldiers marched in their organised units, standards fluttering in the wind, drums pounding and horns blaring as they sounded the beat to which thousands of feet tramped. It wasn't just infantry. Horses whinnied and snorted as they were led by their riders, lances cradled in their arms. Armour sparkled in the sun, glistening and gleaming in a near-blinding column of metal. The silver stream of soldiers marched along with the golden calefin river. He couldn't help but admire the view. The army's rear-guard crossed the grasslands while the vanguard was already far to the south, heading deep into the calefin country. Makeshift ferries had been constructed to ship troops over the Atrael, and these worked continuously to bring more and more units across the waters. His jaw dropped at the sight of a great team of oxen dragging a partially-assembled siege weapon off a ferry to follow the main body of the army.

He heard Gwahl mutter something under his breath but didn't quite make it out. He raised an eyebrow and the daemon leaned closer.

'I said, now we know how they got here. Still, I never expected such a scale. Look there, you see the brambles? They've cut a path through them. Never thought that possible. They cut a path through the bramble plains.'

'How did they get through the marshes?' he whispered back, keeping an eye out for scouts.

'I don't know, they must have found a path, or built one. Stolach managed to cut his way through the brambles, now no feat he accomplishes will surprise me. I can't believe this,' the daemon shook his head, then studied the army heading south. 'Look, Lidan, our trail is the only one turning north. There are...two heading east, and then that one big road heading south. This invasion must have been going on for weeks. A bold move by Stolach... come, my friend, we must return to the others.'

They crawled away from the hill and returned north, running faster than they had on the way south, anxious to return to the rest of the party. It was an unpleasant journey. Neither spoke, too lost in their thoughts to bother making conversation. It was past noon when they finally spotted the first of their company. Gwahl called out when he saw Noswen and Spotal jog from the cover of a small wood and beckoned them over to the riverbank. They were soon followed by the rest, waiting patiently for Widrias to catch his breath.

'What did you find?' he finally asked.

'Bad news for Lleunedd,' began Gwahl, and delivered his report to the stunned expression of the others. 'Must have been planned for a long time, although it's the first I've heard of it.'

'Impossible!' Spotal cried, outraged.

'We should have heard of this from our scouts,' growled Pwtrek.

Widrias held up his hands for silence. 'Tell us more, Gwahl, what else?'

'There's a large army currently crossing the Atrael and heading south. From the trails I could see from our vantage point, this was not the first army to come. Aside from the force that burned that northern village, there seems to have been several other smaller forces heading in various directions across the lands. The main bulk heads south.'

'How many more armies?' demanded Spotal.

'Only one trail headed north, two went east. I can't say how many went south. It's possible the force we saw was the first one to go, but I doubt it.'

'Seems as though Stolach finally decided it was time to expand his borders,' muttered Chekry.

'It seems so,' said Gwahl. 'We even saw siege engines. No prizes for guessing where they're heading.'

'Muranath,' whispered Widrias. Gwahl nodded sombrely.

'What now?' asked Pwtrek. 'Yet another stage in our journey thwarted. Where do we go?'

'Nothing's changed, Pwtrek,' said Widrias. 'I say we continue south, try to reach Muranath before the army does. They'll be slow, we can overtake them, especially when they run into the southern calefin armies. If we keep going as we are now, I'm sure we can reach Lleunedd before them.'

'The army will have outriders, sir,' said Depani. 'They'll run us down as soon as we come close. I think we should consider another option.'

'What options?' snapped the satorr. 'We can't go west to the soldiers, brambles, and marshes. I will not return north to the mountains. There's nothing to the east. South is the only way we can go.'

'I agree,' said Spotal.

'Only because you want to go to your king,' said Depani.

'You're right, I want to see Muranath and stand before my king and commander, is that so bad? I still think it's the safest route, and it gives us a direct heading. As long as we're careful and don't take unnecessary risks, we can remain undetected. Besides, I wish to see this path through the brambles, and Lleunedd must be informed of this breach in our defences.'

'What do you think, Gwahl?' Widrias asked.

Gwahl started, as if surprised his opinion was sought.

'I agree. South. As you said, the other paths are effectively closed to us, and we know we have friends in the south, beyond our enemies. It's also ultimately the fastest route home; to take a ship from Tonnis harbour and get back to the Council. Dangerous as it is, I say we go south.'

'Good,' nodded Widrias. 'In that case it's my order to continue as we are. Gwahl and Lidan can lead us to the crossing of the army and we can further assess that situation when we reach there. Let's go!'

They ran again. Lidan felt the weariness in his limbs, heavy and sluggish, but he kept going. He was now almost used to running with next to no energy. For once, the group did not spread out over a large distance but kept close together for safety. Occasionally, Noswen or Gwahl would run some distance ahead to make sure no enemies were approaching, but the way was always clear.

It felt as though the run back to the ferries was shorter than before. He counted off the landmarks. They'd passed the deep meander of the river, so exaggerated that it was very nearly a full circle, and the four tall rocks shaped like a crown were also behind them, as was the lightning-hewed tree. Finally, they reached the hill upon which he and Gwahl had crouched, and the party edged carefully up to its crest to spy on the river.

The army had since completed the crossing. They could see the silver river a few miles south. Without the hustle and bustle of hundreds of crossing troops, the ferries were easier to assess. There were six, large and sturdy but hastily-made. All of them docked on the far bank. A token army of forty outriders, twenty on each bank, guarded them.

'A shame they're there,' muttered Widrias, 'otherwise I might have been tempted to burn the ferries to prevent any more soldiers from crossing.'

'We could try,' suggested Chekry. 'Depani and I could swim across, light a fire?'

'It'll take too long. On balance, I'd rather they didn't know we were here.'

'I wouldn't mind crossing to the other bank,' said Gwahl. 'I'd like to have a look at this road through the brambles. If I doubled back with Chekry and Depani, we could cross the river further upstream, out of sight of the guards, scout out the brambles, and on the way back the neiads could sabotage the ferries in some way?'

'I don't know, Gwahl,' muttered Widrias, rubbing his beard. 'How long would it take? I don't want to linger here for too long. We need to press on with our journey.'

'We could be done within two hours,' said Depani. 'The rest of you can continue south, skirting around the guards and we'll catch up with you later. It'll be easy if we swim, the current will carry us far swifter than you can jog.'

'Will Gwahl be able to keep up with you if you swim?' asked Spotal.

'He can hold on to one of our backs,' nodded Chekry. Gwahl nodded in agreement.

'You can swim past the ferries undetected, in no danger?' asked Widrias.

'Easily, we'll just keep underwater for a little while when we swim away and they'll never see us.'

'Think of how many soldiers we'd be delaying if we were to destroy them,' said Chekry.

Widrias scratched behind his horns, thinking, before giving the smallest nod.

'But be warned; we won't wait for you, we'll make our camp late in the evening. Find us as soon as you can.'

'What if we're delayed?' asked Gwahl.

'A branch of the Atrael cuts across the land before joining the main flow,' said Spotal, 'we could wait for you there?'

'I'd rather not wait anywhere, Spotal,' said Widrias, frowning.

'We'd be delayed for quite a while anyway while we cross the river, there are only a few flimsy bridges spanning its width,' said Spotal. 'It's good news. Any invading army will be slowed down considerably when they reach it. I don't envy their task of moving their siege engines across it!'

Lidan frowned. 'But... Won't that mean an entire army will be waiting for us by the crossing?'

Spotal paused and turned to Widrias.

The satorr exhaled between his teeth and cursed. 'Winds! How far away is this branch?'

'Around a week and a half away, if we continue at our current pace. I think. I can only estimate,' Spotal played with his amulet absently.

'Well, we should have overtaken the army in well under a week,' said Widrias, confidently.

'We might overtake the army Gwahl and I saw,' said Lidan, 'but what of other armies that have already made the journey? They might be there already?'

'Especially if they have siege engines,' nodded Spotal.

'We don't *know* that there are multiple armies heading south,' said Widrias, unconvincingly. 'The crossings may still be safe.'

'Is it worth taking the risk?' Spotal asked. 'The bridges across the river are narrow and fragile, built of wood and rope and nothing else. It would take an invading army a long time to cross. Think of their supply carts, horses, wagons. An army that has already struck south will almost certainly still be there by the time we arrive.'

'Even if they have passed,' said Gwahl, 'they would not be so absent-minded as to leave the bridges unguarded. There will be blood if we continue on this path.'

'Do we have an alternative?'

Spotal paused. 'We could go east around the river, towards Ahanemis Lake, but that would take us very far from the Atrael, and you'd have difficulty regrouping with us,' he gestured to Gwahl and the neiads.

'It won't be an issue for us,' said Depani. 'If time runs short then we'll just swim the whole way. I can guarantee we'll reach the lake before you.'

'How many weeks will this new route take us? Will we lose much time?' Widrias drew a crude map into the earth, depicting the Atrael River and its eastern tributary. Spotal adjusted the makeshift map slightly, adding Ahanemis Lake, Saraman Woods, the coastline, and Muranath.

'It's not perfectly to scale, but it's close enough,' he muttered in apology. 'If we head to the lake like this, we would reach Muranath maybe two or three days later than if we headed directly south. Taking the southeast route now shouldn't lose us too much time. This way we avoid the enemy.'

Widrias studied the map for a few seconds, chin in on fist, and nodded. 'Very well, this is the path.'

'Actually,' Spotal paused again, 'there's a village here, Duddawl,' he pointed to the map, near the source of the eastern Atrael's tributary. 'Busy, despite its small size. It sits right at the tip of the Atrael. It might be easier to meet you there.'

'Should we wait for you?' asked Gwahl.

'May as well,' shrugged the calef.

'Or we'll wait for you. But it depends on how long you'll take,' corrected Widrias. 'If we reach the village before you, we'll wait two days for you to catch up. If you're not there on time, we head for Ahanemis, where we'll wait for another two days. That should give you enough time to catch up with us if needed.'

'Just let the villagers know we'll be following so they can direct us,' said Depani.

Widrias nodded. 'If you reach there and there's been no word from us, you'll know you got there before us. Wait for us and warn them we're coming.'

'Understood,' Depani nodded.

'Hopefully it won't matter. We'll try to meet up with you before nightfall,' said Gwahl, walking away with the neiads. 'If not, we'll see you in a few days.'

'There's a fishing village on the western side of Ahanemis, virtually in line with Duddawl,' said Spotal. 'Probably the best place to meet you if you're delayed.'

'Good. North winds be with you,' said Widrias, waving them away.

The three nodded and crawled away down the hill, before rushing back upriver, looking for a suitable place to cross. Widrias turned to the rest.

'Right, we need to skirt around these ferries without being seen. The land is mercifully hilly around here so keep to the vales, away from the crests. If they see us, they'll run us down within minutes on those horses.'

Noswen led them east for a few hundred metres, before circling back south, keeping to the shadows and sheltered valleys. They crossed the trails of the two eastern-heading armies. Studying the tracks, he recognised the same signs Gwahl pointed out for him, marking them as cavalry forces. Such outriders would make a nuisance of themselves in these northern reaches, while all the infantry and main body of cavalry headed south to Muranath.

Before long, Noswen led them back to the riverbank. Their boots trod into the soft earth churned up by the passing of thousands of others. It was a strange sensation, walking through an empty country on the trail of a host of enemies, possibly a greater danger than anything he'd ever faced.

Hours of marching passed and Spotal finally stopped. An oxbow lake glittered a few hundred metres away while the river continued its way south. Movement around the lake's shore betrayed the grazing herd of red deer. Four beautiful willows draped their trailing leaves into the lazy lake water while birds, too far away to identify, flit across the surface from their nests in the boughs, seeking the flies and tiny fish at their disposal.

'Time to leave the Atrael behind,' announced the calef, shattering the tranquillity. 'Willow lake marks where it begins its true turn southwest.'

'But Gwahl?' he asked tentatively, turning back upriver. No sign of their return.

'They knew what they got themselves into,' sighed Widrias.

'It won't be too long before we're reunited,' reassured Spotal with a smile.

'Duddawl it is, then. Or, failing that, Ahanemis,' Widrias motioned them forward. Spotal nodded and led them away.

Lidan lingered a moment longer, hoping. But no, the river wound its way through the land, his friends lost. Cursing, he trotted up the column to Spotal.

'Couldn't you have led us just a little further downriver to give them more time?'

Spotal shook his head. 'No, I've already led us too far southwest. Willow lake is actually two miles further downriver than the turn southwest, I lied before. Hoped they'd return to us before then,' he shrugged. 'I couldn't justify taking us any further. I've stretched our journey by a fair bit already, any more would endanger us.'

'What will they do?'

'They might find us by morning. If not, they'll meet us at Duddawl or Ahanemis.'

'Not ideal,' he said, louder than he'd intended, clicking his tongue against his palate.

'No, but it's the best we can do.'

Widrias overheard them and called ahead. 'I warned them against gallivanting across the river, but he had to have it his own way. As you said, it's not ideal, but they chose their path. I wish they were here with us as much as you, but it's unavoidable now.'

'Could we leave markers for them, to show them our path?' he asked, hopefully.

'What would you leave?' asked Spotal.

'Sticks and stones, symbols, I don't know, anything.'

Widrias smiled sadly.

'I understand it must be difficult, Lidan. Gwahl is a fine survivalist and the neiads are the best watermen in Enadir. I'm sure no harm will come to them. We'll see them again before you know it. Leave your signs if it puts your mind at ease, but don't expect them to be seen. Come now, Spotal, lead the way.'

Spotal led them away. None of them looked back.

Lidan spat. Suddenly a foul taste was in his mouth. Curse Gwahl's curiosity! Yes, the road was unusual, impressive even, but was that reason enough to abandon them? He recalled their first ever conversation.

'Curiosity killed the cockatrice.'

He snorted. It seemed that Gwahl ignored his own advice, perhaps he'd fallen foul of the consequences, taking the neiads with him.

Before leaving, he collected a few pebbles from the riverbank and built a little cairn, placing a white stone on its southeast side as a pointer. It was a miserable little thing. He doubted anyone would see it unless they specifically looked for it. About as pathetic a signpost as he'd ever seen. Shrugging in defeat, he turned away, keeping the remaining pebbles in the folds of his cloak.

Leaving the river behind, they walked for the remainder of the day, heading ever deeper into the heart of the country. Although still in the more northern parts of the kingdom, he could already see distinct changes in the surrounding terrain compared to Tarnegrefur's foothills. The grass was considerably softer and longer, which made it infinitely softer and longer than the grass in the Midlands. The ground was also more like soil and less like rock, giving way beneath his feet. There was also more variation in the trees, with the additions of hornbeams, oaks, and maple. All grew tall and broad, sentinels standing guard over their lands. He found a strange comfort in seeing them, dotted singularly or in clusters and small woods across the wilderness. The air itself was warmer. It seemed to lift him, urge him forward, taking the weight off his wearied feet, giving him the strength to go on.

Such changes in the terrain gave them strength to travel a great distance that day, and the red sun was drooping in the sky by the time Widrias told them to set up camp for the night. They found the ideal site at the base of a gnarled oak, standing in solitary pride on a high hill. With a fine view of the country, nobody would easily creep up on them. With the setting sun, the shadows gradually grew longer and darker. A quiet night beckoned.

A fire wasn't permitted, lest some enemy might spot it from afar. He hardly missed it, the very atmosphere of the Kingdom of the calefs provided all the warmth he needed. He settled down in the folds of the oak's roots and was slowly lulled to sleep by the sound of Noswen sharpening her blade.

Before he was lost in the depths of his subconscious, his mind once again strayed to his missing companions, and a frown fixed on his forehead.

Chapter 26

He shifted on his throne. Sometimes, he regretted his decision to have it made so uncomfortably. The marble was cold and hard, the sharp edges dug painfully into his thighs. Of course, the entire purpose of having it uncomfortable was to remind himself, through his own pain, of the pain of his realm. How he hated that notion. Initially, it sounded like such an honourable idea, to bear the suffering and empathise with his subjects. Nowadays he realised such a foolish idea it was. The discomfort did little but set him in a dark mood, and in such a mood then he was harsher, less merciful, unsympathetic. But then again, it discouraged him from making decisions with his heart and let his mind lead, so maybe it wasn't quite so bad after all. He shifted again and his thighs sparked. No, definitely a bad idea.

The old dreyad in front of him was still rambling on. He stopped listening a few minutes ago, who knew what the old buffoon was rattling on about now? He held up his hand for silence. The dreyad's cracked, dolorous voice trailed away.

'I have heard your claims, I have weighed up your arguments,' he began, 'and I have come to a decision. You will give your miners another copper ingot per month, and in return we shall increase the price for which we buy your ores from three silvers per ten tons, to four.'

The dreyad looked confused, 'But, your Majesty, I cannot afford it.'

'Which is exactly why I'm willing to give you more silver for the iron ore you provide. It all works out.'

'Your Majesty doesn't understand, my workers are demanding higher wages, and are getting aggravated, they feel unappreciated-'

'They are getting higher wages,' he cut across. Impudent fool. 'I am increasing their wages by an entire copper ingot per month. That's a lot for a miner. They will be grateful. If you're worried that they're getting, should we say, expressive, in their dissatisfaction over their pay, then take it up with Lord Tunn in Cadaran City. I'm sure he will oblige you with more guards.' The dreyad opened his mouth to protest further, but Stolach raised his voice. 'The matter is done. Your workers will be paid more, and you will get more for your products. Everybody wins, everybody is happy, it is only my treasury that loses.'

He waved the dreyad away and the next subject was escorted forward. Today was his least favourite day in his monthly routine. Only once a month, but still too often for his liking. An entire day spent in the confines of his throne room, listening to the whines and complaints of all his loyal subjects. It was often the same; begging for more money, or a tax reduction, or more protection. Every once in a while, he would have to sit through a man crying for mercy for a son or daughter who'd been arrested, or wrongly accused. Those were the cases he despised most, and they always ended in the same way; the crying men breaking down into violent sobs, led away by stern soldiers. At first, he allowed everyone, whatever their standing, to stand before him and speak, but after the first two sessions he had put an end to such nonsense. The throne room had been packed, with people hemmed in everywhere like cattle. The stench was horrific, his soldiers were hard-pressed to keep order, and it had taken so long. Never again, he vowed, and he never broke a vow. Nowadays, it was only village elders, lords, army officers, or owners of industries – mining, smelting, farming – who were permitted before his throne. There were still more than enough of them. He tried to be as fair as he could, weighing the arguments against the benefits to the realm. Judging appropriately, dismissing short-term for long-term gains, ensuring the needs of the majority were met before the needs of the few, not investing any coin in industries whose custom was failing. He jarred his elbow against the cold marble. Never inappropriately merciful.

This next subject was a hale old man, unshaved, with hard grey eyes and broad shoulders, clad in chainmail, with a sword at his side. Stolach knew that some leaders refused to allow anyone wear arms in their presence, but he was not so fearful. Protected by both unseen assassins and his intimidating personal guard, only the most resilient usurpers would ever reach him. Even if by some miracle they were able to reach him, blade drawn, he was the finest swordsman in the land, nobody would defeat him.

The man spoke. 'Majesty. My name is Ulden Napens. I am head of my village, Nettlehill, we reside in the southern reaches of Dailas,' he paused, as if expecting an answer, but Stolach sat motionless. Ulden continued. 'I have come to you to ask you to send more troops to patrol the lands around my village. Outlaws and thieves live in the surrounding woods. They have taken to stealing our supply carts. Some have grown so bold as to attack Nettlehill itself. Three men have been slain, along with five stolen horses. I have been elected as spokesman for the three other villages within thirty miles of my own, we are all suffering the same problems.'

Stolach nodded. 'I am aware of these outlaws. I have increased my patrols already, but not even my soldiers can cover the whole kingdom. I will send three more platoons of fifteen soldiers to scour the land and bring the men to justice.'

Ulden pursed his lips. 'Forty-five men will not be enough. There are many trees, and many thieves among them. Your soldiers will not be enough to battle them all.'

'They will,' said Stolach, getting annoyed. 'My soldiers are trained. Theses rebels are cowards with swords. How about this, instead of forty-five soldiers, I'll send thirty, and ten of my grey dreyads.'

'You are most gracious, Majesty,' said Ulden, although he still had a sour expression on his face. 'What of my stolen horses and slain men?'

'There's nothing I can do about that. I'm sending soldiers to bring to justice the men who were responsible, that should be enough to satisfy a humble man.

'Before you leave, why is it that you have come as spokesman for four villages? Where are the other elders?'

'The woods have grown wild, Majesty, and the other elders were too fearful to leave the safety of their homes. I am strongest of us, so I came, but still had to travel armed and with a guard of eight men.'

'You had no trouble along the way?'

'None, the thieves must have seen us as too fierce a foe and let us pass.'

He nodded, Ulden certainly had the appearance of a brawler. 'Indeed. You said they were preying on your supply carts? Are your people in need of food?'

Such concern must have caught Ulden by surprise, as he stammered. 'N-no, Majesty, that is most good – most kind, I apologise – of you to offer, but we have plenty of food.'

'Good. This matter is closed. Expect the arrival of my men within a few weeks. They might well use your villages as bases while they scour the surrounding lands for the rogues. You are dismissed.'

Ulden bowed and left. Stolach almost felt insulted by the man's shock at his offer for food. It was, after all, his duty to see his people fed, and if four entire villages were struggling, it would mean many starving mouths. But, Ulden said all was well, and he was happy to accept his word. As the other subjects came and went, he noticed the recent trend in the demands presented to him. More protection, more soldiers, increased frequency of patrols. There were also fewer people present, as had been case the past few months, with more and more people like Ulden coming as spokesmen for several settlements.

When the final subject left, a man asking for justice against soldiers who stole from his larders, he called for his war council. The stoic guards, hidden assassins, scuttling scribes, and yawning pages shuffled out. Once the room was empty, he stretched, massaged the ache from his legs, and sat down on the steps beneath his throne. Much better. He normally held these war councils upstairs, but here was as good as any room today.

Tomon was the first, as always. The juggernaut came striding in confidently, stomping along on flat feet, the sound of his heavy footsteps echoing around the room, bouncing off the marble pillars. He saluted when he reached him. He nodded to acknowledge his presence. Long ago, Tomon's salutes irritated him. The juggernaut should be kneeling, not saluting. He soon realised, however, that it was a mark of respect, in acknowledgment of his military prowess. Nowadays, he didn't mind.

Next to arrive were his highest-ranking commanders. The first was Colonel Autnik Kibend, high commander of his cavalry forces. His presence here was quite trivial, his forces were more useful in the open field of battle, and open battle was not the topic at hand. Not yet, anyway. Shortly afterwards came Commander Teneraso Cawein of the grey dreyads, and General Talto Marbend, who commanded the city guard. Teneraso he had much need for, but Talto's presence, like Autnnik's, was quite unnecessary. He was a cruel bastard, harsh, unnecessarily so. Although, he was admittedly a good commander, and loyal to the end, so he set his reservations aside and tolerated the man's presence. The next three arrived together. General Hemelot Owein of the southern infantry, General Carass Simein of the western infantry, and Field Marshal Lupas Laherr, commander-in-chief of all forces south to the eastern distributary of the Crisiaddwr. Finally, the Chief Assassin. The other men shifted aside as he slid up to the throne, making no sound at all. Named 'the Owl' for the way he hunted his targets, swooping down as if upon muffled wings before striking with his daggers. He was almost as feared as his previous Chief. Almost.

These eight were all of his war council who were present in the city. Five other individuals were not here. Three were across the sea, and the other two; Field Marshal Strikk Inwein, commander in chief of his entire northern forces, and General Denhwyn Nesherr, of the eastern infantry, were away to the east.

Stolach sat up straighter. 'I have a question to ask,' he began, not looking at anyone in particular. 'A few weeks ago, I commanded you, Tomon, to prepare an offensive strategy against the bands of rogues wandering the land, correct?'

Tomon glanced nervously at the others. 'Majesty.'

'And yet here, today, more than two thirds of the people who stood before me were pleading for my help in ridding them of this annoyance. Why has nothing been done?'

Tomon looked uncomfortable. 'Your Majesty, I did my best, increasing the number of patrols, more weapons, more supplies. I even sent a small force of a hundred men to journey through the southern Dailas Forest and try to flush them out. I did my best. Besides, I had that other matter to see to.'

He nodded. 'I'm not blaming you personally, Tomon, don't worry. I know the blame is shared between a few of us present. My people are crying out for help, I won't let them think their cries have fallen on deaf ears. What were the results of these measures you took?'

'Not much, sire, we've caught or killed a few hundred thieves since you gave the order. It's too difficult to find them. Our soldiers are not suited for trudging through Dailas looking for these little bands.'

'It's true, sire,' said Hemelot, a thin fonex, always keen to show how he was as fine a specimen of his race as Stolach himself. What a fool. 'My patrols report the bands are small enough they easily evade capture, but still large enough to threaten the village defences,' he continued, speaking slowly, faintly, his voice as meek as a spring lamb. Were his battle instincts not so sharp, he would have never promoted the pathetic creature to general. 'What few skirmishes we have are easily won, but they are so few and far between that it hardly makes a difference.'

'You're implying the entire concept of sending out patrols is useless?' asked Stolach.

'No, the presence of the patrols is a deterrent to them in the area where the patrols are present, but once they have passed by, the thieves return.'

'How large are these patrols?'

'Not large, between forty and fifty soldiers, usually.'

'That many?' asked Carass, surprised. 'I send out my soldiers out in parties of twenty. I found any more to be unnecessary. The additional men made the patrols slower, and if ever there was a skirmish it would be overkill. Our men are more than capable of defeating the thieves in combat, we don't need so many in each patrol.'

'So you would send out smaller groups?' asked Tomon.

'From what I have heard, these smaller patrols have met with some success in the western woods, and few village elders have been complaining of attacks,' replied Carass.

This was true. Most of the people asking for support against the rogues were from the southern and eastern reaches of Dailas.

'I ordered Hemelot to send out larger patrols,' said Lupas. 'The southernmost woods are teeming with tribes of Hobbs, pine goblins, and Council troops. We lost two entire patrols when we sent them out in groups of twenty. It's unsafe in those woods.'

He nodded slowly, making a note to come back to that point. 'I see. What would you advise? It's obvious that these patrols aren't accomplishing much at present.'

'No fault of mine!' piped Hemelot, his voice shrill.

'I didn't say that,' he replied, 'and you would do well not to interrupt me in future, General,' the fonex quailed under his gaze. 'As I said, they're not much good *at present*. What I was going to say, was to continue the smaller patrols in the western parts of Dailas, in addition to sending our infantry to the larger villages as guards. Only the largest, mind, we cannot afford to guard every cluster of huts that call themselves villages. As for the southern woods, you will command your infantry to cease their patrols altogether and concentrate entirely on guarding the villages and supply carts. Instead of sending common soldiers out on your failing patrols, I want you to send grey dreyads,' he turned to Teneraso. 'Commander? Will that be possible?'

'Of course, sire,' nodded the dreyad. 'How many scouts will you require?'

'How many do you have to spare?'

'My entire forces number just over a thousand, seven hundred of which are out over the country. Three hundred are at your disposal. I wouldn't advise sending away any more than two hundred. You never know when you may have need of them.'

'Very well, I'll use a hundred and eighty. How many are normally in each scouting party?'

'Between four and six, usually.'

'Send them out in troops twice that size. I don't want to lose any more than necessary. Command them to track the thieves to their lairs and kill them.'

'No prisoners, sire?'

'I have no use of prisoners. They don't work for anyone, what possible information could they give me? Kill them all on sight. Concentrate only on the thieves, not the Hobb, not the Council. Only the thieves. Obviously if they do happen to run into some Council members and see an opportunity to defeat them, do so, but they should not go out of their way. There are far too many incidents with these rogue bands for my liking.'

Teneraso nodded. 'Should I go now, sire?'

'No, stay for a moment, we will have other matters to discuss. Does anyone know of the situation in the northern Dailas Forest? There were very few present today from that area, and all of them from its western reaches, no word from the middle or east. Have there been too many rogues for any elders to reach us? What is the current situation there? What information do we have?'

Teneraso spoke first. 'The reports from the northwest are not much different from the rest. Rogues, plenty of them. What few dreyads I deployed there have dealt with the ones they find. The ones who ventured further northeast came with worrying tidings. Villages have been sacked to the ground, some completely taken over by outlaws.'

'The Council?' asked Lupas.

'Rogues. Many village elders have sent their entire inhabitants to Cadaran, looking for sanctuary. I believe Lord Tunn has obliged them all, so far. With the absence of your northern armies, there is little protection in the land for the people, so the bandits are rampant. One patrol reported enemies coming down from the north, monsters and such.'

'I have heard of these monsters. Hydras, direwolves, wyverns. But so long as the villagers are in Cadaran, they are safe from these threats, until the time comes for me to deal with them.' Stolach paused. 'Cadaran still stands strong, I hope? Does it have enough soldiers to defend it, as I ordered?'

'Yes, it is as you commanded, and Tunn has even been bolstering his forces with the refugees capable of fighting. Cadaran is as safe as it always has been, it is only the villages that are in danger,' said Teneraso.

'Can we hold on a minute!' exclaimed Autnik. 'What's this about the absence of your entire northern armies? What's happened to them? Where's Strikk? What's happened to the cavalry I sent him?'

He held up his hands. 'Calm yourself, Colonel, everything is in order. This rise in bandits in the north was to be expected, I was just curious about the extent of the damage done by their absence. I ordered Strikk to leave enough troops in Cadaran to defend the lands surrounding the city, so even with the main body of our forces gone, the north is still safely in our grip. Cadaran is the key to the north, and we hold it.'

'That doesn't explain where Strikk's gone, and neither does it explain why I was not made aware of whatever plans you set in motion. Who else knew?' demanded Autnik, his face like a plum.

'All will be revealed. Of everyone here, only Tomon and Teneraso knew of my latest scheme. And the Owl, obviously. You are not alone in your ignorance, my friend, it was nothing personal against you. Let me explain.

'You should all be aware for several months, I've been gathering and collecting troops in the north. The villages sent men and boys to Strikk to bolster his forces, emissaries were sent to the juggernaut and hanex tribes of the Northlands. Some answered my call. I even gave Strikk enough coin to bribe Hobb clans. His sergeants armed them and trained them. Our northern forces swelled to double its original size. Nearly forty thousand strong. I let out word that the force was intended to sweep down into the southern forest, to smoke out the Council and annihilate them.'

'That's exactly what I thought it was for,' muttered Talto, eerily calm, cold grey eyes staring at him. 'Evidently it's not so. A shame. It was a good plan to rid us of this organisation, this filthy insurgent rebellion.'

'The Council will be dealt with soon enough,' he replied, 'but not by the northern forces. The lie was told so that our real target would not suspect our aim. Before I reveal, let me remind you of the emissaries I sent to Cysgodgors. It was difficult, incredibly difficult, but I was able to convince the troglodyte tribes, many of them, to join forces and strike at the Kingdom of the calefs across their entire southwest border.

'These attacks by the trogs are little more than a feint. It is the Kingdom of the calefs that my northern forces march against. That's where my hammer falls. Lleunedd has ever been sympathetic towards the Council, and in order to defeat these rebels, we must take away their allies. The calefs have always looked down on us, now we shall show them our strength, and further extend my kingdom. Their lands will be mine.'

'From where does the attack come?' asked Lupas, frowning. 'The sea?'

'No. Their fleet is too strong, their ships and captains too able. My sea neiads may be able to match them man-for-man, but they have twice as many galleons as us. There *will* be an attack from sea, but this is yet another feint.'

'So where?' asked Lupas.

'The north, of course.'

Autnik shook his head. 'Won't work. It'll take months to move an entire army across the north. We must account for food and provisions along the way. The Northlands are harsh with little in the way of ready food. A single army of a few hundred might just make it, but forty thousand is impossible. Then you'd have to get past Tarnegrefur Mountains, either walking around them or going through Imhara Pass, which is far too heavily defended. It's a bottleneck. A few hundred calefs would be able to hold off our forty thousand with ease. The north is closed to us, your Majesty.'

He looked at the other commanders. In their eyes, he saw mutual agreement. Good. Exactly as he hoped. It proved his scheme was one nobody would have anticipated. Not Lleunedd, nor Teig, nor any of the Council's high chancellors. It would work. He smiled at his cavalry commander.

'You're right, of course, to attack through the Tarnegrefur Mountains is hopeless, which is why I only send a token force of juggernauts from the Northlands to attack from directly north, my final feint. The true attack comes from elsewhere. Strikk invades the Kingdom of the calefs *south* of the mountains.'

His commanders looked at each other confusedly. Tomon and Teneraso nodded knowingly. Lupas voiced the question on their lips.

'How, sire? There is no road south of the mountains.'

'Wrong. There *was* no road. I built one. While the Council's spies were concentrating on watching Strikk train his new recruits, or watching my scouts probe the Crisiaddwr River, or watching troglodytes attack the southwest borders of Lleunedd's lands, I played my hand elsewhere. Woodsmen, masons, and engineers constructed a road through Cysgodgors, through the bramble plains, and across the Atrael. It's been open for weeks, delivering my troops into the heart of the Kingdom from the unguarded northwest border. Troglodytes will follow Strikk through. Their lands will bleed.'

He looked at his commanders. They looked back in awe, jaws slack. Lupas shook his head in wonder, Autnik whistled between his teeth. 'This is done already? The road is secure and Strikk has made it through?'

Stolach nodded. 'Everything is done. The invasion is underway. Strikk's forty thousand, bolstered by General Denhwyn's eight thousand-strong eastern infantry, are in the Kingdom of the calefs.'

'How did you get through the brambles?' asked Carass.

'A challenge, I admit. Mistakes were made, casualties were suffered. But we learned from our mistakes and the path was cut. It's a dangerous road, but it's passable. Strikk goes from the north, from the sea, the neiads are preparing to launch their fleets. Lupas, you must send a force, three thousand strong, to man my warships and do battle with the calefin fleet. It's not a battle your men are likely to win, but they must be there to prevent escape.'

'It will be done. Should I lead the attack?'

'No. There will be heavy casualties and I can't afford to lose you. No more than three thousand, I doubt the sea neiads' ships will hold many more.'

'Very well, sir, I'll make sure it's done.'

Talto cleared his throat. 'Majesty, what of the Council? I was under the impression our scouts reported they were gathering forces. Shouldn't we do something to counter them? They are, after all, our main foe. Although your invasion of the calefin country is bold and ambitious, I would have thought it far more prudent to carry out this southern offensive.'

'Perhaps such a southern sweep would have driven them out,' he shrugged. 'But at what cost? The Dailas Forest is not a place for two armies to clash. Cavalry would be useless, archers inaccurate, and battle-lines and phalanxes disrupted by the trees. It would have been a campaign of skirmishes. Long and frustrating. Don't forget Commander Afarn. The Crisiaddwr River, although mine by name, truly belongs to the neiad. It would have been a struggle to get my forces across the river. We've already lost hundreds to the neiads, picking them off as they attempt to cross the water. Eventually, we might have prevailed, but a pyrrhic victory is no victory. No, Talto, we won't fight them in the forest.'

'Then where?' Talto sneered.

'As long as they remain in Dailas, we can't do anything. We must wait, bide our time, concentrate on the battle at hand. We take away their allies, one by one. The Southlands are mine, next will be the calefs. When they're alone and broken, the Council will be forced to march against us. When they do, it will be their end.'

'When they do march, they'll head for the South Bridge,' said Lupas.

'Probably, and when they do, they will be met by the bridge's garrison. When they take the bridge, which they will, they will have the Pine Forest to journey through, and must suffer the goblin forces within.'

'How strong is the garrison stationed at the bridge?' asked Autnik.

'Four hundred,' replied Carass. 'They can hold it against a force thrice their number easily enough. Any more than that and they'll be completely overwhelmed.'

'Should we send more?' asked Hemelot.

'If you want,' said Carass. 'Regardless, the bridge will inevitably fall if the Council march against it, no matter how many men we squeeze in. We'd hold the bridge for a few more days, for the price of hundreds of soldiers. Afarn's neiads will see to that.'

'Send another six hundred,' ordered Stolach. 'A thousand men in such a defensible position is not to be ignored.'

'Only a thousand? They'll be facing the entirety of the Council force?' Hemelot asked.

'Only a thousand,' he confirmed. 'As Carass said, it will eventually fall. The ones we send go to their deaths. Besides, if we sent any more, the storerooms would need weekly replenishment to sustain them, it's not worth it. Remember, gentlemen, the Council will not march for a while yet, this talk can wait until the threat is imminent. As I said, concentrate on the enemy at hand, he's our main priority.'

'How does Lleunedd fare?' asked Tomon. 'I know the Guild breached the city defences. Is the calef dead yet?'

He looked to his Chief Assassin. The Owl was a hanex, like Noswen. Her betrayal was one he would never forgive. At times, he saw shadows of Noswen in him, the way he moved, the cold stare, the efficiency with which he killed, infiltrated, sabotaged. But no matter how he tried, no matter how perfect his new Chief may be, there was no replacing her. She proved it time and time again how valuable she was, slipping past his assassins and murdering generals, commanders, advisors, stealing documents, sabotaging equipment. Only a few months ago, she managed to gain entrance to the tower itself. Fortunately, on that occasion, she was discovered and driven away before she could kill anyone of significance, but the fact she came so close was testament to her frightening abilities. That was not to say the Owl had not accomplished incredible feats of stealth and guile as well, but despite his efforts, he lived in her shadow.

The hanex answered in a thin, hissing voice. 'Not yet. I sent ten assassins, ten of my best. All were slain, but not before one got the message out. One made it to the king's bedchamber and scratched him with a poisoned blade, but was killed before he could deal a more serious wound.'

'Will the poison kill the king?'

'Eventually. I don't know exactly when the calef will die, too many variables. How much poison coated the blade, how deep was the cut, where the cut was, whether a vessel was pierced. He could already be dead, or he could die months from now, but yes, he will die.'

'Why don't we send more?' asked Hemelot.

The Owl looked at him, disdain replacing the empty stare. 'It takes weeks to plan such an attack. This was not the first group of assassins I sent to kill the calefin king. I have sent many, and each party, save for that one, have been unsuccessful. Calefs are vigilant and Muranath is heavily defended. It is not simply a matter of sending a group of my best and hoping they stumble on the king. Close to seventy assassins have perished in assaults on the city under my command. Seventy. I have no more to spare at present.'

'Noswen managed to lead her assassins into the heart of the castle to retrieve an artefact,' remarked the general pointedly, stung by the Owl's derisive dismissal of his foolish comment.

'Muranath is heavily-defended,' repeated Lupas, ignoring Hemelot. 'Even with all those soldiers, how will Strikk breach the walls?'

'There are ways of fighting a siege,' muttered Hemelot, struggling to regain his composure.

'Hundreds of ways,' agreed Lupas, icily, 'and I would not fancy my chances using any of them, not against Muranath. Not even Bletta has walls as high.'

'Against fifty thousand men? Plus the hordes of troglodytes? No matter how tall the walls, against such a force they will eventually crack and buckle, like any other wall,' Denhwyn nodded, confidently.

'Not these,' Lupas shook his head. 'Underestimate the calefs at your peril. As ambitious as your offensive is, Majesty, the fifty thousand will be destroyed. Even if they do manage to break through the walls, our forces will be so spent by the effort, we'd be unlikely to hold the city for long.'

'It'll actually be slightly less than forty-eight thousand,' he replied, smiling faintly at the raised eyebrows. 'A fraction of the force will go to Tonnis, to take the harbour, another fraction will simply raid and ravage the lands, while the remainder will go to Muranath. Perhaps around thirty-thousand, plus however many troglodytes, all based on Strikk's discretion.'

'Majesty,' Lupas grimaced, sadly, 'it is too bold.'

He glanced at the others. Hemelot still seethed, but did his best to look disappointed with Lupas, Talto wore a disdainful sneer, Carass, Autnik, and Denhwyn frowned at the Field Marshal. He sniffed, Lupas was right. Under ordinary circumstances, thirty thousand soldiers were not enough, not even when backed by thousands of additional barbarians. The old man was the only one with enough spine to tell him the truth. Talto's resent was borne of disappointment that the Council would survive for a little longer as opposed to any disagreement with his plan.

'Strikk knows how to fight a siege,' he reassured. 'Well enough to hold it for months, years even.'

'Muranath is as well-provisioned as Crastalan,' Lupas shook his head. 'With the additional benefit of easy access to the sea. We will starve before they do.'

'No, measurements are already in place to keep them well-supplied. I have already discussed schemes on how to bring down Muranath's walls. Strikk is well-informed.'

An appropriate silence followed. He nodded approvingly and continued.

'Strikk will employ all the usual methods of siege warfare. Towers, ladders, rams, projectiles, all the rest. It will be as well-run as any other, only on a far larger scale. I sent to him all the documents and old manuscripts from my library written during the city's construction. There are tunnels, countless tunnels in the wastewater systems, dungeons, and old catacombs, waiting to be exploited. Some of these you know about,' he looked at the Owl, 'others you do not.'

'You kept them from me? They might have been useful. Many missions may have been successful with the information?'

'No, no good for your uses, otherwise I'd have given them to you,' he rebuked, sternly. 'Strikk has copies of these documents. Knowledge of the city's foundations will come in use when directing his war machines. We will have an intimate knowledge of the city and will put it to good use.'

'Useful,' agreed Lupas, 'but those manuscripts are likely outdated. Tunnels can be collapsed, doors can be locked. I would not rely on them for victory.'

'No single aspect of this scheme will ensure victory, only when they come together will we defeat the calefs.'

'Is there anything else? Or only the knowledge of the city and the standard siege tactics?' asked Talto.

He frowned at his tone. 'There is more. By splitting our forces, hitting every part of the country, utilising the troglodytes for their barbarism, the calefin army would be stretched thin, looking after their country. Their commanders will have the decision of retreating to support the capital, or remaining to defend their homes. Muranath will not have the support of the full calefin army.'

He paused. They nodded, Lupas included. He continued.

'What's more,' he glanced at Tomon, 'there is a…substance brought to me. Daemon lore. It has a certain…volatile power that would be beneficial.'

'What is it?' asked Autnik, leaning forward, his voice barely a whisper. Such was the effect of anything, any tale associated with daemons.

'A potential weapon. If we can retrieve the components, manufacture it, then it may help us.'

'What kind of weapon?'

'A substance, as I said. Daemon alchemy. Volatile, dangerous. I wouldn't put my faith in it winning us the siege single-handed, but in conjunction with everything else, it will sway the odds in our favour.'

'"If we retrieve the components"?' repeated Talto. 'Surely it would have been more prudent to have everything ready before commencing the invasion?'

'The final components are in the kingdom of the calefs,' snapped Tomon, baring his teeth furiously at the General's insolence. 'They will be collected.'

'You should trust his Majesty,' wheedled Hemelot, staring pointedly at Talto.

'I do, what I don't trust are half-formed schemes,' Talto shrugged.

'Did you not listen?' Hemelot continued. 'The daemon substance is but a boon to the plan, an addition. It is the invasion itself, in its entirety, that is the scheme to break Muranath.'

He blinked. Surprisingly insightful for Hemelot.

'I hope it goes well. I maintain my opinion we should have swept south with all our forces, driven out the Council. Yes, the calefs support them, but if we destroyed them in the forest, the calefs would have nothing to support, would they?' said Talto.

'We already went over this, half our forces would be neutralised by the terrain,' Carass rubbed his eyes.

'We'd have enough to destroy them. If we drew on all our forces,' said Talto.

'And what? Leave the rest of the villages to the rogues?' asked Lupas.

'They could be reclaimed. The Council filth should be exterminated, sweep them out like rodents.'

'My cavalry would be negated,' Autnik rolled his eyes.

'You could dismount and fight on foot, like a real soldier,' grumbled Hemelot.

Stolach sighed. He could feel the meeting slipping away. It was always the case. He would get maybe ten minutes from each council before they began bickering amongst themselves. He rose and they fell silent. He strode past them, up the stairs, to the library.

It was his favourite room. Always quiet and empty, perfect for thinking alone. Tomes and scrolls countless centuries old. Some inscribed on slate, some on wooden tablets, some on waxed paper, to preserve them. But not all. So many times, he'd reached for a scroll, only for it to crumble to dust at the touch of a finger. There were few things as frustrating as finding the perfect title, only for its knowledge to disappear before your very eyes. He had a team of scribes, their sole duty copying the older scrolls and tomes to new parchment. Some of the things they found were extraordinary, not least among them a handful of secret scrolls concerning the construction of the city. But still, they only scratched the surface of the library.

As great as this collection of books was, as beautiful, wonderful, and full of ancient knowledge, it was second to another. The fabled Great Library within the Rhetta Mountains, connected by a subterranean labyrinth to Mount Stohn, the old throne of the giant kings. Its collection of acquired information reportedly dwarfed this one by a hundred-fold. Perhaps, once everything was done, he might make the journey there.

He sat at a random table, idly plucking at a splinter in the wood. Perhaps in that library would be the information on how to manufacture and safely use Gogofaint's fire powder. But perhaps not. After all, the daemon heralded it as a new discovery. If they could get it, Muranath would surely fall in the blink of an eye. If not, then he had his faith in Strikk and the destruction of the invasion.

His thoughts turned to the rogue warriors. What caused such an increase in their numbers? Why were they here? He was bringing order to the land, and yet the people seemed to resent that order, that safety. Were his subjects truly so barbaric as to prefer chaos and anarchy to peace? It was a worrying thought. Perhaps it was because of the Council. Since the growth of the rebellious organisation, it was possible that those disenchanted with his rule felt as though they too could stand against him, like the Council. How wrong they were. Once the Kingdom of the calefs was his, the Council would be next to fall. Once they were gone, he could concentrate on the lone bands of outlaws.

Peace would eventually reign. War came first.

Chapter 27

His eyelids fluttered open. Moving made his head spin. He was in a little room, on a wooden bench with a few sacks of flour beneath his head as a pillow. There was a door to his left. Next to the bench was a wooden crate with a flickering candle. Looking down, he saw his legs were freshly bandaged. The pain was gone. On the stone floor was a pail of water. With shaking hands, he lifted it to his lips and drank deeply.

Sitting back against the wall, he watched the door. His stomach cramped. Too much water, too quickly. Groaning, he leaned forwards, closed his eyes, and wrapped his arms around his middle, trying to squeeze the pain from his abdomen. Somehow, he must have fallen asleep in that position. When he opened his eyes again, the pain was gone and the candle was considerably shorter. There was another person in the room. The fat man in the brown robe.

He stared at him, standing in the opposite corner, studying him with those small blue eyes. He looked like a pig. Bright pink skin, fat, wobbling cheeks. Neither said anything. They just stared. Growing increasingly apprehensive, he cleared his throat and ventured a question.

'Who are you?' he croaked. A voice he barely recognised.

'Colrick,' replied the fat man, his voice deep.

'Where am I?'

'The third level of Crastalan, in the great south infirmary. I am one of the physicians. I found you wandering the corridors behind the main wards. I tended your wounds and saved your life.'

'Why?'

'That's what I do. I heal people. I don't know how you got to those passageways...'

He recognised the implied question.

'I dragged myself there, I wanted to get out, away from the room with the stone beds.'

Colrick's eyes narrowed. 'So that's where you were, the grey ward. I brought you here, to one of our private rooms. The grey ward is where we keep sick prisoners deemed too important to die in their cells. Who are you?'

There was no point concealing his identity. Colrick would surely find out eventually, after his fat gaoler came looking for him.

'My name is Lidan, I tried to kill General Talto and was imprisoned for my insolence, and tortured so I would not forget the price of treason. To attack the king's men is to attack the king himself,' he shuddered as he repeated the cursed words. Memorised through pain, repeated so often throughout his imprisonment, how could he forget them?

Colrick reached into his sleeve and pulled out a little booklet. He flicked through the pages, muttering under his breath and traced his finger. He brightened.

'Here you are. "Lidan Dimarr; insurgent, to be sentenced for correction until broken." Well congratulations, Lidan, you're a dead man. You were reported so three days ago.'

He stared, confused. 'How? I'm here, alive, talking to you. I'm not dead...' he stopped, sudden realization hitting home. 'Unless you mean to kill me now?'

It should have frightened him, but he just felt empty. Death seemed peaceful, an easy escape from his pains.

Colrick smiled. 'That's not what I meant,' he tapped his book. 'My acolytes reported you dead. One of them probably saw your bed empty and assumed you'd been carried off for cremation and someone had forgotten to write it down in the book. Happens often enough, although it's the first time I've ever known the patient to be crawling around the passageways, *alive*,' he peered at Lidan. 'So, what to do with you now?'

'I don't understand,' he said. 'You said correction until death, why would they fix me if I was supposed to die?'

Colrick's smile vanished and he came to sit next to him. The bench creaked in protest at his considerable weight.

'Seems like General Talto was especially displeased with you. Your sentence was for "correction until *broken*". Not death. It's his favourite sentence. It refers to your mind, not your body. You were to be corrected until you descended to madness. Should I return you to your cell, Lidan? Should I let Talto's gaoler complete your sentence?'

He looked at him. Finally afraid, his lips trembled. He tried to answer but the only sound that came from his throat was a hoarse croak. He dipped his head, praying to the four winds to protect him. Death meant peace, the gaoler meant pain.

Colrick sighed and placed his hand on Lidan's cheek, tracing his prisoner's brand.

'I must think on this. You will be kept here until I decide what to do with you. I will give you food and see to your wounds. Nobody else knows your name or who you are. I will keep it that way, until I come to a decision.'

He rose and left. The door slammed shut, a key scraped in the lock. Curling into a ball, alone in his latest cell, he tried to sleep.

*

He woke, and was met by a great eagle perched on a low bough, watching him with amber eyes. Recoiling, he covered his eyes with his arm, for fear of her razor talons. The eagle, however, had no intention of attacking, and was merely observing this stranger.

'A golden eagle,' said Spotal, nodding to the bird, taking a pause from gathering his gear. 'There are many around here.'

'We used to say they brought luck to those travelling in these lands,' said Pwtrek. 'Its gilded crown brings riches flowing to your pockets and the light of its golden eyes repels darkness and evil,' he chuckled.

He nodded, eyeing the bird warily. Even he'd heard of the mystery surrounding them, that they passed good fortune to whoever met them. He couldn't recall what bird brought fortune in the Midlands.

'It's not very golden,' muttered Auran. The bird turned and looked at him, chirping in indignation, ruffling her dark brown feathers and flexing her talons. Auran shrugged and murmured an apology.

Spotal laughed and tossed the bird a scrap of deer meat. She caught it in her dagger-sharp beak and flew away in silence, beating the air with powerful wings, disappearing from sight.

He stood and gazed at the surrounding lands. To the west was nothing but wilderness, the Atrael left far behind as little more than the faintest golden flicker on the horizon. There was no sign of Gwahl or the neiads. South and east were much the same; grass, hills, trees. At first glance, north looked as innocent as the others, with hardly a trace of the brutal secrets beyond the lush grasslands.

Soon enough, Widrias called the order to break camp. Another day's march. Before leaving, he salvaged some fallen branches from the oak and fashioned a makeshift signpost, its arm pointing south. He looked at it for a while, lip curling in distaste. Spotal joined him, chin in his palm, tapping a finger against his lower lip. Snapping his fingers, he selected a stone and carved a symbol on its face. Kneeling, he placed the stone at the foot of the signpost and patted him on his shoulder. Widrias raised an eyebrow, which Spotal ignored, and took his position at the head of the column.

He glanced at the stone. There was nothing remarkable about the carving, a series of lines and swirls. It seemed vaguely familiar, but he couldn't place it. Shrugging, he followed the others.

Around noon, they came to a long, carefully-maintained hedgerow, cutting across their paths from east to west as far as the eye could see. Spotal assured them it was just the border to a farmland and there would be a path through somewhere along its length. True to his word, they found the opening around a kilometre to the east. A partially-concealed tunnel leading through the hedge. Had Spotal not pointed it out to him, he would have walked right past it, so cleverly was it hidden by the leaves above and the long grass beneath.

They walked through a short winding tunnel, testament to how deep the hedgerow really was, and emerged at the opposite side. Awaiting them was a great field, not dissimilar to the open countryside they walked through. The same layout of trees and rocks and long grass was ahead, but Spotal insisted it was farmland. What exactly was farmed here, Lidan couldn't say, but he took his word for it. They trudged on to the next hedgerow, and the one following, and another again.

He was stamping through the grass when Spotal grabbed the back of his brigandine, stopping him in his tracks. He yelped.

'Winds! Why?'

'You nearly stepped on one!' cried Spotal, pointing to the ground. 'Please, everyone stop walking before you crush them!'

'I don't see anything to crush,' said Pwtrek, looking at the ground between his feet.

'That's why I told you to stop. These are Harandale farms. We are standing amidst roots ready for reaping. Look to your feet. You see the little lumps with spiky tufts of grass on top? Dig them out and you'll see the roots.'

Lidan bent low and searched. To his surprise, he saw a slight bulge in the ground. Not a lump per se, but a definite elevation of sorts, with a few blades of coarse grass standing on top, like hairs on an otherwise bald head. He carefully scooped the soil away from around the mound and eventually dug out a root. It had the same familiar pale blue colour, flecked with golden yellow, as he recalled from the start of their journey so long ago. This one was slightly smaller than the ones he remembered, nestling neatly in his palm. He said as much to Spotal.

'Yes, they would be smaller. We're actually a bit far south to be growing Harandale roots, the climate is unfavourable for them. But they'll still provide us with plenty of energy, so gather as many as you can, throw away all other foods in your pack and fill it up with these roots. We've been very fortunate to find such a treasure trove.'

'I'll keep the meat, thanks,' grumbled Pwtrek.

'I heard stealing these roots was punishable by death?' asked Lidan.

'It is, but in times of war and invasion, I doubt anyone would care too much if our own allies took some. So long as they don't fall into the hands of our enemies, all will be well. Anyway, nobody's around to stop us. Take as many as you can.'

They spent the next hour gathering the roots, scrubbing them of dirt in the grass and storing them in their packs. By the time they were finished, his pack weighed pleasantly on his shoulders. Spotal led them on through the fields, finally identifiable as farmlands, judging by the stretches of ploughed turf waiting for seeds to be sown. It wasn't long before they passed the farmstead, abandoned. Spotal suggested staying the night, but Widrias insisted there was still a good few hours of daylight left for them to travel, so they pressed on. Before leaving, the calef borrowed Lidan's knife and cut deep gouges into the farmhouse's door, leaving the familiar symbol.

Lidan stared at it for a few seconds.

'It's a sign for Gwahl,' said Spotal to the unasked question. 'In case he follows us.'

'What does it mean? It seems familiar.'

'Why, it's the symbol of Enadir, Lidan! You must know that!'

He supposed he might have known. It certainly seemed familiar.

'Will Gwahl know to follow it?'

'Without a doubt. If he's on our trail, he'll know we left it for him. Remember it, my friend, one day you may have need to leave a trail of symbols for one of us!'

By the time they reached the final hedgerow, his eyes were heavy, his feet sore. Lazily, he waved away a fly hovering by his ear and followed Auran through the final hidden tunnel. Judging by the ruby sky, the sun was close to setting. Sleep would be welcome tonight. Apparently, Widrias felt much the same and sent Noswen away to find a suitable campsite.

'Is that the end of the farmlands?' he asked Spotal.

'Of this one, but there are more, my friend,' said Spotal. 'We'll certainly cross a fair few more before we reach Muranath.'

He nodded and followed the others after Noswen. As it was, the first suitable campsite was less than two kilometres south of the farm. A fallen apple tree next to a low hill. He knelt with an appreciative sigh between the roots of the tree, brushing away brown and rotten apples from beneath him. Grabbing a root from his pack, he ate it quickly and settled down to sleep.

'Up now, your turn at watch,' Pwtrek shook him awake.

Blinking furiously, he sat up. It was dark, he must have fallen asleep as soon as he'd shut his eyes. Yawning, he picked up his shield and wandered to the northwest slope of the hill and sat with a slump. It was a struggle to keep his eyes open. A dull, uneventful watch awaited, not that he was complaining. Excitement only meant danger, he was happy enough with a boring few hours staring into the silent wilderness. Or not so silent. The thousand sounds of a peaceful night entertained his imagination. The rustle of leaves and grass in the wind, the scuttle of mice and weasels, the far-off howl of a pack of wolves. As pleasant as any night anywhere else in Enadir. Once his time was through, he nudged Auran awake and reclaimed his position within the apple tree's upturned roots.

The morning was a cold, with a light drizzle dampening the land. Looking up, the sun was just strong enough to penetrate the light grey clouds, and the land had a fresh and vibrant palette of colours to greet his bleary eyes. He shivered against the damp and wrapped his cloak tight. After gathering his gear, he helped Spotal write out the symbol of Enadir in fallen apples on the ground. They placed another stick signpost at the top of the hill, pointing its arm southeast. Widrias didn't approve, but did nothing to stop them, barking at them to hurry.

Leaving these little clues for Gwahl to follow, although unlikely to be of any use, was comforting. True, in all likelihood the daemon and neiads were leagues away, swimming along the Atrael, and these signposts were nothing more than a potential trail for any pursuing foes, but it was a way of keeping him with them.

As the day progressed, the clouds grew darker, the rain heavier, and it was a miserable day to be walking across the open countryside. Mud clung to his boots and the hem of his cloak, his sodden clothes hung heavily from his hips and shoulders.

It occurred to him they must all smell worse than pigs. A mixture of mud, bog, damp, sweat, and blood all blended together into a cocktail of unpleasantness. He sniffed his clothes. Nothing new or overly pungent. Clearly, his senses had learned to block out the reek of dirty soldiers. The thought brought a smile. His body was accustomed to life as a Council soldier. It was a good thought.

Day turned to night, and back again in its endless cycle. Eight days flew by without him noticing. Caught up in the monotonous routine of marching, eating, resting, and constructing signposts nobody would follow. That particular morning, their signpost consisted of a moss-covered boulder, lines of vegetation ripped from its surface to carve a crude symbol.

Spotal leaned back, hands on hips, nodding appreciatively.

'This'll be one of our last.'

'Oh?'

He nodded northeast. 'The Cracket Mountains. From their slopes and vales flow the Hostaa Rivers, which break apart and unite in their wild, twisting course, before the western branches come together and empty into Ahanemis Lake. If we can see them, it means the eastern tributary of the Atrael will be a few miles southeast of where we are now. Couple of days and we'll be at Duddawl.'

'Are they like the Tarnegrefur Mountains?' asked Auran, eyeing the distant peaks, little more than a smudge on the horizon.

'No, they aren't nearly as tall. It's mostly farmland. The terrain is ideal for certain livestock. You can walk along those mountains in complete safety.'

The persistent downpour for the past three days made for miserable marching. A southeast wind brought rainclouds from the Great Waters, specifically from the gulf sea between the kingdom of the calefs and the Far Eastlands, flooding the land with fresh water.

'On the bright side,' commented Pwtrek, 'the weather will slow the invaders quite considerably, trapping their siege engines in the mud and all that.'

Lidan snorted. The rain was slowing them down enough, any army would be moving at a painstaking crawl. The rain was not entirely constant, but rather waxed and waned in its ferocity, varying in both size and frequency of its raindrops. After careful thought, he decided that the worse type of rain was when the drops were fat but infrequent, as they had a tendency to wriggle their way down the back of his shirt.

Several hours into their journey, they came to a road. After trudging through wilderness, farmland, and open countryside for so long, the flat dirt road was a thing of beauty. He could have run the rest of the way, but settled instead for a merry skip. Spotal and Pwtrek laughed at his antics. Even Widrias cracked a smile.

'Where does it go?' asked Auran.

'Roads link the villages. Duddawl is the busiest in this area. It's something of a small port for the barges and fishing boats up and down the Atrael. Lots of trade goes through it, and most roads around here lead there, eventually. If we follow this one, we'll reach it soon enough.'

Now on an established road, he expected to find travellers. Calefs riding their tall horses or guiding carts laden with their intricate crafts, maybe a tinker of some sort, leading his mules bearing packs filled with all manner of curiosities. Perhaps even patrols of soldiers, guarding the roads like Stolach's men patrolled the ones of the Midlands. But no, even after two hours, it was as empty as the wilderness. Was the calef population truly so low? A glance at Spotal suggested otherwise.

'Are the roads normally so quiet?' he ventured.

'No. Even with invaders in the lands, I'd have expected to see someone. Traders, performers, soldiers, craftsmen, anyone! Not even refugees. It's abnormal.'

'Are there any forts nearby they might have already fled to?' asked Auran.

'No forts, no. Well,' he paused, 'there might be a tower just beyond Duddawl, some sort of alchemist or something lives there. I think. But it's still days away, and it's not a proper fortification to hold all the travellers from a hundred miles around.'

'Do you think a company has passed this way?' suggested Widrias, directly.

Spotal shrugged, attempting to look nonchalant. His greyish pallor betrayed his concern.

'Might have.'

'Be on your guard. Noswen! Make sure there aren't any patrols waiting ahead,' said Widrias.

She jogged away. Like Gwahl, she seemed to have an endless supply of energy. His initial desire to run the rest of the way was long gone, and seeing her dart away had him shaking his head in admiration.

With only a few hours of daylight left, she returned only twice with reports of a clear road ahead. The third time she returned, they were already camped a few hundred metres from the roadside. Again, the road ahead was clear. That was not to say there were no signs of any travellers over the recent days. Discarded scraps of food, a worn-through boot, discarded lengths of twine, a blunted knife. All lying free and clean on the ground, with barely the faintest covering of dust, betraying their recent fall from the belts of their owners.

An uneasy sleep awaited. Their shelter, a cluster of beech trees, did little to keep out the rain. In the absence of a fire, the risk of being discovered too great, it was a cold and miserable night.

Morning saw no respite to the rain. With spirits as damp as their feet, they set off again, Noswen scouting ahead. Two more days passed by on the road, as empty as ever. Still, the signs of recent travellers preceded them. Noswen surmised they were on the tail of another party, moving quickly, always a few days ahead. Judging by their pace it was probably only small, little more than ten, fifteen at most. Whether friend or foe, it was impossible to say.

The revelation brought excitement, if not a touch of apprehension. A small delay in the other company's journey and they might stumble upon them. Would they be met with drawn blades or open arms? Should they avoid them, flee the other way, or greet them with smiles? Lidan shivered. Despite the potential danger, or perhaps because of it, he wanted to find out.

Noswen returned frowning to their windswept campsite that night.

'Village ahead,' she announced.

'How far?' asked Widrias.

'Half a mile.'

'Anyone there?'

'Seemed empty. Didn't linger for too long.'

'Is it Duddawl?' Widrias asked.

'I don't know the area well,' said Noswen.

'Spotal?' the general turned to the calef.

'Might be,' he nodded. 'I've not been around here for a long time.'

'Alright, it's still light. Shall we have a look?' Widrias heaved himself to his feet.

'Or we could wait until morning?' grumbled Pwtrek, lying on his side.

'No time like the present. Might be more shelter than a dripping branch as well.'

Pwtrek considered for a moment. Shrugging, he rose and extended a hand to help Lidan to his feet. It took only a few seconds to gather their gear and return to the road. Although there was still light, it was fading, and it was dusk by the time they arrived.

Like the razed village, so many miles north, it was built of pretty spires and turrets of twisted, elegant timber and clean white sandstone. Except these were pristine, with no smoke-stains or disfigured corpses. The dusty roads were empty. The windows cold and lifeless. The doors locked. The sconces bare and dark. In all but appearance, this beautiful village was identical to the other.

'Is this it?' Widrias asked.

Spotal shook his head. 'Duddawl is at a fork in the Atrael. I can't even see the river from here. I don't know this village.'

'Doesn't seem like there's anyone to ask, either,' muttered Pwtrek, and blanched. 'Sorry, Spotal, that was crude,' he added hastily.

'It's alright, there's nobody here from the looks of it. Should be a watchman up there,' he gestured to a tall lookout post, a far more beautifully-built structure than its purpose demanded, or indeed deserved.

'Where've they all gone, do you suppose?' asked Lidan. 'The same place as all the travellers?'

'Probably. It's unusual…' his voice trailed away.

'Shall we try the houses?'

Widrias nodded. 'Go in pairs. Nobody goes anywhere alone, we take it a street at a time, don't stray. If someone is here… I'd rather not find out with a dagger at our throats.'

They split into pairs, Widrias and Pwtrek, Spotal and Noswen, and him and Auran. Taking one street each at a time, they explored the delicate houses.

To his surprise, Auran demonstrated considerable efficacy picking locks. Using Lidan's knife, he flipped the window latch on the first house and they jumped through. Landing on the stone floor behind Auran, he took in his surroundings. A large wooden table, carved chairs, an iron grill before a fireplace. Shelves lined the walls, laden with pottery, crockery, and delicate crystal goblets. Down a short flight of steps was a larder with wheels of cheese, dried meats, bundles of herbs, and baskets laden with vegetables all visible from the kitchen. All looked fresh and new. Not the kind of things one would stock before a planned departure.

He glanced at Auran, who placed a finger to his lips and crept to the next room. He held his knife loosely in his hand and followed.

It was a modest parlour, high-backed wooden chairs draped in homespun wool blankets, duck-feather pillows, a reed matt, a second fireplace. In a corner was a harp and stool, intricately carved from different-coloured woods and strung with gut. He resisted the temptation to run his finger along the strings and turned into the narrow corridor leading deeper into the house. Two more doors, one leading to a garden, the other upstairs. They took the stairs, but the neat little bedrooms were empty, the wardrobes half-filled with clothes, but no travelling gear.

He exhaled. 'Well that's that. Empty.'

Auran nodded and led him to the garden. Surprisingly, it was a communal orchard, three apple trees at its heart, fallen leaves at their roots, some floating gently in the little pond they encircled. Flowers and herbs grew around the periphery of the garden in neat little rows. The back doors of the five other houses in the street opened into it. All quiet.

'Probably easier to get in this way,' muttered Auran, moving to the next house.

'Saves us going through more windows,' he agreed.

Auran didn't reply. Dark as it was, it was easy to move stealthily across the grass, hopefully unseen.

Disappointingly, the next five houses were similarly empty. Subtle differences in their layout and furnishings gave each its own character, but with no inhabitants to give them life, they were eerily monotonous.

Shrugging their shoulders, they reconvened with the others. It was a similar story, no inhabitants, fully-stocked houses, empty cloakrooms. All the signs suggestive of a hasty getaway.

Four more streets, all empty. Night was well and truly set, and Widrias kept bending at the waist to rub his calf.

'Alright, we'll have a look at the public buildings. Provided they're all empty, we can find somewhere to sleep.'

'Why not find somewhere to sleep now? Can't see much in this darkness and you need rest,' Pwtrek said, motioning to the general's leg.

'We've come in now, it's more dangerous to leave places unexplored than to search in darkness.'

'Agreed, if anyone's here, chances are they've noticed us,' Spotal rubbed his shoulders, easing his tired muscles. 'If we don't confront them now, we run the risk of a night-time ambush.'

'If we stumble about in darkness, we run the risk of walking straight into one,' rebuked Pwtrek.

'We have a better chance of surviving a skirmish when we're awake,' said Spotal.

'Find a house, set a guard at each entrance, we'd be able to hold off any foes for long enough,' suggested Pwtrek.

'What if they set fire to the building? We'd be cut down as we stagger out the smoke,' said Spotal.

'Then those on watch should be extra vigilant,' said Pwtrek.

'No, Spotal's right,' said Widrias, laying an apologetic hand on Pwtrek's arm. 'We can't run the risk of leaving a building unexplored. Besides, I'd sleep more soundly knowing we were the only ones here.'

Pwtrek shrugged. 'Well at least take it slowly.'

Widrias nodded. 'One more street to explore. Auran and Lidan, take it quickly, the rest of us will be in the watchtower first, then the town hall. You should be done by then to explore the bath-houses, warehouse, and chapel with us. If all's clear, we'll spend the night in the watchtower.'

'Understood,' Auran nodded and turned away.

Lidan followed at his heels while the others made their way to the tall tower.

'I'd be in the watchtower,' he said, glancing over his shoulder.

'Yes. Tactically, best place to be. If they were there, they'd know we were here. Whether they stayed is another matter,' said Auran.

'You think they left?'

'Depends. Might have left the village if they thought we were too strong. Might have found a better place to ambush if not.'

'Where would you ambush from?' he asked.

'Haven't explored the village, have I? But probably...the warehouse. Big building, lots of open spaces. If they had ranged weapons, they could stay on the upper floors and shoot us down as we approached.'

'I'll keep my shield up and ready when we come to it.'

'And I'll be behind you.'

He smiled and jumped the wall into the final communal garden. This one had a pair each of apple and plum trees. It was as silent as any other, barely the faintest whisper of wind through the autumn leaves to disturb it. Auran landed next to him and they moved to the houses.

A quick jiggle of his knife and the door opened. It was clearly an honest village for people to put their trust in such poor locks. Not that it mattered to him. A quick but careful search of the house revealed nothing. They moved on to the next.

This time, Lidan tried his hand at flipping the latch, guided by Auran.

'Get the tip of the blade into the crack, not too much, the taper is too great to thrust it the whole way in, it'll get stuck. Just the point, slide it up until you feel the metal latch. Normally a bit higher than there. Good, looks about right. These are all simple latches, if they were bolts or proper locks, we'd have no chance. Anyway, put it a little further in, lift it slowly. Flick up. Good.'

The door swung open. He smiled, proud of his new-found skill. He motioned grandly for Auran to enter. Auran snorted and walked past, shaking his head.

Walking into the parlour, it was as empty as ever, he started towards the kitchen.

No. A pack next to the fireplace. An oiled travelling cloak. He glanced at Auran, who frowned and placed a finger to his lips. They crept into the kitchen. Empty. The larder had the usual stock of foods, nothing of note. Or was there? A wheel of cheese had a sizeable chunk missing. A razor-sharp knife lay on a chopping board, its surface oily and covered in small crumbs.

'Hello?'

He froze. The sound came from behind, back in the parlour. His eyes met Auran's. The Southlander grabbed the knife, he brandished his own. An enemy was unlikely to announce themselves, but this was too unusual.

Slowly, they crept into the parlour. Each step was a battle to keep as silent as possible while he strained his tired eyes and ears for movement in the dark.

'Hello?' the voice called again. It didn't sound threatening. Indeed, it sounded nervous more than anything.

Auran stopped suddenly. Lidan bumped into his back, making him stumble. The scuffle was as loud as the tolling of bells in the oppressive silence. A flicker of candlelight in the doorway. Auran dropped low. He jumped behind a high-backed seat, crouching, knife at the ready.

The flickering light grew. He saw Auran brace himself.

A hand came through the door, brandishing a taper in its candleholder.

'Hello?'

Auran jumped forward, bludgeoning into the figure. The taper was knocked aside, sending long, bouncing shadows over the walls before extinguishing into a cinder. Disorientated by the sudden darkness, he stumbled around the chair. In the corridor, Auran grappled with the figure, their shadows mingling into an indiscernible mass.

Too scared of striking his friend, he stood over the two, waiting for his eyes to adjust back to darkness. The two tossed and turned on the ground. Now he could recognise Auran, stockier than the other. The Southlander was in control, one hand clamped around the other's arm, his kitchen knife at his throat.

'Check upstairs,' Auran grunted, putting more force on the blade.

He nodded and crept into the corridor. It was too narrow for sabre and shield. Taking a breath, he relaxed his grip on his knife and stole up the stairs. The top one creaked. He froze. Nothing, the only sound was the continued scuffle from below. Keeping his back to a wall, he stole a glance into the first bedroom. And empty bed, an open chest of clothes, empty corners. A quick glance under the bed, but there was nothing. Three more rooms were similarly deserted.

Breathing heavily to still his thundering heart, he descended to the parlour. Auran stood in front of the high-backed seat, arms folded menacingly. A dishevelled figure sat before them.

'All clear.'

Auran nodded. 'He's unarmed. Search his pack.'

Eyeing their adversary warily, he collected the pack from the fireplace. Carefully, he removed its contents, looking for anything suspicious. Provisions, clothes, needle and thread, a water-skin, a short dagger. Nothing suspicious. He handed the dagger to Auran and stood behind his friend, staring at their captive.

Tall and thin, gangly even, with lank hair and scarred, pock-marked skin, he was as different to Spotal as a housecat to a lion. His pointed ears drooped at their tips, his neck was thin and scraggly, his clothes stained and worn.

'Doesn't look like an enemy?' he whispered.

'Nevertheless.'

'Nevertheless what? Please let me go,' the calef croaked. 'I'm sorry I broke in, I thought it was abandoned like everywhere else.'

'Who are you?' Auran barked.

'Banil. I'm from up north.'

'What are you doing here?'

'My village was raided by troglodytes. The north winds only know where they came from, we're miles from the border of the marshes. I came looking for help.'

'Why from here?'

'Not from here, I'm going to Duddawl, if our soldiers are anywhere, it's there. Soldiers and a wise scholar.'

'What does a scholar have to do with it?'

'He's my friend. Lives nearby the village. Do you happen to…?' he looked up, hopefully, curiously.

'No. I'm asking the questions.'

'I promise I'm no threat. Just let me go and I'll be on my way.'

Auran tapped a finger to his lips thoughtfully. 'You know this area well?'

'Well enough.'

'You're coming with us.'

'Where?'

Auran ignored him. 'Repack his things, then we'll head back to the others.'

'What about the other houses?' he asked, hurriedly shoving everything back into the pack.

Auran chewed his cheek. 'Alright. We'll search them quickly, then get back.'

They shuffled from the house, pushing their captive in front of them. In the garden, Auran pushed the calef to his knees and stood behind him, kitchen knife poised.

'You guard him, I'm quicker with the locks,' he ordered. Lidan nodded and took his place. Auran quickly headed to the next house along and a few seconds later was through the newly-open door.

'You on your own?' Lidan asked.

'No,' whispered the calef.

His heart skipped. 'Where are the others?'

'In the Town Hall.'

'Why were you here in the houses?'

'Supplies.'

'On your own?'

'We thought it was abandoned.'

'How many of you?'

'Four others.'

He chewed his lip, unsure whether or not to believe the calef. He watched him with the intensity of a tyrant. Any movement, any shift in balance, was awarded with a touch of the knife to the nape of the neck. Banil soon learned to sit still. Auran reappeared and moved on to the others. Each second, he waited for a cry, a shout, a clash of steel. An excuse to clout this prisoner hard enough to render him unconscious and spring after his friend. It never came. The other houses were empty. Auran jogged back, his expression stern but satisfied.

'He says there are more in the Town Hall.'

'Widrias said they'd be there second! You, on your feet. One excuse and you'll be out cold, you hear? Come on!'

They ran, half-leading, half-dragging the calef through the dusty streets to the central building. It was tall, four storeys, with a central turret of an additional two storeys. The windows were dark, the roof built of red slate. A few short steps led up to the front door, left ajar. The others must already be inside.

Pushing Banil in front, they walked through, breathing heavily from their run.

A crack of light from a closed door in an otherwise black entrance hall. A flicker of shadows. They blundered through the darkness towards it. Empty doorways flanked the corridor, gaping black portals into mystery. All ignored. His concentration was fixed on the light, pooling from the crack beneath the wood.

It was only when he was immediately outside, chest heaving, mouth open, he paused. Auran bumped into him. It was only a firm hand against the solid doorframe that saved him from crashing through. Banil gasped, promptly silenced by Auran's firm hand.

Struggling to control his heavy breathing, he listened. Murmurs from the other side. Muted, soft-spoken. Not the excited whispers of anticipated danger. Too low, too muffled to recognise as any of his friends.

'Caution,' mouthed Auran.

He nodded and drew his knife. Just in case.

Auran nodded to him. He manoeuvred Banil in front of them. They braced their legs against the calef. As one, they pushed.

The crash of the door flying off its hinges was deafening. Banil fell to the floor, limbs splayed. No crossbow bolts met him, no jabs of spear tip or swings of sword-blade. He followed him through, knife at the ready.

It wasn't them. Strangers. Four of them. Two men, a woman, and a fonex. They stood frozen in surprise, not a weapon in sight, mouths open. It was some sort of storeroom or study, shelves of books or ledgers, half-opened crates of pelts, paper, wool. All recently plundered by these four strangers.

Thieves in the night, an empty village, strangers in a foreign land. He needed no other excuse.

Snarling like a wildcat, he sprang forward, battering the nearest stranger to the ground. Behind, he heard Auran jump in and tackle another into a bookshelf.

His opponent was only momentarily distracted. A firm hand clamped around his wrist like a vice, pushing the knife away from his throat. A sharp twist and his wrist sparked in pain. The knife clattered to the ground. Grunting, he shifted his weight, bringing his elbow down into his foe's neck. Their eyes met. His were strikingly blue, bulging ever larger as he pressed harder. The grip on his wrist loosened.

A fist crashed into his temple, knocking him off balance. Blue Eyes sprang to his feet, gasping, rubbing his clenched fist with his opposite hand.

He hardly had time to stagger back to his feet when Blue Eyes was on him again. Disarmed, he saw his foe's bulk. Broad and stocky, with a bulging chest and arms as thick as his legs. Bigger, undoubtedly stronger than him. More suited to wrestle him to the ground.

He seemed to come to the same conclusion. Clean-shaved, with a wide mouth and drooping cheeks, and sallow, hooded eyes, he curled his flabby lips. Lidan blinked. The next moment, he was bent double, solid arms wrapped around his midriff. It was only his shield slung over his back that saved him, too wide to fully encircle.

Blue Eyes tugged and he stumbled. He aimed a knee at his face, but it was deflected by a shrug of his broad shoulders. He grit his teeth and hammered his fists down on his foe's head, neck, shoulders. To no avail. Too strong, too stocky and tough. If anything, the grip grew stronger.

An explosion of pain from his flank. He gasped, winded. Another burst of agony. Blindingly potent. He turned his head in time to see the woman swing another powerful kick at his flank. He dropped his shoulder to intercept, but it did little difference. The pain, the weight of Blue Eyes, too much. He sank to his knees, chest jerking in vain for breath.

On the other side of the room, Auran had his fists up over his temples, shielding himself from the barrage of blows from man and fonex. He swung his fists every once in a while, but was too hard-pressed to land a proper strike. They moved in on him. He had his back to a wall, now batting away their punches with open palms. They circled on both sides. The woman joined them. Auran did his best, but eventually twisted too far to parry an attack. The fonex jumped at the opportunity. His hands clamped down on Auran's shoulders, enough to set him off balance. The other two converged and wrestled him to his knees, to both hands, to one elbow, until he was lying face-down, sweating and grunting like a cornered boar.

'Enough now. They're done.'

'This one's still kicking,' grunted the fonex, still forcing his weight onto Auran's bucking shoulders.

Blue Eyes loosened his grip on him and strode over to Auran. He tried to crawl over to his friend, but the woman stepped in front and placed her foot on his back, forcing his chest to the ground. He could only watch as Blue Eyes aimed a savage kick at Auran's jaw. With a jarring clack of the teeth, his head jerked back, and he lay still, blinking slowly, stunned.

'Now they're done,' grunted Blue Eyes.

'Who are they, Banil?' the other man asked, this one older, wearing a black bandanna, grey stubble on his jaw. He identified him as the first voice, presumably the head of the gang.

'Not sure, they ambushed me in one of the houses.'

'Thought we sent you to ambush them,' sniggered the fonex, his voice nasal and whiny. His skin was a dark grey, like old charcoal, his hair so black it was almost navy. Had he stood still in the shadows, he might have turned nearly invisible. Unnerving.

But not as unnerving as his comment. Twisting his neck, he struggled to lock eyes with the calef. Clearly not the harmless traveller he'd claimed.

'We decided it would be better this way,' said Banil.

'Kimm following you?' asked the woman.

'She's somewhere behind. I saw her on the rooftops on the way over.'

It was difficult to place the tone of his voice. Was there a touch of remorse there? A shred of guilt? Or was it just his imagination, hoping against betrayal.

'Sit them up. We'll have a talk.'

The woman linked her hands beneath his armpits and hoisted him to his feet. His head spun from the sudden movement and he closed his eyes to stave off the rush of nausea. She shoved him against a crate. He sat quietly. Blue Eyes shoved Auran next to him. As soon as the Southlander was sat upright, he started, as if to lunge. The old man pre-empted the jump and swung a stinging slap across his cheek.

Auran sat back, breathing forcefully through flaring nostrils.

'Leuk, make sure this one doesn't try anything else.'

Blue Eyes, Leuk, stepped behind them and placed a menacing hand on Auran's shoulder. A reminder they no longer had the upper hand.

The old man dragged up another crate in front of them and sat with a tired sigh. He regarded them with quiet eyes. His face was lined, rugged, traces of old scars just about visible over the collar of his shirt. Everything he wore was black or dark grey. Breeches, shirt, boots, gambeson. Even the buckles of his belts were of a blackened metal, so as not to gleam in reflected light. Far from the clothes of a simple traveller, excessive even for simple thieves.

'Keep watch, Alach,' he said, after a while. The fonex jumped to attention and left the room.

The silence grew. He swallowed nervously. He didn't know where to look, the staring eyes seemed everywhere. Only once before had he seen such intensity in a look. It had not ended well for Zile.

Beads of sweat formed and trickled down his brow, down his flanks, behind his ears. Mouth dry as the black desert. Heart racing faster than a wild colt.

'Where are the rest of you?' asked the old man.

'Rest?' he choked.

'Where?' the old man repeated.

He shook his head. Cursing inwardly, he wished he could hide his apprehension, but it was too overwhelming. The stare could wilt a rose, curdle fresh milk. He was a mouse in the shadow of an owl.

'They mentioned their companions were coming this way eventually,' muttered Banil, avoiding eye-contact with them.

The man nodded. His eyes never left them, the only movement the methodical, regular flick back and forth between them. Ten seconds of anxiety, ten more of relief, and repeat. Over and over.

'Why are you here?'

He shook his head again. Auran exhaled forcefully again. He saw Leuk push down on his shoulder, silencing him.

'Travellers are no abnormality in this country, especially not in this area. But during war? In the middle of an invasion? Curious.'

He glanced sideways at Auran, but the woman cuffed his ear.

'Eyes front,' she snapped.

'Varied company you keep. Southlander, Midlander, satorr, hanex, juggernaut... calef. Who is he? Your guide?'

He kept his lips sealed.

The man sighed and finally took his eyes from them. Only for a second, to flick to Leuk.

A twist of Auran's arm, and he grunted in pain, bent double, his arm at an awkward angle to his shoulder.

'It won't take much to break his arm. But it'll take less to save it. Just answer a few of my questions.'

'Travellers! As you said!' he blurted, panicking.

Another glance at Leuk. Auran groaned as his arm was twisted further.

'So armed? Unlikely. An honour guard, perhaps? Mercenaries protecting the calef, whoever he might be?'

'No! Just travellers, we're heading to Muranath!' Lidan babbled.

'What do you want in Muranath?' the old man asked.

'Just…trading, visiting. Seeing what opportunities are there for us.'

'Unlikely.'

'Who are you?' he asked, trying to deflect.

The man paused, considering.

'Travellers,' he said, with a slight smirk.

He shuddered. With each passing second, the knowledge they needed saving grew ever more pressing. But Spotal would come soon, he and Pwtrek and the others would come.

'Back to the calef,' he continued, as if reading his mind. 'Who is he?'

'A… guide, like you said. To help us get there,' he said.

'More likely the other way around… but very well, we'll play this charade. Who is he?'

'Our guide, he's from around here.'

'Oh? How lucky of you to come across him. Which village?'

'N- no, not exactly here, just close by,' he floundered. 'Further south.'

'And his village?'

'I don't… remember.'

'Unfortunate. His name?'

'S- Spat…ril,' he caught himself, and conjured the name. He hadn't met many calefs, he didn't know what their names sounded like.

Banil shook his head. 'Made it up. Never heard of a name like it. What's his surname?'

'I don't know, he only ever used his first.'

'Where did you meet him?' asked the old man.

'At Imhara Pass.'

'So, you came from the Northlands?'

'Yes. We've travelled far, you see, wanted to come and see Muranath now we've made it all the way here.'

'And how was the journey through the Pass?'

'A bit…cold,' he guessed.

'And he travelled all the way up there to guide you? Must be paying him well.'

'Our leader is…generous.'

'I'm sure. And what might he be called.'

'W- M- Sto-' he spluttered.

'Shut up, Lidan,' grunted Auran, and was punished with another twist of the arm.

The old man sighed and rose to pace back and forth in front of them.

'Quite. I've had enough of the stories. Worst liar I've met for a while. Makes me wonder why you're protecting him so devotedly.'

'I'm not?'

'Who is he? An academic of some sort? A scholar? An alchemist?'

He waited, gazing with even greater intensity. Lidan blinked, confused. Why in the four winds would they think Spotal was a scholar? He'd never voiced anything more insightful than a comment on the weather. The man searched his face and seemed to come to a conclusion.

'Surprised?' the man asked.

Yes. But evidently not for the reasons he thought.

'We knew we'd find you somewhere around,' he continued.

He tried to swallow, but the walls of his dry throat stuck together too much and he ended up with a lump he couldn't budge. Find them? Could these be the remnants of the mountain garrison, finally caught up with them? No. Impossible. They couldn't have overtaken them so considerably if they were from Tarnegrefur.

'Jonn! Two people approaching. Juggernaut is one of them.'

The older man turned to the door, thrown open by the returned fonex, Alach.

'Kimm with him?'

'Not sure, could've been either her, the satorr, or the hanex.'

'Get ready. Keep them quiet.'

The woman grabbed Lidan's mouth, squeezing his cheeks against his teeth. He opened his mouth to spare the pain, and she shoved a rag into his mouth. Leuk gave Auran a similar treatment.

The strangers took their positions. Leuk and the woman remained where they were, using them as a shield to the door. Banil crouched behind a crate near the door with Alach. Jonn took a seat to one side, commanding a view of the entire room.

He heard them come through the front door. Pwtrek's heavy footsteps, Widrias's shuffling limp. A long wait followed as they explored each room methodically, systematically. He could picture them, clearing each doorway before moving on to the next, ensuring there was no risk of a rear attack. Professional, experienced, clear-headed. The opposite of his and Auran's approach. He had no doubt they knew which door they were behind. Nobody could miss the light spreading beneath it, but they were exercising a greater caution than their panicked, excited dash.

Finally, the floorboards creaked outside. He glanced at Jonn, but the old man's attention was on the door.

Agonisingly slowly, it swung open, its creaking hinges deafening. Waiting, he expected to see them step through, for Alach and Banil to jump forward, wrestle them to the floor, probably a few knives to their throats. Pwtrek would be the difficult one, probably big enough to out-muscle all five of them, but not if Widrias were used as hostage.

Still waiting. The door completed its arc and bumped into the crate concealing Banil. Widrias stood imposingly in the doorway, framed against Pwtrek's looming silhouette behind.

His features were stern, his frown as deep as it had ever been. His sword was in hand, but still safely in his scabbard. He stepped into the room.

'Gentlemen. Marm,' he nodded to the room. Pwtrek squeezed through the narrow doorway, ducking his broad shoulders. In the confined space, already cramped with the excess of bodies, even Lidan felt intimidated by his sheer bulk. It was certainly enough to intimidate Banil, who stepped from his hiding space and quailed away, behind Jonn.

Pwtrek nodded to him reassuringly. Relief flooded through his chest. They'd be alright. He knew they would.

'Out the corner, or I'll drag you out,' Pwtrek growled, looking over his shoulder at Alach.

The fonex sniffed and walked around to Jonn. If he was nervous, he didn't show it. Indeed, he looked as relaxed as ever.

They faced each other. The five strangers, Auran and Lidan gagged beneath them, opposite Widrias and Pwtrek. Jonn bowed slightly to Widrias.

'How can I help you?'

Chapter 28

'Releasing our companions would be a start,' Widrias barked.

'In good time. No harm has come to them,' said Jonn.

'We'll be the judge of that.'

Jonn raised his hands placatingly. 'Relax. No harm will come to any of you if you play along.'

Widrias's eyebrows shot up as high as his frown was deep.

'Play along? I'm in no mood for games. If you want a discussion, let them go. Until you do so, anything you say can and will be perceived as a threat. I do not tolerate threats,' he punctuated each word of the final sentence with a strike of his scabbard to the floor.

'And abandon our leverage? I think not,' Jonn chuckled.

'Leverage is not needed for simple discussion.'

'Well then, you caught us. I was interested in something a little more lucrative than simple discussion.'

Pwtrek's rumbling growl would have made a bear blush.

'Let them go,' Widrias repeated.

'In good time. First, we'd like a little cooperation from you,' said Jonn.

'If you don't-' Pwtrek stepped forward, imposingly.

'What? Save your threats, they mean nothing. We're more than capable of defending ourselves and have your companions at our mercy. All I want is to talk, for now.'

Widrias put his hand on Pwtrek's arm, stopping him from pouncing forward.

'Talk, then, and be done with it.'

Jonn nodded, apparently satisfied. 'You are their leader?'

'Yes.'

'Your name?'

'Unimportant.'

'Really? Well, my name is Jonn. I am the head of my band,' he gestured to the three in black, and finally to Banil. 'Banil here is our guide, been showing us around the area.'

'Good for you.'

'We've just come from Duddawl. I suppose you're familiar with it?'

Widrias paused, his face a stern mask. 'Possibly.'

Jonn nodded again. 'Yes, I'm sure. We've been looking for someone, lives around there.'

'I doubt it was us.'

'Not you personally, no.'

There was a pause. He could see Widrias's frown deepen, his stance shift, trying to figure out the riddle. Again, Jonn seemed to misinterpret the subtleties and smiled confidently.

'What are you doing here? Surely, you'd have known we'd still be around, searching for you? Why not keep running?'

Pwtrek scratched his chin, his eyes meeting Lidan's. He shrugged slightly, Pwtrek nodded slightly in acknowledgement. What were they talking about?

'We are travelling south,' said Widrias, carefully.

'Yes, to Muranath, your friend already tried to sell me your story. We've already moved past it. Are you returning to the tower for supplies? For ingredients and tinctures?'

'The tower?'

Jonn sighed and shook his head frustratedly. 'Where is the calef?'

'The calef? Why? Your own not good enough for you?' asked Widrias.

'You were foolish to return, accept you've been caught and give him up. You were only doing your duty, we won't harm you or him. I can see your limp. Presumably got caught up by Drew and her lot. We'll forgive you for that as well. No bad blood. Just cooperate.'

'I think you're mistaken.'

'I think not. A lone calef travelling through the country with a mercenary bodyguard? The empty tower? We are no fools,' Jonn sneered.

'Debatable. We know of no tower.'

'Enough of this. I've been civil and reasonable,' Jonn clenched his fist. 'Give up the calef.'

'No need!'

The voice called from the corridor and Spotal walked in slowly, taking in the situation with calm eyes. He nodded to Lidan and Auran and came to a halt beside Widrias, where he sized up the strangers.

'I'm here. How can I help you?'

Jonn looked at him, the beginnings of a frown on his brow. 'Who are you?'

'The calef you're so intent on finding, apparently,' Spotal chuckled.

'No. Banil!' he turned to the other calef, a sudden fury in his gaze. 'What is this?'

Banil raised his hands. 'I didn't know! How could I tell in the dark?'

'A child could tell he's not the one!' he turned back to Widrias, grimacing, 'Very well. A mistake. We will not end this violently. Leave the building and we'll return your companions unharmed. The village is yours for the night. Follow us at your peril.'

'No. You've raised too many questions,' Widrias stood firm.

'Leave, or we will hurt them,' Jonn pointed to the door.

'Hurt them, and we will retaliate,' Widrias placed a hand on the scabbard, ready to draw the blade.

'You think you can face us? Outnumbered, outclassed? I'm showing you a mercy many would not,' Jonn sneered.

'Yes, because you know your position is not as strong as you pretend. If it were, I have no doubt they'd already be dead and we'd be fighting for our lives. In such a small room, all it would take is a few swings of my colleague here's claws,' he rested his hand on Pwtrek's arm again, 'and you would all be... worse for wear.'

Jonn flicked his stare back and forth between Widrias and Pwtrek.

'Well, now it seems to be my turn to be coy. You were evasive, I will be too.'

'By the four winds,' Banil suddenly breathed, mouth open, staring at Spotal. 'Captain Spotal.'

Spotal blinked and shifted uncomfortably. Jonn's attention switched instantly to him, gazing at him with a renewed vigour. 'You're sure, Banil?'

'No doubt. I knew I'd seen him before!' Banil nodded excitedly.

'Winds! Last I heard, Spotal was sent to the Council as envoy. Sent directly to the high chancellors,' Jonn's gaze flicked back to Widrias, whose grip was suddenly much tighter around the hilt of his sword. 'A satorr, the leader of this company. You sell yourself short, General Widrias.'

He felt the woman and Leuk shift behind him. Alach glanced between them, a smile on his lips, an excitement in his fidgeting. Jonn stepped forward, approaching the satorr. Pwtrek growled, ready to strike. Spotal's hand shifted to his jian.

Jonn's arm lifted, his hand extended. And waited. An empty palm, extended to Widrias as an offer of peace. Widrias took it hesitantly, and they shook.

'Pleasure to meet you, sir. I've looked forward to this meeting for some time.'

Widrias blinked, caught out by the sudden change in tone.

'You are?'

'Jonn, as I said. We are here on orders from Agral.'

'You are Council?'

'Yes. Leuk, Nan, let them go. Apologies for the mistreatment. We assumed you were rogues, or Stolach's men.'

'An easy mistake.'

The woman, Nan, hoisted him to his feet and brushed him down roughly. He glanced at her, she looked back at him coldly. Uneasy, he shuffled to Spotal and faced them. Auran joined them, unslinging his axe from his back, glaring at Leuk.

'Why are you here?' Widrias stepped back from Jonn, his hand still firmly gripped around his sword.

'Agral sent us.'

'Why?'

'A mission, can't say much more than that.'

'Wrong. Tell me now. If you're truly Council you will obey.'

Jonn shrugged. 'We're looking for a calef. An alchemist. We suspect he may be working for Stolach on something.'

'A traitor?' Spotal sneered, glancing quickly at Banil. The other calef turned his eyes down to his feet, avoiding their looks.

'Yes. We tried to find him in his tower, but it was empty. We looked through Duddawl, but didn't want to draw attention to ourselves, in case the entire town was also in league.'

'Impossible,' Spotal shook his head.

'Unfortunately not. Apparently, your kin aren't as patriotic as you think. There was no welcome for us there as Council soldiers. We had to conduct our work at night.'

'Like thieves in the dark,' muttered Pwtrek.

'Perhaps. But in the name of the Council. Come, let's move to somewhere less cramped to discuss.'

Spotal moved first, turning on his heel to stalk out the door. Auran followed, backing out, keeping his face to these apparent allies. Lidan followed. Pwtrek and Widrias came next, followed by the others. Despite the apparent friendliness, the tension was still palpable. Waiting to be broken as it coiled ever tighter.

They moved down the corridor to another doorway. It was a spacious room, perhaps a venue of some sort. The carefully-tiled floors were what he imagined those of a palace to be like, as even as a still pond. Small round tables dotted the periphery, surrounded by delicate wooden stools. The tall windows were shuttered closed. Leuk brought a torch from the first room and set about lighting the lamps and torches lining the walls.

Standing awkwardly in the middle of the room, they faced each other again.

'So,' Widrias began, still holding his sword and scabbard, 'tell me more about your mission.'

'Not much more to tell. We were sent by Agral to come and capture the alchemist before he made it to Stolach,' said Jonn, smoothly.

'When did you find out about him?' asked Widrias.

'A few weeks ago.'

'Only a few weeks? And you made it all the way here so quickly?'

'It was deemed a matter of importance. Obviously, you yourself have clearly been away for some time…?'

Widrias ignored the implied question.

'How did you get here?'

'By sea.'

'How?'

'A ship from Morgenal, made it to Tonnis, then a barge from Tonnis up the Atrael, and to Duddawl.'

'All the way up the Atrael?'

'Yes.'

'No complications along the way?' Widrias pressed.

'Ah, the invasion. Yes, a complication, but one we circumvented,' Jonn shrugged nonchalantly.

'You've shown remarkable initiative to make it all the way here in such troubled times.'

'Thank you.'

'How long have you been here?'

'Since this morning.'

'Where is everyone?'

'We don't know. We supposed they ran to Duddawl, for protection. Someone must have brought word of the invasion.'

Widrias nodded. 'Who is Drew?'

Jonn paused. 'A colleague. We split into two groups when we found the tower abandoned. We came here, Drew and her group remained around Duddawl, to keep searching for him.'

Widrias rubbed his beard, keeping his eyes on Jonn. 'How are things at the Council?'

'Well, for the most part.'

'Has my presence been missed, these past few weeks?'

Jonn paused, staring, before smiling again. 'Of course. Yours and Spotal's.'

Widrias nodded again and looked around the room, as if in thought. Lidan swallowed nervously. They'd been away for months, not weeks. His unease grew. Why lie? Alach, Leuk, and Nan were staring at them, trying to look friendly. Trying.

'So, what now, Jonn? How do we proceed from here?'

'What do you mean?'

'Do we go with you after this alchemist, or do we continue on our own mission?'

'Well, if you stay with us, we can join forces, complete both our missions. Return to the Council together for another.'

'Yes,' he continued rubbing his beard between thumb and forefinger. 'Yes, maybe. Although, before we do, perhaps you should meet the final member of our group?'

Jonn's jaw bulged as he clenched his teeth. 'Final member? Of course... of course the hanex! Where has he been?'

'Oh, keeping an eye out for us. Just in case.'

'Very wise.'

'So it would seem.'

Widrias gestured to the door. The five strangers turned.

Lidan's lip quivered into a nervous smile. There she was, as silent as ever, bloody falchion in one hand, decapitated head of a dreyad in the other. She stepped through and tossed the head into the room. It rolled to a halt at Banil's feet, a spattering of blood in its grisly wake.

The calef recoiled, disgusted.

'Winds! Kimm!'

'By the four winds,' breathed Alach, staring at Noswen. 'It's her.'

'Impossible...' Nan whispered.

Jonn spun around, his gaze turned into a glare. Growling, his hands shot to his hips. Quick as a flash, there were two dirks in hand. He sprang at Widrias.

No time to pause. Lidan drew his sabre and charged. Banil was closest, so Banil was first. The calef was still recoiling at the sight of the head and barely had time to look up before Lidan struck with his sabre. Once, twice, thrice, he pummelled the hilt into the calef's nose, leaving it a bloody pulp. Banil whimpered and collapsed to the ground, clutching his face.

He considered killing him, all it took would take was a simple swing of the sabre. But too late, Nan sprang before him, sword and hatchet flashing. He stumbled back, caught off-guard by her ferocity. It was all he could do to fend her off. Her blade glanced against his thigh, not enough to penetrate, but knocking him to his knee.

Rolling to the left, he escaped her descending hatchet. Recovering quickly, he was back on his feet, ready to meet her again. But she was gone, dancing away into the melee, now engaging Spotal. Only for a few seconds. The calef's blade caught her hatchet and it spun from her grip across the room. She tried to recover with a backhand slash at his exposed belly, but the jian flashed, too quickly to follow, and intercepted the blade. There was a pause, fractions of a second, as the two blades were held together, only for Spotal to twist again and push her sword away in a sudden rotation.

She spluttered and fell to her knees, clutching her armpit. Lidan shook his head to clear his eyes. He never even saw Spotal's blade touch her, it was all too fast. Nevertheless, there was the blood dribbling between her fingers like a mountain brook in spring. Spotal didn't pause. He placed the tip of his sword on her collarbone and thrust quickly. She fell into an ever-growing puddle.

Shrugging his shield from his back, he rushed up to re-join the fray, but Spotal caught him by the arm.

'No, Lidan. You're outclassed in this fight. Guard the calef.'

'But-'

'No! We can't beat them if we're protecting you too.'

Cursing, he returned to Banil. Not that he needed guarding. He still writhed on the ground, whimpering and clutching his nose pathetically. Lidan kicked his leg half-heartedly.

'Enough of that, or I'll give you something to really complain about.'

He tried to make it sound menacing, but the words seemed weak on his voice. Not that Banil noticed, he was lost in the eye-watering pain of his presumably-broken nose. Placing his foot on his shoulder, he stilled his squirming and watched the skirmish.

Noswen duelled Alach, their swords clashing in a ferocious dance. It ended abruptly. A series of feints built up to a precise lunge that left Alach gasping and clutching his bloodied stomach. In the same movement, she was away, skipping across the stone floor to Auran. The Southlander grappled with Leuk, who'd moved in within the range of his axe. The bigger man used his weight against Auran, muscling him back, his hands firm around the shaft.

With the slightest kick, she jumped on his back, wrapping her legs around his shoulders, leaning back as far as she could. Leuk growled and let go of Auran's axe with one hand, clawing at her legs, struggling to maintain his balance. Auran seized the opportunity and twisted his axe free. Grunting a warning to Noswen, he swung. She disentangled her legs from around their foe, falling to the floor fractions of a second before the battleaxe sank into Leuk's neck, just beneath the angle of the jaw. His bright blue eyes rolled into his head a final time and he clattered in a heap.

Only Jonn left. The old man showed surprising agility, jumping around Pwtrek and Widrias' precise strikes. His twin dirks were always moving, parrying, intercepting, darting forward, as if with a life of their own.

Free from the confines of the first room, the value of such agility proved itself a thousand times. His acrobatic movements were reminiscent of Gwahl, ducking and weaving above and beneath blades, tempting death with each movement.

Spotal, Auran, and Noswen all joined the duel, adding their weapon to the storm of blades. Still, Jonn remained standing, even forcing Spotal to retreat with a barrage of stinging stabs.

Where he first concentrated most of his attacks on Widrias, with Pwtrek more often than not placing himself between him and the satorr, he changed targets with the inclusion of the other three. His attention shifted, and his twisting movements circled Noswen, threatening her with every other strike.

For her part, she held her own, gradually increasing the range and breadth of her attacks, slowly clearing a space between her and her companions. They took the cue and backed away, giving her space to duel, only adding their blades to the fray if Jonn strayed too close.

Dirk in left hand, falchion in right, she faced Jonn's twin blades. The duel seemed to slow, the number of attacks reduced, with only the odd feint between the two. Instead, they duelled with their footwork, matching their positions, advancing and retreating, shuffling their feet, chasséing back and forth, searching for the advantage. It was a complex, entrancing dance between two expert partners.

Finally, they moved together again, exchanged a flurry of blows, and separated, each bleeding from half a dozen new cuts. Jonn wiped a bead of sweat from his forehead, jumped on the spot a few times, and sprang forward again.

Focussed on Noswen, he seemed to forget the others. Without warning, Spotal lunged forward, burying his jian deep into Jonn's thigh. He grunted, stumbling headfirst into Noswen's waiting blade. Pwtrek followed up with a vicious swing of his sword, only narrowly missing Noswen's chin with its sweeping arc.

Jonn fell to the ground, seeping blood, eyes closed. He didn't move again.

Noswen exhaled heavily and nodded to Spotal.

'Swift blade.'

'Not that you needed it,' he replied.

'But always appreciated.'

Spotal smiled and wiped his sword clean.

'They recognised you?' asked Auran, looking at the corpses suspiciously.

'Guild of assassins. This one was with me on a few expeditions,' she turned Jonn's face over with her boot. 'He is one of Stolach's favourites. It must be an important task.'

'Important indeed,' Widrias nodded, leaning on his sword to catch his breath, 'and infinitely curious. But one of Stolach's favourites? His deception was poor.'

'Awful at manipulation,' she agreed. 'Excellent poisoner. One of the best.'

'Poisoner? Interesting. How's the calef?'

'Well enough,' replied Lidan. He supposed it was true. Banil was finally still, breathing raggedly through his mouth, eyes closed, hands still wrapped around his nose.

Pwtrek strode over and hoisted him to his feet, ignoring his muted protests.

'Relax, it's a broken nose at worst.'

'Bring him over,' Widrias turned and took a seat at one of the dainty tables surrounding the room. Banil was thrown to the floor in front of him, towered over by Pwtrek's scowls.

'Well then, where do we begin? Auran, Lidan?' Widrias looked at them sternly.

Lidan jumped forward, eager to tell the tale.

'We were searching the last houses,' he began, excitedly, 'and saw a bag on the floor, next thing we know, we hear this one, Banil, calling out! So Auran tackles him, knocks him down, I make sure there's nobody else about, and Auran ties him up. He said he's from a village up north, attacked by troglodytes, and he's on his way to Duddawl looking for help from any soldiers there. Then he told us he had friends in the Town Hall. We knew you were coming here next after the watchtower, so we tried to head you off, in case they were dangerous. We were ambushed and kept captive, then you came and saved us!'

Widrias nodded, 'I trust you completed your search?'

'Nothing else to report, all other houses empty,' confirmed Auran.

'Well, it was reckless to charge in here, we saw you from the watchtower. Followed oh so stealthily by that one,' he pointed to the decapitated head. 'Obviously, we saw you'd be in need of assistance. Noswen headed off your stalker, Spotal came in from the back, and Pwtrek and I came in the front. All told, an interesting turn of events that could have ended very badly. We are lucky, gentlemen, very lucky indeed.

'So!' he clapped his hands together, suddenly. 'Now for the real questions. Banil. Where are you from?'

Banil licked his lips, his eyes darting from one person to the next. They rested on Lidan for a second, full of fear, before flicking back to Widrias.

'A village further north.'

'That much I suppose may be true,' shrugged the satorr.

'Northern or Southern Kingdom?' barked Spotal, suddenly.

Lidan recoiled in surprise. He'd never heard the calef use such a tone, not unlike how Tanor used to address the Council Guard. Short, harsh, guttural. A tone to demand immediate attention. Compared to Spotal's usual clear, musical voice, it was utterly alien.

'Northern, Captain Spotal, Northern! If I'd known you-'

'What name?' Spotal cut across.

'Casnybain. It's near the Eastern Barrier, at the very northern border. We were-'

'I know it. Razed to the ground. Where have you been since then?'

'By nomads, yes. We fled the village while it burned. Didn't have time to let my dogs out their kennels before-'

'Doesn't matter. It's been eight years since Casnybain. Where have you been since?'

'I went south, to seek help from Muranath. They never let me within a hundred paces of the palace, let alone Lleunedd.'

'So you went to Stolach?'

'I went back home, to what was left of it. Found out the nomads had all been caught, by your army,' he paused, looking at Spotal with a glitter of admiration. Spotal ignored it.

'What then?' Widrias prompted.

Banil blinked. 'I went to Narfen Fortress to see the prisoners, but it didn't help. I left the kingdom, went to the Midlands, eventually ended up in Crastalan. One day I was approached by a woman,' he nodded to Nan's corpse, 'she offered me opportunities to be useful again. I took it. I partnered up with her and we came to Dimrys, a village twenty miles away. Set up as a woodsman and his apprentice.'

'What were the opportunities?'

Banil shook his head, ashamed. 'Spying.'

'On whom?' Spotal barked.

'Nobody in particular, just sending general information over to Crastalan, how crops fared year by year, any natural disasters, rumours and mutterings, public opinions on Lleunedd and Teig. General information about the country.'

'Any reason why?'

'No. I didn't know they were planning to invade, if that's what you're implying,' Banil hung his head in shame.

'Exactly what I'm implying,' Spotal sneered.

'I didn't. I promise. I didn't mean for any harm to come of it.'

'Spying on the country for Stolach? You knew there was some malicious intent,' Widrias scolded, pointing an accusing finger.

'Never!'

'No lies,' growled Pwtrek, roughly pushing the calef to all fours.

'I swear!'

'Alright, well you're guilty of plenty other things in my eyes in any case,' Widrias leaned forward and rubbed his calf. 'How did you end up here with that lot?'

'Nan was my faux-apprentice, she'd been with me for a while. A few weeks ago, the others arrived, said we had an assignment in Duddawl. It was really Nan they needed, they brought me along as a local guide to give the party some credibility by having a calef with them.'

'Assignment?'

'To find some scholar, ask him about something, some alchemy Stolach was after.'

'What for?'

'I don't know. I don't think they knew either. They were to take the scholar down to Field Marshall Strikk, apparently he knew the plans.'

'A weapon of some sort?'

'Presumably, I don't know, I promise.'

'Weapons of alchemy, who'd have thought Stolach would stoop so low?' Pwtrek muttered, shaking his head.

Lidan had to agree. Ever since the scourge of Herikik the Magus, over two hundred years ago, the use of magicks and alchemy in conflict was considered a breach of the rules of war. Not that there was anyone around to enforce such rules, but to stoop to such depths brought back tales of the foul deeds employed by the great goblin, before his demise at the hands of the minotorrs. In all the stories, it ended with the minotorrs tearing his body into a hundred pieces, burning each one and scattering the ashes at a hundred different locations across the Mountains of Iadden. Such was the fear of his conjurings. He remembered a trial once, in Weaverlodge, where a man accused of witchcraft faced the village elders. It lasted two weeks, before the man was acquitted and released. In the end, it was their gwrch, their knowing woman, who provided the evidence to prove his innocence. He left soon after, unable to shake off the mistrust garnered by the accusations.

'And this alchemist is in Duddawl?' asked Widrias.

'Yes, or just outside it,' said Banil.

'You mentioned an alchemist, Spotal?' Widrias looked at the calef questioningly. 'The same one, I would think?'

'Probably,' said Spotal.

'You know him?' Banil asked, suddenly hopeful.

'No. Heard of a tower with someone in it,' said Spotal, turning away from the dishevelled prisoner.

'Ah,' Banil's shoulders slumped again. 'Nobody is there. We searched.'

'That much must be true, then. And the villagers? Where are they?' asked Widrias.

'From what we can – could – tell, Duddawl. Everyone ran there when the first bands of troglodytes were spotted.'

'What of this other group of you? More assassins?' asked Widrias.

Banil nodded enthusiastically, 'Yes. If you go towards Duddawl, you're likely to meet them somewhere on the road. They're less likely to try to play you than Jonn.'

'I'm sure we'll be able to take care of ourselves. Pwtrek, find somewhere to keep him while we discuss.'

The juggernaut grunted and half-pulled, half-carried the calef over to the far corner, and set about tying him up with his own belt.

Lidan watched him for a second, trying to process all the new information. Lies and half-truths, all claimed and disproved within minutes of each other. It was difficult to keep up. Only ten minutes ago, Jonn and Widrias were talking, discussing the Council. Now there were four corpses, a prisoner, and six anxious soldiers. He caught himself, the others were probably calm, having faced such situations a thousand times before. Only one anxious soldier.

'He's lying.'

Spotal's whispered sneer was as unfamiliar as his previous bark. He'd never seen the calef filled with such spite.

'About which part? Or rather, which part is he being truthful about?' muttered Auran.

'He's not from the northern kingdom.'

'How do you know? His accent?'

Spotal shook his head. 'His accent is convincing. He called it Narfen Fortress. Nobody from the northern kingdom calls it that.'

'What is it?' Lidan asked.

'A fortress within the Eastern Barrier. One of two remaining from before the Cataclysmic War. It's notorious for its gaol. Northern calefs refer to it exclusively as The Cage. *Exclusively*. Only those brought up south of Tarnegrefur use its official name.'

'Why lie about it?'

'He mentioned Casnybain and recognised me. It was one of my better-known victories, at least in the south. Probably trying to squeeze some sympathy from me. Manipulative bastard.'

'You're sure he's lying about where he's from?' asked Widrias.

'Nobody calls it Narfen Fortress,' Spotal repeated.

Widrias nodded slowly. 'Alright. I'll accept he's not telling us the truth. But I don't think it's an outright lie. There are some half-truths in there, enough to disguise the fabrications.'

Spotal shrugged in agreement. 'Probably true.'

'Do we think he's dangerous?' asked Auran.

'Probably not,' Widrias frowned. 'He's poor enough in melee to be bested by Lidan, he's no threat to us,' he paused and looked at him. 'No offence.'

Lidan smiled and shook his head. There was no point getting insulted by inconvenient truths. He glanced at the others. Widrias and Spotal studied Banil, the comment apparently already forgotten. Noswen might have smiled at him, it was difficult to tell. Auran caught his eye.

'I'd still be cautious,' the Southlander warned. 'He's stronger than he looks, took me a bit of effort to overpower him. Not as meek and pathetic as he seems at the moment.'

'Yes, well we'll keep two awake at night for as long as we have him. One on watch, one to guard him. Just in case,' Widrias nodded thoughtfully.

Lidan smiled gratefully at Auran, who nodded reassuringly.

'What do you think, Noswen?' asked Widrias.

She stared at Banil intently, then at Jonn's corpse. 'Plausible. If it's alchemy, Jonn would be a good choice of assassin. Mastery of chemicals is integral to poison.'

'You think they were looking to poison something?' asked Widrias.

'Something, someone, developing a new toxin, learning alchemy... all are possible,' she shrugged.

'What will we do with him?' asked Auran.

'Keep him prisoner for now. When we reach Duddawl, we'll see what the locals make of him. First, we have the rest of the village to search.'

*

He woke exhausted. After the night's excitement, followed by a thorough search of the remaining buildings, they'd not had a chance to sleep until the early hours of the morning. Thankfully, his turns on watch and guard-duties had been pleasantly uneventful, with their prisoner asleep the entire time. Widrias even allowed them to sleep until well-past dawn. It was near mid-morning by the time they stirred to activity. But even this prolonged sleep was not enough. Eyes heavy, he tended his things.

Another grey morning. Another miserable drizzle. He took small comfort in the food plundered from the village larders. The cheese was good, the vegetables fresh. There was enough to extend their hospitality to Banil, half his face swollen into an impressive bruise, courtesy of Lidan's beating.

They left the village soon after, leaving its ghostly silence for the next traveller to ponder over. Concern over Jonn's supposed accomplices, the aforementioned Drew and her gang, made for an uneasy walk along the road. More than a few times, Auran suggested going cross-country, but the roads made for easier travel. Noswen resumed her scouting duties, returning every hour.

For the most part, they travelled in silence. If what Banil said were true, there must have been troglodytes near enough the village to make its inhabitants drop everything and leave immediately. Grim memories of the remnants of the *Seascale* crew's fate sprang to mind, and suddenly the thought of meeting these raiders was even worse than coming face-to-face with another squad of assassins.

Even so, despite the dangers, the fears, the apprehensions, the excitement of the journey was second to another in his mind. Banil. A mystery. Everything pointed to him being exactly what he said; a dishonoured calef fallen in with the wrong people after a tragedy. Meek, nervous around the assassins, embarrassed by his shortcomings, berated by Jonn for his mistake with Spotal's identity, awed at the recognition of Spotal's true identity. Everything fit. Everything made sense.

Except for the lie.

It turned everything on its head. Why lie about his origins? What was he hiding?

Looking at him now, stumbling along under Auran's watchful eyes, he didn't seem threatening. Gangly and off-balance by his bonds, it would be a simple enough thing to sweep his legs from under him if he tried anything ambitious. But was there something else? Something deeper, hiding behind this veneer of foolish innocence. Were his stumbles too precise in their clumsiness, his pained sniffles too pitiful, his regretful expression too convincing? Lidan narrowed his eyes. Or was he just looking for things to arouse suspicion? Finding unproven guilt in the accused.

Such things required too much thought. He did his best to dispel his curiosity, to prevent the headache of solving a difficult riddle, but the questions wouldn't go away. Banil's presence was a constant catalyst of questions. All day, he pondered, watching the bound calef like a hawk. On watch that night, he puzzled, searching the darkness for inspiration. When morning came, he greeted it not with a yawn and a stretch, but also a frown that a night's rest hadn't shed any light on the situation.

By late afternoon, he decided to make conversation, try to trip the calef up over his own words to reveal something. True, he wasn't the world's greatest interrogator, he'd never interrogated anyone, but people loved telling stories, and he loved to listen. Any discrepancies, he'd notice them. Each little mistake would be a clue to the truth.

But his conversation never came. The moment he stepped across to engage, Auran brushed him aside, nodding ahead. Irritated, he looked ahead again. The road led up a hill and at its crest stood Noswen, returned a good twenty minutes earlier than usual. Suddenly anxious, he adjusted his belt to make sure his sabre was within easy reach. Banil could wait.

She didn't come down to greet them as she normally would, but waited on the crest, hands on hips. As soon as they drew level, she turned and pointed to the distance.

'Looks about right,' she muttered.

He shielded his eyes with his palm and looked. There was the Atrael, winding its way alongside the road. Not five miles away was the sprawl of a fortified village, at the centre of a web of entangling streams, roads, and bridges. Duddawl.

Chapter 29

'Halt! Come no closer.'

'Peace! We are friends!'

'I said halt!'

'We are allies. Don't you recognise your own kin?'

'One bound, one free. Answers nothing. I said halt! Or we *will* resort to force.'

Lidan chewed his lip, willing Widrias to listen to the guard, her glittering spearpoint less than a foot from the satorr's chest. Another four spears were pointed at them. Behind the weapons, grey-eyed soldiers with tall shields and steady hands.

Widrias shuffled forward again to redistribute his weight off his injured leg. The calef jabbed the spear into his chest as a warning.

'Ignore my warning at your peril, stranger. Otherwise you betray your malicious intent.'

Widrias raised his hands, empty palms facing the guards. The calef, presumably the sergeant, held her spear where it was, its point digging into the cloth of the satorr's tunic. His underlying mail coat would spare him from harm, but the threat remained.

'Consider the warning duly noted,' said Widrias.

'Good,' the calef barked. 'Now consider this second warning. Duddawl is closed to strangers. Leave, or be removed.'

'We mean no harm,' Widrias insisted.

'Leave!'

'Can we not discuss? We seek only respite.'

'Seek it elsewhere. Duddawl is closed.'

'Who is your commanding officer? I would discuss the situation with them.'

'Predisposed.'

'And left the defence of the village in your hands? What rank?'

'Enough! The village is closed.'

The guard pushed and Widrias stumbled back, his knee buckling as the weight was forced to his left leg. His stumble brought his neck down to the spearpoint, leaving a deep scratch where his neck met his jaw.

Pwtrek jumped forward, growling. Five spears were suddenly pointed at the juggernaut.

'Step away, juggernaut. I gave fair warning. You have arms, they won't deter us. Should it come to blows there will be only one victor. Support!' she shouted suddenly. Half a dozen archers appeared at the top of the watchtower, their longbows aimed at them. One struck the bell at the top of the tower. It was answered by the voices of the four other watchtower bells. Reinforcements would be coming.

Lidan stepped back again. It would take a handful of seconds to throw his pack to the ground and get behind the cover of his shield. No doubt too long. He'd be pincushioned before his pack hit the ground. Any sudden movement and the archers might let fly. Auran rested his hand on his shoulder.

'Easy,' he whispered.

He nodded. Nerves made him jumpy, more likely to make a mistake. Taking a deep breath, he did his best to ignore the bows. But perhaps it was too ambitious to do so. He was acutely aware of the second archer from the left, whose arrow followed his every shuffle, unnervingly pointed directly at his chest.

Widrias recovered and turned aside, glancing at Spotal. The calef took the hint and took his place at the head of the party, confidently facing the spears.

'What battalion are you, Lieutenant?' he asked.

Lidan chewed his lip. An officer then, not a sergeant. Presumably there was some marking on her uniform denoting her rank.

'Step away, brother. The warning extends to you as well,' she turned her spear to him.

'I don't doubt it. Before we leave, then, might I ask a favour of you? As your superior officer?'

'No tricks, brother, it will not end well. We give you this chance to leave.'

'No tricks,' echoed Spotal, drawing his amulet from around his neck and holding it forth at an angle, between the curved claws at the tips of forefinger and thumb.

The guard studied it with narrowed eyes before lifting her spear, if somewhat begrudgingly.

'Captain.'

'Indeed. Captain Spotal, at your service.'

'No, mine at yours, it would seem. And my men. Lieutenant Eirlyn. Eighth battalion, second regiment, commanding officer of our detachment is Captain Antil. This is our station, until our relief arrives in two weeks.'

She lifted her arm. The four other spears lifted and the archers eased off the tension from their bows. Lidan sighed heavily, blowing out his cheeks, feeling the nerves drain from his tense muscles. Seems they were safe again, for the time being.

'Your orders?'

'Defend Duddawl. Expected a dull station, Captain, before news of raiding trogs reached us. What's the river patrols playing at, letting them through?'

'It's bigger than that, Lieutenant, much bigger. I wouldn't hold out much hope for that relief.'

'Explain, if you would? Captain,' she added.

'In time, as your captain sees fit, I'm sure. First, the favour.'

'A favour, or an order?'

'Whichever you want, as long as you do it,' smiled Spotal.

'As long as it doesn't conflict with our primary orders,' she stood tall and proud.

'It won't. We have a prisoner,' he gestured over his shoulder to Banil. 'A traitor. Spy for Stolach.'

The spearmen hissed angrily and glared at Banil. Eirlyn looked him up and down.

'Spy, eh? I'll take your word for it for now, but we'll need more proof if you want us to convict.'

'You have all my companions as witnesses. Including our leader, General Widrias of the Council. I'm sure his word counts for something?'

Eirlyn turned her attention to Widrias and bowed her head respectfully.

'I have heard of the general. One of the high chancellors, if I'm not mistaken?'

Auran snorted next to him, making Lidan jump. He cocked his head, questioningly. The Southlander leaned in.

'Considering the identities of the chancellors are meant to be secret, can't be very well-kept. Seems like every other person knows who Widrias is. Jonn knew about Agral as well.'

Lidan smiled faintly. It might have been worrying, but then again, if Stolach had spies in the Kingdom of the calefs, was it that much of a stretch of the imagination to believe he had some in the Council as well?

'Should you want more proof on top of that, at the village a few days' march northwest are five corpses. Stolach's assassins, this one's allies,' Spotal nodded at Banil.

'Your work, I assume?'

'Correct. He mentioned there may be another group of the bastards around here as well. Seen any?'

Eirlyn pursed her lips, nodding slowly. 'We killed them two days ago. They'd been trying to get into the village for nearly a week. Set a trap and caught them, like rats.'

'Do you still have the bodies?'

She shook her head. 'Burned them the night we caught them.'

'How many?'

'Six.'

Spotal turned and looked at Banil. The calef nodded his head, defeatedly. 'That's all of them. Drew and five others.'

Spotal nodded, satisfied.

'My favour, Lieutenant, is to hold him and guard him, until a fair trial can be organised. We'll all write our testimonials against him as evidence, for use when the time comes.'

She nodded and turned, signalling to one of the soldiers in the watchtower. The gates creaked open on their hinges.

'I'll take you in to speak to the captain,' she called over her shoulder. 'I should warn you, it'll be a while before we can hold the trial. Captain Antil is our highest-rank, which, as you know, is insufficient to pass judgement, and if the relief is unlikely to arrive for some time… he might be with us for a while.'

'As long as he's looked after,' Spotal shrugged.

The gates shuddered to a halt, wide enough to allow passage into the village, single file. She beckoned to Lidan and the others to follow.

It was a simple fortification, the curtain wall barely ten feet tall, built of simple grey stone and mortar. The gates were oak, reinforced with iron studs, heavy enough to withstand the combined strength of ten men. The walls circled the village, following its entire circumference like a miniature fortress. Where the rivers and streams cut through the wall, bridges were built, with iron portcullises extending from the underside to the riverbed, maintaining the continuity of the defence. These could presumably be raised to allow passage of boats up and down the waterways. Five slender watchtowers of the more familiar white sandstone apparently favoured by the calefin masons added imposing height to the walls. It certainly was fortified, well enough to hold against a modest enemy, but a larger foe with dedicated siege weapons would surely crush its defences.

As they approached the walls, two guards took Banil's rope from Auran, taking responsibility for the prisoner. Lidan edged through the gate after Pwtrek, who was forced to side-step through the narrow opening. As he stepped through, he saw the walls were roughly two feet thick, paper-thin compared to Crastalan, lacking any murder-holes in the roof of the entrance. No, Duddawl was not built for siege.

Just like that, they were inside. Another town with pretty white buildings and red roofs, decorated with pristine gardens of vivid green and gold. The only difference between this and the two others were the rivers snaking through and the little docks and quays where boats could berth.

The only difference.

Apart from them and the soldiers, it was as devoid of life and activity as any other. No citizens strolling through the streets, no sailors tending their boats, no merchants selling their wares. They were led through a barren market square, the stalls empty skeletons. Windows were shuttered, doors were closed. Buckets creaked eerily on their chains, suspended above their wells, waiting for a hand to cast them to the water below. Who knew for how long, and for how much longer, they'd be waiting?

Eirlyn escorted them to a central building, this one with open shutters and iron bars across the windows. Two spearmen guarded the door. Their heels snapped to attention at Eirlyn's approach and they stared at the party curiously as they were led through the doors.

It was little more than a box of a room, an iron door at one side next to another barred window. A sleepy calef jumped to attention, blinking furiously, a red welt on his chin where he'd been resting against his fist.

'Prisoner for the gaol,' Eirlyn announced, nodding to Banil, 'and these for an audience with the captain.'

'I'll let you through,' the guard mumbled. 'One moment.'

He disappeared. A second later, a series of scrapes, clicks, and thuds sounded from behind the iron door. It swung open smoothly on well-oiled hinges, with barely the faintest scratch of metal on cold metal. The guard beckoned them on.

'Adin, you know the way to the gaol, none of the cells are occupied,' he held up a key to the two guarding Banil. One nodded, took the key, and led their prisoner down a side corridor. As they left, the doorman called out to them again. 'Cell three is the biggest, he can have that! Lieutenant, the captain is currently discussing something with Lieutenant Iego, I'll announce you.'

Eirlyn rolled her eyes. 'It's alright, Samil, I'll announce us myself. Keep to your post.'

The guard, Samil, nodded and returned to his position behind the barred window, where he promptly nestled his chin back to its old position on his closed fist.

Eirlyn shook her head briefly before striding purposefully down the short corridor and led them up two flights of stairs. Another corridor, this one longer, extending lengthways across the building, ended at another door.

Benches lined the passage outside, underneath delicate watercolours of various landscapes. Most were unfamiliar to Lidan, but one might have been an interpretation of the Tarnegrefur Mountains, their grey peaks rising above the deeply-forested foothills. He barely noticed Eirlyn disappearing through the door, lost in the intricate beauty of the paintings. There was the sea, perfectly calm and still, with shores of smooth pebbles, or was it a lake? More mountains, these softer, depicted on a bright summer day, their dark stone a perfect contract to the royal blue sky. A city, no, a harbour, possibly Morgenal? Unlikely, even from his fleeting visit to the city, he could tell it was not the one portrayed here, with a vibrant blue harbour, clean buildings, slender ships. Presumably it must be Tonnis, as seen by a returning sailor as he first came in to port.

The door opened wide, disrupting his daydream. Eirlyn walked out with another calef, this one clad in lighter armour, stained and well-worn by the elements. The stranger strode past them without looking, save for the slightest glance at Spotal. Eirlyn called them forward.

'Captain Antil will see you. I'll be returning to my post. It's been a pleasure.'

They filed into the study. Spacious, organised with military efficiency, everything squarely-placed and fitted perfectly around everything else. Cupboards, drawers, crates, and countless chests circled the room, obscuring any glimpse of the room's panelled wooden walls. An enormous southward-facing bay window flooded the room with natural light, casting it over the sturdy rectangular desk dominating the floor. This desk, polished dark as rich coffee, was the one exception to the rule of order otherwise commanding the rest of the room. Its scratched, stained, used surface was littered with a mess of charts and maps, each one annotated differently. One with circling lines, one with a range of different colours, some intricately detailed, others strikingly simple, one covered in a maze of arrows and crosses, all weighed down at their curling edges with a variety of paperweights, from polished stones to ornate daggers, candleholders, pots of ink, old belt buckles, a clay teapot, anything to keep them from snapping shut.

'Thank you, Eirlyn. You are dismissed.'

Eirlyn saluted and shut the door firmly behind them. Lidan couldn't hear her footsteps retreat down the corridor.

Behind the desk stood the calef who'd issued the order. He considered the maps for a brief few seconds further before turning his attention to them.

'General Widrias, as I understand it? Very pleased to make your acquaintance. I was with Colonel Brawnedd back in the Summer of Sorrow, heard all about how much you helped us back then. I'm Captain Antil, as I'm sure Eirlyn mentioned. She gave me a brief history of your situation, but I'm sure it'll be clearer in your own words.'

'Much obliged, Captain, thank you for having us,' Widrias nodded.

'I would offer you a seat, I noticed your limp, but apart from a chest or crate, I'm afraid there isn't much choice.'

'I can stand for a few hours longer, Captain, but thank you.'

Antil bowed his head respectfully and signalled Widrias to continue. He recalled their quest, briefly skipping over the account of the serpent key, saving the details for their journey south from Tarnegrefur. Antil listened intently, rummaging through his maps as Widrias spoke. Several times, he held up a finger to pause the tale, hunting through chests and crates for more maps, discarding more than half of those selected, unrolling those he kept on the table and tracing a finger along the paper as Widrias continued with the tale. Particular attention was paid to the account of the ferries across the Atrael and the road through the brambles. Spotal chipped in at these moments, lending a hand with the descriptions of the terrain, providing a best-guess as to the position of the invasion on Antil's maps.

He was of average height, his hair cut short, save for a bouncing fringe covering half his forehead. Although slim, his belted gambeson gave the impression of a paunch, exaggerated as he slumped over the desk. Nothing about him suggested a soldier, his shoulders were round and narrow, his arms hid no coiled muscles, and he appeared well-past the age of lightning reflexes. Standing next to Spotal, lithe and athletic as he was, only served to exaggerate his quiet figure. Mild of voice, a hunched posture, an untouched face, he might have been more of an academic than fighter. It was only his sharpness when annotating the maps, his apparent accuracy at tracing their journey from the mountains to the village, that suggested something more. By the time Widrias finished, Antil studied his overlapping maps in complete silence, nodding.

'Well, here's your journey, as best I can place it from your descriptions,' he announced. 'You've made very good time, over two hundred miles in little over two weeks. You must be tired. Be assured, you can rest here for the time being, until you need to move on.'

'Thank you again, Captain, we appreciate the hospitality.'

'Oh, it's not much hospitality, I'm afraid,' Antil shrugged. 'There's nobody around to see to your needs, but you're welcome to stay and use our facilities as required.'

Widrias nodded and scratched his beard. 'On that point. We noticed a distinct lack of...people. Both on the roads and in the villages. Even here. I assumed they'd all migrated here but, apparently not?'

Antil nodded, his expression serious. 'As I'm sure you've guessed, you have the invasion to thank for that. As soon as my scouts first caught sight of trogs, I ordered the evacuation of the surrounding villages. From what we can tell, there are three gangs in a forty-kilometre radius. We've been tracking their movements. I was dealing with the latest report from Iego when you arrived. Updating my maps,' he smiled at the overflowing mess of parchment that was the desk.

'Just tracking them?' asked Pwtrek.

'For now, until I see them heading to ideal terrain for staging a skirmish. Then we'll get them. Plan everything first, then strike. I'm sure you can both appreciate?' he directed the last question to Spotal and Widrias, both of whom nodded sagely.

'But forgive me, Captain, it doesn't explain the absence of people. All we've seen since arriving are soldiers. If everyone migrated here from the surrounding villages, surely the streets should be heaving?' said Widrias.

Antil smiled. 'Exactly. Duddawl presents itself a target, our walls and towers suggest something to defend. It invites a challenge, especially from creatures like trogs, and our walls are neither tall enough, thick enough, nor manned enough to meet that challenge with impunity. I do not doubt at least one mob of trogs will make their way to our walls before we can meet them in the open. I have too few men to combat all three clusters at once. One, perhaps two, will get through. As soon as they're outside our walls, shooting their blowpipes and slinging their stones, there will be casualties. Imagine all those migrants hemmed in to this little village. Collateral damage of innocents would be inevitable. No, let the trogs be drawn to our walls and face soldiers, and soldiers alone, while citizens are safe elsewhere.'

'I was not aware of another fortification nearby?' asked Spotal, grabbing one of the maps.

'Not a fortification, Captain. As I said, walls beckon a challenge. They are hiding, until it's safe to return,' Antil said.

'Where?' asked Widrias.

'Local knowledge of terrain is essential, as I'm sure you know. There are caves and labyrinths around here, beneath our feet. Some are large enough to hold several villages' worth of calefs for weeks, provided they have enough food coming in from above.'

'They're all underground?' Widrias laughed, surprised.

'A natural fortress provided by the Eastlands themselves. Our country defends us, General, better than the walls built by our own hands ever could.'

'I have another question,' said Pwtrek. 'Your guards met us with some hostility. Said Duddawl was closed. Unusual for the place you ordered migrants to flee to?'

Antil bowed his head in apology. 'Yes. But the last villagers arrived four days ago. All identified and tallied up. We were not expecting any more. Even the isolated farmers and woodsmen are accounted for. Anyone else suggested trouble.'

'Like the assassins you killed two days ago,' nodded Widrias.

'Exactly. But their lack of guile was embarrassing. They tried mingling with an incoming village at one point, but we rooted them out and chased them away. After that, it was your typical attempts at scaling walls, picking locks. All very amateurish, not what we'd expect of Stolach's Guild.'

'New recruits, presumably,' whispered Noswen. 'Stolach's been keeping the Guild busy enough recently. Must have been forced to send them out green, apart from Jonn.'

'Presumably,' agreed Antil, looking her up and down.

'Explains why they met us with suspicion, even with Spotal with us. Probably assumed it was some other ploy,' continued Pwtrek.

'Well, we now know you're no assassins. Thank you for your account, it's been very valuable. I'll send a bird to Muranath with news of the invasion straight away. Chances are, someone else has already sent word, but best be safe. I'll let them know you're on your way as well, if you beat the army there.'

'Thank you, Captain. You continue to provide us with favours,' Widrias bowed.

'Allies in war, General. And hopefully friends in peace, when it comes,' Antil smiled.

'I have one more request, if you will?' Widrias asked, suddenly.

'Go on,' Antil raised an eyebrow.

'This scholar. Might we meet him?'

Lidan brightened. He hadn't considered meeting the scholar, but now the request was spoken, his curiosity blazed in a beacon of inquisitiveness. It must be a sage of considerable wisdom to be so revered and valued by the king to send twelve assassins after him. He suppressed a smile. Could this one be the old sage from the stories? The king's old teacher? How many answers to unknown questions would such a person have? Surely, they would know a way to defeat Stolach, some secret to prove the fonex's undoing? The serpent key may have been a lost cause, but their quest led them straight to this scholar, almost as if Enadir and the four winds wished them to find the answer.

Antil rubbed his chin. 'An unusual request. But I understand the curiosity. To find the one Stolach sent his assassins for! Very dramatic. But she is with the other villagers–'

'She?' repeated Widrias.

'Yes, why?'

'The assassins were under the impression it was a he.'

'That's good news, if anything. Means they're even less likely to find her. But nevertheless, to take you to her would be to take you to the villagers. I hesitate to show strangers, esteemed as you are, where they hide.'

His excitement died as suddenly as it was ignited. Perhaps they weren't destined to find the answer to Stolach's undoing.

'Mistrustful?' Pwtrek raised an eyebrow, ending the word in the faintest growl of disapproval. Widrias silenced him with a frown.

Antil shook his head. 'I must apologise, I'm not being rude, only cautious. I have no doubt you are who you claim to be, the captain's pendant is proof enough of that,' he rummaged beneath his gambeson and drew out a pendant nearly identical to Spotal's, held once again at an angle between the claws of forefinger and thumb. 'But the fewer people who know the secret, the better. What if we gave you this information and you were caught, and tortured, and gave up the location of the villagers? Especially with you heading across country in the midst of an invasion. The risk is too great.'

'A no, then,' nodded Widrias. 'Your reasoning is sound, it was only out of curiosity.'

Antil considered for a moment. 'A maybe. Rest for now. I'll see if we can arrange a meeting for you somewhere above ground, away from the other villagers. No promises, but we'll see.'

'Again, my thanks.'

Antil waved dismissively. 'It's nothing, General. When do you think you'll leave? If you pardon the tone of the question.'

'Two days, if you can accommodate us for that long?' said Widrias.

'Of course. Stay for a week if you wish?' Antil offered.

'No, we agreed with our separated companions on two days. Should they come to you after we've left, would you...?'

Antil nodded. 'Of course. We'll direct them to you. Two neiads and a daemon. They'll be hard to miss. I'll let the watch know. Now, if you don't mind? The barracks are for my men, I'm afraid, but the village infirmary will have beds enough for you. I wouldn't encourage sampling the herbs there, Enadir only knows what half of them do, but there are beds aplenty. I'll ask a medic to pop by to tend to your hurts.'

Widrias bowed his head and Antil gestured them to the door. Antil was already considering his maps by the time they were filing out, lost in his little world of lines, dots, and annotations.

'One final thing,' they stopped. Antil was looking at Spotal. 'I would suggest, Captain Spotal, that you keep to yourself. I have nothing but respect for you, but others… well, they are young and foolish. Most won't recognise your face, but your name precedes you. They don't remember what you did for our people before the… umm… before your… ordeal.'

'Understood, I'll keep my head down,' reassured Spotal without batting an eye.

'Very good. As I said, I have nothing but respect for your past endeavours.'

Spotal nodded again and ushered the rest out. Once outside the room, Lidan opened his mouth to ask the obvious questions, but Pwtrek caught his eye and shook his head, sternly. He frowned and closed his mouth.

Stepping outside, he shivered at the surprising chill.

'Three parties of trogs in the surrounding country,' mused Spotal, the final exchange evidently to remain unacknowledged, at least for now. 'We'll have to ask Antil for their last-known positions before we leave, try to avoid them.'

'I'm sure he'll be happy to let us know,' reassured Widrias. 'I, for one, look forward to a warm meal and a safe berth for the night. Rest as much as you can. Take advantage of our situation. We return to reality in two days.'

*

Lieutenant Iego hammered his fist against the door, scowling even more furiously than usual at being made to wait.

'Damn your guts, you'd better be rotting of some stinking infection to keep us in this bloody rain!'

Lidan winced. The scout's barbed tongue had lashed out at each of them at least once during their brief time in his company. Now it was the turn of whoever guarded the tower.

But such a tower! In the gloom of heavy rainfall, it was difficult to fully appreciate its splendour, its upper floors veiled by rain and darkness. What was visible was enough to convince him of its elegance. The pale sandstone walls, expertly chiselled and cut to perfect curves, rose as an unbroken cylinder on its gentle slope. He imagined an intricately-tiled turret at its head, overlooking the land for leagues into the distance, from Duddawl and beyond, all the way back to the Atrael, trickling in the gully at its foot. Leaded windows representing every colour of the spectrum circled the walls, nestled in their deep, vaulted arches. The door, currently assaulted so vehemently by Iego, was of a dark wood, he couldn't tell what kind, with a heavy brass keyhole at its centre. Flanking it on either side were two lanterns, currently extinguished.

Impressive as it was to behold, he secretly shared Iego's frustrations. It would be much nicer to appreciate the tower from the inside.

'By the four winds! Let us in, damn you!'

He glanced at Spotal, who shrugged nonchalantly. At some point during their stay in Duddawl, Spotal had some altercation with the lieutenant. Words were exchanged, threats were made, and their friend stormed back into the infirmary red-faced and seething. Lidan didn't dare ask the exact details, but mumblings about heated words and raised fists soon reached even his ears. Needless to say, they avoided the scowling scout as much as possible.

It was with a mixture of excitement and resentment, therefore, they met the news of their scheduled meeting with the fabled scholar, but were to be escorted there by Iego. Suffice to say, he didn't seem particularly enamoured with the notion, but was a professional nonetheless and followed Antil's orders.

Fortunately, the scholar's tower was less than half a day's walk from Duddawl. Further than initially expected, but only the slightest detour from their planned route to Ahanemis Lake. Antil's latest charts put all three troglodyte bands at least fifteen miles from them, meaning the only adversary on their journey was the heavy autumn downpour.

'Open. The. Damn. Door!'

Each bellow was punctuated with another booming punch to the heavy wood. Iego drew his foot back, snarling, as if to kick the door in, when he stopped. A latch clicked loudly and the door was swung open by another calef, also in light armour similar to Iego.

'Sergeant Shael,' growled the lieutenant. 'Once again, you outdo yourself.'

The calef's initial friendly smile disappeared. He blanched, mouth opening and closing stupidly as he searched for an excuse. Iego growled incomprehensibly and shouldered him out the way to escape the rain.

Lidan followed the others in, instantly struck by the surprising heat inside, and smiled gratefully at Shael, who frowned by the door, oblivious to their thanks as he continued to struggle for an acceptable excuse to pacify the lieutenant.

Unfortunately, pacification didn't seem to be on Pwtrek's mind, as he leaned over to Spotal to whisper loudly enough for everyone to hear.

'You'd think a scout was used to a bit of rain?'

'Take your sarcasm back to the Northlands, you bull. Nothing wrong with rain, my irritation comes at being caught in it for no other reason than satisfying your damned curiosity,' snarled Iego, wiping his forehead.

'You were caught in it because that's where your orders led you, Lieutenant,' sneered Spotal. 'I'd expect you to follow them without complaint.'

'Soldiers blindly following *your* orders are what got you in your current situation, isn't it, *Captain*?'

'At least his men were happy to follow his orders,' spat Pwtrek.

'I'd rather my men frustrated and alive, than happy and *dead*.'

'Silence!' Widrias pounded the pommel of his greatsword against the closed door. 'All of you. We are here for information, not curiosity. We are all wet, we are all cold, it doesn't help with our mood. Let's get warm and dry and do what we came to do. You. Shael, is it? Can you take us to the scholar?'

Shael obliged, beckoning them to the spiralling staircase to their left, built of a deep, rich wood. As they climbed, Lidan glanced from Iego to Spotal and back again. Spotal's men were dead? Was that why he was so secretive about his past, because all his men were killed? But what about blindly following orders? Did Spotal do something, pass or follow a bad order? Now was probably not the time to ask. It never seemed the right time.

He ran his hand along the intricately-carved banister, fingers exploring the ridges and furrows. It was only when he was halfway up, he realised it wasn't a random pattern, but a wonderful zoology. A mighty stag in the hunt, his princely antlers proudly raised as a pack of slavering hounds followed. A leopard lounging in a tree, the carcass of its latest prey in its claws. Wild horses racing one another through a valley of tall grass. Eagles soaring together under a blazing sun. Hares standing tall on a hillside, their snouts turned to the wind. Wild boars turning up the earth, in search of mushrooms or buried acorns. Each scene blended beautifully into one another, as if the whole word were represented in this intricately stylised tapestry. It was a wonder it hadn't worn down from the passing of greasy hands over the years. As the thought struck him, he snapped his hand back quicker than from a sizzling stove. The rest of the way, he appreciated the carvings with his eyes alone.

At the first floor, Shael led them down a short corridor to a door, ajar, with the flickering warmth of an open fire beckoning. As soon as he entered, the heat nearly knocked Lidan back. There was the fireplace, a merry blaze dancing behind the iron rake. A tower of chopped wood flanked each side and the whistle of the heavy copper teapot suspended above the flames welcomed their arrival. The tall windows were shuttered, the walls lined with bookshelves. Beneath the largest window was a heavy table, strewn with glass trinkets, herbs, bottles, pipes, copper pots and delicate iron tongs. A few simple wooden stools surrounded the table, but looked pathetically flimsy compared to the two overstuffed armchairs dominating the space, facing the fireplace.

'Come, dry yourselves,' said someone in one of the chairs, invisible behind the bulging cushions. 'Hang your cloaks by the pipes over there. No, not in front of the fire, Lieutenant, or we won't enjoy its company. By the pipes.'

Lidan followed the others to the left of the fireplace, where a network of iron pipes as wide as his thigh covered the bare wall. Someone had cleverly designed hooks into the rivets of the pipes, perfect for hanging their sodden clothes. His hand accidentally brushed the iron as he hooked his cloak. Yelping, he jumped back. Unlike the banister, the pipe actually *was* like a stove.

'Careful,' said the voice, 'your cloaks wouldn't dry very much if it weren't hot.'

From his new position, he could finally see the speaker. She was old and tiny, wrapped in several wool shawls. Her frame was so thin, Pwtrek could have easily shared the armchair with her, tucked away into the depths of one of its corners as she was. Her skin had deeper wrinkles than a farmer's furrows, and her mouth had a sunken appearance, exaggerated by the shadows of the flames. Spotal's pointed ears stood tall and broad on his head, but hers were drooping and tired. The claws at her fingertips, clutching the shawls around her shoulders, curved sharply into half-circles, their tips blunt and frayed.

'Find yourselves a seat,' she beckoned, 'make yourselves comfortable. There's an awful chill outside, but here is nice and warm. My name is Lenai. I am the master of this tower and keeper of its secrets. Shael? Would you fetch cups for my guests?'

Shael paused, unsure, before Iego nodded. The banging of cupboard doors filled the silence as they searched for seats. Widrias took the other armchair. There weren't enough stools for them all and Lidan found himself standing awkwardly next to the fireplace, trying not to lean too close to either the steaming pipes or the blazing flames.

'Sit with me, my darling,' crooned the calef, patting the expanse of empty cushion by her side. 'I don't take up much space.'

'Thank you, but I'm fine here,' he smiled politely.

'Nonsense, you'll faint if you stand there. I know I like it toasty. Poor Shael never stays here for too long,' she cackled.

'Honestly, thank you, but I'll be alright,' he glanced at Shael, on his hands and knees in front of a cupboard, pulling out all manner of pots and pans in search of the elusive cups.

'I insist. Sit here.'

'Honestly-'

'You'd do me a favour in keeping me company?'

'It's very kind-'

'Poor old woman that I am. I'd love to have a nice boy like you for company.'

'Really, I don't-'

'Lidan,' Widrias interrupted, impatiently. 'Just sit.'

Shrugging, he relented. Admittedly, it was quite unbearably hot next to the fire and pipes, and his clothes were already sticking to the sweat of his back. He carefully sat next to the old woman, who smiled warmly and patted his shoulder. Up close, she smelled of rosemary and lavender, overpoweringly so, as if trying to stifle the smell of something else, more unpleasant. Spotal smirked at him from his seat, as did Pwtrek, looking comically oversized on such a delicate three-legged milking stool.

'Good. Now, I know some names. You're Lidan, was it? Good. A surname?'

'Dimarr,' he replied, trying to drop his shoulder so her hand would slide off. It didn't.

'Ah, from the west of Dailas,' she nodded.

'Yes, the grasslands south of the desert.'

'Lovely. You, of course, are Widrias Gesharr. You need no introduction, my dear. Neither do you, Spotal Lasaai, welcome home. Or would the northern kingdoms be your home now, hmm?'

'Wherever will have me,' he said, jokingly.

'The Council, then, must be your new home,' she pursed her lips thoughtfully. 'Although, I suppose they'll take anything in their plight. No offense, of course, to either of you.'

Lidan frowned. That was unkind of her, this was Spotal's home, to suggest otherwise was cruel. No wonder his friend seemed so haunted when his own kin made such comments. He glanced at Spotal, but the calef wore the resigned half-smile of experience. In many ways, it was worse than a scowl. He regretted taking the seat.

'How about you? Your name, mighty juggernaut?'

'Pwtrek. Mestax,' he added, after her prompting smile.

'And you?'

'Auran Meerl.'

'Well, we can say with some confidence which of you is a Northlander and which a Southlander. Didn't need your names for that. But Mestax… from the far North, are you?'

'Indeed. In the foothills of the Shadil Mountains, by the River of Sekid.'

'How wonderful! Never been myself, must be quite different to these Eastlands?'

'Quite different,' he nodded.

'Almost as different as your Southlands, Auran?'

Auran nodded but remained silent.

'I'm afraid I don't know enough about your homeland to impress with any great knowledge. Did you live in the Daiwen Jungle? Or Maralen, jewel of the south?'

'A village on the Werlit. A few days from Daiwen.'

'Lovely. Ah! Thank you, Shael. Now, fetch the pot from the fire and pour us all some tea, would you?'

'He's not your servant, Lenai!' snapped Iego, suddenly. 'He's here to protect you, not see to your every whim.'

'He is here to do as he is told, Iego,' she replied, coolly. 'That is his station, for as long as he is with me. When that station is over, he returns to your command, as I'm sure he's overjoyed to be reminded. But now, his exact orders are to look after me. If that extends to helping me with my tea, so be it.'

'Antil will know about this,' Iego glowered.

'My dear, I'm sure he already does. He has other things to worry about than a soldier helping an old woman with her day-to-day life,' Lenai smoothed her shawls fastidiously.

'Just pour some tea for her,' said Widrias, rubbing the bridge of his nose.

Iego glared at him, but nodded. Shael filled their cups with the boiling tea, but Lidan was already too hot to drink it and set it aside to cool down. The calef, however, drank deeply, clutching her cup with both hands, greedily taking in the warmth.

'Oh, fetch me the honey, would you, Shael?'

He returned with a clay pot and spoon. She mixed two laden spoons into her cup and drank again, smiling with satisfaction. Lidan blinked in surprise. Where Spotal, Iego, and every other calef he'd met had mouths of gleaming white fangs, hers were black, rotten stumps. She caught his stare, and winked.

'An old woman must have her pleasure from something. Mine is sweetness.'

Smiling weakly, he turned away. Everyone had rotten teeth, from his old village to Crastalan to the soldiers in the Council. Pwtrek was missing more than a few, even Auran had a discoloured tooth in an otherwise pearly smile, but he'd assumed calefs were above it. Spotal's fangs were so pristine, as were every other calef he'd encountered, dead or alive. To see such decay, such rot in her mouth, a member of a race so particular about their delicate beauty, was startling. He'd always assumed they were above such human vices.

With a start, he realised the source of the underlying fetor. The rot took its toll on her breath. No amount of perfume would ever mask it. In the stifling heat, its pungency was overpowering. He turned his head away, searching for an escape. Taking her offered seat was a mistake.

'Perfect,' she purred, after swilling the sweet drink around her mouth before swallowing. 'To what occasion do I owe this visit?'

'I apologise for the interruption to your routine,' began Widrias.

'Nonsense. It is welcome. Any excuse to leave those caves. Far too much of a chill down there,' she sighed.

'Lenai,' growled Iego, disapprovingly.

'What, Iego? I hate them. Making me stay down there when this lovely hearth is right above. Ridiculous.'

'Lenai!' Iego barked, blazing. 'You betray us!'

'I do not. It's true. Why should I stay in those caves when my tower is so well defended? Let the villagers stay down there with the cold and dark, nothing but bats and rats and fungi for company. I should stay in my warm home.'

'The caves are beneath the tower?' asked Widrias.

Iego stood suddenly, sending his stool flying. He pointed an accusatory finger at Lenai, trembling with rage. 'You are despicable. Foul. As untrustworthy as your concoctions and trinkets.'

'I am,' she chuckled.

'You have no shame!' he continued.

'I haven't.'

'All for your own grim entertainment. You would risk the suffering of our people.'

'Oh, what risk, Iego?' she rolled her eyes. 'The Council are our allies. Widrias has commanded our armies before. Spotal is too eager for Lleunedd's approval to do anything wrong. I suspect these others are trustworthy enough.'

'You think so? Spotal's mistakes have already caused the deaths of thousands of innocents. Give him a chance and his blundering will lead to even more.'

Lidan felt his heart quicken. Thousands of innocents? Because of Spotal? He glanced at his friend, to see his reaction, waiting for an explosion of rage, the flash of his jian at such an outrageous lie. It didn't come. He remained as he was, sipping his tea, albeit with a clenched jaw and growing flush of anger.

Pwtrek rose in fury, looming over Iego. But he wasn't finished.

'And the others?' Iego snorted. 'Trustworthy? See her?' he pointed at Noswen, hiding in the shadows by the bookshelves. 'You didn't notice her. The hanex. The black-hearted assassin. Oh yes, I know who you are. Rumours of Stolach's pet nestling under the Council's wing have not escaped us. The calef prisoner you gave us confirmed it.'

'The assassin?' Lenai leaned forward in her chair. She pulled a pair of spectacles from the folds of her shawl and balanced them on the tip of her nose. Shael's hand shot to the short sword at his hip, suddenly tense.

'How interesting,' Lenai continued, taking another swig of tea.

'Not interesting, evil. And you, pretender!' Iego turned on Spotal. 'She killed Major Cetril. Buried the knife into his back with her own hand. But you sit here with her, share her food, and do nothing? A more damning conviction of your character than any other. The killer of your own father, a hero of our race. You are scum.'

'She has paid her penance,' said Spotal, finally standing, raising his voice to meet Iego's challenge. 'She has shown the quality of her character. Her past transgressions were done under the influence of Stolach. He was the evil at her heart, and she left him. I trust her more than you, Iego.'

'More than I?' his face turned beetroot red. 'Than I? I hold my honour. I do no wrong. I fight for my people.'

'As do I!' shouted Spotal.

'Spotal, sit down,' said Widrias, but was ignored.

'You fight for your own agenda. You care nothing for the country, only for your name,' Iego turned his accusatory finger to Spotal.

'You know nothing of me. Everything I do is for my people.'

'Your people? Who are they? Nobody in the Eastlands will have you. You are your only person. You fight for yourself and that's it. You don't even fight for your family, or you would not tolerate her.'

A sudden crack and wave of heat exploded from the hearth, which blazed a magnificent purple for a second. Lidan jumped and recoiled in his chair. It was then he noticed Lenai's outstretched arm, retreating slowly back to the confines of her shawls. A stunned silence replaced the raised voices as they blinked stupidly, trying to comprehend what they'd witnessed.

'Magicks,' whispered Pwtrek.

'Alchemy, my dear,' corrected Lenai. 'To shut up squabbling boys.'

'We weren't squabbling,' snapped Iego. 'And you mustn't use your trickery. It is almost as shameful as this–'

'Enough!' barked Widrias. 'Your behaviour is shameful, Lieutenant. To speak to your superior officer in such a way is an offense worthy of court-martial.'

'He is not my officer.'

'Like it or not, he is still a captain of the calefin army. As are you a lieutenant of the same. Know. Your. Place.' Widrias punctuated each word with a tap of his scabbard against the floor.

Iego curled his lip in distaste. 'Too much of what is happening here is wrong. Lenai betraying our secrets, the assassin, this *captain*,' he shook his head. 'I am far from being the worst offender.'

'Yet you still offend. Be silent, or remove yourself,' Widrias barked.

'My place is here, to keep an eye on these traitors if nothing else.'

'Then silence it is. I have questions and your shouting does nothing but delay,' Widrias turned to Shael. 'You can take that hand away from your sword. For your own sake, don't draw it.'

Shael glanced at Iego. The lieutenant, jaw bulging to control his rage, nodded curtly. Shael slowly moved his hand away.

'Good. Now, shall we discuss?' continued Widrias.

'At your liberty, General Widrias,' smiled Lenai.

'Well, let's start at the basics. I know next to nothing about you, yet clearly you are a woman of some standing. Who are you, Lenai?'

'Difficult question to answer, what are you after? My past? My family history? My favourite flavour of herbal tea?' she chuckled.

'Your role. Your significance to your people,' reiterated Widrias.

'Ah, that would depend on who you ask,' she slurped.

'How about a non-pedantic answer? They said you were a scholar. Spotal mentioned you were an alchemist.'

'Both are true.'

'Lenai. Please. Give us a straight answer,' he shook his head in exasperation. 'Assassins were after you.'

'Truly?' her eyes widened in genuine surprise. 'When was this?'

Widrias leaned forward. 'I will tell you if you answer my simple questions. There's no need to make this difficult.'

'He has no sense of humour,' she said in Lidan's ear in a mock whisper. He suppressed a shudder at her warm breath.

'Scholar, alchemist, teacher, sage, knowing woman, gwrch,' she settled back into her chair. 'They call me many things. I have spent my life in study. I once travelled the lands as an avid student, searching for knowledge. A long time ago, I worked in Muranath. I taught our poor king in a few of his academic studies. There was a time I was entertained as an advisor. But all things end, and I was eventually let go.'

'This is your retirement home?' asked Widrias.

'Winds! No! Far from retired. I came here when released from my tutorial duties to continue my education. This tower has been here for centuries. Its upper levels are filled with books. Most of them duplicate texts, I must admit. It's a pity the libraries of Crastalan and Rhetta Mountains are so inaccessible, otherwise I might have acquired more original texts,' she giggled mischievously.

'What did you hope to learn from here?' asked Widrias.

'Ah. There's a better question. My library may be small and inferior in comparison to the two great libraries, but it is specialised. The subject? Alchemy. An ancient science long abandoned by the rest of Enadir. The old tower-master taught me what he could. Now I have taken over.'

'So you are knowledgeable and experienced, you have an insight into the calefin court, into Lleunedd's education. Plenty of things Stolach would be interested in. But mostly the alchemy,' Widrias rubbed his beard.

'Indeed?'

'Yes. He sent assassins for you,' he repeated.

'Finally, the interesting part!' she seemed to relish in the excitement of the situation.

'Twelve. They searched for you here, but couldn't find you, then went to Duddawl. After that, they split up. One group remained around Duddawl, another explored the surrounding villages for you. Duddawl's garrison dealt with the ones at their doorstep. We ran into the others. They mistook Spotal for you.' He paused. 'At a distance, obviously.'

She chuckled and winked at Spotal. 'An insult to your handsome face, Captain Spotal.'

Widrias ignored her. 'We dealt with them. Kept one alive as prisoner, a treacherous calef named Banil, do you know him?'

She shook her head. 'Never met him.'

Widrias pursed his lips and shrugged. 'Never mind. He said their mission was to find you and take you to Strikk. Apparently you have some sort of alchemical weapon, presumably to use against Muranath?'

'Weapon?' she frowned. 'I know of no such thing.'

'You're sure?' Widrias pressed.

'Absolutely.'

'Lenai,' growled Iego. 'If you're trying to protect one of your little experiments from us…'

'I'm not, Iego,' she replied, firmly. Lidan blinked in surprise at the forcefulness of her denial.

'Because if you are, and are threatening the security of our nation…' Iego continued.

'I told you. I'm not,' she glared at him.

'Then what do you do?' asked Widrias. 'Forgive my ignorance, but alchemy is not a topic I'm familiar with. I doubt any of us have much experience in it. Perhaps if Gwahl were here you could have a better conversation.'

'Gwahl the daemon?' Lenai chuckled, her frown melting away as suddenly as her honey in hot tea. 'Unlikely. Those backwards old things don't want any progression of science. As soon as you mention alchemy or magicks they lose their minds. Entitled old fools. Think they can guard all the secrets forever.'

'Surely if daemons disapprove of alchemy, that should tell you all you need about its pursuit?' muttered Pwtrek, gravely.

'Absolutely not,' she protested. 'I have made advancements you would not believe! All for good.'

'Like turning lead to gold?' joked Spotal, with a smile.

'Cheeky thing,' she winked at him again.

'Like what?' asked Widrias.

'Oh, purified oils of different kinds, used for bodily ointments, some for lamps and such. I make substances to purify water, fertilize our crops, preserve our foods. I've helped make stronger mortar and cement for our buildings, and more. Name it, and I, through the study of alchemy, have assisted in its improvement,' she settled back into her chair, somewhat smugly.

'Including warfare?' Widrias cocked his head.

She exhaled. She might have muttered something under her breath, but too quietly for Lidan to be sure.

'Not directly,' she huffed.

'Ah! Indirectly?' Widrias nodded.

'Purified oils burn well, for one,' she shrugged.

'That might be what they were after?' Widrias tapped his chin, thoughtfully.

She thought for a second, pursing her lips. 'Perhaps. But I don't keep any here, and my discoveries are quite common knowledge in the country. They wouldn't need me for it.'

'Is there anything in particular you are renowned for?' asked Auran, breaking his usual stoical silence. 'Something unobtainable elsewhere.'

She turned her rotting smile to the Southlander. He held her gaze, perhaps a little too well from Lidan's perspective. Clearly, he was not the only one to notice the stumps of her dentition.

'Now you mention it, my dear, there is something,' she murmured.

'What?' asked Widrias.

'Well, you've seen it already! My little colour-changing powder,' she purred.

A pause. They glanced at each other confusedly. Pwtrek gasped, and stared into his mug suspiciously, drawing another giggle from Lenai. Lidan looked into his own mug. No powder, only boiled tea-leaves, in a familiar golden liquid. Her honey, maybe? Changing colour when crystalized? No. His head snapped around as realisation dawned. She caught his eye and her smile reached her ears.

'This young one has it.'

'What you threw into the fire!' he blurted. 'Turned the flames purple!'

'Of course,' nodded Widrias. 'I thought it was just a parlour trick. Foolish.'

'It is what one makes of it,' she replied, draining the last of her tea and brandishing the cup. She held it for a second, before shaking it impatiently. 'Shael! More, please!'

Shael jumped forward, retrieving the proffered mug and returning it a moment later, once again steaming and sickly sweet.

'Explain, please?' prompted Widrias.

'It can be used for a parlour trick, yes, but also so much more' she smiled, as if a mother describing her child. 'It is a substance I invented. In those horrid, now-over-populated caves beneath my tower, to be exact. A little white powder I call saltpetre. If you saw the crystals you'd know why. The purple flames were an incidental finding quite by accident, but they are pretty. Other substances make different colours. Stage magicians often use them to encourage a sense of awe and wonder. I know of at least two who buy my saltpetre for such uses.'

'I doubt Strikk would want it for the spectacle of purple flames,' Widrias shook his head. 'What else?'

'I use it in my fertilizer, probably not much good for a soldier, unless he plans to grow his own crops while at siege. It can be used to make salted meat, again potentially useful for a soldier but not as a weapon,' she mused. 'It has some medical properties if used in certain doses. Perhaps his medics would want it?'

Widrias rubbed his beard. 'I'm not convinced. Anything else?'

She was quiet for a long time, deep in thought, taking the occasional sip from her mug. Lidan's mind wandered. Who'd have thought this one substance could have such a range of properties and uses? What was to say there wasn't another property, currently unknown to its creator, discovered by another? She admitted to selling it to magicians, so there would surely be many throughout

Enadir with access to its mysteries. It was far from a stretch to consider the possibility someone might have experimented with it enough times to discover a deadlier use.

'Not that I know of,' she finally admitted. 'The uses I've already listed are extraordinary enough for this one powder, are they not? It doesn't need anything else to make it wonderful.'

'True,' agreed Widrias. 'I suppose the uses you've given so far could be considered an indirect weapon… they would certainly supplement Strikk's armies. How much of it do you produce?'

'Not much. Its production isn't exactly straightforward, and most of it goes towards the fertilizers, what little is left over I give over to medics and apothecaries, then even less is sold at Tonnis Harbour to travellers, including the aforementioned magicians and illusionists.'

'Perhaps if we could see how it's manufactured?' suggested Widrias.

'Absolutely not!' Iego stepped forward. 'You just want to see the caves! You know too much already, I will not have you see any more.'

'Nonsense, Iego,' scolded Lenai. 'My laboratories are in an entirely different tunnel system to the civilians. You really think I'd let you lump all those people in caves anywhere near my experiments? It could be a disaster. Imagine a child wandering up to my tools… it doesn't bear thinking about. I can take them down with absolutely no risk of seeing any of our poor countrymen.'

'I see no benefit to such a risk.'

'I do,' replied Widrias.

'And what is that?' demanded Iego.

'A general's insight,' he replied, coldly.

Lidan smirked at Iego's expression. He deserved to be put down after behaving like he did to Spotal.

'I can take you there?' Lenai offered, again.

'Gladly, m'lady.'

She snorted, shuffling forward from the depths of the chair until her feet finally reached the floor. 'I'm far from a lady. Come on. I'd put those cloaks back on. Deathly cold down there.'

She led them back to the staircase, but instead of descending, as Lidan expected, she led them up two more flights of the beautifully-carved stairs to a painting at the end of a landing. A magnificent peacock, tail in full flourish, but divided into four sections, to represent each season. Its plumage gradually turned from a pale green, to the traditional rich blue-turquoise, to a deep red and orange, and finally greys and whites. A truly beautiful piece of art. Completely ignored. Lidan's attention was seized by the hidden door opened at the touch of Lenai's hand to the peacock's head, releasing a series of clicks of well-oiled latches to swing open on its smooth hinges in the adjacent wall. The darkness of the hidden passageway beckoned. Spotal laughed, Pwtrek gasped, even Auran whistled softly. It was so well-concealed he'd never have guessed its existence.

'Clever, eh?' smiled Lenai. 'This passageway circles all the way down the circumference of the wall. It's one of the reasons why the rooms feel so much smaller than they should, given the diameter of the tower. A good few feet are lost to the passageway. Inconvenient, but necessary.'

She lit a hand-held lamp and brandished it forth, leading them to darkness. He expected dank, damp, cold, but it was warm. Warmer, even, than the corridor. He realised why when his arm brushed the boiling hot metal of a pipe. This passageway doubled as part of the tower's central heating system.

This in mind, it was immediately obvious when they made the transition from tower wall to underground tunnel. Not that there was a change to the stone of the stairs, or the walls, or the width or height of the tunnel, but the heat disappeared in an instant. Once the great boiler at the heart of the building's cellar was above, it was the dank unpleasantness he'd first anticipated that awaited. He heard Lenai complain from ahead.

'See what I mean? Now you understand the pain of my predicament. Horrible and cold. Watch your footing. Always gets a bit damp underfoot, nothing to be done about it, I'm afraid.'

Despite her warning, he lost his balance a few times. She was so far ahead her dim light hardly reached him, and more often than not each step was taken in blind faith. He might have prayed to the north winds to guide him, but underground, the winds would never hear him.

Their descent finally brought them to a wide chamber and he stumbled a final time as his foot searched for a non-existent step. Spotal caught his arm, steadying him.

'Yes, don't fall on your face now,' cackled Lenai. 'Not much longer, just a few more tunnels.'

It was eerily quiet in the caves. Claustrophobic in the complete darkness, with only Lenai's little lamp to penetrate it. He shivered. He completely understood the scholar's irritation at being confined to this prison when such luxury dangled tantalizingly above. But wait. He frowned and cocked his head. It wasn't silent. The plink-plink of water, clinging to the sharp tips of stalactites before dropping to the flat heads of stalagmites below. Crunching boots on the fine dusting of sediment on top of the smooth rock underfoot. Something else, a shuffle, like leaves in a stiff autumn breeze. And there, underneath it all, a trickle and slap of a stream, somewhere ahead.

He was right. Lenai soon led them through a series of short tunnels and chambers to a wide cavern, this one illuminated by sparse glimpses of natural light from a shallow opening at one end, through which flowed a tributary of the Atrael. The moan of the wind and hammering of rain could be heard beyond the curtain of ferns and shrubs that partly obscured the opening. Its ceiling was high, lost in darkness, with the tips of the largest stalactites hovering twelve feet above the ground. Still, he heard the shuffling. Initially, he suspected the vegetation at the cave opening, but it was too loud for that, too enveloping to be from that one tiny source.

Gradually, more and more of the chamber became visible as Lenai lit several additional lamps. Her laboratory, or at least that's what it appeared to be, was situated in a recess. Three high tables, one wood, one metal, one stone, each strewn with a number of devices similar to those in the tower. There were shelves piled with pots and pouches suspended above sacks and barrels, their contents to be guessed at. Most curious, however, was the tarpaulin stretched taut above it all, held in place by rope, hook, and pole, like a bizarre tent.

Lenai climbed into a high stool by the wooden table and twirled in her seat to face them.

'Well, welcome to my lab.'

'It's certainly a sight,' said Widrias. 'I won't bother trying to guess at the nature of the work you undertake. I'm sure it'll all go straight over my simple head.'

'Undoubtedly,' she cackled.

'But I can guess it culminates in the production of your saltpetre?'

'Very good. It does.'

'Why down here?' asked Spotal, looking around. 'Why not make it upstairs? It would be more comfortable?'

'It would,' she agreed. 'Practicality, however, trumps comfort in this situation.'

'Is the process of its production…volatile?' mused Spotal.

'It can be, yes, but that's not the reason why I do it down here. I tinker with plenty of things upstairs that result in rather impressive conflagrations,' she sniggered. 'Shael will vouch for that.'

Shael rolled his eyes indiscreetly, drawing another snort from the scholar.

'What's practical about working down here?' continued Spotal, tapping his chin thoughtfully.

'I'll let you figure it out,' she settled back into her stool, leaning against the wooden table.

'The cold?' suggested Widrias. 'Does the temperature affect the ingredients or the production?'

'Not quite,' she shook her head.

'Space,' said Pwtrek, assuredly. 'You need space for it. Or air.'

'No, notice how I've confined my laboratory to this crevice. I don't make use of the whole cave for the production.'

'The Atrael,' muttered Auran, kicking a small stone into the river's tributary.

'Yes!' Lenai clapped her hands. 'In part, anyway. Extrapolate on it.'

'You need a constant supply of fresh water for the experiment?'

'No.' she sank back, irritated again.

Lidan frowned. This was pointless. They already knew what she was making. Its use to Stolach may be a mystery, but they'd established its wonderous nature, it had many applications a clever man would find useful. This guessing at its production was unnecessary. Besides, it was cold and he'd rather be away and walking than cooped up here.

He stopped listening to their conversation, each suggestion denied by Lenai, letting it melt into a background drone. The shuffling was still there. Louder than ever before. Maybe there was a forest outside? He couldn't remember passing one on the way, but the wind and rain could easily have obscured his view. Turning away from the others, the regarded the cave again. Nothing unusual, just an ordinary cave. Droplets continued to drop from the stalactites in a steady rhythm. A particularly large droplet hit the floor in front of him. Perhaps it was just an auditory illusion, a small shuffle amplified a thousand times over, bouncing off the high cave walls a thousand times.

He frowned, staring at the fat droplet. It hadn't landed on a stalagmite, but on the floor in between. He crouched for a closer look. It wasn't a droplet at all. Small, black, it looked more like a piece of dirt fallen from the roof. Looking up, his breath caught.

The roof was alive. A pulsating, writhing carpet flowing in the recesses between the stalactites. Like being in the mouth of a beast, seeing its cheeks move between the embrasures of its stone teeth. He rose to his feet. Finally, the source of the constant shuffle was revealed.

'Bats!' he exclaimed.

'Exactly!' Lenai cried, clapping her hands. 'The young one has it right again.'

'Bats?' asked Widrias, dubiously eyeing the colony. 'What have they got to do with saltpetre?'

'Oh, everything. Specifically, these bats, in this colony, in this cave,' she smiled.

'How?' asked Widrias.

'The Atrael is rich in minerals, it's why the bramble plains are so bountiful, why our land is so fruitful, our roots feeding off the rich waters. Some of those minerals make up saltpetre. Bats, all bats, naturally produce a specific compound in their droppings which can be turned to saltpetre. These bats, constantly drinking the waters of the Atrael in this little cave, have an even higher concentration of such minerals within their bodies. Their excrement is a bounty. I collect it from the floor and use it for my pretty white crystals.'

'I understand,' nodded Widrias. 'I won't pretend to understand how you turn one substance to the other, but that is the nature of alchemy.'

'Indeed,' she smiled. 'So! That is it. My secrets exposed. Do you have any further curiosities for me to expel?'

Widrias smiled. 'I think not. We've taken up enough of your time already.'

'Hardly. It was a welcome distraction,' she shuffled down from her stool.

'Although, if it's no trouble, would we be able to keep a small sample of your sal–'

'Absolutely not!' interrupted Iego, blazing.

'It is the scholar's decision to impart what gift she chooses, Lieutenant,' said Widrias, keeping his eyes on the old calef.

Her eyes wrinkled into a deep smile, but she shook her head. 'I'm afraid in this instance I agree with Iego. If my saltpetre is sought by Stolach, for whatever reason, I'd rather not put it into the hands of one travelling through danger. Just to be safe.'

Widrias bowed his head. 'I understand completely.'

'So that's everything?' Iego growled.

'I believe so,' Widrias nodded.

'Finally. Follow me. I'll take you out.'

*

'There's the Atrael. Keep following it east and you'll reach its natural end within a few miles. It's mostly small streams and creeks from then on. When they get to less than half a foot in breadth, stop following them. They wind through the country in all directions, follow them and you'll get lost. Instead, keep heading east and you'll reach Ahanemis.'

'Thank you, Iego,' nodded Widrias.

'Last reports put the nearest trogs three miles away, heading away from you. You shouldn't run across them.'

'Your scouts are truly remarkable. Thank you for your reassurance.'

'Beyond that, I can't tell you anything more,' Iego continued, seemingly ignoring the general's compliments. 'There were sightings of outrider patrols into the distance, but they were too far away to be of concern to us at this moment. We didn't track them, so they could be anywhere. I would be wary if you find evidence of horses.'

'Again, thank you. Extend our thanks to your captain. You have all been very kind to us,' Widrias nodded.

'If your friends arrive, we'll send them your way.'

'If there's anything we can do in return?'

Iego sniffed and flicked his ears, clearing them of the water droplets building up on their pointed tips. The rain quickly replaced them with more.

'You have seen many of our secrets in your short visit. It is only because of your reputation my seniors allowed such breaches of confidentiality. It was unwise of them. I ask only this of you, for the protection of the citizens in those caves, for the secrets of our alchemist. Should you run into any enemies and engage in battle, fight to the death. Don't let them force the secrets from you.'

'We have not seen eye-to-eye on many things, Iego, but I respect your devotion to protecting your people. We will not reveal the secrets.'

Iego nodded. 'May the four winds protect you.'

With a final nod to Widrias, he turned and walked into the darkness, back to Duddawl. He was soon enveloped by the rain and lost from sight.

'Well, that's that,' said Spotal, with a snort. 'A welcome rest and an interesting detour.'

'Detour?' asked Widrias.

'To the tower, and the cave beneath,' clarified Spotal.

'Ah, yes, well, I honestly just wanted to meet the scholar and find out why Stolach wanted her. I only asked to see her lab in the hope it would take us past the villagers in the tunnels. It would have been interesting to see their condition and the condition of their new home.'

'Do you suppose he'll keep searching for her?' asked Pwtrek.

'Possibly. Depends on how much importance he puts on her saltpetre. I wish we knew exactly why he wanted it. It's a shame we couldn't get some,' he sighed in frustration. 'I'm sure Gwahl might have given us some insight.'

'We can ask when he returns,' smiled Spotal.

'Quite. Well, back to it. Noswen, if you'd be so kind to scout ahead? Let's go.'

*

Rain was falling. He couldn't see it. He couldn't even hear it. Nobody came in with damp clothes to give him such information. No, he could smell it beneath the door. He could feel the drum on the roof reverberating through the walls. Rain was good. A storm was better. Thunder and lightning were powerful allies to the anointed. One could hide in near plain sight when the crashing, crackling forks of energy coursed the skies. Today was no storm. The air didn't have the tell-tale heaviness, the ripple of static, or the onerous sense of impending explosiveness to precede a true storm. Today was not the day, but tomorrow, or maybe the day after, the day would come.

Not that it mattered. He was patient. He'd learned patience the hard way. Thieves often learned the hard way. But he was more than a thief. He was thief, burglar, woodsman, traveller, assassin. He was victim, villain, betrayer, betrayed, taker, taken, killer, mourner. His thirst was his relief, his rage his calm. His master, his enemy. His friends, his foe.

He was alone. Always alone.

Stolach didn't understand him. Neither did Lleunedd, or any of the southern scum. How could they? But the northern kingdoms would accept him. One day, they would welcome him back with open arms. When they saw what he'd done for them. And then, when they were free of Muranath and Crastalan and all the other nobilities who blindly pressed their motives on them, the isolated villages of the north would be free to help one another. Free to come to each other's aid.

He scratched at a raised scar on his calf.

Stolach may not have understood him, but he certainly helped. Such things he'd learned in those shadowed halls of the guild of assassins. Of course, he was too old to be fully integrated into the guild, not that he cared. He was a calef, after all, not the pet killer of a fonex. But their subtleties impressed him. As a thief, he knew the crippling impact a light touch could have on a person's life, and the assassins took it to another level. His past experience, his depth of knowledge, much of it handed down from his long-dead father, combined with the new knowledge provided by the guild, moulded him into one of the deftest servants at Stolach's disposal. Even the Owl observed his abilities with thinly-veiled awe.

But greater than his touch, his stealth, his uncanny ability to infiltrate, was his deceit. But that was only natural. The world had deceived him too many times not to learn how to mirror its duplicity. It was a cold, ugly place, dressed in riches and masks of compassion. One had to adapt to avoid its perils.

He kept scratching. His skin burned. He felt blood beneath his fingernails.

If the situation called for kindness, he was kind. If it called for strength, he was strong. If it called for weakness, he would let a boy beat him with the hilt of his sabre, let his companions tie him up, and put him in a calefin gaol.

It was not only his targets whom he deceived. Jonn and his fellow assassins were also enemies. He'd worn this face of weakness throughout the whole mission. Nobody could know his true face. Nobody did. Not on any of his past missions, none of his old companions or enemies. Nobody knew who he truly was. Survival demanded it.

Granted, he'd made an error with the scholar. The Owl, on briefing them of this mission, said the scholar would help Strikk destroy Muranath. Perfect. To see the slimy, filthy, southern scum destroyed in their own cesspit would have been glorious. But his error, an honest mistaken identity, led him to a hero of the north. He could have slipped his bonds and slit the Council members' throats at any point in their journey to Duddawl, but to what purpose? Spotal was a champion. A true hero. A kindred spirit if there ever were one. He simply didn't realise it.

His fingernails caught on something hard within his leg. He wiped his bloody hands on his tunic, dabbed at the oozing scar with the hem of his cloak, and with nimble fingers, grasped the object. With a tug, he pulled it from his own flesh. A gold-plated tube, impregnated into his leg by his own hand, the inert metal coating preventing his body from rejecting it. Holding both ends, he unscrewed it and its contents fell into his lap; a pin, a clip, and thin, hardy tongs. Less practical than his larger set, but that was confiscated in his pack. The lock at his door would eventually give way.

Yes, when the storm came, he would disappear. These fools would never know where he'd gone. His path would cross Spotal's again, one day. When the calefin hero opened his eyes, he would join him. Until then, he was happy to work with Stolach and any task he was given to spread discord in the southern kingdom.

With his lock-pick held gently in his palm, Banil rested his eyes and smiled.

Chapter 30

Dark clouds obscured the sun, making an accurate judgement of time impossible, but the rumble of thunder was enough to put any such concerns to rest. No, not thunder. Lidan cocked his head. It was too constant, too regular. More like the drumming of raindrops on a tarpaulin. He turned, peering into the misty distance, but there was nothing to be seen. Nevertheless, there was something.

Skipping, he drew level with Widrias.

'I heard something, sir,' he said.

'What?' Widrias muttered, out of breath.

'I'm not sure, a rumble.'

'Thunder?'

'No, listen.'

The satorr paused. A few seconds later, he grimaced. 'Yes. Not thunder. Horses.'

'Outriders,' announced Pwtrek.

'More than likely. Let's make it to the crest of that hill. Might be slightly easier to defend than this bloody open ground.'

They ran. It wasn't far. With each step, the drum of hooves grew louder, the reverberation of the damp earth grew greater. Finally, at the crest, they faced their footsteps, gathering close as they awaited the arrival. A forest, a cluster of rocks, an old fence, anything might have been preferable to this open hilltop. But it seemed fate dictated this engagement would take place in possibly the only area of completely open terrain in the whole country. So they waited, hands resting uneasily on the hilts of their arms.

Racing down the slope of a gentle hill, they appeared from the mist. Barely more than a shadow. It would be mere moments before they were upon them. His anxiety grew. Heartrate accelerated. Cold hands sweated inconspicuously. A dry tongue licked even dryer lips. Another skirmish. Another dance with death.

Half a minute later, the outriders were nearly upon them, as was the rain. Fifteen mounted men. He drew his sabre. He crouched behind his shield. Their packs scattered the slope where they'd discarded them in an attempt to break up the open ground.

Lidan narrowed his eyes, confused. Twelve of the horses were without riders. More than that, the three horsemen were reining in their mounts, bringing them to a halt. It couldn't possibly be for fear of their packs. The three fools took it a step further, dismounted, and walked to them with their weapons sheathed.

Shifting his shield to a more comfortable position, he glanced nervously at Spotal, whose hand slowly left his sword to hang harmlessly by his side. He looked again at the approaching figures. Two tall and one short. A sharp breath of realisation. With a short, gasping laugh, he dropped his shield and ran to embrace their returned companions.

Gwahl laughed as Pwtrek grabbed him in a rough embrace. 'Enough, my friend, you'll crush me!'

They laughed and shouted, asking the three where they'd been, how they found them, how they acquired the horses? Widrias held up his hands for silence.

'Give them a chance, by the four winds! Tell us your tale from the start, that would be easiest!'

'Agreed, though it would probably be a more pleasant tale to hear if we were to recount it under cover,' said Depani, blowing a raindrop from the tip of her nose. 'There are enough horses here for everyone, with some to spare to give them rest so we don't wear them out.'

'Good idea,' nodded Widrias. 'Everybody good with horses? Good. Mount up. We'll ride until sundown.'

Lidan took the reins of one, slipped his boot into a stirrup, and jumped to her back. She snorted when he dug his heels lightly into her flanks and followed the rest of the party at a gallop.

Having walked for so long it was a beautiful thing to finally have a horse, although it brought back bitter memories of Saviour and her valiant run from Crastalan. This mare was a rouncey, nothing special, but he was grateful for her nonetheless. She was a light brown colour, with white socks and a dark mane and tail. The saddle was a simple one, the leather covering aged and weathered, riddled with scratches and frays. Perfectly comfortable.

It was not long before he realised that he was at the fore of the party, with only Spotal and Noswen riding ahead of him. Gwahl was a few paces behind, followed by the neiads, then Widrias. Pwtrek and Auran brought up the rear. Pwtrek's horse was holding the juggernaut's weight admirably, but it was obvious it would soon tire. Auran, on the other hand, seemed quite uncomfortable in the saddle and wore a sour expression. The rider-less horses were scatted along the line, whinnying merrily as they ran.

They covered a great distance that day, and by the time the sky blushed with sunset, many miles lay behind them. Unfortunately, no matter how fast their horses galloped, it was never fast enough to outrun the weather. They took shelter under a grove of oaks, hitching their horses to low-hanging branches.

Once settled in the relative dryness beneath the trees, they ate their rations and listened.

'We crossed the Atrael about two kilometres north of the ferries, to give a wide berth of the outriders guarding the boats, and headed for the bramble plains so Gwahl could have a look at the path,' began Depani. 'Not a comfortable journey. We spent the majority of it crawling on our bellies like catfish. Eventually, we penetrated the outermost part of the forest, where the bushes were more widely spaced apart, less risk of getting a whopping big poison thorn in your arse,' she winked at Lidan. 'There was enough room to stand upright and we reached the road.'

'I expected guards at this point,' continued Gwahl. 'I was right. We heard voices ahead. We continued with caution and eventually saw the glimmer of armour through the thorns. I told Chekry and Depani to remain where they were and crept forward for a better look.

'There were only a few, no more than twelve, sitting around in the middle of a pathway pounded hard into the soil by the passing army. This incredible, giant road stretched through the brambles in a near-perfect straight line, from the grassland plains to Cysgodgors. I tried to look for a way past the guards so I could see how they crossed the marshes, but there was none. As for the path through the brambles, aside from its sheer size, it was nothing too special. Broken branches lined the sides of the road, and the thorns on the sides showed signs of axe-blows. Not wanting to delay any longer, I returned to my companions and we headed back north to cross to the Atrael.'

'All this took slightly longer than anticipated,' said Depani. 'Two hours already gone since we'd left you and we hadn't even thought of scuppering the ferries yet.'

'Initially, we considered leaving the boats and returning straight to you, but then that would have negated the very reason why we stayed in the first place. So, we decided to complete our mission,' added Chekry.

'The twins did well with the ferries,' said Gwahl. 'While I waited by the riverbank upstream, hidden from view, these two swam downriver, dived beneath the water, and got to work.'

'They were pretty well-made, all things considered,' nodded Chekry. 'But not good enough. Easy stuff for the likes of us. Even this one has enough brains to dismantle a few rows of logs stacked on top of one another and bound with rope and nail,' he shoved his sister, who shoved him back. 'A few minutes of sawing and wiggling and they were ready to drift apart. We went back to Gwahl and planned to head downriver past the soldiers so we could get back on track.'

'Unfortunately, the twins completed their task slightly too efficiently,' said Gwahl with a smile. 'By the time they reached me, three of the ferries were already destroyed and the logs were getting tangled up in the middle of the river with the loose ropes. Obviously, the soldiers noticed the dissembling of the vessels and after seeing the sawn ends of the ropes, a couple took to the middle of the river in the still-intact ferries to watch out for us. We considered waiting for the remaining ferries to break with the soldiers on them, but had no idea when that would be. Outriders were searching the banks, so time was getting short.

'We swam to the eastern bank and waited for the first outriders to reach us. It wasn't long before those on the far bank spotted us and their colleagues came. These two shot the first few who came at us, so we broke cover and ran. We didn't make it far before they were on us again. Didn't have much choice but to jump back into the water and swim.'

'Swam for the rest of the day, just in case,' said Depani. 'Must have made about twenty miles. When we got out the river, there was nobody around. But we knew it wouldn't be that easy. Next day, we were back in the water.'

'We stuck to the plan and rode the Atrael all the way down,' continued Gwahl. 'We made it to the eastern branch. Everything was going well, all going to plan, until we reached the bridges. We knew it would be a bit of a bottleneck, all those troops crossing all at once, but we never imagined the scale of it.

'Men, horses, war machines, boats, weapons, troglodytes by the tribe-full. The water was heavily-patrolled by boats and rafts. We knew we'd be caught if we remained in the water, but circling back around would take days. Unfortunately, we had no choice. It delayed us massively, but we made it around the rear-guard, avoided their scouts, and kept following the river. By the sheer number of outriders, scouts, and troglodyte raiding parties flooding the land, it's a wonder we made it to Duddawl.

'They were expecting us. You were two days gone. We decided to rest for a little while, we were exhausted, you see, then pressed on the next day.

'Before we left, the captain, Antil, warned us a patrol of outriders were sweeping quite close. He sent a Lieutenant Iego with us, along with a contingent of scouts, in case we ran into them.'

'Grumpy pike,' muttered Depani.

Gwahl ignored her. 'Incredibly lucky he was with us. We saw them coming early one morning, ambushed them, and won the ensuing skirmish. I think Iego took us on a bit of a detour to ensure we intercepted them, but he also let us keep the horses, so we can't complain too much. After that, we kept heading east and found you.'

'Horses make us easier to track, mind,' said Auran. 'It's one of their disadvantages.'

'Another being you dislike riding?' laughed Depani.

Gwahl smiled. 'No, you're right, my friend, but secrecy has been sacrificed for the sake of speed. I believe it necessary.'

They nodded and one of the trounces neighed, as if in agreement.

Lidan chuckled. 'Where to now? Now we're reunited do we keep going to Ahanami Lake or do we go south?'

'We'll continue to *Ahanemis* Lake,' corrected Spotal. 'Probably less chance of running into any armies.'

'How long will that take?' he asked.

'Now we have horses, we should arrive tomorrow, provided we maintain our pace,' Spotal reassured.

'How long then from the lake to Muranath?' he asked again.

'I'm not sure. Couple of weeks?' said Spotal.

Two weeks wasn't too long, he supposed. It would be good to see the great calefin city with his own eyes. In his old village, he had often heard tales of its majesty. Even in Crastalan folk would speak enviously of the capital of the Kingdom of the calefs, of its orchards, its fountains, its high walls glimmering with the light of purity.

Something rustled above them. Among the sodden leaves, drooping branches, and late acorns was a golden eagle, taking shelter from the wind. It regarded Lidan with is piercing frown. He imagined it was the same one they'd met all that time ago.

He nudged Gwahl and gestured to the bird.

'The golden eagle is lucky here, what bird is supposed to be lucky in the Midlands?'

'Where did that question come from?' asked the daemon, surprised.

'We saw an eagle the first morning without you, now there's one here. It just made me think maybe there is some truth in their myth.'

'There certainly is truth in these tales,' said Pwtrek, eavesdropping. 'The golden eagle is for the Eastlands, including the uninhabited wilderness of the far east, and the Kingdom of the calefs. It is the white-tailed eagle that brings fortune to the Northlands, and I believe it's the buzzard that guards the Midlands? The Westlands belongs to,' he paused, chewing his cheek as he searched his memory, 'either the peregrine or the kestrel.'

'The peregrine,' said Gwahl, nodding. 'What's the lucky bird of the Southlands, Auran?'

'Eagle owl,' he replied, curled up at the foot of an oak.

'That's the one, and the one of the Jagged isles is the albatross. Those are all that I know,' said Pwtrek.

'On the great isle of Alnaitack, far to the south, they say their lucky bird is the giant petrel,' continued Gwahl. 'On Daemon Isle it was always the red kite we associated with fortune. On Uffernen I believe it to be the cinereous vulture, although I can't see anything that resides on that land bringing you anything but pain.'

'When did you go to Uffernen?' asked Pwtrek.

'Many years past,' replied Gwahl, shaking his head. 'Won't go back in a hurry.'

'What's there?' asked Lidan.

'Death and darkness. A ruined continent with rancid air full of forgotten history. I'd rather not talk about it. Get some sleep, all of you, I'll take first watch.'

*

'Ahanemis Lake,' declared Spotal, pulling back on the reins of his mount as he came to the crest of the hill. 'See how she glitters with light. Evil has not reached this jewel.'

'I wouldn't be so sure,' muttered Widrias, leading his horse next to the calef. 'Are there any towns surrounding the lake? You mentioned a fishing village, if my memory serves?'

'Yes,' confirmed Spotal. 'Most of the calefs here are fishermen. We might have veered off course slightly, but I can just about see the one I meant over there,' he gestured to a slight blur on the shoreline to the south. 'We can warn them of the impending danger.'

'They may not require our warning of approaching armies.'

Spotal considered for a moment, nodded, and rode down the slope. He probably didn't think anyone would notice his bowed head and hunched shoulders.

Lidan followed his descent with the others. The soldiers at Duddawl seemed to revive Spotal somewhat of his previous depression. Indeed, learning so many escaped the clutches of the trogs must have filled him with hope that the desolation of his country was not as awful as he'd initially feared. But of course not. Duddawl was an exception. A military-based village with a sharp captain, prepared to take necessary initiative. Lidan doubted there were many such villages.

It was still morning by the time they reached their destination. White shores of a serene silver plate in the middle of surrounding chaos. Had someone told him this was the eastern coast he would have believed them. The far shore was lost in the horizon. An endless, perfect sight of tranquil beauty.

He shifted uncomfortably in his saddle as he observed the burnt village a few hundred metres south of their position. Noswen left half an hour ago to scout the place and search for survivors. She was not yet returned. He glanced at Spotal, sat at the shore, the waves gently lapping his boots as he played with the pebbles by his side. To be fair to him, upon seeing the charred buildings on the horizon, he simply sighed, shook his head, and smiled wanly at Widrias, who clasped him on the shoulder. There were no tears this time, finally accepting his lands were torn apart. There would be no comfort.

Finally, Depani announced Noswen's return. She saluted Widrias.

'A few corpses in the homes but not enough to account for an entire village. The earth is too churned and confused to tell if they were taken or fled.'

'Troglodytes or soldiers?' asked Widrias.

'Soldiers. Outriders,' she added.

'How fresh?'

'A few days.'

Spotal rose wordlessly and threw a pebble as far as he could into the lake, destroying the stillness with the spreading ripples.

'Where to, Spotal?' asked Widrias.

'South, past the village. All we have to do is follow the lake until we come to the southwest Ahanemis River. We'll cross it when we come to a fjord and continue south to Muranath.'

As they followed his instruction, they passed another ransacked village and a collapsed watchtower. Widrias didn't bother stopping to search the ruins. Spotal never asked. It took a day's ride to reach the river, where they camped at its shore. It had little in common with the Atrael, narrow, deep, and slow-moving, with the same silver water as the lake.

By midday the following day, they splashed across a wide, pebbled fjord and continued south.

*

Patience was a virtue Lidan always lacked, and the monotony of the southward journey bored him. It was not that the land was unpleasant, indeed it was as beautiful as it had ever been, but after seeing so many tranquil valleys and wondrous little woods, it was difficult for any of the landscape to catch his attention. The only feature to spark his curiosity was the idea of passing the Saraman woods. To his disappointment, they were too far to the east for him to catch even the slightest glimpse of them. He might even have accepted a run-in with outriders, scout, or trogs. A pursuit on horseback would be exhilarating, something to get his heart racing.

But no, Spotal purposefully led them across country, avoiding the main roads and villages at all costs. Obviously, this had the advantage of avoiding any targets for raiders, but at the disadvantage of a more difficult ride. Game trails provided adequate pathways and the calef appeared to be leading the from one to the other, his hunting experience proving its worth, but it was the parts in between, navigating wild forests, steep hills, and boggy valleys that proved troublesome. He guessed at Spotal's personal desire to avoid any more desecrated homes as another motivation for their chosen route,. He never complained.

Night-time, however, was a constant reminder of the invasion. The wind carried faint cries, beats of war drums, wails of horns, and the tramping of feet countless leagues away. From time to time, a faint glow on the horizon suggested a distant campsite at best, or another burning settlement at worst. The faint taste of smoke in the morning mists made breakfast a bitter experience.

Ten days after leaving Ahanemis Lake, he sensed a familiar smell tickling his nose. He flared his nostrils and sniffed loudly,

546

searching. Yes! There it was again. The fresh, clean smell of saltwater.

'I can smell the sea!' he cried, pulling his reins to bring his horse beside Spotal.

'Only now?' asked the calef. 'I caught the scent half an hour ago!'

Lidan rolled his eyes. 'Alright well done, but does this mean we're near Muranath?'

'Less than half a day's ride,' confirmed the calef. 'It's a few miles southwest. I think we trailed a little bit to the east on our journey.'

'Should we veer away to the southwest to get there?' asked Auran.

'We could, or we could just keep south until we reach the coastline and then follow it west to the city. I think that would be easier.'

A few hours later, he caught the first glimmer of the sea on the horizon. Whooping with delight, he dug his heels into the horse's flanks and raced away. The others followed with a laugh, even Widrias allowed himself a happy chuckle when the wind tugged at the hem of his cloak as they raced.

When they reached the coast, he pulled the reins in surprise. There were no beaches, only a steep cliff with a sheer drop to the crashing sea below. He sat still and breathed deeply, savouring the wonderful smell of salt, seaweed, and soaking rocks. Gwahl tapped him on the shoulder and pointed to the west along the cliffs. Far in the distance was the smallest smudge.

'Muranath,' declared Gwahl. 'It stands at the very edge of the land, at the southernmost point of Nefarwy, apart from the Far Eastlands, of course. The fortress is bounded by the cliffs and sea from the south and its curtain wall to the north. Arguably the most easily-defended fortress in Enadir, which is fortunate for us.'

'Seems quite small from here,' smiled Lidan, knowing such a comment would irk Spotal. He was not disappointed.

'It's a great city!' cried the calef haughtily. 'Far greater than any of the villages of the inhabitants of the Midlands. The only reason you aren't gasping in awe at its majesty is because your inferior human eyes cannot see its beauty from so far away!'

'I was only teasing!' laughed Lidan, holding up his hands in defence.

'I suppose we'd better get there as soon as we can, should we not, Spotal?' said Widrias. 'That way, our inferior eyes might bask in the glory of your city?'

Spotal smiled and nodded. Kicking his heels into his horse's flanks, he led them away at a gallop to his capital.

*

They were still miles away from the city when the first sounds of battle reached their ears. Widrias ground his teeth loudly enough for him to be heard above even the coastal winds. Everyone else was silent. Despite knowing what lay ahead, Widrias ordered them on to see the full extent of the battle. On the crest of a hill a safe distance from the city, Lidan's eyes took in all that lay before him.

There was not much to see of the city itself, its great, semi-circular outer wall hid the majority of the buildings. Compared to Crastalan, it was higher and cleaner, built of blocks of grey sandstone covered in shining steel, in an imitation of the giant's city. One or two towers of the city were visible above the walls, and right at the southernmost point stood a high watchtower, but apart from these rarities all he could see were the walls, teeming with soldiers. Rank upon rank of calefs stood in defence, raining arrows, quarrels, and javelins on their enemy. Some operated ballistae and trebuchets, others tended huge cauldrons, presumably filled with boiling tar and water. Bright banners fluttered in the wind, straining at their poles. At the heart of the wall were the gates. Even from this distance, he marvelled at their enormity, reaching nearly a third of the way up the wall. The wood was charred and blackened, pitted with countless arrows, spears, and all manner of missiles. They stood firm.

Surrounding the city were the invaders, their army larger than anything he could have ever imagined. Countless ranks of archers squatted behind shields, returning fire at the defenders. Scattered among them were the invaders' catapults and siege engines. Even as they watched, four enormous siege towers rolled up to the walls, pushed by teams of oxen and enormous blocks of infantry. Near the main gates lay the charred remains of two battering rams. Around the enemy camp a mile or so from the city, teams of woodsmen felled the towering trees from the surrounding countryside to provide more wood to fuel the machine of war. The camp itself was enormous, filled with tents and pavilions, surrounded by hastily-constructed walls as protection. Around its peripheries cavalry units milled, waiting for the gates to be broken so that they could finally play a part in the battle.

'Is there any way inside?' asked Pwtrek.

'None,' replied Spotal, glumly. 'Not unless you fancy your chances climbing the cliffs to get to the city from the south side,' he laughed bitterly and spat.

'How many do you think there are?' asked Lidan.

'More soldiers there than I've ever seen in my life,' muttered Chekry.

'I'd estimate thirty thousand,' said Gwahl. 'Minimum. But look north, another relief force approaches. Then there's the army at the river on top of that.'

'And the cavalry forces scattered around the country,' added Spotal, angrily.

'Who's their leader?' asked Auran. 'How did we not hear of such a large force?'

'We did know of it,' said Widrias. 'We just didn't know its purpose. These are Stolach's northern armies, led by Field Marshal Strikk. The purple standard with a white oak leaf is his. I can see it everywhere. Back at the Council, Pwtrek reported recruits flocking to the northern forces. I never considered this would be their mission. We were so focussed on our own survival, we forgot Stolach's greed.'

'Strikk. What kind of a man is he?' asked Auran.

'Ruthless and capable,' replied Pwtrek. 'Stolach chose his commander wisely.'

'Denhwyn is there too,' said Gwahl. 'See the yellow banner with three red feathers? It's not just the northern forces. The eastern infantry as well.'

'How many soldiers can Teig muster?' asked Widrias.

Spotal shrugged, 'Depends on whether she's willing to abandon our defences at the Atrael, request reinforcements from Tonnis Harbour, or call down our northern forces. If she decides to leave those armies where they are, she has roughly fifteen thousand calefs at her command. Should she call for aid and they all reply, then we're looking at forty to fifty thousand.'

Lidan looked around sadly. He'd so dearly hoped for some respite in Muranath, some safety, some semblance of hope for the future. Witnessing the battle before him, it all crumbled away. Stolach was greedily swallowing up the whole world, and the Council's plight seemed all the more impossible to accomplish.

Chapter 31

The glowing log hissed and crackled as fat dripped from the roasting deer carcass above. Spotal clutched his cloak tighter around him, eyes on the campfire. Tonight was a large meal, something to fill their empty bellies. Except no amount of food would ever fill the deepening pit in his stomach. The hunt with Gwahl and Noswen provided momentary distraction from the horrors of the ravaged lands. Still, the roasted meat would provide a welcome change to Harandale roots and travel rations provided by Duddawl, both already running thin after their four week journey north from Muranath. Now, once again, the towering silhouette of the Tarnegrefur Mountains loomed above. He shivered. Plenty of danger in the peaks, plenty of sorrow beyond them.

A hard four weeks. Among the hardest of his life. First was a dangerous journey around the siege to Tonnis, evading scouts and outriders in completely congested lands. As expected, the city was assaulted from land and sea, caught in Stolach's pincers. The calefin navy would win, he was certain of it, but would they win in time to support the harbour and its people from the land army? By the grace of the four winds it would be so. But the harbour was closed, with no hope of reaching its gates undetected. Widrias made a hard decision, the only decision.

'Strikk's forces are invading the south,' the general said. 'Which means the north is undefended. We'll travel back the way we came, through Imhara Pass, through the northern kingdom, and back to Dailas. Once we reach the Crisiaddwr, neiad scouts will eventually pick us up and we'll be safely returned to the Council. Any objections?'

There were none. Who could object to the only path available to them? Weeks of travel, wasted. Weeks of exhaustion and misery at the sight of his tortured country for nothing. Horror after horror, sleepless nights and anxious days, weeks of teetering on a knife-edge, the abyss on either side calling his name. All the while heading to the northern kingdom, to agony.

They considered returning to Duddawl to seek Antil and Iego's help, but it was hopeless. Each time they tried, another foe blocked their path. Trogs, outriders, scouts, a whole platoon at one point, spears on shoulders as they marched to Duddawl. The captain would soon have his maps overwhelmed with new annotations, his tiring guard crying ever louder for the non-existent relief force.

Alone, unsupported and with dwindling supplies, they continued north. Ahanemis Lake was left behind, as were the Cracket Mountains, they crossed the borders of five duchies on their journey, countless empty villages, without a friend or ally to lend their support. A bleak time, made worse by the knowledge of what awaited. Tarnegrefur, and beyond.

'Pass some deer, would you? Must be cooked by now.' grunted Pwtrek, shoving the flattened stone he was using as a plate to Gwahl turning the ramshackle spit. The daemon ignored the plate and wrenched an entire hind leg off the carcass.

'Have this, there's plenty for everyone, we may as well eat well while we have the chance.'

'Don't mind if I do!' Pwtrek took the leg with a grin.

'Remember to save some for supplies,' said Auran.

'Plenty, this is only half the thing,' muttered Gwahl. 'I'll smoke the rest. I took more than my fair share of the strength so I won't be eating, there's more than enough for the rest of you.'

He grimaced. The daemon's disappointed look as he stomached only a cursory mouthful of blood grated on him. Not that he said anything. For all his judgment and consternation, the daemon knew when to speak and when to hold his tongue, he supposed he was grateful for that, at least.

'Good, we'll need those supplies. I don't fancy another few weeks of starving in those freezing mountains, especially with winter on its way,' muttered Chekry.

'We won't be going over the mountains, Chekry,' he sighed. 'We'll be travelling through the pass. Nice and sheltered.'

'Fine, but how about when we're past the mountains? Won't the northern kingdom be harsh?' asked Chekry.

He shrugged. They would be harsh, but not for the reasons the neiad supposed.

'Yes,' he mumbled. 'But not as harsh as the Northlands. As long as we're in my country, there'll be food available to those who know how to find it.'

'There's food in the Northlands,' snuffled Pwtrek in between mouthfuls of steaming meat. 'It's just not as abundant as here. As long as you have me with you, you won't starve up there either.'

'What kind of food will be on the menu, Pwtrek?' asked Lidan, one of his infectious smiles breaking through their frowns.

'A feast, little one,' winked the juggernaut. 'Flans, pies, broths, stews, and mountains of delicious tropical fruits!' Lidan laughed, then Pwtrek turned serious. 'No, in all honesty it'll be foul-tasting roots, small goats, rabbits, and moose. If you're feeling especially adventurous you can try to slay a few wyverns or direwolves for an added kick, but I wouldn't recommend it.'

'What are wyverns like?' asked Auran.

'Big, ugly lizards,' said Gwahl, carving some meat for Widrias. 'Stocky bodies, thick necks, small heads, a long spiky tail, and enormous wings to finish it off.'

'So...dragons?' asked Auran.

Gwahl chuckled. 'No, no. Dragons are no more, gone before the time of the giants. Think of wyverns like... reptilian manticores. They're usually found on high mountaintops above the clouds where they can soak up the sun's rays. Or pillaging livestock.'

'I'm surprised they live in the north, being cold-blooded reptiles,' said Auran.

Gwahl nodded. 'Good observation. It's not their natural habitat. They used to live in the Midlands, Westlands, and Eastlands, but were driven to the Far Eastlands by the giants. Since their demise, they've slowly been creeping back across the Eastern Barrier. Most are dealt with by the calefs, but as the northlands are emptier, a number have settled there. Fortunately for us, these northern-dwelling wyverns are smaller and more docile than their Eastland relatives.'

'They seem pretty big to me!' exclaimed Pwtrek.

'You wait until you see a real wyvern,' chuckled Gwahl.

'If they're as bad as you say, I'd rather not know,' Pwtrek shivered.

'What are direwolves like?' asked Lidan, innocently. Spotal flinched and closed his eyes. Cruel memories sprang forth so readily with such an innocent question. Pwtrek gave Lidan a brief description, sensitively describing them as concisely as possible. He caught his eye and nodded gratefully. Lidan was the only one who didn't know his past. Everyone else did. He guessed most people in Nefarwy knew his tragedy, even Auran, probably.

Gwahl handed him a plate and clasped his shoulder reassuringly.

'I'll be fine when we get through Imhara,' he said, forcing a smile. 'You don't have to worry about me. I appreciate the concern, but I'm alright. No need to tiptoe around me.'

'How far north were you when it happened?' asked Pwtrek.

'On the very border of my kingdom. The roads will lead us past the villages, but I don't mind, it's the quickest way to the northlands.'

'We could always take a slight detour to avoid them?' suggested Gwahl.

'No detours,' barked Widrias. 'If Spotal says he's fine, I believe him. I don't want to lose time skirting around graveyards for the sake of one soldier. No offense.'

Spotal shook his head. 'None taken,' he said truthfully. 'It would be disrespectful not to visit them.'

'Thank you, Captain,' said Widrias, 'your men would be proud.'

He saw Lidan's confused expression, looking from one person to the next for explanation. Nobody met his gaze, and he was wise enough not to ask. One day, he would let the boy know, but not today.

*

'How far away is it?' shouted Depani as they rode in the grey morning, their cloaks flapping in the wind.

'Less than a day's ride,' he shouted back, gracefully riding his rouncey. The horses were nothing compared to the magnificent destriers and palfreys he was used to. Nevertheless, under his gentle guidance, even these average mounts glided smoothly over the ground, in stark contrast to the jolting lopes of everyone else's horses. Not even Gwahl or Noswen rode as well as he. Lidan, who'd often boasted of his riding capabilities, seemed disappointingly rough in the saddle, too much tugging at the reins, not enough guidance with he thighs. Then again, perhaps it was a bit much to expect anyone to match him, he'd been trained by the best, after all.

As if to prove his point, there was a loud clatter behind him, making him jump. He swivelled in his saddle, guiding the rouncey around to investigate. Auran lay spread-eagled on the ground. He remained motionless for several seconds before heaving himself up to one elbow and rubbing his head.

He smiled at Gwahl, and was about to make a sarcastic comment when he realised the daemon wasn't paying him or Auran any attention, but was scanning the surrounding slopes of the foothills. He steered his horse beside him.

'What is it? I thought Auran just fell?'

The daemon shook his head. 'Struck by a stone, probably from a sling.'

'A party of outriders?'

'More than likely, but from which army?'

He stared dumbly at the daemon, missing the implication. When it dawned, he smiled.

'Calefs?'

'I can't imagine one of Strikk's newly-trained recruits hitting a moving target with a sling from so far away... unless they're dreyads.'

They didn't wait long to find out. As soon as Auran clambered back on the horse, three figures strolled down a hill towards them. Calefs indeed. He relaxed. The others waited a few additional seconds before letting their hands fall from their sword-hilts. Noswen kept one hand beneath her cloak, on her dirk. Perhaps she was afraid. Perhaps Banil was still at the forefront of her memory. But he was an exception. Few calefs betrayed their people. Banil was scum, an abhorrent freak of nature who came around perhaps once in every generation. Nevertheless, he hoped she'd relax her hand. The scouts would surely notice it. He wanted them relaxed, friendly, easy to communicate with.

He sometimes felt strange to hold no ill feeling towards his father's killer. It should be a gulf between them, a gloom to mar every conversation they had, but it somehow wasn't. He had every right to hate her, yet considered her a friend. Maybe it was because he knew at the time of the assassination, the hanex was a soldier carrying out orders, much like how he hadn't been there to fight alongside his father on account of his orders. She was a different person back then. A tortured puppet on the strings of her master. It wasn't her fault.

As the calefs approached, he forgot about Noswen and concentrated on his kinsmen. All three wore the same kind of leather brigandine as his, indicating their roles as scouts. However, theirs were far simpler than his eloquent white leather. Two held unstrung bows in their hands, the third held a sling, all wore slim arming swords at their waists. Each had the same dark brown hair tied up in a neat ponytail. The style never suited him, he preferred to wear his down, as was fashionable in Muranath.

They stopped ten paces away. Widrias swung his horse around to greet them. One of the archers bowed his head to the satorr.

'The northern winds have blessed us to find such a noteworthy individual wandering our lands, General Widrias. My father served you in the Summer of Sorrows. It's an honour.'

'It is us who are blessed to have been found,' replied Widrias with a salute. 'Who are you?'

'I am Stilnim Cahal, and these are Turilihan and Antelebwy, we're scouts from the northern armies. We'll take you to our commander, if you will.'

'Are you not curious as to why we're here?' asked Widrias, surprised.

Stilnim shook his head. 'My curiosity is of no importance, it isn't my place to ask such things of *you*, General. Though the company you keep is... alarming in times like these, you command enough respect in our armies to be treated graciously. Our commander, however, will certainly have questions.'

The calef's eyes pierced each member of the party, lingering on Noswen and Pwtrek especially. When he caught Spotal's eye he raised an eyebrow and bowed his head slightly. Spotal returned the gesture. Widrias offered the calefs their spare horses to hasten their return to their main force, and they obliged.

'My apologies to you, sir,' said Turilihan, the slingsman, to Auran. 'We saw you travelling to the pass and didn't recognise Widrias straight away. Had I known, I wouldn't have struck you.'

'Forgiven,' Auran grimaced. 'A good shot.'

'A glancing hit, only,' Turilihan bowed his head. 'A good shot wouldn't let us have this conversation.'

'Ah. Then I'm glad you've not been practicing.'

Turilihan smiled and re-joined his kinsmen.

As they rode north to Imhara, Spotal watched the scouts. Why would scouts from the northern armies be wandering south of Tarnegrefur? Unless this was a relief force coming to assist the defenders of Muranath? Maybe it was a retreat from an even larger threat sweeping in from the Northlands? Whatever the reason, his questions would soon be answered. The cleft in the mountains grew closer. Imhara Pass.

*

'Impressive,' nodded Depani as they stood at the opening of the pass. Spotal smiled in agreement. It was an incredible natural wonder, a clean cleft that cut through an entire range of the mountains. A great canyon that eroded its way through the rock, providing a pathway, a gateway, between the northern and southern reaches of the Kingdom of the calefs. Although for the majority of its length it was bordered by steep, impassable cliffs, there were areas where the slopes were gentle and easy to climb, allowing access to the mountainous peaks.

The scouts urged them on. Several more calefs appeared before them, halting their progress. Stilnim exchanged a few words with the soldiers, pointing to Widrias and Pwtrek, too quiet to eavesdrop. An agreement was reached and the new group stepped aside, sending a runner ahead. A couple nodded to Spotal as he passed. One even saluted and breathed his name. The recognition sent

557

a quick shiver down his back. It was different to the recognition in Duddawl. He didn't know why.

A few hundred metres into the pass, they came face to face with the first of two fortifications. Two curtain walls, one north and one south, stretched across the entire canyon. It was a formidable defence, with fortified gates at the base of each wall through which one would gain access. It was years since he last walked through them, in shame and sorrow, now it was finally time to do so again. Hundreds of eyes peered at them from the battlements. How many on him? Looking, judging. Bad enough in the southern kingdom, now he'd be judged again by the very people he'd failed.

Approaching the fortress, funnelled to a narrow pass by the near-vertical slopes on either side, he couldn't help but feel horribly exposed. All it would take was a volley from the parapet and they'd be skewered. Hemmed in by the mountain walls, it was a death corridor. And here he was approaching it as a fellow calef, how intimidating would it feel to approach as an enemy?

He narrowed his eyes as he steered his rouncey through the gate, glancing upwards furtively at the murder-holes above. Straining his eyes, he could see cauldrons and fireplaces next to the holes, but thankfully, felt no heat. As suspicious as these calefs seemed to be, they weren't suspicious enough as to fully prepare their defences against them.

Blinking, he rode into the sunlight at the other end, through the inner gates. His breath caught. An enormous encampment of soldiers, tents and standards everywhere. Ordered into neat rows and columns, each tent would house five men, and there were easily over four hundred tents. Calefs milled around, going about their business as they prepared to break camp. They were planning on moving on soon. Carts were stacked, provisions handed out, boots repaired for the march ahead, horses given new shoes. He took note of the standards around him. Most simply bore the royal crest, a green lion on a yellow field. Several, however, also bore an all-too familiar sigil, the golden hawk on a white sky.

His jaw dropped at the sight of the standard. His mind went blank. It was all he could do not to fall off his horse as he sat there, paralyzed, waiting for the inevitable. His agitation must have been noticeable, and Auran leaned across.

'Everything alright?' he asked, gently.

'Fine,' he lied, mouth dry as bone. 'It's just being around my people again. Not seen any since Duddawl. I get nervous.'

Auran nodded grimly. 'There is an air of mistrust here. I don't like the way they stare. What've we done to merit such hostility?'

He shook his head. He didn't know, he didn't even notice any hostility, and only half listened as his friend rambled on about how strange their reception was.

Eventually Stilnim halted before a tent set slightly apart from the others and knocked on the post outside. They waited for a few seconds for a reply. It felt like an age, an age which set his heart hammering at his ribcage. Finally, the tent flaps flew open and out she came. Silwei.

She was of average height, athletically built, wearing light travelling armour. Her face was as lovely as he remembered, with typically large eyes and long lashes, a small chin and tanned skin, dotted with freckles. Her chestnut hair was bound in a tight ponytail, and she pursed her lips as she examined them.

'You are the commander of this army?' asked Widrias, curtly.

'I am,' she replied. Her voice sent a shock through his body. He breathed deeply. Relax. By the four winds, just relax.

'Very well, I'm General Widrias Gesharr, I've fought alongside your kinsmen numerous times in the past, including your scout's father, apparently,' he gestured to Stilnim. 'I have commanded your armies in battles and am a friend to both King Lleunedd and General Teig.'

'I recognise you, General, but your past does not protect you from the company you hold.'

Her comment stung. He didn't think she'd insult him in such a way. The last time they'd spoken was before his loss of honour, it seemed as though his losses cost him his friendship as well.

'The company I hold is of great soldiers,' said the satorr, sternly. 'There is nothing wrong with my men. I believe this encounter will go far more pleasantly if you spare the insults and state your mind. Now please, give me your name.'

Silwei looked at him coolly, a look he recognised all too well. She'd often regarded him with the same judging eyes whenever he did something she disapproved of.

'My name is Lieutenant Silwei Ganelia, acting commander of this northern calefin force. The company I refer to is the juggernaut. And who is the calef–' she stopped suddenly, finally catching Spotal's eye. She blinked in surprise. 'Spotal! What're you doing here?'

'My lady,' he croaked, with all the grace he could muster, which was about as much as a toad swimming in treacle. Winds! Of all places to see her again. He cleared his throat. 'General Widrias asked me to accompany him on this journey. It's taken a few twists and turns, and we've ended up far from where we expected to be.'

'Far from where *I* expected you to be as well. I thought you'd be in Muranath?' she asked, a smile tugging at the corners of her lips.

'That isn't the task I was assigned,' he replied, keeping as calm as he could.

'We must catch up soon,' she said and turned back to Widrias, watching them with raised eyebrows. 'So General, would you tell me why you're wandering our lands with a juggernaut? You have much explaining to do, it seems.'

'As do you,' replied Widrias, frowning. 'Pwtrek is a loyal servant to me and the Council, he has no quarrel with you. He's served our purpose for many years. What do you hold against him?'

Silwei looked him up and down.

'Come, join me in my tent. I can explain everything. Your men can wait outside, they won't be harmed.'

She turned and walked inside. Widrias grunted and heaved himself off his horse, wincing as his leg hit the ground, and limped inside, motioning for Gwahl and Spotal to follow.

By the four winds! Of all officers to lead this force, why her? It could have been anyone, anyone at all. Why her? He shook his head and followed them inside.

There was nothing in the tent save for a weapons rack, against which leaned Silwei's silver spear and a travelling pack filled with all her gear. She glanced up at the trio.

'I told you to leave your men outside.'

'You and Spotal know each other, so I'd like someone present who can verify what you say. Gwahl is one of my advisors. Anything you say to me you can say to him,' Widrias said sternly, unslinging his sword from his back and leaning against the scabbard.

'Very well, valid enough reasons, I suppose. I recognise your name, Gwahl,' she said. 'I'm honoured to meet such an esteemed individual.'

'My thanks,' Gwahl bowed his head respectfully.

'You're the first daemon I've ever met. Your race is dying, I fear Spotal and I will soon share your loneliness,' she looked at Widrias. 'You tell me first why you're here. Then I'll answer your questions, if I see fit.'

Spotal sat in silence as Widrias recounted their tale, skimming over the details, but telling everything Silwei needed to know. When the tale reached the slaughtered villages and Muranath's siege, the calef gritted her teeth in frustration. Once the satorr finished, she nodded stiffly.

'Thank you, General. So Spotal led you here to get to the Northlands, head east into the Dailas, and travel south back to the Council. You have a long journey ahead of you. Would you consider remaining with us for a while?'

'To what end?' asked Widrias, frowning.

'The army you see here is all we could spare from Dorfen Fortress on the Barrier. A skeleton guard is all that remains. We march south to Muranath to strike back at our enemies and save our capital.'

Spotal looked hopefully at Widrias. Maybe if he were at the head of the army that broke the siege and drove away the invaders from Muranath, then Lleunedd would forgive him and he would be returned to glory! He pictured himself hacking his way through hordes of soldiers to the gates of Muranath, planting the king's standard in the ground and declaring that this was calefin land, that no invader would ever set foot upon it again!

'No,' Widrias shook his head, and Spotal's picture faded. 'My duty is to return to the Council. I cannot come with you, nor can any of my soldiers, before you try to recruit them.'

'We could use a commander of your reputation. I would appreciate it greatly.'

'My apologies, but the answer is no. My battle lies elsewhere.'

'We are your allies, General,' her voice was steady, but Spotal could hear her silent anger building. 'Our battles are your battles. If the Kingdom of the calefs is destroyed, as seems increasingly likely, you lose a powerful ally.'

'You will not fail, Lieutenant,' said Widrias. 'You do not need me to direct your battle. Destroy their camp, shoot into their ranks to scatter the men and hit the disorganised lines hard from the rear with your cavalry. I'm needed back with my people.'

Silwei stared at the satorr for a while, and he stared back, unblinking. Spotal shifted uncomfortably in the silence. Eventually she nodded.

'You seemed surprised when the general told you about the siege,' said Gwahl, breaking the silence. 'You clearly didn't know about it before we told you. Why then, is this army here? You intended to travel south before we came, what drove you?'

'We knew Stolach had invaded, but we didn't realise the extent of his campaign.'

'How did you know? Did you receive a message?'

'Of sorts. A message from Stolach, from the north, in the form of an army of several hundred juggernauts, all of them armed and intent on slaughter. They swept aside two entire battalions before we managed to rally here. It was at the northern wall we made our stand, two and a half thousand calefs against six hundred juggernauts. The battle was hard-fought and bloody, but we emerged victorious. We managed to capture a few of the enemy and extracted a thimbleful of information from them, enough to establish an invasion was underway. We prepared to set south to rid the land of hostiles. That's why my scouts were initially suspicious of your party, seeing the juggernaut south of Imhara was startling. You can't blame them.'

She continued. 'Anyway, we'll be breaking camp within a few hours and heading south. You're free to travel northwards. I'll give you a letter with my seal to show the soldiers guarding the wall you have my blessing.'

'Might I ask for your healers to tend to some of our wounds?' asked Widrias.

'I'll ask if they can spare the time. Remember my army stands in the wake of a battle. My wounded soldiers take precedence over yours, I'm afraid. Now go, find a place to rest, or feel free to leave whenever you wish.'

They rose and bowed to her. Before he walked out, Spotal stole a quick glance over his shoulder. Silwei gave him the faintest smile before he left.

He followed Widrias back to their horses and the satorr led them beyond the last tent to the side of the canyon, where they waited for the army's healers. Everyone was wounded in some way or another. The general's chronic pain in his leg, Pwtrek's exhaustion, Auran's bruised temple, Lidan's old wounds. The list went on, not a single one of them was fully fit. He wondered how many more wounds they would suffer before another fell, following Tanor, Mostyn, and all the others.

As they waited, he watched his kinsmen go about their business, preparing themselves for the long march ahead. In another life, perhaps he would be with them, leading them on to the glorious battle to save king and country. The unfamiliar faces fleeting past his eyes would have names to them, brave soldiers who trusted him with their lives. It was cruel how even the calefs of the north, his calefs, no longer revered his name.

'I'm going for a walk,' he announced, rising. They acknowledged him with nods.

'Be back within two hours,' said Widrias. 'Try convincing someone to come and tend to us. Work your charms.'

'I'll do my best,' he nodded with a smile, strolling leisurely into the camp.

Wandering aimlessly through the throng of calefs busying themselves with preparations for war, and yet doing nothing to help them, was odd. He wanted to load the carts, unhitch the tents, distribute provisions, but whenever he approached them and offered, they would always refuse, stating it was their duty not his. Most of them didn't recognise him, some didn't even realise he wasn't a part of their army. Strange. In Duddawl, they all knew him. His failures were hundreds of miles from that town, but still they knew him. How could so many of these not? Was he truly forgotten? Of course not. Iego was the likely source of the hostility at Duddawl, spreading the news of his presence in their little town. Some of these recognised him. He knew straight away the ones who did. They stopped and stared, mouths open, some remembering to salute out of courtesy. It hurt to have their stares. And yet… there was something different. Softer, kinder than Duddawl. Or was it just imagination?

To his right, he was distracted by a young calef struggling with a spirited destrier, furiously tugging at the reins in an attempt to lead the mighty horse to his destination. The destrier, a beautiful grey creature, was having none of it, throwing her head and snorting angrily as the young squire fought with her. Spotal smiled and tapped the young calef on his shoulder to offer his assistance, expecting a rejection.

'I wouldn't mind, thank you!' gasped the calef breathlessly, not looking at Spotal, concentrating on the horse.

'Certainly,' Finally! A chance to help. 'Just keep hold of the reins, I'll calm her down.'

Gripping the reins tightly with one hand, he approached cautiously, staring into the mare's black eyes. He inched forwards until his hand rested on her shoulder, and he slowly stroked her mane and rubbed her neck. She snorted and threw her head at him, irritated. He stooped low and gripped her foreleg, pressing gently just in front of the chestnut. Almost immediately her temper dissipated and she stood still, breathing heavily and flicking her tail.

Smiling, he glanced at the young squire. 'Should be easier to lead from now on. Who gave you charge of this horse? You're not experienced enough to handle her.'

'I gave her!' someone shouted from behind him. He turned to see a tall, handsome calef stride towards him. He wore beautiful clothes. High riding boots, brown trousers, a loose silk shirt, and a black leather waistcoat with golden buttons. On his left hip was a long, curved sabre, and in his right was a white riding crop. His silver hair was about his shoulders and his young eyes stared at Spotal sourly. He spoke again, in a quieter tone.

'She's my horse, and Gleren in my squire. I gave *him* charge of her while I was preparing to leave. She should have been at the gates with the other horses an hour ago.'

'Maybe next time you should see to her yourself, and leave your other preparations to your squire,' suggested Spotal.

The calef bristled. 'I would appreciate it if you did not tell me what tasks to give my own servant.'

'I think you'd appreciate it if you knew what tasks your squire was capable of. That way, you can be sure your horse is never late again.'

'I appreciate your concern, I'm sure,' the calef replied, coldly. 'But he must learn through experience. Besides, who are you to touch a knight's horse without his permission?'

'He is a captain,' Silwei's voice floated through the air. Spotal glanced around and saw her walking towards them, smiling. 'As your superior officer, when you're on duty he can do whatever he sees fit with your horse. Be grateful, Anall, that he doesn't choose to trade his scraggly rouncey for your mighty destrier.'

Anall looked Spotal up and down. Spotal reached inside his brigandine and held his captain's pendant aloft. Anall glanced at it and bowed his head. 'In which case I am grateful, Captain, that you would take the time out of your day to assist my squire in the handling of my horse. Forgive me for not recognising your rank. I wasn't even aware we had an officer higher than lieutenant present in this army. When did you arrive?'

'I'm not a part of this force,' he replied. 'Just passing through with my companions.'

Anall paused. 'I see, so you came with General Widrias and the juggernaut. You must be Captain Spotal Lasaai. Tales of your past... *campaigns* have reached most soldiers.'

'Very good, Anall,' said Silwei with a wave of her hand. 'Take your horse and go to your station.'

Anall saluted her and Spotal, turned on his heel, and led his horse away. As he walked away, Silwei called after him. 'And next time, don't give charge of your horse to your new squire until you've taught him how to handle her!' she laughed as Anall turned and smiled through his teeth.

She turned to Spotal. 'Forgive Anall, he's a fine knight, but headstrong and overconfident. He'll learn humility soon. He's from *down south*. Do you have a minute to talk?'

'Of course,' he said, heart fluttering as she took his arm in hers and walked him through the camp.

'I'm from *down south*,' he reminded her as they strolled.

'I know. We all have our flaws,' she nudged him. 'Oh! I'm glad to see you again, my friend,' she sighed. 'How long's it been? Nearly a decade, surely?'

'Close to that.'

'Where's the time gone? Tell me about your life these past ten years!'

Spotal sighed. 'You know what it's become. Four years ago, I was... disgraced. Now I'm ambassador for the calefs in the Council.'

'That's an honourable position! Lleunedd would only send an experienced, capable soldier and commander for such a task!'

Spotal laughed bitterly. 'No, Silwei, I'm out of his way in the Midlands, to be kept out of sight as punishment for my shame.'

She shook her head. 'You lost your army to a horde of monsters. How many armies do you think General Teig has lost? Or Captain Ffeleb? Or Colonel Oli? How many soldiers do you think have died under their command? Lleunedd isn't punishing you.'

'He made me wear a bag over my head whenever I was in his presence.'

She was silent for a while. 'He did that?'

'He said my hands were stained with the blood of the innocents mauled by the wolves. He said I was unfit to wear the armour of the Calefin Guard.'

'The Calefin Guard are overrated, pompous soldiers,' said Silwei. 'You don't need to be associated with them. The true heart of the calefin army is the battalions of soldiers who fill the battlefield, not those regiments of sanctimonious fencers.'

'My father was the head of the Guard. It was one of the happiest moments of my life when I was accepted into their ranks. Don't insult them, I beg you,' he sighed. 'This failed mission was my last chance to get back into Lleunedd's favour. My honour's gone for good.'

'Get over yourself,' she huffed, making him flinch. 'There's more to life than honour on the battlefield. All you southern highborn calefs are so narrow-minded in your pursuit for glory and fame. Happiness is more glorious than a famous, miserable old soldier whose only accomplishment in life are the medals on his breast. You say this was your last chance to get back into Lleunedd's favour, so what? I've never met the calef and I'm none the worse for it, but I'm happy.'

'I must honour my father's name!'

'Honour him by living. You were undoubtedly his greatest victory, eclipsing all battles won and enemies defeated. Don't throw away his honour by killing yourself trying to live up to this ideal you have built him up to be.'

'You insult him?'

'No, you do. You've become twisted by the death of your army and by Lleunedd's pettiness. You've put Cetril on a pedestal, worshipping his memory as the greatest ever soldier our race has seen. He *was* a good soldier, Spotal, but you are equally good, if not better! I know you refused promotion so many times before because you felt as though you hadn't quite done enough to hold the same rank as him, but you have. Had you accepted promotion to major, then you wouldn't have been up north when the... attack occurred. You would have been in Muranath, on the Barrier, or on the Atrael along with the other majors.'

'Why are you saying this?'

'I'm giving you a hard truth. Trying to show you how no matter what 'honour' you earn, or think you earn, on the battlefield, it'll never be enough. You don't understand how good you were, how good you *are*. There's something in your head stopping you from accepting it. You're as fine a soldier as your father was, some sort of inferiority complex that makes you overlook everything good you've done and focus on your apparent failings.'

'You can't deny my kin have lost all respect for me, while Major Cetril is one of the most respected names in military history.'

'I can. You're a legend in the north. One mistake doesn't overshadow the countless victories you won. The villagers still adore you up there. They lament the ones lost, of course, but you forget the scores of others you saved from other threats. These soldiers around us, many grew up on stories of your victories.'

'Had you seen the reception I received in Muranath upon my return, you would not say this. Duddawl was the same. They had nothing but contempt for my name.'

She snorted. 'Who cares what those southerners think? They're all almost as stuck-up as Lleunedd. Look at Anall, he's an arrogant toad, all because of his upbringing in Muranath. He only got sent up north because someone caught him sleeping with his colonel's daughter. A big scandal, as far as I understand. Think now, I'm sure that not everyone in the king's court showed you such disrespect?'

Spotal thought for a while. 'General Teig argued for my case,' he mumbled.

Silwei smiled a victorious smile. 'She's from the north.'

He sighed and forced a grin. 'So what, should I march up to Lleunedd and demand to be reassigned back to one of the northern armies? I was lucky to keep my rank.'

She shook her head and smiled sadly. 'No, my friend, I'm saying you don't need to be so concerned about what Lleunedd thinks of you. Complete your time with the Council. When this war is won, come back to your people with pride.'

'My people would not look at me.'

'Your people are the villagers in the north. I'm sure Teig would assign you to an army up here, and you'll be happy.'

He shuffled his feet awkwardly, thinking about everything she'd said. If ever there were someone to call him out on his mood swings or petulance, it was her. How many times had she spoken out of turn in strategic meetings, or questioned a strange order? He could always count on her to be honest and true, unapologetically standing by what she believed.

But did he believe it? No. Her outlook was flawed, simplistic, *idealistic*. Reality was different, harsh. She wasn't the one to suffer the shame of defeat. She wasn't the one to tarnish the honour of her family.

Swallowing the lump in his throat, he sought lighter topics, and spotted Anall again, striding purposefully to the gate with a beautiful saddle under his arm.

'Sleeping with a colonel's daughter?' he smirked. 'I'm surprised you let him in!'

'Oh, I had to,' she leaned close. 'I had to know all the details!'

He grinned wider, her hair smelled of jasmine. Funny, she never used to enjoy tea. 'Which colonel was it?'

'Colonel Panai,' she sniggered.

'Winds! Which one? His eldest? I thought she was engaged to some earl near Saraman woods?'

'His *youngest*!'

He grimaced and looked at her. 'His youngest? The one with the…?' he gestured to his nose.

'The very one!' she giggled.

'Wow…' he looked after Anall. 'The more you know!'

'I've not got the rest of the details yet,' she whispered. 'But I'll get them. Otherwise our young knight will find himself scheduled for a suspicious amount of latrine duties in his spare time.'

'You know how to turn up the pressure!'

'Expert hand. I'm out for promotion to the spy network,' she winked.

He smiled. It was so easy, falling back in line with her, pointless conversations and laughing over nothing. As if they'd never been apart. If only duties hadn't set them apart, if only their careers weren't so important, the last decade might have been spent in each other's company. But no, his honour demanded sacrifice, and he did what had to be done, as did she.

'Thank you for trying to comfort me, Silwei. I'm tired of talking about me, what have you been up to?'

She smiled, accepting his reluctance. 'After Issil and I were married, we remained in the south for a while, not my choice, I assure you. We were both assigned to one of the river patrols. It was a good enough life, not especially exciting, with only the odd few troglodytes attempting to cross every few weeks. Then, seven years ago, we decided to have a child.'

It was like a punch to the gut. 'You're a mother?'

'A proud one.'

His heart skipped. 'Congratulations! I'm so pleased for you! What's the child's name?'

'Anaali.'

He forced a smile. 'A good name, may he live up to it.'

Silwei laughed. 'Unless he becomes an impromptu king, that'll be difficult! He's strong and bright, wants to be just like his parents.'

He was silent for a moment. 'Where is he now?'

Silwei looked at him seriously. 'Safe. Three years ago, Issil and I decided we wanted to move back north and were reassigned to our respective forces up here. Anaali is safe in our village, next to Dorfen. Issil is there with the skeleton guard while we move south.'

'Our kingdom is destroyed,' said Spotal, sadly, suddenly wanting nothing more than to change the subject. 'The things I've seen as I travelled up and down the country... the slaughtered villages reminded me of the ones I failed. Avoid them at all costs, Silwei, if you see a burned village in the distance, don't march into it.'

'I might have to, my friend. There's no avoiding the horrors of this war.'

'You know, at the beginning, the only reason I was fighting was to prove myself. But now? I want to fight. He has to pay for what he's done. I still can't believe he actually invaded.'

'I can. Stolach is greedy and hungry for power. The Council are a threat so he attack us, their allies. Besides, he's always hated us for all those years resisting him.'

'Do you think you can drive out his forces?' he asked, seriously.

'As Widrias said, we must. I have over two thousand calefs with me and we'll collect reinforcements as we travel south. How many other armies did you meet on the way here?'

He looked at her. 'None, Silwei, you're the first. There might be a few river patrols who've not yet joined the fight, but they're well out of your way. You're the only relief force of any real size Lleunedd can expect.'

She frowned. 'Well, that's unfortunate. But you're wrong about us being the only ones. I sent emissaries to the Cage before coming. Hopefully they'll be following soon.'

'Would they come?' asked Spotal, eyebrow raised. 'Can they spare the bodies?'

'Our country is being invaded. They'll answer my call.'

'But they'd lose honour for abandoning their posts!'

Silwei tutted and shoved him playfully. 'Come on, these are northern calefs! We put more important things before honour.'

He rolled his eyes. 'How many do you think would come?'

'Well if you ask me, the Barrier is hopelessly overprotected anyway, so I'd say a good seven thousand should come, but it's more realistic to expect some five thousand.'

'Winds, I wish it were so overprotected! You'll be lucky to get a fraction of that. Even if you did, you'd still be outnumbered.'

'How many men has Stolach sent?'

'His entire northern armies and the eastern infantry, however many men that is, around forty-odd thousand? Possibly more. Strikk's been recruiting for a while, plus the thousands of troglodytes from the marshes. Back at the Council they assumed the northern forces were preparing an offensive against them. How wrong they were.'

They reached the end of the encampment, where the knights were gathered with their horses. Spotal spotted Anall in the throng, feeding carrots to his destrier. Looking around at the soldiers, he noticed a trend in their characteristics.

'Your men are young, Silwei. How experienced is this army?'

She clicked her tongue and murmured. 'The battle with the juggernauts was their first real engagement, aside from the skirmishes fought against marauders from the north. This will be a hard campaign for them, but they'll exceed.'

'Where are the veterans? Speaking of which, why are you the commanding officer? Massive army for a lieutenant, no offence.'

'There's no offence in the truth,' she said sadly. 'You remember the two battalions I said were destroyed by the juggernauts? They were our seasoned fighters. Captain Mali commanded them. She bought us enough time to reach Imhara before the invaders. Took our best men and women with her to meet the juggernauts on an open field. I don't know whether any survived, but they took down several hundred of our enemy with them. I dread to think what the outcome of our battle would have been had there been any more of those beasts hammering our gates.'

'I thought the battle went well? Hard-fought, but well? At least that's the impression you gave Widrias.'

'In theory it did, but you'll see the full extent of the damage to the northern gates when you get there. They were splintering by the end. That's why I ordered them open and charged out with our knights, arrows flying around our heads.'

He raised his eyebrows. 'Bold.'

'Yes, it was, but I had no choice. Either open the gates and take them head-on with the element of surprise, or wait for the gates to finally splinter and face them in the pass. If I were commanding seasoned warriors then I might have held inside the wall and let the terrain come to our aid, but with these jittery young things, I felt a glorious charge was likelier to succeed.'

'You know your army,' he smiled.

'A commander should,' she laughed. She looked around at the camp. There were only a couple of tents left standing, and they collapsed as she watched. She looked at Spotal again. 'It's time for me to leave, my friend. Good luck on your travels, and take care back in the Midlands, especially the northern forests. From what I've heard, the very shadows up there will try to kill you.'

She embraced Spotal and turned to call for her horse. He stood next to her as she mounted.

'You be careful as well, Silwei,' he said. 'Fight for Anaali. Beware the dead villages, they'll only bring you pain. Our kingdom is not the bright land it once was.'

She nodded and turned to her waiting army. 'Now begins our true campaign, my friends,' she shouted. 'Be wary of Stolach's armies, they scurry across the land like flies over carrion. We head south!'

With one last look at Spotal, she rode away.

Chapter 32

'Good, you're back,' said Widrias, heaving himself to his feet, 'now we can move again.'

'Apologies if I kept you waiting,' replied Spotal.

'Yes, well, at least you're back now. Mount up!'

Lidan jumped into the saddle and they set off again. It was pleasant in the canyon. There was no wind to cut through them and the high walls provided shade from the sun. Although this led to a slight chill, Gwahl reassured it was better than the alternative. Apparently at the height of summer, the entire Pass was flooded with sunlight for a brief few hours, but those few hours were of unbearable heat as the sunlight bounced off the rocks to be magnified a thousand-fold. Thankfully, they greyness of the autumn morning carried into the afternoon, with no such sweltering conditions to endure.

He guided his rouncey beside Spotal. 'Who was the woman you were speaking to?'

'Her name is Silwei, Lieutenant Silwei Ganelia.'

'She was your lover?'

Spotal smiled. 'No, we were only ever friends. We met some twenty years ago, when I was stationed with my army at the northern borders. She served as one of my lieutenants for a few years, and we developed a good friendship. When we weren't on duty we used to spend much time together, hunting, exploring Tarnegrefur, sparring, wandering through the lands... She's from one of the villages up north. Took me to meet her family a few times, excellent cooks. I often promised to take them down south to meet my own family, but alas, my parents died before I was able. They were all so welcoming though, and I'd dare say they admired me a great deal!'

Lidan raised an eyebrow. 'You're sure she wasn't your lover?'

Spotal sighed. 'I'll admit, once upon a time I adored her in my juvenile, superficial way, gazing at her from afar, too frightened of rejection to ever approach her with my true feelings. I'm not sure if she knew. She certainly didn't feel the same. One day I realised she had strong feelings for a good friend of mine and they ended up as partners. For a long time, I tortured myself by comparing myself to him, Lieutenant Issil Edenahal. Taller, stronger, a broader jaw and brighter eyes... Yes, I held a higher rank, but what good is a rank to a lover? Eventually I realised such comparison was futile, that my grief was a lie. I was never going to approach her, never going to wed her, so what did I really lose? My love for her was naught but the immature dream of a young calef, an artificial emotion constructed from superficial attraction. Of course, that's not to say she's ever been anything less than beautiful.'

He whistled between his teeth. 'So, you don't think you like her anymore?'

'As I said, it was an artificial love.'

'It's just that you seemed a little bit lost back there in the camp, wandering around with your head in the clouds, coming back with a thunderous frown after she left.'

'I just didn't expect to see her!' Spotal shrugged.

'If you say so. There's no shame in it,' he winked knowingly.

'I didn't realise you were such an expert, Lidan. Who'd have put you down as a master matchmaker, a leading mind in the field of courting and romance?' Spotal laughed as the blood rushed to his face.

'I'm just stating the obvious. Didn't want to see you unhappy.'

'Well I appreciate it, but you looked too much into it.'

Lidan settled back into the saddle. Best to leave him alone, spare him any more awkward questions. He patted his midriff absentmindedly. A few calefs eventually came to take a look at their wounds before they left, but hadn't done much. They had a quick look at Widrias' leg, but decided it was healing as well as could be expected, all things considered, and his own wounds were announced fully-healed. Aside from that, Auran's head was examined, and everyone else was given a quick patch-up. Pwtrek, however, was taken to one side with Widrias following his examination, where the calefs discussed something with him in hushed tones. Throughout the conversation the satorr glanced repeatedly at his companion, who stood with an iron jaw.

Swivelling in his saddle to look behind him, he stole a quick glance at the juggernaut. He looked the same as ever. Tired, irritated with the horse, but strong. Settling back into a sensible riding position, he watched the canyon pass them by. Spotal pointed out to them a couple of places where gentle paths led up to the mountains themselves. Maybe they could have continued along the peaks to here on their initial descent from the plateau as Spotal suggested, instead of following the Atrael. It all seemed so long ago now, their flight from the army, searching for the source of the river, the waterfall... Reminiscing about the previous legs of this quest reminded him of the unfamiliar sounds heard in the night, of Gwahl's apparent fear of something following them. He should ask him again what gave him such cause for concern, what horrors lay in the snowy peaks.

They reached the north gates. The mountain range itself was only a few miles wide at this point, although many leagues long, and it was only mid-afternoon by the time the fortification came into sight.

To say the north wall was in a sorry state would be an understatement. The gates themselves were on their very last legs, clinging to the walls by their battered hinges. The ground was churned following the chaos of battle, uncollected arrows still peppering the earth. Above the walls could be seen a thick column of acrid black smoke, enough to sting the nostrils with the reek of burning hair and flesh.

A couple of calefs hailed them from the parapet. Twenty soldiers marched out the gates, weapons drawn, while archers sighted down drawn bows from the walls. Widrias leaned down and handed the leading calef Silwei's parchment. The calef gave it a quick read, and signalled his men to stand down.

'The battle is down south, friend,' he said, leading them to the gates.

'Not ours. We have needs to travel north.'

'I won't question your motives. I apologise for the smell.'

Five calefs stepped forwards to heave the inner gates open, creaking and groaning against their miserable hinges. Once again, they rode through the tunnel beneath the wall, murder-holes gaping above. Even in the gloom, bloodstains on the walls were all too visible. He raised his eyebrows as they passed the outer gate, wrought to nothing but timbers of splintered wood and twisted metal.

They passed the battered defences and were finally free of Imhara Pass. To one side was an enormous, smoking mound of juggernaut corpses. On the other side was a smaller, neater funeral pyre, long since burned to ash. He glanced again at Pwtrek. The juggernaut stared sadly at the undignified mound of carcasses. He caught Lidan's eye and smiled weakly, flicking his eyebrows. He smiled back. It must be difficult for him. Brothers in blood but enemies in war.

Corpses were odd things. A human corpse left a gnawing pit in his stomach, but a troglodyte, goblin, or even calefin corpse was somehow easier to bear. In battle, killing troglodytes, neiads, goblins, even the Hobb, twisted by Vapour and covered in a tapestry of tattoos, they all left him drained. But in the cave, against another man, it felt so much more like murder.

What was the fate of the murderers of murderers? Would they be rewarded as heroes for ridding Enadir of filth, or were they themselves condemned to be hunted by other bidding heroes? Maybe those soldiers had families, brothers left alone in a hateful, tortured world. Was it possible that his plight for vengeance against Stolach and Grey Eyes was doing more harm than good? Creating more lost, angry men such as himself to roam the world in search of blood? The memory of his past companions, lost so long ago, answered his question. He clenched his jaw. No, there was no murder in his quest, not against troglodytes, dreyads, satorrs, juggernauts, or men. There was only retribution.

Nevertheless, he had no desire to be a mindless killer. Frowning, he fished for a name, an important name for an unimportant hanex. Dirdin. Praise the north winds.

They left the burning bodies behind. To the west were the northern ridges of Tarnegrefur. They would follow these mountains until the end, where they could turn west through the northlands and return, at last, to Dailas Forest.

*

It took them fifteen days to finally clear the mountains. Morning of the second day had them pass a fresh battlefield, the bodies of fallen soldiers sprawled in twisted heaps along the rocky land. Tattered banners flickered in the morning wind, grim reminders of the outcome of the melee. At a distance, juggernaut and calef were indistinguishable, enclosed in their final fatal embrace. It was impossible to count how many had fallen, for all Lidan could tell there could have been a thousand soldiers, waiting to decompose. As they approached, a cloud of crows rose to the air, crying their indignation at the disturbance. To the north, a pack of wolves pricked their ears at their approach and watched their passing with wary eyes and raised heckles.

Eventually their path took a turn and they rode through the sea of bodies, picking their way between friend and foe. From the corner of his eye he saw Spotal scanning the battleground, taking in the sight of his slaughtered kin. Each calef he passed, he raised a hand to his chest in salute, honouring them for their noble sacrifice, buying time for their companions to escape.

With wide eyes, Lidan passed a fallen juggernaut, surrounded on all sides by dead calefs. He was terrifyingly bulky, bigger even than Pwtrek, bolstered by his heavy iron armour, flecked with rust and splattered in gore. His head was concealed by a visored helm crested with four ice blue feathers, hiding what he imagined to be empty, lifeless eyes. Comparing this monster to the surrounding calefs, seemingly so small and fragile next to him, he recognised the courage they demonstrated facing the juggernauts on an open field.

Ahead, Spotal dismounted and walked a few paces to their left. He knelt next to a body and laid a hand on her head.

'Captain Mali Rhelanai,' he said, loudly.

'She gave her life nobly,' said Pwtrek, resting a heavy hand on the calef's shoulder. 'As did all of your kin here.'

'They did, as honourable an act as one could ever ask for,' nodded Spotal. He clasped Pwtrek's hand and rose. 'I'm sorry so many of your countrymen lie here as well.'

The juggernaut nodded, and together they walked back to the main column. Spotal turned to the fallen captain once more, and saluted.

*

With the mountains behind them, Lidan quite enjoyed their ride through the northern kingdom. The terrain was different enough from the south to make it an interesting journey while still being uneventful enough to feel safe. The lands were far rockier and rougher than the rolling hills of the south. Pines dominated the forests, and countless rocky gullies and valleys cut through the land. The water was always ice cold and fresh, originating from melted snow on high peaks. If the southern lands were easy to hunt in, then up north the animals practically presented themselves on silver platters. They soon had several carcasses hanging from their saddles, supplies for the waiting Northlands.

'Bloody easy hunting,' chuckled Chekry, tying the latest rabbit to his saddle.

'Easy enough. Fewer calefs around, aren't there?' said Spotal. 'More resources for the wild animals. Animals in the south are likelier to live in herds for whatever reason, so although there are still plenty down there, they're a bit harder to isolate and kill individually. Remember as well this is the natural environment for the harandale root. With such a nutritious food source, populations are always going to boom.'

'It's also closer to the Far Eastlands, not separated by the sea,' added Gwahl. 'The Eastern Barrier was destroyed long ago in the Cataclysmic War. Although the calefs have rebuilt it as well as they can, there are countless places where creatures can break through.'

'I wouldn't say "countless",' muttered Spotal.

'Perhaps not countless,' admitted Gwahl, 'but plenty.'

'I'd like to see the Far Eastlands one day,' said Auran. 'Must be good hunting.'

Gwahl's laugh was one Lidan recognised well. It was not mocking, per se, but there was a certain condescension to it, as the daemon asserted his knowledge and experience.

'You'd be the hunted one, Auran,' he laughed. 'The monsters there are like no other. They aren't simple creatures to hunt and kill and bring home as trophies. They're cunning and malicious. They stalk and wait, play games with you, paralyse you with fear, then strike you down before you knew they were there. Back in the times of the giants, banishment into the Far Eastlands was a death sentence reserved only for the cruellest of criminals.'

'Perhaps not then,' Auran flicked his eyebrow.

'You're right though, it's a treasure of a country. Beautiful as these lands may be, compared to the Far East they are like dogs to wolves, house cats to lions. You probably wouldn't return from the journey, but the experience would be worth it,' Gwahl smiled.

'Now you're giving mixed messages,' Auran shook his head.

'Nothing new there, then,' Pwtrek grinned to Lidan.

'He said he wanted to see the Far Eastlands. I'm just giving him fair warning of the risks!' Gwahl protested, smiling.

'Consider me warned,' Auran snorted.

'Aye, him and all of us,' said Pwtrek. 'Pretty sights and populated by monsters. Not for me.'

'I didn't say it was *only* populated by monsters,' Gwahl smirked.

'Now you're pushing it,' Pwtrek shook his head with a disbelieving grin. 'I won't accept that any living person lives beyond a few miles of the Barrier, and even that's a stretch.'

'I never said person either, although there are colonies surviving the wilderness' Gwahl's smirk broadened. 'But there are creatures you know nothing of, Pwtrek Mestax. Beyond that barrier, animals are greater than here, they have grown and evolved into things you'd find unfamiliar. Direwolves are an example of one who made it across the barrier, before they were corrupted by the cockatrice.'

'Well that's convinced me, if anything else like them exist, you won't see me marching about their land.'

Lidan watched the daemon as he trotted ahead to Noswen, engaging in whispered conversation. At times he infuriated him with his arrogance and know-it-all attitude, and sometimes his words stung when another lesson was taught, but the bond he felt to the small daemon was the closest he felt to anyone since his cousins. Gwahl wasn't the only one, either. Pwtrek, Spotal, both like protective older brothers. The neiads were kind and playful, but too close to each other to let anyone else in. Noswen was too different, Auran too solemn, Widrias too stern.

Shifting his heavy shield across his back, he let his mind wander as they headed ever northwards, towards the grim desolation of the Northlands.

As they sat around their campfire that night, the conversation turned once again towards their past lives, and he listened earnestly, eager to find out more about these heroes he knew so well.

'When did you fight with the calefs, General?' asked Depani.

'Several times, I've even commanded some of their armies.'

'What battles?'

Widrias shrugged. 'They weren't large encounters, just small armies of troglodytes crossing the Atrael.'

'Not all of them,' smiled Spotal. 'I recall word making its way all the way up here of one great victory we had with you leading our army. This was some ten, fifteen years ago? In the midst of the Summer of Sorrow. Probably the one Silwei's scout mentioned.'

The satorr smiled. 'Ah, I know the one. I'd already made a name for myself as a capable commander beforehand, after many adventures with Mostyn among the Jagged Isles. Back then Stolach's rule hadn't reached them, and it was only recently that the Midlands had fallen to him, so there were plenty of foes to fight.

'Anyway, I was in Muranath by invitation of General Teig, who'd heard of my exploits and wished to meet me, maybe even tutor me in the arts of warfare. I bet you didn't know that, Captain?' the satorr's eyes twinkled in a way Lidan hadn't seen since entering Cysgodgors. 'Well anyway, I was with her when the attacks began. You see, the summer Spotal called "the Summer of Sorrow" was a season in which we met a certain ambitious troglodyte called Gluss-edd, or maybe Gluss-add, I forget his name...'

'Gluss-edd,' confirmed Gwahl, nodding.

'There we go. Gluss-edd was an ambitious, if misguided, tribal leader who decided his people had dwelt in the marshes for too long and would now move out. With Stolach the new name in the lands and many still smarting from crushing defeats at his hand, Gluss-edd decided to attack the Kingdom of the calefs, whom he perceived as a softer foe. Throughout the summer, time after time he led his forces against the calefs, with many lives lost on both sides. Hundreds of other tribes joined his cause, and the calefin armies were stretched thin.

'Word reached us the trogs had split apart into three large armies and would attempt to cross the Atrael at three different points. General Teig therefore needed three armies to counter them and split her forces evenly. She took command of the southern force, Colonel Menerai commanded the northern army, and I was given the middle.'

'Did the calefs not have another commander?' asked Auran. 'Where were you, Spotal?'

'I was with my company defending our northern borders from marauders.'

'They did have more commanders; Colonel Panai, Major Toli, Captain Ffeleb, Captain Hwylian...' Widrias ticked them off on his fingers

'Major Heddim?' suggested Gwahl.

Widrias shook his head. 'No, he was away on some voyage. Anyway, you get the idea, there were enough commanders, and many of them were with me to aid and assist in my direction of the battle. However, Teig decided a good way to improve my abilities in leading an army was through experience, so she gave me command of this force. Major Toli wasn't too pleased to be following my orders, but he didn't complain. He even offered some solid pieces of advice as the battle raged on.

'What a battle it was! Their force lined up on the west bank, and we were on the east. Arrows whipped through the air like wasps, croaking trogs lusting for blood. It was the first time I'd ever seen them attack in such an organised manner, I didn't even think it possible. When Spotal told us at the Council about how the same was happening again... I could hardly believe it.

'We did our best to repel the invaders, burning their rafts as they came across, battling them on the shores, but there were just too many. We were being pushed back. Four hours into the battle, the first trogs set foot on the east bank, followed by hundreds more. It was then I carried out my final strategy.

'Feigning panic, I ordered a tactical retreat of my forces, and we peeled away from the riverbank, battling as we went. The enemy went wild with excitement and pushed our battle line as hard as they could. Eventually my entire army reached high ground. At this point, outriders threw lit torches to intersecting lines of tar I'd painted across the ground. The field burst into flames, incinerating many of the brutes and spreading panic among the others. All the while my archers continued pouring arrows into the savages. Blinded by smoke and fire, the troglodytes returned shots in all directions, hitting each other more often than they hit one of us. By the time the flames died down, there was enough discord for me to send in the cavalry, breaking their entire army, routing them, and drive them hissing back into the Atrael. On the far bank the remaining trogs had already fled into the stinking swamp.

'It was a crushing victory. I lost many soldiers, but ten times as many enemies lay dead or dying. I found out later Gluss-edd led the attack from the northern army and was killed by an arrow as he tried to cross the Atrael on one of the rafts.'

'That was your first battle?' asked Lidan.

'It was my largest battle. Still is, in fact. As I said I'd already made a name for myself among the Jagged Isles with Mostyn.'

'Would you tell us about one of them?' asked Lidan.

Widrias smiled again. 'There are too many for me to recount. Mostyn and I used to be good friends, before certain events drove a wedge between us.'

'I wouldn't have guessed you were friends, considering how cold your reunion was back in Morgenal,' said Auran. 'It was more like the meeting of two old enemies who had long since forgotten their hate for each other.'

'You're not wrong, Auran, we certainly were enemies by the end. I suppose my new friendship with General Teig and the calefs was the beginning of our separation. You see, Mostyn always labelled himself as a pirate, a rogue, a ruffian, but above all else a free man. The thought of subjecting himself to anyone's rule was abhorrent to him, and he knew that if he followed me to the calefs, then he would be forced into the calefin fleet, to be commanded by higher-ranking officers. Ironic, of course, because he ultimately had to grovel to Morgenal's barons for protection from Stolach.'

'Fleet masters,' nodded Spotal. 'But surely you must have known he would never be allowed into our fleet? Our captains would have killed him as soon as his ship appeared on the horizon.'

'No, you're right, I knew this, and he knew this, and it was the main reason why he didn't follow me; because he couldn't. Through his insistence on naming himself a pirate, he made himself an enemy of the calefs.

'As the years went by, I saw less and less of him, occasionally meeting up whenever I left the Kingdom of the calefs for Morgenal, but I had work to do with the Council, and finding time for him was difficult. Once or twice we'd go on adventures together, but they'd lost their carefree appeal. I saw a change in the man. He was more reckless, foolhardy, attacking the king's galleons with impunity.'

'Surely that was a good thing? To have an ally at sea battling the king's fleet?'

'In some ways it was good. He was able to sink or capture ships far larger than his own, and his name was feared on the Great Waters. It was a profitable time for him too, as the ships he did not sink were sold to the barons, sometimes the Southlanders, sometimes to the Jagged Isles. But it was never a controlled attack, never carefully planned. He would simply see a sail on the horizon and attack. I was with him once when he walked straight into a trap. A merchant's ship with its cargo holds packed with the king's soldiers. He sailed in, carefree as you like, declared the enemy vessel his own, and as his crew went about looting, the enemy soldiers burst forth from below deck for a bloody battle. We barely escaped with our lives.

'I asked him several times to rein in on these stupid raids, to become a valuable member of the Council. He wouldn't listen, spouting his usual rubbish about being a free pirate. I pointed out he was not as free as he liked to think, shackled by the barons. He took offense, and we didn't speak for some time.

'A few years ago, I needed to travel to the Jagged Isles and I approached him again. Reluctantly, he agreed to take me, on the condition it would be the last time I ever set foot on the *Seascale*. My mission, set by the other chancellors, was to attempt to recruit as many of the inhabitants of the Jagged Isles to our cause.'

'How did that go?' asked Pwtrek.

'Well at first, quite a few of the independent lords promised me their armies. Of course, none of those promises mean anything now, they're all either dead or with Stolach. Anyway, we were on one island when the lord invited me and Mostyn to his hall. We went, feasted, and talked. The lord was a greedy little fellow, a fat little man who'd covered himself in cheap jewellery in a pathetic bid to look powerful. Anyway, the price that he set for his allegiance was Mostyn's ship and all its contents, in addition to several other demands. You must understand, this pompous little fool, although pathetic himself, had a very large army at his back, nearly two thousand soldiers. It would have been a massive boon to the Council to secure this ally.

'Obviously I was never going to give him Mostyn's ship. I knew the pirate would never allow it, and I had no particular wish to see him lose his dear vessel. After all, he was my friend. Nevertheless, I thanked the lord for his offer and told him I would think it over during the night and negotiate a deal in the morning. We left, Mostyn ready to burst with anger, anger he turned on me. He claimed I betrayed him, that this was my plan all along to get him out the way. No matter how much I tried to reassure him, he wouldn't listen, eventually storming off to his cabin. Tired myself, I went to my hammock and slept.

'When I woke the ship was moving. I heard sounds of battle overhead. I rushed to deck and saw Mostyn had commanded his men to leave the dock under the cover of night and attack the island's fortifications from sea. His war engines were screaming, the arbalests were thrumming, and men died in droves. The lord sent some of his own, lesser ships to attack the *Seascale* and a slaughter commenced, with Mostyn's experienced pirates butchering the opposing sailors.

'I rushed to the poop deck and ordered Mostyn to stand down, but he laughed in my face and struck me in the head with a cudgel. I didn't take kindly to this and drew my sword. He drew his cutlass, and we fought. Normally he would not be a match for me, but the waters were rough, I was still half-asleep, and my head was spinning from the cudgel-blow. Eventually I got the better of him. I stood over him, my sword at his gut, and ordered him one last time to stand down. He decided to pull out a dagger and swipe at my legs, so I stabbed him in the stomach.

'His crew were watching and went wild. I cut down the first few who rushed at me, but I knew I would fall if I stayed, so I jumped overboard and swam back to the dock while the *Seascale* sailed away. It took some doing for me to convince the lord not to kill me for treachery, but eventually not only did I convince him to let me live and take me back to Nefarwy, but I also secured his allegiance.

'When I arrived back, I heard word in Morgenal that Mostyn was indeed alive, and I returned to the Council. That was our last voyage. Now you know why our reunion was not a particularly happy one.'

'I'm not sure I'd have agreed to set foot on his ship had I known about his turbid past,' said Auran, scratching his head

'Maybe we shouldn't have,' nodded Widrias, sadly. 'Maybe we should have sought a different route to the plateau. In fact, we should never have even set out on this mission, and for that I apologise.'

Lidan blinked in surprise, taken aback by the unexpected apology.

'Nothing to apologise for, sir,' assured Pwtrek. 'The serpent key would have been a beautiful asset to our cause, and you were right to look for it. I'm sure the Council is getting along fine without us for the moment. It's not like we're the only ones capable of fighting against Stolach, no offense meant, of course.'

'It doesn't matter that we're miles away from our companions, because we're expendable?' Depani said with an air of indignation.

'No, Depani,' Pwtrek replied, wearily. 'It's just there is a great depth of knowledge and skill within the Council. Although we are all valuable, if we do perish, at least there are others who can take our place. It's a good thing that even if we die, our cause lives on.'

An uncomfortable silence followed. It was all so easy to forget there was so much going on in the war outside their mission. Lidan had become so completely engrossed in this quest that for him, their little band of warriors *was* the Council, and that they alone were fighting against Stolach. What Pwtrek just said reminded him of the scale of what was going on. There were undoubtedly countless other bands of brothers-in-arms trudging across the countryside on their own quests, and theirs was just another leaf in an autumn gale. The true beating heart of the Council were the remaining high chancellors back in Dailas, pushing their minds to come up with schemes to drag Stolach from the throne.

'What will happen when we return?' he asked.

'We'll discuss what happened with the other chancellors, listen as they tell us what has happened in our absence, and see what steps to take next,' said Widrias.

'And what will those steps be?'

'Well that depends on what's happened while we've been away,' the satorr raised his hands in exasperation.

'Will we be sent on another mission, do you think?' he pressed.

'I don't know, if there's need for one, maybe.'

'Will we remain together or be sent away to different branches of our forces?' he asked, worried.

'Lidan, I don't know. For all I know by the time we reach the Council they'll have already begun their march against Crastalan, or everything might be exactly as it was when we left. Patience! Concentrate on getting back first.'

He grimaced and threw a blade of grass into the fire. He didn't want them splitting up, they were in it together. Besides, not knowing things always irritated him, it's why he was always so inquisitive, so curious. He glanced at Spotal. He'd been so sombre lately. Everyone else knew why, but they wouldn't tell him. He didn't understand why.

Mustering his courage, he asked what he'd wanted to ask for months.

'Spotal? What happened to you up here? I know it's painful for you–'

'Lidan!' scolded Pwtrek. 'You shouldn't pry into things.'

'I know, I was just curious, I know something–'

'What do you know? Not enough to be asking such things,' said Pwtrek.

'No, no,' Spotal raised his hands placatingly. 'It's alright. While we're in the mood for storytelling… you may as well know. We'll be passing the results of my exploits soon anyway.'

'Oh, no it's alright,' he stammered, suddenly guilty at the haunted expression Spotal wore. 'I was being insensitive.'

'No. I… I should relive it. Now more than ever. You should all hear it from my perspective before you see… what I caused.'

Spotal rubbed his eyes, composing himself. Lidan glanced nervously at his companions, expecting disapproving glares, but their attention was on the calef.

'I'll start from the beginning. Give you a bit of context. From what I know about you, Lidan, your knowledge of the wider world beyond your own village isn't exactly extensive,' he snorted. 'Anyway, my childhood was largely uneventful, my parents were kind and caring and everything anyone could ever ask their parents to be. My father was the great Major Cetril, my mother Lady Anharel. They provided me with warmth and happiness and I adored them.

'Each and every calef knows which vocation to pursue from a very young age, for we suffer not the ambiguity of men as to what we should do in life. It is set before our eyes. Some calefs will aspire to be craftsmen, fishermen, physicians, farmers, poets, whatever. Obviously, I chose to be a soldier, like my father.

'I am not entirely familiar with how other races are trained in combat but for us it's a long and arduous affair, often going weeks with little sleep as we hone our skills. Even when I was sent home for recuperation, my father would constantly drive me to improve, to perfect and sharpen my wits. He taught me how soldiery is not only about how you handle a weapon, but it requires intelligence and wit, the greatest soldiers of all hiding unimaginable amounts of knowledge within their helms. Thus, much of my training was in our library as I read countless tomes on philosophy and complex theories on a myriad of subjects. My father and I would spar for hours as he worked to improve my swordsmanship.

'I was the best at what I did. It sounds arrogant, but it's the truth. Even after my official training was complete, my father would send for swordsmen throughout Enadir to come and teach me more, to ensure I was adept in as many different styles of combat as possible. He taught me how to command a battlefield, what strategies and feints to use in order to win the day. He showed me the honour that is to be won upon the field of battle, whether in noble sacrifice or a perfect victory.

'He pushed me to be the very best that I could be. All the pain and sleepless nights were necessary to give me the opportunity to be great.

'When I was forty, I was ready to join the Calefin Guard. Ten years older than most of the soldiers in my regiment due to my extended training. Thanks to my father's rank and standing, I was offered an officer rank as soon as I joined the regiment. I refused, instead deciding to make my own name. My father was proud of me for that. I was proud of myself.

'Most of the time my regiment was stationed as a border patrol between our land and the Marshes. One of the river patrols. You've heard of them, yes? Our famous river patrols? We fought many skirmishes with invading troglodytes. I distinguished myself in those battles, and soon found myself rising through the ranks to corporal, sergeant, made the jump to lieutenant, and eventually captain. I was given command of a unit of fifty. My father called it the best day of his life. My mother wept with pride.

'General Teig would often send my unit very far away from Muranath, up north past those bloody mountains, to protect our northern villages from the horrors of the Northlands. It was during this time that Stolach sent his assassins to steal a key, and my father was killed.'

Lidan glanced at Noswen. Pwtrek, Chekry, and Depani did the same. She ignored them. Spotal didn't pause. There was no accusation in his story, only simple fact.

'My duties prevented me from returning to my home and attending the cremation. I was not ashamed of this. My father would have scolded me had I abandoned my men to see him away. My troops held a token ceremony for my benefit. I appreciated that. They were good soldiers.

'What I regret is not being there to comfort my mother, who died soon after. A combination of grief, loneliness, and pneumonia. Or so they say. The loss was unnecessary and weighed heavily on my conscience. Still does. But once again, my brothers in arms reassured me I did the right thing in remaining, protecting the villages.

'I admit, my father's death affected me more than I would have originally anticipated, as I refused King Lleunedd's offers of promotion to major. I just hadn't done enough to deserve the rank my father held when he died. So, I remained captain for years, although the size of my force grew to well over two hundred calefs. My own small army. My victories over invaders from the north were being talked about, and I was becoming a well-known figure in the Kingdom. Whenever I returned to Muranath, they would run after me in the street and give me flowers. Women adored me. My peers treated me as their equals. General Teig assured me my father would be proud. She said I commanded great respect in the court of the king.'

He paused. He wore a smile that never reached his eyes as he idly played with his captain's talisman.

'Four years ago, a village was destroyed by a pack of direwolves sweeping down from the Northlands in a frenzy of blood. I was ordered to destroy them. I set out with my army of loyal soldiers and chose the field where we would meet them in battle. Because of my experience fighting against bands of marauders attacking our villages, I thought these animals would be easily culled. I swaggered in, expecting a swift slaughter. In a way it's what I got.

'I underestimated my enemy. The giant, savage wolves massacred each and every soldier under my command. They were stronger, faster, more powerful than anything I've ever seen, and there were so many of them. I know Pwtrek described them to you, Lidan, but he did it too sensitively for you to appreciate what they are. Each wolf easily ten feet long from snout to tail, their shoulders five feet tall. Each a crazed, hunger-driven monster imbued with madness which gives them strength like lightning. Their fangs are deformed, each canine so long it rips holes in their bottom lips when they close their mouths. Their eyes are burning and malevolent. They fought with the cockatrice against the giants in the Cataclysmic War, you know? They're possessed with a need to gorge on the hearts of the living, a grim reminder of what might assail our lands if we do not protect our borders.

'They broke apart our phalanxes and tore through the throng of bodies in a disgusting orgy of carnage. I… picked my battlefield poorly. Too much space for them to surround us, exposed our flanks. Treated them like an infantry rabble where I should have treated them like a light cavalry force. A thin phalanx open at the flanks and archers exposed. The wolves just ran around my line, massacred the archers, then smashed through the middle of my thin lines from both sides. I lost every single one of my troops that day. I survived because a wolf I'd slain fell on my body and knocked me unconscious. Trapped beneath it, it saved my life. Hours later, when I finally pushed the carcass away, I saw what the beasts had done to my kind, brave, perfect friends. Devoured heads and hearts, bodies left to rot.

'That pack of wolves proceeded to devour the entire population of three more villages before the relief force arrived and killed them all. Trapped them in a vale, poured boiling tar into their midst and set them alight. Had I done that, then I wouldn't have thrown away the lives of so many soldiers and innocent villagers. My army was dead and my honour was lost.

'When I returned to Muranath, the king could hardly look at me. He was so disgusted I was ordered to wear a black bag over my head when I was in his presence. He said I was to blame, that the blood of hundreds of innocents now stained my hands, that I was unfit to wear the armour of the Calefin Guard. He was right. The humiliation was unbearable. I would wander the streets of the city, and every calef knew of my failure and judged me for it. Where children presented me with flowers they now scurried to the other side of the road, parents would regard me with malcontent, or worse, pity.

'Lleunedd wished for me to be cast out of the army, but General Teig stood up for me and ensured that I was able to keep my undeserved rank. She used the memory of my father against the king, and told him that they should not allow my family's name to be forever tarnished after the great deeds of Major Cetril. Despite this, Lleunedd refused me permission to have anything to do with the Calefin Guard, correctly judging me to be inadequate. So, I would remain in my parents' home in my loneliness, only venturing out to collect food to sustain my miserable life. A soldier in name and rank alone, forbidden from having anything to do with our armies.'

He sighed and hid the talisman within his brigandine once again.

'My home was a grand house, a prominent building in the Kingdom due to the accomplishments of my family. Young calefs would come to see the home of Major Cetril, but no more. It was shunned, I was pushed to one side. Nevertheless, I could not be forgotten. People still knew my name, they knew I remained locked behind iron gates, enduring my own shame. I was a thorn of dishonour in Lleunedd's side.

'When the king was approached for aid by the Council, he was pressed for time, short on troops, our armies stretched thin by the threat of the trogs. He found a way out and gave me the role of ambassador between the royal court and the Council. On the surface it seems like an honourable role. In reality, it is a way for Lleunedd to be rid of me, and for me to be forgotten, unless I'm able to somehow honour myself once more with my actions in my new role. He's essentially given me an ultimatum; regain my honour by defeating Stolach with you, or accept that my name will at last be lost, freeing the king of any further obligation to me or my father.

'I've been disgraced and humiliated, mostly by my own hand. This was my final opportunity to regain my honour and pull myself back from this pit. The serpent key was more to me than a tool to defeat Stolach. It was my lifeline. Now it's lost, everything I've ever lived for is lost, and Stolach is as strong as ever.'

He fell silent, his cheeks flushed with embarrassment. He didn't meet Lidan's gaze, perhaps too afraid of what his reaction would be.

It was a lot to process. Obviously, much of the tale was glossed over, but Lidan didn't want to press him for further details. His hooded eyes, thin mouth, and slumped shoulders were testament to his misery. Probing him further would do no good. Perhaps an attempt at comfort?

'You're not a disgrace, Spotal,' he said, softly. 'You're one of the finest soldiers I've ever met.'

'Then your experience has been sadly lacking,' spat Spotal, bitterly.

'I don't see any loss of honour in your actions. You did your best, which is all anyone can ask of you.'

'My best? All those years studying, learning, thrown aside by my own arrogance. My father would die of shame if he knew. I suppose that's the only consolation I can take, that neither of my parents were alive to see their only child fail.'

'But people make mistakes! How many mistakes has Teig made? I'm sure she's committed several tactical blunders? You shouldn't be so hard on yourself.'

Spotal blinked slowly, controlling his anger. 'You didn't listen to what I said. I was the cause of the murder of three entire villages. Teig may have lost the odd battle, lost soldiers, but was never the cause of the deaths of innocents. These were villagers, Lidan. Children, gardeners, artists, scholars, cooks. War was not their business. It was mine. And I failed. I let it march right up to their doors and kill them all.'

'You made a mistake. At least you tried to stop them, your men died fighting to protect their lands.'

'They died because of my incompetence. Do you know how many of the relief force were killed? Four. Compare that to my two hundred.'

He paused. It was certainly a costly mistake. He understood his guilt, but it was a mistake nonetheless. There was no malice, no purposeful evil, only cruel misfortune. But it was difficult to put into words.

'I'm sorry, it's a sad tale,' he began, struggling to find the appropriate words.

'It's not for you to be sorry. It's my shame to bear,' Spotal shrugged.

'But you shouldn't have been treated so cruelly! All this with wearing a black bag…'

'Cruelly?' he snapped. 'Deservedly. My honour gone, my family name in tatters, I deserved that black bag, that humiliation. Three villages of innocents, two hundred soldiers…'

'Well, from what I've seen, you're one of the bravest people I know,' he insisted.

'No,' Spotal shook his head.

'I still respect you.'

'You mustn't. I am no role model.'

'The way I see it, you lost this "honour" because of a costly mistake, fighting against monsters. But you still fight, you're still here by our side, helping us through this war,' he smiled, trying to meet his gaze. 'You could've stayed hiding in your home until you were old and grey, but you agreed to come to us. It shows you understand there's more at stake than petty concepts of glory.'

'Careful, Lidan,' he flashed his fangs. 'Why do you think I came, if not to regain my honour? Seeing what's been done to my country may have…invigorated my efforts, but still. I am the reason for hundreds of innocent graves. As guilty as Stolach. You, or you, or Silwei may not understand that'

'But it isn't your responsibility to stop Stolach on your own!'

He glanced at the others, imploringly. Auran nodded furiously in agreement, Gwahl simply cocked his head.

'Leave him, Lidan,' said Gwahl, tiredly. 'You don't understand the politics of Muranath. Spotal fights for his family name, their memory. His mistake was, as you said, costly. Don't begrudge him the right to mourn, especially not here.'

Reaching out, he patted the calef on the shoulder. Spotal closed his eyes and turned away.

Lidan caught Gwahl's eye, and the daemon flicked his eyebrows. He nodded. Presumably, it was a conversation they'd had several times over, one the daemon had long since given up on. Spotal was too set in his ways to listen to them, the wounds still too fresh to heal.

'Enough excitement for tonight,' said Gwahl. 'Time to sleep.'

*

The following day, with the jaws of Tarnegrefur still visible to the south, Spotal fell silent. He conferred with none save for Gwahl. The daemon rode next to him, constantly whispering words of comfort to the increasingly-distressed calef. Even Widrias rode back a few times to exchange a few words. Lidan was no fool. The reason for Spotal's silence was obvious; they were approaching one of the villages.

He was not the only one to recognise the reason for Spotal's silence, and a brooding mood descended over the party. Each reflected over their own personal failings, the bitterness and remorse of those memories weighing heavily on their shoulders. To him, it was the reason for his initial imprisonment that haunted him. Foolish decision after foolish decision, half-thought actions and their inevitable consequences, culminating in tragedy. Just as Spotal felt responsible for the loss of his soldiers, Lidan knew he was, in part, equally responsible for the loss of his friends. It was an ugly truth he preferred not to face, but here in the shadow of Spotal's wretched guilt, he could not so easily avert his eyes. He looked at Gwahl longingly. If only he'd ride back and whisper a comforting word to him too. He shook himself, ashamed of such petty jealousy. Spotal needed Gwahl more than him at this moment, especially if what he could see on the horizon were true. At present it was nothing more than a blur against the grey sky, but soon enough it would be all too clear.

Sure enough, two hours later, they rode past the village. Widrias initially tried to steer them clear of the settlement, taking a detour to spare Spotal's pain, but the calef refused, determined to face his past. Thankfully, he didn't make them ride through the village, but they passed close enough to see the extent of the damage.

Time and cold had preserved the buildings somewhat, and despite being uninhabited for four years, they still stood as they were, or at least, as they were after the direwolves. Even with his limited knowledge of calefin architecture, Lidan could see the buildings had suffered damage. Holes were torn through walls, doors lay askew, and trees lay collapsed and dead on the ground.

It was the overwhelming silence that struck him most. Not a bird sang, no mice rustled, no timbers creaked, no hinges squeaked. Enadir herself had entombed the village in a respectful hush, a tribute to the voices of the village's inhabitants, permanently silenced by the wolves.

He shifted in his seat, straining his eyes to catch a glimpse of any old bloodstains, or skeletal corpses, but there were none. If anything, the lack of blood or bones was more chilling than had it been a gore-encrusted settlement filled to the brim with jet black carrion crows, screeching their morbid calls to the sky. Unsettlingly clean and mild, this lifeless shell of a village, once a happy home for so many, was a ghost.

His nostrils flared as his rouncey stomped the ground impatiently, sending up a cloud of dust and a foul aroma. Choking, he was tempted to lean over and spit, in an attempt to clear his throat of the cloying smell, but felt it would be disrespectful. Agitated, the other horses nickered softly, tossing their heads in an attempt to clear their nostrils. Eventually the dust settled back down, but the smell lingered. It had been present ever since they approached the boundaries of the village. Musky and sickly, the direwolves had marked this village as their own, and to this day it belonged to them.

'This is Abrenelan,' announced Spotal. 'The third village the direwolves desecrated, after Abrenefain, Talbonain, and before Carnelan.'

'How many lived here?' asked Pwtrek, gently.

'No less than eighty,' replied Spotal. 'All gone now, basking in the fields beyond the clouds.'

They stood in silence for a few minutes, saying nothing, staring solemnly at the ruined village. Faced with the actual buildings, Spotal's tale suddenly became real, and he could finally appreciate why he bore such overwhelming guilt. How it would feel to know your failings were the reason why so many innocents were dead? Could he live with that level of remorse? Probably not. But he wasn't as strong as Spotal. Even though this ghost village showed the true extent of Spotal's terrible defeat, it also proved his strength and determination to carry on.

Shaking his head sadly, Widrias turned to the calef and nodded.

'It's time to continue, Spotal. Put this village behind you once more. Concentrate on succeeding in this latest campaign.'

The calef was the first to turn away, digging his heels into his rouncey's flanks to a brisk trot. One by one, Lidan and the others followed, leaving behind the ruined village.

Chapter 33

'This isn't the time of year for shearing my sheep, they'll freeze in the coming months, especially if this winter is to be as cold as it promises!'

Stolach chewed his cheek thoughtfully. The grizzled old farmer was right, of course, but then again, his people needed the wool to clothe themselves in the aforementioned harsh winter they expected.

'I understand your concerns for your livestock, but people come before animals, and I will not see anyone freeze when I could have done something about it.'

'Your Majesty, I cannot do what you ask. It would be the equivalent of sending them to the slaughterhouse.'

'That is what they are ultimately bred for, is it not?'

'Eventually, yes, but I need at least seven seasons of wool out of them before I send them away, otherwise my business wouldn't be sustainable.'

'Then only shear the ones who are old enough for you to justify sending away to be slaughtered.'

'I don't have enough to make up the amount of wool you require.'

He closed his eyes and rubbed his eyelids wearily. Preparing his realm for winter was stressful at the best of times, but preparing for one in the midst of a war was even worse. The amount of clothing, food, armour, weapons, and livestock that had been sent across the border to the Kingdom of the calefs was both staggering and crippling. If he had half of the resources he'd sent away, then these seasonal concerns would be negligible. As it was, this was an exhausting weight on his shoulders.

'Very well, here's my proposition to you. Send away half of your stock for slaughter, and you'll be paid in full for them, with an additional half on top of that.'

The old man grimaced and rubbed his chin, before nodding glumly. 'That is a good arrangement, thank you, your Majesty.'

Stolach nodded and waved him away, and the farmer was escorted out of the throne room by his guards. Stretching, he rose from the throne and wandered to the spiral staircase. Another day of listening to his subjects done, now he needed sleep. Later today, he had another council of war with his commanders, but he would have to reschedule that for another day. He had no taste to hear the latest terrible losses suffered at the hands of the calefs.

He climbed the stairs, passing floor after floor, past the great library he loved so much, up to the final landing, the twentieth storey. Out of the depths of his cloak he pulled an iron key. From the other side he heard the familiar old latch click and pushed the heavy, iron-studded door open.

His living quarters. A large bedroom, a spacious cleaning room decked with a large copper tub, and several small cloakrooms and storerooms to keep his various possessions. Behind one door was a ladder leading to a viewing platform where he had a perfect three-hundred-and-sixty-degree view of the surrounding country.

But now was not the time for star-gazing. Today, he only had eyes for his comfortable bed and the person lying upon it.

Stroking her hair lightly, she stirred beneath his touch. Soft, like the finest Southland silk.

She opened her almond eyes and looked at him. His heart fluttered, as it always did when those wondrous amber eyes met his. He smiled.

'Hello, my darling,' she whispered, propping herself up onto her elbow. 'What time is it?'

'The sun will rise within the hour,' he whispered back, pulling off his boots and lying down beside her. 'You're in bed early?'

'I was exhausted. The city nobles and master-merchants are such tiresome company.'

'Everything alright with them?'

'For now. Trade is still good from Morgenal, despite the Council's efforts. A couple are complaining about Baron Allut, as always. I promised them a stronger military presence around his docks to make sure their ships aren't taxed unfairly,' she yawned.

'Little good it'll do. The baron thinks he's king of that city,' he shook his head.

'I know, but it made them feel better,' she shrugged. 'Are you not supposed to meet with your generals later?'

'Yes,' he said, with a sigh, 'but I'm not in the mood for it now.'

'Is it not important? I thought they were going to report to you the latest on the war to the east?'

'I get reports every hour, I have no need for yet another arduous meeting with my generals, telling me things I already know.'

'They might give you some good advice?'

'What advice could they give me? One is inept, one is a bloodthirsty maniac, one is blinded with vain ambition-'

'And *all* are fine commanders, otherwise you wouldn't have appointed them. Don't be so proud, Stolach, you need to listen to them. What's the point of having advisors if you won't entertain their ideas?'

'It's not just that,' he yawned. 'War is tiring, I forgot just how tiring it really was.'

'You can't complain about that, you made this one yourself. Nobody forced you to invade.'

He cuffed her playfully around the ear. 'You don't understand.'

'Yes I do, you want more power, so you attacked the calefs.'

'If you understood you wouldn't say that, and you're no fool, by the four winds. I've been at war with Lleunedd for nearly eighteen years, my invasion is just another advancement. It's all moves and counter-moves. He saw my rise in the Midlands as a threat, which is why he wouldn't give me the lion key, which is why I sent Noswen and her assassins, and that's how my conflict with them began. A little while later the Council rose, and to this day Lleunedd openly supports them. So you see, it is not only for power I constructed the invasion, it's retaliation for various other attacks, direct and indirect, the calefs have made against me.'

'And the troglodytes?'

He looked at her, and saw she was frowning. 'We've discussed this. I don't have enough soldiers to defeat the calefs alone. I needed their hordes.'

'But they're barbarians, killers, cannibals! I still find it difficult. Why you would throw your lot in with them…?'

Shaking his head, he took her hand and interlaced his fingers with hers. 'Try to look at it from this perspective. The troglodytes *are* barbarians, they *are* killers and cannibals, and for as long as we can remember they've lived in chaos in their swamps and mud-holes. But look at what I've achieved. I've united them and directed them towards a goal, a cause. I brought order to their chaos, just as I brought order to the Midlands. And that's why I do this. Order and peace out of chaos.'

'Perhaps, but what will happen once the war is over?'

'What do you mean?'

'They're united, for now, but only under the banner of war. As savages, what more can you expect? But once this war is over, do you really expect them to form stable societies in their swamps? They'll regress to their barbaric ways because that's their nature. If the giants of old couldn't direct them to order, what hope do you have?'

'The giants didn't have the same conviction as I do,' he bristled.

'They had the very same conviction. Your cause is a twin to theirs. They fought for peace and unity, and they succeeded in everyone except the troglodytes, whom they were only able to suppress and keep to the swamps. You've read the history books. How many wars were fought between those monsters and the civilised folk? Countless. It's because they multiply so quickly. Within a decade there are five new generations of savages crying for blood as they were not there to see the destruction of their previous wars.'

'Those uprisings only occurred in the times of weaker rulers; Haled Hementirion, Nimiha, Affedin Huy.'

'You forget the very first war against the troglodytes, when Arekellor Anaali was king. He was strong. From what I've read, he reminds me of you,' she took his face in her hands. 'A brave fighter, rising from the chaos to unite the lands. His name and fearsome reputation did little to quell the troglodytes, and it was only after they tasted his fury that their uprisings ceased.'

'It won't come to that. At least not yet. As I said, I need them for now. Besides, I can succeed where the giants failed. After all, they're all dead and gone whereas we're still alive, centuries after the Cataclysmic war.'

'Don't feed the trogs with war, otherwise they'll only become more and more violent. You'll make them an even greater enemy for when the time comes to face them across the battlefield.'

'Vixel, please, I can't defeat all my enemies without the support of mercenaries.'

She huffed and turned away. He understood her frustration. He'd met her seven years ago on one of his rare adventures across the Midlands, in a village a mere half mile from the borders of Tarin Swamp. Troglodyte raiding parties were running amok, and after several unsuccessful attempts by his inept captains to catch them, the voices of his subjects finally called out loud enough for him to take personal action. Vixel's village had been destroyed and she was among the four survivors who crouched tenaciously in the ruins of their homes. Stolach saved them, riding in with his personal guard and taking them back to his camp. He fed them, clothed them, and extracted vital information about the raiding party. Their contribution to this small campaign was invaluable. He used their reports to figure out the number of the enemy, where they'd come from, where they went. A week later the thirty troglodytes lay rotting at the border of Tarin swamp as a stark warning to the rest of them. He would not tolerate raids into his lands. Afterwards, he bought Vixel and her companions back to Crastalan. A great friendship soon developed into something more.

He understood her hatred of the troglodytes, but was not prepared to let it cloud his judgement as well, at least not until they served their purpose.

'Do you not believe in me?' he asked sadly.

'Of course I do,' she soothed in a gentle tone, 'but I don't want to see you crushed when you underestimate their savagery. I believe you are a commander who is more than capable of winning this war without the support of monsters.'

'When all is done, if I cannot bring them to order, then I will eliminate them from Nefarwy.'

'Genocide?'

'The giants did it with the cockatrice, I will do what I must to our enemies. I know they are barbaric and wild, and this attempt to tame them will be the final one. Should my efforts prove unsuccessful, then there is no place for them in my world of order.'

She shifted her position to rest her head against his chest and held him tight. He settled his arms around her shoulders and breathed in the scent of her hair. Cinnamon oil from the Southlands, warm and sweet.

'I had a dream you went away to fight with the calefs,' she whispered. 'You stood on the slopes of a mountain, sword and shield in hand, your tall helm upon your head, and swathes of enemies fell before you. But then at the eve of your victory, a shadow crept up to the summit of the mountains and created an avalanche that buried you all, and you suffocated, and left me here alone.'

'That will not happen,' he whispered. 'I will not fight across the borders. The only time my sword will taste blood is if they should ever attack us here.'

'I want this war to end.'

'So do I, and it will, once all threats are eliminated.'

'All threats... There will always be a threat. As long as your kingdom grows there will be threats.'

'If it grows it grows in strength, and those threats become smaller and smaller until they are hardly threats at all.'

'No matter how large your kingdom grows, all it will ever take is a single assassin's poisoned blade, the smallest of cuts, and everything you have built will crash down.'

'My legacy will live on, someone else will stand up and take my place.'

'Whom? I don't know anyone with the same willpower as you to bring peace to the kingdom.'

'I know of one.'

He felt her jaw clench against his chest. 'He is no ruler. His kind were never rulers. You need an heir, someone you've mentored their entire life, someone who can command as much respect as you.'

Stolach paused. 'What about Tomon? He might be able to take it up, provided he had someone by his side to guide him in the politics of ruling a land. You could be that person.'

'Tomon is not a ruler either, and I am not a political advisor. You know what I'm getting at.'

He knew.

'Now is not the time for children, Vixel, not in the midst of a war.'

'I agree. But you said yourself, you've been at war for nearly eighteen years. For all we know, you'll be at war for the rest of our lives. If not now, when?'

'I would not know what to do with the child, and neither would you.'

'Instinct will guide me, as it will guide you.'

'I do not wish to discuss this right now.'

'You never want to discuss it.'

'You're right, I don't.'

'This isn't some maternal brooding. It's common sense. You need someone to follow your footsteps. If we raise one from birth, instil our values in their core, your work will be immortalised. It will herald back to the time of the giants; succession of a royal bloodline. The people *need* the stability of a ruling family. I want this for your sake.'

'For my sake?'

'Yes. We need to think about the bigger picture. Expansion and conquering is only worth it if there's a long-term plan in place. We need cities for stability, agriculture and trade routes for sustainability, and a lineage for survivability. I don't especially want to put my body through it, but I see its necessity. I'm willing to make the sacrifice. Are you?'

He didn't reply. They lay in silence as he struggled to find the words. Vixel waited patiently. He could practically hear her brain working to construct another argument.

Finally, he spoke in a hesitant voice that would have sounded so alien to everyone else, such a contrast to his usual cold, assertive tone.

'Eventually, we will conceive. But at a time when I can devote my full attention to the child, to raise them to be as strong and wise as we are. But not now. There is too much conflict, a war on too many fronts. I cannot divide my attention between the two. Perhaps when the calefs or the Council are defeated. Any expansion is essentially halted until those goals are reached anyway.'

'What if you lose?'

'If I lose, it won't matter.'

She nodded slowly. 'I'll keep taking my herbs until the time comes, don't worry. It won't happen until we're in a better position.'

He shifted and sat up, and she sat up as well. Unlocking his hands from hers, he cupped her face. 'It will happen. The calefs will fall, the Council will be crushed, the Southland resistance will be purged, and the rogues of Dailas Forest will be brought to justice. We will build a better future for Nefarwy together, I promise. Our legacy will be greater than the giants. Have faith in me.'

'You know I do.'

He nodded slowly and lay back down, willing himself to sleep away the day's weariness.

*

As always, he awoke as soon as the sun's final scarlet rays filled the sky. Carefully untangling himself from Vixel's arms, he washed his face from the ceramic basin at the bedside. He brushed his teeth with a stiff-bristled brush, removing the cloying film from their surface. Once dressed, he climbed the ladder to the viewing platform.

The scarlet sky made an impressive backdrop to the black dunes, framing each one with a ruddy outline. Trading caravans came from the south, scouting parties returned from the east and north, columns of soldiers marched from the west.

He allowed himself a wry smile. How fortunate he'd been to finally gain the allegiance of the Westlands. They were steadfast and resolute. A nobility born of struggle, a resilience nurtured by the

605

wilderness, something beyond the grasps of the Midlands. He should have approached them so much sooner than what he did. The Burning Eye of the West and Dreclan Mountains seemed like the end of the world. How wrong. He's set his boundaries too small. But Enadir was large. With their support, his new order could reach beyond the borders of all his maps. First the Jagged Isles and the Southlands, then the Eastlands, then the barren Northlands.

It hadn't been an easy task to secure their allegiance. Barely a quarter of his men returned, bearing news of fertile lands and brooding men. They'd been treated first with suspicion, then with hospitality. Recently returned from the Jagged Isles, he'd felt in an adventurous mood and made the personal journey beyond the mountains.

It wasn't a journey he was likely to make again. After countless days of riding through ash storms, skirting around roasting lakes of lava, then braving the freezing mountain peaks beyond, they made it to lush forests and open plains. They were met by the Westlanders.

Their meeting was unusual. The Westlanders were curiously aware of events in the Midlands, despite his ignorance of their affairs. Relatively few in number compared to the Midlands, they'd managed to maintain order. An order and peace the likes of which the Midlands hadn't enjoyed since before the Cataclysmic war. Each settlement was aware of the other, working together to maintain their people, pooling resources and knowledge. A balance. Made possible for its seclusion. He would bring that balance to the rest of Nefarwy.

Despite its order, there was also danger. Fearsome creatures swept down from the north, came from the western seas, and burst forth from the Stenn Wood. It was these constant battles that hardened the people and maintained their sparse population.

Of course, to have order, a population needed a ruling figure of some sort. In the case of the Westlanders it was an order of wise elders and, to his personal distaste, daemons. Setting aside his bitterness towards these creatures, he met with them, conversed with them, and forged their allegiance. It took surprisingly little effort. The only thing they asked in return was aid in building defences from the wilderness.

He recalled the parting words of the ugly, grizzled daemon called Gogofaint.

'As elders of the Westland, we strive for peace and order, and are successful in our cause. We see in you, King Stolach, a kindred spirit. You fight for peace. We must support you as you bring the order of our small land to the vast world beyond.'

The vindication in those words! How foolish those treacherous, so-called high chancellors would feel if they heard this daemon tell such stark truths about his campaign. They'd see the truth. *They* were the true enemy of the Midlands, tearing it apart from within. If it was war they wanted, then they should have joined his armies. There would always be battles to be fought on the borders, to defend the country from neighbouring enemies. Something that Vixel didn't understand was his kingdom required constant expansion, to absorb enemy states in order to secure peace for the future. It was difficult, undoubtedly so, but in the long term, it was worth it.

Thinking back to their conversation last night, he sighed. She was right, he needed an heir to ensure the longevity of his kingdom, but not now. Truthfully, he didn't know whether he even wanted an heir. He knew all too well how sons could kill fathers. Then again, without an heir everything he'd built would fall apart. He could always name someone else as his successor, but whom? As Vixel said, Tomon was no ruler by any stretch of the word, and he didn't trust any of his other commanders, not even Strikk. The lords of the court were even worse, bureaucratic fools. One of the minotorrs might be a suitable choice, provided he were under his tutelage.

He shook his head. All of this was irrelevant if he lost the war. Now wasn't the time for this. With a final glance at his glorious kingdom, he descended the ladder and returned to the bedroom. Stepping carefully so as not to make a sound, he took his sword belt and left the quarters.

At the bottom of the stairs leading to the library stood a girl, shifting nervously from foot to foot. Stolach raised his eyebrow. Unusual. Nobody visited so early in the day.

'Your Majesty, there is a visitor waiting on you,' she stuttered. 'He arrived yesterday evening. He wasn't very happy when told you were unavailable.'

'Who?'

'A messenger from the minotorrs, will you meet with him now?'

'I will not. Do you know the reason for this visit? Does he carry a message?'

'None was given to me, other than to ask you to meet him, with great urgency.'

'And he gave no suggestion as to why he's here? The nature of his message?'

'None, your Majesty, other than it has something to do with the war.'

'I wouldn't expect it to be for anything else. No, I will not meet with him now, tell him I'll see him with my council of war at midday.'

She scurried away, apparently relieved to have delivered her message successfully. He pursed his lips. A messenger from the minotorrs. What could they have to say that was so urgent? Perhaps the Council were attacking the northern forests in the absence of his armies? But that wasn't important. As long as he held Cadaran then the north was his. Unless it was the city itself that was the subject of the message? Was it being attacked? Or worse, had old disagreements resurfaced between the minotorrs and the rulers of Cadaran? But that shouldn't happen. Lord Tunn was renowned for his clarity of thought. It's the reason why he named him lord of the city. He wouldn't do anything so foolish. Perhaps it was to do with the wild beasts and monsters in the northern woods?

Only time would tell. No use pondering over it. He set about his usual daily routine, the message pushed to the back of his mind. His day began in the basement levels, in the large training rooms where he could practice his swordplay. He did it religiously, no matter how tired he felt or what the day promised, his practice every morning was a constant ritual. It began with a complex sword-dance, moving gracefully across the floor, eyes closed, executing the steps with the ease of a master. It lasted half an hour, stomach and shoulders burning by the end. After a quick rest, he moved to another room, filled with training dummies. He stayed here for the remainder of the hour, stabbing and hacking at straw, wood, and cloth, improving the speed, strength, endurance, and precision of his attacks. It was a tiring and constant exercise, one that demanded dedication and ability. He had an abundance of both.

Next, he sent for his five sparring partners. Picked from the Guild of assassins, he never kept the same partners for longer than two weeks to ensure variability. It served a dual purpose as a valuable training lesson for the assassins themselves, and was considered a great honour among them to be selected by the Owl to train with him. More often than not, his partners' performance impressed him, but occasionally they were found to be grossly incompetent, and their lack of skill would soon be corrected.

Fortunately, his current sparring partners were more than capable. They duelled for thirty minutes. They varied between single combat, pairs, threes, and ended with all five assassins battling him alone.

Exercise done, he washed his body of sweat and grime, dressed in fresh clothes, and returned to the library, where he lost himself in the tomes for a few hours, carefully reading some of the latest reports written by his scribes concerning the running of the kingdom. This was not something he did regularly. There were many others charged with the responsibility of reading the reports, consolidating the results, and analysing them in detail before presenting him the systemic analyses. Sometimes, however, he liked to have a first-hand experience of what was written, seeing how individual farmers, or villages, or mills, or smithies, were coping in the current climate.

Midnight finally arrived, and he left the library for the third level, which housed the main council room. Leaving the staircase, he walked across the torch-lit corridor, dark and cool, to the council room's heavy iron-studded door.

It was not a large room by any standards, made to look even smaller by the presence of a large table that cut it lengthways in two.

Around the table were his advisors and generals. Tomon, Colonel Autnik, Captain Teneraso, General Talto, General Hemelot, General Carass, Field Marshal Lupas, the Owl, and General Keren Maebis-Fawe, returned from across the seas.

This room was brighter than the corridor, illuminated by numerous torches set in sconces on the wall, with large mirrors on three of the four walls to give the illusion of space. He sat at head of the table. Behind him was the only wall without a mirror. Instead, it concealed a hidden door set into the stone, leading to a hidden passageway. It connected to a network of tunnels within the walls of the Tower, interlaced like a complex web opening up into the library. Few knew of its existence. Certainly nobody else in the city knew about it, as he'd personally destroyed the one and only record of its existence from the tower's library. It was this system of passages weaving through the walls that gave him the idea to construct the tale of secret passageways opened by the fabled serpent key. It seemed even the giants were unaware of their existence, as they'd been cut into the walls *after* the tower's completion. The culprits were the daemons, of course, specifically the great Deia, chief advisor throughout the ages to the giant kings. The record, a single forgotten scroll, hidden behind a false wall beyond one of the less accessible library stacks, was written by Deia himself. It was by simple chance he found it, exploring the depths of his library one sleepless night. The secret scroll claimed this system of passages took several centuries to complete, as it was vital to keep it hidden, and was originally conceived as a method for the daemons to keep a careful eye on their rulers. He knew from his old teacher that similar passages had also been tunnelled into the northern fortress of Rhetta Mountains, Mount Stohn. Clearly, treachery was ingrained into their very nature. The passageways originally opened into the seventeenth level, which was originally given over completely to the daemons. When the upper levels were converted to a library, some five hundred years after the building of the tower, Deia and the daemons insisted on making the changes themselves for fear of their passages being discovered. The poor, naïve giants who ruled Nefarwy never suspected a thing.

Over twenty centuries later, the passages remained, and Stolach discovered them. He seldom used them. Indeed, he could count on one hand the number of times he'd entered those tunnels, but it was comforting to know they were there, waiting to protect him and sweep him away to wherever he wished within Crastalan Tower.

'I apologise for delaying this meeting,' he said, resting his elbows on the arms of his chair. 'I'm sure you all have much to say. We have a surprise visitor joining us at some point; a messenger from the minotorrs.'

'A messenger?' Lupas raised his eyebrows. 'What does he have to say?'

'I'm sure we'll all find out when he gets here. Now, deliver your reports. Let's get them done before the messenger arrives.'

'The war goes badly, sir,' began Tomon nervously. 'Weeks of siege and Muranath still holds strong. Our supply lines remain open, for now, but it's only a matter of time before they're shut down.'

'The naval battle has also been met with…difficulties,' continued Lupas. 'The sea neiads had too few ships compared to the calefin fleet, and many galleons have been sunk or captured. The armies we had attacking Tonnis Harbour were routed two days ago. Fortunately, our commanders managed to rally them and direct them to Muranath to aid in the siege, but many of the troglodytes were lost, fleeing back to their swamps and across the Kingdom, to pillage and devour what they can.'

'Can we rally them?' he asked.

'We're doing what we can, but a siege is not their kind of warfare. Those who returned grow restless with no foes to sink their weapons into,' Tomon replied.

'Let them pillage as they see fit. If we can keep a few hundred around the siege it'll be enough. It's always good to have a few expendables around in case the situation calls for them,' he turned to the Owl. 'Any news from your men? The daemon substance?'

'Nearly a month since their last message,' hissed the hanex.

'We can assume the worst, then. A shame. Any chance of sending another band to continue their mission?' he spoke in a low tone, so the others would be hard-pressed to hear. It was a force of habit, to keep the affairs of the assassins within the Guild. The others could have an idea of what was being discussed, but a sense of mystery and suspicion should always be retained.

'Not without recalling them from another. There will be a delay,' the Owl replied, equally quietly. A few of the others leaned forward unconsciously, straining to hear the private conversation.

'Send them. I want that weapon. What of the north?' he addressed the room.

'The juggernauts? All destroyed at Imhara,' Tomon shrugged.

'No real surprise. I didn't expect much from them. This does, however, pose us a problem. If the northern forces of the calefs come down to reinforce their besieged kinsmen at Muranath, then our army will be caught on two fronts and our supply trains will be destroyed. Strikk sent coin to the Northland clans before heading to Muranath. There's another army of mercenaries on its way to attack the northern kingdom, but there's no guarantee they didn't take the gold and leave it at that. We need something more reliable.'

'We could have some barges sail up the Atrael and ferry them down to avoid the calefin forces?' Hemelot piped up.

'Ridiculous suggestion,' spat Stolach, shooting the fonex an irritated stare. 'Our barges would be destroyed by the calefin fleet before they made it halfway up the estuary. The question is where to find the soldiers to defend the trains.'

'How many men?' hissed Talto.

'We should not need to send too many,' mused Lupas. 'The juggernauts would have made quite a dent in the calefin armies, despite being defeated, so I can't imagine there being too many of them. They'll be weak and tired, so an additional four thousand or so should suffice.'

'Where will we get these soldiers, Lupas?' Hemelot asked, an arrogant tone to his voice. 'This campaign in the east is not our only front. The Council grows ever stronger, and the Dailas Forest is growing ever wilder. You cannot draw soldiers from the Midlands. We need everyone we have.'

'We could direct the troglodytes up there,' suggested Tomon, 'if they grow impatient with the siege, letting them loose on calefin relief forces would be a good use for them.'

'They're too unreliable. It's a good idea to send them up there, but not alone. We'll still need soldiers to form a solid spine to any army, and I would never trust troglodytes to protect our supply trains,' said Lupas.

'I have a solution there,' said Maebis-Fawe. He was of average height, broad, and had the slightest hint of a gut drooping over his belt. The stubble over his jaw was unkempt, and he spoke with a slight lisp owing to the large gap in his dentition where all four upper incisors were missing. Nevertheless, the fifty-year old man was a good leader.

'Despite the challenges the calefs have posed,' he continued, 'I'm pleased to report the campaigns across the seas are a resounding success. All of the resisting states of the Jagged Isles have been defeated, with their armies either dead or fighting with us, and their leaders... disposed of. The Southlands have also been purged. Lord Belia-stobai was caught and killed. The coward was hiding in the Daiwen Jungle for the past few months, holed up in the Setarack Temple, but we found him. Made him sing.'

'You found the Temple?' exclaimed Autnik, impressed.

'Indeed, General Hanem himself led the final push. Personally slew a dozen of the enemy, including Belia-stobai.'

'And what does Hanem do now?' asked Stolach, staring at Maebis-Fawe intently.

'He maintains the Southlands for you, your Majesty, ensuring your kingdom across the seas is safe and secure. But now the remaining rebels have finally been eliminated, many of our forces can return-'

He was cut short by a loud knock on the door. Everyone looked at Stolach, who indicated to Autnik, sitting closest to the door, to open it. In stepped a servant, pale and trembling with anxiety upon facing so many high-ranking officers.

'The messenger from the minotorrs awaits your audience, your Majesty,' he trembled, fidgeting nervously.

'I'll call him in when we're ready,' said Stolach.

Maebis-Fawe coughed lightly, and continued. 'As I was saying, many of our forces can come home, providing a handy solution to the issue of insufficient forces to protect the supply trains.'

'How soon can they return?' asked Lupas.

'A small force came with me, but more can come as soon as we send the ships.'

'How many?' Lupas asked, again.

'All are eager to come home, so as many as we need.'

'Could you be more specific, General?' asked Stolach. 'Exactly how many troops are left in the Southlands, how many are in the Jagged Isles, and how many need to remain there to maintain my rule?'

The man paused for a moment, in thought, then took out a small scroll and a length of charcoal, and scribbled a few calculations as he worked out the mathematics. They waited patiently for him to finish. Eventually, he cleared his throat.

'As of now, I estimate forty-seven thousand soldiers in the Jagged isles, if you count the recent additions from the surrendered armies, but only twenty-five thousand are needed to maintain them. In the Southlands are another thirty thousand troops, but twenty should be enough to hold those lands. So we have around thirty-two thousand troops at the ready, waiting to come home.'

'Twenty thousand men needed to hold the Southlands?' asked Talto, dubiously. 'Seems like an over-estimation to me, especially if the rebels are completely destroyed, as you claimed.'

'The Southlands are far larger than you might think, Talto, and twenty thousand is what is needed,' Maebis-Fawe bristled.

Stolach thought for a moment, eyes narrowed. There were alternate motives at play here. He respected Maebis-Fawe. Not only for his leadership skills, but also his ruthlessness in battle, his ability to motivate his men, his wisdom, his ambition. But it was this ambition that made him wary, because Talto was right. Twenty thousand soldiers were far too many to hold the sparsely-populated Southlands. General Hanem was also a slippery character. Given the opportunity, these two would jump at the chance to take the Southlands for their own.

'Here is my decision,' he announced, coolly. 'Twenty-two thousand men will be taken from the Jagged Isles, as you suggested, but from the Southlands I will recall another twenty thousand, leaving ten thousand.'

Maebis-Fawe had always credited himself with an impressive ability to hide his true emotions, and was able to conceal them from nearly everyone in the room, save for two. Stolach saw the flicker of anger flit across the general's features, the slight clench of the jaw, the subtle narrowing of the eyes, the twitch of the fingers. He shared a glance with the Owl. He'd seen it too. He went a step further.

'You've done well, Maebis-Fawe, and deserve time here, away from the glaring climate of the Southlands. You need not return with this message across the Great Waters, I'll send another.'

To the general's credit, he composed himself admirably, and nodded in agreement, seemingly accepting the decision with grace and appreciation. Stolach could have laughed. That this man ever thought to usurp his rule was ridiculous, nevertheless, it was best if he and General Hanem were kept apart and dealt with once the war was over.

'Now, these forty-two thousand will be put to good use. Five thousand will protect Strikk's supply trains, as discussed. Another ten thousand will be sent to Muranath, to replenish our forces. Five thousand will go to Cadaran to reinforce our weakened north, and the rest will remain here in anticipation of what is surely to come.'

Everyone nodded, knowing full well to what he was referring.

Teneraso looked around the table. 'Since the matter's been brought up, we may as well discuss it now. The Dailas Forest is teeming with enemies. The Council's taken over a large portion of the southernmost woods, and ninety-percent of the scouting parties I send there never return. Of those who do, half of them have nothing to report, and the rest can only give troubling news. People are flocking to their banners, mostly villagers dissatisfied with the protection offered by the crown from the marauders of the forests.'

'These marauders have still not been disposed of?' sneered Maebis-Fawe. 'We heard of them back in the Southlands when we were dealing with our own bands of ruffians in Daiwen. I'm surprised you've not managed to flush them out yet.'

'We always knew it would be a difficult task,' said Tomon, angrily. 'Since our attention has been focused on the Kingdom of the calefs, you can understand why this threat hasn't been dealt with.'

'If you want my humble opinion, as an individual who has been away during the majority of these times, I would say that your attack on the calefs was premature,' Maebis-Fawe crossed his arms. 'You should have secured your own lands before trying to spread your borders.'

'I agree,' hissed Talto. 'The Council should have been dealt with first. Traitors and betrayers are the lowest scum. We should never tolerate them in our lands.'

Stolach stared at both with a blank face. He often found an expressionless gaze far more unsettling than a glowering glare, and soon enough both men were shifting uncomfortably in their seats, doing everything they could to avoid eye contact. Finally, he replied.

'The Council *is* being dealt with, dear generals, because I am striking at their allies. Once we remove their support, then we shall eliminate them. The thieves of the woods are notoriously difficult to combat, because unlike the insurgents you encountered in Daiwen, Maebis-Fawe, these rogues have no leader, no base of operations. You were trying to catch smoke in Daiwen, all you needed to do was find the fire. In Dailas, we are trying to catch mist; a vapour born of the land itself with no source or base of operations, but an all-encompassing, surrounding entity that coils around every bough of every tree in the forest. Let us not argue over who is most efficient at catching criminals, rather we should think on how to complete the task at hand.

'Now,' he turned to Teneraso, 'the very southernmost woods belong to the Council, what of the rest of the forest? Exactly how saturated with thieves has it become?'

'To be honest, the presence of the Council in those woods has actually done some good, as they are nearly completely devoid of any thieves or Hobbs, so that's one small consolation.'

'I wouldn't call it a consolation to see how proficient they've become,' said Lupas.

'Quite right,' nodded Hemelot. 'They're worryingly organised. The southwest forest is, as Teneraso said, teeming with foes. However, our villages and supply trains remain secure. Your strategy to concentrate only on the defence of the villages and supply trains was well-conceived, your Majesty.'

Stolach let the empty flattery pass over his head without acknowledgment. 'What of the rest of the southern forest?'

'The same again,' said Lupas, 'the larger villages are secured, the supply trains are safe, and in between is a sea of death. Some of the smaller settlements have emigrated to the larger villages where we can offer them protection, others are fleeing south to the Council. Some are even going to Morgenal Harbour in their desperation. Supplies are holding up for now, but we're losing farmlands and industries as more and more flee their homes. It could turn ugly.'

'In that case I encourage you to order your captains to continue with the defence of the larger villages and try to move as many of my people there as you can. Undoubtedly you will be met with opposition, but it's far easier to defend a few large settlements that many small ones. How about the lands around the Crisiaddwr? What's Commander Afarn been up to?'

'More of the same,' said Lupas. 'Neiads attack our men and scupper our rafts whenever they can, but less frequently now than they have been.'

'Less frequently? Why?' asked Autnik.

'Who can tell? I like to think it's because we've whittled their numbers down to the point where they can no longer sustain such a ferocious guerrilla war against us. However, my instincts tell me it's because they're pulling away from Crisiaddwr and regrouping with the Council.'

'Concerning,' mused Stolach, 'but for now it works to our advantage. Less trouble for our supply trains as they cross the river to make their way to the Kingdom of the calefs. But what about the northern forests?'

'Practically overrun,' Teneraso shook his head in frustration. 'We still have some semblance of control over the north-western reaches, thanks to the contribution of the minotorrs, but the rest is a warzone. Marauding bands fall on one another with as much ferocity as they fall on our villages, and my dreyads have plenty of tales of packs of direwolves sweeping across the forest, screaming banshee tribes running rampant, hydras burning scores of rogues with one breath, and other, fouler, unnamed creatures of malice. Essentially, the northeast forests are lost.'

'Cadaran, however, is still strong. Lord Tunn keeps the surrounding lands safe and the city is secure,' assured Tomon. 'According to the latest reports, he's been sending out large patrols to the surrounding forests, clearing what villages he can of bandits, rescuing those who wish to be rescued, and safeguarding the mills, forges, tanners, and any other trades that remain. Doing well.'

'Glad to hear. I'll be sure to make the journey to Cadaran soon to congratulate him and see the extent of this success. Now, I'm afraid I grow impatient and wish to hear what our messenger from Iadden has to say. Autnik, would you send for him, please?'

Autnik rose again and opened the door, where Stolach heard him mumble a few words to the servant waiting outside. Half a minute later there was another knock. Autnik rose again, and the messenger entered.

The messenger was no minotorr. A red dreyad, his face as old and grizzled as a thousand-year oak, amber eyes glinting from the shadows beneath his heavy brows. Like their grey cousins, the red dreyads had rough bark-like skin and long fingers, perfect for gripping branches. Although their stature was typically rounder and shorter than the grey kind, they were no less athletic. They were a rare breed and few clans remained, but those who did were mostly found in the forested foothills of Iadden, hence their friendship with minotorrs.

He sensed Lupas stir beside him, and Tomon shifted uncomfortably in his seat. Their unease was warranted. The minotorrs were an honourable people. For them to send a messenger who was not of their blood to treat with the king was a stark message in itself. A statement. An act of defiance. An insult.

Keeping his composure, he stood and nodded politely to the dreyad, who gave a stiff bow in return, and took the offered seat beside Hemelot. From the corner of his eye, he saw Teneraso sneering at the messenger. Hopefully, the petty rivalry between their species would not leave a sour taste on this meeting. Certainly, he hoped the words the dreyad carried would not leave an even sourer taste.

'Greetings, friend, I thank you for travelling so far to reach us with your message. Might I ask for your name, dreyad?'

'Greetings, your Majesty,' replied the dreyad, his voice like the rustling of a thousand ruby leaves in autumn. 'My name is Tibaduy Menwein, I was sent here by the High Marshal Nostiir Zanmekh, to bring you a message from him and his court, regarding your war.'

'Forgive me, Tibaduy, but why do *you* bring this message? Surely you must know how this looks, for the high officer to send a messenger who is not of his own race to treat with his king? Is there a reason for this?'

'Your Majesty, the absence of a minotorr in this room will be explained by the contents of the message with which I was entrusted. I am well aware of the possible implications behind the nature of the messenger, myself, and hope that you will reserve any judgment, justly or unjustly held, until the message has been delivered.'

He nodded, with a faint smile. The dreyad seemed to enjoy the sound of his own voice, and with good reason, for there was a comfort to be had in his crackling tones.

'My message is an important one,' continued Tibaduy. 'One you would all do well to take due note of, for it concerns you all. It concerns the decisions made by this council of war, to deal a blow to the Kingdom of the calefs.'

'That was a strategy in war, surely the minotorrs must understand? A clash with the calefs was an inevitable occurrence,' Lupas said, leaning forward uneasily.

'There are strategies and there are strategies, Field Marshal. The high officer understands the calefs are your enemies, and in war, enemies tend to be met at the tip of a spear, but it is not the attack itself that has alarmed the minotorrs. Rather, it is the events that have taken place during the invasion they find disturbing.

'You see, by the time word of the attack found its way to Bletta Castle, the invasion was, regrettably, well underway. News of allegiances formed with troglodytes gave the high officer apprehension, as the minotorrs know as well as any race the horrors that these people can unleash. "Why were the minotorrs not included in the invasion?" was the question that echoed through the halls of the castle. To be sure, the inclusion of such a powerful army would have greatly improved your chances of emerging victorious from the east, with their skill, superior tactics, and most importantly – discipline.

'"Why discipline?" you might ask, well I shall tell you, for it is a lack of discipline that has brought me to this meeting. Every minotorr in the mountains of Iadden spit at the mention of the disastrous invasion of the Kingdom of the calefs, because of the tales of horror that have emerged from there. Villages ransacked and razed to the ground, while your soldiers rape and pillage and murder to their black-hearted content. Worse still are the whispers of gangs of your faithful troglodytes devouring men, women, and children even as their pitiful screams beg for some semblance of mercy.'

'From whose mouths come these reports? Are the calefs sending for aid?' asked Teneraso. 'My scouts should have intercepted anyone attempting to enter or leave the kingdom.'

'The calefs are too proud, and require no aid to win this war. By the four winds I cannot say why there is even a single soldier of yours still alive beyond the Cysgodgors marshes, why Lleunedd entertains this siege of Muranath is beyond me. No, no messengers were sent from the calefs, but you cannot possibly believe Iadden is blind to all that occurs in the land? Admittedly our eyes were turned away from the neighbouring country, as we never had reason to believe that such an attack would occur so soon, hence us only finding out recently, but eventually, our scouts throughout the land delivered their reports, and we now know.'

'Red dreyads, I assume?' said Tomon.

'Indeed.'

'Tibaduy,' said Stolach, rubbing his chin wearily. 'This business with the deaths of innocents is regrettable, but this is war. Innocents will die. When our enemies eventually march upon this city, then civilians will die here too, that is inevitable. You claim this to be due to lack of discipline by my soldiers, but they were acting under my orders. I *wanted* them to spread panic and discord, to hamstring the calefin people in such a way that they would no longer threaten me.'

'You ordered your soldiers to mutilate innocents like this?'

'I did not order them to kill children or rape women. I ordered them to spread fear throughout the land. Clearly the best way that they know of spreading fear is through these unsavoury acts. As for the inclusion of troglodytes over minotorrs, their savagery is perfect for spreading fear and panic, and while the cold discipline of the minotorrs is fearsome in itself, the armies of Iadden are pathetically dwarfed by the sheer flood of bodies I can call upon from Cysgodgors. *Fear* is the name of this invasion. Fear of my armies, my vengeance, my anger. It is as much a message to the entire population of Nefarwy as it is a strategy to eliminate my enemies; I do not tolerate uprisings.

'You called the invasion "disastrous", but it is nothing of the sort. Fear has taken their hearts. Victory for the calefs is not so clear-cut as you evidently perceive it to be, especially when terror and rage blinds their judgement, leading them to hide behind their high walls and hope to survive my fury. Even if they win, if my attempts prove futile and my armies crash helplessly against the walls of Muranath, they will be riled for war. If they defeat Strikk, they will not stop there, they will come to the Midlands, and on these open fields, without their high walls, our armies will destroy them.'

'What you have done is monstrous, and Nostiir will have no hand in such a dishonourable battle.'

Stolach narrowed his eyes, bracing himself for the news that would surely follow. 'He will have no hand in it?'

'None. The slaughter of innocents stains the souls of everyone here, and as such disgraceful crimes have been committed, you no longer have the support of the minotorrs in your war.'

Silence followed the dreyad's announcement, and the eyes of Stolach's commanders shifted between him and the dreyad, who stared at each other with dark eyes.

'The minotorrs are turning sides against me?'

'No. They are simply withdrawing from the war, they will not aid you, and nor will they oppose you. You have no new enemies, only fewer friends.'

'Is it only in war they have abandoned the crown, or in trade as well?'

Tibaduy paused. 'That I cannot say, as they gave me no message regarding anything save their new position in the war. I can return to them with your enquiry regarding trade. Understand me, they are not opposed to your idea of uniting the lands under one banner, so I do not doubt they *will* remain your allies in trade and such, to aid in building a better future for the land. But they refuse to play a direct hand in this war, where deeds of notoriety have been committed. Do not look for their banners on the battlefield, they will not be there.'

Stolach nodded, and stood. 'I've heard enough. You will stay here, Tibaduy, while I construct a reply to your masters. There are plenty of empty quarters for you in the Tower, ask one of the servants to show you the way. Now, leave.'

Tibaduy stood, gave the slightest bow, and walked out the room. Tomon opened his mouth to say something, but Stolach raised a hand to silence him.

'I'm sure you all have your opinions on this matter. Let me know in a week's time, after you've given it more thought. There is no more to discuss for today, you may all leave.'

In silence, they shuffled out the door. Out in the corridor, they were venting their rage to one another, calling the minotorrs every name under the sun, cursing Tibaduy, praying the calefs suffered even worse horrors than what they had already experienced. For his part, he stood still, gazing thoughtfully into the heart of a torch.

Chapter 34

Peaceful nights were beginning to feel like something of a myth to Spotal, as he lay curled up and shivering in his cloak. Their fire had long since burnt to ashes, its heat lost to the biting wind, growing ever stronger as they progressed north. But the wind wasn't the only reason for his insomnia. Anger, grief, frustration, they all kept him awake as much as the gales, as did Lidan's constant whimpering, lost in yet another haunting dream. Restraining himself from kicking the boy quiet, he breathed deeply, trying to find that elusive state of relaxation sleep demanded.

It didn't work. His mind was too active. He remained as he was; awake, tired, irritated. When the others finally arose two hours later, he was still annoyed, and his mood only worsened as the day went on.

Rain fell in its irritating spitting way, just enough to dampen them to the point where the cold northern wind snapped like a starving wolf. Ever since they reached the Northlands, things had only been getting worse.

At first, there wasn't much difference between the Northlands and the northern kingdom, the ground looked the same, the trees were the same, the wind was just as cold. Spotal, however, knew immediately that his land lay behind, just as did Pwtrek and Noswen must know theirs lay ahead. It was an intuitive feeling, an instinct that told him he'd left home again. To anyone else there would have been nothing to differentiate, nothing to distinguish the invisible borders, but to the ones who made their homes in these places, it was as obvious as stepping from a bank into a freezing river.

Several miles beyond his country, the changes were more obvious, noticeable even to the others. Smaller, sharper trees with a miserable appearance, never clustered in more than two or three. Indeed, the majority stood alone, solitary wardens surveying the north. What little grass was also sharper, like a bed of needles stuck into the ground, dotted with spiky heather. Beneath the sharp grass was a hard, unforgiving ground of cold stone and rubble. Boulders and rocky outcrops were commonplace, dotting the earth like pockmarks on skin. It was a flat land, with few hills or vales, covered instead in a network of steep gullies and sharp gorges. Of course, it was the wind that was the greatest difference. Without any hills or forests to break up the gales, it tore through the land with a vengeance. The rocky clusters channelled the gusts between them into vicious streams of razor-sharp cold.

The first night they spent was horrid, the second worse, last night was mild in comparison to the others, but it still hadn't given him any rest. He bent down in his saddle and patted his rouncey comfortingly. She whinnied miserably in reply. The poor creatures were suffering in these climates. They lacked the thick hair and long manes of the wild horses who survived here, and the wiry grass gave them little sustenance. With their heads bent against the winds, they bore their riders ever westwards at a walk, for they had not the energy to gallop, and the risk of misplacing a hoof into one of the deep gullies was too great. To make matters worse, heavy rainfall the night before filled some of the gullies to the brim, disguising them as innocuous puddles. Efforts were made to avoid anything that wasn't clear firm ground, which was itself complicated by the slick rocks underfoot. The going was slow, far slower than they would have liked, but they had no choice. Prayers were whispered and heads were lowered, continuing doggedly on.

Overhead, a solitary bird cried in the rain. From its high-pitched voice, he guessed it was a buzzard, but when he turned to look he could hardly see it, the rain filling his eyes in moments. Eventually he caught sight of it, A tiny line high in the sky, gliding on the air currents that bore it ever westwards. Although the buzzard was nowhere near as majestic as a golden eagle, its cry was certainly more rousing than the eagle's squawk. Its piercing calls made him smile, and he followed its flight for as long as he could. It was soon lost from sight.

Contrary to Pwtrek's assurances, food was far less easily come by in the Northlands than expected, and he could tell his companions were swiftly losing their taste for Harandale roots, judging from their grimaces whenever they bit into them. Personally, he found them both nourishing and refreshing, with a comfort in their earthy taste, but his opinion wasn't shared. Depani managed to shoot a rare wild rabbit, and this tiny morsel of meat was shared raw between them.

There was soon meat for everyone, without any hunting needed.

Despite his concerns, his rouncey was not the first to die. Such a privilege went to one of Pwtrek's. The poor creature collapsed without warning and lay still, dead on the spot from exhaustion. The juggernaut was clearly upset, flatly refusing to take another. With their pace as slow as it was, even in his exhaustion, Pwtrek could comfortably keep up with them, and was only breathing slightly more heavily at the end of the day than on previous nights.

But the death of the first was like the falling of a first rock in an avalanche. Four more died by the end of the day, including Spotal's. It happened an hour before sunset. He sensed her falter beneath him, and managed to jump clear before she fell. He lay a hand on her neck as she gasped for air. Relief seemed to fill her great dark eyes as she rasped her final breath and was freed of the torment of their arduous journey.

It was Auran who had the idea of butchering them after the third fell an hour before Spotal's, so their packs were already full of horse-meat from the previous two. As such, they could only fit a few chunks of his mare into their packs and had to leave the half-butchered carcass for the wilderness to claim for its own. If the other horses were alarmed by the treatment of their dead kin, they didn't show it. He suspected they were too worn-out to feel anything but pain and weariness. There was no dry wood anywhere to be found, so they dined on raw horsemeat that night.

Two days later, they were down to their last five horses. The decision was made that Widrias would take one to spare his leg, while the other four were given their packs. At least walking kept him warmer than riding.

Soon, their trail of carcasses drew the attention of unwanted followers, and the next day, their wild shadows were spotted.

Around midday, he saw Noswen turn to look behind them, pausing with narrowed eyes. Wordlessly, she approached Widrias and whispered something to him. Turning in his saddle, the general shielded his eyes to the horizon, before glancing quickly at Spotal and whispering something back.

'Is something wrong?' asked Spotal, suspicious. He couldn't see anything.

'Noswen saw something. Nothing to worry about.'

'What is it?' he asked again.

'As I said, nothing to worry about,' reassured Widrias.

'Anything that follows us gives me some concern,' he said, raising an eyebrow expectantly.

'They don't pose us any threat, so don't worry about it,' insisted Widrias, flicking the reins and urging his horse on.

'Sir, what did she see?' he called after him.

'There is a pack of direwolves behind us,' said Noswen, looking at Spotal intently. 'About a mile away.'

He froze in his tracks. He narrowed his eyes. Too much rain, damn it. Climbing the nearest boulder, he looked again. The others watched from below. Sure enough, dark shapes walked in their footsteps. They were too far away to say for sure how many, but it looked between seven and ten. He played with his talisman. Of everything it could be, why these?

'Widrias is right, they don't seem to be a threat,' said Gwahl, climbing up beside him without him noticing. 'They must've found our dead horses and are following to scavenge an easy meal.'

'You should know better than to ignore direwolves in our wake,' he warned, quietly.

'I'm not ignoring them. I'm recognising the truth. They're clearly not hunting us, their formation shows that much, and their pace is about the same as ours. Besides, there are at least as many of us as there are of them. If they do attack, for whatever reason, we'll be able to fend them off without any trouble.'

'That's the kind of thinking that got me here. We should quicken our pace to lose them.'

'Now you should know better, we'd never outrun them.'

'Then we should turn and face them, meet them head on instead of waiting for them to snap at our heels.'

'The best thing we can do is keep going,' said Pwtrek, offering them a hand down. 'Direwolves are more complicated than you give them justice. It'll be a small pack, not one of the ravenous murder-herds that you encountered with your army. There is a different psyche among them when found in fewer numbers, they are far more similar to ordinary wolves than bloodthirsty killers.'

'I know more about the horrors of direwolves than you, Pwtrek,' he grumbled, clambering off the rock to follow the rest of the party, who had continued past them.

The juggernaut laughed and shook his head. 'The Northlands are my home. I can assure you, I know much more about them than you do. Just as you have a deeper knowledge of the Kingdom of the calefs, so do I have a deeper knowledge of my lands, including its inhabitants.'

'You're saying the "murder-herd" that destroyed so many of my people was a freak incident of some sort?'

'Not a freak incident, but not common either. Direwolves *are* more ferocious than ordinary wolves, they are far more dangerous and frightening, but for most of the time they're still animals, with the same instincts for survival and self-preservation.'

'So what changes with the "murder-herds"?' asked Lidan. 'I've never heard of it.'

'I was once told it stems back to the cockatrice, and how they used their powers to cajole beasts into joining them in the Cataclysmic War,' explained Pwtrek. 'The subtle urges impinged upon their primal minds by the cockatrice left a permanent mark, which has passed down through the generations.'

Spotal glanced at Gwahl, who nodded in agreement.

'That's what I heard too. Note how the direwolves in these murder-herds consume the hearts of their slain foe, mimicking the actions of the cockatrice. It is also only in the presence of great numbers of direwolves that the herds form, numbers large enough to be viewed as armies. A minotorr once suggested to me the imperfection, the anomaly, in their minds is only activated when they gather in great numbers, but when they are few, it is dormant.'

He glanced over his shoulder, but the wolves were once again lost in the drizzle. Invisible ghouls of his past haunting his footsteps.

'Say what you like, but I'll sleep uneasily tonight,' he said, irritated at their brazen attitude.

'I was under the impression you've slept uneasily since we arrived in my country,' said Pwtrek.

'How did you know? I've not complained!'

'Your body complains for you,' chuckled the juggernaut. 'The bags under your eyes could have been used to carry all of our dead horses, eliminating the problem of our followers.'

Smiling, he shook his head, irritation dissipated, grateful for his friends' company.

*

True to his word, he was uneasy that night. As soon as he lay down, all he could hear was the snapping jaws of wolves, the cries of his dying men, all he could smell was the stench of their steaming fur, saturated with blood, and each time he closed his lids, furious eyes blazed from the darkness.

Unable to bear such torment, he gave up on sleep and joined Noswen on watch. For a while, neither said anything, staring into the night. Relentless, the wind blew as swiftly as ever around them, whipping their hair and setting their noses running. Thankfully, there was no rain, and the clear sky boasted a bright moon and a thousand stars, illuminating the Northlands in a soft silver glow. To his relief, the shapes of the direwolves could not be picked out among the silver-lined boulders and trees.

'A gentle night for the Northlands,' he muttered.

Noswen smiled and looked up from her lovingly-polished dirk. 'This is an average night for these parts. We're still far from the true north. This barely qualifies as my home. Were we in the true Northlands, a night such as this would cause mass panic for its unnatural peacefulness.'

Spotal smiled. 'Panic and hysteria over a moonlit evening?'

'Like you've never seen.'

They both chuckled. 'How long has it been since last you were home?'

Noswen thought for a while. 'Nearly nineteen years since I was taken to Crastalan. I've not returned to my village since.'

'Do you think you will?'

'Maybe. But I don't think I'll find anything there for me. I've been changed too much by my actions to return.'

He nodded. 'I know what you mean. But we're not alone, this war will change the Midlands as we know them.'

'Not just the Midlands, all of Nefarwy.'

'All because of one fonex's foolish ambition.'

Noswen was silent for a while. 'Do you think we can win?'

Spotal looked at her, surprised by the question. It was difficult to read the hanex's voice, emotionless as it was, and her face was the same unchanging mask of stillness. 'I believe we can. It'll be difficult, we will lose friends, but in the end, I think we can win. If we don't, at least we'll fail fighting for what we know is right.'

'Stolach is no fool, he won't bring the fight to us. Eventually we'll have to go to Crastalan.'

'All fortresses have weak points. We need only find one.'

'Like the serpent key?'

'Secret passages and hidden doors are fantasy. I'm talking about real weaknesses that we can exploit. Old mortar, weather-damaged walls, drains, rusted hinges on the city gates. These things can be found in all defences.'

'Even Muranath?'

'Yes,' he admitted. 'But our walls are exquisitely constructed and well-tended. Besides, you of all people should know the weaknesses in Muranath's defences.'

He looked up suddenly, realising what he'd said, but she didn't react.

'Weaknesses I hope were corrected since my visit. Even so, I doubt your walls are stronger than the ones built by the giants, and General Talto is not the kind of man to leave his walls untended.'

'Then I don't know how we'll win, but we'll fight on regardless. Do *you* think we can win?'

'I hope so. As for Crastalan, I know a lot about the city. I can think of ways in for me but not an army.'

Spotal rolled his talisman between his fingers. 'He really pulled one on us with the serpent key.'

'I believed it too. Stupid, really,' she snorted.

'He fooled us all. Even Gwahl.'

'Gwahl knows a lot, more than anyone I've ever met, but he doesn't know everything. He's often come to me asking for details about Crastalan, any discoveries I made during my time there. It seems like it's something of a void in his vast field of knowledge. We can't blame him for this.'

'I would never hold anything against him. He's done too much good to ever tarnish his name in my eyes.'

'He's not perfect, you know.'

'I know, but he is as good as he can be, which is as much as I can ask of him.'

'Stolach seems to hate him, and all daemons. I never found out why...'

Noswen's voice trailed away as she stared into the distance. Spotal followed her gaze. Nothing but dark lands and a starlit sky. The direwolves? Marauders? No, an oddity. One star was moving towards them, growing larger and brighter.

He glanced at Noswen and motioned for her to wake the others. Not a star. A torch, wielded by a hooded figure.

Watching carefully, he sensed a presence by his side.

'Where is it?' whispered Widrias.

'Northeast, around two hundred paces away,' he whispered.

'Coming towards us?'

'Not directly, but if it follows its current path it'll come quite close.'

'Looks like a torch,' said Widrias after a second.

'Aye. Can't tell who's carrying it.'

'We'll find out soon enough. Noswen?'

Spotal heard the swish of her cloak as she raced away into the darkness.

Straining his eyes, he could just about see her circle the bleak country to the torch. A shadow against darkness, silent as an owl. All the while, the torch approached, seemingly unaware of the eyes watching it.

Barely a minute later, Noswen was back among them. She materialised out of the darkness, throwing a cursory glance over her shoulder to the light, now barely a hundred paces from their position. She seemed unconcerned, but then again, she'd always been impossible to read.

'A man,' she announced. 'Looks like he's carrying weapons beneath his cloak, but I couldn't be sure. The light comes from a simple torch.'

'Does he know we're here?' asked Widrias.

'Undoubtedly. He was looking in our direction. I don't think he'll pose much of a threat. He looks quite aged, and has no friends skulking in the night.'

'Should we go and greet him?' asked Lidan excitedly.

'No, he'll be upon us soon enough. May as well wait,' said Widrias.

They did not have long to wait. Less than a minute later, Spotal squinted against the torchlight shining in his eyes, trying to take measure of its bearer. The light dipped from his eyes, sparing them from the blinding beam.

Before them stood a man. Aged as Noswen said, but by no means old. He placed him at around fifty years old, with deep lines in his grey face. He was tall and broad, with the hint of a belly jutting over the belt about his waist. Had Spotal been alone, he would have been more wary, as he had an air of a formidable warrior about him, from the width of his back and shoulders to the hardness of his grey eyes. It was the form of a man who'd seen and survived many battles. The leather cloak was battered and stained, barely concealing the sword at his hip. Not that it mattered, his right hand still gripped the lowered torch. Of greater interest were his clothes. A white surcoat emblazoned with a black, tilted semicircle with four spikes, the topmost spike coloured in gold. The symbol of the northern winds, worn by holy men. Priests were forbidden from carrying blades, so this one must be a brother of one of the fabled knightly orders of Nefarwy.

The knight regarded them with his hard eyes, taking in their characters. For some time, nobody spoke, but finally Widrias broke the tense silence.

'Good evening.'

'It is,' he replied in a deep voice, a voice that demanded silence whenever it sounded. 'Yours are the footsteps in which direwolves prowl.'

'Yes, they've been following us.'

'With good reason, when you leave so many dead horses behind you, they can hardly be blamed.'

'And why do you walk in our footsteps?' asked Pwtrek, standing behind Widrias protectively, his hand on the hilt of his sword.

'To see who is feeding the direwolves. They will not follow you any more, I scared them away. You are a child of the Northlands, juggernaut, you should know the wolves require no feeding. They will fend for themselves well enough to survive. Why do you journey through these lands with these creatures and your sister hanex, who approached me with such stealth as I came to you?'

Spotal glanced at Noswen, who blinked in surprise. She seemed suitably impressed the knight had sensed her presence in the darkness.

'We journey to the Dailas Forest,' said Pwtrek.

'Where did your journey begin?'

'Why is it important to you?' asked Widrias, frowning.

The knight's lips twitched in a half-smile. 'It is not, simple curiosity as to why a juggernaut and a hanex should lead a calef, two men, two neiads, a satorr, and a…daemon,' he paused and looked at Gwahl carefully. 'You are… Dwerel? Or maybe Gwahl.'

Spotal looked at his friend in surprise, but if the daemon was startled this old knight knew his name, he did not show it.

'Indeed, I am Gwahl,' he replied coolly. 'Would you indulge us with your name?'

'Brother Leam Pranah, of the Order of the Winter Snow.'

'An honour, sir knight,' said Gwahl, politely, but oddly coldly.

'An honour. I have lodgings, should you care to join me? Shelter from the weather. I fear a storm approaches. You would not have a merry time caught here in such conditions.'

'How far is it?' asked Widrias.

'Three miles. A slight detour from your chosen path, but what's a few miles when you have so many leagues yet to go?'

'Very well,' said Widrias. 'We will stay the night, but in the morning, we'll continue on our journey.'

Leam nodded and led them away. It took a few minutes for everyone to gather their belongings and collect the horses, but they were soon on their way, following the knight into the dark lands.

Chapter 35

'Look at this map, Stolach. Point to me where the safest places in Nefarwy are right now.'

'Now's not the time for games, Vixel.'

'It's not a game. It's a truth that must be told.'

Stolach rubbed his eyes and wandered over to the opposite side of the table. They were in the library, him pouring over old tomes, her scouring over a recently-drawn map of the Midlands. New maps were constantly being drawn, refining details, noting changes in the boundaries of countries, altering the courses of the landscape as it changed with time. It sometimes amused him to look at the older maps and see how much the land had changed, especially comparing the landscapes before and after the Cataclysmic war. Those before were wonderfully drawn, beautiful and full of detail, drawn by the giants of old, whereas the ones after were cruder, rushed, confusing. But they were getting better. It was no small comfort to him that as time wore on, they were slowly clawing back to the mighty civilisation they once were under the rule of the giants. It took time, but eventually they would get there.

The map in Vixel's hands was a relatively recent one, written in the past year, but was clearly lacking the road through the bramble plains and the bridges across the Crisiaddwr. Aside from that, it was accurate enough. With a sigh, he took the parchment from her and started pointing at various points on the map.

'Crastalan, Cadaran, the southern grassland plains, Bletta Castle, the black desert, the Westlands to an extent...'

'Include our enemies as well, they've also found protection in places,' she encouraged.

'I suppose the southern reaches of the Dailas forest are quite safe.'

'As is Muranath.'

'Apart from the siege, you mean? Yes, it's perfectly safe,' he rolled his eyes. 'What's your point? Do you mean to complain again about the invasion?'

'No, I was making a point. The places you named all have something in common.'

'What?'

'They're all cities, or close to cities.'

'I don't remember any cities south of here, or in southern Dailas.'

'Crastalan is the city of the southern grasslands, and the Council have essentially formed a city within those southern woods, have they not? That's why you find it so difficult to drive them out.'

'There are far more reasons than that, Vixel.'

'But it's still a reason.'

'It's one reason, yes, but I fail to see your point.'

'My point is, cities are safe.'

He looked at her blankly. She did this at times, she said overly simplistic things in an attempt to draw some inspiration from him, but this time there was none forthcoming. He was tired, irritated, and in no mood for her games. Raising an eyebrow, he prompted her to elaborate.

'You told me about the situation in Dailas, how the smaller villages should flock to the larger ones for protection, and how in the north Cadaran is an island of peace amidst the sea of carnage. It's because there's safety in numbers, especially against petty gangs of rogues.'

Again, he couldn't think of a reply. There was something she was trying to get across, no doubt, otherwise she wouldn't have bothered him. At least she provided a safe medium to practice his patience.

'Must I spell this out for you?' she asked.

'It would help.'

'You've been doing this without realising it; encouraging the foundation of more cities.'

'How? By encouraging villages to stick together? That's for protection, once the rogues are dealt with they'll return to their homes.'

'Until another uprising occurs, and they'll flock together again. You always say Cadaran is the key to the north, because its walls and its people have such strength together. If you establish more cities throughout the land, you'll establish your presence in more places and have more strongholds from which to rule.'

Stolach pursed his lips. 'I've considered this before,' he said truthfully, 'but it can't be done, at least not to the scale of Cadaran.'

'Why not?'

'There's not enough money,' he said, simply. 'It would take an unimaginable wealth to build something that lasts, and it would be many years before anything truly formidable were constructed.'

'So you won't even try?'

'Once the war is done. We've had this conversation. Cities will come with expansion, not before.'

'The Council managed it.'

'Have you seen this "city" of theirs? No. Neither have I, but I've seen reports from Teneraso's scouts, and it's not a city as you imagine it. It's a hybrid overgrown army barrack and campsite, nothing more.'

'Then why haven't you taken it?'

'Terrain, war on other fronts, grander plans. Pick a reason. The Dailas Forest is no place for an open battle, we've been over this,' he handed the map back to her.

'But it *is* a place to build a city. We could use the foundations of the Council as a place where a new stronghold can spring forth, to hold the southern forests in your name.'

'Their "city" is a collection of tents and pavilions, there are no walls or towers or strongholds. Where would they get the stone and mortar? A wooden wall won't stand the test of time.'

'But it's built on the foundations of an old village!' she scrambled for another map, one of the ancient ones, and pointed to a corresponding spot in the land. 'See? Obviously the Dailas Forest isn't there, but it's the same distance from the coast and Tarnegrefur, see? I'll bet you anything that's why they built it there, whether they knew it or not. Even if it is only ruins, we can enlist the aid of Cadaran and the minotorrs, and the barons of Morgenal. That way we could ship all the necessary supplies from elsewhere.'

His back ached from bending down over the table for so long, so drew a chair from under the table and sat next to her.

'Perhaps.'

She looked at him excitedly. 'Not perhaps, my dearest. If you want to expand your kingdoms, first you secure what you already have. The lands to the west of Crisiaddwr are relatively safe already, it's only Dailas that proves difficult to control. If we were to build a city where the Council now stands, and perhaps another in the northeast to twin Cadaran, then you'd have a much more secure grip on your country. As for the money, it would be expensive, I'm sure, but your people would rejoice in safety. No thieving band of rogues, or rebels, or vicious troglodyte would ever be able to destroy their homes again.'

'It would also spare many of them the journey from Dailas to Crastalan,' he mused, turning the idea over and over in his mind. 'And something not even the giants achieved.'

'So you agree?' she said excitedly. 'You'll attempt it?'

'Yes, Vixel, I'll try. But it'll take time. We'll both be old souls by the time even one of them is complete. War is expensive, and it cripples lands. People will be tired for many years after.'

'I think they'll find a vigour within themselves, putting their hands to building instead of destroying. Even if we only see one city complete, then our children will be here to complete the task.'

'It'll take a lot of planning. I'll have to rebuild relations with the minotorrs, possibly even the calefs, if they surrender. In fact, we could even try to rebuild Denran? It would give us a good hold on the Eastlands.'

She shook her head. 'You know as well as I do the city is cursed. We should stay away from it.'

'The foundations are there? As are the building materials, all we'd have to do it patch it up. It would take but a fraction of the time compared to an entirely new city.'

'Look to your history books, it's already fallen five times. Leave Denran alone.'

He sighed and rolled his eyes. He'd never believed the ghost stories told of the city, but the majority of the land did, even the calefs shied away from the ruined city's walls. Even if he did build it, he supposed nobody would be brave enough to live there. She was probably right.

'Alright, not Denran, just the ones we discussed.'

'Is the dreyad still here?' she asked. 'The one who brought the message?'

Stolach nodded. Tibaduy remained for longer than expected, and ten days had passed since their meeting, but Stolach still had not granted permission to leave. Now he would need another meeting with the plump little dreyad, to put together an appropriate response to the minotorrs for their insult, and still ask for their assistance. It would require eloquent wording.

'He's still here. I'll send for him.'

Vixel smiled, 'When?'

'Today. He's surely anxious to be back with his masters. I've been delaying constructing an appropriate reply to their message. Now, I have more motivation to send a response.'

She squeezed his hand lovingly and left the library. Stolach remained where he was, the tomes across the table forgotten as he stared at the map. Vixel was right; cities meant safety. It *was* what he'd been unwittingly doing by gathering settlements together, and it *did* provide a point from which one could mount defensive attacks against any rogues, as evident with Cadaran and, unfortunately, the Council's headquarters. The more he thought about it, the more the idea grew on him. He would undoubtedly be the greatest ever ruler in Enadir if he succeeded. The security provided to the people of the Midlands by two additional fortified cities would be incredible, and in what way could one measure a ruler's greatness if not in their ability to protect their people? All he had to do was defeat the uprisings in the land and he would be free to accomplish this greatest of acts.

*

'Two cities,' repeated Tibaduy, slowly, looking down on the map.

'One in the southern woods, another in the northern,' said Stolach.

'Without a doubt, it would be a great accomplishment.'

They were sitting in the council room once again, darker and more brooding than usual, given the fact only two torches were lit. It was only Stolach, Vixel, and Tibaduy at the large oaken table, covered in maps, plans, and crude designs for the building of the cities. A jug of wine and three empty goblets stood on one corner, as yet untouched. Following his conversation with Vixel two days past, Stolach devoted the majority of his waking hours to the design of these cities, poring over old architectural scriptures and geographical reports of the lands. He was not so proud to believe he was capable of planning them alone, that would be arrogance bordering on madness, but he liked to have a hand in their design. Until he knew these cities could come to life, nobody else was to know of his plans.

'In times such as these, people need to keep together. Cities are the embodiment of safety, giving protection with their high walls and locked gates.'

'I am aware of the benefits of cities, your Majesty. But it is an ambitious project, remind me where they will be built. I am no architect and have never in my life called any city home, but I know they need space and firm ground to lay the foundations.'

Stolach pointed to the map. 'The first will be in the south, where the Council have already built a settlement. We may as well use what they've already accomplished and build upon it.'

'A good place to start,' agreed Tibaduy. 'Of course, what they have currently built will have to be completely taken down; there are no foundations to it. Loose earth and loam is no place to build stone walls upon, not if you would have them last.'

'There are foundations, see?' Vixel, pointed to the ancient map. 'Old giant village.'

'They picked their spot well,' Stolach admitted, begrudging the compliment to the outlaws, but Tibaduy might appreciate it. 'It might have been coincidence they picked the place, but I doubt it.'

'Those cunning rebels,' commented Tibaduy, sarcastically.

'The location is favourable too,' continued Stolach. 'Close enough to Morgenal and the Gwenal River to be able to use its port, and far enough away from the Cysgodgors Marshes so that there would be little threat of troglodytes to the masons and builders.'

'On the topic of Morgenal, it would be especially advantageous to have a city so close, so the barons are reminded of our presence,' said Vixel, smiling at him.

Tibaduy observed her from beneath his heavy brows. 'It is a fine location. With this new, southern city, Crastalan, and Cadaran, you will have a triangle of cities, each eliciting control over different points in the Midlands, each separated by the Crisiaddwr River. Three finely positioned settlements for the inhabitants of your country to call their own.'

'And one other,' said Vixel.

'Where will this second city go, your Majesty?'

Stolach now moved his hand to the northeast, and indicated an area to the east of Cadaran, at the fringes of the Dailas Forest and in line with the northwest stretch of the Tarnegrefur Mountains, 'Here. This location will turn my triangle into a diamond, with a city at each point of the compass. It's outside the forest, so there'll be plenty of space to build, but still close enough to call on its resources. Stone for the walls can be mined from Tarnegrefur, and the surrounding lands can be utilised for farming. Note also it is close to the great road through the bramble plains. An adjoining road could connect the two to allow continued trade across the lands.'

Tibaduy's frown deepened. 'Close to Cysgodgors.'

'Too far north for the troglodytes to attack, they have no love for the cold.'

'Neither do the people of the Midlands,' snorted the dreyad. 'It *is* far north, and close to the Kingdom of the calefs… are you trying to expand your borders, King?'

Stolach ignored the insolent jibe. 'It's further south than Cadaran.'

'Then why do you need it? You don't have much to rule to the east, and the other cities' radius of influence should be large enough to cover the majority of the forest.'

'As you said at our last meeting, Iadden is not blind. You know the influence of Cadaran ends within a few leagues east of its walls.

The northeast woods are dangerous, its people cry out for salvation, which I will provide in the guise of this city.'

'And what of the Kingdom of the calefs? Were you to raise a city so close to their northern lands, they would not take kindly to it. They would see it as I saw it; an attempt to expand your borders.'

'By the time I come around to building this city the war with the calefs will be over. They will no longer have the influence to deny its construction. As I said, if I can connect the city to the road through the brambles, then we will have a properly united land, with ease of access between the Midlands and the Eastlands. I suppose it is a way of expanding my borders, but necessarily so. At this moment the calefs are my enemies, and it's within my interests to name their lands my own.'

Tibaduy glanced at him, his eyes now almost completely lost beneath his brows. 'You have told me the basics of your plans, I understand it is only recently conceived, and so the basics are all I can expect to hear. Although you have not said the words, I can see a proposition when it is laid before me. You wish to ask for the aid of the minotorrs in building them. There are a few things you must consider before I leave with your message.

'Firstly, I would say your relations with High Officer Nostiir are, at the present, somewhat strained. This I made clear to you with my message from Bletta Castle. I shall repeat what I said regarding whether they will offer any support at all; to my knowledge, their segregation from the crown was limited only to acts of war. I do not know whether this would include aiding you in building and development, indeed I would say they are still open to aid you in these matters as they wish to see the land united. As such, with this in mind, I believe they will aid you. Obviously, I cannot speak for them, but rest assured, when I deliver your reply, I will be sure to underline the fact these cities will be an important step in uniting the lands in peace.

'However,' he paused, as if for dramatic effect, 'there are many things I believe the court at Bletta Castle would find... unappealing. First is the proposition of building two cities at once. That is both naïve and foolish, it simply cannot be done. Can you imagine how much money, how much force, it would take to accomplish such a task properly?'

'Not once did I say they would both be built simultaneously,' said Stolach. 'That would be doomed to fail, just as King Haled Hementirion nearly bankrupted himself attempting to build two cities at once. I am not such a foolish ruler.'

'Indeed, then which would you choose to be built first? Remember, you will not be alive to see both cities complete, King Stolach, you will have spent many years in the fields beyond the clouds before both are bustling with life.'

'The southern city will be built first,' answered Vixel. 'As already established. We might as well use what's there already before moving to an entirely new settlement.'

'A wise choice, it's the one I would have humbly recommended. It also leads to another point; history. Remember the last time minotorrs assisted the people of the Midlands in building a city? Slavery and oppression followed by a war. It was not so long ago they were still at war with Cadaran, and it is possible they would regard any new city with an element of mistrust.'

'They were indeed wronged,' said Stolach, 'but they shouldn't forget *who* brought those responsible to justice. For a hundred and fourteen years were the minotorrs at war with the rulers of the city. It took me two years to conquer it and bring justice to the corrupt, evil descendants of the treacherous rulers who imprisoned the minotorrs after they did nothing but aid them. It is I who ended that war and brought peace to the north.'

'Indeed it was, and they will not forget it, but I must warn you, old wounds heal slowly, especially when poisoned with the festering filth of slavery. That is why it is better to build in the south first, for another northern city would surely bring back painful memories for my masters. Another consideration would be their concern over whom you select as master of the city. They would not readily build a city for a man who rules as a tyrant. Do you have a candidate in mind?'

'It's too soon to think of such matters, but I can assure you it will be an individual capable of taking on such responsibility with grace and proficiency.'

He saw the dreyad's mouth twitch at the corners as he restrained a smile, before continuing. 'I can accept it is a long way to go before the city is complete, but you should give it some thought, your Majesty. Yet another point I feel necessary to raise is that of these expanding borders. The proximity of the northern city to the calefin lands will not sit kindly with the minotorrs. Their races are different in most aspects, but also quite startlingly similar in others. One such aspect it their respect for one another, and the desire to see the preservation of one another, especially after the loss of their beloved giants.'

'This we could surmise from their lack of support towards the invasion,' murmured Vixel.

'Among other reasons. But this is not the sole reason why your expansion will not sit kindly with them. They will see you reaching out for more lands, grasping and clutching at the neighbouring countries in a desperate attempt to gain more power and influence over Nefarwy, and will wonder why.'

Stolach glanced at Vixel. 'To bring the peace and order of my kingdom to as much of Enadir as is possible, to return the world to the way it was before the Cataclysmic War.'

'They will disagree, as I do. You are stretching too far, trying to claim too much for your own. If you stretch yourself too thinly you will not be able to maintain order in what you currently have. The exact situation you currently find yourself in. They want unity, not tyranny. The lands must work together.'

'I only invaded because they were already at war with me. Once I defeat them and quell the uprisings in the land, all will be well. The new northern city is important to secure safety, peace, and tranquillity to those northeast woods. Its presence is eventually needed.'

'You know as well as I do those woods are scarcely populated by civilised men. It is the realm of the barbaric and fearsome, and few villages would feel the benefit of your new city.'

'Surely that's a reason to build one there?' exclaimed Vixel. 'If the land is as wild as you say, we should be fighting to tame it, drive out the barbaric and make room for civilisation? Few would feel its benefit now, but once we clear those woods of their dangers, people will flock to build villages, and will later move to the city.'

'Nonetheless,' said Tibaduy, 'all I do is warn you what I believe High Officer Nostiir will say.'

Stolach smiled, knowing he and Vixel won that argument. 'Are there any further points to warn me of?'

'Two more. First is the question of who would be allowed to live in these cities?'

'All who would have safety.'

'Impossible. That would be everyone in the Midlands, and your cities would not be able to hold them. What would result would be another shanty town, just like the one I see outside Crastalan. This would not do.'

Stolach paused. It was another issue he'd considered several times, but the solution continued to evade him. Granted, there were plenty of half-formed plans, but nothing substantial, nothing solid. The ever-growing shanty town of Crastalan, as Tibaduy said, was testament to that.

'There will always be slums outside of cities, such is a truth that cannot be altered, especially in times where cities offer such protection and opportunity to its inhabitants,' he said, slowly. 'There are ways around this, of course, such as expanding the city slowly every few decades to accommodate the swollen populations, but this is expensive and resource-heavy. What I believe to be the best solution at present is to imitate Cadaran. What I instructed Lord Tunn to do, and he has done so admirably, is to keep close council with the elders of the surrounding villages. In crises such as war, plague, natural disasters, then those elders lead their villagers to live temporarily within the city walls, until such a time they're able to safely return to their villages.'

'So the inhabitants of the Midlands will *not* be allowed to live in the city, only in times of crisis?'

'No, many of them will, but the ones who cannot will live in large villages surrounding the city, close enough to feel the comfort of its protection, and close enough to flee behind its walls when necessary, but not so close they end up forming these shanty towns.'

'Well how would you decide who lives there and who does not? These are the things one must consider.'

'Taxes,' said Vixel, and the two turned to her, both with the same expression of confusion, 'there will be different tax rates. The ones in the city will be higher, as they have permanent protection and residence, while those in the surrounding villages will be less, as they only come when needed!'

'Many would prefer to live in their forest villages instead of the cities, as is true right now. Not everyone in Nefarwy has come to Crastalan, Cadaran, or Morgenal, many are more than happy to stay in their ancestral homes,' said Stolach, sensing Tibaduy's trepidation at the prospect of one's wealth determining the degree of their safety.

'It is an imperfect solution,' said the dreyad, sadly, 'and you will have to discuss it at length with your advisors, the ruler of the city, and your allies. I will let the high officer know you have thought of this issue, and are at least *trying* to find ways around it.'

There was a brief pause, before Vixel asked. 'What was the final point of note?'

'An uncomfortable one to bring up, but necessary. At present, as I told you earlier, your relationship with Nostiir is, to put it delicately, unsound. For the simple reason it is *your* proposal, I fear the high officer may refuse, simply because he doesn't wish to be associated with you at present.'

Vixel hissed between her teeth, but he ignored her. 'We've gone over this. I accept he won't play a direct hand in the war, but you said he would aid us in other ventures. You said it a few minutes ago.'

'Those were my musings over the situation, yes, but I obviously cannot speak for such an esteemed individual as Nostiir. His thoughts may well be to aid you in the building of the cities, however the fact *you* yourself are involved, might make him pause and reconsider,' said Tibaduy.

'What is he, a petty child?' sneered Vixel. 'He won't protect the people of the Midlands because he has a quarrel with their king? It's not what one would expect of a good ruler.'

'That might be your opinion, others would say it is sensible to distance oneself from an individual who sanctions the destruction of innocent lives by barbarians... but it is not for me to judge. I can only advise,' said Tibaduy.

'What would your advice be?' she sneered.

Tibaduy paused, and turned his gaze to Vixel. 'I would advise that I approach Nostiir with these plans under the pretence it is *your* idea, m'lady. If I were to say that you, not his Majesty, are the head behind them, and that the king is only there as an advisory role, then it could well work to your advantage.'

From the corner of his eye, Stolach could see Vixel's lips curl into an involuntary smile. 'You think this would work?' he asked. 'Vixel's not on any of my Councils, she's not an advisor or a general, not an architect or builder. Would Nostiir put his faith in her?'

'Not an advisor?' repeated Vixel. He closed his eyes. That would come back to sting him over the next few days, no doubt about it. She could turn a careless word into a hornet's nest at a whim. 'I might not sit at your meetings, but I'm your foremost advisor in all matters. Nostiir would be wise to put his faith in me, the one who originally conceived this idea!'

The dreyad raised his eyebrows, a smirk playing on his features. 'Your Majesty?'

He took a breath and nodded quickly. 'She's right, she's more than capable of heading this project. I trust her judgement.'

It was easier to just let her have it and avoid unnecessary conflict. Taking a chief advisory role as opposed to a definitive lead would also take a load off his shoulders and give him time to pursue other ends. An easier life.

'Excellent,' said Tibaduy. 'I will relay this information to the high officer. Lady Vixel is the head of this project, and it is with her that dealings will be made, with the king as an advisor and supervisor.'

'Good,' he said. 'I'll have provisions packed for you and your horse made ready to leave as soon as possible.'

The dreyad nodded his thanks.

'You're a wise advisor, Tibaduy,' continued Stolach as they walked to the door, maps and charts bundled beneath his arm. 'Do you sit with other advisors in Bletta Castle?'

'No, I am a scout, I belong with my people in the woods, not locked behind stone walls in high mountains. I long for the touch of leaves on my cheek and bark beneath my fingers.'

'A pity,' he sniffed. 'I might have invited you to return here sometimes as an advisor for me.'

'That would not do,' smiled the dreyad. 'The closest forest to us here is the Pine Wood, leagues away. Your own advisors will have to make do for now, your Majesty, and I do not think you lack wisdom among them.'

Stolach looked behind them at Vixel, who gathered up the goblets and jug of wine, and extinguished the torches, plunging the room into momentary darkness. Light flooded in once more when he opened the door, and they stepped out into the corridor.

He turned to the dreyad a final time. 'Luck be with you on your journeys, Tibaduy. I'm glad we met.'

'Indeed. I am sure you will hear from Bletta Castle with your answers soon. Farewell.'

One of the servants led the dreyad away down the corridor, and Stolach and Vixel walked in the opposite direction, each absorbed in their thoughts.

Chapter 36

Leam's lodgings were far more than Lidan ever expected in the barren Northlands. In his mind, the ageing knight would have made his home in a humble little hut, with barely enough room for himself, and no furnishings aside from a simple cot, perhaps an uncomfortable wooden stool if he were lucky. He couldn't have been further from the truth.

They were led to a small chapel, built of stone and mortar, surrounded by a waist-high boundary wall. To one side was a small stable, where two horses grazed on dried grass. The chapel itself was roughly rectangular, no more than eight metres wide and fifteen long, with an arched roof covered in slate and flint. A single oaken door in one of the shorter walls served as the entrance. Its humble exterior hid the wealth within. Fourteen wooden benches on each side formed an aisle through the middle, with a final smaller bench at the far end before the altar. A round stone table, a foot in diameter at most, with a white marble plate on top. These humble furnishings were where the frugality ended, as the walls and ceiling were draped in a wealth of cloth. Beautiful tapestries garnished the walls, suspended on heavy brass rings and iron poles, the rich embroidery glittering with cloth of gold and silver, a dozen landscapes, stories, and characters woven in thread. From above hung a multitude of old battle standards, some frayed and ancient, others younger, all bearing the same weight of history and grandeur. Nestled in the alcoves between these masterpieces were candles and torches to hidden shrines, each dutifully lit by Leam as he passed them.

Turning to them, the knight nodded to their horses, ambling outside beyond the open door. 'Take them to the stables, they'll be warm there. You can rest on the benches. Take off your cloaks, use them as blankets, and put your arms to one side, no harm will come to you here. Should you feel the urge to pray, feel free to come to the altar and I shall lead your ceremony.'

Lidan shifted nervously as everyone ambled away to find seats. Unsure what to do, Lidan followed and sat next to Spotal, gazing at the adorning tapestries and standards. The majority bore the symbol of the northern winds, the same as Leam's surcoat, in addition to the other unrecognisable crests and heraldry. Well, unrecognisable to him. Spotal could probably tell him the history behind each one.

He felt a sudden chill, and was surprised to see an open window behind the fluttering standards above their heads, the only window in the entire building, set high into the wall above the stone altar. Their chapel in Weaverlodge had a similar feature, but it was warm down there, having a permanently open window at the border to the Northlands just seemed ridiculous.

He must have been staring, and Leam sat at his side.

'The window is to let the northern wind in to bless this holy place. At times it can get a little cold, but it's better to be cold and blessed than warm and damned.'

'Do you live here alone?' he asked, quietly, shyly. As a boy, he'd been told stories of the knightly orders, of the quests they set out on in the name of their holy worships. He and his cousins often played knights and mercenaries, beating each other with sticks and proclaiming themselves the bravest in the land. To meet such a figure in person...

'Yes, I alone am protector of this chapel and our holy altar.'

'Why have a chapel here? Surely you can't have many visitors?' commented Widrias from nearby, rubbing his leg. 'Not much of a community to guide.'

'We have one or two, people who've felt the call of the northern winds and wish to make the holy pilgrimage to the far north. Some of these brave souls will visit my chapel on their way.'

'What lies in the far north?' asked Lidan, wide-eyed.

'What you find differs from person to person. Some find enlightenment, others find clarity, most find unity with the wind as they shed their mortal bodies and unite with its might.'

'You mean they die,' said Spotal, bluntly.

Leam smiled his half-smile. 'How else would you unite with the wind?'

'Have you ever made the pilgrimage yourself?' asked Lidan.

'Of course, one cannot become a member of our Order without completing the pilgrimage,' said Leam.

'How far is far north?' asked Pwtrek with a chuckle. 'Perhaps I qualify as a knight, I've travelled far up there quite a few times.'

'Each pilgrim knows for himself how far is far enough. Personally, I travelled beyond the East Jaws of the North, past both the Zarhanoq Mountains and Shadil Mountains, beyond the Gorge of Khakarah, and to the foothills of the Koaa Mountains. That was where my journey came to an end, as I was not permitted to travel any further.'

'What stopped you?' breathed Lidan.

'Enlightenment. I saw the tips of the great mountains rise above me, and as I stared at their lofty peaks a great storm descended their slopes, and I was beset by snow and lightning. As I battled forward, I heard the north wind whisper my name and warn me of approaching danger. Barely an hour later, a fearsome beast attacked me with fang and claw and tail. In the light of the flashing storm I did battle with it, and by my sword and shield, I struck it down. Within minutes, the storm had passed, and I knew my test was over. Stronger, wiser, blessed, I returned.'

'And now you protect a chapel?' he asked.

'Indeed, I offer assistance to travellers in the land, I bless holy pilgrims on their journeys, and I protect the altar of the northern winds.'

'How've you amassed such riches? I thought your order was against personal wealth?' asked Spotal, gesturing to the walls.

'The tapestries and the banners? They are not mine, they belong to all who worship the northern winds, to revel in their beauty, and to gather behind them should we march into battle.'

'What do they depict?' asked Lidan, standing to gaze at the tapestry above him. In the torchlight it was difficult to properly see exactly what was shown, and he had to strain his eyes before recognising the heavily-stylized depiction of a priest, holding a basket of food above his head.

'This one shows the liberation of Nefarwy of starvation after the Cataclysmic War,' replied Leam, pointing to the far end of the tapestry. With the eye of faith, Lidan could just about make out the shapes of armoured soldiers battling winged snakes with fierce beaks, as fire raged about them. 'After the giants defeated their enemy for the last time, the land was barren, and Enadir refused to provide its inhabitants with food, as punishment for the death and destruction of the war. It was during this time the northern wind came to our salvation, driving storms from the sea to the land, so rain would fall and give us water and life. Eventually the efforts of the northern winds proved successful, and Enadir bounded into a new age of prosperity.'

From across the chapel, Gwahl snorted loudly. Lidan turned and saw the daemon blush, embarrassed by the unconscious reaction to Leam's tale. The knight didn't seem insulted. Indeed, he seemed to expect such a reaction, and approached the daemon with his hands raised.

'I do apologise, Gwahl the daemon, I know your race are opposed to the teachings of the holy orders.'

'How would you know that? More to the point, how do you know my name? I've never before come to your chapel. How do you know me?'

Lidan couldn't see the knight's face, but knew he was smiling as he replied. 'The answer to both your questions; I was told it by an old knight. He described many of your kin to me, including yourself, and much about the characteristics of your race.'

'How did the knight come by this information?' asked Gwahl.

'He read it in a tome,' said Leam.

'What tome?' the daemon's tone was defensive, aggressive, like a cornered animal spitting at a tormentor.

'One that he found in the far north. My brother knight was permitted to travel further than I, and he found himself led to a Great Library beneath the Rhetta Mountains, where he found a tome on the daemons of Enadir, written recently, within the last few centuries.'

'A man of your order found the Great Library of Knowledge? Alone and uninvited?' Gwahl nearly spat the words from his mouth. Lidan had never seen the daemon so agitated.

'Indeed, but it is not such a Great Library after all. He searched for weeks, but only ever found that single book.'

For some reason this pleased the daemon, and Gwahl visibly relaxed, but still held Leam in a furious stare. Lidan wished he knew what was happening, what information lay beneath the icy conversation held before his eyes.

'What did this book say of daemons?' asked Gwahl.

'Too much, or too little. Enough to pique the curiosity of anyone who read it, but left too many unanswered questions for anyone to understand your race. My brother spent years trying to answer the questions raised by that tome, and died before he could do so.'

'What did it say?' repeated Gwahl. Lidan listened intently, eager to find out more about his mysterious friend. He sensed everyone else doing the same, sitting on the edge of their seats in complete silence, barely daring to breathe lest the sound might distract the knight and the daemon and end their conversation.

'It described many of your people, including your names and brief descriptions of your appearance; Deia, Godan, Gwahl, Dwerel, Dwrelian, Aani, Lloniwr, Gogofaint, Karanydd, Corusul… hundreds of names and descriptions for us to memorise. More importantly it spoke of mysterious things, of Enadir and nature, giants, cockatrice, dragons, and other… things. An infuriatingly, *purposefully*, incomplete history of your race. My Order, and all Orders, have always been scorned by the daemons, but we know it is *you* who hold the answers to our questions, but guard them too jealously to share.'

'Is the book in your possession?'

'Not mine. It lies where it was found, for its covers were bound in iron, and my brother knight could not carry it home, so he memorised as much as he could before returning.'

'I cannot give you the answers you want to hear,' replied Gwahl, coldly.

'I thought not,' said Leam, turning away, dejectedly. 'My old brother knight told me in all his years searching for answers, he came across three daemons. Elnydd, Carydoedd, and Synwewyn, neither of these answered any of his questions.

'You will not aid me, that much is clear, but please do not scorn me or my faith. I do you no harm in my beliefs, do me no harm in yours.'

Gwahl nodded in apology and turned away, curling up on the bench to sleep.

Lidan sat back, disappointed more hadn't been revealed. One piece of information stuck with him; the book was written within the last few centuries. If it included a description of Gwahl, that must make him impossibly old.

Spotal raised his eyebrows at Lidan, mirroring his own disappointment at the outcome of the conversation.

'So aside from the pilgrimage to the north, what else do you need to become a knight?' he asked. Gwahl may be a closed book on the mysteries of his race, but Leam seemed open to share.

'First, you must be a recognised member of the faith, a priest of some kind, then you must complete the pilgrimage. Then, you must prove to a current knight your worth.'

'How do you do that?'

'It depends on what the knight deems to be worthy. Only then will you be recited the sacred passage and be anointed a Knight Garia; a knight of the Order of the Winter Snow, holy warrior of the northern winds.'

'Seems a bit subjective,' commented Spotal. 'The deeds one knight perceives as worthy might be utterly different from another. As Pwtrek said, he's been quite far north, what's to say he shouldn't be a knight?'

'Perhaps, but ultimately, we all comply to the same teachings. By extension, all knights who understand the rites of the northern winds will recognise worthiness wherever it is demonstrated. But if Pwtrek were to join the faith and make an official pilgrimage, I'm sure I'd be happy to assess him,' he smiled.

'Seems a bit convoluted to me,' shrugged Spotal. 'How many pilgrims have you anointed to your order?'

Leam considered for a moment. 'Two.'

'How many have approached you?'

'Twelve brothers have approached me.'

'And you refused ten of them?'

Leam shook his head. 'I did not refuse them, I merely pointed out they were not yet ready to join our ranks.'

'How did they feel?' asked Lidan.

'Most of them knew in their hearts that my decision was true, that the northern winds had not yet felt the need for their swords. Only one reacted with bitterness.'

'What did he do?'

'He abandoned the northern winds, and set it upon himself to desecrate this altar,' the knight looked sadly at the open window. 'I was forced to defend the faith and hasten his ultimate fate.'

Lidan understood. Looking around, he noticed on the eastern wall a discoloured stone with carvings etched onto the surface, below which rested a battered old kite shield, bearing the symbol of the order.

'What does that engraving say?'

Leam glanced at the wall and approached it slowly. Standing in front of the stone he lightly touched the words. 'These are the rites I would read when ordaining another to our ranks. I would stand behind the altar and they would kneel before it, sword held in both palms. I would then take a pendant, like this,' he rummaged inside his tunic and held aloft a silver pendant at the end of a cord around his neck; a solid circle engraved with the mark of the northern winds. 'I would then recite the vow. "*You are about to receive the honour of entering the Order of the Winter Snow. Countless others have stood in your place, each one a noble warrior and devout servant of the Northern Winds. This pendant is an ancient relic of our order, a talisman blessed by the Wind to protect its holder. Wear it on your breast with a pious heart, and you will be spared from all but the deadliest blows. Wear it to defend the faith, the weak, the lost, by your sword and shield, in the name of the Northern Winds. You are gentle as a breeze, and as fierce as a storm. You are frost. You are iron. Rise, Knight Garia. Rise, brother.*" With the pendant about their necks, they would rise and become a protector of the faith.'

Lidan pondered the words for some time after. It seemed far-fetched that such a small token would actually protect the knight from any blow, he would put far more trust in a shield or breastplate. But perhaps that wasn't to be considered literally, but rather as a symbol that if you carried the pendant, you carried your faith on your breast, and your faith protected you in a metaphorical sense, that you had no more fear of death. He shrugged, it was all too philosophical for him. The days of playing knights and mercenaries were dead and gone, now reality was all the adventure he needed.

'Would your Order march against the king?' asked Widrias, suddenly.

Leam frowned at him, and rubbed his chin. 'An unwelcome question. We do not participate in wars of politics, our sole purpose is protection, not destruction.'

'No, the vow that you took states you must defend the weak and the lost. The war that Stolach fights is only creating more souls in need of charity to survive. Had you only seen the horrors we witnessed in the Kingdom of the calefs, a land that once shone as bright as a star now shrouded in darkness, due to the destruction that Stolach wrought upon it. Where were the knightly orders then? I saw no fallen knights, slain protecting the weak.'

'Did Stolach initiate this war? Or did you, high chancellor of the Council? Yes, I know who you are, the great General Widrias cannot hide from his reputation. There was no war until the Council rose up against the king.'

'We rose up to protect the inhabitant of the Midlands. Stolach was ruling as a tyrant, oppressing, persecuting, discriminating, abusing his power. We had to stand up because nobody else would.'

'Now the war you fight has only bred more suffering. So many innocents dead, so many lost souls turning to thieving and murder to survive. Have you considered what would have happened had you left it all alone?'

'Stolach would have still attacked my country,' said Spotal. 'The Council only hastened his hand, an attack on the Kingdom of the calefs was inevitable. The fonex is hungry for power; that's why we must stop him.'

'People would have still turned to murder and thieving,' continued Widrias, passionately. 'With so little money they would have been forced to steal to survive. When a greedy mind sits upon a throne, it is only a matter of time before war breaks.'

'Believe me when I say I meant to offence,' said Leam, slowly, 'but the fact remains, the order will not march in a war of politics.'

'This is not a war of politics, or of faith, or of greed or thirst for power. We fight for the right to live as we should, in peace and prosperity, as we once did before the Cataclysmic War. Stolach must be removed from power before his shroud covers all of Enadir. It is your duty to fight in this war.'

'You would have me and my brothers fight alongside you, I'm sure Stolach could conjure an argument just as convincing to fight against you.'

'So you side with the king?' demanded Widrias.

'I take no sides. My order acts only to protect the weak, and our work will be cut out for us in the aftermath of this war,' said Leam.

Widrias shook his head. 'You would be more efficient in protecting the weak if you joined us.'

'I doubt anyone from my order would agree with that sentiment.'

A thought seemed to strike the satorr and he looked up, a glint in his eye. 'Perhaps not from your order, but others would.'

Leam's frown deepened. 'The business of the other orders are their own. Why mention them?'

'You know my name, you know I am a high chancellor, what other chancellors do you know?'

Leam shook his head. 'Yours was the only name I knew, and Tuulik, who has been a chancellor for longest.'

'One of us is Chaplain Stegil Mawein, of the Order of the Mountain Air. His entire order will fight with us should they be called upon, all the Knights Mynaw, fighting alongside the Council.'

Leam paused. 'The chaplain sits on the Council? This is news. I will pray through the night for guidance. Rest now, we have talked for long enough.'

*

Lidan lay on the bench, his arms resting behind his head as he stared at the ceiling. Shadows from his little candle caught the various imperfections in the stone, creating strange shapes that swirled before him, blending together in an everlasting chaos. He sighed. It was nearly a month since Colrick saved him, and he was still stuck in this little prison beneath the great south infirmary, waiting.

By now he was quite sure Colrick meant him no harm, and the healer spent much of his free time down with Lidan, tending his wounds, feeding him, keeping him company. Not much conversation was held between the two, and the fat man would often come down with large tomes, quills, and pots of ink, and spent hours scratching away at the pages as he wrote down his accounts of his day's work. Once, Lidan asked him why he had to document everything.

'It's our protocol,' he replied. 'We write down everything we do during treatment of our patients, from the time we saw them to the time we left, what ointments we used, what surgery we carried out, what instruments need to be cleaned after use. There's a lot to do. Unfortunately, I have no time during the day to make a truly detailed account, so I write down the basics on spare parchment, and copy it down in greater detail into my case volumes. Everything needs to be regulated so we know what work goes on in this place.'

It made sense, but it wasn't something that he personally would have the patience to do. Writing down the exact details of his contact with his patients was clearly tedious and long-winded work, but something Colrick insisted was essential. He smiled as he wondered whether his rescuer included him in those volumes.

Swinging his legs off the bench, he stretched and arched his back. With so little to do in such a cramped space, his rehabilitation following his grisly wounds had been difficult at best, but the healer gave him a series of stretches to do throughout the day to keep limber.

'Exercise is important as well,' he remembered Colrick saying. 'I know there is not much room here for you to be running around, so you could try a method some of the assassins use?'

'What is it?'

'Isometric exercises. It's when you use an immovable object as your resistance, imparting force on that object while keeping your muscle and joint length consistent. I'll demonstrate a few for you...'

The few basic exercises that Colrick showed him were useful, and Lidan had since modified and built upon them to create an entirely new workout routine of his own, to build his strength as he waited for the time to leave Crastalan. That thought was the constant motivation, it never waned nor faltered like the little taper next to his bed, but burned as fierce as a beacon. Resting his hands against the wall, he braced his body, enjoying his returning strength.

A few hours after his exercise, his company returned. Something was different. No books, no quills. Colrick's piggish face was sweatier and more flushed than usual. Behind his back was a large knapsack, tied at the neck with a rope.

Colrick shut the door carefully behind him, untied the neck of the sack, and emptied its contents. Lidan watched with curiosity as he took out a brown robe, a length of cord, and a thin cloak. He handed him the robe first.

'Put that on, Lidan, the time has come to leave. We must be discreet and swift. Fortunately for us, nobody is looking for you, but on the off chance someone *does* recognise you... well, I would rather they didn't. This should disguise you as an acolyte, a trainee shadowing the footsteps of a chief healer. Quickly now!'

He rushed to do as told, throwing the robe over his head and tying it around his middle with the cord, the cloak over his shoulders completed the disguise. Colrick looked him up and down.

'Good, you look passable. Nobody will suspect anything. Now, follow me.'

He turned on his heel, picked up the knapsack, and strode away down the dimly-lit passageway. Heart in throat, Lidan followed, stumbling every so often on his flowing brown robe. For ten minutes he scurried through the passages, turning this way and that as the healer led him ever onwards. Eventually they came to the great circular passageway in which Lidan had been lost. It seemed so long ago.

'How did you get rid of the blood?' he breathed.

'Elbow-grease,' Colrick replied. 'A pail of water and a stiff-bristled brush was all it needed.'

They reached a door, the same as any other door, leading down yet another stone passageway. He felt an unfamiliar sensation. The faintest chill of the wind caressing his frail body. He shivered, whether from the cold breeze or excitement he couldn't tell. Probably a mixture of both.

At the end of the passage was a solid oak door, studded with iron bolts. The healer stopped and glanced back, looking him over one last time. Satisfied with the disguise, he opened the door and stepped outside.

Cautiously, he followed, stumbling ever so slightly over the threshold, out into the cold air. Sunrise was nearly upon them, and the sky was losing its pitch-black colour, adopting a more comforting navy. After another searching look, Colrick took him by the arm down an alley.

His breath came in ragged gasps. Outside, after so long! Freedom. It was almost too much. His heart hammered and his breath came quickly, eyes flicking, gazing frightfully at the few people who were still about at this hour. Fortunately, the disguise served its purpose, and of the few who acknowledged them, none paid any attention to the thin little acolyte scampering like a puppy at the senior healer's heels.

After walking for a good ten minutes through the streets, Colrick finally pulled him to one side into a shadowy alcove.

'The southern gates to the second level are ahead of us. This is where it gets particularly dangerous. It's time to change your disguise once again,' he reached into the knapsack and took out a long bandage.

'Why? This one seems to be working well.'

'We need to get past the guards. If two healers go through the gates then they'll expect two healers to come back. If only one of us returns, then it'll arouse suspicion, and they'll be suspicious enough as it is to see anyone about at this hour. However, if they see a healer leading a blind patient back to his home, hopefully they won't think too much of it. Here, take off the robe.'

Lidan did as he was told and handed the fat man the disguise. Colrick then returned to the knapsack and took out a small leather purse, which he handed to Lidan.

'There should be enough money in there for you to survive a few nights in the second level. Use it to buy some food, a place to stay, and keep some coins for the tolls out the city. Don't sleep on these streets, it's not worth the risk of getting robbed or caught by guards. Beggars aren't welcome. Now, we need to cover the brand. Let me tie this bandage around your eyes, don't worry, I'll guide you through.'

He couldn't stop shaking as the bandage was wrapped around his head. Fear tightened its grip. He should just run. Take his chances. Live his final few days of freedom. No. It would work. Colrick was with him. He'd led him this far, why would he abandon him now?

Holding out his arms, he felt a large, warm hand enclose his thin wrist and guide him onwards. They barely walked two dozen steps when he heard someone call out,

'Who goes there? Identify yourselves!'

'I'm Colrick, a chief healer from the great south infirmary. This is one of my patients. I'm leading him to his home in the second level.'

They halted, presumably in front of the gates. Lidan nearly jumped when another voice sounded, barely two feet away from him,

'Why are you coming so late? The gates are about to close for the day.'

'I was treating him all day, and he cannot stay in the infirmary overnight. We have too many patients and not enough beds.'

Another voice. 'That's true, you know, my cousin's wife had a horrible chest pain, gasping for air, but they wouldn't let her stay the night there because there wasn't enough room. Poor girl was dead by the morning.'

The first voice spoke again. 'You should sort that out. Poor people are dropping dead and you lot don't have the resources to treat them. What's wrong with this one then?'

'Blind.'

'I can see that – shame he can't,' there was an unpleasant snort at the comment. 'But being blind isn't a reason to go to the infirmary.'

'He had a sore gut, ate too many sour apples.'

A third voice piped up. 'Ooh I feel for you, Blindey, I've done that before.'

'Yes, well, should it ever happen again just come to see one of us, the treatment is a simple solution to ease the acid in your stomach.'

'How much does it cost?' asked the same voice.

'I'm afraid I don't know, finances aren't my area,' said Colrick.

'Probably too much, you lot charge through your noses for some things, I'm telling you now. Alright that's enough chatter, it's two coppers each to go through.'

'Actually, as a chief healer, it's only one copper for me.'

'Honestly there's no end to the perks you people get... fine, give me the three and go on through. Will you be staying the day in the second circle?'

'No, I'm only seeing him to his home and then I'll return.'

Lidan heard the jingle of money as Colrick handed the guard the fees.

'Well be quick about it. Remember we'll be charging you again on your way back. Can't dodge out of that one. Now go, go.'

He felt himself be ushered on, and nearly stumbled again, drawing a series of chuckles from the soldiers. Thankfully, Colrick was still there to steady him, and he led him through to the second level. They kept walking for a few minutes, before stopping.

Relieved, he felt the bandage unwrapping itself from around his head. Sight returned, he took stock of his surroundings. A cold black stone road surrounded by black granite buildings, some of them with rickety wooden extensions to provide more living space. There were crates and barrels outside the buildings, presumably filled with water or some other goods, the possessions of the inhabitants. He smiled, each step took him that much closer to freedom.

Colrick clasped him on the shoulder and looked at him sternly.

'This is where I leave you, my friend. Remember what I said, find an inn, keep healthy, and save some money for the main gates. You'll have to be cautious around soldiers, if they see your mark then you'll be back in the dungeons. Get out of here, get away from Crastalan and start a new life in peace. I don't know what you did to get yourself thrown into those cells, but whatever it was, forget about it and live your life. Will you promise me that?'

'I'll try,' mumbled Lidan, trying to sound convincing.

The fat man saw right through him. He sighed. 'The man who seeks revenge should dig two graves, Lidan. Remember that. I wish you the best of luck on whatever path you choose.'

'I can't thank you enough for saving me. I owe you my life.'

'I know, so please don't throw it away. Goodbye,' he clasped his hand on Lidan's shoulder one last time, then turned and scurried back to the gates. Lidan walked down the deserted street, alone again.

*

Morning brought the rain. It wasn't a heavy downpour, but a light drizzle which might have been pleasant in the Dailas Forest. In the Northlands, however, the wind gave the raindrops a sharpness, and they fell in stinging diagonal sheets. The open window in the northern wall gave the weather an entrance to the chapel, and Lidan was awoken by the waspish fall of rain on his unprotected face.

Yawning, he rolled his feet off the bench and sat upright. He was the last to wake, as always, and he could see the others milling about the yard, fetching the horses. It didn't take long, and within minutes they were back inside, shaking the rain from their hair as they helped themselves to the food Leam prepared. There wasn't much. A thick stew of some sort thickened with oats, but it was hot and satisfying, and they thanked the old knight for his consideration.

Having eaten, they prepared to leave, but not before Leam requested they join him in his morning prayers. Everyone obliged him out of politeness, save for Auran and Gwahl, who stepped outside. With the short sermon done, in which Leam prayed for protection and guidance on their journey, they left the chapel.

Widrias paused at the gate and turned to the old knight. 'What did the northern winds say to you on the matter of joining the Council?'

Leam sighed. 'They were silent, but that is an answer in itself. Perhaps they tell me this is a decision I must make myself. The fact the Northern Winds already fight with you through the Order of the Mountain Air is significant. I will send messages to the head of my order and tell him of this news. I can make no promises, but the Knights Garia cannot truly stand by when the Knights Mynaw die in battle. They are a different order, but servants of the Northern Winds nonetheless, and we must protect our devout brothers.'

'You might join us?'

'I cannot promise you anything, our chaplain might see otherwise. It is possible it is the Knights Mynaw who are misguided, and the Northern Winds will depend on us once their order is destroyed in war.'

'When will we know?'

'I will set out the next time a pilgrim arrives at my chapel.'

'That might be weeks from now!'

'Yes, but it cannot be helped. I have no birds with me to carry my messages.'

'We might have marched for the final encounter before you return to us.'

'I do not think this war will end with one battle, the two opposing forces are too large for that. Even if we do miss the climactic battle you seem to expect, you might have need of us later. Besides, we are no army. The inclusion of the Knights Garia into the Council force will hardly make a difference. An additional hundred-or-so soldiers will not swing the tide of a large battle.'

'It might. It's not just the bodies you bring, but the symbol of your order that will make a difference. If people see us marching with the holy banner of your order, in addition to that of the Knights Mynaw, they will believe in our cause that much more.'

'As I said, I'll get the word to you as soon as I can. Farewell, General Widrias.'

Widrias opened his mouth to say something, but thought better of it. With a final nod of farewell, he flicked the reins of his horse and led the party away. Lidan stole one final glance over his shoulder, and Leam raised a hand to him as he watched them walk away from his beloved chapel.

'Do you think they'll join us?' he asked Pwtrek.

'He seemed convinced once he knew another order were already with us,' Pwtrek shrugged.

'How many orders are there?'

'More than you might think. The four largest are the Winter Snow, the Mountain Air, the Peaceful Night, and the Burning Skies. After that you have lots of other, more obscure ones, like the Order of the Maelstrom, the Serene Forest…'

'The Blazing Stone,' added Depani, 'the Mirror.'

'Yes, those too.'

'What do they worship? They can't all worship the northern winds, otherwise there wouldn't be any point in having so many different ones, would there?'

'The Winter Snow and Mountain Air both worship the northern winds, the Peaceful Night worship the four winds, and the Burning Skies worship the Sun – they're mostly Southlanders. The others worship the Great Waters, the southern winds, the Burning Eyes, and I think it's the Order of the Mirror, the Knights Darrych, who worship the long-dead dragons.'

'How many knights do you think there are? Leam said his order has around a hundred.'

Pwtrek laughed. 'I think that was somewhat of an exaggeration. I'd be surprised if there were many more than seventy in each of the four largest orders, and the others can't have many more than thirty each. He was right to say they're no army, but Widrias is also right to say they're a powerful symbol to fight alongside.'

*

A week later, a soaking company of travellers, stained up to their ears in mud, stood shivering before the northeast fringes of the Dailas Forest. Their shoulders were rounded, their backs hunched, and their legs trembled with exhaustion. The satorr shrugged off his pack and limped up to the nearest tree to lay a weary hand on its trunk. Had a stranger been watching, he might have wondered why such tired individuals would not travel with horses, to share the load of their heavy arms. This stranger might also have wondered what reason they might have had to be in the Northlands at such a perilous time, with so much chaos reigning in these woods. One thing was unmistakeable; the fierce joy of individuals who had finally reached the end, or near-end, of a desperate journey.

Chapter 37

Treading through the forest, Lidan was taken by just how different these woods were to those in the south. The ground was hard, quite the polar opposite to the rich loam he was used to. Pine and cedar trees dominated, with the odd redwood towering above everything like sentinels of the north. More than this was the atmosphere. Tense as a taut bowstring, with a heavy silence, broken occasionally by the snuffling of rodents and the half-hearted chirps of finches and sparrows in agitated flight to find food.

Despite the cold, sweat trickled down his flank and neck. His mouth was miserably dry. No matter how many sips he took from his water-skin, that cloying, parched sensation would always return. What made him so uneasy? Judging by the frowns and clenched jaws of his companions, he was not alone in his sentiments.

In many ways, he was glad the horses were all dead. They would have suffered in this these woods. From experience, he knew there were few things as difficult as leading a reluctant horse.

Night brought additional discomforts, howling wolves in the distance, a screaming rabbit caught by an owl, the rumble of thunder. Thankfully, the storm was not above them, and they slept beneath dry skies, illuminated every few seconds by flashes of lightning within the dark clouds.

By morning the storm reached them, but by expending its energy during the night, only an irritating drizzle beset them. The covering canopy received the worst of it, so he was only slightly damp that day. Nobody spoke much since leaving the Northlands, it was almost as if voices were forbidden here. This perceived law against sound was what made the screaming so much worse.

It started during the third night, during his time on watch. He first heard scuffling somewhere in the darkness, but being unable to see very far, given the moon's difficulty in penetrating the canopy, he raised no alarm, assuming it to be some fox or badger. An unease took hold when he sensed watching eyes, but again saw no enemy. He drew his sword and held it before him, hoping to intimidate any spying creature and drive them away. For a while it seemed to work, as the night returned to its normal quiet. The hooting of an owl settled his nerves, and he sat back down with a sense of relief. Not five minutes later, he heard moans, quickly followed by sobs, broken apart by screams. There was no need to wake anyone. They were on their feet, weapons drawn, eyes wide. For a moment nobody moved, they just stared ahead of them, searching for movement in the shadows.

It was difficult to listen beyond the screams, to shut them out and concentrate on any other sounds lurking beneath. Lidan did his best. But he could only hear the pain. They bounced from tree to tree, ringing horribly in his ears. Winds! Let it stop. Be merciful and end this cacophony.

'Noswen!' called Widrias, raising his voice to be heard. 'Do you see anything?'

'Nothing,' she hissed. 'But I feel something. Malicious eyes in the dark.'

'Lidan, did you see anything?' asked Widrias.

'Nothing. I heard a few scuffles but thought it was just an animal,' he muttered.

'It might be, we don't know anything yet.'

'Should we go and see what it is? We might be able to put them out of their misery,' said Spotal.

'Noswen! Go.'

'She shouldn't go alone,' said Gwahl. 'I'll go with her.'

'I'll go too!' said Lidan, morbid curiosity overcoming any anxiety.

'No, stay and guard the camp. Stealth is required for this,' said Gwahl, gently pushing him away.

'It makes no difference if he comes,' whispered Noswen, materialising beside him. 'Whoever is doing this knows we're here and will expect us to investigate. Let him come, he can watch our backs.'

Gwahl glanced at Widrias, who nodded in agreement. The daemon grimaced and motioned for Lidan to follow.

They tread cautiously, straining their senses. Noswen skilfully wove a path through the trees, placing each foot carefully, making as little sound as possible. Gwahl followed next, then Lidan, constantly sweeping his eyes back and forth, finding nothing. Each wail sent beads of sweat running down his nose. He licked his dry lips in anticipation, eager to see what lay ahead. Suddenly, Noswen held up a fist and slowly pointed ahead to a redwood, its vast trunk easily two metres in diameter. Tied around that trunk was the source of the screaming.

Three men, little more than boys, bound to the tree with painfully tight ropes. Each one barbarically mutilated. One was half-skinned, the red-raw flesh beneath shining in the sparse moonlight. All were missing limbs, and blood still pumped from their severed vessels to feed the blood-slicked ground beneath. Two were blinded, their eyes gouged out and left to dangle on their cheeks beneath gaping sockets. One of the blinded ones had his abdomen sliced open, spilling his innards to the floor in a messy heap. The only boy still alive breathed laboriously as blood poured from his severed arms, and frightening, lidless eyes rolled wildly in their sockets, blinded by blood.

Gwahl and Noswen largely ignored him, instead concentrating on the surrounding wood for signs of their tormentors. Lidan was transfixed in horror. He was no stranger to torture, and endured enough pain to drive him half-mad, but Colrick's gentle hand guided him back to health. All that suffering, all that agony, seemed like nothing compared to the mutilation these poor creatures suffered.

Eventually, Noswen stalked forwards to the living one, and whispered something to him. The poor boy sobbed, delirious in pain. She waited a moment longer for an answer. Only a moment. She killed him with a swift stab to the chest. Lidan breathed in relief, relishing in the merciful silence. Noswen returned to them, wiping her blade clean, but not returning it to its sheath.

'I'll have a look around for tracks.'

'No time,' replied Gwahl, as a shout rang out from behind them. 'Back at the camp!'

They ran back, crashing through the forest to their friends, as more and more sounds of battle rang in the night.

'Why would someone do that?'

'A distraction. Dividing our forces,' replied Gwahl, angrily. 'Some barbarian out for blood.'

Fifty paces from their camp, they saw their first enemy. A thin, filthy creature with yellow eyes and brown teeth. Wispy hair covered its limbs. It was clad in filthy rags made of a thin, stinking material. It was not particularly tall, or small, but an average height, its hunched back taking a few inches off its true height. The goblin screeched at them when it saw them approach, and charged with a crude stone-tipped spear. As fierce and bloodthirsty as it may have been, it never stood a chance against Noswen, who easily knocked aside the jabbing spear with her falchion and buried her dirk into its belly. Collapsing, the goblin rolled on the floor in agony as the three jumped over it, leaving it to bleed to death.

Of course it was goblins. Who else were cruel enough for such desecration?

A gang of them separated them from their companions, huddled together in defence. Backs to a grove of pine trees, tightly clustered boughs providing an impenetrable wall, they fought fiercely, killing many and wounding more. It was a desperate situation, as more and more goblins poured out of the woods, screeching battle-cries as they waved their weapons.

Gwahl and Noswen fell upon them with a vengeance, Lidan trailing close behind, covering their backs as they tried to push through the throng. With the initial momentum of their charge lost, they fell into an ugly brawl. His left arm ached from the countless jabs and cuts hammering his shield. Eventually, he saw an opening in the knot of bodies and rushed through, barrelling goblins out the way. He sensed Gwahl and Noswen following behind. They burst through the horde like a battering ram, finally reaching the pines.

A quick glance showed they were too late, as the defensive line was broken. Now the company fought in isolated clusters, back-to-back, holding off the enemy. He and Gwahl did the same, and there was a comfort to be felt in the daemon's back pressed against his, knowing such a warrior was with him. If he expected Noswen's back too, he was to be disappointed, as the hanex danced away into the enemy, flicking her falchion and twirling her dirk, delivering death to any who stood up against her.

'We need to regroup!' shouted Gwahl, grunting as he thrust and parried, making extraordinary use of his short blade. The daemon had long since mastered the technique of ducking inside the opponent's effective range, knocking aside the tips of spears or longswords and advancing quickly to attack. Against these fierce, but untrained goblins, it was all too easy to land his blows.

'Who's closest?' asked Lidan, bashing an approaching goblin with his shield. Nose rendered a mushy pulp, the goblin fell to the ground clutching its mangled face.

'Spotal and Pwtrek, five paces to your left.'

Lidan nodded and slowly edged his way to the calef. Gwahl followed closely, keeping his back pressed against Lidan. Closer and closer they moved, shoving aside their enemies, hacking, lunging, and stabbing. Eventually only two goblins stood between them, and no sooner had Lidan raised his sabre to strike, both fell down with choking gurgles. Spotal stepped over their bodies, bloodstained jian in hand. The calef nodded to them breathlessly and they hurried to re-join Pwtrek. With such accomplished warriors beside him, Lidan was sure they would emerge victorious.

*

A powerful kick to the fork of the legs sent her enemy keeling, and Noswen cut him down. Seeing the trail of death lying in the wake of the hanex, the goblins were cautious when it came to engaging her. The amount of space they gave her was foolish, as it provided more than enough time to execute perfect swordplay. She struck down each brave, foolish enemy who stood to meet her. Screams of agony rose from the ground all around as her beaten opponents desperately tried to staunch their wounds. It was no use. If it took a few minutes or a few hours, they would all bleed to death if they stayed on this battlefield.

With an ease that bordered on laziness she parried the clumsy slash of the next goblin, deftly turning the blade aside to cut harmlessly at the rancid air of the battle. Barging her shoulder against him, she sent him stumbling backwards and cut forcefully across his chest. Shrieking, the goblin fell to the floor, dark blood pumping through his dirty rags as he desperately clutched the wound. With her enemy incapacitated, she surveyed the battlefield.

Her companions drew together, fighting side by side against the rapidly-dwindling enemy forces. Goblins had never been considered the most courageous of fighters, and seeing the wanton destruction at the hands of these soldiers, many lost heart and slinked back to their hovels.

Gwahl, Spotal, Lidan, and Pwtrek stood together as one unit, while Widrias, Auran, Chekry, and Depani formed another. Once they were back together, she was certain the battle would soon be over.

Just as the thought entered her mind, it was immediately lost, as Depani broke ranks, forgetting herself as she furiously fenced a goblin with a swift spear. Immediately the foe closed in, and their unit was broken apart into individuals, beset on all sides. Spotal's unit couldn't see them. It was up to her to help.

There was no need to worry about Depani, as Chekry was soon by her side, protecting his sister. Auran managed to work himself to a strong defensive position, moving swiftly and smoothly, never exposing his back to any opponent for longer than necessary. He was still in danger, but not compared to Widrias.

He was ten paces away, standing awkwardly. His left leg buckled uncomfortably under his weight as he fought, holding the blade of his sword like a polearm. Noswen fought over to him, but goblins kept springing in her path, jabbing at her with their crude spears and rusted swords, gnarled faces twisted in rage. One eye was always kept on the general as she ducked and parried and cut down foe after foe, and slowly, so slowly, she was getting closer.

Battles had always been places of madness and despair, with moments of triumph eclipsed by the blood-stained destruction of lives. Noswen's triumph upon finally cutting down the last enemy standing between her and Widrias was equally cast in shadow.

Even as she tugged her sword from the dead-weight of the goblin kneeling in front of her, she saw him stumble slightly on his injured leg, his sword falling to the ground. The satorr winced in pain as spasms seized his muscles. Behind him loomed a goblin, spear raised, wicked intent etched into his features, and she knew sorrow would soon be upon them.

*

Pwtrek swept his sword before him, cutting through foes like a scythe through grain. Despite the many who fell, he was losing this battle. Fatigue from their long journey had worn him thin, and he was losing energy. Occasionally a goblin would duck beneath his swinging blade, step inside his sword to assail him with needle-like weapons, which always seemed to find the smallest gaps between the plates of his armour, or the skin beneath his once-thick pelt. Soon, he was bleeding from a dozen cuts. In the past, his pelt would have protected him, negating the attacks to nothing more than pinpricks, but now it was thin and brittle, easily penetrated, even by rusted iron.

In the heat of battle, he saw Noswen fighting, an air of desperation surrounding her. Following her gaze, he spotted Widrias, isolated, struggling on his poor leg. By the grace of the north winds! He'd abandoned his post as the general's guardian! His oath would count for nothing. His leader, his friend, would die.

Another spear bit into his flank. Growling in fury, he swiped the goblin aside and felt his claws rip into the soft flesh of its stomach. No! This scum would not come between him and his friend. Not after so long, after enduring so much. Today was not the day to fail.

Doubling his efforts, he swung his sword. One hand on the hilt, the other on the ricasso. He was no longer looking at his enemies. They were nothing. Mere objects between him and Widrias. An axe sank into his hip, jarring against his bone. He howled in pain, and the goblin's head disintegrated into a cloud of blood and bone by his sword.

It hurt. Funny, none of the others seemed to. Through the red haze of battle, he could faintly make out several spears sinking into his flesh, withdrawing in spurts of blood, and jabbing forward again. But he couldn't feel them. Only that one axe, the blade grating against his hip bone with each step.

It didn't matter. Only reaching Widrias mattered. Protecting his friend. He would make it. Noswen was fighting too. He needed to reach him before she did.

Widrias stumbled, just as Noswen cleared the last goblin between them.

No! Treachery! He could only gaze in horror as the hanex pulled her dirk from its sheath, holding it by the tip of the blade to throw. Aimed at Widrias.

Horrified, he bellowed with fury. The pain in his hip disappeared. Time slowed. Rage coursed like lightning through his veins.

Like a charging bull, he crashed through his remaining foes, sending them flying. From the corner of his eye, he saw Noswen's arm whip forward, just as he reached Widrias.

Throwing his arms wide, he tackled him to the ground, covering him with his body. He made it. He protected his friend.

*

There was no time to run to the general's aid, she wasn't fast enough. There was no use calling out, as he wouldn't hear over the sound of the battle. Flipping her dirk in her hand, she held it by its blade, and threw.

In all her years as Stolach's assassin, she mastered most forms of combat. Her skill with a sword was rivalled by only a handful, her agility was legendary, her accuracy with bows and crossbows feared, and her proficiency with thrown knives was cited by scholars as faultless. The dirk flew like a silver star. Its path would take it deep into the goblin's chest.

Her smile disappeared when Pwtrek's massive body crashed through the melee and clattered into Widrias. The satorr fell like a rag doll just as Noswen's dirk would have passed over his shoulder. Instead, the dirk buried itself deep into Pwtrek's back, just below the shoulder blade.

The goblin was strong, fast, and still alive. With so much momentum behind his thrust, he couldn't change the direction of his spear, which sank deep into Pwtrek's flank. Nearly a foot of the shaft was lost in the juggernaut's body. The goblin snarled and tried to twist it free, but the spear was stuck too deep. It wouldn't budge.

As the goblin tugged, her eyes caught Pwtrek's. Rage gave way to sorrow. Snapping out of her momentary paralysis, she sprinted to her companion. Her leap took her over Pwtrek, landing behind the goblin. He was fast. She was faster. Her falchion's edge was sharp and bright. Her swing found the goblin's throat. Her arm jarred as the blade met bone.

One brief look at the spear in Pwtrek's back was enough to tell her all she needed to know. She turned away, facing the surrounding enemy. Her sword flashed red, and she took a firm stance, ready to protect her two fallen companions.

*

When Pwtrek charged away, Lidan moved quickly to close the gap left behind by the juggernaut. Spotal and Gwahl followed, drawing together into a tight triangle. He was tired, panting heavily, and could feel his sword-arm growing sluggish, his shield-hand numb from the constant trauma. Sweeping his sword above his shield, he felt it cut through flesh. A spurt of blood splattered his face. The wounded goblin was thrown aside by its companions as they surged forwards with a renewed vigour, emboldened by something. He didn't consider the reason behind this rejuvenation in morale, instead concentrating on repelling his attackers and staying alive. This thoughtless fight for survival was lost as soon as he saw Pwtrek lying motionless on the ground, Widrias struggling beneath him.

'Pwtrek!' he cried, now pushing through the sea of rusted swords and flailing limbs to his friend. Spotal and Gwahl followed, once again using him and his shield as a battering ram, lending their strength to crash through the foe. Within seconds they were next to the juggernaut. Lidan took a position beside Noswen, trying to ignore the motionless body. Despite the hanex's valiant attempts to protect Pwtrek, she couldn't defend him from so many enemies while still looking out for Widrias. His fallen frame was covered in desecrating wounds, brutally hacked apart by sword and axe.

Gwahl knelt to pull Widrias from beneath him. The satorr gasped in pain. Pwtrek's considerable bulk crushed his leg, now cruelly twisted beneath him. Gwahl handed him his sword, instructing him to rest on it.

'Pwtrek?' Lidan called. 'Is he alive?'

'Dead,' said Noswen, quietly. 'Or soon to be.'

'Can't we help him?' he shouted desperately, hacking wildly at any goblin who approached.

'No.'

'Gwahl?' he looked desperately at the daemon, praying for a contradiction.

'He's dead, Lidan, let Gwahl look after Widrias,' said Noswen.

'We need to get away from here,' yelled Spotal. 'There are too many!'

'There's no way Widrias is outrunning anyone,' said Gwahl. 'He'd be cut down within ten paces! We fight!'

Suddenly, out of the throng thundered an enraged bellow, and Auran crashed through, swinging his mighty axe. His skin was slick with sweat, his gauntlets and arms stained with blood. Their foe fell away from him, like blades of grass kneeling before a gust of wind. Following behind him was Depani, struggling to support her brother. Chekry had a deep gash in his forehead, the blood gushing into his eyes to blind him, and his left hand clutched his opposite shoulder tightly, trying in vain to staunch a heavily-bleeding stab-wound.

Lidan nodded to the Southlander, who nodded at Pwtrek questioningly. Lidan shook his head, jaw clenched, and Auran turned back to face the teeming horde, breathing heavily, like an exhausted dog.

'Chekry's wounded,' shouted Depani. 'Gwahl, help him!'

'There's nothing I can do right now,' spat the daemon, grappling a goblin with his left hand and fencing another with his right. With a snarl, his hand closed around the first goblin's throat, crushing its gullet with a squelch, while simultaneously lunging forwards to stab the second's gut. His foe fell to his knees, wheezing in pain, only to be silenced when Gwahl's dirk rammed into his eye.

'He's losing blood!'

'There is nothing I can do!' shouted the daemon. 'Put pressure on it, that's all we can do for now. Concentrate on your own survival!'

Lidan could hear the tension in his voice, the fear. It filled him too, giving him the energy to keep swinging his sabre long after his natural strength was spent. Gradually, the tide of foes dwindled, their recklessness ebbing away as they realised that these stalwart warriors would not give any more ground. Facing an opponent ready to die could be a daunting task, too daunting for the faint-hearted goblins, who slithered away, leaving only the boldest, most violent of their kind to face the wrath of the company. It was Spotal who slew the final one, turning aside a clumsy slash to cut a deep wound into his enemy's stomach. The goblin fell with a whimper, to be silenced by the calef's sword.

Gasping for air, Lidan collapsed to one knee. He remained as he was for a few seconds, preparing himself for what was to come, and turned to look at Pwtrek. A few seconds was all he could bear. He turned away, tears welling in the corners of his eyes. It seemed impossible in such a short space of time for a person of his might and courage to be reduced to an empty, bloodied carcass. All he once was was gone. Now just a dead body, like the dozens of others.

Behind him, Gwahl whispered soothing words to Chekry, easing off his shirt to have a better look at the wound. It looked bad. An ugly tear in the flesh surrounded by congealed blood, just where the shoulder met the chest. Gwahl cleaned it carefully. Without the caking of blood, it immediately seemed better. The daemon, however, did not seem impressed. He asked Chekry to gently raise his arm, to make small movements, to hold his sword. The neiad tried his best, but was in too much pain, his hand clumsy and slow.

'Enough, now,' said Gwahl, 'someone get me those medicine-packs. I'm going to stitch and bandage it, your scalp too. Your right arm will be in a sling across your body.'

'Will he be alright?' asked Depani, anxiously hovering over Gwahl's shoulder.

'He'll live if we keep it clean. No major blood vessels were cut, otherwise he'd be in a very dire situation. Chekry. Your life as a warrior may well be over. I cannot predict the true prognosis of your arm, but it seems like tendons and nerves were cut, so sword-fighting and shooting will be… difficult.'

'How do you know? Because he found it difficult to move his arm? Might that not be due to the pain?' asked Depani, anxiously.

'It almost certainly is because of the pain. I'm just warning you. Palpating his shoulder, the movements felt odd, out of place, and his hand isn't working properly. We'll know more when we return to the Council.'

'What about Pwtrek?' asked Lidan, quietly. Whether the others ignored him or didn't hear, he couldn't tell, but nobody reacted.

Gwahl turned to Widrias. 'How's your leg?'

The satorr shook his head, gripping his sword with white knuckles as he fought to control the pain. Gwahl gently prodded his leg, and he nearly screamed.

'Can you put any weight on it?' Widrias shook his head again. Gwahl tutted softy. 'I didn't think so. It's badly sprained, possibly dislocated too, I can't tell. Needless to say, you won't be scouting ever again.'

'What about Pwtrek?' Lidan asked again, louder. Again, he was ignored.

'At least it's on the one that's already wrecked,' said Widrias through gritted teeth. 'Otherwise I'd have two useless legs.'

'We can splint it and look for something to use as a crutch. Apart from that there's not much I can do.'

'It's enough, thank you, my friend. Go and see to the others.'

'What's wrong with you all?' shouted Lidan, gesturing to Pwtrek. 'Look at him! He's the worst wounded. Gwahl!'

'He's gone, Lidan. We treat the living first,' Gwahl said, sternly.

'At least look at him!'

'I have! I don't need to look again. I don't want to look again. He's gone,' Gwahl retrieved the medicine-pouch from his pack, avoiding his glowering stare.

He knew he was dead. Of course he was. He hadn't moved since he'd first fallen. There was barely an inch of his body untouched by a blade. But he couldn't accept it. He wouldn't.

Walking over to him, he fell to his knees and cradled his head in his hands.

'Please,' he whispered.

'Stop, Lidan,' said Spotal, gently.

'Please!' he screamed, clutching Pwtrek's face, his eyes still open in their final, haunting stare.

'It's alright,' soothed Spotal, his arms around Lidan's shoulders. 'It's alright.'

'No…' he sobbed. He pulled at his friend's features, trying to animate them. Useless. He knew it was useless. He knew his friend would never smile again. But what else could he do? Accept it with the cold indifference of his companions? No. This was his friend. They'd been through so much. It wasn't fair.

'He was brave, he fought well,' whispered Spotal, comfortingly.

'I don't care!' he wailed. 'Gwahl please just have a look at him! There might be something you can do? If we stitch up the wounds and take out the spear?'

'It's alright,' soothed Spotal again, gently rocking him back and forth.

'No…' he moaned, his fatigue preventing him from struggling free from the calef's hold.

'I know, it's alright.'

He tried to lean forward, to inspect Pwtrek's wounds, but Spotal pulled him back, now resting a hand against his forehead, shushing and crooning in his attempts at comfort.

'Let me go,' he wept, wriggling feebly. 'I need to see him.'

'You can see him. It's alright,' whispered Spotal.

'Let me go.'

'Shush. It's alright.'

'Let me go!' he shouted, kicking against him.

Spotal relaxed his grip and Lidan fell forward, covering Pwtrek's head with his body. His face buried in his mane, he breathed deeply. Memories of being carried on his back through Tarnegrefur came flooding back. He protected him. He always protected him and everyone else. Why couldn't he protect himself?

But the smell was soured by the metallic stench of blood. So much blood. It congealed within his mane, matting the hair, staining it.

'Please, Gwahl,' he pleaded, quietly.

He felt Spotal's arms on his shoulders again and he shrugged them away. He persisted, slowly prising him away from the carcass. He snarled and threw his fists behind him. Again, Spotal persisted, dragging him away.

He turned, fist drawn back to strike. It dropped by his side. It was Gwahl, black eyes filled with sorrow, his hands on his shoulders.

'He was my friend too.'

He shook his head, tears flowing unchecked. He let Gwahl pull him into an embrace.

'He was my friend too,' repeated Gwahl, holding him.

*

Eventually the sobs ceased, and he was able to stand away from the carcass.

Gwahl inspected their other injuries. Nobody emerged from the battle untouched. Spotal had an ugly bruise on his flank, Auran's little finger was dislocated, Depani and Noswen both had a number of small scratches and grazes, and Lidan had a cut on his right forearm. He blinked in surprise when Gwahl pointed it out to him.

'I can't even feel it,' he murmured, watching the daemon wrap it in a length of bandage.

'You seldom do. There are more important things to consider during combat than a flesh-wound. It looks worse than it is, you'll be fine.'

'Can we leave?'

'Yes.' Gwahl turned to Widrias. 'Sir, might I suggest that we get on our way as soon as possible?'

'We leave now,' nodded the satorr, leaning heavily on his sword.

'What should we do about Pwtrek?' Lidan asked, quietly.

There was a brief silence, before Spotal answered. 'We burn him, of course. The winds can take his ashes to the fields above the sky. I'll get some wood.'

He returned a moment later with an armful of pine branches. With care, he piled the branches on top of Pwtrek, along with a scattering of dried pine needles and cones. Solemnly, the calef struck a flint, showering the makeshift pyre with sparks. It took light. After a pause, he bent over the flames and tugged Noswen's dirk from the juggernaut's shoulder, handing it back to the hanex. She took it without a word and sheathed it immediately, watching the hungry flames lick the carcass within them.

'Why was your blade in his shoulder?' Depani demanded, angrily, 'Did you stab him in the back?'

'I was trying to save the general,' she replied, flatly. 'I threw the dirk to kill a goblin and Pwtrek dived in front of it. I suppose he thought I was aiming for Widrias'

Depani snorted. 'A likely story. You never liked each other.'

'If I wanted him dead, I would have killed him long ago, in quieter circumstances.'

'Oh aye? A battlefield is the perfect place to commit murder, with so much death around, who would notice?' Depani spat, angrily.

'Enough!' cried Gwahl, furiously. 'Pwtrek is dead. Have some respect. I will say this one last time; Noswen is not an enemy. Shame on you for accusing her so. I trust her, Spotal trusts her, Tanor trusted her, Widrias and the other chancellors all trust her. Normally I wouldn't care whether you do too, but right now, in our present situation, we need to hold together. Squabbling like this does nothing to aid us.'

Depani blinked, taken aback by Gwahl's furious tirade, and was about to reply when Widrias cut across her.

'Well said, Gwahl. Pwtrek was my friend. He was a loyal soldier, strong and considerate, but his prejudice against Noswen was foolish. We should grieve him, not point blame at others. Now, say your final farewells. We must move on.'

One by one, they each peeled away from the fire, leaving behind the juggernaut who lay at its heart. Lidan was last to leave. He could have stood there for hours, until the flames died down to ash, and the ash was blown away. He didn't relive memories of the juggernaut. He didn't recall any conversations, or meals shared. He simply stood and stared at the lapping flames.

But it was time to go. He followed the others. A movement caught his eye and Noswen stepped from the shadows behind. It turned out he wasn't the last to leave, after all.

*

It was slow going. Painfully slow. Even he was frustrated by the snail's pace at which they crawled. Walking so slowly gave far too much time for free thought, and time and again his mind would drift back. Could he have saved Pwtrek? Could Gwahl have done more? How many goblins had he killed? How many lay on beds, shivering from fever as infection took hold of their wounds? It was impossible to tell. It frightened him how many lives ended that night. What frightened him more was the lack of regret he felt, the lack of emotion towards such slaughter. He didn't care about the ones dead by his hand. He was hollow, numb, frozen in the heat of death and emptiness of sorrow.

'Dirdin,' he whispered, praying he would not lose himself in those deaths.

Regarding his companions, they were all equally frustrated at the slow pace. Spotal strolled lazily, kicking pine cones in an attempt to amuse himself on the slow journey. Auran had an empty expression and dull eyes, as if he were in a trance. Gwahl was the most restless, constantly running up and down the column, checking on everyone. Depani stuck with Chekry, while Noswen took over Pwtrek's role in supporting Widrias, and walked with his arm slung around her shoulder.

The next morning, while they prepared for the day's travel, Gwahl approached Widrias.

'Should I scout ahead? Take in the lay of the land, make sure we don't stumble on any other foes.'

'That would be an idea,' said Widrias. 'When can we expect you back?'

'I'll report back immediately if I find anything. If not, I'll meet you when you camp for the night.'

'You'll be able to find us easily enough, I trust?'

'Yes. Just keep heading south,' Gwahl nodded, and left, disappearing into the trees without another word.

As promised, he returned that night, reporting the path was clear for ten miles to the south. At their current pace, ten miles a day was about all they could manage, so there was no need to report on anything further away. This continued for the next few days, with him returning each night with his reports, occasionally instructing them to modify their path slightly southwest or southeast, but no more than that. Once he returned with a roe deer fawn around his shoulders, and they had a wholesome meal around their fire. Another time he returned with an ugly cut beneath his eye, but he didn't offer an explanation, simply stating the path south was clear. One night, he didn't return.

At first, they were unconcerned. The daemon was more than capable of looking after himself. As the night wore on, they heard a terrible moan in the distance, carried many miles by the wind to their campsite. It was a hideous wail, completely different to the wail of the tortured boys, who'd screamed in agony. It was like the wrenching, sorrowful cry of a mother mourning a child, a desperate lament for a lost loved one. Lidan felt like weeping, to share the despair of this individual to hopefully lessen their loss, to share with them the loss of Pwtrek and find compassion in their painful emptiness. A few minutes later it was over, but the lingering sadness remained.

Come morning, the haggard expressions of his companions showed they too heard the wails. When Lidan asked whether they should seek out the source of the noise, Spotal shook his head furiously.

'We go nowhere near those sounds.'

'Why? It's no trap. I know it isn't. There's a person suffering, like us. We should go to them, weep with them, tell them tales of Pwtrek and listen to their tales of their own loved ones.'

'Those were the cries of a banshee, Lidan, a hunting banshee. Let us pray it wasn't Gwahl they hunted,' Spotal shuddered.

'No, it was someone else in pain! Their cries echo my heart, we should go!'

'He's delirious,' Depani shook her head.

'I'm not, I know their loss, I feel it now, I need to comfort them,' he was close to tears, having worked himself up into the grief of the night before.

'It's alright, Lidan,' soothed Spotal, approaching him. 'You've never encountered one before.'

'I know what it was, Spotal,' he pleaded. 'They've lost someone, just like us... like us.'

The calef embraced him, shushing him as he continued his muffled tirade, before the sorrow finally became too much, and great sobs wracked his body in heaving spasms. He knew the others were watching him, but did not judge him for weeping. They all needed the release he was experiencing, and maybe watching him embrace those emotions would help. Even Widrias was willing to wait, using this moment of silence to remember Pwtrek, missing his gruffness, courage, loyalty, and friendship. Eventually the tears ceased, and he pushed himself away from Spotal, drying his eyes with his palms. But something was wrong. He shook his head in frustration.

'Why do I still feel so awful?' he asked pitifully.

'Pwtrek was dear to us all, we'll weep many times before we're well.'

'I know, but normally you find some... relief in tears? I don't feel any difference.'

'The banshees,' said Noswen.

'Yes,' agreed Spotal, sadly. 'Their aura still saturates the air, we'll find no solace until we're away from here, where their cries were so vivid.'

'I've never heard anything like it,' he whispered.

'Hopefully you'll never hear it again,' said Spotal.

'It was like pure sadness embodied in a single note,' said Auran, shaking his head. 'Brought back cruel memories.'

'Were we closer to it, depression isn't the only thing you'd have felt. Fear is the underlying melody of their call. Pure terror hitting you like an arrow, freezing you where you stand as the pale, spectral forms of these hunters bear down upon you. The further away you are, the less fear their call instils, but the anguish remains.'

'Are they primal like troglodytes, or are they like us?' he asked, sniffing.

Spotal paused for a moment. 'It's difficult to say. They're too solitary to interact normally with other races, but are not barbarians like troglodytes. Besides, they regard us as prey, so having a conversation with one is impossible.'

'Can we kill them if they attack?'

Widrias laughed bitterly. 'Easily. They have some deficiency in their blood which prevents it from clotting. It makes them pathetically vulnerable, that's why they need their howls to transfix their prey.'

'Nevertheless, they're dangerous. There's a reason why their race still exists, despite their physical weaknesses,' continued Spotal.

'Yes, we should leave. I doubt they were particularly close, but it's best if we put as much distance as we can between us,' said Widrias. 'You might start to feel better as we move away from here, Lidan. In fact, I'm sure we all will.'

'We're not waiting for Gwahl?' he asked

'There's nothing we can do. If he's alive, he'll find us. There's no point waiting around for him,' replied Widrias.

'I'll scout ahead in his place,' said Spotal, and Widrias nodded in confirmation.

All day, Lidan listened for the daemon's voice, jokingly scolding them for abandoning him. He never heard it, and their journey felt that much more hopeless without him. Spotal returned to them more often than Gwahl, delivering his reports in the same detail to guide them south to safety. They steered clear of any settlements, not that there were many, and avoided contact with anyone whenever possible. As they struck further and further south, far away from Gwahl and Pwtrek, this became increasingly more difficult.

Eventually, Spotal requested Auran join him to clear the path south. Lidan lost count of the times they returned, breathlessly telling them to change course to avoid a gang of rogues. Several times they returned with bloodstains on their clothes. Lidan hardly noticed them. His eyes were dull and his shoulders slumped, walking in a daze. Initially he thought the cries of the banshee might have had a lasting effect on him, but no, his sorrow came from within, from the loss of his friends. The nights were worse. Fires were no longer lit, for fear of drawing attention of unwelcome visitors. He slept fitfully, dreaming of goblins, prison cells, dead calefs, stinking swamps, raging seas, and pain. Chekry was in a poor state, and although the wound was healing reasonably well, the damage was done. Moving the arm was a torture for the neiad, and it hung limp and useless in front of his chest in a sling. Widrias was equally bad. His leg was so damaged now, it was impossible for him to put any weight on it, and he moved carefully on his makeshift crutches. Noswen would often have to lend him her strength to cross certain parts of the forest, small streams, fallen trees, dense undergrowth, small slopes and ledges, all of these had become difficult obstacles for the satorr. Truthfully, it was pathetic. Lidan hated being reminded of how far they'd fallen. These were supposed to be the ones to defeat the king, the ones strong enough to stand up and rally the support of the people of the Midlands. They were supposed to be the ones to outmanoeuvre him, break his armies, cast him off the throne, and make Nefarwy a better place. Instead, it was Stolach who outthought them, sending them away to the Tarnegrefur Mountains, chasing a desperate dream. A sad tale of pathetic hope.

Each day he left a signpost for Gwahl, just as Spotal had done in the Kingdom of the calefs. Cairns, bent twigs, stones carved with the symbol of Enadir. Initially, he left them with a hopeful heart, but now they were simply another part of his morning routine. He didn't expect them to be followed, but it was a comfort to pretend.

*

The northeast reaches of the Dailas Forest were being torn apart by chaos. Order had always stood on precariously flimsy foundations in those lands, constantly fighting to maintain its balance as anarchy pushed and pulled at its feet. Eventually it buckled and fell, and was consumed by madness, madness into which Lidan and the others stumbled.

So far, with the exception of a few scraps fought by Spotal and Auran, their passage had been silent, smooth, easy. One might notice that such an occurrence happens often, when the uninformed breeze through an impossible situation simply because they are unaware of its impossibility. Of course, eventually the uninformed notice the signs surrounding them, the tell-tale whispers of the environment that betray its deadliness, and the illusion is blown apart, giving way to the truth and all its lethality.

This truth made itself known to Lidan first of all. A week passed since Gwahl's disappearance, twelve days since the goblins and Pwtrek. He walked with slumped shoulders, misery and defeat branded on his forehead. Wounds long forgotten suddenly started bothering him again, and he found himself clutching his stomach and rubbing his cheek as he marched, trying to ease the pain of their memory.

With the absence of Spotal and Auran, the remaining five walked slowly and exhaustedly, hardly paying attention to their route as they blundered their way through the forest. If it was cold, they didn't notice, each of them too deeply buried in their thoughts to pay much attention to such trivial things as warmth. Pain was their main concern, of both mind and body, for themselves and their companions.

Distracted as they were, it was not until they were within fifty feet of danger when he paused and looked up. He was unsure why he looked up. Certainly, he had no reason to look anywhere but the ground three feet in front of him, but look he did at the surrounding forest. In looking, he saw, and his heart caught in his throat. In an instant his stomach eased and his cheek settled, and with the ease of a stalking cat, he settled into a crouch and retreated to find his trailing companions.

Noswen and Widrias were barely twenty feet behind him. With a finger to his lips, he approached, gesturing to the trees beyond.

'There are people up ahead, where are the twins?'

'Somewhere close behind,' whispered Widrias grimacing as he tried to stand comfortably. 'We'll wait here.'

Lidan nodded. He found them within seconds and beckoned them over, again with a finger to his lips. Depani immediately drew her rapier, while Chekry attempted to hold his crossbow left-handed, but the motion was ugly, awkward, like a child. Together, they returned to Noswen and Widrias. Widrias held his sword low, its point buried in the loam as he used its length to support his body weight. One look from Noswen was all it took for the satorr to wearily lift the sword and return it to its scabbard, before reclaiming his crutch and leaning heavily against the trunk of a long-dead pine.

'Where, Lidan?' asked Noswen in her deathly-still voice.

'Less than a hundred feet ahead. I saw four men, but there might be more. Auran and Spotal must have just missed them.'

'Armed?' she hissed.

'I saw swords and daggers at their hips.'

'Sheathed? Good, they won't be expecting us in that case.'

'Pray, what do you intend to do, Noswen?' asked Chekry, somewhat breathlessly. 'We're in no fit state to fight them.'

'Agreed,' nodded Widrias. 'We should hide and let them pass.'

Noswen blinked slowly. 'We do not yet have enough information to decide on a definitive course of action. I'll approach them, unseen, discover how many there are, and we'll proceed from there.'

Widrias didn't contradict her, so she silently melted away into the trees. Lidan made as if to join her, but the general's hand clasped about his forearm.

'She doesn't need your aid, Lidan, but I do. Until her return we will hide, and I need you and Depani here to protect us,' he motioned to Chekry. 'We cannot hope to defend ourselves in our current condition.'

'I can't see many places to hide, sir,' he replied, scanning the surrounding trees for ledges, overhangs, fallen logs.

'There was a little holly bush further back,' suggested Chekry. 'We could hole up in there until she returns?'

Widrias nodded, and they retreated some twenty feet to the holly. It wasn't especially big, and the leaves were sharp and irritating, but it was the best the forest had to offer. Lidan helped Widrias ease to one knee, his left leg jutting awkwardly to one side as he tried to keep as much weight to his right as possible. With a quick shrug, Lidan eased his shield off his shoulder and drew his sabre, anticipating the worst.

Barely a minute passed and Noswen was back among them. Lidan saw no sign of her until she was almost upon them, at which point she coughed lightly to alert them of her presence. He started in surprise at the sound, and nearly jumped to engage her before realising who it was. An unreadable expression masked her face as she crouched next to them behind the bush.

'We must hide,' she declared. 'But keep our weapons at the ready, should they find us.'

'How many are there?' asked Widrias through gritted teeth.

'Fourteen, all bearing light arms. Swords, daggers, maces, as Lidan said.'

'Soldiers?' Widrias asked.

She shook her head.

'Rogues,' the satorr spat the word with venom. 'Are they coming towards us?'

'If they continue on their current course, yes. They walk slowly, without purpose, ambling and shambling in their arrogant swagger. If they find us it will be the worse for us, I can assure you. They have the look of violent men about them. I've seen countless others like them, all hungry for blood.'

'Would we have a better chance of fighting them off if Auran and Spotal were with us?' asked Lidan.

'No. They'd still outnumber us two-to-one, and they seem well-rested and well-fed, we are neither. They would overwhelm us.'

'Surely you and Spotal have more skill than they?'

'Undoubtedly, but they would still overwhelm us. Right now, it's Depani, you, and I, Lidan, against fourteen enemies. You lack the experience to engage multiple opponents of this calibre and come away unscathed, especially not when defending your companions.'

He flushed, but couldn't deny her argument. 'So, what do we do? Sit here and wait for them to find us?'

'Normally I would advise us to circle around them, but right now you wouldn't be able to do that,' she looked at Widrias. 'Not if we wished to remain unseen, at least. The other option is to wait here, as you said, but again, the risk of discovery is too great.'

'What's your idea?' Widrias asked, with a tone that suggested he knew what the hanex was about to suggest. She nodded. Widrias sighed. 'I don't want to lose you as we did Gwahl, Noswen. Take no unnecessary risks.'

Again, she nodded, and slipped away into the forest, gliding silently over the dried leaves in her stealth. Lidan looked at the general questioningly, and he turned away, eyes closed in acceptance. Seconds later, he heard shouts, startlingly close to their holly bush. Gruff voices rose in outrage, followed by a single, painful scream. The forest exploded into noise as the approaching rogues bellowed incomprehensibly to one another, followed by the thundering of footsteps as they gave chase. Soon, the voices trailed away west, and after a minute of silence, Widrias heaved himself to his feet and motioned the other three to follow, heading south as fast as his crippled leg would allow.

Lidan stole a quick glance behind. A man was stretched out next to the dead pine against which Widrias leaned only minutes before. The front of his tunic, once yellow, was stained brown by blood from his cut throat.

'Will she be alright?' he asked Widrias, quietly.

'She'll lead them as far away from us as she can. Maybe she'll be able to pick a few off if they stray too far from the others. Whatever happens, those rogues will no longer bother us.'

Lidan didn't say anything. Widrias soon put his arm around his shoulders for support, and with the neiads close behind, they struggled on through the forest.

*

With their illusion of safety shattered, the party saw the danger of the northern forest. Every foul bastard north of the Crisiaddwr placed themselves between them and their destination. That very day,

690

after the first encounter with the rogues Noswen led away, they were forced to conceal themselves from two other bands of thieves, and fled for their lives before a snarling direwolf, feasting on the warm carcass of its recent prey.

As soon as Auran and Spotal returned, Widrias forbade them from further scouting, for fear of being separated and lost. Horrified that such a large gang of enemies slipped past them, they agreed, ashamed by their failure. Not that they should be. There were so many around, one or two were bound to fall through the net. Night brought a fresh array of horrors as the silence was constantly broken by shouts and screams, some distant, some near, as man and beast were caught by crueller, deadlier man and beast.

Morning saw the weary, sleep-deprived travellers stir uncomfortably to their feet and continue on their journey. The day brought yet more danger and anxiety as more and more rogues blocked their path south, forcing them to cower in ditches or, if safe, attempt to skirt around their foes, only to lose themselves in the endless woods. Once, they stumbled into three children, their wiry frames slumped like stunted apes as they crouched around an ensnared rabbit, its legs kicking furiously as its life slowly strangled away. The three looked up at them, skeletal faces alight with excitement. They kept their hands close to their weapons, just in case. As Depani passed, she drew her rapier and ended the rabbit's torment, throwing a pointed look at the children. One look at their dark eyes, glaring, and she sheathed her sword, quickly catching up with her companions.

Throughout the day, Lidan heard the three following them, their childish giggles ringing eerily through the trees as they played and stalked through the undergrowth. At one point, Spotal turned and drew his jian, pointing it at the woods behind them, commanding the children to return home, lest they run into peril. His warning was ignored, as the three continued to follow for hours afterwards, growing bolder with each mile. Stones and pine cones were thrown from the shadows at the party, once striking Lidan on the chin. He supposed they might have lost their families and had nowhere to call home, as they had travelled many miles from where they first came across them. Orphans of the forest, they didn't fear the threats of their sorry company.

It was only when another danger made its menace known that the children left them, scampering away like startled squirrels. With barely an hour of daylight left, a roar echoed through the darkening sky, shaking the earth with its resonating dread. Lidan's breath caught in his throat, making him stumble. Auran shakily took his arm and brought him to his feet.

'A mighty creature indeed,' said the southlander.

'What was it?' he asked, fumbling to draw his sabre.

'I don't know.'

'A hydra,' said Spotal, breathing quickly, worriedly. 'Sheath your sword, Lidan, it's no protection here.'

'What should we do?' asked Widrias, face pale.

'Run!'

With fear clawing their hearts, they fled, ears straining for the sounds of pursuit. Another roar shook the forest a few minutes later. They hastened their flight, desperate to get away from the monster at their heels. Lidan practically dragged Widrias, cursing his hobbled leg. He didn't scold him for it, didn't deny his frustrations.

Apparently, the hydra grew bored with the chase. Subsequent roars were fainter and more distant, but lost none of their malice as it pursued another quarry. He hoped it wasn't the children. As irritating as they may have been, they didn't deserve to be devoured.

Sleep that night, when it came at all, was fitful. After waking from nightmares of monstrous shadows chasing him through forest and city, he decided it was better to stay awake until morning. Looking around at his companions, it seemed they came to the same conclusion. Auran slowly polished his axe, Spotal sat on watch, Chekry was lying far too still to be asleep, and Depani kept rummaging through her backpack, looking for something. Widrias sat upright against a tree, eyes closed, but the way his hands caressed his sword betrayed his wakefulness.

Morning couldn't have come soon enough. They were on their feet and ready to leave as soon as the sun's first rays stained the sky a hazy orange. The days dragged on with their feet. Within a week of avoiding rogues and direwolves and monsters, that first encounter with a hydra hardly seemed as frightening as it once did. Five more prowled the woods somewhere behind them, and by now they knew how easily avoided they were if one kept his wits about him. Although their roars were terrifying, their hides like chainmail, their heads a mass of eyes and fangs, their breath a blazing inferno, their bodies as big and strong as half a dozen bulls, they were slow. In short bursts they could be fast, horrifyingly so, but they didn't possess the stamina to drag their massive scaled bodies for long. They had two distinct methods of hunting; either roaring to startle and terrify their prey into freezing in fear, or stalking them like snakes before pouncing. The second method was by far the most dangerous, and twice they were nearly caught, saved only by Spotal's sharp eyes and ears picking out the danger mere moments before it struck.

It was midday on the eighth day after the first hydra when a welcome face materialised from the trees.

'General,' saluted Noswen, calm and collected as ever.

'By the north winds, you're back!' exclaimed Widrias, stumbling forward to embrace her.

If she was surprised by the gesture, she didn't show it, but stood still with her familiar emotionless mask. Widrias stood back and nodded. 'What do you have to report, Noswen?'

'I led the rogues far away from us. They'll never bother us again. As I returned, several others stood in my way, none of them are of concern to us now. Your trail was easily followed.'

'How so? I wouldn't think we left such a mark in the woods to show our passing?'

'Only because of the trail markers left by Lidan,' she reached into her cloak and held forth one of Lidan's signposts for Gwahl; a series of twigs bent and twisted into a crude symbol of Enadir.

Widrias took the sign and raised an eyebrow at Lidan. 'Still leaving these for all the world to follow? He's lost to us, Lidan, accept it. He would've returned by now if not. We're lucky it's only Noswen who followed the trail. How many markers were you leaving?'

'One, sometimes two each day,' he replied, head hung.

'Each marker I found I destroyed,' said Noswen, 'there weren't many.'

'You destroyed them?' exclaimed Lidan, cheeks flushed. 'How will he find us now?'

'Lidan,' Widrias put a hand on his shoulder. 'If Gwahl were on our trail, it would not have taken him this long to find us. He's lost to us.'

'I don't believe he's dead.'

'Neither do I, I said he's lost, not dead. Should he reunite with us, it will be by a different path,' he turned back to Noswen. 'What else did you find on your journey? Anything of interest?'

'Not much,' she replied. 'I passed many abandoned villages, some destroyed, some just empty. These woods have lost civilisation. It's chaos out there. The rogues who roam the land do so with rage and ferocity born of fear and desperation. We would do well to be clear of them.'

'Then let us waste no more time, come, my friends, there cannot be much further to travel.'

*

Crisiaddwr was the largest river in Nefarwy. Its origins were within the Mountains of Iadden, bringing crystal-clear water to the Midlands. After running for many leagues south, the river divided into its two main branches. The larger branch continued south, bordering the Pine Woods and rushing through Tarin Swamp before reaching its estuary. Its second branch turned at a sharp angle to run east into the Dailas Forest, dividing the trees into northern and southern woods, before emptying into the Cysgodgors Marshes. It was the life source of the Midlands, just as the Atrael was for the Bramble Plains and Kingdom of the calefs.

Three weeks after Noswen's return, and they were finally clear of the northern woods. At the start of each day, Widrias would tell them the same seven words; 'There cannot be much further to travel.' Day by day, the words became emptier and emptier, as each new day bought only more trees, more rocks, more ice, until finally they found the Crisiaddwr. The neiads were the first to sense it, heads lifting in anticipation. Spotal was next, his sharp ears picking out the sounds of the water. Lidan didn't sense it until they were barely a hundred feet away, and when he finally saw its wonderful, rippling water, he smiled. It was the first smile for a long time. Flowing broad and steady, its waters were crystal clear, clear enough to see the riverbed, the weeds, the glittering scales of fish. The gentle waves caught the rays of the midday sun, sparkling like the most precious of treasure troves, beckoning them, welcoming them to its wonderful waters.

Depani eased herself into the water and disappeared from sight, swimming upriver at a furious pace to seek her kin. Upon her return, they would follow the neiads to their base, where Commander Afarn would aid them. After that, it was a final push through the southern woods to the Council. What welcome they would receive was anyone's guess. The fact they returned at all seemed a miracle.

Casting aside their clothes, the exhausted company fell into the river, gasping as the icy water hit their weary bodies and washed away the filth of many months' travel. Lidan watched the water around them turn brown and foul, polluted by the grime that clung to their skin. He washed himself thoroughly and breathlessly, clawing away the cloying muck from his hair and scrubbing his body clean, then grabbed his clothes and washed them too. Eventually the surrounding water returned to its perfect state, carrying all the filth back to Cysgodgors. Staring at his reflection, he traced a finger over his scars. He lingered on his left cheek, his most painful scar, and explored the ridges and wrinkles of the granulated mutilation. When the time came to return to Crastalan, he would finally have retribution, and the skin beneath his fingers would feel smooth again.

With their clothes hanging to dry behind them, they sat on the riverbank with their breath coiling around their heads as a fine mist. To their backs were the northern woods, and beyond them were the Northlands and the Tarnegrefur Mountains. Had they turned their heads to the left, they would have been gazing in the direction of the Kingdom of the calefs, the bramble plains, and the dreaded marshes. All these lands lay in their footsteps, to be returned to in tortured memory. Nobody said a word. They waited.

End of part 2